Praise for the Wayfarer Redemption series

The Wayfarer Redemption

"Storyelling at its best, with fast-paced action, gritty realism, powerful characters, magic, and romance."

—*Romantic Times BOOKreviews*

"Epic storytelling on a par with Terry Goodkind and Robert Jordan."

—*Library Journal*

Enchanter

"With three races, licit and illicit lovers, prophecy, fraternal hatred, and enough battles for several campaigns, Douglass has whipped up enough raw material to avoid short-changing readers throughout her vast undertaking."

—*Booklist*

"Sara Douglass is a powerful voice in high fantasy that readers can equate to the likes of Robert Jordan, Marion Zimmer Bradley, and Anne McCaffrey."

—*Romantic Times BOOKreviews* (4½ stars)

Starman

"A superior adventure fantasy right to the last." —*Booklist*

"Should satisfy a fantasy readership hungry for strong female characters."

—*Publishers Weekly*

"Exciting writing with emotional highs and lows! Ms. Douglass has created a mystical world populated with many vividly portrayed races."

—*Romantic Times BOOKreviews* (4½ stars)

BY SARA DOUGLASS
FROM TOM DOHERTY ASSOCIATES

Beyond the Hanging Wall
Threshold

THE WAYFARER REDEMPTION SERIES
The Wayfarer Redemption
Enchanter
Starman
Sinner
Pilgrim
Crusader

THE TROY GAME SERIES
Hades' Daughter
Gods' Concubine
Darkwitch Rising
Druid's Sword

THE CRUCIBLE TRILOGY
The Nameless Day
The Wounded Hawk
The Crippled Angel

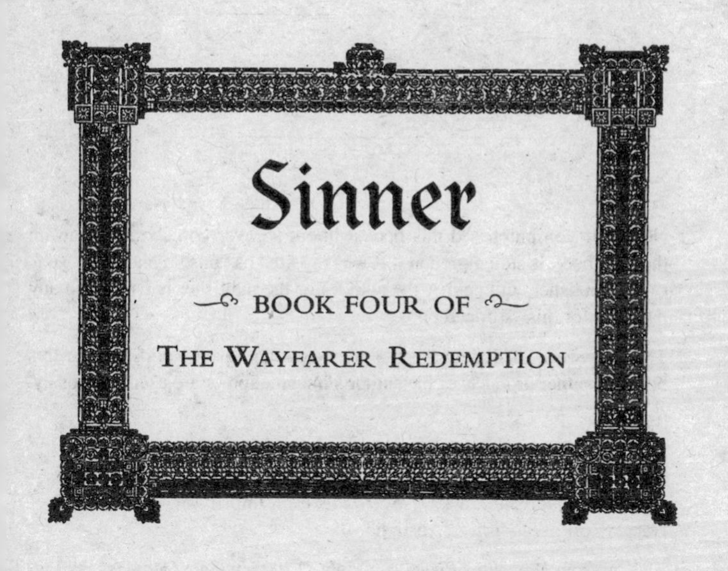

Sinner

BOOK FOUR OF

THE WAYFARER REDEMPTION

Sara Douglass

A TOM DOHERTY ASSOCIATES BOOK
NEW YORK

This is a work of fiction. All the characters and events portrayed in this book are either products of the author's imagination or are used fictitiously.

SINNER

Originally published in 1997 by *Voyager*, an imprint of HarperCollins*Publishers*, Australia

A Tor Book
Published by Tom Doherty Associates, LLC
175 Fifth Avenue
New York, NY 10010

www.tor-forge.com

ISBN-13: 978-0-7653-4278-2
ISBN-10: 0-7653-4278-2

First Tor Edition: September 2004
First Tor Mass Market Edition: May 2005

Library of Congress Catalog Card Number: 2004048033

Printed in the United States of America

0 9 8 7 6 5 4

The six books of *The Wayfarer Redemption* are for
A. Lynn Martin, Tim Stretton, and Frances Thiele,
who have regarded with amiable tolerance
their colleague's slow drift into the Star Dance.

If poisonous minerals, and if that tree
Whose fruit threw death on else immortal us,
If lecherous goats, if serpents envious
Cannot be damned, alas, why should I be?
Why should intent or reason, born in me,
Make sins, else equal, in me more heinous?

—John Donne, *Holy Sonnet* no. V

Contents

	Fire-Night	1
	Prologue	3
1	West and North	9
2	Master Goldman's Soiree	22
3	StarSon Caelum	29
4	Beggars on the Floor, Travelers o'er the Bridge	38
5	Speaking Treason	47
6	The SunSoars at Home	56
7	Disturbing Arrivals	62
8	Maze Gate	70
9	WolfStar's Explanation	76
10	Pastry Magics	93
11	Niah's Legacy	99
12	Council of the Five Families	113
13	The Throne of Achar	121
14	A Moot Point	129
15	Murder!	134
16	SunSoar Justice	141
17	The Lake Guard on Duty	152
18	Hunting Drago	161
19	The Fugitive	167
20	Icebear Coast Camp	177
21	Traveling Home	182
22	Impatient Love	192
23	Minstrelsea	201
24	StarDrifter	211
25	DragonStar	216
26	The Sack (1)	222
27	Niah Triumphant	227
28	River Crossing	230
29	The Ancient Barrows	236
30	The Rainbow Scepter	243
31	New Existences	250
32	The Questors	257

33 StarLaughter 263
34 Of What Is Lost 270
35 SpikeFeather's Search 278
36 Kastaleon 285
37 The Leap 291
38 Zenith Lost 298
39 The Maze 302
40 The Maze Gate's Message 306
41 A Town Gained, a Scepter Lost 313
42 ForestFlight's Betrayal 324
43 Faraday's Lie 332
44 . . . And Sixty-Nine Fat Pigs 338
45 The Enemy 344
46 The TimeKeepers 348
47 Niah's Grove 359
48 Carlon's Welcome 364
49 Caelum amid the Ruins 370
50 The Shadow-Lands 378
51 The King of Achar 381
52 Voices in the Night 392
53 An Army for the Asking 398
54 Journeying through the Night 412
55 The Blighted Beacon 417
56 Discussing Salvation 422
57 While WolfStar Lay Sleeping 426
58 As Clear as a Temple Bell 433
59 Zenith 439
60 Old Friends 445
61 An Army of Norsmen 451
62 The Warding of the Star Gate 456
63 Leagh's Loyalties Divided 464
64 A Dagger from Behind 469
65 A Brother to Die For 473
66 In Caelum's Camp 479
67 Caelum's Judgment 484
68 Toward the Star Gate 490
69 The Fading of the Dance 501

70 Leap to the Edge 507
71 The Sack (2) 513
Epilogue: The Wasteland 529
Glossary 533

Fire-Night

The four craft crashed through the barriers between the outer universe and the planet, exploding in raging flames, creating the portal that later races would call the Star Gate.

The creatures inside fought for control of the craft, fought even knowing it was a lost cause—the craft had ceased to listen to them hundreds of years previously. But even when death was only moments away, their hands clung to navigation mechanisms, hoping to somehow save their cargo . . . and maybe even save the world to which they plummeted from their cargo.

It was useless. Most of them were drifting ashes by the time their flaming craft smashed deep into the surface of the planet.

Most of them. One, like the four craft, survived.

Within days the craft had shifted comfortably into the pits created by their violent arrival, accepting the waters that closed over their surface. For three thousand years they dreamed. Then they woke and began to grow, spreading their tentacles deep beneath the land, reaching out, each to the other. Their metaled surfaces and walkways and panels and compartments hummed with the music they had learned in the millennia they'd traveled the universe. But this music the craft kept to themselves, not letting it mix with the sound of the Star Dance that filtered through the Star Gate.

* * *

The Survivor occasionally woke from his own deep sleep, wandering the corridors of the craft and those hallways that extended between each craft, looking, looking, looking, but never finding.

"Katie!" he would cry, "Katie! I don't know where it is!"

His searching always left him physically and emotionally exhausted, and within days of waking he would wander disconsolately back to his chamber, and there lie down to sleep yet again.

His dreams were disturbed, wondering why he'd survived, and yet not his comrades.

Wondering what the craft needed him to do.

Wondering whether the cargo was safe.

Wondering whether it would ever be claimed.

Wondering.

Aeons passed.

Prologue

Enchanter-Talon WolfStar SunSoar wrapped his wings tighter about his body and slipped deeper into the madness that consumed him. He stood at the very lip of the Star Gate itself, his body swaying gently to the sounds of the Star Dance that pounded through the Gate.

Come to me, come to me, join me, dance with me! Come!

Oh! How WolfStar wanted to! How he wanted to fling himself through the Gate, discover the mysteries and adventures of the universe, immerse himself completely in the loveliness of the Star Dance.

Yet WolfStar also wanted the pleasures of this life. The power he wielded as Talon over all Tencendor, the awe of the masses of Icarii, Avar and Acharite, and the firmness of StarLaughter's body in his bed at night. He was not yet ready to give all that up. He had come young to the Talon throne, and wanted to enjoy it for as long as he could. But how the Star Gate tempted him . . .

Come! Join me! Be my lover! I have all the power you crave!

WolfStar could feel the indecision tearing him apart. Stars! What sorcery could be his if he managed to discover the full power of the Star Dance *and* ruled this mortal realm of Tencendor!

I want it *all*, he thought, *all!* But how?

If he surrendered to the almost irresistible lure of the Star Gate and threw himself in, then WolfStar also wanted to know he could come back. Return and flaunt his new-found power and knowledge. *Revel* in it. Use it. Of what use was power if it could not be used in life?

WolfStar was destined for legendary greatness. He knew it.

He shifted on the lip of the Star Gate and his mouth twisted in anger and frustration. What *more* could he do?

Over the past weeks he had selected the most powerful of the young Enchanters among the Icarii and had thrown them through the Star Gate. Come back, he had ordered, with the secrets of the universe in your hand. Share them with me. Tell me how *I* can step through the Star Gate and yet come back.

They were young, and their lives could be wasted, if waste it was.

But none had returned, and WolfStar was consumed with rage. How was he to learn the secrets and mysteries of the Star Gate, of the very universe itself, if they did not come back? Why did they refuse to come back?

Their weakness, their lack of courage, and their consummate failure meant that the mysteries of the stars were denied WolfStar until after his death. No, no, no . . . he could not countenance that. He *couldn't*!

"WolfStar?"

WolfStar's body stiffened and he barely restrained himself from letting his power bolt in anger about the chamber. "My title is Talon, CloudBurst. I command that you use it."

"Brother, you must stop this madness. Nothing gives you the right to murder so many—"

"Murder?" WolfStar leaped down from the lip of the Gate and grasped his brother's hair, wrenching CloudBurst's head back. "Murder? They are adventurers, CloudBurst, and they have a duty to their Talon. And they are doing that duty *badly*!"

"WolfStar—"

"My title is Talon!" WolfStar screamed and twisted CloudBurst's head until the birdman's neck creaked and his face contorted in agony.

"Talon," CloudBurst whispered, and WolfStar's grip loosened. "Talon, you are throwing these children to their deaths. How many lives have been wasted now? Two hundred? More, Talon, *more!*"

"They would not die if they crawled back through the Star Gate. They have wasted themselves, not I. *They* have failed. *Their* blame, not mine."

"No-one has ever come back through the—"

"That is not to say no-one can, CloudBurst." WolfStar finally let CloudBurst go and stood back. "Perhaps they are not strong enough. I need young Enchanters of powerful blood. Very powerful." His eyes locked with CloudBurst's.

"No!" CloudBurst sank to his knees, quivering hands outstretched in appeal. "No! I beg you. Not—"

"Bring me your daughter, CloudBurst. StarGrace has SunSoar power. Part of her shares my blood. Perhaps she will succeed where others have failed."

"No! WolfStar, I cannot—"

"I am *Talon,*" WolfStar hissed. "I am WolfStar SunSoar, and I *command* you! Obey me!"

But StarGrace did not return, either. WolfStar muttered instructions and orders to the terrified, sobbing sixteen-year-old girl as he seized her by her wings and hurled her into the Star Gate. But like all the others, she only cartwheeled into the pit of the universe to vanish completely. WolfStar stood at the lip of the Star Gate for two full days, watching and waiting, taking neither food nor drink, before he cursed StarGrace for all eternity for her weakness and failure and stepped back.

He jumped, startled.

"You are tired, my husband. Will you not take some rest?"

StarLaughter stepped forward from the shadows of the arches. "Come with me, my love, and let me warm and soothe you to sleep."

WolfStar reached out and smoothed his wife's dark hair back from her face. She was his first cousin, close SunSoar blood, and second only to him in Enchanter power. So powerful.

Perhaps too powerful. For months now WolfStar had good

reason to suspect StarLaughter plotted against him, plotted to take the title of Talon for herself.

WolfStar almost laughed. She must be mad to think she could wrest power from him.

He caressed her cheek, his fingers gentle, and StarLaughter forced herself to smile, even though her love for her husband was long dead.

WolfStar leaned forward and kissed her softly, allowing his hand to slide down over her body until he felt the energy throbbing through her swollen belly. His son, and so powerful, so powerful . . . did his unborn son conspire with StarLaughter? Was their son the reason she thought she could best him?

WolfStar's hand stilled. His son. Even unborn he wielded more power than any other Enchanter he'd sent through the Star Gate. His son.

Perhaps *he* could succeed . . . his *son*. And it would certainly solve the more immediate problem of StarLaughter's treachery.

StarLaughter's hands closed over his and wrenched it away from her body.

No! she screamed through his mind.

"I need to know, beloved," WolfStar whispered. "I need to know if I can come back. I need someone to show me the way. Who better than our son?"

"You would throw a newborn infant through? *You would murder our son?*"

StarLaughter took a step back. The birth was only weeks away—how far could she get in that time? Far enough to save her son's life? Far enough to save her *own* life? What did WolfStar know? How much *could* he know?

"Too much!" WolfStar cried, and leaped forward and grabbed her. "Consider yourself a fit sacrifice for your son, StarLaughter. Your body will protect him from the ravages of passage through the Gate, my lovely. Will you not do this for our son? *He* will come back, I am sure of it."

And once he does, WolfStar thought, I shall divest him of his knowledge and then of his life.

Now so terrified she could not even speak with the mind voice, StarLaughter shook her head in denial, her eyes huge and round, her hands clasped protectively over her belly.

"WolfStar, not your *wife*! Not StarLaughter!" CloudBurst stepped into the chamber, accompanied by several Crest-Leaders from the Icarii Strike Force.

WolfStar growled in fury and lashed out with his power, pinning them to the floor. "Anyone I choose . . . *anyone!*"

He dragged StarLaughter across to the Star Gate. In her extremity of fear she found her voice and screamed as she felt her legs touch the low wall surrounding the Star Gate. "No! WolfStar! No! No! *No!*"

It was the last thing anyone heard from StarLaughter for a very, very long time.

Five days later CloudBurst's remorse and grief gave him the courage to plunge the twin-bladed knife into WolfStar's back in the center of the Icarii Assembly on the Island of Mist and Memory.

He gave one sobbing, hiccuping sigh as WolfStar sank to the mosaic floor, and then he relaxed. It was over. The horror was finally over.

There was no grief among the peoples of Tencendor when WolfStar SunSoar's body was laid to rest in his hastily constructed Barrow above the Chamber of the Star Gate. With WolfStar dead, entombed, and on his own way through the Star Gate, Tencendor was at last safe from his madness.

Four thousand years passed. Tencendor was riven apart by the Seneschal and then restored by the StarMan, Axis SunSoar. The Icarii and the Avar returned to the southern lands, and the Star Gods, Axis and Azhure among them, were free to roam as they willed. Even though WolfStar had managed to come back through the Star Gate, he vanished once Axis had won his struggle with Gorgrael. Control of Tencendor, and the Throne of the Stars itself, passed from Axis to his son and heir, Caelum. Tencendor waxed bright and strong under the House of the Stars. All was well.

1

West and North

His wing-span as wide as a man was tall, the speckled blue eagle floated high in the sky above the silvery waters of Grail Lake. The day was calm and warm, the thermals inviting, but for the moment the eagle resisted climbing any higher. He tilted his head slightly, his predatory gaze undimmed by his vast age, taking in the pink and cream stone walls and the gold- and silver-plated roofs of the city of Carlon. The eagle's gaze was only casual, for it was almost noon, and the streets so busy that all rodents would have secreted themselves deep in their lairs many hours previously. The eagle was not particularly concerned. He had feasted well on fish earlier, and now he tilted his wings, sweeping over the white-walled seven-sided tower of Spiredore.

The power emanating from the tower vibrated the eagle's wings pleasantly, and made the old bird reflect momentarily on the changes in this land over his lifetime. When he had been newly feathered and only just able to stay aloft, he'd flown over this same lake and tower with the eagle who had fathered him. Then the tower had been still and silent, and the land treeless. Men had scurried below, axes in their hands and the Plough God Artor in their hearts. Ice had invaded from the north and Gryphon—creatures whom even eagles feared—had darkened the skies. But all that had changed. A great battle had been fought in the icy tundra far to the north, the ice had retreated and the Gryphon had disappeared from the thermals. In the west, enchanted forests had reached for the sky, and the white tower below had reverberated with power and song. The armies that had crawled about the land in destructive, serpentine trails disbanded, and now the peoples of this enchanted land—those who called themselves human, Icarii and Avar—shared their lives shoulder to shoulder in apparent harmony.

Contented, knowing that the score of chicks he had raised over his lifetime would have nothing more to fear than the anger of a sudden storm, the eagle tipped his wings and spiraled higher and higher until he was no more than a distant speck in the sky.

Leagh stood at the open windows of her apartments in the north wing of the Prince of the West's palace in Carlon, watching the eagle fade from sight. Sighing, for watching the bird had calmed the ache in her heart, she dropped her gaze slightly to the ancient Icarii palace that loomed above the entire city. It seemed to Leagh that the palace looked lonely and sad in the bright sunshine. And so it should, she thought, for StarSon Caelum so rarely leaves Sigholt now that he only uses his palace in Carlon every three or four years.

Leagh did not covet the magnificent Icarii palace. Her older brother Askam's palace was spacious and elegant, and grand enough for Leagh, who was a woman of conservative tastes and temperate habits. She dropped her eyes yet further, down to the gently lapping waters of the lake. A gentle easterly breeze blew across the waves, lifting the glossy nutbrown hair from her brow and sweeping it back over her shoulders in tumbling waves. Leagh had the dark blue eyes of her mother, Cazna, but had inherited her hair, good looks and calm temperament from her father, Belial. She had loved her father dearly, and still missed him, even though he'd been dead a decade. He'd been her best friend when she was growing up, and to lose him when she'd been sixteen had been a cruel blow.

"Stop it!" she murmured to herself. "Why heap yet more sadness and loneliness on your heart?"

Gods, why could she not have been born a simple peasant girl rather than a princess? Surely peasant women had more luck in following their hearts! Here she was at twenty-six, all but locked into her brother's palace, when most women her age were married with toddlers clinging to their skirts.

Leagh turned back into the chamber, and sat at her work table. It was littered with scraps of silk and pieces of embroidery that she had convinced herself she would one day sew into a waistcoat for the man she loved—but when everyone around her apparently conspired to keep them as far apart as possible, what was the point? Would she ever have the chance to give it to him? Her fingers wandered aimlessly among several scraps, turning them over and about as if in an attempt to form a pattern, but Leagh's thoughts were now so far distant that she did not even see what her fingers were doing.

Leagh's only wish in life was to marry the man she loved—Zared, Prince of the North, son of Rivkah and Magariz. Yet it would have been easier for me, she thought wryly, if I'd fallen in love with a common carter.

The problem was not that Zared did not love her, for he did, and with a quiet passion that sometimes left her trembling when she caught his eyes across a banquet table. Yet how long was it since they'd had the chance to share even a glance? A year? More like two, she thought miserably, and had to struggle to contain her tears. More like two.

Nay, the problem was not only that Zared and she loved too well, but that a marriage between them was fraught with so many potential political problems that her brother, Askam, had yet to agree to it. (Though doubtless he would have let her marry a carter long ago!) Leagh loved her brother dearly, but he tried her patience—and gave her long, sleepless nights—with his continued reluctance to grant approval of the marriage.

Leagh's eyes slowly cleared, and she picked up a star-shaped piece of golden silk and turned it slowly over and over in her hands. Power in the western and northern territories of Tencendor was delicately balanced between their two respective princes, Askam and Zared. Should she marry Zared, then the grave potential was there that one day West and North would be united under one prince. Askam had married eight years ago, but his wife Bethiam had yet to produce an heir. For the moment Leagh's womb carried within it the entire inheritance of the West.

And, with its burden of responsibility and inheritance, thus did her womb entrap her.

If I *were* a peasant woman, Leagh suddenly thought, I would only have to bed the man of my choice and get with his child for all familial objections to our marriage to be dropped. She crushed the golden silk star into a tight ball, and tears of anger and heartache filled her eyes. Askam would not let her get within speaking distance of Zared, let alone bedding distance!

Frustrated with herself for allowing her emotions to so carry her away, Leagh smoothed out the silken patch and laid it with the others. The political problems were only the start of Askam's objections, for Askam not only disliked Zared personally, but resented and felt threatened by Zared's success in the North. The West encompassed much of the old Achar—the provinces of Romsdale, Avonsdale and Aldeni. Each year the lands produced rich harvests, and for decades Carlon had grown fat on the trade with the rest of Tencendor and the Corolean Empire to the far south. But despite its natural abundance, the West was riven with huge economic problems. As Prince of the West, Askam had managed to mire himself deep in debt over the past seven years. For three years he had entertained the entire eight-score strong retinue of the Corolean Ambassador while, on Caelum's behalf, he had thrashed out an agreement for Tencendorian fishing rights in the Sea of Tyrre. When the agreement had finally been concluded, and the Ambassador and his well-fattened train once more in Coroleas, Askam had personally funded the outfit of a massive fishing fleet, only to have three-quarters of the boats lost in a devastating storm in their first season. Thinking to recoup his losses, Askam had loaned the King of Escator, a small kingdom across the Widowmaker Sea, a vast sum to refurbish the Escatorian gloam mines in return for half the profit from the sale of gloam, only to have the mines flooded in a disaster of epic proportions, and the new king—the previous having drowned in the mine itself—completely repudiate any monies his predecessor had borrowed.

These were only two of the investment disasters Askam had made over the past few years. There were a score of others, if not so large. Smaller projects had failed, other deals had fallen through after considerable cash outlay. Askam had been forced to raise taxes within the West over the past two years which, though they made but a small dent into the amount he owed, had caused hardship among farmers and traders alike. Yet who could blame Askam for the economic misfortune of the West? Sheer bad luck seemed to dog his best endeavors.

In total contrast, Zared's North—the old province of Ichtar—had blossomed in unrivaled prosperity. In the days before Axis had reunited Tencendor, the old Ichtar had been rich, true, but it had relied mainly on its gem mines for wealth. The gem mines still produced—and a dozen more had opened in the past ten years—but Zared had also opened up vast amounts of previous wasteland for cropping and grazing. Zared had enticed the most skilled engineers to his capital of Severin, in the elbow of the Ichtar and Azle Rivers, with high wages and the promise of roomy housing and good schooling for their children. These engineers had designed, and then caused to be built, massive irrigation systems in the western and northern parts of the realm. Zared had then attracted settlers from all over Tencendor to these vast and newly watered lands by offering them generous land leases and the promise of minimal—and in some cases no—taxation for the first twenty-five years of their lease. Unlike the West, all farmers, traders and craftsmen in the North were free to dispose of their surplus as they chose. As a result, a brisk trade in furs had grown with the Ravensbundmen in the extreme north, which were then re-traded to the southern regions of Tencendor. And add to that the trade in beef, lamb, gems and grain . . .

The mood of the North was buoyant and optimistic. The income of families grew each year, and men and women knew their futures were strong and certain. Trade, working and taxation restrictions were so slight as to be negligible, and success waited for all who wished to avail themselves of it.

The picture could not have contrasted more with the West, where it seemed that month after month Askam was forced to increase taxes to meet debt repayments.

It was *not* his fault, Leagh told herself, willing herself to believe it. Who could have foreseen that a storm would virtually destroy Askam's entire fishing fleet, or that the gloam mines of Escator would be flooded? But Askam's misfortunes did not help her situation. Especially not when Askam was aware that each week saw more skilled craftsmen and independent farmers of the West slip across the border to avail themselves of the opportunities created by Zared's policies.

"Leagh?"

She jumped, startled from her thoughts. Askam had entered her chamber, and now walked toward her.

"You wanted to see me, sister?"

"Yes." Leagh stood up and smiled. "I trust I have not disturbed you from important council?"

Askam waved a hand for her to sit back down, and took a seat across the table. "Nothing that cannot wait, Leagh."

His tone turned brisk, belying his words. "What is it I can do for you?"

Leagh kept her own voice light, not wanting to antagonize her brother any more than she had to. "Askam, it is many weeks since you have made any mention of my marriage—"

Askam's face tightened and he looked away.

"—to Zared." Leagh shifted slightly, impatiently. "Askam, time passes, and neither Zared nor myself grow any younger! I long to be by his side, and—"

"Leagh, be still. You are noble born and raised, and you understand the negotiations that must be endured for such a marriage to be agreed to."

"Negotiations that have been going on for five *years*!"

Askam looked back at his sister, his eyes narrowed and unreadable. "And for that you can only thank yourself for choosing such a marriage partner. Dammit, Leagh, could you not have chosen another man? Three nobles from the West have asked for your hand. Why not choose one of them? They cannot *all* be covered with warts and possessed of foul breath!"

"I love Zared," Leagh said quietly. "I choose *Zared*."

Askam's face, so like his father's with its mop of fine brown hair and hazel eyes, closed over at the mention of love. "Love has no place in the choosing of a noble marriage partner, Leagh. Forget love. Think instead of a marriage with a man which would keep the West intact *and* independent."

He paused, let vent an exasperated sigh, then smiled, trying to take the tension out of their conversation. "Leagh, listen to me, and listen to *reason,* for the gods' sakes. I wish you only happiness in life, but I must temper that wish with knowing that I, as *you,*" his tone hardened slightly, "must always do what is best for our people, not what is best for our hearts."

Leagh did not reply, but held her brother's gaze with determined eyes.

Askam let another minute slide by before he resumed speaking. "Leagh, it is time you knew that the yea or nay to this marriage has been taken from my hands."

"What? By *whom*?" But even as she asked, Leagh knew.

"Caelum. He is as disturbed as I by the implications of a union between you and Zared. Last week I received word from him to delay a decision until he could meet with me personally to—"

"And yet he does not wish to speak to *me,* or to *Zared*?"

"Caelum sits the Throne of the Stars, Leagh. He has heavier responsibilities than you can imagine."

Leagh bridled at her brother's school-masterish tone, but held her tongue.

"Caelum knows well that the continued well-being of Tencendor matters before the wishes of any single person. Leagh, you are a Princess of Tencendor. As such you enjoy rights and privileges beyond those enjoyed by other Tencendorians. But these rights and privileges mean you also carry more responsibility. You simply can *not* live your life to the dictates of your heart, only to the dictates of Tencendor. I have tried these past five years to discourage you from choosing Zared, but you have not listened. Now, perhaps, you will listen to Caelum."

Both his words and his tone told Leagh everything she needed to know. Caelum would not assent to the marriage either.

As Askam rose and left the room, Leagh finally gave in to her heartache and let tears slide down her cheeks. The very worst thing to bear was that she understood everything that stood in the way of her marriage. Why *couldn't* she have accepted the hand of a nobleman from the West? It would be so much easier, so much more acceptable for the current balance of power. But what she understood intellectually didn't matter when she'd totally given her heart to Zared. All she wanted in life was the man she loved.

Far to the north Zared straightened his back, refusing to let weariness slump his shoulders. He'd spent an entire week clambering over the ruins of Hsingard with several of his engineers to see if there was any point in trying to rebuild the town, only to come to the conclusion that the Skraelings had so destroyed the buildings that all Hsingard could be used for was as a stone quarry. Now he'd spent ten days riding hard for Severin, and even though he was lean and fit, the week at Hsingard and the arduous ride home had exhausted him.

But now Severin rose before Zared and, in spite of his tiredness, a small smile tugged at the corners of his mouth. It was a beautiful town, built not only with sandstone and red brick to withstand the harsh winters of the north, but also with skill and imagination, so that the structural strength of each building was perfectly married with grace of line and beauty of feature. Severin was a town built to satisfy the spirits as much as it was to harbor the bodies of those who lived within.

Thank the gods for my parents' foresight, he thought. Rivkah and Magariz had lived out the final twenty-five years of their lives in the town they'd had built, and had loved it almost as much as they had loved each other and the son they'd made between them. His parents had not only laid the foundation stones of Severin, but also of the territory Zared had inherited from them. The North had been the most severely ravaged region of Tencendor during the wars between Axis SunSoar and his brothers Borneheld and Gorgrael. Once it had crawled with ice, and worse—IceWorms, Skraelings, and Gryphon. Now fields ripened and cattle fattened, and any man, woman or child could travel from the Fortress Ranges to the coast of the Andeis Sea and encounter nothing more dangerous than the chill of a northern breeze.

Zared pulled his horse in slightly, waiting for his escort to catch up with him. He was a tall, spare but striking man with his father's dark good looks and his mother's light gray eyes. Even though he was now in early middle-age, Zared was as agile as most young men, and could still best any swordsman in the country. He had been bred in an age of war, and his father had spent many years training him in the arts of war, although for what, Zared was not sure. For forty years, since Axis had finally bested Gorgrael, Tencendor had lain peaceful and largely prosperous in the sun. Axis had ruled well and wisely—a glib enough statement, but true. And since, nine years ago, Axis had handed over control of Tencendor to his eldest son, Caelum had continued to lead Tencendor with the integrity that was the hallmark of the House of the Stars. And yet . . . and yet Zared would rest the easier once Caelum had proved his worth in true crisis.

His escort now directly behind him, Zared rode his horse through the gates in the town walls, returning the salutes of the guards standing to either side. For an instant the walls blocked out the noon-day sun and, as their shadow settled over Zared, so his mind turned to the one shadow in his own life—Askam.

He drove the thought from his mind almost as soon as it had surfaced, reining back his horse to a walk in the crowded streets. It was too warm a day to let thoughts of Askam cloud it over.

Zared's path back to his palace on the hill overlooking the town was slowed, not only by the crowds, but by the individuals who called out greetings and, occasionally, stopped him for a quick word. Zared had never been a distant prince, not only holding open court in his palace every Thursday afternoon when he was in residence so that any citizen of the North had the chance to gain his ear, but making sure that he did not ride the streets of Severin so encased by retainers that all his people ever saw of him was a brief glimpse of a linen shirt or glittering sword hilt.

Now a man—a carpenter, Zared thought, by the tools at his belt—called out a cheerful greeting in unmistakable southern brogue. Zared grinned widely as he nodded back at him. That man was from Romsdale. Yet another who had chosen Zared over Askam.

It cheered Zared to think that so many skilled craftsmen and farmers chose to relocate to the North, but at the same time it concerned him. The tension between himself and Askam was a decade old, and growing stronger with each passing year. Every carpenter, every brickworker, every field-hand who moved north deepened the tension just that fraction more.

Ah! There was Askam again, intruding on his thoughts! Zared's face lost its humor, and he pushed as quickly as was polite through the remaining streets to reach his palace. There, after a few words to the captain of the guard and a smile of thanks for his escort, Zared handed the reins of his horse over to a stableboy and hurried inside.

A bath and a meal later, Zared felt more refreshed. As his personal manservant cleared his table, Zared took a glass of wine and wandered into the reception gallery of his residence. His home was a palace in name only, a term designated by his subjects who somehow thought that as a prince he ought to live in a palace. Built initially by Rivkah and Magariz, the house was a roomy, elegant mansion that spread over the hill which rose on the northern borders of the town. When Zared was twenty-seven he had taken a wife, Isabeau, sister of Earl Herme of Avonsdale, and had added on a light and airy southern wing that together they'd planned to fill with the laughter of their children.

Zared's steps slowed at the first portrait that lined the gallery. Isabeau. Her dark red hair cascaded about her shoulders, her mouth curled in secret laughter, her bright eyes danced with love for him. The portrait had been painted eighteen months into their marriage. Two weeks after it had been finished Isabeau was dead, crushed beneath the body of her horse which had slipped and fallen during the excitement of the hunt.

She had been five months pregnant with their first child.

Zared had never forgiven himself for her death. He should never have given her that horse—but she was so skilled a horsewoman. She should never have been riding at that stage in her pregnancy—but she was so healthy, so vibrant. He should have forbidden her to follow the hounds and hawks—but she did so love the hunt.

He'd never ridden to the hunt again. The day after her death Zared had given away his hawks, and the hunting horses in his stable. His huntmaster had drifted away, seeking employment with lords to the south.

And Zared had promised himself never to love so deeply again, and never again to expose himself to such hurt.

He took a mouthful of wine and moved along to the next portrait. His father, Magariz. And next to his portrait, that of his mother, Rivkah.

They were, Zared supposed, the reason he *had* succumbed to love again. Magariz and Rivkah had lived life so completely in love, and so contented in that love, that Zared just could not imagine living himself without a soulmate to share his life with. For years after Isabeau's death he'd kept himself distant from women, keeping to his promise . . . and then he'd met Leagh.

Re-met her, actually, for Zared had known Leagh as a tiny girl in Belial's arms. But once he'd assumed the Princedom of the North, his responsibilities had kept Zared away from Carlon, and he didn't see Leagh again until she was twenty-one.

They'd met, not at Carlon, but at Sigholt. Wreathed in its magical blue mists, Sigholt was normally the province only of the enchanted SunSoar family, but the year Leagh turned twenty-one she'd traveled to Sigholt with Askam for a meeting of the Council of the Five First Families. Askam and Zared, as the heads of the two leading families, had attended, along with FreeFall SunSoar, the Icarii Talon, Sa'-Domai, the Ravensbund Chief, and Prince Yllgaine of Nor. Leagh had gone, partly at Caelum's invitation—a gift for her coming of age—and partly because she was close friends with Caelum's youngest sister, Zenith.

Zared had found himself alone with her late one night atop the Keep of Sigholt, both there for the night air. They'd spent the night talking, laughing, and—as they both discovered to their amazement—falling deeply in love.

Loving her was the easy part, Zared reflected. Being together, spending their lives together, seemed all but impossible. He'd come home from that Council so optimistically in love that he'd ordered the private apartments of his residence to be redecorated in the blue of Leagh's eyes.

Almost immediately he'd opened the diplomatic negotiations needed for such a high-ranking marriage, only to be confronted with a wall of distrust from Askam. Certainly the two had never liked each other, and they'd been economic rivals for years, but Zared had never thought that such matters would come between him and Leagh.

It was naive of him. *Stupid* of him.

Zared's fingers tightened about his wineglass, and he moved a little farther down the gallery. He didn't want to be so close to his parents' portraits. Now the likenesses only reminded him that his parents had spent some thirty years apart, and Zared didn't want to think that he and Leagh might have to endure a similar separation.

Damn Askam! If he hadn't got himself into such dire debt, if he hadn't imposed such heavy taxes, then maybe the West would prosper as much as did Zared's North. And maybe Askam would not feel so threatened by a marriage between his sister and Zared.

Zared was not a proud man, but neither was he foolishly modest. He knew that if he had been Prince of the West, he would not have made such risky investments as had Askam, nor would he have made his subjects pay for his mistakes. If he was Prince of the West as well as of North, then virtually the entire human population of Tencendor would live lives of heady prosperity. If. If. *Damned* ifs!

Now Zared stood in front of portraits of Rivkah's brother, Priam, and her father, Karel. They had once ruled as kings of Achar, a vast realm that had stretched between the Andeis and Widowmaker seas and from the Icescarp Alps to the Sea of Tyrre.

But as Achar was no more, so too had the monarchy died. Acharite lands had been split up between Avar, Icarii and human, its territory incorporated into the larger Tencendor, its peoples divested of their king.

As he stared at the portraits of his uncle and grandfather, Zared remembered how well both had reigned. True, they had supported the Brotherhood of the Seneschal, an organization that had brought only evil to all those who lived in the land, but in their own way Priam and Karel had ruled well and wisely. The monarchy had been brought into disrepute only when Zared's older half-brother, Borneheld, had murdered Priam and taken the throne.

There was no portrait of Borneheld. Zared's mouth quirked. Borneheld was a son and brother best forgotten.

He swallowed the last of his wine, still staring at the likenesses of Priam and Karel. What *would* it be like to govern (Zared's mind shied away from the word "reign") over such a large territory? What would he do with it? How would he improve it? How might he best help the West recover from the debts Askam had saddled it with?

Ah! These thoughts were treason!

Zared blinked, and started to turn away, but as he did so his eyes were caught by the golden circlet on Priam's brow, and he stopped, his thoughtful gaze lingering on the gleam of gold as the shadows of dusk gathered about him.

2

Master Goldman's Soiree

"Curse the Corolean Emperor to all the fire pits of the AfterLife," Askam seethed, and tore the parchment he held into tiny pieces. "Why does he hound my life so?"

Askam's four advisers, two minor noblemen, the Master of the Guilds of Carlon and the Chamberlain of Askam's household, stood diplomatically silent. One million, three hundred and eighty-five thousand gold pieces was the reason the Corolean Emperor so hounded Askam. To be precise, one million, three hundred and eighty-five gold pieces that *Askam* owed the Emperor.

Jannymire Goldman, the Master of the Guilds, dropped his gaze to his thick-fingered hands folded politely before him. He'd advised Askam not to take out such a massive loan with the Emperor, but Askam had needed the money badly, and the Emperor had been willing to lend.

Now he wanted it back.

And what if Askam could not pay (and Goldman *knew* Askam could not pay)? What then? What might the Emperor demand as recompense? Goldman shuddered to think. The Coroleans would not invade, never that, but they certainly might lay claim to some lands or, gods forbid, to Carlon itself.

Would that make StarSon Caelum finally take a more personal hand in the West's affairs? Caelum, although concerned about Askam's increasing debt, had thus far preferred to see if Askam could not solve his problems himself, but Goldman knew that Caelum would never stand by and allow the Coroleans to assume control of even the most barren of fields in Tencendor.

"Well, there's nothing for it," Askam said in a milder tone of voice, "but to pay the damned man."

Goldman raised his eyes in surprise, as did the other three advisers. Pay? How?

Askam took a very deep breath and sat back in his chair, staring at the four men ranged before his desk. All the gods in the universe knew he hated to do this but . . . not only would it solve most of his financial problems, it would also stop the flow of his people north.

And, perhaps, wipe the smirk off Zared's face.

"Gentlemen," Askam said softly, "I have no option. From fifth-day next week the taxes on goods moving up and down the Nordra, as goods moving along all inland roads in the West, will be raised to a third of the total value of the goods so moved."

Goldman could not believe he'd heard right. A *third*? A

third tax on all goods moved would cripple most merchants and traders, but it would *destroy* any peasant bringing a meager bag of grain to the market. And what of the man who thought to take a basket of eggs to his widowed mother in the next village? Would that also be taxed a third?

He opened his mouth to object, but Askam forestalled him.

"Gentlemen, I know this is an onerous burden for all western Tencendorians to bear, but it should last only a year, perhaps two."

A year or two would be enough to drive most to starvation, Goldman thought, on top of the taxes they already had to pay.

"And," Askam continued, "think of the rewards we will reap from those . . ." he hesitated slightly, ". . . others who move their goods through our territory. For years they have taken advantage of our roads and riverboats to move their goods to market, whether here in Carlon or farther south to Coroleas. It is high time they paid for the maintenance of the roads and boats they use."

And by "others" Goldman and his three companions knew precisely whom Askam meant. Zared. Zared, who moved the wealth of his grain and gems and furs along the Nordra down to the markets that made him—and his people—prosperous.

"Sir Prince," Goldman said, "this is indeed a weighty tax. If I might advise against it, I—"

"I have made up my mind, Goldman," Askam said. "I called you here, as the Chamberlain Roscic and Barons Jessup and Berin, not to ask you for advice, but to inform you of the measures that must be taken."

Roscic exchanged a glance with Goldman, then spoke very carefully. "Sir Prince, perhaps it might be best if you talked this over with StarSon Cae—"

"I will *inform* Caelum of my decision, Roscic!"

The Chamberlain subsided. He had already said too much, considering that his very position relied on Askam's goodwill. Goldman, however, had no such qualms.

"These taxes are so grievous, Sir Prince, that perhaps they *should* be discussed with—"

"StarMan Axis SunSoar himself gave my father the right to tax the West as he willed, Master Goldman! I will inform StarSon Caelum, but I have every right to impose these taxes without his assent. Is that understood?"

The four bowed their heads.

Askam looked at them a moment, then resumed. "There is one other thing. Over the past eighteen months, if not more, over two thousand men have moved their families north of the Azle."

Askam shrugged a little. "If they want to subject their families to the northern winters, then so be it, but the fact remains that most of those two thousand have been men skilled in their crafts, professional businessmen, or successful farmers. They have left a considerable gap in the West's resources—no wonder I have so much trouble trying to meet debt repayments."

No, no, Goldman pleaded silently, don't do it! Don't—

"In order to stem the tide I have instructed the border guards at the Azle and Jervois Landing to exact the equivalent of ten thousand gold pieces from each family that intends to leave for the North."

But that is ten times *my* annual income, Goldman thought. How will an ordinary craftsman pay it?

"That should go some way toward balancing the loss of their skills," Askam said. "That is all, gentlemen, you have my permission to leave."

That evening Goldman called more than a score of men to his townhouse in upper Carlon, all of them leading citizens and tradesmen, and there he spoke volubly about the new taxes and their implications.

"I will be ruined!" cried Netherem Pumster, Master Bell-Maker. "How else can I transport my bells if not by riverboat?"

"And I!" said Karl Hurst, one of the leading wool traders in Tencendor. "As will most of the peasants in the West! All rely on transporting their wool bales across the roadways of the West to the Icarii markets in the Minaret Peaks!"

His voice was joined by a dozen others, all increasingly angry and indignant as the implications of the tax sank in.

"As will *everyone* eventually be ruined," Goldman said quietly into the hubbub. He held up his hands. "Gentlemen, please . . ."

Men slowly subsided into their seats, worry replacing anger.

"I should have moved north last year, when my brother went," Hurst said as he sat down. "The North may be farther from the markets than I'd like, but at least Zared wouldn't try to take my soul to put meat on his table."

"More like," put in a stout silversmith, "he'd give *his* soul if he thought it might put meat on *your* table."

Goldman nodded to himself, pleased with the direction the conversation had taken, content now to sit back and let the treason take its course.

Treason? he asked himself. Nay, natural justice, more like.

"Things have never been the same since Priam died," said a fine-metal worker.

"Not the same since Axis SunSoar proclaimed Tencendor on the shores of our lake," said another.

"Now, now," Goldman demurred. "The SunSoars have done us proud. Have you ever known life to be better? More peaceful? Who dislikes trading with the beauty-loving and generous-spirited Icarii? Or even the Avar?"

There was a small silence, then Hurst spoke up again. "Our quarrel is not with Tencendor as such, nor with the Icarii or the Avar. I, for one, admire the SunSoars greatly for what they have done for our land."

"Oh, aye!" a dozen voices echoed fervently.

"Aye," Hurst repeated. "I voice no wish to resurrect the hatreds of the past."

"Nay!" came the resounding cry.

"Nay," Hurst echoed again, then looked about and licked his lips. "But these taxes . . . I cannot believe them! It never would have happened under King Priam, or even King Karel, from what I have heard of the man! Askam will destroy the West in his attempts to solve *his* debts!"

No-one missed the emphasis.

"Of course, Askam was not bred for such responsibility," said a merchant named Bransom Heavorand. He was one of Goldman's closest friends, and he knew the way the Master of the Guilds' mind was traveling. "He has not the blood for it. No wonder he missteps so badly."

"Yet his father, Belial, base-born as he was, was a kind and effective prince," Goldman said, working as closely with Heavorand as two voices in a duet. "And he was Axis SunSoar's right-hand man. Surely he deserved the reward of Princedom of the West?"

"Askam is not the man his father was," Heavorand said. "Unlike Belial, he's lived a life of ease. He's not had to fight for his life, nor the life of his country. He's not been tempered by the sacrifice and loss Belial endured. Nor has he inherited his father's courage and fairness."

Men nodded about the room.

"Given an estate to run, no doubt he would prove capable enough," Heavorand finished. "But so large a responsibility as the Princedom of the West has Askam flummoxed."

"And us bankrupt," someone muttered, and the room broke into subdued laughter.

"Yet the North prospers," Goldman said. "Zared, as his parents before him, has built steadily on solid foundations. He is generous but firm, courageous but conservative in the risks he takes—or exposes his people to. His people love him."

"Many among *our* people love him, too," said one of the men.

"And there's the nub of the matter," said Heavorand, speaking only at the slight nod of Goldman's head. "Zared was born of the blood of kings, Askam was not. Thus the North prospers while the West strangles."

Silence.

"Born of the blood of kings," said a voice far back in a darkened corner. "Are you saying what I think you say? Zared was born to *rule*?"

"What I say is only fact," Heavorand replied. "Zared is born of Rivkah, last princess of Achar, and Magariz, one of the highest-ranking nobles Achar had ever seen. They were legally married. Borneheld, Rivkah's eldest, was illegitimate, and thus his attempts to claim the throne of Achar met with disaster. Axis, may he live forever, was also illegitimate, and while he founded the Throne of the Stars, he rightly made no claim to the Acharite throne. Zared was Rivkah's only legitimate child. Zared," he paused, reluctant to speak these words even among friends, before finally gathering his courage, "is the legitimate heir to the throne of Achar."

"But Achar no longer exists," Goldman put in. "The throne no longer exists. Axis destroyed both. Surely Zared is heir to nothing but memories?"

There was a moment of silence, then Hurst spoke up, his face red. "But is that *right*? The Icarii have their Talon, the Ravensbund have their Chief, and now the Avar even have *their* head, the Mage-King Isfrael! Why should the Acharites not have their head . . . nay, their *pride* back?"

The room broke into uproar, and Goldman was once again forced to stand and hold up his hands for quiet.

"May I remind you, my friends," he said very softly, "that the term 'Acharites' is no longer lawful." One of Caelum's first edicts on taking the Throne of the Stars had been to ban the use of the term "Acharites" for the human population of Tencendor. To him it smacked too much of the hatreds that had torn Tencendor apart in the first instance.

"Whether we are Acharites, or Tencendorians, or bloody Manmallians," said the silversmith angrily, "doesn't change the fact that I'd prefer to have a *King* Zared ruling my life than a petty Prince Askam. No! Wait . . . there's more. It doesn't change the fact that whether prince or king or pauper for all I care, Zared is the man I'd prefer to have at my back in a street brawl, in a war, or as a drinking companion in a tavern. I respect Zared, I *like* Zared, and what I think of Askam doesn't bear spoken word in this company!"

"And what's more," cried a voice, "Zared is the rightful ruler, not Askam!"

"Gentlemen! Gentlemen!" Goldman cried. "Please . . . *listen* to me! Quiet down now! Yes . . . yes . . . thank you, that's better. Gentlemen, I am Master of the Guilds of Carlon. I am your spokesman, your voice. What would you have me do?"

Silence.

"I think," Heavorand said quietly, "that a little visit to Zared might be in order. I think the Prince needs to know just how his people—"

No-one in the room missed the use of the phrase "his people."

"—feel about a number of issues."

"Will he act?" said a voice. "Or will he back away?"

"If it is your wish," Goldman said, "then I, with Heavorand, will make my way north . . . on a trading trip, should Askam inquire. Once with Zared, I am sure I can phrase matters in such a way that Zared will be hard put *not* to act."

He regarded the room silently, then grinned conspiratorially.

3

StarSon Caelum

The great silvery keep of Sigholt sat quiet in the night air, reflecting stray moonbeams across the Lake of Life. At this time of night few people were about. Two or three guards moved about its walls, a servant trotted silently through the courtyard from barracks to kitchens, an Icarii Enchanter stood on the roof, mesmerized by the stars. Around the crescent of the lake, the town of Lakesview sat fat and secure on the shoreline. It was a well-established town now, its people indulging in some trading, some agriculture and much contentment. The nearby valleys and slopes of the Urqhart Hills in the immediate vicinity of Sigholt gave them all they wanted in food and recreation; few within the town pushed themselves to do much more than enjoy what proximity to the wondrous lake was given to them by the magical Keep and the extended family of SunSoars resident within its luminous gray walls.

Almost perfectly centered on the strip of shore between Lakesview and Sigholt was a substantial stone building. Over five storeys high, most of its large unglassed windows and permanently open doors faced the lake, as if the building wished to absorb as much of the breeze, or perhaps as much of the lake, as it could.

From one of the ground-floor doors two Icarii birdmen emerged. They walked slowly toward the lake, eventually standing in close conversation as the waters lapped at their feet. One wore an ivory-colored uniform with an embroidered device that resembled a twisted knot of golden braid centered on his chest. The other birdman had striking red plumage and hair, the skin of his face and hands so white they seemed to glow in the moonlight.

StarSon Caelum SunSoar, supreme ruler of Tencendor, stood at one of the windows in the map-room of Sigholt, wondering what they talked about so quietly. Caelum was one of the most powerful Icarii Enchanters born, a child of the Star Gods, and even though his keen eyesight could easily pick out the birdmen so far below, he balked at using his powers to listen to their actual words. Caelum was ever polite, and he trusted the two men below as few others.

Still, they were an enigmatic pair. WingRidge CurlClaw, the birdman in the ivory uniform, was captain of the Lake Guard, a somewhat eccentric force who had dedicated themselves entirely to the service and protection of the StarSon. Even so, Caelum sometimes felt they kept themselves at a distance, not only from the life of Sigholt, but even from himself.

But in itself that distance, and its essential peculiarity, was not surprising—and had a great deal to do with the birdman WingRidge currently conversed with, SpikeFeather TrueSong. The Lake Guard was formed exclusively from the six hundred children SpikeFeather had rescued from Talon Spike many years ago. Rather than risk the children to possible Gryphon attack on the ice trails of Talon Spike, SpikeFeather had pleaded with the Ferryman to take the children to safety via the waterways. The children had reached Sigholt safely, but they had been subtly changed by the experiences in the waterways with Orr, and when they reached their majorities they had formed the Lake Guard. They announced their complete dedication to the service of the StarSon, and chose as their uniform breeches and plain ivory tunics with the strange emblem on their chests.

None of the Lake Guard ever explained it.

If no-one quite understood the Lake Guard, then all trusted them. Again and again the Guard pledged their loyalty to the StarSon. Their lives were dedicated to his word, their hearts to his cause. They might disappear for days, sometimes weeks on end, but they claimed their ultimate duty was always to the StarSon. Caelum, as everyone else, did not doubt it. They were an accepted part of Sigholt, and as mysterious as the Keep itself.

SpikeFeather was almost as enigmatic. He, too, had been changed by his contact with Orr the Ferryman. As payment for Orr transporting the children to Sigholt, SpikeFeather had dedicated his life to the Ferryman, and for the past twenty years had spent much of his time in the waterways with Orr. What SpikeFeather did down there, or what Orr did to the birdman, Caelum did not know.

As Caelum watched, WingRidge and SpikeFeather parted company, WingRidge rising slowly in the air toward the walls of Sigholt where Caelum supposed he would inspect the members of the Lake Guard stationed there, Spike-Feather walking slowly about the shoreline of the lake, apparently deep in thought.

Caelum sighed and turned back into the circular map-room. The center table was covered with documents, piles of accounts, reports from several of the major towns, and ledgers bound with ribbon and stuffed with loose pages. Caelum fought the urge to sigh again and wandered slowly over to the table, running a hand through his thick, close-cropped black curly hair. Was there never an end to the paperwork? Sigholt sometimes seemed full of secretaries and notaries and bureaucrats, all of them there supposedly to keep track of the vast amount of paperwork that governing Tencendor somehow generated, but Caelum sometimes wondered if they were of any use—his desk never seemed to clear of the damned stuff.

No wonder Axis had handed control of Tencendor over to him! Caelum smiled softly, thinking of his parents, and knowing in his heart that it was far more than paperwork that had seen them leave. Axis and Azhure had remained at Sigholt while their children grew into adulthood, but when Zenith, their youngest, had reached the age of twenty-five, they had increasingly turned to their fellow Star Gods for companionship. Nine years ago, growing ever more inclined to the ethereal and wanting to spend more time exploring the mysteries of the stars, Axis had handed over full control of Tencendor to Caelum in a magnificent ceremony on the shores of Grail Lake, where Axis had proclaimed Tencendor so many years ago. In the years since then Caelum had seen his parents only three or four times. They kept themselves remote, as befitted their status as gods, and left Caelum to manage the realm of mortals.

Even though he had steered Tencendor for nine years, and seen it successfully through several peaceful disputes, Caelum still felt slightly uncomfortable about his position as supreme ruler. Axis had won his right to rule through sheer courage, through years spent on the fighting trail, through heartache and loss and grief. Caelum had been given the realm, almost literally, on a golden platter. Oh, he'd been trained and guided and counseled for years beforehand. Axis had sent him for several six-month periods to the great southern empire of Coroleas, and once for seven months to the intriguing little kingdom of Escator. At the hands, not only of Axis himself, but other petty kings and grand emperors, Caelum had studied the art of governance in depth.

But still Caelum sometimes felt that he should have *won* his right to sit the Throne of the Stars as his father had. Was the sheer luck of birth order enough to guarantee that a son had the skills and wisdom needed to govern so large a realm? What did his people actually *think* of him?

"I should get out more often," Caelum said to himself. "Actually see what's going on and not rely on reports. How long is it since I've left Sigholt?"

"Too long," a soft voice put in from the window, and Caelum turned about, unsurprised. He'd known who it was even before she spoke, for he'd felt her presence coalesce in the window as he'd muttered to himself.

"Zenith." He grinned and held out his hands. "It's been days! Where have you been?"

His youngest sister jumped lightly down from the windowsill and hugged her brother tight. Unlike Caelum, who remained bare-backed like their parents, Zenith had glossy wings, as raven-black as her hair. She was a beautiful birdwoman, even more stunning than her mother, Azhure. Mysterious, intriguing, and yet somehow sad, always apart from the life of Sigholt. Caelum held the hug, wondering why. Even as a child Zenith had seemed troubled. She had often slept badly, suffering formless nightmares, and on many days was withdrawn and uncommunicative. And sometimes . . . sometimes Caelum had caught her looking at him with an expression that was so unlike her that he'd wondered if . . .

"Why the frown?" Zenith leaned back and took her

brother's face briefly in her hands, kissing him lightly on the lips.

Caelum folded her wings against her back and stroked them softly. "I was thinking, loveliest of sisters, that it is high time you also thought about fleeing—"

Why had he used that word? Caelum stumbled slightly, but managed to carry on before Zenith could speak. "—leaving Sigholt. How many years since you left? No, don't answer! Too many, that I know."

Zenith quietened in that strange way she had, and Caelum sensed a slight withdrawal.

He stood back a little, but kept his hand lightly on her shoulders. "Zenith? StarDrifter would love to see you, I'm sure. You spent a great deal of time with him when you were a child, and the Island of Mist and Memory is a wondrous place."

"Maybe." She suddenly grinned, her dark blue eyes mischievous. "Should I take Drago with me, as I did when a child?" Zenith more than half suspected that Caelum's suggestion was a roundabout way of ridding Sigholt of Drago's presence for a while.

Caelum dropped his hands and walked away from her. "As you wish," he said, his voice toneless. "But that wasn't what I meant."

Zenith instantly regretted trying to joke about Drago. He was a constant note of disharmony within Sigholt, although he never said or did anything that could be in any way construed as sinister or hurtful. It was just that he was so different from his brothers and sisters. Caelum, RiverStar and Zenith (as also Isfrael, their half-brother) were the children of gods. They were highly magical beings, and their enchanted lives would likely stretch into infinity before they ended. Once Drago had been like them. Briefly. Drago had been born the second child of Axis and Azhure, the elder twin of RiverStar, and potentially one of the most powerful Enchanters ever birthed. But even as a mewling infant he had abused that power, allying himself with his father's foe,

Gorgrael, and plotting to murder Caelum so that Drago might inherit his place.

As punishment Azhure had disinherited him of his Icarii powers. Now, forty years on, Drago wandered the corridors of Sigholt a dark and enigmatic mortal, aging into useless thin-faced middle years as he watched his brothers and sisters glory in their youth and enchanted powers.

Caelum was never able to trust him, even knowing his powers had gone. It was Caelum who had been the object of Drago's infant ambitions, who had been subject to the terror of kidnap and abuse by Gorgrael, and it was Caelum who was daily reminded of that horror every time he caught sight of Drago from the corner of his eyes. Zenith knew that Caelum made every effort to avoid Drago whenever he could, but even in a place as large as Sigholt the brothers constantly ran into each other.

"I'm sorry," she said softly to Caelum's back. "I did not mean to jest."

He turned his head her way, and smiled slightly. "It does not matter, Zenith. Drago does not—"

There was a knock at the door, and it opened without waiting for Caelum's word. WingRidge CurlClaw entered, stopped after precisely five paces, and saluted Caelum. "StarSon."

"WingRidge. What is it?"

WingRidge glanced at Zenith, but made no comment on her presence. "StarSon, a courier bird has just arrived from Carlon with a message from Prince Askam."

Caelum took the proffered parchment, unrolled it with a snap of his wrist, and ran his eyes over the text.

"Curse him to . . . to . . . oh, *damn* him!" he cried, and Zenith laid a concerned hand on his arm.

"Caelum? What is—"

"That cursed fool has just levied a third . . . a third . . . tax on all goods moved along the Nordra and along the roadways of the West. *And* slapped a tax on any and every man and family who wants to move north to live. Gods! Look at the amount! That figure must have come to him when he was suffering a nightmare caused by chronic constipation. Oh! I can't *believe* this!"

He threw the parchment on the table and stalked away to the window, standing and staring out as he fought to regain his temper. Gods, but Askam and Zared gave him more trouble combined than Borneheld and Gorgrael had ever given his father, he was sure of it! How many times had he had to draw one or the other aside for some diplomatic advice? Between them they controlled half the territory of Tencendor—was it too much to ask of them to try and do that in something even *vaguely* resembling peace?

Zenith looked at WingRidge, who remained completely expressionless, then picked up the parchment and briefly scanned the contents herself. Her eyes widened as she slowly put it down—no wonder Caelum had reacted so strongly.

"Caelum?" she said, and waited for her brother to look at her.

"Caelum . . . this time something needs to be done to solve their problems. And Leagh, you must surely end her misery soon." Although Zenith had not seen Leagh in some four years, they remained in close touch; Zenith not only knew how much Leagh hungered for Zared, she understood why Caelum and Askam were going to deny Leagh her heart's desire. Poor Leagh, she thought, it's time she was told to move on with her life. Five years of alternating between misery and gut-wrenching hope was too long for anyone.

Caelum nodded slowly, and rubbed his face with one hand. He suddenly looked very, very tired. "The time *has* come to solve this. Askam has gone too far with his debt—and Zared should have been astute enough in the first instance to know that a marriage between him and Leagh, especially with Bethiam remaining so stubbornly barren, would be a political impossibility."

He drew a deep breath. "This needs not only my authority, but the weight of the Council of Five."

Zenith's eyes widened. The heads of the leading five families of Tencendor only met on a biennual basis; to call them in now, not eight months since their last meeting, bespoke how serious Caelum thought the problem was. As ruler of Tencendor, Caelum's final word was law—legally he did not need to call the Council on this matter—but he obviously felt both Zared and Askam needed the judgment of their peers as well as his own word.

"WingRidge?"

WingRidge snapped to attention.

"Send couriers to Zared, Sa'Domai, FreeFall, Yllgaine and Askam. We meet with the utmost haste—no later than seventh-day three weeks from now. And send for Isfrael as well."

Isfrael, now Mage-King of the Avar, was not officially a member of the Council of Five and did not have a vote, but for the past ten years he had attended all the meetings, and given and listened to advice. As Caelum's half-brother and leader of one of Tencendor's three main races, he was usually invited as a courtesy.

Besides, no-one particularly liked to make a decision in Isfrael's absence that might subsequently annoy him.

As WingRidge put his hand to the doorknob, Caelum called him back. "No, wait. Leave Askam. I will send a personal courier rather than one of yours."

WingRidge nodded, and was gone.

"Zenith?" Caelum smiled at his sister, although his eyes remained tired and careworn. "Why don't *you* tell Askam?"

"Me? But—"

"The bridge can connect you to Spiredore easily enough, and from there it's only a short flight across Grail Lake to Carlon."

"But why me?"

"Because I think Leagh should be here as well. I need to tell her my decision, and I'd rather do it to her face than by courier bird. Don't you want to see her? Bring them both back by Spiredore. Askam can send his escort north by more conventional means."

"I don't know that I want to leave—"

Caelum's voice hardened into command. "You need to be more involved with Tencendor, Zenith. I am asking you to go, but if you wish I can make your departure slightly more compulsory."

Zenith's chin tilted up, and in that movement Caelum saw all of his mother's fire and determination. "As you wish, brother. I shall leave before sunrise."

And with a slight but noticeable twitch of her shoulders, she brushed past him and left the room.

4

Beggars on the Floor, Travelers o'er the Bridge

She preened before the mirror in her chamber, running her hands down her lightly clad body, liking what she saw, what she felt.

RiverStar SunSoar was a lovely, alluring birdwoman, and she knew it. What man had ever been able to resist her?

She lifted her hands to her fine golden curls and shook them out. How they complemented her violet eyes! Her pale skin!

"I *am* irresistible," she said, then laughed, low and husky.

Irresistible indeed—except to the one who continually resisted her.

She froze at a subtle touch. Power.

His. It stroked at her arms, lifted the material from her breasts, rippled down over her belly, her legs.

Her lover. He was close.

She did not move, pretending not to notice. She would make him beg. She would!

Except he never begged. Always *she* ended on the floor

before him, her hands clinging to his legs, her golden wings spread out in appeal behind her, begging him to bed her.

She would writhe before him, sobbing and shrieking, until he had her so completely in his power that she would scream her gratitude when he finally lifted her and threw her to the mattress.

RiverStar frowned at her reflection. She did not like to have to beg . . . but, oh gods, how could she withstand him when his power stroked her, caressed her, penetrated her?

As it did now. She shuddered, tears filling her eyes, and when he opened the door and entered the chamber she fell to the floor and begged, begged, begged . . .

"You are unlike any other," she whispered into his ear when it was finally done and they lay sweat-tangled amid the sheets. "None."

"I was made for a purpose," he said, smiling, and kissed her brow.

"Let me stand by your side as your lover," she said. "Please. Let all see how good we are together."

"No."

"Why not?" she screamed, hate for him contorting her beautiful face. *"Why not? You can do anything you—"*

His hand caught at her face, his fingers digging deep, hurting so badly she whimpered.

"You will tell *no-one* about us," he hissed. "No-one! *Do you understand?*"

"Yes, yes, yes," she whispered. "I will tell no-one. Never tell. No. Please, love me again. Please . . . please . . . please . . ."

Zenith stopped in her chambers to change into a vivid robe and to give her face and hair a cursory check in her mirror. Caelum was right, it was time she left Sigholt for a while. She'd been thinking much the same thing—thus her reaction when Caelum had verbalized the unspoken thoughts that had consumed her for almost a week.

Something was wrong. She couldn't say what, or even what it might be related to, only that for the past few days a feeling of formless dread had been growing in her. Dread, and a sense of loss so deep that for three nights in a row she'd woken drenched in sweat, her hands clawing at the sheets.

Thus the reason she'd been wandering about Sigholt so late tonight.

These nightmares reminded her of those she'd had when she was much younger. Nights when she'd woken screaming, nights when the only way she'd agree to go back to sleep was sandwiched between the comfort of her parents. Axis had always questioned her closely about the dreams, but Zenith could never remember their details—maybe didn't *want* to remember—and Azhure had refused to let Axis use the Song of Recall to summon them from her murky subconscious.

"Leave the child be," her mother would say softly, stroking the hair back from Zenith's brow. "She doesn't need to remember them, only to be reassured of our love."

And somehow that love *had* helped Zenith through. The dreams had begun to fade when she was eighteen or nineteen, and were gone completely by the time she'd reached her majority.

Although there was still the problem of the lost hours.

This was something she'd never told her parents about—why, she could not say. But some days she would suddenly find herself in a distant part of Sigholt, or even in a nearby valley of the Urqhart Hills, and have no knowledge of how she had arrived there. Hours, sometimes even half a day, would have been lost to her.

These episodes had also lessened as she grew older, but Zenith still had one or two a year.

And, in the past week, three.

This was the reason she'd hesitated when Caelum had suggested she go to Carlon.

What if she "lost herself" somewhere in Spiredore and came to her senses sitting on an icefloe in the Iskruel Ocean? How would she explain that to Caelum? How could she explain it to *herself*?

Zenith hesitated in the center of her chamber, a stunningly beautiful, slim birdwoman, robed in scarlet that contrasted vividly with the darkness of her wings and hair.

Taking a huge breath, Zenith tried to calm her nerves, wrapping herself so deep with magic it literally blurred the outlines of her figure.

An image formed before her: her grandfather, StarDrifter. It was a memory only, not the actual person; StarDrifter lived far south on the Island of Mist and Memory, devoted to his duties among the priestesses of Temple Mount.

This was a memory that Zenith had carried with her for some thirty years, a memory of a day when she'd been staying with her grandfather on the island, and had found herself wandering the southern cliff faces of Temple Mount with no idea how she'd got there.

She'd been young then, and she'd been growing her wings only a year. They'd still felt strange to her, and she still fumbled on her infrequent flights, so that suddenly coming to awareness at the crumbling edge of a thousand-pace drop had been terrifying.

She'd screamed, sure she was going to die, and then StarDrifter was there, wrapping her in his arms and wings, pulling her back, holding her and singing to her and telling her she was safe, safe, safe.

From that moment on Zenith had adored StarDrifter, treasured him beyond the usual love of a granddaughter for her grandfather.

Now she recalled the image of StarDrifter, his beautiful face full of love, a gentle hand cupping her chin so he could look in her eyes.

"I'll always be there to catch you," he'd said. "I'll always be there for you."

"Always . . ." Zenith whispered, and the image faltered and then faded.

"Very pretty."

She whirled about, furious that anyone should have seen the vision.

Drago was leaning nonchalantly against the doorway that led into her private washroom. His thin face was unreadable, his eyes narrowed, his arms carefully folded across his chest.

A towel was tucked over one arm, and Zenith noticed that Drago's coppery hair was damp and newly combed back into its tail in the nape of his neck.

"Why not use your own chambers to wash?" she snapped.

"I'd been down in the stables," he said, standing up straight and throwing the towel back inside the washroom, "helping Stephain with the gray mare. She foaled tonight. Difficult birth."

"But that doesn't excuse why—"

"I would have used my own chambers, save that Caelum is stamping and striding about the upper-floor corridors, and frankly the last thing I needed tonight was to run into him. So I thought I'd ask you if I could use your washroom. You weren't here, so . . ."

He shrugged, walking over to stand before Zenith. "I heard you come in just as I was finishing up. If you're concerned, I didn't stand and watch you change. I may be many things, sister mine, but I am not a voyeur."

"Yet you saw my memory of StarDrifter."

"I thought I heard his voice—it made me come to the door. Zenith, I like him too . . . remember?"

Zenith was rapidly losing her temper which, truth be told, was mainly a product of her shock. And Drago *did* like StarDrifter. She was unsure about so many things regarding Drago, but his genuine feeling for StarDrifter was not one of them. As a child, Drago had enjoyed his months with StarDrifter almost as much as she had. For some reason

StarDrifter had been able to reach the uncommunicative youth in a way Axis and Azhure could not—or could not be bothered to.

She looked at her brother, and for an instant emotion threatened to choke her. What could he have grown into if he had been given love instead of rejection? Their parents had, if not ignored him, then favored all their other children before him. His punishment for plotting against Caelum had left him with little of his rich Icarii heritage: his coppery hair, still thick but kept pulled back into its tight tail, and his violet eyes, although they had faded with age. Against his vivid and powerful siblings he was just a thin, rather plain man, age and frustrated life marking his face with deep lines.

Drago had done wrong, no-one could deny that, but Zenith often wished their mother could have found some other way to punish him that would not have resulted in the destruction of so much potential, the annihilation of so many dreams.

She caught herself before Drago thought to ask why she took so long to respond.

"Well, if you don't want to run into Caelum—and he *is* in a fearful temper—then you can use my bed for the night."

Drago arched an inquiring eyebrow.

Briefly Zenith told him what she and Caelum had learned.

"And so now, good girl that you are, you go to do StarSon's bidding." Drago yawned theatrically. "Well, off you go now. That bed *does* look inviting."

Not trusting her temper, Zenith stalked over to the door. Just as she reached it, Drago said softly, "That was a beautiful memory you conjured up into flesh, Zenith. I wish I had that skill."

Zenith turned and stared at him, not knowing how to take his words. Was he expressing resentment that he no longer had the power to do similar feats, or was he expressing genuine regret?

But Drago gave her no clue. He'd dropped across the bed, his face away from her, and so Zenith left the room, not knowing whether to feel sorry for him, or angry.

By the time Zenith reached the courtyard Drago had slipped far from her mind. Instead she felt the first tingle of excitement. It *was* good to get away, even if only for a day or so.

The guards at the massive gate in Sigholt's walls nodded to her, and then Zenith was through and on the short space of roadway leading to the bridge that guarded Sigholt's entrance.

"A good evening to you, bridge," she called softly as she stepped onto its cobbled carriageway.

"And a good evening to you, Zenith," the bridge said in her deep, melodious voice. No-one ever understood the bridge, what she truly was, or what magic had created her. She simply existed, and her sole purpose in her existence was to guard all entrances into Sigholt. All visitors, whether by foot, hoof or air, were challenged by the bridge as to whether they were true or not.

No-one ever knew what she really meant by that, either.

But the bridge generally kept Sigholt safe—apart from the one notable exception when the infant Drago had tricked her into allowing Gorgrael access to Sigholt—and she was good company for nights when sleep refused to come.

"Do you wish to pass an hour or so with me, Zenith?" the bridge asked hopefully. Even so fey a creation as the bridge still liked to gossip whenever the opportunity presented itself.

"No, bridge. I am sorry. Tonight I must go to Spiredore. Can you lead me there?"

"Of course. Where are you going?"

"Carlon."

"Ah," the bridge sighed. "I have heard many wondrous tales about Carlon. But wait . . . there. Spiredore awaits you."

Zenith looked across the bridge. Normally it led to the roadway that ran the length of HoldHard Pass, but now the other side of the bridge connected into a misty blue tunnel at the end of which Zenith could see the stairway of Spiredore.

"I thank you, friend bridge," she said, and stepped across.

If the bridge was unknown magic, then Spiredore was a hundred times the puzzlement and even more the magic. The tower that stood on the opposite shoreline of Grail Lake to Carlon belonged to Azhure, although it was as ancient, some whispered, as Grail Lake itself. Its interior was a maze of seemingly disconnected stairwells and corridors, but if one knew how to use Spiredore's magic, those stairwells and corridors could take you just about anywhere you wished. Azhure had taught all her children—save Drago, of course—how to use the tower, and how particularly to enter it via the bridge at Sigholt.

Now Zenith stepped off the bridge and into the short corridor of blue mist that led to the interior of Spiredore. As powerful and knowledgeable an Enchanter as she was, all Zenith understood of this process was that somehow the bridge had called across the scores of leagues separating her from Spiredore, and the tower itself had reached out and formed this connection.

From the misty corridor Zenith entered Spiredore at one of its myriad balconies. Glancing quickly up and down, she saw a bizarre outcropping of disconnected balconies and stairs—and even some ladders—that lined the circular interior of the tower. None of them appeared to go anywhere.

"Spiredore," she said firmly, "I wish to go to Carlon."

And she walked to the nearest stairwell and stepped down.

Azhure had always impressed on her two winged daughters that they must never fly in Spiredore, as it was so strangely magical they might easily become disoriented and crash into a balcony, or even the floor of the tower. Zenith walked until she felt her calves begin to ache and then, just as she paused to rub them, she saw that around the next curve of the stairs was a flat floor.

Zenith smiled to herself. It was ever so in Spiredore. Just when you thought you could go no farther, Spiredore delivered you to your destination.

Once on the floor Zenith saw a door before her, and through that door . . . through the door was the dawning air about Grail Lake, the harsh cries of the lake birds filling the air as they rose to meet the sun.

"I thank you, Spiredore," she said as she passed through, closing the door gently behind her.

Outside the tower looked plain, even though it imposed with its height. Completely windowless, it climbed some one hundred paces into the crimson sky—the sun ascending almost directly behind it.

Zenith stood motionless for long minutes, drinking in the view of the tower, the lake, the stunning city rising on the far shore.

"How wrong I have been to so secrete myself in Sigholt," she whispered, then sprang into the air with a glad cry, her arms wide as if to embrace the entire world.

Leagh was sitting at her mirror-table, brushing the tangles from her hair and trying to stop yawning.

There was a rush at the window, as if it had been struck by a great gust of air, and then a small pale fist was tapping impatiently at the panes of glass.

"Leagh!" a muffled voice called, "Leagh! Let me in!"

Leagh sat and stared for long minutes, unable to believe what she saw, before she finally roused herself enough to walk over and open the windows.

Zenith almost fell through, enveloping her friend in a great hug.

"Leagh! Leagh! You and Askam are to come to Sigholt—can you believe it?"

Leagh just stared at her.

"And Zared is to be there, too! Come, sleepy-eyes, what shall you wear?"

Zenith did not think it wrong to give Leagh a day of hope and excitement. And it *was* true. After at least two years, Leagh would finally see Zared again.

5

Speaking Treason

Zared sat on his chair on the slightly raised dais in his reception gallery, trying to hold his temper. Generally he enjoyed holding open court, but this Thursday afternoon had brought such evil news he knew there would be little delight left in the day.

Ranged before him were six men, four peasants from his southern border with the West, and—for the gods' sakes—Jannymire Goldman, the Master of the Carlonese Guilds himself, and one of his merchant cronies, Bransom Heavorand. The tidings they had brought would sour anyone's day, Zared thought, let alone mine.

"A third . . . a third!" he muttered yet again. Obviously the guilds, as the merchants, would be crippled by the tax, but these peasants . . . gods! They'd had a third of their year's grain confiscated!

"Gustus!" Zared called, and his captain of the guard stepped forward. "See that these peasants receive recompense from my treasury for their losses."

Gustus nodded, and moved off. The peasants effused thanks to their Prince, then scurried after the captain.

Zared eyed Goldman thoughtfully. As Master of the Carlonese Guilds, Goldman was one of the most powerful non-noble men in Tencendor. He controlled not only great wealth, but was the voice of the traders, craftsmen and businessmen of Carlon and, by default, most of Tencendor. Why come north himself? And why complain to *Zared*? Surely his complaints would be more effective directed at Caelum?

"Askam will grow rich at your expense, good sirs," Zared remarked.

"As yours," murmured Heavorand.

Yes, as mine, Zared thought, his dark face remaining carefully neutral. Shall I now risk sending my goods to the southern markets via the Andeis Sea? But even pirates would not risk those treacherous waters, and Zared knew he'd lose considerably more than a third of his goods if they went south via the Andeis. Askam had him trapped. He had no choice but to send his goods via road, where they would be snaggled in the web of crossroad taxation posts, while his river transports would not escape the castle of Kastaleon, which sat with its brood of archers on the great central bend of the Nordra like a rabid spider itching to spit its venom at tax evaders.

Gods, what was Askam doing to the people of his own province if he could inflict this hardship on the North?

"It is strange to see you so far north," Zared said to Goldman. "And at *my* house."

Goldman shrugged expressively. "It is a long story, my Prince, and one not suited to this reception gallery." He looked meaningfully at Zared.

Zared hesitated slightly before he spoke. "My dinner table is ever lacking in long stories, gentlemen. May I perhaps invite you to dine with me this evening?"

Goldman bowed. "I thank you, Sir Prince. Heavorand and I will be pleased to accept your—"

The twin doors at the end of the gallery burst open and two men strode through, Gustus at their heels.

Zared's mouth sagged, then he snapped it shut, keeping his seat only with an extraordinary effort as Herme, Earl of Avonsdale, and Theod, Duke of Aldeni, stopped three paces away from the dais, saluting and bowing.

Goldman and Heavorand, who had quickly stepped aside

for the noblemen, shared a glance that was both surprised and knowing.

"Herme? Theod? What brings you here in such haste? I had no warning that you—"

"Forgive us, Zared, but this news cannot wait," Herme said. More formality should have been employed, but Herme had something to say, and he wished to waste no time. Besides, Zared was an old friend and one-time family member; Isabeau had been Herme's sister.

To one side Theod fidgeted. He, too, was a close friend of Zared's, and his higher ranking than Herme should have seen him speak first. But Herme was older and had the longer acquaintance with Zared.

"Sir?" Gustus put in to one side, but no-one listened to him.

"If it's about Askam's new taxes, then I have already heard it," Zared said, gesturing toward Goldman and Heavorand.

Herme and Theod glanced at them, then looked back at Zared.

"My friend," Herme said, "matters have come to a head. We cannot—"

"Sir?" Gustus said again, but was again ignored.

"—endure under such taxation! Belial must be turning over in his grave! I suggest, and Theod agrees with me, that we must take this matter to Caelum instantly."

"Sir!" Gustus all but shouted.

"Gustus, what is it?" Zared said shortly. Never had he had open court like this! Were half the merchants and nobles of the West en route to complain to him?"

"Sir," Gustus said, "one of the Lake Guard has this minute landed with a summons from StarSon Caelum."

Every eye in the reception gallery was riveted on the captain of the guard.

"A summons?" Zared asked quietly.

"Sir Prince, StarSon Caelum summons the heads of the Five to Council, to be held at Sigholt three weeks hence."

Zared stared at him, then shifted his gaze back to Herme

and Theod. "I seem to be holding a dinner party this evening. Would you two gentlemen care to join me?"

Goldman placed his fork and knife across his plate, and decided it was time to direct the conversation to more important matters. So far they'd discussed everything from the weave of Corolean silk to the exceptional salinity of the Widowmaker Sea, and Goldman was tired of the niceties. He smiled at the young, impish Duke Theod across the table. Theod was a rascal, but good-hearted, and once he'd grown five or six more years, and survived a tragedy or two, he would become as fine a Duke as his grandfather, Roland, whom Goldman remembered well from his youth.

"You must have ridden hard to reach Severin from Aldeni, Duke Theod, as must," Goldman glanced at Herme, "your companion . . . who had to come yet farther."

"Herme and I were both at my home estates, Goldman. We share a common interest in the management of the Western Ranges."

Goldman nodded to himself; Theod's home estates were close to his northern border with Zared. No wonder they'd managed to get here so quickly. "And no doubt you were both as horrified as Heavorand and myself to hear of Askam's new taxes."

"No doubt," Herme said carefully. He was not quite sure of Goldman, nor of the motives which saw him at Zared's court.

"Enough," Zared said, throwing his napkin on the table and leaning back in his chair. "Goldman, you came north to say something. Say it."

"Sir Prince, as you know, Prince Askam's taxation measures will place an unfair burden on many Tencendorians, rich as well as poor, traders as well as peasants."

Goldman paused and looked about the room, pretending to gather his thoughts.

"Yet if Askam's taxation measures affect poor and wealthy, peasant and noble alike," he continued, "these taxes *do* differentiate between *types* of people."

The entire table stilled. Heavorand, who knew what was coming, looked hard at the napkin in his lap. But the other three men's eyes were riveted on Goldman's face.

"Continue, good Master Goldman," Zared said.

"Sir Prince, Askam's measures affect those people living in the West and North, not those living in the rest of Tencendor."

"And your point is . . .?"

Goldman took a deep breath. "Sir Prince, the Icarii and Avar do not feel the strain of Askam's petty taxation, yet the Acharites—"

"Be careful with your phraseology," Zared said quietly.

"—yet the human population of the West and the North, good Prince, are direly affected by it. Sir Prince, there are many among the Achar—ah, the western and northern populations of Tencendor—who stoutly believe that Askam's taxations are unfair in that they discriminate against one race out of three."

"The Ravensbundmen are affected by it as well," Herme put in carefully.

"Sir Duke, the Ravensbund only trade with the people of the North. They care not if Askam starts demanding a life per cargo of goods transported through the West."

Zared steepled his fingers before his face and pretended an interest in them. "And so your request is . . .?"

"That you raise the issue with StarSon Caelum at the Council of Five, Sir Prince. StarSon is the only one with the authority to rebuke Askam. To force him to rescind the tax."

That had not been the original request that Goldman and Heavorand had come north with. Their plans had been hastily revised with the news of the Council of Five. But they were not dismayed. Far from it. StarSon Caelum had played right into their hands.

"The tax is the very reason Caelum has called the Council, and Caelum is a reasonable man," Zared said. "I am sure he will listen to what I have to say. So your lengthy trip north was needless, Goldman. I have ever intended to raise this issue."

"Zared," Herme began, "I will not rest until I know that Caelum has clearly understood what hardship this tax will impose—"

"Do you doubt my ability to state the case, Herme?"

"Not at all, my friend. But I think it important that Caelum listens to someone from Askam's own province, as well as your objections. If only you speak against it, well . . ."

All knew what he meant. The history of conflict between Askam and Zared was well known.

Zared opened his mouth to speak, but was forestalled by Goldman.

"Sir Prince, Earl Herme speaks wisely. Caelum needs to hear from the peoples of the West, as much as from you. I suggest that Heavorand and myself will be as suitable witnesses as the Duke and Earl."

"Are you saying that I should take you *all* with me to Sigholt?"

Zared's four guests looked at him steadily.

"Ah!" he said, giving in. "Very well. Your support will be useful."

"There is one other associated issue, Sir Prince." Goldman's voice was tense, and Zared looked at him sharply.

"Out with it, then." He waved his servants forward to clean away the plates.

Goldman waited until the men had gone. "Sir Prince, many among the human race of Tencendor, the *Acharites,* my Lord Zared, for I am not afraid to use the term, feel that Askam's taxes are not only unfair, but illegal."

"And why is that, Goldman?"

"The talk of the taverns and the streets of Carlon argues that Askam is not the legal overlord of the West, Sir Prince."

Goldman paused, gathered his courage and spoke his treason. "Most Acharites believe that you are."

Silence.

Zared's eyes regarded Goldman closely over his fingers. "Yes?"

"Sir Prince, when Axis created the nation of Tencendor he created Belial as Prince of the West. Few were loath to speak out against that. Belial was a loved man, and remains a loved memory. But his elevation essentially replaced the office of King of Achar. Axis destroyed the throne of Achar after he defeated his brother, Borneheld. Zared, *you* are the only legitimate heir to the throne of Achar."

Herme leaned back in his chair. True, true and true, good Goldman, he thought. I could not have put it better myself. Speak on, man.

Goldman did indeed hurry on. "Sir Prince, you may have been disinherited of a crown, but more importantly, the Acharites have been disinherited of their throne and their nationhood."

Zared spoke again, his voice now noticeably tight. "Continue."

"Have not the Icarii, the Avar and the Ravensbund their leaders, their titular heads? Yet the Acharites have lost their monarchy and, in so losing, their pride. Sir Prince, why is it that the Icarii, Avar and Ravensbund retained or gained kings when the Acharites lost theirs?"

"Perhaps," Herme put in carefully, for this was something Zared could not say without proving disloyal to at least one of his brothers, "it is because Borneheld, as King of Achar, was far too closely allied with the Seneschal and pursued a policy of hatred and war toward the Avar and Icarii. Axis rightly wanted to ensure that would never happen again."

Goldman looked directly at Zared. "Sir Prince, I am not asking you to resurrect the beliefs of the Seneschal, only your people's pride and nationhood. Prince Zared," his voice slowed and he stressed every word, "your people want you back. They want their King. With few exceptions, western Tencendor would rise up to back your claim."

Goldman glanced at Herme and Theod, hoping he had not read them incorrectly. "True, Sir Duke? Sir Earl?"

"We would not speak against it," Theod said slowly.

Herme hesitated, then said curtly, "No king of Achar ever treated us as vilely as Askam does."

"You all mouth treason!" Zared said, and pushed his chair back as if he intended to stand. "I do not intend to—"

"Treason?" Heavorand repeated. "Is it treason to speak of that which is our wish and your *inheritance*?"

Zared had stilled, his face expressionless.

"They are right, Zared," Theod added. "*Right!* Achar needs its King back! Look how Askam is tearing the heart and soul out of the West!"

"May I remind you, Theod," Zared said very carefully, "that as a Duke of the West, you are under Askam's direct overlordship?"

"As am I," Herme said, "and yet I find myself agreeing with both Theod and these two good merchants here."

"Re-creating the position of King of Achar would tear Tencendor apart," Zared observed, but his tone was milder, and his eyes thoughtful.

"It is going to tear apart anyway," Goldman said very quietly. "The tensions between Acharite and the other races would see war within a generation. You understand the Acharite perception of injustice, Zared. You share it. Sir Prince, you *are* rightful heir to the throne of Achar. Take it. Take it and direct some of this tension rather than letting it swell out of control. Take it . . . sire."

When Goldman and Heavorand retired, Zared waved at Herme and Theod to remain.

He sat motionless, silent, for a long time before he finally spoke.

"My friends, I do not know what to think. My parents raised me to believe in Tencendor, in Axis' and then Caelum's right to rule over all races. They raised me to believe that the Achar nation, and its monarchy, was dead."

"Zared," Herme said. "Re-establishing the monarchy of Achar is not treason. As with FreeFall, Isfrael and Sa'Domai, an Acharite king would still owe homage and fealty to the Throne of the Stars. Any discussion of reclaiming the throne of Achar is *not* mouthing treason against Caelum, only discussing what many—nay, most—people in the West and North want."

Zared was silent, remembering how he had looked at the circlet on Priam's brow and wondered how well it—and the throne—would fit him.

"Where do your loyalties lie, Herme? Theod?" he eventually asked. "With whom?"

"With StarSon Caelum," Herme said unhesitatingly. "First."

"And then with you," Theod finished. "Goldman has said much of what was in our hearts as well. Zared, if both the Master of the Guilds in Carlon, as well as two of the West's most powerful nobles, have come to your doorstep with the same speeches on their lips and hopes in their hearts, how can you refuse to consider their words?"

"This whole issue has been prompted by Askam's taxes," Zared said. "What happens if Caelum forces him to rescind them? What then?"

"No!" Theod said. "These taxes are but the final straw. Zared, the 'issue' is fed by the fact that for decades resentment has grown among the Acharites at the way they have been treated. Yes, the SunSoar order is great and good, but it doesn't change the fact that the Acharites have been denuded of their monarch and their nationhood. Man, listen to me! In you they can see the legitimate heir, and in the North they can see what prosperity awaits them under your rule!"

"This problem is not going to go away, Zared," Herme said. "Not so long as Askam—or a Prince of the West—remains."

"I will think on what you have said this evening," Zared said, then raised his eyes from the fork he'd been fidgeting with. "There is something else I think should be considered."

"Yes?" Herme asked.

"How will Askam react at this Council? We all know how bad his debts are, we know he *needs* the monies the taxes will raise."

"And we all know how he hates you . . . and your success," Theod said. "Look how he has striven to frustrate your heart these past years."

Zared looked at him sharply, then chose to ignore the last remark. He did not like to think of what implications this evening's conversation had for himself and Leagh, nor even for the peace of Tencendor itself. *How would Caelum react?* "My friends, I think it best to be prepared for whatever this Council might bring."

Zared paused, then spoke his own treason. "I have given orders to move the bulk of my troops out of Severin to within several leagues of Jervois Landing. If I might suggest . . ."

Herme grinned. "Where would you like *our* troops moved?"

6

The SunSoars at Home

Leagh sat with Zenith, watching RiverStar preen before her mirror. Leagh wished she were in any chamber but this one—even Drago must surely be a less disagreeable companion than Zenith's elder sister! She shifted herself into a more comfortable position in her chair, and let her mind wander from the sisters' conversation.

She had been in Sigholt over two weeks. Waiting. Waiting for the other heads of the Five Families to arrive. Waiting for

Caelum to put her out of her misery and tell her his decision regarding her marriage. Waiting for Zared.

Once Askam had sent his escort north via riverboat and horse, Zenith had led Leagh, Askam and their two body servants into Spiredore. Leagh had never been in the tower previously, and its magic—as also the evidence of Zenith's power—had almost overwhelmed her. Askam had remained stoutly silent, but Leagh had noticed that even he had paled when, emerging at the top of one of the bizarre stairwells, they had beheld Sigholt at the end of an enchanted corridor of blue mist.

On her first day in Sigholt, Leagh had been consumed with excitement. What would Caelum say? Where was Zared? But apparently it was only she and Askam granted such an unconventional (and speedy) conveyance to Sigholt; everyone else called to the Council had to arrive by more mundane means. Zared was still far distant. And Caelum proved as great a disappointment. At first Leagh had managed to convince herself that Caelum had asked her to Sigholt for good news—surely he would have preferred to have sent bad via a courier? But Caelum remained steadfastly silent at her repeated pleas for his word. He would wait until Zared was here. Then he would inform them of his decision.

Bad news, then. Leagh was miserably sure of it.

So she spent her days either wandering the shores of the lake by herself, or talking with Zenith. Askam was almost as unreachable as Caelum; her brother spent many hours each day either closeted with Caelum, or at weapon practice with Sigholt's master-of-arms.

But surely her waiting was almost over. Over the past two days FreeFall SunSoar, Talon of the Icarii, Prince Yllgaine of Nor and the Ravensbund Chief Sa'Domai had all arrived. Sigholt awaited only Isfrael (if he chose to appear) and Zared—how far could he be?

Zared. How could she live life without him?

Leagh could not answer that question, and preferred not to

think on it, thus here she was this afternoon, sitting with Zenith, listening to RiverStar prattle on about love.

RiverStar tilted her lovely head before her looking glass, admiring the curve of her throat. Her fingers lingered at the base of throat and breast, remembering the touch of her lover. She smiled and shifted her gaze in the glass, first looking at Leagh, sitting still and disconsolate, and then her sister.

"Poor Leagh is in no position to discuss the arts of love, Zenith," she said. "But tell me, sister, have you taken a lover yet, or do you yet cling to your chastity?"

"I have not yet met the man of my heart, sister," Zenith said, sitting by a small fire.

RiverStar's eyes hardened at the implied criticism in Zenith's tone. Zenith was truly a prude if she did not while away the time at Sigholt with a lover. Stars! But what else was there to do in Sigholt? And what else was the body for but to be used? All Zenith ever did was murmur incoherent words about the *right* lover every time some birdman dared touch her flesh or invite her into his bed.

RiverStar twisted about on her stool and stared at her younger sister. Zenith had all of their mother's dark good looks, and more. So where had she inherited the reluctance to put them to enjoyable use?

"All this yearning for your imaginary lover will see you in your grave before you are bedded, Zenith. Let *me* find you a lover." RiverStar paused. "And you, too, Leagh. Zared is a lean man, and reaching mortal middle age. No doubt he will tire early in bed. Let me find you an Icarii lover."

Embarrassed, Leagh dropped her eyes, and Zenith glanced at her before responding to RiverStar's taunt. "Spare your energies, sister, and find one for yourself."

RiverStar chuckled deep in her throat. "I *have* found me a lover. The best yet. He kept me awake far into last night and exhausted me all over again at first light. There is none that can match him."

Zenith was not very interested. RiverStar claimed every month that she had found a better lover than the last. Besides, this conversation could hardly be doing Leagh any good. Before she could say anything to redirect RiverStar's mind, her sister continued.

"I think I shall wed him," she said, and smiled in satisfaction as she watched Zenith's surprise.

"Marry him? Is he an Enchanter? What is his name?"

RiverStar toyed with a curl of her hair and tried to look mysterious. "Well . . . he is an Enchanter of sorts, and he has unimaginable power. Can you guess his name?"

Zenith frowned and shook her head. "RiverStar, come on, tell me. Are you serious about taking a husband?" She couldn't imagine RiverStar making anything but a very bad wife. What vows of fidelity she managed to mouth at the marriage would undoubtedly be broken within weeks.

"No, you are wrong, Zenith. I could be faithful to this man for an eternity. He is . . ." she shivered theatrically, and ran one hand down her thigh, " . . . more than enough to keep me satisfied. Dangerous. Darkly esoteric. Insatiable." She almost growled the last word, and ran her tongue about her lips.

Gods, thought Leagh. He must have the stamina of an ox and a wall of steel about his heart to survive RiverStar! Leagh hoped RiverStar did not think to use her Enchanter powers to read her mind—the images jumbling about there were not very complimentary to RiverStar.

"Surely such a lover could only be a SunSoar," Zenith observed, more than a little suspicious. "Who?"

Zenith was sure RiverStar was making this up. SunSoars were fated to truly love only another SunSoar, cursed to desire only their own blood. RiverStar could not be this satisfied with anyone *but* a SunSoar male—and who was available for them in Sigholt? No-one but first blood, their brothers and their father, and first blood was Forbidden.

She paused with her mouth half-open. No, not quite. There was always—

"Perhaps, perhaps not," RiverStar said, and Zenith stood up in frustration, determined to find another topic of conversation. Did RiverStar think of nothing but the pleasures of a bedding?

"What else is there to think of in this foggy palace?" RiverStar asked, looking out the window to where the magical blue mists shrouded Sigholt.

"There are mysteries to contemplate," Zenith said quietly, moving over to the window. "Dreams to examine." Her voice had faded, and she was lost in her own thoughts now, not listening to RiverStar.

"Mysteries, bah!" RiverStar waved her hand impatiently. "The only mystery I wish to explore exists in the junction of—"

"In you the Icarii inclination toward obscenity has flowered into its full, foul-smelling ripeness, RiverStar," a man's voice said from the doorway.

"Drago," RiverStar said, and leaned back in her chair, smoothing her filmy gown over her body. "My dear, sweet twin brother, what bitterness you display! Ever since our mother reversed your blood order and disinherited you from your Icarii powers you have been absolutely incapable of bedding anyone save the girls who sweep the kitchens. Think, Zenith, of all the Icarii female Enchanters he must covet," she ran her hand over a breast, "and yet whom he cannot hope to bed in the face of their laughter and rejection."

"RiverStar—" Zenith began.

"Would you *beg* to have me, Drago?" RiverStar pinched out her nipple. "Would you roll on the floor before me and *beg*?"

"Whore," Drago said flatly, and stepped into the room. He turned as if to speak to Leagh, sitting in such embarrassed silence she wished all the SunSoar siblings would just go and find somewhere else to quarrel, but RiverStar had not yet finished with her brother.

"Wouldn't he have made a useless Enchanter, Zenith?" she said, pretending a thoughtful expression. "But perhaps he would have expended his power using the Star Dance to burn up beetles on the parapets."

Zenith opened her mouth, and then closed it again. What could she do now that she hadn't tried previously? The gulf between RiverStar and Drago had grown over the past ten years as Drago had felt the first stirrings of age within his human body. RiverStar—shallow creature that she was—could not help but taunt his mortality. Drago could do nothing but meet her taunts with either the pretence of indifferent silence or the uselessness of sarcasm. That they had once shared a womb meant nothing to them now.

She saw Drago turn his gaze from Leagh to her, and watched his own eyes harden as he saw the sympathy in hers. Drago did not want anyone fighting his wars for him.

"But there is SunSoar blood in you yet," RiverStar murmured, and her hand slid down her belly, her fingers daring, "and perhaps it craves SunSoar blood. Methinks you do not find *that* among your kitchen maids."

Drago took a great breath, held it, and turned his back on RiverStar. "Leagh, Caelum would like you to—"

"Aha!" RiverStar laughed. "Our splendid leader has found a purpose for this all but useless man who stands before us. A messenger boy. Not an occupation imbued with pride, Drago, but perhaps it gives you some small purpose in life."

Her barb finally found its mark. Drago whipped round to face his sister. "You're nothing but a cold bitch, RiverStar," he said with icy flatness. "You'd be happy enough left with a hound to couple with."

He, in his turn, had stung deeply.

"You pathetic little *human* man!" RiverStar hissed, her

face twisted with loathing. "I shall laugh over your grave! I will enjoy my lover on the sods above your moldering flesh! I will—"

"That is *enough*," Zenith said sharply. "Drago, what is it?"

Drago wrenched his eyes away from RiverStar, two red spots of anger in his cheeks, and half bowed to Leagh. To Zenith's amazement his voice came out soft, almost gentle, and she wondered at the effort it must have cost him.

"Princess Leagh, I was walking up the main staircase when my brother Caelum called me to find you. He wishes your presence in the courtyard. The word from the sentries is that Zared and his escort ride toward the bridge."

And then he stepped forward, and with the grace of a courtier offered a shocked and pale Leagh his arm and support.

7

Disturbing Arrivals

Leagh could not control the skidding of her heart, nor the sudden cramp in her chest that made each breath a painful effort. Calm down! she berated herself, but it did not help. Zared was only moments away, and it had been so long since she'd seen him.

Drago did not say a word as he led her down the corridors and stairwells of Sigholt. Leagh leaned on him without embarrassment—without him, she thought, she could not walk—and Drago made no complaint.

It was late afternoon, and the Keep threw a deep shadow over the courtyard. Leagh stumbled slightly as she and Drago walked outside, and he tightened his arm and drew her in a little closer.

"Hope," she thought she heard him say, but when she

glanced at his face it was expressionless, his eyes elsewhere, and so she thought she had imagined it.

There were several ranks of soldiers lined up in the courtyard, their hands ready on the hilts of their swords to provide a welcoming salute. Caelum, dressed all in black, walked forward to greet her.

Askam was two or three steps behind.

Leagh saw Caelum exchange a hard glance with Drago, and she felt Drago stiffen at her side, but she had no time for further observation of the brothers' enmity.

"Zared?" she asked Caelum, and was stunned to hear her voice come out cool. Calm, even.

"A minute away," Caelum said. "No more."

And, indeed, at that moment Leagh heard the bridge call out to Zared, welcoming him. The bridge did not challenge him, for Zared had been born within Sigholt's walls, and she knew him well.

Almost before the bridge had finished her greeting there came the clatter of many hooves on the bridge, and Leagh had a moment of panic.

Gods, what was she wearing? A pale blue linen gown that could be called serviceable, nothing more. And her hair! Leagh's free hand patted at her head, remembering with horror that this morning she'd left her hair in nothing but a single thick braid down her back.

"Leagh," Zenith's soft voice said behind her, "you look lovely. Do not fret."

I should be greeting Zared in the audience chamber of our palace in Carlon, Leagh thought, resplendent in satins and jewels, not here in this dairymaid's gown—and she had no more time for thought, for at that moment Zared rode into the courtyard.

She was the first thing he saw. Absolutely stunned, Zared pulled his horse to such a sudden, skittery halt that Herme and Theod, who rode directly behind him, had to rein their own mounts sharply to one side to avoid him.

"Leagh?" he whispered.

At that precise moment the ranked soldiers presented their swords and standards, and a trio of trumpeters high in Sigholt's walls blew out a clarion of welcome.

In the sudden presentation of arms, and the flags and banners fluttering about, Zared lost sight of Leagh.

Frustrated, he leaped from his horse, ducked under its neck . . . and came face to face with an impassive StarSon Caelum.

"Prince Zared, I welcome you to Sigholt. May its doors always swing wide to greet you, and its bridge always sing you a greeting."

Damn these polite receptions! Zared cursed. He tried to see past Caelum, but he only saw Askam farther back in the gloom, and the first of the ranks of stony-faced soldiers.

"I thank you, StarSon," he replied evenly. "I, as must my other companions among the Five, find myself somewhat surprised to be so suddenly called to Council."

"You know why you are here," Caelum said, his voice toneless, and Zared wondered how long Askam had been in Sigholt, and what he'd managed to whisper into Caelum's ear. While not as close as their fathers had been, Caelum and Askam were nevertheless friends. "This disunity between you and Askam must finally be put to rest."

Askam had whispered nothing complimentary, Zared thought. "Then I welcome the summons, StarSon. I wish for nothing more than peace and harmony within Tencendor."

Caelum's eyes had slipped behind Zared. "Herme? Theod? Why do you travel with Zared?"

"We met the Prince of the North coming through the lower Urqhart Hills," Herme said easily, "and chose to ride the final leagues with him. Theod and myself thought to have our voices heard at this Council, as the weighty matter before it affects all those living in the West. As in the North."

Far back in the column of Zared's escort, Goldman and

Heavorand pulled their hoods a little closer over their faces. No doubt Caelum's enchanted eyesight could spot them if he chose, but they did not want Askam to see them. Their business was best conducted without their Prince knowing they were at Sigholt.

"Who gave you permission to attend this Council?" Askam stepped forward to Caelum's shoulder. "Theod? You should be at home, attending your seasonal county courts. Herme? *You* should know better than to present your uninvited self at Sigholt!"

Theod was lost for words, but Herme replied smoothly. "I did not realize our freedom of movement—our *choice* of movement—was also subject to your whim, Sir Prince."

"Enough!" Caelum snapped. Truly, Theod and Herme should have known better than to ride in with Zared as if *he* were their prince, not Askam! But Herme had also made a telling point, and Caelum did not regret the chance to hear from someone other than Askam how the West was responding to the taxes.

"You may stay, Sir Duke and Sir Earl," he said, his tone more even now. "I shall organize an afternoon to speak with you, but I also reserve the right to invite you or bar you from Council as I please."

He turned slightly and called to his steward. "Runton? Prepare chambers suitable for the Duke and Earl. Zared, perhaps you might like to dine with me tonight?"

Zared ignored his invitation. "Caelum," he said softly. "What is Leagh doing here?"

Caelum stared at him a moment, then waved Leagh forward.

She hesitated, and the man at her side—Zared noticed with some surprise who it was—spoke softly in her ear. Leagh gave the smallest of nods, and then walked forward calmly to stand at Caelum's side.

"Zared," she said simply, her eyes fixed on his.

Zared opened his mouth, found he could say nothing, and so stepped forward, took her hand, and kissed her palm.

"I think we will resolve many things in Council," Caelum said softly. "Not only the issue of taxes."

The evening meal, held with due pomp in the Great Hall of Sigholt, was the longest Zared had ever endured in his life. All the heads of the Five were there, as were their captains, their lieutenants, Caelum's brother and sisters, DareWing FullHeart and the other Crest-Leaders of the Strike Force, the mayor and entire council of Lakesview, their wives, as well as WingRidge CurlClaw, SpikeFeather TrueSong and fifteen assorted Enchanters.

Leagh . . . Leagh was seated not only *across* the broad banquet table, but *seven places down!* Zared had not the chance to speak one word to her, let alone touch her, hold her.

If the decision on their marriage was to be discussed—and then determined—in Council, then Zared knew what that decision would be. Damn Caelum—and every other member of the Council—to everlasting crippling arthritis for what they were going to do to him and Leagh! Did they not bed as they chose? Had not every one of them picked their own mate . . . save Caelum, of course, who yet lingered unmarried.

Zared went through the meal in a state resembling an angry fugue, replying only in monosyllables when he was addressed, pushing his meat about his plate until it went cold and congealed in its gravy, then tapping his fingers irritably against the linen-clothed table until Caelum finally rose and departed.

As the rest of the company scraped back chairs and got to their feet, Zared managed to catch Leagh's eye, but no more. Askam placed a tight hand about her elbow and whisked her away before Zared could slip about the table to speak to her.

He stood, fuming with silent rage, as Herme paused behind him.

"Think how marriage to her would cement your claim to

the throne, my prince," he whispered. "Askam will never sire an heir. *She* would bring Achar to your marriage bed."

Zared turned to stare at Herme, a muscle working in his cheek. "I want her as my wife because I love her!" he finally seethed. "Not for her inheritance!"

He pushed past the Earl of Avonsdale and strode away, but all he could think about on the long walk back to his chambers was whether or not, on that night atop Sigholt five years ago, his unspeaking mind had only seen Leagh standing before him . . . or the rich acres of the West as well.

Zenith was preparing for sleep when the gentle knock came at her door. Surprised, not knowing who could wish to speak with her this late, she slipped a wrap over her shoulders and opened the door.

Zared stood there, his face lined and tired, his eyes dark with unreadable emotion. "Zenith, you and I have always understood each other. Please, bring Leagh to me."

Zenith stared at him, her mind in turmoil. By the gods, how she felt for both of them! Surely they deserved at least a private word—but, if left in private, how far might that "word" go? Their love was fraught with so much political tension, it carried such enormous consequences, that to even let them see each other . . .

Should she tell him that Caelum would not let the marriage take place? That there was no hope? No, there was no need. She could see by the pain in Zared's eyes that he already understood.

"Zenith," he said, reaching out and placing a hand on her arm. "Do this for me, and do it for Leagh."

Zenith hesitated only a heartbeat longer, then she gave a curt nod. "Come with me."

The corridors were darkened, only a few subdued torches lit to cast pitiful pools of light in isolated corners. Shadows flickered and lifted, seeming to envelop them in waves and then retreat, as if they had moved too far from the total darkness for their own comfort. Zenith led Zared to a room on the floor above his, at the end of the corridor.

He stopped, surprised. "This was my mother's chamber!"

"And so here came Magariz to Rivkah, before they confessed their love to the world. Now, Zared, *listen* to me. I will wait outside. Keeping watch—but not only for those who might tread this way. I can also sense you, and what you do . . . do you understand?"

Zared nodded, his expression bitter.

"If you try to bed with her," Zenith continued, her tone now as hard as Zared's eyes, "I will know and I will stop you. You may speak with her, you may hold her, but you will not have the chance to win the West via the trickery of an illegitimate child!"

"Caelum has an utterly loyal sister in you!" Zared hissed, furious that Zenith would intrude upon them with her power.

"I am utterly loyal to Tencendor," Zenith said quietly, holding Zared's stare. "Treat Leagh with the respect that I have for the peace of our land."

"Let me in, damn you!"

And Zenith opened the door.

The chamber was even darker than the corridor, for Leagh had apparently shuttered her windows tightly closed. Zared stood, trying to get his bearings, wondering if Leagh had heard his whispered conversation with Zenith.

Apparently not, for the room was quiet save for the soft sound of gentle breathing, and Zared moved carefully toward the source.

His hip banged into the corner of a table, and Zared halted, his eyes stinging with the pain, his ears straining to hear if Leagh had woken.

No, she still breathed deep in sleep across the room, and Zared resumed his movement, now with a slight limp. He'd never wished Enchanter powers for himself until this moment. By all the stars above, he wished he could see where he was going!

But even as he thought that, a pale bed cover resolved itself from the darkness, and under it Zared could see the still form of Leagh.

He moved closer—how could he best wake her without startling her into a loud cry? It would hardly do his cause good to have Caelum—or Askam, gods forbid!—burst in on them.

But even as he hesitatingly reached down a hand, Leagh sighed, turned her head, and opened her eyes.

"Am I dreaming," she whispered, "or do you truly stand before me, Zared?"

"Oh, gods, Leagh!" he cried softly, brokenly, and he sat down on the bed and gathered her into his arms.

Outside, Zenith tensed, but she gradually relaxed, tears coming to her eyes. What *would* it be like to love like this? To be loved this deeply? She withdrew her presence a little from the chamber to give them more privacy, although she still maintained watch. They could spend the hours before dawn together, but then she would interrupt, and take Zared from Leagh.

The tears trickled down her cheeks. This was likely to be the only time they would ever have together.

Then, without warning, a sense of doom so profound it left her gasping washed over her.

Zenith groaned and bent almost double, clutching at the wall for support.

What was wrong, what had disturbed her this deeply? Zared and Leagh? No, they were close, but not too close. It was something else. Something . . . something so fundamentally wrong that the very Star Dance seemed to waver before it beat on as strong as ever.

The sensation of imminent doom faded almost as soon as it had washed through her, but it left Zenith with a feeling of such fright that she spent the rest of that night crouched outside Leagh's door, wrapped in enchantment so thick that a spear would have bounced off an arm's distance away before it could have touched her.

Zared, Leagh and Zenith were not the only wakeful ones that night. Caelum also paced the corridors, returning to his own chambers from whatever nocturnal mission he'd set himself to.

He also felt the sudden alteration in the Star Dance, but Caelum was of infinitely more power than Zenith, and he knew that it had been caused by the sudden intrusion of a powerful Enchanter somewhere in Tencendor.

There was someone different about. Who?

Who?

Caelum stood in the center of his chamber, seeking, probing through Tencendor with his power . . . feeling out whoever it was who had so suddenly disturbed the Star Dance.

He twitched, and an expression of utter horror came over his face.

"WolfStar!" he whispered, then he tipped back his head and screamed. "*WolfStar!*"

And then he vanished.

8

Maze Gate

In unconscious imitation of the ancient madness of WolfStar SunSoar, the Ferryman stood wrapped in his ruby cloak at the lip of the Star Gate. Even though the Icarii had reclaimed the Star Gate, few visited there except on ceremonial occasions, and Orr was alone in the circular chamber.

Blue light chased about the dome, and the sound of the universe roared through, demanding, seductive, entreating.

Orr ignored all of it. "There . . . again!" he whispered, and trembled. *"Again!"*

There was a sound beyond that of the Star Dance, beyond that of the interstellar winds of the universe. A whisper, but a whisper of many voices.

Maddened voices. Demanding voices.

Orr shivered. What was it, this ravening pack of voices? Who were they? Why did they cry so?

What did they want?

"And again," he said, his hands tightening about his cloak. "Who are they to disturb the peace of the stars so?"

"They claim to be my judgment, friend Ferryman."

Orr jumped so badly he almost fell into the Star Gate. A hand closed about his arm, steadying him.

Orr turned to see who had surprised him, then squealed in terror and stumbled back several paces. "WolfStar!"

Was anyone safe about the Star Gate with this renegade present?

"Peace, Ferryman," WolfStar said. "I am not the same madman who cast so many children to their deaths."

Orr was not so sure. Could four thousand years abate such madness? WolfStar may have assisted Axis SunSoar defeat Gorgrael, but Orr's fear of him was still strong. He carefully backed away yet farther.

WolfStar ignored him and stepped over to the Star Gate. Its pulsing blue light washed over his face, turning his copper curls almost as violet as his eyes. For several minutes he stood silent, tense, then his shoulders relaxed slightly and he gave Orr a small, humorless smile.

"They call themselves my judgment," he said again, "but they are yet far away. We are safe. They will never find the Star Gate again."

"They?" Orr said. "They? I hear voices. Many voices. And they are angry voices. There is . . ." He searched for the right word. "There is a *pack* of them."

WolfStar's eyes narrowed. "A 'pack,' Ferryman?"

"They hunt," Orr said very quietly, beginning to understand. "They hunt for you." He was silent briefly, turning a sudden thought over in his mind. "They are those you murdered."

WolfStar's mouth twisted slightly and he looked back into the Star Gate. "Yes," he said. "They yearn for my blood. And perhaps I do not blame them. But I am safe. They do not have the power or the skills to find their way back through the Star Gate. They will drift for eternity, calling my name."

He did not seem distressed at the thought of what he'd condemned the children to.

"I have never heard them before." Orr walked closer to the Star Gate, but he still kept a prudent distance from WolfStar.

WolfStar shrugged slightly. "They knew I would die eventually, and that—as all Enchanter-Talons—I would step through the Star Gate for my eternal rest. So they drift on the interstellar winds, looking for me. This is the first time they've drifted this close to the Star Gate."

"But you evaded them before. You stepped back through into this world."

"Yes, I did. When I died, and then stepped through, the children were in a far part of the universe, utterly lost. Before they drifted back my way I found the knowledge in death that returned me to life."

That was only a very mild lie on WolfStar's part. In truth, the power that had allowed him to return had actively sought him out.

Orr accepted WolfStar's words. He had no doubt the Enchanter never wanted to re-encounter the hundreds of children—or his own wife—whom he had hurled to their deaths.

There was a movement in the shadow of one of the archways that circled the chamber, and both WolfStar and Orr turned toward it.

Caelum SunSoar, StarSon of Tencendor, stepped into the

light. "Well, lonely wolf of the night," he said softly, his gaze fixed on WolfStar, "it has been over forty years since you peered into my cradle and then crushed MorningStar's head for the temerity of witnessing. Forty years for you to work your mischief. I know of you, WolfStar. You can accomplish a great deal in forty years."

WolfStar sat down on the low wall of the Star Gate, unperturbed by Caelum's abrupt appearance. His golden wings spread out to either side of his body, and he tilted his head quizzically, looking Caelum up and down. The intervening years have grown a great man, he decided, and power sits him easily.

And yet WolfStar wondered if Caelum had yet learned the power it would take to best *him*. He grinned. He doubted it.

"Well?" Caelum snapped, irritated by WolfStar's demeanor.

"Well, what?"

WolfStar!

All three in the chamber heard it. WolfStar leaped off the wall and across the chamber in a single bound, and Caelum's eyes narrowed. So frightened, WolfStar? Why? Why?

We're coming, we're coming . . . we hunger . . .

"They're lying," WolfStar said, recovering his poise. "Bluffing. They cannot come through."

There was a sound in the chamber. Unusual, but rather like . . . a flock of birds sweeping through the sky.

Caelum locked eyes with Orr momentarily, sharing knowledge, then turned his gaze back to WolfStar. "And how can you be so sure? If you could step back through, then why can't they?"

Orr faded back underneath one of the arches. He wanted nothing to do with the confrontation between these two.

WolfStar stared at Caelum before he answered. "You want answers, StarSon? Then I will give you some. But not here."

"Not here where they can hear you, WolfStar? What is it that you have brought upon Tencendor now, renegade?"

Caelum took a step forward, but WolfStar only smiled at the implied threat. No-one could touch *him*. Except, perhaps . . .

"I have a fancy to see my grandchildren and a fancy to see what you have made of Sigholt," he said, forcing his mind away from what *else* might be accompanying the children.

We're coming, we're coming . . . we hunger . . .

And pray all gods in creation it is only you who shout my name!

"WolfStar! I *demand* answers! Do you think I am going to stand aside while your troubles tear Tencendor apart yet again?"

"Sigholt!" said WolfStar. "I will meet you and yours at Sigholt."

"When?"

"Soon. A day. Wait."

And then he vanished.

Caelum took a deep breath. Stars, what was going on? He peered into the Star Gate, becoming one with the Star Dance briefly, then shook himself and looked at Orr, still secreted in the shadows. "Have you heard these voices before?"

Orr shook his head. "Today was the first time. StarSon, they are not strong, and . . ."

"And?"

"And, perhaps to be expected. WolfStar murdered some two hundred and twelve Enchanters, including StarLaughter and the child she carried. I can well imagine that their souls have drifted four thousand years seeking vengeance. Pray their vengeance is directed only at WolfStar."

"I shall throw the Enchanter through myself if it will appease their need," Caelum said. "I think I will ask WingRidge to mount a guard here. I would not like us to be . . . surprised."

"No need," said the Ferryman. "I shall stand watch."

* * *

WolfStar stood before the gate. The gate to the Maze, not the Star Gate. Its wooden doors were closed—thankfully. WolfStar hoped to be far, far away if ever they opened.

Did anything else follow those voices toward the Star Gate?

His hands drifted over the strange inscription in the stone archway surrounding the gate. It had taken him many years to understand this language. The language of the ancients, or the Enemy, as *their* enemies referred to them.

The Enemy that had crashed through from the universe so many millennia ago, creating the Star Gate.

Leaving behind its deadly cargo.

He silently cursed, and concentrated on the inscription. Yes, there, there and there. StarSon. As it had been for the past forty years. For three thousand years before that the inscription had only mentioned the vague term "Crusader," but a year after the birth of Caelum the Maze had changed its mind and substituted "StarSon" for "Crusader."

Now the symbol for StarSon trumpeted forth, again, and again, leaping out from the gate's inscription.

This time the Maze was certain.

Well might it be. It was the Maze which had taught WolfStar the Prophecy of the Destroyer, and then commanded him to write it down and do all in his power to ensure its eventual realization. After he defeated Gorgrael, Axis had asked WolfStar if the Prophecy was nothing but idiot gabble for his own amusement. Then WolfStar had hedged. He'd said that certain knowledges had come to him beyond the Star Gate that made his return imperative—true enough. However, it was not the Prophecy itself that had persuaded him back through the Star Gate, but rather the Prophecy's true author. The Maze.

The Prophecy had a very clear and direct purpose, and it had nothing at all to do with protecting Tencendor from Gorgrael.

Its *only* purpose had been to breed the champion the Maze needed. The Crusader.

WolfStar had always assumed that the Crusader would be Axis, but the Maze had never named him. Instead it had chosen Axis and Azhure's son Caelum.

WolfStar nodded. Of course. He should have realized that the Crusader would need both Axis' and Azhure's blood.

Then a chill swept through WolfStar. If the Crusader had been born and was now named by the Maze, it meant the hour of need must be nigh.

What else followed those voices toward the Star Gate?

He'd had three thousand years to prepare himself for this moment, and yet WolfStar wished he had three score more three thousand years.

StarSon! StarSon! StarSon! the inscription about the Maze screamed. *Aid me now!*

WolfStar turned very slightly so he could see the row upon row of seated birdmen and women behind him. There were hundreds of them, seated in orderly ranks, slowly swaying from side to side in perfect unison as they regarded the gate with part reverence, part fear, part love.

"Are you true?" WolfStar asked softly.

"True to the StarSon," replied the hundreds of voices.

On each of their chests glowed the golden knot.

9

WolfStar's Explanation

Zared caught up with the Ravensbund Chief, Sa'Domai, on Sigholt's main staircase.

"What's wrong, my friend? Why has Caelum summoned us this early?" Gods, he'd only been back in his private chamber a few minutes before the impassive Lake Guard was banging on his door!

Sa'Domai shrugged, the tiny bells in his braided hair jingling merrily. "I can think of no reason Caelum would pull us from our beds this early, Zared."

"Not for Council, surely?"

His question was effectively answered as RiverStar and Zenith joined them from one of the landings. Neither had a seat on the Council. Zenith, Zared noticed, looked as haggard as he felt.

She shook her head at Zared's inquiring glance, while RiverStar ignored both him and Sa'Domai. RiverStar had her own reasons for feeling tired this morning.

Below them Zared heard FreeFall softly greet Yllgaine of Nor, then both the Icarii Talon and the Nors Prince were behind them. Zared nodded greetings at them, noting that both wore worried expressions.

What was wrong? Invasion? Surely not—who would invade?

Have farflight scouts reported the troops I have mustering west of Jervois Landing? Zared wondered, fear turning his belly to ice. But he quelled the thought quickly, filling his mind with jumbling images of the landscape between Severin and Sigholt. This place was full of Enchanters—and the most powerful of all would be in this hastily convened gathering. Zared needed none of them reading his mind. Even Zenith had indicated last night that she owed her highest loyalty to Tencendor itself.

Where were Herme and Theod? Not called to this meeting, that was apparent. Were they already in chains in the dungeons? Were their confessions already being signed with their blood?

Stop it! Zared carefully arranged his face in a neutral expression. Rivkah had carefully nurtured her son's vivid imagination, now Zared cursed it.

Caelum lived in the spacious apartments that had once belonged to his parents. The central chamber was large, but it now seemed crowded with people moving about, finding themselves seats or stools, murmuring greetings, raising eyebrows in puzzled anxiety.

"By the stars themselves," muttered FreeFall SunSoar behind Zared, clapping a friendly hand on the prince's shoulder. "I hope my nephew has had the foresight to order us breakfast!"

Zared nodded, smiling slightly. He respected FreeFall greatly. The Icarii Talon was an extraordinary birdman, not only because, as most of the SunSoars, he was exceptionally beautiful with his violet eyes and silvery white wings, but because he had once died for Axis, only to have the Star God himself plead for the return of his soul with the GateKeeper in the realms of the Underworld. FreeFall's journey to the gates of death had changed the birdman. He was still fun-loving and quick-witted, but there was a depth of experience and knowledge about him, even an eerie stillness, that touched the souls of all in his presence.

FreeFall found a stool to sit on, folding his wings neatly behind him and his hands patiently in his lap. Yllgaine of Nor, his dark eyes mischievous and his person beautifully clothed and jeweled even this early in the morning, touched Zared on the elbow. "There, a couch . . . if we leap and shove and scream I believe we can get there before Askam drapes himself along it."

Zared bit his cheek to stop himself grinning and followed Yllgaine, decorous and polite despite his words, across the room, and sat down next to him.

He chatted quietly with Yllgaine about inconsequential matters while looking about the chamber. Caelum, who had called everyone so hastily from their beds, had yet to make an appearance. All the Five were here. Askam was lounging against a window, and Sa'Domai had taken a stool next to FreeFall. As well as RiverStar and Zenith (who, Zared was amused to note, had sat as far away from her sister as possible), Caelum had also invited SpikeFeather TrueSong and

WingRidge CurlClaw. Zared did not know either very well. Both, if not aloof, were in some undefinable way unapproachable. Besides, SpikeFeather now spent so much time with Orr the Ferryman it was little wonder that few among the Achari—*human, dammit!*—race knew him well.

The gathering had arranged themselves comfortably and were either quiet, or murmuring softly to their neighbors, when Caelum entered from a door hidden behind a curtain.

Zared's eyes widened a little at the sight of him—Caelum had also spent a sleepless night, it seemed. He was dressed and groomed perfectly, but his eyes were lined and weary.

Something was worrying Caelum badly.

A knot of fear coiled about Zared's belly. Had he seen any guards stationed in the main stairwell or the corridors as he'd come to Caelum's chambers? No, but they could now be lining the walls, and the Strike Force could be wheeling outside the windows, for all he knew.

He caught eyes with Zenith. She shrugged slightly, but indicated with a small gesture of her head not to worry. Caelum had not discovered that Zared had spent so many hours with Leagh last night.

Maybe not that, Zared thought, but what else? Gods! Where was Herme? Theod?

Caelum walked to a spot before the unlit fireplace, so large and extensive that its mantel loomed above his head. "I am sorry to have called you here so early," he said, "but something has happened that—"

The outer door opened and Drago walked through. Two steps inside he stopped, apparently astonished at the gathering in Caelum's apartment.

He ran his eyes slowly about those assembled, his eyes lingering on Zenith and RiverStar, then he looked questioningly at Caelum. "Brother? I do beg your forgiveness for so intruding—"

Zared thought he sounded anything but apologetic. In fact Drago's voice was so carefully neutral, so perfectly modulated, that his words sounded like a speech he'd carefully rehearsed walking up the stairwell.

"—but I was searching for Zenith and one of the guards told me I could find her here."

Drago paused, as if waiting for someone to say something. When no-one did, he carried on. "If I may ask, why so many people crowded into your chamber, Caelum? This all seems a trifle . . . unusual."

Caelum stared at his brother, his eyes blazing, but Drago held his stare easily, his own face carefully set into an expression of inquiry.

Zared thought it extraordinary. Few people could hold Caelum's gaze when he was angry, as he so obviously was now, but Drago apparently had no difficulty.

"Every member of our family who is currently in Sigholt seems to be present," Drago said very softly, "and yet I wonder why it is that you forgot to extend me an invitation as well."

Zared had to repress a small, hard smile. There was the crux of the matter. Drago had heard about this hastily convened meeting, and decided to attend as well. He'd put Caelum in a difficult position. If he asked Drago to leave, Caelum would look petty; if he asked him to stay, it would be clear that Drago had forced him to back down.

"Perhaps as Drago has business with me," Zenith said into the silence, "he could stand with me here until this meeting is over . . . unless your errand is so important you suggest I leave with you now, Drago."

Drago finally dragged his gaze away from his brother. "No, it was but a trivial idea I had for a new board game, Zenith. But, as I find the rest of the family here, I might as well stay."

And he walked over to his sister, stepping around FreeFall and Sa'Domai as he did so.

Caelum looked at Zenith, looked at Drago, then took a deep breath and noticeably bit down his temper. Zared thought it must have taken a particular effort, for Drago had verged on the insolent—but Zared also had to admire Drago's nerve, and sympathize with the man for being so obviously excluded from the life of Sigholt. For a SunSoar, that would indeed be galling treatment.

Despite the terrible deeds of Drago's youth, Zared rather liked the man, and had always got on well with him. Drago was quick-witted and fast on his feet, and often spent a morning at weapon practice with Zared when the Prince stayed at Sigholt; Zared had good cause to rue the occasional lapse of concentration that had seen Drago give him a deserved nick with the sword blade. Watching him slip in beside Zenith, giving her a small smile, Zared decided that Drago was talent and intellect ignored and wasted by most of his family.

Then Caelum spoke again, and Zared turned his eyes back toward him.

"WolfStar has reappeared," Caelum said, and watched the faces of everyone in the room. All wore varying expressions of horror, amazement, and shock. All, Caelum noted with disquiet, save Drago, who managed to combine shock with a certain degree of thoughtfulness, as if weighing up the possibilities for mischief in this development.

Caelum shifted his gaze to Zenith, who was so pale as to be ashen, and held a trembling hand to her throat as if deeply disturbed, and then he looked at RiverStar. She had recovered quickly from her shock, it seemed, for she held his gaze easily, her lips curled in one of her secretive smiles.

The gathering was quickly recovering from its surprise, and now voices rose and fell, asking questions, demanding explanations. WolfStar was a name well known throughout Tencendor, and equally deeply distrusted. The renegade Enchanter-Talon had not only murdered hundreds of Icarii children, but had—to all intents and purposes—allied himself with Gorgrael, enabling the frightful creature to all but destroy Tencendor with his ice and Skraelings.

True, he had fathered Azhure, and she had been instrumental in enabling Axis to eventually defeat Gorgrael, and true, the word was that WolfStar had been fighting on behalf of Axis all the time he had stood at Gorgrael's side.

But that was almost beside the point. WolfStar was an Enchanter of frightening power—enough to see him come back from death through the Star Gate—and who worked only for his own purposes. And even if WolfStar's purposes might ultimately be for Tencendor's well-being, they had an appalling habit of causing the death of tens of thousands in their unraveling.

FreeFall locked eyes with Caelum. "I like this not!" he spat. "What mischief does WolfStar now?"

Caelum shrugged, made as if to say something, and then turned to Zenith as she spoke.

"I felt a horror last night," she said, her eyes huge and round, her cheeks still pasty. "A sense of doom, as if the stars were falling in. Was this WolfStar?"

"Undoubtedly, Zenith." Caelum swept his eyes about the room. "He appeared at the Star Gate, while Orr was there. And what they heard, and then what I heard, needs to be told so that—"

"Has Council been called already? Without my presence?"

An extraordinary figure had appeared in their midst. No-one was sure if he had slipped in through the door unnoticed or had simply used his extensive powers, a combination of both the Earth magic and the Star Dance, to materialize among them.

The man was tall, slender, bare-footed, bare-chested and smooth-backed, his lower body wrapped in a cloth that, although it hung gracefully about him, looked as if it had been woven from bark and twigs. His eyes were emerald green, and fierce, as if he might snap at any moment. His hair was a tangle of wild curls the color of sun-faded wheat, and at his hairline, on each side of his forehead, curled two unmistakable horns.

Isfrael, hope of the Avar, conceived of Axis StarMan and Faraday, when she had been Tree Friend.

Zenith shifted nervously, as did most others in the room.

She was slightly apprehensive of her older brother. Although he was only a few years older than her, and although they had shared a childhood at Sigholt, Isfrael had changed since leaving to live with the Avar in the great forests to the east. Where once had been laughter was now only studied silence. Where once had been shared warmth was now only wary distance. Now Isfrael was all forest, all for the Avar. Alien, as if he had never shared a childhood with the other SunSoar children. There was a darkness, almost violent in its intensity, about the Mage-King. A tension within him, as if he would uncoil and strike at any moment.

His mother, the creature that had once been Faraday, still roamed the Minstrelsea and Avarinheim forests, but was so fey and so shy that Zenith did not know anyone who had seen her over the past thirty years.

"Isfrael," Caelum finally said with commendable calmness. "This is not a Council, but rather a hastily convened gathering to discuss my late-night meeting with WolfStar."

Isfrael's eyebrows rose almost to his horns. "Then I am indeed glad I made the effort to arrive a day or so ahead of schedule. I have long held a wish to meet this demon of myth."

"You should have spoken earlier, Isfrael. Had I known, I would have walked the paths of the Sacred Groves to meet you long before now."

Barely over the shock of Isfrael's sudden appearance, everyone in the room now looked toward the gloomy, shadowy fireplace at Caelum's back; Caelum himself whipped about, and stepped to one side.

There was a movement within the vast interior of the hearth, and then a figure stepped out.

WolfStar. For everyone in the room who had never seen him—and that was most—it was immediately apparent from whom so many of the present-day SunSoars had inherited their copper hair and violet eyes. With his coloring and his golden wings, WolfStar was not only remarkably handsome, but radiated such power that everyone in the room found themselves either stepping back, or inching as far down in their seats as they could.

Zenith cringed against a far wall, her knees threatening to buckle, her heart thumping erratically in her chest, barely able to breathe. The doom that had surrounded her last night had returned thrice-fold the instant WolfStar had spoken, and now Zenith did not know how anyone else in the room could stay so calm, when to her the entire universe seemed in danger of self-destruction.

A hand grasped her arm and prevented her sliding to the floor.

Drago.

Zenith tried to speak, to thank him, but could not, for now WolfStar was staring at her, now walking toward her, and Drago had to slide his arm about her waist to stop her toppling over in the extremity of her horror.

"Zenith," WolfStar said, stopping a pace away. It was not a question, not a greeting, just a statement, but Zenith felt as if he had somehow taken command of her soul with that one word.

What was wrong with her? Why fear him so much? *Why did he affect her this badly?*

Zenith, be calm. I am with you, I will protect you.

Caelum, speaking to her with the mind voice that all Enchanters used. Together with Drago's arm about her waist, it saved Zenith from fainting completely away.

WolfStar's eyes moved fractionally; he had also caught Caelum's thought.

No-one can best me, fool boy! His mind moved back to the birdwoman before him. *Zenith, do not fear me. Never fear me.*

And he reached out and touched her cheek.

Some of the unreasoning fear vanished with that touch, but with it came a muddle of confused thoughts and images: the Dome of Stars on the Island of Mist and Memory, but seen from the interior, where Zenith had never been; a room in a peasant house, a man advancing to her, his hands outstretched in anger; a child, a raven-haired girl, nursing at her breast.

WolfStar's fingers dropped from her cheek, and with them went the images.

WolfStar smiled, his eyes tender, then turned slightly to Drago—and snarled.

It was a horrible, harsh, totally aggressive sound, and it appalled everyone in the room. Drago himself literally thudded back against the wall, and no-one watching knew if it was simply his own fear and shock that had caused him to leap backward, or WolfStar's power.

"*Vile creature!*" WolfStar spat at him, his hands twitching. "Azhure should have killed you for your efforts in trying to murder Caelum!"

"Why quibble about a few years between deed and execution?" Drago shot back. "My mother may not have killed me then, but she ensured my *inevitable* death!"

Zared, watching, was consumed with two equally strong reactions. First, incredulity that Drago should have so quickly recovered to meet such frightening anger, and secondly, a sudden insight into how Drago must feel living with virtually immortal siblings—and knowing he had once shared that future—while he lined and aged day by day.

WolfStar hissed in Drago's face, but this time the man did not flinch, holding WolfStar's furious eyes with the ease that he'd previously held Caelum's.

By the gods of Earth and Stars, Zared thought, that man has more courage than a battalion of battle-hardened soldiers put together!

"WolfStar!" Caelum snapped, and the Enchanter turned about, rearranging his expression into one of genial goodwill as he did so.

"But there is one more I must yet greet," he said, as he stepped over to RiverStar and kissed her full on the lips.

Zared blinked, then decided to be unsurprised. RiverStar's lusts were so widely gossiped about that no doubt even WolfStar had heard of her escapades. And, as sexual liaisons between grandparent and grandchild within the SunSoar clan were not forbidden, he supposed WolfStar had full right to so lingeringly enjoy RiverStar's mouth.

Certainly RiverStar was in no hurry to end the kiss.

About the room eyes dropped and cheeks reddened. Zared himself eventually looked away; even high Tencendorian society has its pruderies, he thought, although both WolfStar and RiverStar seemed intent on making an exhibition of themselves.

"What a beautiful girl Azhure birthed," WolfStar whispered. "And so practiced."

RiverStar almost visibly preened.

"WolfStar!" Caelum's voice cut across the tableau, and WolfStar straightened and looked about, locking eyes here and there, smiling as people shifted and dropped their own gazes, acknowledging FreeFall and Sa'Domai with a nod.

Zared himself felt WolfStar's power as the Enchanter's eyes swept over him, but WolfStar apparently thought Zared of no account, for he spared him nothing more than a fleeting glance.

For the first time since he'd entered the room, Zared let himself relax. Caelum knew nothing about the troop movements to the west (and of course, Zared told himself, they are only there in case Askam moves against me), and even if WolfStar had reappeared, no-one yet had been burned to ashes, and Sigholt still stood as solid as ever.

But Zared flicked a glance at Zenith. She had recovered somewhat, but still appeared nervous and shaky.

Isfrael, who of all in the room appeared least put out by WolfStar's presence, now stood with his arms folded across his chest and his feet well apart. "Where have you been, WolfStar? The last anyone heard of you was when you confounded my father amid the icy drifts of the northern tundra forty years ago."

WolfStar grinned at the memory. "Axis thought to best

me. He failed. But to answer your question, I have been . . ." he paused, his face set in a theatrical expression of thoughtfulness, ". . . about. Drifting."

"That explanation will hardly relieve any minds within this room," Caelum said. "Much can be accomplished in forty years."

"But no mischief, Caelum. No mischief. Now, would you like me to explain to this group of open-eyed and slack-mouthed listeners what we—"

"What we heard," Caelum interrupted, obviously increasingly irritated by the way WolfStar so effortlessly commanded the room, "was something beyond the Star Gate. Something that whispers. Something that has caused WolfStar to reappear. Whatever it is, or they are, it calls for WolfStar."

Voices again rose in shock and bewilderment. Something beyond the Star Gate?

Caelum's voice cut across the murmuring. "WolfStar, will you speak? Will you offer, for once, some degree of explanation?"

WolfStar, whose eyes had drifted back to Zenith, her own gaze now firmly on the floor, sighed and looked about.

"I threw two hundred and twelve Icarii through the Star Gate," he said bluntly, horrifyingly, into the slight silence that had followed Caelum's request. "I killed them. Including my wife, StarLaughter."

"And her son," FreeFall put in grimly. The SunSoar Talons had long lived with the guilt that one of their number had committed such atrocities.

"We had named him . . ." WolfStar shifted his weight slightly, hiding the momentary gleam of amusement in his eyes. "We had named him DragonStar."

Utter, horrible silence.

Zared could not believe his ears. DragonStar had been Drago's birth name, given to him by his grandfather StarDrifter, and stripped from him by Azhure when she'd also taken his Enchanter powers and Icarii heritage. Zared risked a look at Drago—the man appeared as frozen as a trapped hare, his eyes locked with WolfStar's.

"Imagine my amusement," WolfStar continued, now moving his gaze about the room, "when I discovered that StarDrifter, insipid fool that he is, had unwittingly named *you* after my lost son."

Caelum took a step forward, his eyes sharp, his voice heavy with angry power. "Is this your manipulation, WolfStar? Did you twist StarDrifter's mind so that you could enjoy your amusement and our discomfort so many years later?"

WolfStar laughed merrily, driving the witting cruelty yet deeper into Drago's heart, and waved a casual hand. "No. It was sheer coincidence. Or maybe Fate. I do not know."

He looked back at Drago. "I believe, Drago, that had you not mishandled your infancy so badly you would have grown into an Enchanter unparalleled in the history of the Icarii. As my DragonStar would have done."

Drago was now staring fixedly at a lamp far across the room, as if he could not trust himself to look at WolfStar.

"And yet here my unfortunate brother is," RiverStar said, unable even in this crisis to control her vicious tongue, "a cripple in every sense save the physical one. Even then, I hear the kitchen girls laugh behind his—"

"Hold your tongue, girl!" Zared had heard enough, and gods knew what Drago was going through. "Enough, RiverStar! Can you not see or understand what Drago is feeling? Can you not feel his *pain*?"

Drago looked at Zared with complete astonishment, and Zared wondered if this was the first time in his life someone had actually spoken on his behalf.

RiverStar slowly stood to her feet, furious that this . . . this *mortal* had spoken so harshly to her. "Do not forget, uncle," she hissed, "that I also witnessed Gorgrael tear Caelum from Imibe's arms because of Drago's persistent jealousy, and I watched as Gorgrael sliced the flesh from Imibe's bones. I believed then," she turned her gaze to Drago, "that he would direct Gorgrael to my murder as well. I feared for my own life. That is a fear, Zared, that twists and warps."

Along with everyone else, Caelum was looking at his sister. But he had lost all sense and understanding of being in this chamber. All he could see was the horror of Gorgrael plummeting from the sky, all he could feel was the terror of knowing his *brother* had plotted to kill him by the vilest means possible.

For decades Caelum had fought to bury that memory, fought to forget the frightful weeks he'd spent trapped in Gorgrael's Ice Fortress, fought to heal himself of the scars on his soul as his body had healed itself of the scars inflicted by Gorgrael's talons.

But now the emotions and words of this room had called it all back, brought the fear and the pain and the uncertainty slithering to the surface again.

He blinked, blinked again, and finally managed to control himself. He was beyond that now, *far* beyond it. Surely. His eyes drifted to Drago, and a lump of unreasoning fear rose in his throat.

And Zared thought to defend Drago? Why? Was he in league with Drago?

FreeFall watched the emotions flow over the faces of Axis' children. Fear, hatred, bitterness, sadness—all were evident. How is it, FreeFall thought, that Axis and Azhure united a land so deeply divided, yet left a brood of children separated by such appalling antipathy that they can barely keep themselves from each other's throats?

He sighed, and spoke. "WolfStar, is this coincidence of naming of any consequence?"

"No, FreeFall. None. It is not even surprising, when you think about it. The son whom StarLaughter carried was very, very powerful, and DragonStar was an appropriate name for him. Azhure also carried an immensely powerful son, and DragonStar was also an appropriate name for that baby."

"And yet as I was stripped of name *and* heritage," Drago said, his voice under tight control, "so was he. *Both* DragonStars doomed just before or just after birth."

Caelum stared flatly at him. "WolfStar's son did not deserve his fate, Drago. You did."

Drago visibly winced, and dropped his eyes. But WolfStar grinned impishly at him. *Oh, but he did, he did*, he thought, his mind masked from all the other Enchanters in the room. *Like you, Drago, my son plotted to steal my heritage as you plotted to steal Caelum's. Maybe it is something to do with the name . . .*

"Continue, WolfStar," Caelum said, his eyes still on Drago. "We have not yet got beyond the front gate of your explanation."

WolfStar shook himself from his entertaining train of thought. "I killed two hundred and twelve," he repeated. "I threw them through the Star Gate in my obsession to discover a way back. I thought that if one of those children, just one, managed to come back, then I would be able to do so as well."

"You wasted two hundred and twelve lives," FreeFall said flatly.

"At the time I thought it was necessary," WolfStar replied. "I was afraid that the Star Gate held more terrors than wonders. What if someone, some *thing,* crawled through that could threaten Tencendor?"

"An admirable sentiment," Caelum interrupted, "if only it were true. My father told me you were also intent on expanding your own power."

WolfStar smiled humorlessly. "No, not entirely. I was genuinely afraid of the potential threat that the Star Gate posed. I wanted to understand all its mysteries, not only to expand my own power, but also to ensure Tencendor's protection.

"Well, to continue. Every Icarii birdman and birdwoman

in this room has the right, as the Icarii nation has the right, to sit in judgment for that act. None of the two hundred and twelve came back, and I had lost the two I valued most dearly, StarLaughter and our son. Before I could commit acts of even greater horror, CloudBurst ended my misery, and the misery of the entire Icarii people, with a heavy dagger thrust to my back."

WolfStar twisted in his seat, clearly remembering the feel of the blade sliding in, the taste in his mouth as his lungs filled with blood. "I died, I was entombed, and I walked through the Star Gate."

"What did you find there, WolfStar?" Caelum's voice was very, very soft.

"I found . . . other existences. I found knowledge. I found that life, as death, are but passing dreams." *And there were other things I found and that found me, Caelum StarSon, that I am unwilling to disclose. Not until I am sure there is the need.* But this thought WolfStar shared with no-one.

From the corner of his eyes, Zared noticed that Drago had leaned forward slightly, as if caught by the magic of WolfStar's voice, or perhaps the vistas the Enchanter's words had prompted in his mind.

"And other worlds, WolfStar," Caelum asked. "Did you find other worlds?"

"They exist, Caelum. I experienced them—I cannot put it in any other way—but I did not physically visit them. But they are there, yes."

"Do they harbor races who might invade?" Zared ventured to ask, leaving the enigma of Drago for the moment.

WolfStar blinked. "Races from other worlds? No, no, I think not. I did not sense any threat—"

"Then what of the children you murdered?" Zenith said. Zared was surprised to hear that although her voice was soft, it was strong. "For surely it is they who whispered beyond the Star Gate. Will they come back?"

Her question made WolfStar turn and stare at her for long

minutes, as if he were trying to burn every angle, every plane of her face into his mind.

"Yes," he finally managed, "you are right. They are those I killed."

"Do they pose a danger to Tencendor?" Caelum asked.

"No, they do not. They yearn for my blood, but I am here and they are lost beyond the Star Gate. As far as I am concerned, that is the way it will stay."

Isfrael shifted irritably. "Then why do we hear their voices now, and never before?"

WolfStar shrugged, not willing to take his eyes from Zenith. "They drift, lost. It is not surprising that they would eventually drift slightly closer to the Star Gate than they had been previously."

"Should we help them come home?" FreeFall asked.

His question was enough to make WolfStar drag his eyes away from Zenith. "No! No, we cannot do that!"

"And why not, WolfStar?" FreeFall's voice was very tight.

WolfStar took a deep breath. "They have changed. Being thrown through the Star Gate as they were, alive, terrified, into a cosmos to drift for thousands of years, has altered them. They are not what they were. If they *were* to come through, then yes, I would fear. Please, believe me in this."

No-one in the room noticed Drago's eyes narrow.

"But you said there was *no* danger," Caelum said.

"As long as they remain beyond the Star Gate," WolfStar replied testily. "And I can see no way they can step through."

"*You* could," Caelum reminded him. "You came back."

"Yes, I came back, but I went through under very different circumstances," WolfStar explained, unwilling to disclose what it was that had helped him back. It wouldn't help the children, would it? "I was a powerful and fully trained Enchanter when I went through. I came back, but they *will not*. They do not have the skills, and they do not have the power. Believe me. They will never come back. In time the interstellar tides will carry them far away from the Star Gate. In a week or two their voices will be gone."

Caelum stared at WolfStar a moment longer, then he turned to SpikeFeather.

"My friend, get you to the Star Gate and keep watch with Orr. If those voices come closer, if *anything* happens, then let me know."

SpikeFeather nodded, and slipped from the room.

WolfStar raised his eyes above the gathered heads and looked at WingRidge CurlClaw.

10

Pastry Magics

At some point, when people had grouped into ones and twos to discuss WolfStar's words, the Enchanter himself had disappeared. Zenith, who'd made sure she kept a close eye on him, had no idea how he had done it. He'd been close to the fireplace, but she could have sworn he had not stepped back into it. Neither had he used any Song of Movement, because she would have felt it had he done so.

He was there one heartbeat, gone the next.

And Zenith had allowed herself to breathe a little more easily.

Of the others, Drago had been the next to leave, his exit far more noticeable. He'd pushed bluntly past those in his way and stalked from the room, every eye following him.

Zenith felt for Drago, and wished she'd had the courage Zared showed in leaping to his defense when RiverStar's cruel tongue had been working its damage. Zenith had felt so ashamed that she'd later made the effort to join in the conversation, even asking WolfStar a question.

He'd stared at her, but this time there had been nothing but the stare, nothing but the roiling and yet unreadable emotion in his eyes.

Once Drago had gone, the rest of the group had been fairly quick to break up. There was much to be discussed and debated in the privacy of individual chambers, and even breakfasts to be had, for the initial shock of WolfStar's appearance, and then his news, had long gone, and stomachs were now complaining.

Most of the servants within Sigholt, as well as the heads of the Five and their advisers, were busy with preparations for Council, which was to commence the next morning, so Zenith spent most of the day with Leagh. She felt restless, and useless in the current hive of activity, and Leagh was always comfortable company. Zenith told Leagh all that had happened in Caelum's chambers, for she thought the woman had as much right to know as Askam or Zared, and then she asked what had transpired between her and Zared the night previously.

"Oh, Zenith! I saw more of him last night than I swear I have in the past four years. Thank you, *thank you!*"

Leagh's eyes had glimmered with emotion, and Zenith had to fight back the tears herself.

Having passed the evening meal with Leagh, Zenith wandered back to her own chamber, but could not settle. Every time a drape moved in a draft, or a shadow flickered, Zenith jumped, thinking it was WolfStar.

She was sure he would come after her—

Why use that phraseology?

—why, she could not tell. But something in his touch, something in his eyes . . . he wanted something from her. But what? Surely it was not lust, for what WolfStar had shown her was not the wantonness he'd displayed with RiverStar.

But something else.

Something . . . deeper.

But that was ridiculous. She'd never met him, she was sure. WolfStar had disappeared long years before she'd even been born. Why should he spare her even a passing thought? She was nothing in the power games and mysteries currently being played out in Tencendor.

The images—memories?—that had flooded Zenith's mind when WolfStar touched her cheek now came back and assailed her again, though with less force this time. She'd seen the inside of the Dome of Stars—but that was the province only of the First Priestess of the Temple, and Zenith had never been there. She'd seen inside that peasant hut, seen the angry, nameless man advance on her, murder in his eyes—but neither had she seen hut nor man previously. And the child . . . the child. Who?

Ah! Zenith shook herself. She would go mad left alone in this room to think!

She wondered again about Drago, how he felt after enduring his own personal trauma that morning, and determined to find him.

She found him, as she thought she would, in the kitchens.

RiverStar goaded Drago about affairs with the kitchen girls, but Zenith knew the real reason Drago spent so much time in the kitchens of Sigholt.

She'd discovered his secret one night seven years ago when she could not sleep and had thought to heat herself a glass of warm milk. She'd come in the kitchen doors, and then halted, astounded.

Drago had been standing at one of the worktables, dicing a huge mound of vegetables.

For some obscure reason, Drago loved to cook. He spent an hour or two down here most days, and longer if he was particularly upset over something. It was no mystery to Zenith that he would be here now.

This late at night the fires were damped down, and the

staff had long gone to bed. Even so, the air was still warm, and the great metal ranges against the far wall radiated a comforting glow.

Drago was standing at a table before one of the ranges, several bowls before him, the tabletop strewn with flour and pieces of discarded meat.

"Drago?"

His head whipped up and a bowl rattled as he jumped. "What is it?"

Zenith walked farther into the room. "I thought you might like to talk about this morning."

Her brother dropped his eyes and kneaded some dough in a bowl, unspeaking.

Zenith walked over to the range, keeping her wings carefully tucked away but rubbing her hands before its warmth. "What did you think about WolfStar?"

Drago did not answer.

Now Zenith hugged her arms to herself, her eyes unfocused. "He scares me, Drago. I did not like the way he looked at me. The way he touched me."

"I am sure there are some dozen or more people within Sigholt today who could say they do not like the way WolfStar looks at them." He still had not raised his eyes from the bowl.

Zenith studied Drago carefully. He was kneading dough as if he wanted to bruise it.

"Drago . . ." She hesitated, but thought it needed to be discussed. "How did it make you feel to learn the name of WolfStar's son?"

Drago lifted the mass of dough out of the bowl and slammed it down on the table, sending flour drifting in a cloud about him. He lifted his eyes and stared at Zenith.

"If he did not lie—and from the tales we've heard we know how WolfStar can lie—then all I can say is that DragonStar is a cursed name. Both of us condemned to our different deaths."

"Drago—"

"Except that I think WolfStar's son died far more gently than I!" He started to roll the dough back and forth, back and forth.

"Drago—"

"I do not want to talk about it!" He chopped the dough in two with the side of his hand, played at shaping one of the pieces into a pie crust, then suddenly threw it into a corner of the kitchen with all the strength he could.

"I do not want to talk about it!"

"Damn you, Drago! You must talk sometime!"

Drago rounded on her. "Look at you, Zenith! You are beautiful, vital, and you revel in your Enchanter powers. You have an aeon to live. Look at *me*!"

His fingers pinched at his body, then his face. "*Look* at me! I am wrinkling and aging. I get out of breath climbing the stairs to the roof. All the magic *I* can perform is getting this . . . this . . . this arse-blasted lump of pastry to rise in the oven! And all I ever hear about this cursed Keep is how vile I am, how much air is wasted on my breath, and how I can never be trusted or loved or relied upon!"

Unable to bear her brother's pain, Zenith lowered her eyes and toyed with the handle of a pot on the range hotplate. She could not blame Drago for feeling angry or resentful. No-one in their family seemed willing to harbor a single positive thought for the man or to consider that perhaps he had been punished enough. No-one seemed to entertain the idea that Drago might be so consumed by bitterness that his very punishment might drive him to ill-considered action.

And no-one save she had ever seemed to think through the implications of what Azhure had done to him. Icarii babies were very different from human babies in that they were completely aware from the moment of their birth and, indeed, many months before it. All Icarii memories stretched back to events pre-birth. But when Drago was only a few months old, Azhure had stripped him of his Icarii heritage, and had plunged his mind into the dim murkiness of human infancy. Drago's memories could not date from anything earlier than his second or third year of life.

Drago would have no memory of the events that had seen him so cruelly punished. He was largely reviled, mistrusted, unloved and, above all, condemned to a life of only some three or four score of years, when he could have expected hundreds at least, *for a crime he could not remember!*

No-one cared about how Drago might be feeling or what kind of man lay buried beneath all the years of built-up bitterness. Zenith alone of the immediate family rather liked Drago; perhaps because she'd not yet been conceived when he had arranged Caelum's kidnapping. Drago had a sharp wit and was, in odd, unexpected moments, kind and thoughtful.

He is trapped here in Sigholt, Zenith realized suddenly. Trapped by *other* people's memories of what he did as a child.

As I am trapped by another's memories.

Zenith went ice cold. Was that what it was? Why she had such unexplained memories invading her mind? *Were they someone else's? But whose?*

"Perhaps we should both leave Sigholt for a while," she said softly.

"What?" Drago had given up his efforts at cooking and was piling bowls into the sink with loud, angry rattles.

"Drago, how long is it since you left Sigholt?" Zenith moved forward but stopped as Drago's face tightened. "I don't think you've left in at least eight years. Drago . . . *why?*"

He stared at her, not answering.

"There is nothing keeping either of us here . . . why don't we visit StarDrifter? Escape the tensions in this Keep?"

"Why should *you* want to leave?"

Why indeed? Zenith almost said, "Because of WolfStar," but stopped, knowing she couldn't explain to Drago, let alone herself, her deep-seated fright of the Enchanter, her unsettling visions, or her recurring gaps in consciousness.

"Because there is a world of purpose out there," she said

eventually, "and because neither of us has a purpose in here."

"If I have no purpose it is because my life has been made deliberately purposeless! I am not trusted enough to be given the responsibility of a purpose."

"Then why *not* leave, Drago? StarDrifter would enjoy seeing both of us."

He looked at her, his violet eyes soft, almost gentle in this light, and she knew he was remembering the image of StarDrifter she had conjured up, and the happy months they had spent on the Island of Mist and Memory as children.

"I have no purpose *anywhere,*" he finally said, his voice weary with resignation. "Wherever I go I will always be the vile traitor."

"You can remake your life if you leave Sigholt. Please, Drago."

He seized her shoulders, and Zenith was astounded to see tears in his eyes. "I can never escape, Zenith! *Never!* Word would spread that Axis' untrustworthy and evil son Drago is traveling the land. Doors everywhere would be closed to me. I have no life here in Sigholt, but I would have no life anywhere. Now, will you leave me alone?"

And he strode from the kitchen.

11

Niah's Legacy

Even more troubled now, Zenith climbed to the rooftop of Sigholt. She stood and watched the lights shut out one by one in the town of Lakesview on the other side of the lake. She let the warm breeze caress her, and briefly contemplated a flight over the lake and hills. But she was tired, her mind full of problems, and she preferred just to lean over the wall of the roof and let the view soothe her.

Determined not to think of WolfStar, or Zared and Leagh's troubles, or even of Drago, Zenith fixed her thoughts on RiverStar's claim to have found a new lover. And one she might wed? Zenith almost laughed aloud. Maybe her lover considered marrying RiverStar, but Zenith doubted seriously that her sister would ever go that far. She enjoyed her freedoms too much to discard them for fidelity.

Unless . . . unless her lover were SunSoar. A SunSoar might well tempt RiverStar, but who was available to her here in Sigholt if not first blood?

Zenith frowned. FreeFall . . . but FreeFall was impossible. He and his wife EvenSong were virtually inseparable, and EvenSong was here with him. Besides, who could ever think of FreeFall and RiverStar . . . no, that was laughable. Surely.

And WolfStar. WolfStar was here—how much longer had he been about before he made his presence known? His penchant for disguises was legendary. If he was RiverStar's new lover, had he been coming to her in the guise of a stableboy, or himself?

No, no, not WolfStar. Zenith did not want to think of him at all.

Although remember the way he'd kissed RiverStar this morning; was that boldness, or familiarity?

Isfrael! Zenith forced her mind as far from WolfStar as she could. Was Isfrael first blood? She supposed he was, for he and RiverStar shared a SunSoar father. But then Isfrael had changed so much since he'd become Mage-King of the Avar that it was as if his SunSoar link was gone.

Although he still had the blood to satisfy RiverStar, if indeed it were him.

No, surely not Isfrael. He had only been here since this morning . . . hadn't he? When *had* Isfrael arrived?

"Oh, for the sweet Stars' sakes," Zenith murmured. "RiverStar is probably just making it all up, anyway."

She looked down to the far courtyard, her Enchanter vision

having no trouble picking out every detail in the thick night shadow. A guard moved from barrack to gate, another checked the doors to the weapons room off the main building.

A movement. Drago. Zenith sharpened her vision, then smiled gently, her eyes soft. He was feeding scraps of meat to the courtyard cats. Five or six had gathered, mewling about his legs, reaching up to pat his knees with their paws. He laughed, and squatted down to scratch them, their heads butting against his arms and chest affectionately.

Zenith had never realized he liked cats so much—nor that they so obviously adored him. All the food was gone, but still they stayed, winding about him. Her face softened yet more. Someone besides herself in this great Keep liked the man.

Drago stood up, extracted himself from the cats, and stepped back inside.

Zenith watched for a few more minutes, but he did not reappear. She sighed, and moved to the parapets that overlooked the lake, resting her elbows on the wall, her chin in her hands, lost in thought.

Sigholt was now completely quiet. The dogs were curled in sleep, the guards seemed to have turned to stone at their posts.

Silence and stillness reigned.

Zenith felt as if she had been transported to another world. Even the breeze had disappeared.

Her wings relaxed and drifted over the flagstones behind her. She sank into a greater lethargy, leaning her full weight on the wall, watching the waves ripple across the moonlit Lake of Life.

Zenith did not notice the tiniest of movements in the air about her, nor catch the enchantment that rippled over the rooftop.

"I find it not strange that I have discovered you atop Sigholt," WolfStar said, and she whirled around, her heart pounding.

He stood relaxed and easy, his wings drooping behind him in the traditional Icarii gesture of goodwill. "For so once StarDrifter found Rivkah, and loved her, and so Axis once found Azhure, and loved her, too. No, do not lift off. Stay and talk to me, Zenith. You have nothing to fear."

Then why does my heart race so, Zenith thought, and my breast heave with such fright? She steadied herself, although her eyes flickered about, seeking the reassurance of another person close by.

There was no-one save her and WolfStar.

A movement above her, against the Dome.

Zenith gasped, her eyes involuntarily jerking upward. There was nothing there save the swirling stars. Nothing.

"Do you remember, sweet Zenith," WolfStar said very softly, "when last you saw me? Do you remember that night so long ago?"

A shadow spiraling down from the roof of the Dome.

"No," Zenith whispered, grabbing at the parapets for support. "No! We have never met before this morning!"

Something was happening. The night air of Sigholt was swirling about her, and every few heartbeats it seemed to solidify until she felt as if she were inside . . . inside an empty building . . . a dome.

"No!"

"Zenith, do not fear. You are only remembering. Accept."

WolfStar walked slowly toward her, and as he did so he lifted his hand in the demanding gesture of seduction that male Enchanters used to will women to their bed.

"No!" She could not move, and her mind voice seemed to have vanished. She was trapped, trapped . . . he was too powerful . . .

"Yes! Zenith . . . here . . . let me remind you."

He was close now, gathering her stiff body in his arms, and Zenith struggled uselessly, wondering if he was intent on rape.

She felt his arms about her, and it was good.

No, no it *wasn't* good! Yet something seemed to have taken possession of her, some part of her mind willed her to cease resisting and let WolfStar slide her to the floor, some part of her was saying . . . *you have bedded with him previously.*

No! She twisted her head away but WolfStar was too powerful for her, both his body and his power were too strong, and she felt his mouth close over hers . . .

And something happened. Something broke free, something *struggled* free within her. Memories, voices, scents, laughter not her own crowded her mind. Faces, experiences, songs she'd never seen or heard before leaped out of hiding. A desire she'd never felt flooded her body. She . . .

felt him enter her body, move within her, and she had never believed it could feel this good, had never believed that such intimacy could engender such feeling, and . . .

No! No, what was wrong with her? His mouth was on hers, that was all. All? She could not escape it, she could not escape him, she . . .

twisted under him, encouraging him with body and voice, willing him on to even greater effort, willing him to merge so completely with her body and soul that they would indeed become one and not just two bodies briefly conjoined in an act designed only for child engendering.

Zenith tore her mouth from his. "No!" Broke away from him, yet even as she stumbled five or six paces away from him she felt . . .

the fire that he had seeded in her womb explode into new life and . . .

She screamed and fell to the floor, doubling over, clutching at her belly. Her wings beat futilely behind her, and almost knocked WolfStar over as he leaned down and grabbed her, holding her tightly against him, trying to stifle her sobs.

"Zenith, your mother was wrong not to tell you this before—"

"Tell me *what*?"

"That you were born to be my lover, Zenith. Meant for noone else. Why else are you still a virgin at your age? Here I am, Zenith. Accept me. Zenith, you love me . . . accept me."

And the dreadful thing was Zenith could *feel* that love, could remember the nights she had lain in her lonely bed, wishing he would return to her, crying as the night lightened to dawn and he had not appeared. She could remember years spent loving him, and she could remember months spent watching her belly swell with his child.

"No!" she shouted once more, and lunged from his arms, using both limbs and wings. Her hip struck the sharp edge of the parapet over the courtyard, and she cried out, her arms flailing. WolfStar lunged for her, but he was too late, and Zenith tumbled over the edge of the roof, gaining control of her wings only within feet of the ground and landing roughly enough to scrape hands and knees.

Help me! Help me!

And suddenly, Drago was there.

"Oh, Stars!" he cried, and fell to his knees, gathering her in his arms. Two guards from the gate had started to run toward them, but Drago waved them back. "A slip! Nothing more!"

Then, her sobbing face pressed into his chest, he held her tight, rocking her back and forth. "Zenith, what is it? What is it?"

Zenith clung to her brother, sobbing, letting his closeness and warmth and touch drive away her memories and the feel of WolfStar.

In the rectangle of light behind Drago another figure appeared. "Zenith!"

Caelum.

"Zenith! Drago, what have you done to her? *Let her go!*"

"Caelum," Zenith sobbed, trying to say it was all right, that Drago was helping, not hurting, but the words would not come, and Caelum reached down and literally tore her from Drago's arms.

"Get you gone from here!" Caelum snarled at Drago, who had backed away, his eyes swinging between Caelum's face and Zenith, now clinging to her eldest brother.

"I was only helping—" he began, but Caelum reached out with his power and cut off Drago's words.

"I do not want to hear your excuses! *Get you gone from here!*"

Drago's face twisted, trying to form words, but Caelum would not let them come, and with a gesture of half rage, half frustration, he disappeared inside the kitchen door.

"Sweetheart," Caelum whispered, gathering Zenith more tightly into his arms, and then the music of a Song of Movement rippled about them, and they disappeared from the courtyard.

She came to her senses, still wrapped in Caelum's arms, but now sitting on one of the commodious couches in the inner private chamber of his apartments.

"Where's Drago?" she said, sniffing and wiping her nose with a cloth Caelum handed her.

"He fled. Did he push you?"

"No! No, I stumbled from the rooftop. WolfStar . . . WolfStar was there."

"Ah! WolfStar! He is truly the bane of our lives. Did he hurt you?"

"No," Zenith said, but she spoke so hesitatingly that Caelum took her shoulders and pushed her back a little so he could see her face.

"He did," he said slowly. "He did hurt you. How?"

Zenith probably would have confessed to the first person who showed her kindness, be it Caelum or unknown dairy maid. Words came tumbling out of her mouth.

"WolfStar . . . on the roof . . . kissed me . . . thoughts, images, not mine . . . crowded me . . . frightened me."

Caelum pulled her close again, stroking her hair. "Go on." His eyes were distant.

Zenith gripped her hands together in an effort to stop them shaking. "He appeared suddenly, and that surprised me, but then I felt as if I was in a . . . chamber of some kind. The Dome of the Moon. It was very dark. I felt there was something there, clinging to the roof. It frightened me, terrified me, I was *there,* I *saw* that place—and yet I have never been inside it in my life!"

She raised her head, enough to look Caelum in the eyes. "I felt as though I was someone else. Memories crowded my mind. Memories that were not mine! Oh, Caelum . . . !"

And in another flood she told him of the lost hours and the nightmares and the fears. Who was this who crowded her mind, and who sometimes took such possession of her that she could not remember what she had done? Who?

"Caelum, I do not know what to think, what to do!"

"Hush," Caelum said, holding her tight, stroking her hair, her back, kissing the crown of her head. "Hush."

Thoughts and memories crowded his own mind, but they were not of someone else's making. He remembered the time, nine years ago, when Axis and Azhure had handed control of Tencendor over to him. True, there had been a glittering ceremony on the shores of Grail Lake, but there had been a far more private afternoon, when his parents had handed into his keeping some of the most precious items of their lives.

The Rainbow Scepter, now carefully secreted within Sigholt.

The Wolven Bow, for Azhure had said she no longer needed to ride to the hunt.

The enchanted quiver of arrows, which never ran out.

A Moonwildflower.

And a letter. A letter addressed to Azhure, and written by her long dead mother, Niah.

No-one save Azhure could remember Niah, for she had died when Azhure was only about six. Niah had been the First Priestess on the Island of Mist and Memory when one night WolfStar had appeared to her, lain with her, and got Azhure upon her.

Within seven years Niah was dead, burned alive at the hands of her Plough-Keeper husband, Hagen, in the cursed village of Smyrton. But she had left Azhure a letter, and when Azhure had given it to Caelum she'd told him that one day he must hand it to Zenith.

"You will know when, Caelum. You will know the moment."

And this *was* the moment. Trembling, for he had never read the letter, and did not know what was in it, Caelum gently disengaged himself, and left the room.

Zenith sat up straight, dried her eyes, and shook her hair out, grateful for the support and love Caelum had shown her, but wishing she could have explained about Drago.

Caelum was back within a few minutes, holding an envelope in his hands.

"Caelum. Drago was only—"

"Hush. Let us not speak of him, Zenith. Read this. Maybe it will help you understand."

Puzzled, Zenith took the letter. Across the envelope there was a word scratched in bold ink. *Azhure*.

Even more bewildered, Zenith looked at Caelum. The writing was in Zenith's own hand. "Who wrote this?"

"Niah, Azhure's mother."

Niah?

"Read it, Zenith."

Zenith dropped her eyes to the letter. Quashing the sudden wave of apprehension that almost engulfed her, she opened the envelope and took the letter out. Hands trembling, she unfolded it and began to read, her eyes skipping over the irrelevant passages.

My dearest daughter Azhure, may long life and joy be yours forever . . .

Five nights ago you were conceived and tonight, after I put down my pen and seal this letter, I will leave this blessed isle. I will not return—but one day I hope you will come back.

Five nights ago your father came to me.

It was the fullness of the moon, and it was my privi-

lege, as First Priestess, to sit and let its light and life wash over me in the Dome of the Moon. I heard his voice before I saw him.

"Niah," a voice resonant with power whispered through the Dome, and I started, because it was many years since I had heard my birth name.

"Niah," the voice whispered again, and I trembled in fear. Were the gods displeased with me? Had I not honored them correctly during my years on this sacred isle and in this sacred Temple?

"Niah," the voice whispered yet again, and my trembling increased, for despite my lifetime of chastity I recognized the timbre of barely controlled desire . . . and I was afraid.

I stood . . . my eyes frantically searched the roof overhead and for long moments I could see nothing, then a faint movement caught my eye.

A shadow was spiraling down from the roof of the Dome . . . The shadow laughed and spoke my name again as he alighted before me.

"I have chosen you to bear my daughter," he said, and he held out his hand, his fingers flaring. "Her name will be Azhure."

At that moment my fear vanished as if it had never existed. Azhure . . . Azhure . . . I had never seen such a man as your father and I know I will not again during this life . . . His wings shone gold, even in the dark night of the Dome, and his hair glowed with copper fire. His eyes were violet, and they were hungry with magic.

Azhure, as Priestesses of the Stars we are taught to accede to every desire of the gods, even if we are bewildered by their wishes, but I went to him with willingness, not with duty. I wore but a simple shift, and as his eyes and fingers flared wider I stepped out of it and walked to meet his hand.

As his hand grasped mine it was as if I was sur-

rounded by Song, and as his mouth captured mine it was as if I was enveloped by the surge of the Stars in their Dance. His power was so all-consuming that I knew he could have snuffed out my life with only a thought. Perhaps I should have been terrified, but he was gentle for a god—not what I might have expected—and if he caused me any pain that night I do not remember it. But what I do remember . . . ah, Azhure, perhaps you have had your own lover by now, but do you know what it feels like to lie with one who can wield the power of the Stars through his body? At times I know he took me perilously close to death as he wove his enchantments through me and made you within my womb, but I trusted him and let him do what he wanted and lay back in his wings as he wrapped them about me and yielded with delight and garnered delight five-fold in return.

Zenith blinked, for it was as if she were there, *feeling* this, not reading about it. She . . . she could remember writing these words, remember sitting there for almost an hour at this point, her mouth curling softly in memory of that night of passion and loving. She had not known his name then, but that had not mattered very much, not when she had his body to grasp to her, not when both she and he burned with such virulent desire.

Zenith shuddered. Gods! What was happening to her?

Even as he withdrew from my body I could feel the fire that he had seeded in my womb erupt into new life. He laughed gently at the cry that escaped my lips and at the expression in my eyes, but I could see his own eyes widen to mirror the wonder that filled mine. For a long time we lay still, his body heavy on mine, our eyes staring into each other's depths, as we felt you spring to life within my womb.

Zenith's mouth formed the word "No," but she did not voice it. She was no longer in her mother's chamber in Sigholt, but lying on the cold floor of the Dome of the Moon, staring into WolfStar's eyes as he lay atop her.

After a moment she managed to regain enough control so she could resume reading the letter. Niah wrote of how the "god"—WolfStar—had told her she would have to travel to Smyrton, wed the local Plough-Keeper, Hagen, and bear her child. There the child, Azhure, would eventually meet the StarMan.

I know that I will die in Smyrton, and I know that the man your father sends me to meet and to marry will also be my murderer. I know that my days will be numbered from the hour that I give you birth. It is a harsh thing that your father makes me do, for how will I be able to submit to this Plough-Keeper Hagen, knowing I will die at his hands, and keep a smile light on my face and my body willing? How can I submit to any man, having known the god who fathered you? How can I submit to a life dominated by the hated Brotherhood of the Seneschal, when I have been First Priestess of the Order of the Stars?

Your father saw my doubts and saw my future pain, and he told me that one day I will be reborn to be his lover forever.

"No, no, no, no." Zenith shook as the implications of what she was reading began to sink in. "*No!*"

He said that he had died and yet lived again, and that I would follow a similar path.

He said that he loved me.

Perhaps he lied, but I choose not to think so. To do otherwise would be to submit to despair. His promise, as your life, will keep me through and past my death into my next existence.

"I do not believe it," Zenith said with all the calmness she could muster. She carefully folded the letter in half and handed it back to Caelum. "Read it. But do not believe it. It is a mistake. A lie."

Caelum walked slowly over to the fire, standing with his back to the flames as he read through the letter once, then once more, far more slowly.

"I knew some of this," he said, finally looking up. "I knew that WolfStar came to Niah in the Dome of the Moon. I knew how Niah died. But this . . . this promise that WolfStar made to Niah . . . that she would live again . . . that I did not know."

"But Mother *did* know. She knew . . . all these years! Knew and never told me! Why?"

Is that why Mother did not give me a Star name? Zenith wondered. Because she knew I was Niah reborn?

"Why?" Caelum shrugged helplessly, spreading his hands out. "Zenith, I don't know. Maybe she felt there was no point telling you until . . . until WolfStar reappeared. Gods! I don't know!"

"So she let me find out *this* way?"

"Zenith." Caelum came back to sit by her side, his voice gentle. "If there is one thing I have learned from my parents' lives, and from my own, it is that we are all born with a destiny. My parents were into their third decades before their destinies became clear to them, and—"

"No!" Zenith took the letter from Caelum's hand and began to turn it over and over in her own. "I will *not* accept it!"

"—and I have had to accept that my destiny is as StarSon, and my burden is Tencendor."

"I am *Zenith*! No-one else!"

"Yes, my dear, yes. But . . . but it is apparent that you also have Niah's soul and many of her memories, and—"

"No!" How many times had she shouted that negative tonight, Zenith numbly wondered in a dark recess of her mind, and how many *more* times would she have to shout it?

"—and," Caelum continued, speaking over Zenith's increasing denials, "you still have life. You have all of your own memories and experiences. You must only come to terms with the fact that you also have a set of memories and experiences that stretch back before your birth."

"No!" Zenith leaped to her feet and began pacing restlessly about the room. What now was truly, truly terrifying was the fact that as she had shouted that "No!" some part of her mind had whispered back, *Yes!*

She was Niah reborn . . . born to live out Niah's yearnings, Niah's life.

No!

She was Niah, reborn, both mother and daughter to Azhure.

No!

She was Niah reborn, and what that meant was that she no longer had any say in her own life, because her life would now be lived according to Niah's dictates, Niah's dreams.

"No!"

She would live her life locked in the arms of *Niah's* lover.

"I am *not* Niah!" she whispered, low and fierce. How *could* she be?

"Zenith! Listen to me!" Now Caelum was before her, his face was determined, his voice hard. "Zenith, you will have to adjust, but you will be able to—"

"No! No! No!" Zenith wrenched herself from Caelum's grasp and stumbled across the room. With vicious movements she tore the letter into shreds and threw the pieces into the fire.

"Niah is *dead*!" Not living in her. Not! Had this misplaced ghost always been hiding in her bodily spaces, waiting for a moment when she could—no! She could not even *think* it!

"No!" Zenith screamed one last time and fled from the chamber.

Caelum stood in the middle of his chamber, staring after her, trying to make sense of her reaction. It had been a shock, of course . . . but surely if she calmed down, thought it through, and accepted it, then it would be easier. Perhaps she'd best be left alone for a while. Perhaps all she needed was time.

Then Caelum remembered how WolfStar had kissed RiverStar, and his eyes clouded over. Not RiverStar! No! Better Zenith, better by far. Zenith must learn to accept WolfStar, and WolfStar surely would not harm her if he loved her.

But . . .

"Leave her alone for a few days, WolfStar," he said into the empty room, but he spread the words over and through Tencendor with his power, seeking out the Enchanter. "Give her time."

Somehow he felt, if not saw, WolfStar's predatory grin.

12

Council of the Five Families

The Great Hall of Sigholt sat silent, waiting, as the morning sun danced down through the high arched windows set among the massive roof beams. Banners, pennants and standards hung from walls and beams, their fields and borders rippling slightly in the warming air. From the windows the silvery-gray walls fell unfettered for twenty paces, eventually dividing into immense arched columns, behind which shifted the shadowy spaces of the cloisters. The floor was utterly bare, the newly scrubbed and sanded flagstones gleaming almost ivory in this bright light.

In the very center of the Hall sat a great circular golden oak table. Seven chairs were arranged about it.

About eight paces from this great table, and between it and the empty fireplace, were arranged some three smaller tables, each draped with black cloth and with a dozen chairs behind them.

The notaries were first to enter, their faces solemn with

importance, their scarlet robes stiff with self-worth. Behind them came their secretaries—arms bustling with ledgers, accounts, papers, scrolls and the minutiae of a nation's life—and their scribes, carrying the quills and inkwells of final judgment. Finally there was a brief scuttling of messenger boys, too overcome with the occasion to be anything but round-eyed and obedient.

Once the bureaucracy had arranged themselves at the black-draped tables, the messenger boys waiting behind them amid the columns, the honor guard entered. Three Wing of the Strike Force, unarmed, stood about the walls of the Great Hall, their black uniforms merging with the dimness behind the columns. When they were still, WingRidge led in twenty-five of the Lake Guard, who took a prominent position, standing in a ring ten paces back from the central circular table.

All the Council needed now were the main actors.

Of those, StarSon Caelum entered first. He wore black, as was his custom, but his face was far more careworn than usual. Without fuss he seated himself at the table. And then, in a procedure initiated by Caelum when he first assumed the Throne of the Stars, the heads of the Five Families entered simultaneously, each from a different door. They strode to the central table, their boot heels clicking, arriving to stand behind their chairs as simultaneously as they had entered the hall. All were unarmed, their swords left back in their chambers.

They waited. From the central doors Isfrael emerged.

As one they all turned to Caelum, and bowed.

"I thank you for your attendance here this day," he said. "Be seated."

Askam sat on Caelum's immediate right, Zared his left. FreeFall sat next to Askam, Isfrael next to Zared. Sa'Domai and Yllgaine took the seats immediately opposite Caelum. There was nothing on the table before the men, save their differences.

"My friends," Caelum said in a voice that, although soft, was so well modulated it carried easily to the men at the table, and to the notaries and secretaries eight paces away. "I bid you welcome to Sigholt for this Council, and I express my regrets that it should be convened so hastily and so soon after our last Council.

"However, as you are all aware, there are matters which need to be discussed and decided among us. Chief among these matters is the issue of the taxes that Prince Askam has been forced to levy on the West. Over the past few weeks Askam has imposed taxation on goods moved by land or water through his territory, as well as on those families deciding to emigrate to the North."

"'Forced' is hardly the word I'd use," Zared muttered, his gray eyes on Askam.

"I had every right to impose those taxes—" Askam began, but Caelum silenced them both with an angry look.

"We are all aware of how onerous these taxes are," he said. "A third of the value of goods is . . . exorbitant. Ten thousand gold pieces per family moving north is incomprehensible."

Zared relaxed slightly.

"I wish to hear from the principals involved, then from Duke Theod and Earl Herme who were kind enough to ride to Sigholt to offer their views, then from the rest of you about this table. Askam, will you speak?"

Askam took a deep breath. "My friends, I am as aware as any of you how draconian these taxes sound. However, consider my position. For years I have worked tirelessly on Tencendor's behalf, and on StarSon Caelum's behalf. These efforts have cost me dearly. My creditors push for the return of their funds. These taxes will clear the West of debt within two years—"

"And two years is more than enough to drive your people into *starvation,* Askam!" Zared cried. "Curse you! There are better ways of raising revenue than stealing it from the mouths of those who can least afford to—"

"Oh, god's arse, Zared!" Askam said. "This is all about *you*! Have you not been transporting *your* ore and gems and furs free of charge down to the southern markets at a handsome profit for decades? This talk of starving peasants is nonsense. Your purse has been dented—you who can *well* afford it—and thus you complain. I have not seen *you* spend more than a copper piece entertaining diplomats and foreign missions, nor founding the schools or universities that I have."

"Be quiet, Askam," Caelum said, then shifted his eyes slightly. "Zared, Askam *has* got a point there. You have indeed made free use of his extensive system of roads and riverboats for many years now."

"I have paid full price for their passage, StarSon," Zared said.

"Still, Askam does have the right to impose taxes on external goods moving through his territory. The fact is, he could have levied this tax only on your goods, not on those of his own people."

Zared held his breath for a moment, then spoke very deliberately. "The fact *is,* Caelum, that Askam has imposed a tax which directly hurts the West, and indirectly hurts another province. And the . . . human . . . populations of the West and North feel that they have been inordinately imposed upon. If these taxes are the result of debt run up in your cause, Caelum, then why do not *all* the peoples of Tencendor help retrieve the situation?"

"The Avar do not pay taxes," Isfrael said, very low.

"And yet *my* people must!" Zared cried. "Can you not all of you see how dangerous this is? One race pays the debts of a nation of three races?"

"Enough," Caelum said. "Before I ask the views of the Avar, Icarii and Ravensbund, I would have Herme and Theod enter."

He nodded at the side tables, and one of the secretaries hurried to open the doors, whisper urgently, and escort the Duke and Earl to the table.

Herme and Theod stood slightly to the right of Sa'Domai's chair, where all could see them. Both wore tightly restrained expressions, both avoided looking at either Askam or Zared.

"Your views, gentlemen?" Caelum asked.

Herme spoke first, detailing how the taxes had impacted

upon his own county of Avonsdale. All had been crippled, not only those with business moving goods on the road, but even the lowly farmers or laborers who moved neither stock nor fodder from their land.

"They can hardly afford food now, StarSon," Herme finished. "If they cannot grow it, then they certainly cannot buy it, for merchants have been forced to increase the cost of all merchandise to cover the taxes."

Which naturally, Zared thought, then increases the taxes in direct proportion to the inflated value of the goods.

Theod told a similar tale. The people of Jervois Landing, of whom almost all relied on trade to survive, would be destitute within the year. And yet they could look across the Nordra, look into eastern Tencendor under FreeFall's control, and see free markets, and round, rosy cheeks on the children.

"As, of course, they can in the North," he said finally. "Many among the people of the West are moving north, and if they cannot afford to pay the border tax, then most of them will become homeless, destitute, and a burden on those already struggling to survive."

"I thank you, gentlemen," Caelum said, just as Herme had opened his mouth to say something else. "You may retire."

He waited until the doors had closed behind them, then he looked at Isfrael, FreeFall, Yllgaine and Sa'Domai. "My friends?"

FreeFall spoke first. "There can be no doubt that these taxes are onerous, StarSon. But . . ."

"But obviously *something* must be done to relieve Askam of the burden of debt he ran up in your service, Caelum," Yllgaine said. "The tax on goods moved through the West seems the best way to do it."

Zared bit his tongue to keep his anger from spilling out in unreasoned words. Yllgaine undoubtedly would not want *his* trading rights taxed!

Isfrael's only comment was to repeat that the Avar had never been taxed, and would not consent to being taxed now. "And how would they pay it? In twigs? In acorns?"

Sa'Domai shrugged. "I can sympathize with Zared in that his people also suffer . . . but I note Askam's point that this debt was largely run up in Tencendor's service—"

Zared could no longer contain himself. "*And* some appalling investments! Gloam mines, for the gods' sakes!"

Caelum hit the table with the flat of his hand. "Be still, Zared! Or would *you* like to entertain the Corolean Ambassador and his train the next time he decides on a three-year stay?"

Zared leaned back in his chair, his eyes carefully blank, listening to the conversation waft about him. Those of the Five not directly affected by the taxes first spoke of the weight of the taxes, then of Askam's pressing (and understandable) need for money.

Caelum listened, nodded occasionally, and was careful not to give the impression that he was for one side or the other. Finally he held up his hand for silence.

"The issue of placing a border tax on those families wishing to move north must also be resolved."

"The *issue* is one of the freedom of a man to move his family to where they can *eat,* Caelum," Zared snapped, tired of the discussion, but not willing to let such an important point pass with no debate.

"The *issue,*" Askam shot back, "is whether or not you have the right to entice the most skilled of my workers and craftsmen north. I hear rumor that you pay well for such men to settle in Severin. Well enough, I think, to levy a tax on each of their departing heads for the troubles their loss causes me."

"I pay them nothing! They journey north only because they know their families will have a future with—"

"*Enough!*" Now Caelum stood, furious. "I have heard sufficient to judge in this matter."

He sat down again, but his eyes were still flinty. "Askam. You may have the right to levy taxes as you will in the West, but you do not have the right to deprive people of the means of survival. Zared, your people have suffered too, and that is wrong, but what is also wrong is the fact that for many years . . . too many years, you have grown fat on the riches of Ichtar which you have shipped, free of any levy, to market via the West.

"This is my judgment. The border tax must go. It *is* an injustice to so deprive people of their freedom of movement, their freedom of choice to move."

"But—" Askam began.

"However, I hope that my decision on the other tax will go some way to alleviate your financial troubles, Prince of the West. The third tax on goods carried through the West must be lowered to one-tenth, still onerous, but enough for your people to bear."

Askam's face went dark with anger. How did that help him? A tenth would never bring in—

"But, Askam," and Caelum's eyes slid fractionally toward him, "I am fully aware that most of your debt was accomplished in my service, and for that I am more than grateful. While the people of the West must only pay one-tenth in tax, anyone else moving their goods through the West must pay half value in levy."

Zared's mouth dropped open in astonishment. *What was Caelum doing?* "No-one else moves goods through the West save the people of the North," he finally managed. "That is a tax aimed directly at me and mine!"

Caelum turned to look him full in the eye. "And when have *you* run into debt to aid me, Zared? *When?* This is a fair way, as I see it, of making sure that all contribute toward—"

"But none of them have to pay!" Zared shouted, flinging an angry arm at the others. "When do they contribute toward—"

"Are you asking what the Icarii contribute?" Caelum seethed, "*when they spent a thousand years in exile due to* . . . due to . . ."

Due to your people. Caelum may not have spoken the words, but all heard his thoughts in their minds.

"Do you ask what Nor contributes, when for a thousand years his family maintained the Island of Mist and Memory?"

And for a thousand years your people desecrated every sacred site in Tencendor they could lay a plow to?

"Do you ask what the Avar contribute, when they had to watch their homelands slaughtered, their children burned?"

And for a thousand years your people took the axe to every tree they could find, and murdered those who did not conform to the Way of the Plough?

Zared had gone white with shock. He stared at Caelum, absolutely incapable of speech.

How could Caelum send those thoughts careering through all of their heads, and still claim that he didn't want the term "Acharite" used because it stank of the hatreds of the past?

Caelum held his stare, then waved one of the Lake Guard over. "Bring in the Princess Leagh," he said.

"No," whispered Zared. "Not after that, not—"

The doors opened, and Leagh walked in. She had dressed herself in a gown of silk that precisely matched the gray of Zared's eyes, and her face was as ashen as his, for she had heard the shouting of the previous minutes.

Even so, she was composed, and she did not tremble or falter as she curtsied before Caelum. "StarSon."

"Princess Leagh," Caelum said, his tone now far more gentle. "You and Zared are aware of why I have called you here."

She stood, and gazed calmly at him. "I am, StarSon. Is it yea or nay?"

Caelum was taken aback at such bluntness. He had meant to put this matter before the entire Council as well, even though he had made up his mind weeks ago, because he'd felt that both Zared and Leagh would take it better if his decision was backed by the weight of the Council.

But after the previous "discussion," Caelum did not trust this gathering, nor even himself, to be able to keep a debate calm and reasoned.

"Leagh . . . Zared," he risked a quick glance at Zared, but turned back to Leagh. "Leagh, it is nay. It *must* be nay. There are good reasons for my—"

He got no further. Zared leaped to his feet. "Good reasons, Caelum? Good reasons to deny Leagh and myself our hearts' desire? Why? Is there a tax on her I have neglected to pay?"

He turned to Askam. "How much, man? A third? A half?"

Askam leaped to his feet, his chair crashing behind him. He made as if to lunge across the table, but FreeFall was quick enough, and strong enough, to seize his arm and drag him back.

"Peace!" Caelum shouted. He signaled one of the Lake Guard. "Please escort the Princess Leagh from this Hall. I have words to speak that I would not like her to hear."

Leagh shot one frightened, stricken look at Zared, but then the birdman had her by the elbow and was pulling her back.

"Leagh!" Zared cried, but he was restrained by Isfrael, and the door closed behind Leagh with no further word or look being exchanged.

Caelum whipped about to face Zared. "You have gone too far, Prince!"

As have you, Zared thought. He was icy calm now, and he shook off Isfrael's hold.

Caelum sat down. "I will close this Council within minutes, Zared, but first I need to say that—"

"You cannot close this Council yet," Zared said. "There is one more item of business we need to discuss."

Caelum stared at him. "And what might that be?"

"We need," Zared said, his hand absently hovering where his sword normally hung from his weapons belt, "to discuss restoring the throne of Achar."

13

The Throne of Achar

The entire Hall was silent, stunned. The notaries and secretaries had paused in their incessant hunt for precedents in their documents to stare openmouthed at the central table. The scribes' quills had dipped unnoticed to scratch uselessly against cloth instead of parchment. The messenger boys were rigid with terror, incapable of moving.

The guards, already rigid and expressionless, still somehow managed to register their outrage.

Restore the throne of Achar?

"And so now the traitor speaks," Askam said softly into the silence. "Is this what you have wanted all along, Zared? Is this the reason you so pursued Leagh?"

"I am no traitor," Zared said, just as quietly, "to want for the Acharites what every other race in Tencendor has—their own head. Their own pride."

"Sit down, Zared," Caelum said. Nothing about his demeanor revealed the intense shock, even fear, Zared's words had caused.

Caelum set his hands flat on the table before him, stared at them a long moment, then raised his eyes to the six men about the table. "Speak to me," he said.

"Well," Yllgaine said, "technically this conversation is academic only. The throne of Achar no longer exists. It is a relic of the past. It cannot be revived."

"*Achar* no longer exists!" Askam exclaimed. His body was stiff with outrage, his eyes bright with indignant anger. As Prince of the West, Askam had the most to lose if the realm of Achar was re-created. Achar had once covered most of the territory he now governed, and had included Carlon, the richest and most populous city in Tencendor. "And thus the 'Acharites' don't exist. Have you not read your *Edicts of the First Year of StarSon Caelum's Reign,* Zared?"

Zared ignored him. "This is not how I wished to raise the issue—" he began, when Caelum interrupted.

"Nevertheless, this *is* how you raised it! I—nay, all of us here at this table—would be grateful if you would enlighten us as to the motives . . . the desires . . . behind your words."

"But now that the issue *has* been raised," Zared continued regardless, refusing to look at Caelum, "may I speak without interruption?"

Askam started to say something more, but Caelum held up his hand for silence. "Let him speak."

"My friends, when Axis reunited Tencendor he righted a massive wrong. I cannot deny that. Former Acharite kings and the Seneschal had riven the ancient realm apart with their lies and hatred. Borneheld only made matters worse, and I have no quarrel with the fact that Axis killed our brother in fair duel in the Chamber of the Moons in Carlon.

"But I do have some reservations about his choices immediately after winning that duel. He reproclaimed Tencendor, yes, but in doing so he destroyed the ancient kingdom of Achar."

"It had no place in Tencendor!" Askam said, looking about the table for support. "It was ever an aberration!"

Two or three other heads about the table nodded.

"Peace," Caelum said, laying a hand on Askam's arm. "Let us hear what Zared has to say." His eyes were very watchful.

"That day on the shores of Grail Lake," Zared continued, "Axis proclaimed Tencendor and created the Five Families representing the Icarii, Ravensbund and Acharite races."

"*Human* races," Yllgaine murmured. Zared ignored the interruption.

"He created the House of the Stars as supreme over all others, and created the Throne of the Stars, the throne that you now sit, Caelum. Supreme over Tencendor, below only the Star Gods themselves.

"But," Zared's tone became harsher, and he leaned forward slightly, "Axis left the Icarii with their Talon," he nodded at FreeFall, "he left the Ravensbund with their Chieftain," he indicated Sa'Domai, "and he eventually gave the Avar their own Mage-King, Isfrael.

"What this means," Zared's tone now hardened, "is that all races in Tencendor, all cultural groups, if you prefer that phrase, have a 'king,' save the Acharites—and, *yes!* I *insist* on using that term! Both their throne and their identity were destroyed. Damn it, you have even banned the word

'Acharite'! Caelum, whether you want to hear it or not, that has created dissent and distrust among the Acharites."

"Nonsense!" Askam looked angrily at Zared. "I am Prince of the West, and you Prince of the North, Zared. Between us we provide the Acharites—the peoples of the West and North, *dammit!*—all the royalty they need. This talk of the throne of Achar is—"

"Necessary!" Zared said.

Askam slammed his fist on the table, but before he could speak Caelum shouted, "Enough!

"Enough," he repeated in a more reasonable tone. He waited until Askam and Zared had calmed themselves. "Zared, what exactly are you saying?"

"I am saying that the Acharites have paid enough," he said. "They do not have to keep on paying. They look about and they see that all other racial groups have their kings and leaders, but the Acharites have been denied that right. They look about and they see that *they* are the *only* ones to carry any heavy burden of taxes. Caelum, they are feeling persecuted. That is dangerous. Very dangerous."

"So what are you saying that you *want*?" Caelum said very quietly, his gaze riveted on Zared's face.

"I, as so many of the Acharites, want the throne of Achar restored."

Utter silence greeted his words.

Finally FreeFall dropped his head into his hand, rubbed the bridge of his nose, then looked up. "Axis should have foreseen this," he said quietly.

"Listen," Zared said, "I want only for the Acharites what every other race in Tencendor has got—its own leadership, its own pride. As with every other race and seat of power, the throne of Achar would be subject to the Throne of the Stars. To you, Caelum. I am in no way disputing your claim to overlordship."

"And I suppose you want all the land west of the Nordra back to go with your throne, Zared! And Carlon! And the *palace* in Carlon!" Askam yelled.

No-one missed Askam's inflection of the "your."

"No, I do not, Askam," Zared said hurriedly. "There is no need to give up any land or any of your power. A ceremonial throne, nothing more. But something to give the Acharites their pride back."

"And when they have their pride, will they again take up their axes and come after the Avar and the Icarii?" Isfrael asked.

"There was no need for that remark!" Zared retorted. "The Wars of the Axe are long gone, Isfrael. The Seneschal is dead. I talk only of resurrecting a people's self-worth, not of ancient hatreds. Do not confuse my request with the mistakes of the past."

"And I say there was *every* need for that remark!" Isfrael's lips curled, as if he were about to snarl. "The 'Acharites' have been feeling persecuted for *how* long? Forty years, if that? Why don't you ask *FreeFall,* Zared, or any one of my people, what it was like to be repressed for a thousand years! What it was like to have to haunt the shadows and the ice caves to escape the murderous axes of your . . . of the Acharites! And why not let Sa'Domai speak of the generations *his* people were reviled as carrion-eating barbarians? I feel no pity for your cause."

His last words came out almost as a growl, and everyone at the table stared at him, mesmerized by his wild anger.

Caelum finally dropped his eyes to the table where he traced a forefinger through imaginary dust on its gleaming surface. "Are you saying you want to be King of Achar, Zared?"

Zared just stared at him.

Caelum raised his eyes, very calm now. "The line is *dead,* Zared. It died with Borneheld on the floor of the Chamber of the Moons."

"No," Zared said quietly. "The line lives. There is a legitimate heir. I am the *only* son of the Princess Royal's *only* legitimate marriage! Borneheld was illegitimate, Axis is illegitimate, and I—"

"You can't prove Rivkah's marriage to Magariz," Askam said. "There are no records."

"Does anyone at this table call Rivkah a liar?" Zared asked, his eyebrows raised.

Silence again, and eyes dropped to the table. Both Rivkah and Magariz had been honorable people. No-one doubted their claim to their teenage marriage.

"So," Caelum said very slowly, back to his irritating play with his forefinger. "Zared wants the circlet and ring of office back."

Zared gave a bark of harsh laughter. "I *have* the circlet and the ring, Caelum! Did you forget that Axis gave both to Rivkah? What I am asking is that you give the throne back to the Acharites."

"It's too dangerous, Zared. You must realize that."

"Dangerous to *whom,* Caelum? Can you not see that it is dangerous if you do *not* give it back?"

"No wonder you want my sister," Askam said. "She would almost guarantee you the entire territories of Achar."

"Not if you weren't so lax about getting yourself an heir, Askam."

Askam leaped to his feet, as did Caelum, who had to physically restrain the Prince. "Askam, sit down! I command it!"

Askam sank resentfully back in his chair. "And as ever again," he muttered, "the devious brother from Ichtar shall seize the throne of Achar."

"That is *enough*!" Caelum shouted, then turned back to Zared. "Have you no idea what dissent you have created with your request, Zared? Have you no idea of the fears you have resurrected?"

He threw a hand about him. "Stars damn you! Look at what has happened about this table, then multiply that one hundred thousand times!"

"I know only of the dissent and anger that will be roused if you refuse, Caelum." Zared paused. "I can see that I have created uncertainty and discomfort among my fellows—for that I express my regrets. But I do not regret having mooted the possibility of a restored King of Achar. It should have been discussed years ago."

"Zared, if you will remain silent a few minutes," Caelum said, then he took a deep breath and looked about the table. "Talk to me."

Sa'Domai raised his eyebrows, and Caelum nodded at him.

"Zared has a point," the Ravensbund chief said. At Askam's irritated gesture, Sa'Domai hurried on. "Certainly regarding the human population feeling victimized, and probably about the need for a throne as well. What he says makes sense, and yet I understand the concerns that go with the idea of a restored Acharite King."

Askam scowled at him, wondering if Zared had paid the Ravensbund Chief for those words.

"FreeFall?" Caelum asked. "What do you say?"

The Talon of the Icarii hesitated. He had never foreseen the possible resurrection of Achar, and the thought filled him with foreboding. Yet he liked and respected Zared. Trusted him. But what if, several generations into the future, another Borneheld was born? Or if the Acharites, having got their throne back, started to hunger once again for the Seneschal? Could he accede to a request which might eventually result in yet another devastating civil war? Another forest burning? Another exile for the Icarii?

"I say the restored throne is too dangerous," he said. "It is too soon. The scars of the past could too easily reopen. Achar is best left a memory."

Askam nodded. "Yes. Exactly."

"Isfrael?" Caelum asked. "Your people bear as many scars as FreeFall's, and must have the same fears."

The Mage-King had quietened since his previous outburst. He sat in silence a moment, his eyes introspective. "I must protect my people," he finally said, "as also the infinitely precious souls who roam the magical Minstrelsea. I must think of the forests, and of the pain and blood that my mother, Faraday Tree Friend, expended in planting those forests. She was once Queen of Achar, but she abandoned her place for the trees. I say," and now his eyes sharpened and he looked about the table, "that the peoples of the West and the North have their respective heads in the two Princes of those regions. I say they should look for their pride to both Zared and Askam. I say the throne of Achar is too dangerous. Let it stay buried."

Zared turned his head away slightly, his mouth twisting.

"Yllgaine?" Caelum turned to the last of the Five.

Yllgaine sighed. "Like Sa'Domai I can see both sides of the issue. I have myself heard murmurings among the peoples of the West, but I can also," he looked at FreeFall, "understand the fears generated by the past. If a marriage bed is too dangerous an item with which to unite the West and North, then how much more dangerous a throne? I say no."

Caelum nodded. Only Sa'Domai had come out in favor, if it could be called that, of Zared's request. Caelum knew he had to refuse—Stars damn it! He had no choice! What was Zared thinking of? But what would happen when he *did* refuse? Was Zared likely to mount a rebellion? Was it inevitable war if he granted the request, or inevitable war if he refused?

No, Zared could never hope to mount a rebellion. He had the resources of the North, true, but that did not stretch to such massive manpower that it could defeat a combined army from the rest of Tencendor, or the Lake Guard and Strike Force combined, if it came to that.

No, Zared would sulk, but he would not fight the issue.

But, by the Stars! Caelum decided, he had to do something about Zared. How many people in the West and North *did* see him as a possible heir to the dismantled throne? If Zared wived, and then bred, then how long might that line continue to haunt Tencendor?

Caelum, as his father had so many times before him, silently cursed Rivkah for producing an heir to the line when by rights she should have been too old to breed.

"Your request was foolish in the extreme, Zared," Caelum said. "Gods, man! Why resurrect the hatreds of the past?"

"I was *not* trying to resurrect the—"

"Your request is refused, Zared. You will never mention it again. Isfrael was right. The peoples of the West and North have their respective Princes as their source of pride."

He stood up. "So I have said and so it shall be done," he stated formally, nodding at the notaries and secretaries. "This Council of the Five is formally disbanded."

14

A Moot Point

Herme, Theod and Jannymire Goldman awaited Zared in his chambers. It was risky, perhaps, but they'd felt it better to wait there than lurk about corridors.

The three men were silent, apprehensive. None of them could sit: Theod leaned against the mantelpiece of the fireplace, playing with a candlestick; Herme stared out a window, his hands clasped behind his back; Goldman stood behind a great wing-backed chair to one side of the chamber, his hand resting on its high back, his fingers drumming restlessly.

No word had come from the Great Hall, although one of Goldman's new-found friends among Sigholt's servants relayed that the Princess Leagh had been hastened from the hall, her face stricken, and had not emerged from her chamber the entire afternoon.

Now it was approaching dusk.

What was happening? What had been decided?

The door flung open, and all three men jumped.

Zared strode in, stared at them, then slammed the door behind him.

"Nay, nay and nay!" he snarled, and poured himself a

drink from a wine decanter on a sideboard. His hands shook so badly, fat red rivulets of the wine ran down his fingers and pooled on the sideboard, but no-one noticed.

Herme glanced at Theod, then both nobles looked at Goldman.

"The taxes?" Goldman asked softly.

"Oh, you will do well, good Goldman," Zared said, his tone harsh, and he gulped down half his wine. "For those residing in the West the tax has been reduced to one-tenth."

Goldman visibly relaxed, as did Herme and Theod.

"But . . ." Herme said, noting well the anger radiating out of Zared's eyes.

"*But* for everyone else the tax has been raised to a half. One-half!"

None of the others missed the new tax's significance.

"Caelum must think you are made of diamonds," Goldman said carefully.

"Caelum," and the way Zared said it, the word became a curse, "believes that Askam has become indebted only because of his service to the Throne of the Stars. Thus it is only fair that someone else help shoulder the burden of that debt. Me, no less! I ask you, gentlemen, would I have received more sympathy if I had lost all my wealth in flooded gloam mines as well? No—don't answer that!"

He refilled his glass and swallowed some more wine. "The border tax has gone. At least Caelum managed to right *that* wrong."

"Nevertheless," Herme said evenly. "It seems that only the Acharites must bear the burden of the tax, and of the debt Askam accrued in Caelum's name. I assume the Icarii and the Avar, even the Ravensbund, will contribute nothing to its repayment?"

Zared shook his head. "The Acharites only." He paused. "My friends . . . I tried to argue against this, but . . . but, *gods, I cannot believe this!* . . . Caelum spoke such words into our minds that I am still reeling. He said this was only right as the Acharites had spent a thousand years persecuting everyone else, desecrating this land. We are repaying the debts of our forefathers, my friends, not Askam's debts."

Silence, then . . .

"May his liver burn with the heat of sunfire," Theod muttered savagely, "and his testicles feel the nibble of—"

"Silence!" Zared cried. "Speak not against Caelum in this enchanted Keep!"

Theod took a deep breath and half-turned away, but if he held his tongue, then his fury was shared by all in the chamber.

"And Leagh?" Goldman eventually asked.

"Nay," Zared said. "She and I must bed elsewhere, it seems."

Again the three men exchanged looks.

"And our pride?" Herme said very, very quietly. "What judgment did Caelum make on the throne?"

Zared raised his head and looked at him. "Nay, my friend. What else?"

Then, in a movement so sudden and vicious it shocked everyone else in the room, he turned on one heel and threw his glass into the fireplace.

It shattered into a thousand pieces, glittering like raindrops across the cold, gray stone.

"In Caelum's eyes, inevitably a king of Achar would lead the Acharites east with axes," Zared said, his voice rising until he was almost shouting. "Slashing and burning and murdering until again we drive the magical races from this land! *There* lies his reasoning! Curse his reasoning, I say! Does he think I would bring Artor the Plough God back from his ethereal grave as well?

"Herme, Theod." Zared swung about and faced them. "And you, Goldman. I need to know how you stand. I need to know where your loyalties lie. With Caelum? With Askam? Or . . ."

Herme picked something up from a low table and walked over to Zared, holding the object out in his hands.

It was Zared's sword.

"Our loyalties lie with the Acharites, Zared, and with the

man legitimately born to lead them. Take the sword, take us, and take hold of your destiny."

Zared stared at Herme, then his eyes slowly dropped to the sword.

"Whatever words Caelum mouths," Goldman said very quietly, "whatever he argues, Achar and Leagh are still within your grasp. Once they are yours, you can right the wrongs done to our people."

Zared reached out and grasped the sword, but he did not lift it from Herme's hands. He looked about the room. "I pledged Axis my loyalty when I came into my inheritance, and then the same to Caelum when he assumed the Throne of the Stars. Must I now turn my back on my pledges and become another Borneheld to tear Tencendor apart?"

"Axis turned his back on the Acharites by destroying their monarchy and their pride," Herme said. "Caelum has done the same by insisting that only Acharites pay taxes to save Askam from beggarhood."

"Caelum's disregard for the needs, wishes and pride of the Acharites is insulting, my Prince," Goldman added. "What a town is on fire, do the citizens petition the mayor for permission to put the flames out? No! They see the fire and they rush to remedy it. My Lord Zared, the Acharite people are on fire and you have the ability and the means to douse their agony. *Do it!*"

"You will not tear Tencendor apart," Theod said, with more wisdom than his years suggested, "but simply rebuild its integrity. Only with Acharite pride restored can all races share equally, and bear the burdens equally."

Zared stared long moments at his sword, then sighed, and picked it up, buckling it to his weapons belt with swift economical movements. "You three have encouraged me, now you must advise me. Our troops are stationed—surely you do not counsel war against the StarSon?"

"Nay," Herme said, his voice now brisk. "Caelum has erred in not realizing the severity of the situation, and the depth of Acharite feeling."

"And so . . ."

"And so you—we—must do something to make the StarSon realize just how serious Acharite needs are."

"Yes?"

"Kastaleon."

Zared stared at him, then slowly smiled. "You counsel well. Kastaleon it is. If we seize that, then not only will it free trade along the Nordra, but Caelum will realize the need for dialogue."

"And, of course," Goldman said, "Caelum will appreciate that you could have done much worse. The entire West lies for the taking, but you content yourself with Kastaleon."

"You have been wasted in the guilds, good Master Goldman," Zared said. "You are a diplomat born and bred."

Goldman shrugged depreciatingly, but his eyes glinted. "'Tis the very reason I *am* Master of the Guilds, my Prince."

Zared looked at the other two. "How *will* Caelum react? With dialogue, another Council, or with war? If Caelum raises the resources of Tencendor against us, we will be crushed within a day."

"I think not," Herme said. "Goldman spoke well. Caelum will do *everything* he can to avoid war. You will be reprimanded, yes, but you will also be listened to. Caelum is not his father. He has not been trained and bred in war and he will most certainly not rush into it. Zared," he said very quietly and with the insight of his years. "Caelum feels insecure on that throne. He will do *anything* to avoid a serious confrontation."

Zared narrowed his eyes at Herme. Caelum felt insecure on the throne? He'd never thought about it, but it just might be true. Axis had been a superb war leader and an equally good peace-time ruler. It must be hard for Caelum to wonder every day if his subjects compared him to Axis, or to pause before every action to agonize, "Is this how Axis would have done it?"

Finally he gave a single nod. "What force does Askam have at Kastaleon?"

"Small, my Prince," Theod said, then grinned wolfishly. "Tencendor *is* at peace, after all."

"I want this bloodless," Zared said. "I am, after all, only making a point."

A moot point, my lord, Herme thought cynically, for we *are* going to war! His blood leaped in joy at the thought. War. Herme had been too young to participate in the wars that had gripped Tencendor forty years ago, and yet he had been trained for war all his life. He longed for it, and he longed to see the Acharites regain their rightful place in this new world that Axis SunSoar had created.

"I leave first thing in the morning," Zared said. "You two follow in three days. I do not want Caelum to see us ride out together."

He paused. "Leagh. I cannot leave her behind . . ."

"You most assuredly should not," Goldman said, "for she will be as important a conquest as Kastaleon. But you cannot seize her and carry her off with you."

"I was not *quite* thinking in those terms, Goldman," Zared said. "What do you suggest?"

"I have the perfect plan, my Prince," Goldman said, and smiled. "I will travel from Sigholt with you, and then head straight for Carlon to prepare the way. But you, Sirs Duke and Earl, shall carry a little something extra on your ride from Sigholt . . . don't you think?"

15

Murder!

It was late, but Zared could not settle. He moved restlessly about his chamber, picking up a boot here, a book there, eventually discarding them all. He had given Gustus his orders, and in the early morning they would ride out.

Ostensibly for Severin.

Zared would be very glad to get out of this Keep. Its bewitched air was all very well for the SunSoars and Icarii Enchanters, but Zared longed for the smell of the grass plains, and the homey bustle of Severin.

When would he see it again?

He sighed and decided that wandering about his chamber was doing him no good. He needed to see Leagh and, failing that, to find Zenith and ask her to give Leagh a message for him.

"I *will* fight for you, Leagh," Zared whispered into the room, then he turned for the door.

The corridors were very quiet. Most people would be asleep by this time. Zared walked to the main stairwell and was preparing to mount to the next floor when Zenith appeared, coming down.

She halted at the sight of him, and Zared held out a hand in concern.

"Zenith, what is wrong?"

Her cheeks were flushed, her eyes unnaturally bright, and her own hand trembled as she took his.

"I *am* Zenith," she said, her voice almost harsh. "I *am*!"

Zared's concern deepened and he drew her closer, putting an arm about her waist. "Sweetheart? What is wrong?"

"I—"

He gently folded her wings and stroked them with one hand. "Come now, Zenith, what's wrong?"

Zared's voice calmed her. He had always been a close friend, and Zenith trusted him more than most. But . . . "I cannot speak of it, Zared, Please, do not—"

The sound of feet drumming on the stairs above them stopped her mid-sentence. She and Zared looked up. It was Caelum, coming down the stairs at a pace that was almost a run. He crashed into Zared and Zenith before he could bring himself to a halt.

"What do you here?" he snapped.

"What do *you* do, almost falling down these stairs?" Zared asked.

Caelum ignored him. "Zenith, I've been looking for you. We need to talk. I don't want you to think that—"

And then, before he could finish, the disturbed peace of the stairwell was further shattered by a roar of anger from the level above them.

"Murder! Murder! A *foul* murder!"

It was Isfrael's voice.

"Isfrael?" Zared muttered. "Did he say—"

"Murder?" Caelum cried, then leaped for the stairwell. "His voice came from RiverStar's room!"

Zenith roused in Zared's arms. "No, no . . . Stars! *No!*"

Zared hurried with her after Caelum. By the gods! Zared thought, all of Sigholt's windows and doors need to be flung open to rid it of the ill-feeling floating about its spaces!

By the time Caelum, Zared and Zenith had climbed the stairs and reached RiverStar's open door the night was still and quiet.

The faint glow of a lamp shone through the doorway, and Caelum strode through without a word or a knock.

He halted two strides in. Immediately before him stood FreeFall and Isfrael, both stiff with shock. Caelum pushed them to one side, then stilled at the horror revealed.

Behind him Zared's and Zenith's faces went slack with disbelief.

Drago knelt on the far side of the chamber, a bloodied kitchen knife in his hand. On the floor before him lay River-Star, her limbs and wings flung wide, her dress torn and rent, her body smeared with blood that even as they watched pud-dled in dull pools about her.

Her eyes were wide, staring at the ceiling. They were blank. Uncaring. Dead.

Caelum slowly raised his eyes toward Drago's face. As in his chamber when WolfStar had told the gathering about what he'd heard at the Star Gate, all Caelum could see was

Gorgrael hurtling out of the sky, following DragonStar's call. He remembered the agony of Gorgrael's claws wrapped about his body. He remembered DragonStar's triumph as he had thought he'd finally rid himself of his hated brother.

And now here lay RiverStar, murdered, and his hated brother crouched in undeniable guilt over her corpse.

All could now see his damnable treachery. And *this* time, Caelum thought, we will finally do away with you, brother.

"No doubt I shall be blamed for this," Drago said with extraordinary calmness. He stood up, but he did not drop the knife. His eyes were fixed on Caelum's face.

Zenith pushed past Isfrael, FreeFall and Caelum and sank to her knees before her sister's body. "RiverStar?" she said uselessly. "RiverStar?" Her hands trembled badly. She clenched them, then reached out and closed RiverStar's eyelids.

"Isn't there something you can do?" Zared asked, looking between the two Enchanters and Isfrael. "Surely . . ."

"There is nothing we can do," Zenith said. "Nothing! The Song of Recreation can work only on the dying. Not even the gods can resurrect the dead."

She turned to Drago. "Drago? What happened?"

There was a silence, and when Drago responded he looked only at Caelum. "I don't know. It is as if . . . as if I can't remember . . ."

He frowned suddenly, and looked at Zenith. "It is as if I have a dark hole in my memory. I heard Isfrael cry out, and I blinked, and here I was."

Zenith went cold at his words. You too? she thought.

"You don't *know*?" Caelum said. His tone was angry, yet somehow almost mocking.

"We found them like this," FreeFall said, his voice hoarse with shock. "Isfrael had just joined me in my chamber down the corridor. We heard . . . felt . . ."

"Despair," Isfrael said, his voice so even it was almost detached. "We felt despair from this room, so we investigated."

Yet if Isfrael's voice seemed detached, his body was so taut he appeared as if he would uncoil and strike at any moment.

"When we stumbled in," he continued, "we found Drago kneeling before our sister's bloodied corpse."

"And so you shouted out," Zared said. He shifted uneasily, glancing at the two small horns that curled out of Isfrael's hair.

Isfrael swept his eyes back to Drago and managed to bare his teeth and hiss at the same time. "Murderer!"

"Murderer," Caelum repeated flatly.

"No," Zenith and Drago said almost as one.

"No," Drago said again. "I did not do it. That I swear."

Zenith reached out with her power, testing his response, and sensed that he spoke the truth. She looked at Caelum, about to speak, but her eldest brother responded first.

"*Liar!* You were ever the murderer! You tried to kill me, and you have finally succeeded with RiverStar!" He turned to the door and used both voice and power in his summoning. "Guards!"

Drago finally dropped the knife. It fell softly, almost apologetically, on RiverStar's body.

"No!" he shouted, and Zenith winced at the negative reverberating around the room. You too?

"No," Drago said more quietly, his voice surprising in its dignity. "I did not murder RiverStar. I may have hated her, but I did not murder her. I will *not* admit to something I did not do. But I do not expect you of all people to believe me, Caelum."

His face was very, very calm.

Again, silence.

Then Zared spoke. "Caelum, the guards are here. What do you want them to—"

"They will take Drago and they will chain him—"

"Caelum, please—" Zenith began.

"—and they will throw him into the most secure cell we have. There," Caelum's voice hardened, "he will rot until this time *I* decide how he shall be punished!"

"Perhaps you would give him to me for an Avar trial," Isfrael said, a gleam in his eyes. "I can ensure he would receive due justice."

"No," FreeFall said. "Leave him with Caelum, Isfrael. Caelum will see that he gets—"

"Caelum," Zared interrupted, "Drago should be kept under watch, surely, but is there need for such measures? He has denied RiverStar's murder—"

"*You* were not the one to suffer days under Gorgrael's claws!" Caelum shouted. "How dare *you* preach to me how this . . . this traitor should be handled?"

Zenith rose, and reached across RiverStar's body for Drago's hand. It was sticky with his sister's blood. "Drago," she said quietly, "what did you mean when you said you had a dark hole in your memory? Tell me."

Suddenly she felt an angry hand about her arm and she was wrenched backward.

"You will stay away from him, Zenith!" Caelum said, waving the guards forward to take Drago into their custody. He opened his mouth to say more, but there was a step in the doorway.

Everyone in the room looked to see who it was.

Everyone in the room stilled, their emotions a mixture of fear, awe and, for some, gladness.

In the doorway stood Axis, God of Song, and his wife, Azhure, Goddess of Moon. Although they were dressed in simple robes, they exuded unimaginable power. All felt it and, feeling it, feared it.

Axis and Azhure—parents of RiverStar. They looked only at her body, strewn so carelessly on the floor. Both their faces had paled, and Azhure had a hand clasped over her mouth.

Axis slowly raised his eyes from his daughter's corpse to Drago. "Do you know what I said to your mother, Drago, when she recounted how she had punished you for your part in Caelum's kidnapping? I said that if I had been there I would have killed you."

He paused. "This time I *will* see that you are put to death."

* * *

Caelum stood with his parents in his chamber. They held each other, their tears streaming freely. RiverStar had not been the most lovable of children, and as an adult she had spurned her parents' love, but that had not stopped Axis and Azhure loving her with all the strength they had, and that did not stop their grief now.

Azhure was trembling and still very pale, tears flowing freely down her cheeks. On one side, Axis had an arm about her, on the other, Caelum, both giving her all the support and love they could.

Azhure had struggled so hard to keep RiverStar when she had been but a babe in the womb. To see her so brutally murdered was almost more than she could absorb.

Axis was the first to recover, and he wiped his tears away with the back of his hand, and looked at Caelum.

"He must die."

Caelum nodded. "He will, Father. This time he *will* die."

They stood there a long time, holding each other in silent comfort. Then Axis and Azhure made their way back to RiverStar's chamber where her body, now cleaned of its blood, was upon her bed. They were gods, but they could do nothing but grieve as parents.

They stood long minutes, staring, then Azhure reached out a hand and ran it down RiverStar's cold face.

"Good-bye," she whispered.

And then she and Axis vanished.

16

SunSoar Justice

Having hosted the Council of Five three days earlier, now the Great Hall of Sigholt was arrayed for a trial.

About the dais at the far end of the Hall a plain wooden throne, several chairs and a table had been arranged. Before the dais were set several smaller tables. To either side were seats for the SunSoar family, the four remaining heads of the Five Families, their lieutenants and assistants. The body of the Hall was filled with curious, murmuring people from Lakesview, a goodly number of the Icarii Strike Force who were stationed in Sigholt, and most of Sigholt's servants.

Standing in ranks down either side of the Hall, and behind the seats of the Five and the SunSoar Families, were several hundred silent members of the Lake Guard. Here, as always, to serve StarSon in whatever manner they saw fit. WingRidge CurlClaw stood several paces in front of their leading ranks, only a pace or two behind the Throne of the Stars itself.

At noon the heads of the Five Families filed silently onto the dais and took their seats, and behind them came Isfrael. He looked tense and unhappy in the stone hall, surrounded by so many people, and he hesitated briefly before finally taking his seat. The SunSoar family then moved into their places: EvenSong, FreeFall's wife and Axis' sister, and Zenith. Princess Leagh of the West sat next to Zenith. As the heads of the Five arranged themselves in their seats, Caelum entered the Hall and stepped onto the dais. He glanced at the assembled crowd, then walked over to the throne and sat down silently.

As always he was dressed entirely in black, save for a golden sun that blazed from the center panel of his tunic. With his black hair and his angry, dark blue eyes, he looked exactly what he was supposed to look like—a dispatcher of justice, and the ultimate authority in the realm.

Zenith looked about for WolfStar but could not see him. She heaved a sigh of relief, and her hands relaxed from the claws they had been bunched into. She had not seen the Enchanter for three days, not since the night he'd kissed her above Sigholt.

She had not slept well since. Her eyes were ringed with dark shadows, her skin pasty. Every time she slept she would find herself on the Island of Mist and Memory, reading the rites at Yuletide, moving familiarly about the quarters of the First Priestess, sitting at her desk to write to her unborn daughter.

The nights were unendurable, and Zenith had taken to drinking stimulants to keep herself awake.

To keep Niah at bay.

Beside her, Leagh was torn between observing the huge crowd gathering in the Hall, and watching her friend with concern. Zenith was not herself, something seemed to be worrying her to the point where the Enchanter virtually refused to eat, and Leagh had almost forgotten her own troubles in the strength of her anxiety for Zenith.

But every so often Leagh would remember Zared's stricken face as she'd been dragged from this very Hall, and remember the love and the desperation she'd seen there. She blinked back tears. Zared had ridden out two days ago. She'd heard the clatter of hooves early in the morning, but had not been able to see him from her window. He had gone, and they had not even been able to say good-bye.

Not personally that is, although one of the Lake Guard, somewhat unusually, Leagh thought, had relayed messages between them. "He will fight for you," the birdman had told her. "Never fear."

There was a movement in the Hall, and Leagh refocused her eyes on the present.

Caelum had signaled, and now a Strike Force member carried forth a plain wooden chair and placed it in a clear space before the dais.

It faced Caelum.

Again Caelum signaled, and a guard of four Strike Force members escorted Drago into the Hall and to the chair.

Drago glanced about him, blinking in the light, and then he slowly faced Caelum. Leagh drew in her breath at the sight of him. His face was shadowed with beard, his hair and clothes unkempt, his eyes sunken but bright with hostility.

They could at least have given him water to wash with, Leagh thought, and then wondered if he'd even been given water to drink.

"Your name?" Caelum asked softly, but in a voice that carried throughout the Hall.

"My name is Drago SunSoar." Drago paused. "It *was* once DragonStar SunSoar."

Caelum's face tightened in anger.

"Your birth name," Caelum said, "was stripped from you, and you have no right to mouth it now. Today we sit in judgment to decide whether your life will be stripped from you as well."

Leagh's immediate reaction to this initial brief—but highly charged—exchange was a sense of wonderment that Drago's life had not *already* been taken. Had Drago sat in his cell for the past three nights, watching the shadows about the cell door, expecting assassins with each breath he drew?

"My sister RiverStar is dead," Caelum said, his eyes locked with Drago's. "She was your sister, too, and you shared the bond of the womb. It is abhorrent," Caelum almost spat the word, "to me that you could murder not only your own sister but a sister with whom you shared the womb bond."

Beside Leagh, Zenith roused and opened her mouth to speak, obviously as perturbed as Leagh that Caelum was not even going to pretend impartiality. But EvenSong also saw her movement, and laid a restraining hand on Zenith's arm.

Sadness overwhelmed Leagh. She remembered how kind Drago had been when helping her down to meet Zared in the courtyard. Without his support that day, Leagh did not think she would have been as calm or composed. Yet all she could feel here in this Hall was a communal hatred toward Drago that was as stunning in its blindness as it was in its intensity.

They *should* have killed him earlier, she thought, surreptitiously brushing away a tear, for that would have been kinder than this public spectacle.

"Your predilection for violence is legendary," Caelum continued, his voice more controlled but his hands white where they gripped the arms of the throne. "You allied yourself with Gorgrael the Destroyer against your parents and the realm of Tencendor. Your single betrayal was almost enough to prove the undoing of this entire nation!"

"How am I supposed to believe that this happened?" Drago cried, stung into response. "I am told this tale, but I remember none of it! As far as I am concerned it is an excuse made up to justify our father's own misjudgments and his almost failure to stop Gorgrael!"

A murmuring arose from the body of the Hall. Caelum's face was rigid with anger, but before he could speak Drago forged on, his own face lined and pale, his violet eyes darkened by intense emotion.

"Remember that I am not on trial here and now for what *may* have happened forty years ago! Have I not paid enough?"

"*You?* Well may *we* ask, have *we* not paid enough for your past crime? Don't you have any idea how it continues to plague . . . Ah! Enough of that! You are on trial here and now for your present crime and for your *life*!" Caelum paused, controlled himself, then waved at a guard. "Sit him down."

A guard laid a hand on his shoulder and Drago sank down into his chair. Leagh thought he wore the face of a man who knew he was dead. Why this public charade, Caelum? she thought. Why?

As Drago sat down, Caelum stood and spoke to the assembly. All those present who could remember Axis addressing the crowd outside Carlon when he had proclaimed Tencendor could instantly see his father's blood in Caelum. He had, if not quite the same aura of command, then the beauty, grace, and presence of his father.

"My friends," he said, and held out his hand in supplication, "let me tell you what I know. Three nights ago I was talking with my father's brother, Zared, and my remaining sister Zenith. We heard the Mage-King Isfrael cry out from the direction of RiverStar's chamber and we rushed to investigate. When we reached her chamber, we found Isfrael and Talon FreeFall standing before Drago, who was crouched in undeniable guilt over RiverStar's body, the vile blade he had used to murder her still clutched in his hand. FreeFall, will you explain how you came to find Drago?"

FreeFall stood and, speaking in an even tone, but keeping his eyes away from Drago, told how he and Isfrael had been conversing in his rooms when they'd felt, as Isfrael had said, a despair emanating from RiverStar's chamber. On investigating, they'd found Drago crouched over her body. When he'd finished speaking he sat down.

"I thank you, Talon," Caelum said, then turned to Isfrael. "My Lord Mage-King, did Talon FreeFall speak truly?"

Isfrael stood. "He did, StarSon."

"I thank you, Mage-King." And Isfrael sat down.

Now Caelum turned his attention to his sister. "Zenith, have I described what we heard and saw accurately?"

Hesitant and uncomfortable, Zenith slowly rose to her feet. She opened her mouth, but had to lick her lips before any sound came out. "We heard Isfrael cry out, and when we reached RiverStar's chamber we found the Mage-King and FreeFall. And we saw Drago SunSoar before RiverStar's corpse."

"And he clutched the murderous knife in his hand?"

"He clutched a knife in his hand, yes. But—"

"I thank you, Zenith. You may sit."

Zenith sank down, and Leagh took her arm, trying to give her friend some comfort. No-one liked testifying against a brother, and surely not against one as unfairly treated as this.

Caelum faced Drago once more. "Stand, if you please."

Leagh's face hardened. This was more than ridiculous! Drago was up and down like a child's string puppet.

Drago stood.

"Face those here assembled, if you please."

Drago did not move, a muscle working in his cheek.

"Face those here assembled!"

A guard's hand fell on Drago's shoulder, but Drago wrenched himself about on his own. Slowly he raised his eyes. Before him a thousand pitiless eyes stared back.

"Did I speak the truth, Drago? Did I tell it how it was? Answer!"

Drago fought to suppress his fury. Did Caelum want him to stand forth and admit to his own sister's murder?

Apparently so. *"Answer!"*

"Isfrael, FreeFall and then Caelum, Zenith and Zared found me in RiverStar's chamber," he finally said. "Kneeling over RiverStar's body. A knife in my hand."

"And is it not true that you murdered RiverStar?"

Drago took a huge breath. "I cannot remember, but I cannot believe that I killed her."

Caelum paused, as if considering the idiocy of that denial. His mouth curled sardonically. "I cannot remember," he repeated, shaking his head slightly.

Then he addressed FreeFall and Isfrael once more. "My Lords, you say that you felt a 'wrongness' that led you to discover Drago over RiverStar's corpse. Do you think that 'wrongness' indicates the time of her death?"

FreeFall indicated that Isfrael should answer. He was the one with the magical ability, not FreeFall.

Isfrael considered carefully. "StarSon, the sense of wrongness hit very suddenly. I assume that it indicated the moment of RiverStar's death."

"Good," Caelum said. "How long was the time interval between feeling the wrongness and discovering Drago in RiverStar's chamber?"

"Very short," Isfrael said. "We ran as soon as we felt it. Seven or eight heartbeats' space, no more. RiverStar's chamber is only two doors from FreeFall's."

Caelum nodded, as if considering. "Then, brother Isfrael, do you consider there was enough time in these seven or eight heartbeats for someone else to have escaped River-Star's chamber?"

Isfrael shook his head. "We would have seen another person. We were out of FreeFall's chamber almost instantly. Of course," he added, "someone winged could have left via her window. Or," and he cast his eyes slowly about the hall, "someone with sufficient magical ability could have just vanished."

"I do thank you," Caelum said, nodding as if considering Isfrael's words, then turned back to Drago. "The time between RiverStar's death and the discovery of you with her corpse was tiny, Drago. Yet you say you did not murder her. If *not*, then mayhap you saw who *did*. Who, Drago? Who vanished or dropped from the window?"

Caelum paused melodramatically. "Who?"

Drago swung back to look at Caelum. "My memory is blank, brother! Can you not understand that?"

"You have a very agreeable memory to so forget your own sister's murder." Caelum's voice was heavy with sarcasm.

"StarSon."

Caelum—as Leagh—leaped in surprise as Zenith's clear voice rang through the chamber. He glared at her, his eyes dark with anger. "Zenith, you have no right to—"

"Caelum," Zenith interrupted, shaking off Leagh's hand and standing. "You are correct in saying that Drago might have seen the true murderer. If so, then any one of the Sun-Soar Enchanters can easily solve this mystery. Yet he says he cannot remember. How easily this can be solved! We could employ the Song of Recall to see what happened with Drago's own eyes. Witness with him."

"You would witness your own sister's death?" Caelum took a horrified step back.

"If it would reveal her true murderer, then yes," Zenith said.

Caelum stared at her. "You are right," he said eventually, "the Song of Recall will clearly show whether Drago is lying or not." His tone clearly indicated which one he thought it would be.

Zenith shot Drago a smile of encouragement as she sat down. He returned her look, but his face was unreadable.

"Drago!" Caelum stepped down from the Throne of the Stars and moved forward, within a pace of Drago. "Drago," he said more softly, "attend my power!"

A hint of music brushed through the air. Leagh knew what was happening, Caelum was using a thread of music from the Star Dance to create a Song of Recall. She could barely hear it herself, but knew the Song must be thundering through every Enchanter in the Hall.

Zenith trembled at her side, and Leagh glanced at her. Zenith seemed all right, her eyes fixed on Drago, and Leagh turned back to look.

Drago had stiffened. His eyes slowly closed, and then his head snapped back.

Caelum half stepped forward, a hand outstretched. Leagh noticed with some bewilderment that his face was contorted as if with massive effort; Leagh had been about Enchanters all her life and knew this Song should be an easy one for Caelum to manipulate.

Caelum's breath hissed out between his teeth, and Drago jerked and shuddered.

Caelum seemed to put more effort into his enchantment. A gleam of sweat appeared on his brow, and his outstretched hand trembled.

"It is of no use!" he cried suddenly. "I cannot retrieve it! He has placed a block over his memory."

"A block?" Zenith murmured at Leagh's side. "A block?

No-one can do that, surely, and least of all Drago, who has no Enchanter powers left!"

"Let me try!" a voice rang out above them, and Zenith uttered a small cry and clutched at Leagh's arm.

"WolfStar!" she whispered, and Leagh was horrified to see stark terror in Zenith's eyes.

She looked up, as did everyone else in the Hall.

From the roof beams far overhead an Icarii birdman was slowly spiraling down. Leagh caught her breath—he was so beautiful! His wings were gold, reflecting the sunlight, his hair seemed almost to be on fire, and his face . . . his face was rippling with power and sensuality.

If Leagh was breathless with admiration, then Zenith was nauseous with shock and horror. As if a light flickered, she first saw WolfStar spiraling down from the roof of the Hall, and then saw him descending from the roof of the Dome. One part of her wanted to flee, another wanted to rush forward into his arms.

"Let me try," WolfStar repeated as he alighted on the floor by Caelum.

Caelum, although he looked startled, stepped aside immediately. "Gladly, WolfStar. I bow to your greater power. Retrieve the murderer's memory for us."

And Caelum shot Drago a look of pure triumph.

WolfStar stepped close to Drago, but did not outstretch his hand as Caelum had. He just stood there, a slight smile on his face, his eyes fixed on Drago, his wings slowly relaxing onto the flagstones behind him.

Zenith trembled, and clutched at Leagh. "Is *he* the murderer, do you think?" she whispered, so low Leagh could hardly hear her. "Is *he* RiverStar's SunSoar lover?"

Leagh could not take her eyes off WolfStar. He radiated power so potent she could feel her very bones vibrate with it. Stars alone knew what it was doing to Drago.

The man had his eyes still bravely fixed on WolfStar's, but his entire body was shaking; Leagh assumed only WolfStar's power was holding him upright, because otherwise she could not see how Drago's legs could possibly hold him.

Then WolfStar whispered.

"No-one bests *me,* manling!"

And everyone in the Hall heard that whisper, *felt* it, and felt (if not heard) the Star Dance surge through the windows and stones and seemingly coalesce on WolfStar.

The Enchanter's hands clenched into fists by his side. *"No-one bests me!"* he screamed, and then Drago screamed also, his arms flailing at his side, and in the space behind him a gray mist materialized, and in this gray mist formed horror.

A ghostly Drago, stepping into RiverStar's chamber. She turned, and spoke, taunted. Drago shouted back, and raised a fist. RiverStar laughed, spoke again, and turned her back dismissively. Drago reached into his robe and withdrew a kitchen knife. He stepped across the space between them and plunged it into RiverStar's back. She half collapsed, screaming, and then Drago had her by the hair, turning her half about, plunging the knife into her flanks, her breasts, her belly. RiverStar's hands beat futilely; nothing could stop Drago's murderous frenzy. Eventually she slipped to the floor, her eyes wide, her mouth opening and closing in the shock of her agonizing dying. Drago let her go and stood above her, panting. His face wore a malicious expression of triumph. He watched her die. He laughed.

Leagh herself was gasping after the horror of the vision, and she only dimly realized that someone was screaming.

She blinked, clearing her eyes and mind.

It was Drago. *"No! No! No! No!"* WolfStar had released him from his enchantment, and the man had slumped to the floor. But still he screamed. *"No! No! No!"*

Zenith burst into tears, and Leagh realized she was crying as well.

Before them, both Caelum and WolfStar relaxed.

Time to do away with this murderous canker in our family, WolfStar? Caelum used his mind voice so that only WolfStar could hear it. So consumed was he by his fear of Drago, Caelum would have allied himself with the most loathsome demon if it meant he'd finally see the last of his brother.

Far more than time. That block was . . . robust. Where did he get the power for that? Yes, definitely time to dispose of him. Azhure should have done it forty years ago. Now, StarSon, you can march into the future with confidence. Forget the horrors of the past.

And face the trial which is ahead of you, WolfStar thought, screening it from Caelum. For that, it is definitely best that Drago be dead.

Caelum had resumed the Throne of the Stars, and WolfStar stepped to the side so that the StarSon could pass judgment on his brother, still kneeling before him.

"Drago, your memory, once so conveniently blank, has admitted to your sister's murder, and you must suffer the sentence imposed on all murderers."

"No!" Drago cried hoarsely, "that 'memory' was a phantasm of someone else's imagination. *I did not kill RiverStar!*"

"The Song of Recall never lies," Caelum said very calmly. "You are sentenced to death, Drago SunSoar. An arrow to the heart as the sun rises in the morning. Thus I speak, thus shall it be so." He paused, and gestured to the four guards from the Strike Force. "Take him away."

As Caelum stepped down from the dais and Drago was led from the Hall, the Lake Guard snapped to attention, swords to foreheads.

17

The Lake Guard on Duty

Zenith sank down onto the floor by her bed and rubbed her head. "Go away, go away, go away," she murmured.

But Niah refused to go. She had been buried in Zenith since birth, content until now with sending only the odd memory bubbling to the surface of Zenith's conscious mind, and enjoying the occasional excursion in something like control of Zenith's mind. But since WolfStar's kiss, since his insistence, Niah was prepared to fight for supremacy.

All the tales Zenith had heard of Niah were of a sweet-natured woman who had willingly given her life for Azhure. But this presence she felt within her was anything but sweet-natured. Had death done this to Niah?

Whatever Caelum had said, Zenith *knew* in the very pits of her soul—*her* soul, dammit!—that the Niah presence was a very different being to herself. There were two of them, not one.

I am not Niah! she thought, and then cried aloud as the Niah voice responded, biting like fire into her mind.

I am you—do either of us have any choice?

"I am *not* you and I have *every* choice, damn you!"

You want what I want. You always have.

"Has all my life thus far been a lie?" Zenith cried to the empty room. "Have none of my decisions been my own, only what this Niah-voice has whispered to me?"

Who could help her against this insistent voice? And even if someone *wanted* to help, then what could they do? Over the past few days Zenith had tried everything she could, used every one of her not inconsiderable powers, and yet nothing had dampened Niah's insistence—or curbed her growing strength. And if Zenith could not repress her . . . who could? Caelum, maybe, but Caelum believed that accepting Niah was Zenith's destiny. That she would just have to "adjust."

"No! Never!"

Desperate for comfort, Zenith tried to conjure the image of StarDrifter. She wanted to hear him say again that all would be well, and that he would always be there for her.

But no matter how hard she tried, all Zenith could manage was a flickering, insubstantial image that faded after only moments.

Was this Niah who so interfered with her power, or something, someone else?

Briefly Zenith remembered the apparent difficulty Caelum had in using the Song of Recall, but at that moment Niah made a renewed surge for supremacy, and Zenith forgot everything save the struggle for her sanity.

She searched frantically for something to hold on to, some thought that was even stronger than Niah.

What?

Drago! Yes, she had to concentrate on Drago. His problems were far worse than hers, for he had only hours to live; already the night had quietened into absolute stillness.

"Drago," she muttered through clenched teeth, clinging to his name and his plight as a charm against the incursions of this hated voice within her. "Drago."

WolfStar . . . where is he now, I wonder?

She fought to think of Drago . . .

Think of how you will enjoy his embrace, my dear. He is SunSoar. He has the blood you crave . . .

In desperation, Zenith concentrated on the horrific vision WolfStar had summoned, and that finally blocked out the Niah-voice. The Song of Recall never lied, all Enchanters knew that . . . but Zenith found it difficult to believe that the vision had been entirely the truth, either. Especially when it was a vision conjured through WolfStar's magic. WolfStar was capable of anything, and he loathed Drago as much as Caelum did.

Neither Caelum nor WolfStar had been prepared to believe anything save that Drago must have killed his sister.

No-one had been prepared to believe anything but that, it seemed.

And so now Drago had to die. He had been condemned, not for what he may or may not have done to RiverStar, but for what he'd done to Caelum all those years ago.

What could she do to help Drago? It was no use going to Caelum. The only other person who still believed in Drago was Leagh, and as sweet as she might be, Leagh would be little help here in Sigholt. Stars, but Caelum had her under almost as close a guard as Drago!

Zared might have helped, but Zared was not here.

Zenith's mouth twisted bitterly. The only people left who had any power to help were her parents, but they distrusted Drago as much as Caelum did, and Zenith was astute enough to realize Drago's sentence was as much their work as Caelum's or WolfStar's.

That left her. She was the only one who could help him. Again her mouth twisted. Both she and Drago were condemned to their different fates by events decades old.

Well, she wasn't going to succumb to her fate without a struggle, and damned if she was going to see Drago condemned to his, either. Sigholt was a prison and a death for both of them. In the morning an arrow waited for Drago's heart, and no doubt WolfStar would appear to claim hers, too.

Both she and Drago would die if they stayed.

No.

Again, Zenith suppressed the voice, thankful to find it easier now. Yes, Drago must be saved. And in saving Drago perhaps she would help herself.

Zenith wrapped a cloak about her shoulders and slipped from the room. There was only one place they could go, one person who might yet help them. StarDrifter. *He* would listen to them, and maybe he knew the magics needed to extinguish Niah's bid for freedom. Zenith wasn't sure how they would manage to get there—she didn't dare use the enchantments of the bridge and Spiredore, for Caelum would be able to follow them that way—but they would manage somehow.

The upper corridors were deserted. All were in bed. Sleeping soundly, no doubt, Zenith thought, before the final threat to their peace of mind was put away in the morning.

But the lower corridors leading to the holding cells in the foundations of Sigholt were deserted as well, and Zenith frowned.

Why no guards?

She moved carefully, peering about corners before slipping down each corridor. Few torches were lit, and those that were guttered in a faint draft that came from nowhere.

No-one? Why? Was she in a dream? Surely Drago merited a guard? Zenith thought Caelum would have posted them at least six deep.

She turned around the final corner and jerked to a halt, her eyes wide and frightened.

One of the Lake Guard stood there, his ivory uniform gleaming in the dim light, the golden knot emblem seeming to leap out at her. He stood straight, but not at attention, his wings carefully folded behind his back. Zenith did not know his name. The Lake Guard might be a constant presence about Sigholt, but they kept to themselves.

"What do you do here, my Lady Zenith?"

She clutched the cloak a little more tightly to her, and kept her own wings folded against her back. "I have come to see my brother. He dies in the morning."

"So I have heard," the guard said. "Well, it is good that you are here. We have been waiting for someone."

What a curious remark, Zenith thought, but then forgot it as the guard unlocked the cell door and pushed it open. "He waits."

Odd, odd people, she thought vaguely, then pushed past him into the cell.

Drago sat crouched in a corner, his back to the wall, staring at her. Everything about him radiated bitterness, directed even at her. She would live in the morning, and he would not.

"I do not deserve to die," he said.

"You surely deserve to have some sense battered into you," Zenith said. "Drago, are you prepared to help yourself?"

His eyes narrowed. "What do you mean?"

"The corridors are deserted, and only one guard stands outside this cell. Sigholt sleeps. If I call the guard in, could you tackle him? Perhaps stand behind the door, so, and leap at him as he enters?"

Something other than bitterness gleamed in Drago's eyes, but Zenith wasn't sure what it was. "Why help *me,* Zenith?"

"Because we both need to get out of this prison, but mostly because you are my brother and I love you," she said softly.

"No-one loves *me*!" he said. "I am *Drago*!"

She gazed levelly at him. "If you want to live, then I am your only chance."

"Why help me?" he asked again. "Caelum is going to be more than upset with you."

"I cannot stay here either, Drago. We each have our fates to escape."

"What do you mean?"

"I cannot explain here and now, Drago. *Do* you want to escape?"

He waited a moment longer, studying her. She had the appearance of calmness, but there was something she was holding in. Drago realized she was only a breath away from snapping completely. "Yes. Yes, I do want to escape."

He pushed himself to his feet, taking a moment to stretch cramped muscles, then moved behind the door. "Call the guard."

Zenith stood in the center of the cell and faced the door. "I am ready to leave now, guard," she called.

Silence.

Her eyes moved to Drago, and he jerked his head to the door. "Again," he whispered.

Zenith called out again, her voice now clearly strained, but again her request was met only by silence.

She trembled, and Drago shifted in irritation. "Once more!"

So she called once more, but still only silence.

Drago cursed softly, and banged on the door with his fist.

Nothing.

Zenith glanced at Drago, trembled, then walked to the door. She hesitated, then banged on it with the flat of her hand. "Open up! Please!"

Stillness.

Again Zenith hesitated, then, suddenly making up her mind, she seized the handle and pulled.

The door swung open, and Zenith almost fell over. She leaped back, giving Drago room to subdue the guard when he entered, but beyond the open doorway there was only flickering light and waiting silence.

Zenith took a step into the corridor and looked about. The guard had disappeared.

Why?

But no time for questions now, time only to seize the chance offered.

"Come on!" she hissed, reaching back into the cell and hauling Drago's sleeve. "Come *on*!"

He crept out of the cell, huddling in the shadow of the wall, his eyes suspicious. "Where are the guards?"

"You don't know? Well, neither do I. Drago, get moving. Now!"

"It's a trick. They're waiting farther down the corridor. I know it."

"Well, my Enchanter powers tell me the way is clear. There is nothing."

"I *know* it is a trap! Caelum will be waiting—"

She almost hit him in her frustration. "Move! Now! Or I swear I will do no more to help you!"

And without a further look she marched down the corridor.

Still Drago hesitated. Then suddenly the concept finally hit home. *Escape!* Escape—and if he escaped, would he then finally be able to seize control of his own destiny and heritage?

Yes, he would damn well *make* the opportunity! Drago straightened and ran after Zenith.

The corridors remained empty, and Zenith led Drago toward a small door in the side wall of Sigholt. But as they turned down the final corridor, Drago caught at his sister's arm.

He had the most curious expression on his face, and his head was tilted, almost as if he were listening to something.

"Wait," he said.

"What?"

"There's something I have to get."

"What?"

"Zenith, for forty years I have been punished for my infant escapade. For forty years I have been denied my heritage. Now I want to snatch a piece of it back."

"Damn you to all the black pits of the interstellar wastes, Drago! We have no time for this!"

Drago seized Zenith's chin in his hand. She stiffened in both affront and fright, but although he had pulled her close, he did not hurt her. "Was I treated fairly in that trial, Zenith. *Was* I?"

"No," she said.

"Have I ever been given a chance to redeem myself?"

"You have had forty years to redeem yourself, Drago," she said. "Do not blame that lack on Caelum as well."

His face twisted and he stepped back. "Wait here for me, Zenith."

"Drago—" She reached out a hand, but he had already gone.

Damn him! In her frustration and anger, Zenith slammed a fist into the rough stone wall, then bit down a cry of pain as the stone bruised her flesh. What was Drago up to?

She waited, the uncertainty agonizing. Then, when she had made up her mind to go after him, she heard his soft footfalls approach.

"What were you doing?" she hissed as Drago rejoined her. He carried a bundle, a small hessian sack bulging with something Zenith could not see, even when she probed it with her mind.

"What is in the sack, Drago? And how is it no-one saw or felt you?"

He laughed humorlessly. "I know how to creep about these corridors undetected, Zenith. Being naturally sly has its uses."

"The sack?"

He shrugged. "Nothing important."

Important enough to risk recapture, Zenith thought, and strange enough that I cannot scry out its contents.

You have done your best, girl. Now go back to bed and wait for our lover. WolfStar can warm the hours before dawn. He waits. I can feel him. I want to feel him.

Zenith gave a low cry and clutched at her head.

"Zenith? What is it?"

"We've got to get out of here, Drago. We *must*!"

Drago stared at her, but she seemed to have recovered from her momentary lapse, and what she said was sensible enough. He had already dared too much and wasted too much time in retrieving this . . . this insurance.

"Then move!" He grabbed her elbow and pushed through the door into the night.

There were a few guards about the central courtyard, but Zenith held her head high and smiled, and pulled Drago close, his head against her shoulder and her arm about his waist. The guards paid them little attention. Zenith and . . . a lover perhaps . . . out for a night stroll.

Through the gate, and to the bridge.

The bridge. The magical guardian of the way into Sigholt. Would she challenge them? Stop them?

"Greetings, lovely Zenith," the bridge remarked, and then her voice tightened. "And you, treacherous son."

Drago stiffened. Even the bridge knew how to hurt.

Zenith spoke rapidly, hoping the bridge would continue to

keep her voice down. "We are out for a stroll, bridge. Do not concern yourself about us."

"There has been trouble in the past few days," the bridge said. "And Drago has been amid the thick of it. I cannot let you pass. I *will* not let you past. He tricked me once before."

"No!" Zenith said. "Please, bridge, we mean no—"

"No."

Zenith could feel Drago rigid next to her, and was terrified he would attempt to run across the bridge, regardless of the consequences.

"We can always swim the moat," she whispered.

"No matter what you do," the bridge said, her voice implacable, "you will not get past. Especially with what you carry, hated son."

Zenith looked again at the sack Drago had under his arm. *What was it?*

"You seem to have misunderstood, bridge," said a low voice, and Zenith and Drago swiveled about in shock.

WingRidge CurlClaw walked slowly toward the bridge from the Keep. He nodded at them, and then spoke again to the bridge.

"Drago walks as one with that sack. Let him pass—"

"I do not believe it!" the bridge hissed. *"Him?"*

"Always," WingRidge said.

There was utter silence. Zenith couldn't believe what was happening—what was WingRidge doing? What was he saying? Why hadn't guards swarmed out of Sigholt to seize them? Why—

"Then pass," the bridge said grumpily.

"Go on," WingRidge said, and pushed Zenith. "Go!"

Drago needed no further prompting. He set off across the bridge at a run, and after a moment's hesitation Zenith followed him.

"It would help," WingRidge said to the bridge, "if you did not mention what has just happened or what I have just told you."

The bridge thought about that. "I find it difficult to believe that Drago—"

"The Maze unwinds in many and varied ways," WingRidge said, "and few understand its conundrums."

18

Hunting Drago

Caelum had called Askam, Herme and Theod to the map-room just before dawn to arrange the final details for Drago's execution, when WingRidge and another of the Lake Guard knocked and entered.

The Lake Guardsman stepped past his captain, and bowed. "Drago is no longer there, StarSon."

"What?" Caelum stopped himself from seizing the birdman's tunic only with the most strenuous of efforts. "What do you mean—'Drago is no longer there'?"

The birdman's face remained expressionless. "StarSon, when we opened the cell this morning he was gone."

Herme and Theod exchanged looks, neither sure what to think, and Askam muttered under his breath.

Caelum looked at WingRidge. "How could this have happened?"

"As yet I cannot say, StarSon. Perhaps SkyLazer," he indicated the birdman who'd entered with him, "can further enlighten us. He was in charge of Drago's guard last night."

"SkyLazer? Well, man, *you* tell us how this could have happened!"

"StarSon, we had guards posted the entire length of the corridors leading to the cell. Three guards stood outside Drago's cell itself. They have reported that there were no visitors and no sounds throughout the night. They are good men all, StarSon, but if you like I can summon them and you can test the truth of their report for yourself."

"No, SkyLazer." Caelum subsided. "That will not be necessary. Askam? I want you to mount a search of the Keep. Take whoever you need, and send several units around the shore to Lakesview as well. He could be hiding in the town."

"As you will, StarSon. And if we should find him?"

Caelum regarded him steadily. "I do not care what condition he is returned in, Askam. Breathing or not. Just make sure he is returned."

Askam understood perfectly. His mouth tightened into a small smile as he bowed to Caelum and then left the room.

Caelum turned to the other two noblemen. "Herme? Theod?"

The two somewhat reluctantly stood forth. Both wanted nothing more than to escape themselves; important business awaited them to the west. Would this delay their departure?

Curse the SunSoars' curious attraction for deep crisis, Theod thought, keeping his face neutral. It was a remarkable achievement if they managed to get through a child's name-day feast without the need for a war council in the middle of it.

"Yes, Caelum?" Herme said.

"I want you two to lead a patrol through the closer Urqhart Hills. If he managed to get past the bridge . . . *damn* . . . the bridge! She must know what has happened! I should have thought of that sooner!"

WingRidge's face tightened a little, but no-one noticed.

Caelum turned back to the birdman from the Lake Guard. "SkyLazer, see to it!"

"My Lord," said SkyLazer, and he stepped to the window and spiraled down.

"The bridge has aided Drago before now," Caelum said to WingRidge. "I'll see her torn apart brick by brick if she has done so again."

I wish you luck, WingRidge thought. More powerful mages than you mortared her together. "She was duped that time, Caelum."

"Then she could be duped again. *Damn* that bridge! Is she not supposed to protect us? Herme, Theod, what are you still doing here?"

"We thought to wait for the bridge's news," Theod said. "It would be pointless for us to scour the hills if the bridge knows where he is."

"Yes, yes, of course," Caelum muttered irritably. He stared at the window. "What can be keeping SkyLazer?"

At his very words, SkyLazer fluttered at the window, grasping the frame and swinging in.

"Well?" Caelum snapped.

"Nothing," SkyLazer said, and unnoticed to one side WingRidge visibly relaxed, relieved the bridge had remained silent. "The night and morning were quiet. The only ones who passed were routine patrols."

"Then we won't be needed—" Herme started, but Caelum interrupted.

"No. I still want you to search the hills. I . . . I want to be certain he has not escaped this Keep. Get to it."

Theod waited on his fidgeting horse as Herme mounted.

"We came to Sigholt for a Council, Herme," Theod observed roughly, "not a manhunt."

"Still, it gives us a chance for a morning's ride, my friend," Herme said, settling himself in his saddle, "and a further chance for you to whittle down that bulk of yours."

Theod put aside his ill humor and laughed good-naturedly. His grandfather, Roland, had been famously fat, but Theod was a slender man whose frame nevertheless belied a whipcord-taut strength.

"And now we are set to hunt one of the famed SunSoar brood?" Theod said as Herme reined in beside him. "I can hardly blame Drago for slicing the lovely RiverStar to bits. Her tongue could cut roast beef from a distance of thirty paces."

"Theod!" Herme said, looking about anxiously. "The very walls can hear! Watch your tongue!"

"Well." Theod shrugged. "I suppose we'd best set off on this manhunt His Starriness has given—"

"Theod!" Herme's voice hissed between them. "Be silent!"

Theod grinned at him, but he kicked his horse forward and said no more.

The hills surrounding Sigholt were not overly high, but there were scores of ravines and gorges within two hours' walk from the lake and Keep, and a thousand more shadowy spaces amid the tree ferns and undergrowth that could hide a man. Herme and Theod rode for the morning and part-way into the afternoon, dividing the thirty-strong company into three groups to scour as much territory as they could, but the blue enchanted mist was thick and the hills secretive, and by mid-afternoon they had found no trace of Drago.

"I think Drago must still be creeping about in Sigholt's cellars," Theod said, reining up next to Herme's mount. "My friend, the sun sinks and we have all missed our lunch. Might I suggest—"

They were interrupted by a shout. One of the forward riders was trotting back toward them from a small ravine to the south-east.

"Sir Duke? Sir Earl? There is a track in that ravine. Someone has walked down it recently. A man, by the size and depth of his boot marks, and a woman. A birdwoman, for wings have left faint trail marks after her footfalls."

Herme and Theod glanced at each other, and spurred their horses forward.

The tracks appeared for about fifteen paces just inside the ravine where there was a patch of soft ground.

Theod swung down from his horse to inspect them more closely. Eventually he looked up, his eyes excited. "Herme? These are—"

"Not Drago's?" Herme said smoothly. "Well, we have done our best."

He waved away the rider who'd accompanied them. "-Ride back to the patrol and tell them to turn for Sigholt. This manhunt is useless. Drago must still be in Sigholt or its surrounds."

"Yes, my Lord," the man said, and wheeled his horse about.

Theod waited until he was out of earshot, and then stood straight. "Herme? What are you doing? These are clearly Drago's tracks. Look, there is the distinctive square heel of those boots of his."

"So what would you have us do, Theod? Ride after him and hunt him down for Caelum?"

Theod frowned, and looked uncertain. "Well . . ."

"Well, no, my boy. Drago suits our purpose far more on the loose than shut up in Sigholt, or buried in a corpse yard."

Theod's face cleared. "Of course! Caelum might spend weeks searching for him."

"Or at the least be so consumed with worry about him that he won't think clearly on 'other' issues. A free Drago will create fear and uncertainty and confusion, and that cannot suit us better."

Theod tore a small gorse bush from the damp soil and wiped out the tracks.

"Then it is just as well we found no trace of him, eh, Herme?" he said, as he finally remounted his horse.

Herme grinned, his face appearing years younger. "Just as well, Theod. We must impress that fact on the man who thought he'd found tracks here. Now, let's ride back and eat."

"Nothing," Herme reported to Caelum, his face weary with the effort he'd expended on the search.

He and Theod still sat their horses in Sigholt's courtyard, Caelum and Askam standing before them.

Caelum nodded, his own face lined with worry. "I thank you, Herme, Theod."

"Our patrols found nothing in Sigholt or Lakesview, either," Askam told them. "Where could the snake be coiled?"

"Stars knows what mischief he could get up to out there," Caelum muttered. "What is he doing? *Where is he?*"

The silence dragged out four or five heartbeats before Theod spoke up.

"We, ah, we would ride out in the morning," he said, "with your permission, StarSon."

"What? Oh yes, I suppose so. Askam, will you stay a while? I may yet need a mounted force to help the Strike Force search."

Askam half bowed. "As you wish, StarSon."

"Perhaps Theod and myself could escort the Princess Leagh home," Herme said.

Both Caelum and Askam looked up sharply, first at the two horsemen before them, then at each other.

Askam shrugged. "I don't see why not, Caelum."

"I'd prefer Zenith to take her back via Spiredore," Caelum said. "It's quicker and safer."

"She would be no trouble for us to escort—" Herme began, but Caelum waved him into silence.

"No. Zenith can take her. Now, gentlemen, if you would like to wash and eat, I would see you in the map-room at dusk."

But Caelum could not find Zenith anywhere. Having spent the morning and afternoon searching for Drago, the Lake Guard spent the evening looking for Zenith, as did every soldier in Sigholt. Nothing.

Finally, late at night, Caelum called the search off.

"Well, maybe it is best you take Leagh with you in the morning," he said wearily to Herme and Theod, and the two noblemen nodded, hiding their relief.

"As you will," Theod said, and they bowed and left.

Caelum was sure he knew where Zenith was. As soon as he had the map-room to himself he sent his power surging out.

WolfStar! WolfStar! WolfStar!

And the Enchanter appeared, curious at the desperation in Caelum's call. "Yes?"

Caelum stared at WolfStar balefully. Again he had appeared out of thin air; that was an enchantment Caelum could only accomplish with the utmost concentration and power, and yet WolfStar made it look like a five-year-old child's accomplishment.

"Where's Zenith?"

WolfStar raised an eyebrow. "Zenith? You told me to stay away from her. I have done nothing to her."

He turned and walked away slightly, his golden wings rustling irritably, his back stiff as if with affront.

"She's not in Sigholt," Caelum said. "Neither . . . neither is Drago."

WolfStar whipped about. "What? He is not dead?"

"Both have disappeared. I . . . I had not thought to connect their disappearances until this moment."

WolfStar stared, chewing his lip, as Caelum told him what had happened since dawn.

"I will find them," he said once Caelum had finished. "They will not escape *me*!"

19

The Fugitive

They ran south and east through the Urqhart Hills, Drago leading, Zenith some paces behind. They had plunged into Sigholt's protective blue mists almost immediately on leaving the bridge, and Drago wanted to get through them before the alarm was raised. He didn't understand the enchantments that had created the mist, and he was afraid the mist could trap them as easily as it could hide them.

As he ran, he kept the sack tightly under one arm.

Two hours after dawn it was clear that Zenith needed to rest. She was heaving for breath, stumbling along, catching at anything she could for support. Drago pulled her under the overhang of a cliff and almost pushed her to the ground as she still protested she could go on.

"Damn it, Zenith. Why didn't you tell me you were so exhausted! We will sit here a while."

"Only a few minutes, Drago. I just need to catch my breath."

He looked at her. "As long as you need."

She nodded, dropping her head into her hands and heaving as much air into her distressed lungs as she could. She was normally so fit, but her struggle with Niah had weakened her physically as well as spiritually.

Drago studied her silently. He didn't know why she had helped him, or why she was even still with him. She had wings, and could have been leagues away by this stage. On foot, those wings were far more hindrance than help.

She said she'd done it for love, but Drago could not quite bring himself to believe that.

"Can this mist trap us?" he asked, once Zenith was breathing easier.

"I don't fully understand it, but, yes . . . I think that it could."

"How much farther does it extend?"

Zenith ran her hands back through her hair, lifting it out of her eyes. "Another hour or two on foot, perhaps."

"And then where?" he asked softly.

She was silent for a while before she answered. "The Island of Mist and Memory."

"What? Gods, Zenith! How do you expect us to get there? It's a hundred leagues . . . more!"

"Drago—"

"*Stars!* You might as well have left me back in the—"

She grabbed his wrist, furious at him. "Back in your cell? Except you wouldn't be in the cell now, would you, Drago?

You'd be a skewered mess on a litter being carried to the corpse yard!"

He pulled his wrist away, but he did so gently, and when he resumed speaking his voice was more even. "Why the Island of Mist and Memory?"

"StarDrifter is there."

Drago sat and thought about that. StarDrifter might well be pleased to see Zenith, and gods alone knew she'd be glad to see him, but would their grandfather be pleased to see *him*?

But where else could he go? At the least he could hide in the jungles that covered the greater part of the island.

He grunted, thinking of living his life as a wild man of the jungle. He was sure many would think it a fit end for Drago the Treacherous. Stay away from the jungle, children, or Drago the Treacherous will eat you!

"I thought we would go through the forests," Zenith said softly. "Cut across into Minstrelsea once we are out of the Urqhart Hills."

"They'll have captured us long before then."

"Maybe, maybe not. Drago . . ."

"I know. WingRidge."

"Why did he help us? He is supposed to be devoted to Caelum."

Drago chuckled, and Zenith caught her breath. Drago so rarely smiled that she'd forgotten how it lit up his face.

"Then I admire WingRidge's 'devotion,'" Drago said, still grinning, and Zenith found that her mouth also had curved in a small smile.

"But I don't know, Zenith," Drago continued, his grin fading. "WingRidge was ever the mystery. Frankly, I have never understood him. Sometimes I caught him staring at me with such a strange expression on his face . . ."

It was the strangeness of that expression that had unsettled Drago the most. He'd learned to deal with looks of loathing, contempt and even fear—but WingRidge had been so unreadable that Drago had avoided him whenever possible.

Zenith noted the discomfort in her brother's eyes and decided to change the subject.

"We'll get to the forest, Drago. We will," she said firmly.

"And it will protect us," Drago said slowly. "No armed patrol is going to be able to ride through it, and Caelum can't send hunting hounds through there. And shadows are ever good for fugitives. We'll be safer there than anywhere else."

The trees of Minstrelsea hated weapons above all else—save, perhaps, hunting. The magical forest was full of creatures so fey and precious that any man who went near the forest with a weapon or a hound rarely survived the touch of the first shadow along the forest's shaded walks.

Zenith's eyes slipped to the sack Drago still held tight under one arm. "What's in that sack, Drago? I cannot scry it out."

That brought a smile to Drago's lips. "Well, well, so the SunSoar power *does* have its limits, does it? And as to what this sack contains, that's neither here nor there for the moment, and I have no intention of opening it within this enchanted fog."

He looked at his sister. "Come," he said, rising to his feet and holding out a hand to Zenith. "It's time to go."

For another hour they struggled through the mist. The sunlight penetrated the fog, but only weakly. Rocks and chasms alike loomed up suddenly, so that both had to be careful that an unwary step did not plunge them into a gorge. Zenith moaned occasionally and clutched at her head, but whenever Drago asked she insisted she was well enough to continue.

But just as they reached a deeply shadowed section of the rocky valley they were traversing, Zenith suddenly groaned and, falling forward, clutched desperately at the back of Drago's tunic.

"Zenith! What is—"

He broke off as he saw her face. It was deathly pale, and shone with a sickly sheen that couldn't be totally blamed on the mist.

"Zenith?" He slipped an arm about her.

He could feel her heart thudding crazily against the wall of her chest. *"Zenith?"*

"Zenith," she whispered. "Is that my name? No, no, it sounds wrong somehow."

Drago tightened his arm about her. "What are you saying?"

She raised her head and stared at him. "What am I doing here? I have my duties to attend to. The First should not be so far away from the Mount."

She wriggled in his grasp. "Who are you to touch me as you do?"

And then she moaned as if sick almost to death, and half collapsed onto the ground. "No! No! My name is *Zenith*!"

She took a deep breath, shuddering with the effort, and then she managed to straighten and smile at her brother. "Why do we stand here? Come, there are surely only a few more minutes left of this mist."

Two long hours later, almost mid-morning, they broke free of the mist. Drago did not know whether to stand and take great gulps of the sun-drenched air, or crouch down to peer overhead for the Strike Force scouts he was certain would be searching for him.

Behind him Zenith stumbled into the sunshine. Her fine gown was shredded about the hemline, and her cloak had a great tear in it, but she had managed to regain some of her composure. "Where are we?"

"In the hills above Gundealga Ford, I think," Drago replied slowly, although he wasn't completely sure. It had been years since he'd ridden through these ranges. He studied Zenith carefully. There was something badly wrong with her. Her mind, he thought, because apart from a few scratches and bruises there was nothing wrong with her body.

"Zenith, look, there is a sheltered spot in the glade beyond the rock outcrop. You need to rest. We both do. We are free of the damned mist, and perhaps it would be better to wait for the night to continue moving."

She didn't even hesitate. "Yes . . . will you take my arm, Drago? I do not know how much longer I can walk."

He helped her across the rocks and into the dappled shade of a small grove of golden ash trees. As soon as she sank to the ground, Zenith curled into a tight ball.

"And when you wake, Zenith," Drago said quietly, "you are going to tell me what is wrong."

"Mmmm," she murmured, and let sleep claim her.

Hugging his sack tightly to him, Drago sat by his sister through the hours of the day, watching her, wondering, watching the sky and the lower Urqhart Hills, wondering.

Thinking.

Here he was a fugitive, running from those determined to kill him.

He had never felt freer in all his life.

His fingers tightened momentarily about the sack, and he smiled slightly.

Drago relaxed against the trunk of a tree, daring to think that he and Zenith might escape, daring to think that he might actually have a chance to take control of his own life. What would that be like, to be whoever he wanted?

He'd said to Zenith in the kitchens that even if he left Sigholt, word would spread that Axis' untrustworthy and evil son, Drago, was traveling the land and that doors everywhere would be closed to him. He'd said he would have no chance at a life anywhere.

But was that true? What if he dyed his hair, grew a beard, assumed a new name, a new identity? What would it be like to wander as a traveling peddler, or seasonal laborer?

What would it be like to be *liked*?

Apart from Zenith, and to a lesser degree Leagh and Zared, Drago had never known what it was like to be extended friendship and love. He'd first come to an awareness of his unenviable spot in Sigholt's life when he was about three. He could remember the day clearly. He'd been playing alone in the courtyards of Sigholt, toddling about among the piles of hay and manure the stable lads were mucking out of the horse stalls, when he'd suddenly spotted the cook's wife carrying her six-month-old infant into the sunshine.

She'd had a blanket over one arm, and she spread it out and sat herself and her baby upon it. After a few minutes the cook had called from the kitchen, and the woman had gone inside after checking that her baby was safely asleep.

Curious, for Drago had not seen a baby this small previously, he toddled over. His face was set in a frown of concentration and his fists clenched with effort, for the stable lads had left the cobbles wet and he did not want to slip over. He was about four or five paces from the blanket when the mother had re-emerged from the kitchen.

She'd taken one look at his frown and fists, then screamed in total panic.

Her baby had woken and begun to scream as well, and so also did Drago, as thoroughly frightened as mother and baby.

The woman had snatched her baby to her, and then literally spat at Drago. "*Get you gone from my child! If you come near him again I will kill you!*"

At the commotion a dozen people had come running, including his parents and Caelum, then about four or five.

At that time Azhure was heavily pregnant with Zenith, and when she had seen the woman and screaming baby, both staring terrified at Drago, she had cried out herself, and caught Drago by the shoulders, spinning him about.

"You will *never* go near any baby! Do you understand, Drago? When my baby is born you will *never* go near her . . . *do you hear me?*"

In fact, Drago could hardly hear her above his own sobs, but he nodded violently anyway. Even worse than the screams and the words was the ring of people about him, all wearing varying degrees of revulsion, disgust and fury on their faces.

You will never harm another baby again, Drago . . .
Think to kill again and you will be killed yourself . . .
You will never be allowed to harm again . . .
We will never forget what you did . . .
Against Caelum . . .
Against Tencendor . . .
We will never trust you . . .
Never . . .
Never . . .

The thoughts and words of accusation and hate rang about him and Drago began to spasm with his own hiccuping sobs. What was happening? Why did everyone stare at him with such hate? Why? Why? Why? He fell to the ground and hid his face in his arms.

Eventually they'd left him there, curled up into a tight ball—as tight as Zenith was now—against the hatred and disgust.

Caelum had been the last to leave, and Drago had caught a peek at his face from under his own arm.

It was such a mixture of terror—terror of *him*—and hatred and disgust that Drago had closed his eyes as tight as he could. Closed them against the world and everyone in it.

There he'd lain, wishing somehow he'd wake from this frightful nightmare, when a small cat had bumped her head against his arm. Reaching out to the only thing that had shown him affection, Drago had hugged the cat to him, and she'd snuggled into his chest, her body reverberating with the strength of her purring, and Drago had sobbed anew.

No, Drago had never forgotten that day.

He'd grown silent and withdrawn. Sullen, his parents said. Zenith had been born shortly after that event, and all Drago had known of his sister for the first four years of her life was her distant cry, or tiny footfall. His parents had never let him near her until she was four.

When he was five it was RiverStar who'd finally told him why everyone hated him so much. She'd told him with a smirk on her face, reveling in his hurt. Drago hadn't believed her, hadn't *wanted* to believe her, and had in fact asked Axis to tell him it wasn't true.

Axis had stared at him, silent, and turned away.

Drago hugged his sack tighter to him, tears glinting in his eyes. He had hated himself for a while, hated himself for what he'd done to Caelum, but over the years that self-hatred had been turned back out against the world that hated him. He'd spent his teenage years deep in bitterness, then his twenties and thirties as deep in resentment. How was he to know if he'd actually done what legend stated?

And finally, by the time he'd reached thirty-five, his mortality had struck deep. His siblings were all highly magical, enchanted creatures, reveling in youth and power and the adoration of all who saw them.

Here he was, rejected, hated, loathed by all . . .

Well, not quite all. The cats continued to adore him, and as a child and even a youth Drago had spent many nights curled in the hay with the courtyard cats.

And Zenith liked him. That was unbelievable. She was the child he was never allowed near, she was the one everyone feared he would hurt, and yet Zenith had never regarded him with anything except friendship—and perhaps even love.

Unbidden, a memory crashed through his mind. A night racked with violent storms long ago when the SunSoar children had all been staying with their grandfather StarDrifter in the Temple complex on the Island of Mist and Memory. He had been about twelve then, battling to reconcile his approaching puberty with his ever-increasing resentment, only to realize they complemented each other. He had been lying in bed, watching lightning streak across the night sky, when the door had opened and Zenith, only six or seven, had scampered across the room and flung herself into his arms.

"Please," she had whispered then, "I'm scared."

And she had clung to him all through the night and Drago, so rarely hugged or cuddled himself, had lain there, holding her tight, wondering that she had come to him first of all in her fright.

Zenith whimpered in her sleep, and the sound broke Drago out of his reverie. "Zenith?"

But Zenith was trapped in her own nightmare and did not hear him.

She was in a house, and the man who approached her had death in his eyes. He forced her to her knees, and then to the floor, and then he'd begun pushing her back.

Back toward the fire.

Oh, how she'd fought him! Her terror had given her abnormal strength, but she could not fight her way free.

Heat lapped at her head, and then flames at her hair. She could feel them crackling amid her hair, she could smell them, and then with a great roar her entire head had been enveloped in a ball of fire.

The agony was extraordinary.

Fire lifted her skin in massive blisters that burst and caught fire themselves. Fire seared through her throat and lungs when she took breath to scream. She tried to beat it out, but her hands caught fire, and then she somehow comprehended that her entire dress was aflame, and she knew she was going to die slowly, horribly, from the outside in, and that the agony would take its own sweet time in killing her.

She'd called out to her daughter, but those words did not mean very much now, not when her entire body was such a mass of torment, and her spirit inside was aware, aware, aware . . .

Drago jumped back, almost crying out. Zenith had abruptly rolled over and screamed, beating at her body with her hands as if she were consumed by fire. She screamed again, her body convulsing with the strength of it, and Drago gathered her into his arms and tried to calm her.

She struggled against him for a long time, and then finally lay quiet, crying a little.

Caught as she had been in Niah's torment, Zenith had realized why the sweet-natured woman had changed in death. It had been the manner of her death—the suffering, the fear, the knowledge that no-one would come to save her. She had lain there, helpless, hearing and smelling and *feeling* as she burned into blackened meat that crackled and joints that popped in the heat.

And all the time she had remained aware. Right to the end, when her heart finally gave out.

But her sweet nature had given out first. That had been destroyed along with her body. Even in rebirth, Niah would never be the same again.

"Zenith?"

At Drago's soft query, Zenith raised her head and smiled.

"Will you tell me what is wrong?"

Her smile faded, but finally she nodded and spoke. "Do you remember the stories of our grandmother Niah? Then listen . . ."

20

Icebear Coast Camp

In the east of Tencendor the Fortress Ranges rose from an undersea range and then stretched north in wildly undulating ridges, dividing forest from plain, and the haunts of the Avar from those of the human plain-dwellers. After a score of leagues the Fortress Ranges thickened, then leaped for the sky in a series of massive, almost vertical, razor-backed ridges until they merged with the permanently cloud-shrouded Icescarp Alps. For generations these Alps had been the haunt of the Icarii, condemned to a bitter exile by the Brotherhood of the Seneschal, but now few of the brilliantly colored birdpeople fluttered about the ice-capped mountains, preferring the milder climes of the Minaret Peaks far to the south.

Each one of the peaks in the Icescarp Alps was a majesty in itself, but of them all the fabled Star Finger was the most exalted. Once it had been called Talon Spike, and had been the home of the Icarii during their exile, but it was now a place of contemplation and study, where the most powerful and knowledgeable among the Icarii Enchanters studied the mysteries of the stars. The mountain had become a place of libraries and halls, of music and enchantments, and of tremulous discoveries and lingering silences.

Star Finger's hauntingly beautiful ice-shrouded cliffs and ethereal mists cast a shadow, if not literally then metaphorically, over all of Tencendor.

From the northern and eastern faces of Star Finger a great glacier ground its way yet farther north to calve its icebergs in the Iskruel Ocean. Here curved the extraordinary landscape of the Icebear Coast. To the south the alps rose sheer and black, while to the north the gray–blue sea crashed onto the pebbled beach, the icepack grinding behind it, the seabirds wheeling and crying with eerie voices above.

Few mortal steps ever trod the Icebear Coast. Sometimes a tribe of Ravensbund would move silently along the shoreline, seeking seaweed to make their Tekawai tea, very occasionally a fur trader from the plains far to the south would stand overawed on the pebbles, staring over the unknown waters that extended farther north.

More often the pebbles rasped and rattled beneath the great paws of the strange icebear Urbeth as she chased down seabirds and seals, scattering their blood over the shoreline before she retreated to her ice den and her waiting cubs.

And sometimes the Icebear Coast played host to beings far stranger and far more powerful than Urbeth.

* * *

They sat about a campfire somewhere on the Icebear Coast. Nine of them, the complete Circle of the Star Gods. Adamon, turning a roasting partridge and smiling about the fire. Xanon, his wife, and Goddess of the Firmament. Zest, Goddess of Earth, and her companion, Narcis, God of the Sun. Across from them sat Flulia, Goddess of Water, Pors, God of Air, and Silton, God of Fire. Making up the Nine were Axis, Song, and Azhure, Moon.

"You frown, Axis," Adamon said. "Why?"

Axis sighed. "I worry."

"The worries of Tencendor should be far behind you."

"I fought for that land, I watched those who fought with me die. It is hard now to just sit, and watch."

"Axis," Adamon said gently, handing him a piece of roast bird. "You are one of us now, and you must let Tencendor and Caelum find their own feet."

"The weight of Tencendor rests on Caelum's shoulders. What if he falters? Am I to let Tencendor falter with him?"

"Oh, Axis!" Azhure said shortly. "Caelum will *not* falter! Trust your own son."

"We understand how you feel, Axis," Xanon said in her gentle voice. "That Tencendor relives, and that we are Nine, is so much due to your and Azhure's efforts. But now you are not what you once were. You must move on."

"You let me deal with Gorgrael. You were happy enough to let me wander the plains and mountains of Tencendor then."

"Gorgrael was personal, Axis," Adamon said, "and your battle with him concerned us greatly. If you had lost then *he* would have taken his place among us as God of Song. Now we must *all* move on, and you must let Caelum rule from the Throne of the Stars. Leave mortal worries for mortal shoulders."

"You are right," Axis said after a small silence. "It is just that the past few days have been so disturbing. I long to be there. To help in some way. Stars! Our daughter is dead!"

"We grieve with you and Azhure for RiverStar's death," Pors said, and by his side Flulia took Azhure's hand, and stroked it.

Axis nodded, unable for the moment to speak.

"I knew here," Azhure touched her head, "that Axis and I would eventually outlive our children. But we thought that we had hundreds of years . . . that we could watch them grow and love and give us grandchildren. To see RiverStar die, and so cruelly, and," her voice hardened, "at her own brother's hands makes it hard for Axis and me to sit and watch."

Her hand now touched her breast. "My heart cannot let go my mortal concerns so easily."

There was silence as the other gods shared their grief, and tried to impart comfort. They were much older than Axis and Azhure, and had seen their own mortal families die into dust thousands of years previously. They had come to terms with their immortality—Axis and Azhure still had to embrace unending life with equanimity.

"And now Drago has run," Axis said. All the gods were aware of the search for Drago.

"Leave it, Axis," Xanon said, and touched his knee. "Leave it. They inhabit a different world to you and I. Leave them to that world and all the pain it contains."

"There *is* one problem we should not discard so quickly," Azhure said, and looked about the Circle. "WolfStar."

The others nodded slowly. WolfStar. His reappearance was disturbing. For all their powers, the Star Gods still could not entirely understand WolfStar, nor where he went for so many years or what he did when he was gone.

Anything they did not understand made them wonder if they should fear it.

"We will watch," Adamon said eventually. "It is all we can do."

"And the Star Gate?" Azhure asked. "Should we watch that, too?"

"The voices," Adamon reflected. "The Icarii nation's murdered children, come back to haunt their killer."

"There is something wrong," Axis said, and he suddenly leaped to his feet and paced back and forth just inside the circle of light from the fire. "There is something wrong!"

"Axis?" Azhure glanced worriedly at Adamon, then rose to her feet and took Axis' arm, bringing him to a halt. "What?"

"I don't know!" Axis cried, and kicked at a pebble in utter frustration. "I don't know *what* it is, but there *is* something wrong. The Star Dance seems . . . not quite as it should."

"It is your grief and worry about your family that so disturbs you," Xanon said soothingly. "The voices are nothing. They will not hurt us, nor this wondrous land."

"We heard them occasionally during the time when Artor imprisoned us in the interstellar wastes," Silton said. "Trifling voices."

"They are there," Zest agreed, "but they are harmless enough."

"Are you *certain*?" Axis said.

"Absolutely," Adamon replied. "They drift about the interstellar spaces calling WolfStar's name, looking for vengeance." He suddenly laughed. "No wonder he chose to return from his death so quickly! I would not like to have such as these on my tail!"

"And they will not come back through the Star Gate?" Axis asked.

"WolfStar was right when he told Caelum they do not have the skills to step back through," Adamon said as firmly as he could. "They are relatively powerless, kept alive only by their need for revenge. Axis, leave it be. Drift with us. We are your home now, not Sigholt. We are your family, not Caelum."

21

Traveling Home

Leagh dressed herself in the dawn chill, despondent and apathetic. She was to go home with Herme and Theod, it seemed, and there wait for however Askam and Caelum decided to dispose of her future.

Over the past few days she had wept until she'd realized that weeping did no good. Then she had sat and wiped her eyes and decided that her only choice was to accept what life had dealt her. She loved Zared, but she was not to be allowed to consummate that love. Well, that was the lot of a princess. It was foolish to dream of being a peasant woman and choosing as her mate a man she loved. She was not. She had been raised in privilege, and lived in privilege, and for that privilege she had to mate with whomever her brother and Caelum decided would be best.

"I must trust them," she muttered as she laced her boots over her breeches—Leagh always rode astride—"and I must believe that they will choose a man kind and compassionate." Her mouth curled bitterly. "As well as politically acceptable."

She must forget Zared. She would rarely, if ever, see him again anyway. "Gods, let Caelum find me a husband a thousand leagues away from Zared," she said, staring at the door. "For I could not bear to meet with him again."

Mentally shaking herself from her thoughts, Leagh looked about the room, finally picking up a blue cloak. There was nothing else to take home, for she'd brought nothing with her. In the time she'd been in Sigholt, she had shared with Zenith.

Gods! Where was Zenith? If anything served to take her

mind away from her own problems, it was fear for her friend. Where could Zenith have got to? Something had been troubling her in the past few days, but Zenith had not been able to speak of it, and now she had gone. Had Drago been involved? Having killed one sister, had he then stolen his other one?

But Leagh could not quite believe that Drago *had* killed RiverStar, despite the vision WolfStar had conjured. And despite his aura of diffidence, Leagh truly thought that Drago cared for Zenith. He could not have done her harm.

Yet none of this solved the problem of Zenith's disappearance. Where was—

There was a knock at the door, and Leagh jumped. Hurriedly stuffing her hair into a cap, she opened the door to find Duke Theod standing there.

He bowed theatrically. "My Lady? May I escort you to your mount?"

Leagh smiled, for she liked Theod, and the thought of a week or more in his company was no hardship.

Then her smile died a little, for behind Theod stood Askam, and though Leagh loved her brother, he was so closely tied to her loss of Zared that his presence made her heart ache.

"Leagh," he said gently as she exited her chamber. "I am sorry that Caelum and I have caused you so much sorrow, but—"

"But say no more," Leagh said, and laid a finger on his mouth, "for to do so would only break my heart. Leave it, Askam. I will accept in time."

He nodded. "Would you like me to come down to the courtyard?"

She smiled, knowing that even though Askam hated Zared, he truly did feel for her own pain. "No. Wave me farewell from the parapets. When will you come home to Carlon?"

Askam shrugged. "Caelum wants me to stay for a while, lead a few more patrols through the Urqhart Hills in case—" his eyes slid fractionally toward Theod, "—any track has been overlooked."

"I assure you, my Lord," Theod said stiffly, "that Herme and I were *most* thorough."

"I am sure you were," Askam soothed. "But Caelum wants to be certain. What if Drago hid in the Keep for a few hours, and then slipped out after your patrol had left?"

"Is Caelum up?" Leagh asked.

"Yes, but he is closeted with FreeFall and Isfrael, who also depart within the hour," Askam said. "Sa'Domai left late last night. Caelum asked me to farewell you for him." Askam kissed her on one cheek, then the other. "There, that's from Caelum, and that's from me."

"My Lord, my Lady," Theod said, "the sun grows warm, and we have a long way to go."

"Farewell," Askam whispered, kissing Leagh's cheek once more, then he turned to Theod. "Do not lose her," he said, his voice hard, "for she is precious to me."

No doubt, thought Theod, but he bowed. "I will take the utmost care of her, my Lord. I know her value."

Then he had Leagh by the elbow, and they were descending the stairs.

Despite her sadness over Zared, and her worries about Zenith, Leagh found that her heart lifted as they exited the Keep and clattered over the bridge.

"Farewell, lovely Leagh!" the bridge cried, and Leagh laughed.

"Farewell to thee also, fair bridge. May your arches never crumble."

"And your spirits never falter," the bridge responded, and then Leagh, with Herme to one side and Theod to the other, was over the bridge and into the blue mists.

They rode south for many hours, then turned slightly east, heading for the trail that would lead them through the southern Urqhart Hills to Jervois Landing. They broke clear of the mist mid-afternoon, to find the hills bathed in sunshine and the skies awash with migrating brown Skelder birds, heading south from the Icescarp Alps toward their wintering fields in Coroleas.

"You always know when autumn bites deep," Herme remarked, his eyes to the sky, "when the Skelder birds abandon Tencendor."

Yet even though it was DeadLeaf-month, the sun was still strong, and Leagh let her cloak flare back from her shoulders in the westerly wind.

"Theod, will you take the riverboat south with us at Jervois Landing, or will you ride west to your home estates?"

Theod hesitated, glancing at Herme. "I still have to make my plans, Leagh. I will stay with you a while yet, though."

Leagh nodded, and let the topic slide. It would be a ride of perhaps two or three days to Jervois Landing, and at the moment she was so excited at the thought that they would camp this evening in the ruins of Hsingard that she could think of little else.

Hsingard had once been a lovely and substantial stone city, the capital of Ichtar. But during Axis' war with Gorgrael, the Destroyer's Skraelings had invaded it, destroyed it, and built themselves massive breeding hatcheries in its basements. In some wondrous manner that Leagh did not quite understand, Azhure had in a single night destroyed all the Skraelings and hatchlings, and now Hsingard lay a sad sprawl of tumbled ruins.

There might be no life in it, but it made a good camp site.

Four of Herme and Theod's men stretched canvas covers over several piles of stones, creating a spacious and deeply shadowed shelter removed from the camp of the thirty-six men of the escort. Leagh sat and watched as Theod made a fire. A man fetched food from one of the packs on the supply mules, and within a half-hour of pulling their horses into the ruins everyone was seated, eating.

There was little conversation. It had been a hard ride to get from Sigholt to Hsingard in one day and Leagh soon found herself wishing Herme and Theod would move off to their sleeping rolls so she could curl up and get as much rest as she could on the hard ground. But they seemed curiously reluctant, even when the rest of the camp had settled for the night, and they sat tossing sticks into the fire, and occasionally looking about into the night.

"Gentlemen, are you afraid that there are Skraelings left within the ruins?"

Herme jumped slightly, and looked at Leagh. "Nay, sweet lady. It's just that you never know whether or not brigands might creep by in the night, and—"

"You have posted no guards."

"Foolish of us," Herme said, and turned to Theod. "Why didn't you think of that?"

"Me? I . . . ah . . ."

Theod was saved from further comment by the sound of a distant horse.

Leagh tensed a little. "Who could that be?"

"I'll look," Theod said hurriedly, rising and walking off into the night.

Leagh noticed he hadn't taken his sword. "Herme, what's going on?"

"There's nothing to worry about," Herme said soothingly, and was about to say something more when they heard Theod talking quietly with someone in the distance.

Herme hesitated, then rose to his feet. "Leagh, stay here. Whatever happens, do not move."

And he was gone.

Leagh pulled her cloak about her nervously and stared before her. Despite Herme's caution, she was tempted to move farther back into the ruins. The only thing that stopped her was the thought that she didn't know what might be behind her, awaiting her arrival.

Whoever Theod had found to talk to had now been joined by Herme. Leagh could hear low voices, now so far away she couldn't really distinguish them.

They stopped, and she tensed.

Silence.

Then the sound of someone walking toward her.

She swallowed, suddenly aware of how vulnerable she was. The nearest forms of sleeping soldiers were at least twenty paces away, and the cul-de-sac of tumbled stones that the men had stretched a canvas over for her was as much a trap as it was a shelter.

The steps came closer, and slowly she rose to her feet, prepared to run if she had to.

Then she froze, her eyes wide and disbelieving.

Zared had stepped into the flickering circle of firelight. "Hello, Leagh," he said. "May I join you?"

She just stared stupidly.

"Leagh?" He stepped forward.

"What are you doing here?" Shock had made her voice harsh, and Zared faltered.

"Leagh?"

"Zared . . . *what are you doing here?*"

He grinned, and walked around the fire toward her. "That is a stupid question to ask the man who loves you."

And then he had his arms wrapped about her, and was kissing her, but Leagh was still too shocked and bewildered to play the lover, and she pushed her hands against his chest until her mouth was free.

"Zared, what are you—"

He sighed, and his arms loosened a little. "I said I would fight for you, Leagh . . . but I didn't realize the battle would be so hard."

"But—"

"Theod and Herme said they would bring you to Hsingard. I've been waiting here for some three or four days."

"Why?"

Zared sighed. "Why do you think? Did *you* accept Caelum's decision?"

"We have no choice, Zared. Caelum is—"

"*Do* we have no choice?" he interrupted softly, then his hand was buried in her hair and he stopped her protests with a kiss that was considerably deeper and more thorough than the last.

"Come back to Severin with me," he whispered eventually. "Come with me and be my wife."

"But Caelum said—"

"What in curses' sakes can Caelum do once we *are* married?"

She was silent, thinking.

Zared held her as close as he could, rocking her gently back and forth. "Be my wife, Leagh. Be courageous enough to be my wife."

Leagh's head was swimming with conflicting ideas and emotions. Zared, so close, so warm, offering her what she so desperately wanted. But she was Leagh, Princess of the West, and she couldn't just run off with a man her overlord had expressly forbidden her to marry. And what would Askam say? What would Askam *do*? Would she ever see Carlon again? Was Zared worth being totally ostracized from elite Tencendorian society—for Leagh had no doubt that was what would happen.

And then she was overcome with remorse for thinking that. Here was the man who loved her, and she him. He would only ever be her true chance for happiness, and she was worried about her social standing?

But how deeply would she hurt Askam? And what would Caelum do?

"Sweetheart." Zared kissed her cheek, her ear, her neck. "What say you? Will you come back to Severin with me, will you be my wife?"

He didn't give her a chance to answer, but kissed her again, molding her body to his.

It was too much. Leagh just didn't have the courage to say no.

"Yes?" Zared asked, and she simply nodded her head, her

eyes swimming with tears, both for love of Zared, and fear of what her actions would do to Askam.

He smiled, and Leagh frowned slightly, thinking it an odd expression, almost one of triumph.

He shifted slightly, and Leagh realized he was pulling her back into the canvas-covered rock shelter.

"No," she said, and she truly meant it.

"What does a week or two matter, my love?" he asked, his strength too much for her. "The public notary in Severin can marry us soon enough, and I can assure you there will be no physical inspection of the goods beforehand."

Leagh blushed a deep red. "No."

And yet now here they were, deep within the shelter, and Zared had pulled the flap to, shutting them into an almost total darkness.

"Don't rush me—" she started, but he laughed softly.

"Rush? Why rush? We have a long autumn night ahead of us, my love, and I am in no mood to rush."

His fingers were at her throat, and suddenly her cloak fell away, and then his hands, his insistent, strong hands, had pushed her jacket over her shoulders and halfway down her arms.

Then he stopped and Leagh, her arms trapped, could do nothing as he unbuttoned her linen shirt and ran his hands and then his lips over her bared breasts.

She considered screaming—but was deeply embarrassed at the thought of what the men who answered her scream would find.

"No," she said yet again, but her voice was weakened with indecision, and he heard it.

He laughed again, low, and held her to him, running his mouth from her breast to her throat and then to her own mouth. His hands finally jerked off her jacket and shirt, and then she was somehow lying on her back amid the blankets and he was a dark shape and weight above her.

He murmured in her ear, sweet words that meant nothing

but nevertheless relaxed her, and she lifted her hips of her own accord when he pulled at the waistband of her breeches, and let him slide them off.

"You are so beautiful, Leagh," he whispered, "so precious."

And she closed her eyes and wrapped her arms about him, and like the peasant woman she had always dreamed of being, she let the man she loved enter her body and love her. If there was a child from this, she thought, then so be it, and Askam and Caelum must accept it.

Then there was no more space for coherent thought, and she cried out, and clutched at his back, and hoped that the night would never end.

It was dawn when he finally let her drift off to sleep. But Zared stayed wakeful, holding her against him, still running an exploratory hand over her body, marveling at his love for her.

Yet there was more to it than that, and Zared was honest enough to admit it. It was not just Leagh he had seduced that night, but the West. It was not just Leagh's body he had invaded, but Askam's lands of the West.

His hand stilled, and he smiled into the faint light filtering past the canvas flap. Whatever Askam and Caelum might do to him, there was nothing they could do to undo last night.

"Is it done?" Herme asked when Zared emerged.

Zared nodded, and Herme grunted, relieved. "What will she do when she finds out?"

Zared's hands stilled in the act of buckling his weapons belt. "There is nothing she *can* do, Herme. Not now."

There was a movement, and Leagh emerged. She blushed faintly and dropped her eyes when she saw Herme, and he turned away to give her privacy.

* * *

They rode south that morning, but some eight leagues above Jervois Landing they swung due west.

Leagh found it hard to believe what she had done—she knew that had she been given an hour alone to consider Zared's request she would have refused. After all, she couldn't submit to her dreams at the expense of her duty . . . but that was exactly what she *had* done.

Gods! *What had she done?* She loved Zared, she truly did, but Leagh was also very much afraid of the consequences of her seduction.

And what were Herme and Theod doing riding with Zared? That thought was too frightening to think through to its natural conclusion, so Leagh left it well enough alone.

I won't lie with him again, she said to herself. I won't. I will find a way to slip away . . . and if there is no child, then last night can be forgotten . . .

But there was no chance to slip away, and when that night Zared again drew her down to the ground, she submitted meekly enough.

And so again the next night, and by then, Leagh knew she was committed to Zared. She had no choice. By that stage there were some three dozen tongues of the escort willing to testify that Leagh was a maiden no longer, and that it was Zared, Prince of the North, who had so possessed her.

On their fourth day from Hsingard they splashed their horses across the wide and shallow upper reaches of the River Azle, riding toward a small valley to the northeast.

Leagh was daydreaming, wondering what Zared's palace in Severin would be like, when she was suddenly snapped out of her reverie by a glint of steel in the distance.

And again.

"Zared—" she began.

But he silenced her with a raised hand. "It is safe, Leagh. Those are my men."

"An escort to see us back to Severin? Do we part with Herme and Theod here?"

He spurred his horse forward and did not answer.

Angry, Leagh urged her own mount after him, but as they drew closer she drew rein, aghast.

True, the standard that many of the men wore was Zared's . . . but there was a unit of Herme's, and there one of Theod's. And there, more of Herme's men!

What was happening? Why were Herme's and Theod's men waiting so neatly arrayed in battle gear with Zared's troops?

"Oh no," she whispered, and then Zared rejoined her.

"Leagh . . . Leagh, we will not be riding for Severin after all. There is some . . . business that we must attend in the south."

"Where?" she asked, her eyes bright, her hands clenched into fists about her reins.

Zared thought about not telling her, then decided it wouldn't matter. She would have no chance to . . . no chance to escape.

"Kastaleon."

22

Impatient Love

For a week Drago and Zenith moved slowly southeast toward Minstrelsea. They kept to uninhabited areas and rarely trodden pathways, and Zenith cloaked them as best she could with enchantments from curious eyes.

Even so, she could not understand why farflight scouts had not spotted them. Whether it was Niah, or some sickness battling within her, Zenith found that the cloaking enchantments had abnormally taxed her strength—and even then, the enchantments were weak.

Zenith glanced at the sack in Drago's arms.

Whatever their luck at evading capture so far, Zenith and Drago both believed they ran only on borrowed time. Scouts would spot them, a peasant on his way to market would stop and ask them their business, or WolfStar would finally arrive to claim his bride.

Both hoped they could still escape.

Drago managed to snare a rabbit the evening before they approached the ferry that crossed the Nordra above the site where once had stood the village of Smyrton. It had been days since they'd eaten, and even though Zenith produced a fire with her Enchanter powers, they gobbled down the meat half-raw, burning fingers and mouths.

"We'll get to Minstrelsea by tomorrow," Drago said as he regretfully regarded the well-chewed bone in his hand. "We'll be safe there."

Brave words, thought Zenith, but she nodded dispiritedly anyway.

Drago lifted his eyes. He could not imagine what it must be like to live with another inside you. Zenith had told him how she had been fated to be the reborn future of Niah, their grandmother. WolfStar's reborn lover. Fate? Drago imperceptibly shook his head. SunSoar manipulation, more like.

Damn all SunSoars to eternal fire! Drago thought, throwing the bone to one side with a jerky motion. Both of us left to run through the night by events out of our control!

As Drago reached for the final morsel of rabbit flesh, Zenith dropped her face into her hands and began to cry silently. Drago dropped the meat, scrambled about the fire, and put his arm about her.

"Shush, Zenith. I am here."

She let him hold her for a while, then she made an effort to wipe her eyes and sat up a little.

"I know what you have been thinking, Drago," she said.

"You have been damning all the SunSoars to a particularly nasty fate."

Drago tried to smile for her, but the effort failed dismally. "And curse your Enchanter powers, too, Zenith."

That did raise a small smile from his sister. "Drago, I hope you never know what it is like to have another being battling for control of you. There is this *thing*," she hissed the word, "coiling about in my mind, trying to tell me that she is me, and I her."

Drago was silent.

"But . . . *no!* I refuse to believe it. I am Zenith, and this thing inside me is foreign and unwelcome and completely *apart* from me. But she writhes and calls to me, and begs me to lay down in WolfStar's arms!"

"Can you cast her aside?"

Zenith shook her head miserably. "I have tried every trick I know, used all of my powers. I have even begged her. But she has sunk such determined claws into my mind and soul that I do not know how to remove her."

Drago thought of how death had changed Niah into the grasping demon she was now. "I do not ever want to die, if this is what death means," he remarked.

Zenith shrugged a little. "She is determined for life, and she cares not that she snatches mine in the process."

"And she calls to WolfStar?"

"Constantly. I try to dampen her call, but . . . oh Stars, Drago! I am terrified he will hear, and find us!"

"Shush, Zenith. No-one has found us yet, and soon we will be in the forest."

She didn't answer, and after a moment she turned away and curled up for the night.

Zenith woke in the early hours of the morning, shivering with the cold. She sat up, wrapping her wings more closely about her, and threw some more wood on the glowing coals.

She shivered again, and this time Zenith realized it was something other than the cold.

Something else. Somewhere out there in the darkness.

Coming closer.

Fast.

She whimpered and hugged her arms about her, and this time Zenith was so frightened she leaned over to shake Drago awake.

Niah! Ah, my love! I have found you!

Stars! Zenith froze in the act of leaning over to Drago. It was WolfStar! Close . . . very, very close, but not yet here.

She stared at Drago, knowing he was dead if WolfStar found him.

Without a thought for her own safety, she lurched to her feet and ran into the night.

She ran, not knowing where she could run, but knowing she could not outrun WolfStar. He was still in the ethereal, not the physical, and that meant she had a few minutes to put as much distance between the camp site and herself as possible.

His voice followed her, homing in on her, homing in on the Niah-voice's call—now almost thundering through Zenith's mind, threatening to swamp her completely—but Zenith knew she had to hang on as long as she could, hang on until she was far, far from Drago.

She tried to lift into the air, but she was weak, and her wings failed her, and the next instant her foot caught in a fox's burrow and she was falling, falling, tumbling down an incline.

"My love!"

Strong arms grasped her and prevented her crashing into the rocks at the foot of the gully.

WolfStar.

"My love," he said again, and Zenith knew she was lost, she could not fight him and Niah at the same time.

"My love," he said yet one more time, and his hands ripped at her gown, bruising her flesh.

She bit her tongue, knowing if she cried out Drago might wake and come looking for her, and then she felt a knee force itself between her legs.

WolfStar grunted, and settled himself upon her. He had waited too long. Far too long.

WolfStar thrust, and Zenith moaned. Again he thrust, and Zenith twisted her head to one side, hoping that Drago had not woken, hoping she had run far enough.

She could do nothing but endure this rape. Something—*someone*—else now controlled her arms, her entire body. Appalled, Zenith found that her hands now grabbed at Wolf-Star's shoulders and back, encouraging him, and her body writhed under his, her hips arching to meet him, her voice now strangely demanding that he expend greater effort upon her satisfaction.

And the true horror of it was that she found herself enjoying this, enjoying the feel of him, the fire of him inside her.

I wish he would never stop.

No! But she did not have the strength or the control for the cry. WolfStar was playing to her SunSoar blood, and playing to the Niah-soul within her, and so finally she gave up the struggle, and allowed WolfStar and her own body their independent ways.

He jerked and shuddered, and she felt the extension of his own life fill her womb.

And something else.

No, no, no, no . . .

Even as he withdrew from my body I could feel the fire that he had seeded in my womb erupt into new life. He laughed gently at the cry that escaped my lips and at the expression in my eyes, but I could see his own eyes widen to mirror the wonder that filled mine. For a long time we lay still, his body heavy on mine, our eyes star-

ing into each other's depths, as we felt you spring to life within my womb.

It was happening all over again! He lay hot and oppressive over her, the stickiness and dampness of his body where it touched hers repulsive, his eyes fixed on hers, and both felt the new life leap in her womb.

"Our magical, magical daughter," he whispered, a hand now pressed into her belly. "Do you feel her?"

Zenith could not find the strength to speak. Again she turned her head to one side, trying to ignore him, hoping he would go away now that he'd used her.

WolfStar thought her movement only the languor of love. He kissed her, and rubbed and pinched her nipple, and he lay still longer, enjoying her warmth and what he thought was her love.

Zenith moved, trying to ease off his weight, but her movement only aroused WolfStar once more, and then again he was atop her and moving within her. Again she found her hands encouraging him, and her body writhing wantonly under his, again her voice moaning and calling out to him, and Zenith let go, the only thing she could do, and slipped completely into the pits of oblivion, leaving Niah to enjoy her lover.

Drago woke suddenly, thinking he'd heard a faint cry. He lay, wrapped in his cloak, watching the flames leap in the fire, listening.

There, again. The hoarse cry of a man—and Drago was old enough and experienced enough to recognize that cry for what it was.

Puzzled, he pushed himself into a sitting position, glancing over to make sure Zenith was asleep . . . and saw nothing but the flattened grass where she had once lain.

"Oh gods!" he whispered, appalled, and struggled to his feet.

Where had that sound come from? Where?

Ah, there . . . again!

Drago hurried into the night.

"Ah," WolfStar breathed, and then cried, and then shuddered again.

Go away, go away, go away, Zenith thought in a litany of repugnance. Go away! When would he have done? *When?*

WolfStar sighed and rolled off her, leaning up on an elbow and stroking her face. "Under the stars," he whispered. "Perfect."

Zenith tried to smile, but found it difficult.

WolfStar smiled and kissed her. "Now that I have found you . . ." he whispered, then sighed again—in impatience this time—and sat up. "I wish I could stay, but I must away. Damn your brother—did you know he has escaped?"

Zenith looked at him, but did not speak.

WolfStar, busy rearranging his breeches, did not notice. "I have tried to scry him out, but I cannot find him. I *must* find him, for I cannot allow him to live through *this* crime."

He paused, his face puzzled. "But I cannot scry him out. Has he refound his power? *Has he?*"

And he swiveled to look Zenith direct in the eye.

She managed to find her voice. "How can I know? I have not seen him for many days."

He frowned. "And why are you running, my lovely? Why? Where?"

She smiled for him, although it cost her dearly to do so. "I have been struggling to come to terms with what you told me, WolfStar. I . . . I thought to go south . . . south to . . ."

"Ah, the Island of Mist and Memory," WolfStar said. "Yes, that would indeed be best for you."

He rose. "I will see you there, Niah. Wait for me."

And he shimmered and vanished.

* * *

Drago got to the lip of the gully just in time to see WolfStar lift himself from Zenith's side and then disappear.

"Zenith!" he cried, and started to clamber down the side of the gully.

She lay curled on her side, naked, bruised and bloodied, her hands over her belly.

Her eyes were wide open, staring.

"Zenith?" Drago hesitantly touched her shoulder. "Zenith?"

She didn't move, or even acknowledge his presence.

"Zenith . . . come." He pulled gently on one arm, and finally managed to get her to sit up.

She blinked, as if seeing him for the first time, then she burst into tears and hugged him tight.

"Oh gods, Drago," she sobbed, "you're alive!"

He carried her back to their makeshift camp, wrapped her in her cloak, and sat her by the fire. He had no idea what to say to her, what she wanted to hear.

She kept her face averted, her eyes on the fire, apparently lost in thought.

She hardly blinked.

But when the sun rose, so too did Zenith, wrapping the cloak more closely about her nakedness.

"The ferry is only a few hours away," she said, and walked off.

Stunned, Drago stared after her, then after a minute snatched at his sack and got to his feet.

They had to wait over an hour for the ferry to come back to their side of the shore, and when the ramp had been dropped, they stepped as silently onto the ferry as they had walked the last three hours.

"Fare," grunted the ferryman, a man as thin and insipid as the waterweed he plied his craft through.

"Zenith," Drago murmured. "Zenith, you need to do something. I have no coin."

Zenith lifted her head and stared at Drago, then she shifted her eyes back to the waters of the river disinterestedly.

Drago opened his mouth, then closed it again. He thought frantically—what could he do? He fumbled with the sack, sliding his hand in as if he was going to withdraw money.

"No fare and I don't move this craft," the ferryman said, and now there was a gleam of malice in his eyes. At the other end of the ferry two muscular assistants picked up short, thick poles and hefted them menacingly.

Drago groped about in the sack, pretending to search for a sack. Maybe he could hit the ferryman with it and jump off. Maybe he could . . . his eyes widened, and he slowly withdrew his hand. In his palm lay a newly minted silver piece.

The ferryman leaned forward and snatched it.

"That's more than the fare," Drago said.

"Aye, but I've had to wait for it," the ferryman said. "Want to argue the matter with my sons?"

The two assistants stepped yet closer.

Drago retreated. "Just get us to the other side as fast as you can."

"Aye, my lord," and the ferryman gave a mock bow.

Drago waited until he had moved away, then whispered to Zenith. "Thank you. I did not know how I was going to pay him."

She looked at him, frowning. "It was not my doing," she said, and turned back to the water.

She stood at the railing, where Drago could not see her, and wept. She felt so alone, and yet she felt more crowded than ever before. Trapped.

WolfStar was so good! You enjoyed it, I know you did. Ac-

cept it, Zenith. You are me and I am you, and WolfStar is our future. There can be no other way.

No. There *must* be another way.

I have been reborn SunSoar so that WolfStar will never leave me. Our blood will sing to each other through an eternity of nights. Accept.

No. No, I will not allow it.

You have no choice.

Worse still than that insistent voice was the distinct feeling of fire eating into the lining of her womb. New life. A magical daughter. Who? Who? Another Azhure? No. Another Azhure to birth another daughter to live out this hell all over again? No, no, no!

What could she do? Zenith tried to keep her thoughts private, tried to think what to do, but it was no use. All she could see was WolfStar leering into her face, and all she could feel was the thrust of his body.

23

Minstrelsea

They stumbled toward the forest, Drago with one arm about Zenith, now constantly mumbling to herself, the other wrapped about his sack.

Drago didn't know what to do. Zenith obviously couldn't go much farther—but where could he leave her? Who could he leave her *with*? Drago loved his sister, and was terrified for her, but he also knew that he was no help to her. She needed more powerful magic than his concern to evict this Niah creature.

Besides, there was a compulsion growing within him. Get south. Get south fast.

Where? Where? The Island of Mist and Memory? No. That didn't feel right.

"Where? *Where?*" he muttered, tense with frustration and worry.

"What?" Zenith whispered, rousing slightly. "What did you say?"

"Nothing. Look, the forest is not far away. A few more minutes only."

"The forest?" she said. "What forest?"

Drago stopped and wrapped his arm more securely about her. "Minstrelsea. Remember? You wanted to come here."

"I did?" She struggled a little against his arm, but did not have the strength to break free.

"I'll find help," he said. But help against what? Niah? Or the shock of WolfStar's rape?

"No, no," Zenith whispered, again struggling feebly. "Not Minstrelsea. Not here . . . no . . . no . . . no . . ."

"It won't hurt you, Zenith! Be still now, I can hardly hold you!"

Here is where Niah died! Zenith wanted to scream at him, but her voice was no longer her own. *Here is where she is strongest! Not here! Not—*

Yes, here, Zenith. Here is where you *die, at last.*

She choked, and Drago stopped in alarm. "Zenith? Zenith?"

But she was no longer responding, and Drago, sure now that the only way to help her was to somehow get her deep into the forest, hauled her onward.

Minstrelsea loomed before them. There was no thin scattering of brush and seedling trees to blur the demarcation between plain and forest. Behind them and to the west lay leagues of rolling grass and grain land, while before them reared a wall of trees. The trees hummed, singing softly to themselves, and between their trunks peered the curious eyes of the strange, fey creatures that populated the forest.

Drago could not help a shiver of apprehension as the trees

loomed above him. He'd been in Minstrelsea only once or twice previously, although Zenith and Caelum had visited regularly.

And Isfrael, of course, had come with Axis to meet with his mother Faraday.

No wonder Isfrael was so strange, Drago thought feverishly, to have a doe as a mother.

But even if Drago had hardly ever been here, and even if he no longer had the use of his Icarii powers, he knew those trees were far more than they appeared. Each one was a living entity capable of anger or of love. Combined as the forest, the trees could wipe out an army if they wished, or midwife the birth of a butterfly.

He paused just before committing himself and his sister to the forest. Then, because he had nothing left to do, and nowhere else to go, he plunged into the trees as if he were running into a burning building.

As so many others had before him, Drago stopped in utter amazement within five or six paces.

Despite its forbidding aura, Minstrelsea was a pool of light and music. The trunks of the trees grew far apart, and sunlight filtered down through the green canopy at least a hundred paces above. Birds—strange birds—sang from the branches of the immense trees, and even stranger creatures gambolled about the glades, paths and in the rivulets that wound their way through the trees.

Peaceful. It was peaceful. Drago dared to take a deep breath and let his shoulders relax for the first time in days.

Even Zenith seemed to revive slightly, and Drago found he did not have to support so much of her weight.

They began to walk slowly down the forest track, Drago lost amid the beauty of the forest, Zenith lost in *(losing)* the battle in her mind.

This forest is so beautiful. I loved it when Azhure brought us here as a child.

No, no, no, no . . .

Look! There is a diamond-eyed bird! Remember how we loved to watch them flutter from branch to branch?

No, no, no, no . . .

You know where he is taking us, don't you, Zenith? My grove. Poor girl, soon it will be your burial ground, not mine.

No, no, no, no . . .

But Zenith was now very, very tired of saying "no." She thought it would be good to lie down. Rest a while. Perhaps just to let Niah have her way for a few days, a week at the most. Then, once she had rested . . .

You go to sleep now, dear. You have been good. Go to sleep . . .

And Zenith tottered along by Drago's side, losing the strength to maintain her grip on life.

They walked for an hour or more, deep into the forest, Drago unaware of, and Zenith ignoring, the thousand fey eyes that watched their passing from the shadows.

It was only when they approached a large grove that Zenith's head whipped up and she stopped, aware at last, her eyes wide. "No!"

Drago turned wearily to her. "Zenith, we need to rest, and this grove has sunlit spaces we can warm ourselves in. Come on now, we're almost there."

He pulled her forward.

The instant they stepped into the grove, Zenith felt Niah *lunge* within her. She screamed in terror—Niah was too strong here! Ah! *Stars!* Niah was penetrating and invading her soul, tearing it apart, a rape more painful, more humiliating than WolfStar's invasion of her body.

And she could do nothing to stop Niah—she was so powerful, so vigorous, so certain!

"Zenith!" Drago tried to hold her, but she wrenched away from him, falling against a tree.

"Zenith!" Again Drago reached for her, but recoiled in horror as his sister convulsed.

Her hands beat frantically at her bare breasts where the cloak had fallen away, and she whimpered. "Help me! Oh, Stars, *help me!*" Her voice ended on a thin wail of terror.

Drago tried to grab his sister to him, but she kept rolling out of his arms. What was going on?

"Oh Gods, it hurts, it *hurts*!" Zenith's hands were now patting at her head, now her abdomen, now clasped about her shoulders. "Put it out, please . . . put it out! It *hurts*!"

Drago stared wildly about, desperate for help, taking in the large grove ringed by nine trees and covered in Moon-wildflowers, Azhure's mark.

A coldness overwhelmed him as he realized where they were. What had he done? He'd led Zenith right into Niah's Grove, the place where Azhure's mother had burned to death—when this site had once been the village of Smyrton—and the place where her body lay buried.

"Oh Stars!" he cried. "What have I done?"

Zenith no longer spoke or cried out, but her eyes and mouth were circles of horror reflecting the agony that the Niah within was visiting upon her.

Suddenly Drago was very, very angry. *Damn their parents into every eternity of unhappiness for visiting such pain on their children!*

He finally managed to grab Zenith to him, trying as best he could to give her some reassurance, trying to touch her mind, to break the horror that had consumed—*was consuming*—her.

The sack fell to one side, but Drago ignored it. "Zenith," he murmured. "Zenith!"

Zenith was no longer aware of him. She writhed and struggled, and was now gasping and choking so much that Drago thought she would, in truth, die.

I wish Niah's soul would stay in its damned AfterLife! Drago thought, and then cursed aloud, panicked that he could do nothing to help Zenith.

"'Tis no use getting so angry, my boy," said a voice firmly to one side. "It will not help your sister."

Startled, Drago looked up, and Zenith almost rolled out of his grip. He managed to hold on to her, then continued to watch the other side of the grove warily. A peasant woman had stepped forth, rubbing her hands anxiously above her large belly. She was in her mid-thirties, with roughened skin and thick limbs. She was clean and well-kept, but she was dressed simply in a worsted dress and enveloping black apron, and her expression was that of a simpleton.

"Who are you?" he snapped. "Stay away!" His arms tightened about Zenith.

The woman ignored him and advanced a little more. Drago wondered if she was indeed dim-witted, or if she used that expression to mask more dangerous thoughts. Stars knew what mad creatures these woods contained! "Stay away! I—"

"You need help, m'lad." And ignoring his angry expression she sank down on the other side of the still-writhing Zenith. "Tell me what's wrong with her."

Drago had no intention of telling her. What? This peasant woman who at best knew how to curdle milk? No! He wasn't going to—

The woman raised her eyes from Zenith and stared at Drago.

Drago may have had no residual Icarii power himself, but he had lived his life among Enchanters and Gods, and he recognized power when he saw it.

This woman's eyes blazed with it, although it was such power that Drago had never seen before.

"It is the power of the Mother," the woman said, and now her voice had dropped its simple brogue and throbbed with power as well. "Come to help your sister, if it can. Now, be still."

She dropped her eyes back to Zenith, and patted at her arm with one work-roughened hand.

Suddenly Drago knew who this woman was; not only had his mother talked of her, but she was a legend among the Icarii and Avar. She was Goodwife Renkin, the peasant woman who had helped Faraday plant Minstrelsea, and the woman who also acted as a conduit for the voice and power of the Mother, the being who personified the power of the earth and nature. When Faraday had completed her planting, the Goodwife had wandered off into the forest, never to be seen again.

Not by human eyes, anyway.

Now here she was. Sitting before him, patting Zenith's arm and singing a trifling lullaby to her.

Much good that was doing, Drago thought. He trusted no-one, and certainly not this odd woman before him now.

"She is in great pain," the Goodwife said, her voice still carrying its power. "Why is that, older brother?" She raised her eyes back to Drago.

He considered again if he should tell her or not, then found to his amazement that the words were flooding out of him. "She battles the reborn soul of Niah within her," he said. "It is a trouble she should not have to bear, for she is innocent of any wrongdoing."

"Unlike you," the Goodwife observed.

Drago's mouth twisted. "Have the tales of my misdeeds penetrated even this green haven?"

"All know your story, Drago. You betrayed your brother for your own gain."

"So I have been *told,*" Drago said, angry beyond measure. "And to be perfectly frank with you, Goodwife, I wish I had been more successful at it! Maybe then I could have saved Zenith this pain!"

Her head jerked up. "Do you still covet your brother's place?" she asked softly. "Would *you* like to sit the Throne of the Stars?"

He stared at her, frightened, because suddenly that *was* what he wanted—very much. What *would* it have been like to have been born first? To have been born heir?

"It is not good to covet your brother's place," the woman said, babbling again in peasantish brogue rather than the power of the Mother, and with her eyes focused on something other than Drago. "Is it, m'Lady?"

Drago looked over his shoulder where the woman was gazing and froze.

A doe stepped from the far side of the grove, her russet skin trembling with apprehension, her great, dark eyes flickering from the tableau before her to the forest. Drago was unsure whether she'd stay or flee.

"Come, come, m'Lady," the woman said. "This child here needs your help. I find I can do little for her."

Drago glanced at the woman. Not even with *your* power? he thought. But just then the doe took a hesitant step forward, and Drago's eyes flew back to her.

Again he knew who this was. Faraday. Once Queen of Achar, now trapped in animal form.

All of us betrayed in one way or another, Drago thought suddenly. All of us trapped in flesh we don't want.

"Nay," the Goodwife said quietly before him, her brogue again gone. "This girlie before me is betrayed, surely, and Faraday has betrayal branded into her very bones, but you are a betrayer. It is what you were born to. You have *sin* branded into your bones."

Appalled and hurt rather than angry, Drago stared at her. "No, no . . ."

There was a quiet movement at his shoulder. The doe had crept up to them, and was now standing a pace away from the sack, staring at it.

She was trembling almost uncontrollably. Slowly she raised her great eyes from the sack and stared at Drago.

And he understood with that look that she knew what it contained.

"The girlie," the Goodwife said gently to the doe. "She needs your help."

For a heartbeat longer the doe continued to stare at Drago, then she broke the stare and edged about him to Zenith. She lowered her head and nuzzled the woman's face with her nose, then sank gracefully down at her head.

Drago could not take his eyes from her. He had never seen the doe—Faraday—before. The tale of this woman was so legendary, so lovely, that even Drago had found himself touched by it.

Particularly because Faraday had been so betrayed by his father, and yet still she had died for him.

Drago could not imagine loving anyone that much. Was her agony worth it? Surely she must now regret her devotion to Axis. Surely?

The doe raised her eyes from her contemplation of Zenith and stared briefly at Drago.

It was only a brief look, but in that moment Drago saw something that took his breath away.

As the doe had raised her head he had seen in the curve of the animal throat the grace of a beautiful woman's neck, and he had seen in the rough reddish hair of the doe's coat the gleam of tangled chestnut hair, and for an instant he had seen a tortured woman's soul behind the creature's dark eyes.

The doe glanced once more at the sack, trembled, then bent her attention back to Zenith.

She is losing her battle. She descends toward madness. This place is too Niah-strong for her already weakened and saddened state.

The voice, so soft and gentle, whispered through Drago's mind, and he stifled a cry.

"M'Lady?" the Goodwife said. "Isn't there something you can do? My herbs cannot mend this malady."

How can I evict this presence that torments her so? The doe lowered her nose to Zenith's forehead. *She fights, and it fights within her, and I can see no help, no solution.*

"WolfStar found her, and raped her," Drago put in suddenly, wanting them to know all the horror.

"And what did you do as WolfStar raped her?" the Goodwife asked.

"I . . . I did not know what was happening. She'd run from camp. I did not know until it was too late."

The Goodwife lowered her eyes contemptuously.

Was he to be blamed for *all* Tencendor's woes, Drago wondered, then turned to the doe.

"Help her, please," he said, and extended a hand toward her.

The doe flinched, and he dropped it.

I can do nothing, she said.

"I can do nothing," the Goodwife echoed.

"But what can *I* do? I can't leave her here! I—"

"Where do you go?" the Goodwife asked. "What sin do you plan next?"

"I plan to save my own life!" Drago shouted. "Is that such a sin?"

He took a huge breath, trying to bring his anger under control. "She wanted to go to the Island of Mist and Memory. To StarDrifter."

StarDrifter?

"He said once . . . he said he would always be there to catch her."

Ah. The doe tilted her head and considered Drago. *Perhaps I can summon StarDrifter here. Zenith will never survive the trip to the Isle.*

Drago hesitated, then leaned down and touched Zenith's cheek a last time. He could do no more for her, and he knew that she was better left in the care of these two than struggling farther south with him.

"Take care of her, please." He let her weight fall into the arms of the Goodwife, picked up the sack, and stood up, retreating several paces.

Where are you going?

Where? Where? Drago didn't know. He retreated another pace, the sack clutched tight to his chest.

Why that? the doe asked sadly.

"I don't know," Drago muttered, staring at her. "I don't know."

It has its own purpose.

"It has no thought of its own!"

It seeks . . . it seeks a home.

"No!" Now Drago had reached the far edge of the grove.

Take it back.

"No!" Drago yelled one last time, staring frantically for a moment at Zenith, and then was gone.

24

StarDrifter

After his son defeated Gorgrael, StarDrifter had made his home on the Island of Mist and Memory. There he studied and dreamed, conducted the rites of Star worship, and was generally content. He lived on Temple Mount, establishing an academy for Icarii children with Enchanter powers, and teaching what he knew and what he'd come to understand. He had mellowed in the tranquillity of the island, and became more patient and serene, although StarDrifter did not fully realize this change in himself.

He did not lack for company, either. Although the population of the Mount itself had not grown appreciably over the past years, the Icarii had built themselves a spreading town about the foot of the mountain. From there, they could rise on the jungle thermals to the peak to attend rites, or just to come and absorb the power that washed about the great Temple of the Stars.

At first StarDrifter had visited his family in Sigholt once or twice a year, but as time had passed, and Axis and Azhure's children grew into adulthood, his visits had become more infrequent, sometimes once every two years, more often longer. Axis and Azhure came to him on Temple Mount now and then, but their visits had become rare since they had drifted more with their Star God companions; StarDrifter had not seen them in some three years.

He missed them, but he missed his grandchildren more,

and every few weeks guilt made him vow to himself to go to Sigholt *this* Yuletide. But he somehow knew that Yuletide would come and go, and his grandchildren would remain unseen. Caelum was now too busy ruling Tencendor to leave, RiverStar too self-absorbed, Isfrael and Zenith had their own lives, and Drago . . . well, Drago had so little in common with the other SunSoars that he was the last person StarDrifter expected to visit the island.

All his grandchildren had spent time with StarDrifter when they were growing up. StarDrifter even missed Drago who, despite his outwardly sullen appearance, had a lively mind and had spent hours following StarDrifter about the complex, asking questions. StarDrifter missed them all . . . except RiverStar. He was glad she no longer came. StarDrifter had once promised himself that he would have Azhure's eldest daughter if he could not have Azhure, but RiverStar had herself crept into his bed when she was thirteen, her hands knowing and bold, and StarDrifter had been so repelled by the experience that he had lost any desire for her.

StarDrifter was lonely, although he did not recognize it. He had let Rivkah go, and he had lost contact with his son and his grandchildren. Even FreeFall and his wife, EvenSong, StarDrifter's daughter, were too busy to attend to him.

So this day he wandered the orchard above the Dome of the Stars, his wings fluttering out behind him, eyes half closed, his head lifted slightly to the sea breeze as it rushed over the cliffs, and he wondered why he felt so melancholy.

It was a warm day, and yet StarDrifter found his flesh creeping with a strange chill. He opened his eyes fully, and stood still, looking about.

There was something wrong.

A knot of nervousness twisted about in his belly. He had not felt anything like this for years . . . many years. What was it?

He turned about in a slow circle, his wings now half extended, ready for flight.

StarDrifter . . .

That voice! He knew it, but could not place it. Who?

StarDrifter . . .

Calling, calling to him. Worried, but so far away. Who?

And then power hit him like a blast of turbulent wind. StarDrifter cried out, almost fell over, then managed to regain his balance. He looked about, not understanding. He was surrounded by vibrant, pulsing emerald light. So vibrant it lived, shadowing and shifting . . .

"Stars," he whispered, and saw that one section of the emerald light was changing, reshaping so that it became a tunnel of swirling silver and emerald light, and at the end of this tunnel stood two women, one holding out her hand.

One was a pleasant-faced woman in late middle-age, dark brown hair graying and coiled loosely about her head. She was dressed in a soft pale blue robe, belted about with a rainbow-striped band. From her came most of this power.

The Mother. StarDrifter had never seen her personified, but he recognized her power from years of conducting joint rites with the Avar.

The other woman was Faraday. StarDrifter could not believe it. When had he last seen her? At Axis' side in Carlon, smiling and cheerful, not yet knowing that Axis had betrayed her with Azhure.

She held out her hand, and she smiled. "StarDrifter." Her voice came from very far away. "StarDrifter, I have need of you as you once had need of me. Will you aid me?"

"Gladly," StarDrifter said without hesitation, and stepped into the spiraling tunnel.

He spread his wings to the power, letting it carry him toward the two women. He felt earth and stars rush by him, knowing it carried him a great distance, and when it finally let him go and he stepped into Niah's Grove, he was not truly surprised.

There waited before him a doe and a peasant woman. Like Drago before him, StarDrifter knew instantly who these two represented. But his eyes were caught by the twisting, moaning figure between them.

"Zenith!" And with one great flap of his wings he was at their side, falling to his knees beside Zenith. "What's wrong? What's happened to her?"

"Drago," the Goodwife began, and StarDrifter's head snapped up at the name of his grandson, "told us her body and mind is tormented by Niah's reborn soul. Zenith fights it."

The Goodwife shrugged. "But m'Lady and I can do nothing for the poor sweet girl. The Niah-soul wins."

Niah's reborn soul? Azhure had once shown Niah's letter to StarDrifter, and he knew what the Goodwife alluded to. Niah? In *Zenith*?

He looked again at his granddaughter. She appeared unconscious, but was obviously in anguish. Her skin was pale and sweating, her muscles twitching, her breath jerking in her breast.

And why was she naked under this cloak, and with the marks of some assault upon her?

"The poor sweeting," the Goodwife said. "Not only does she battle the dead soul within her, but her body and spirit were raped by WolfStar—"

StarDrifter gave a great cry and leaped to his feet. *WolfStar!* He had known that malevolent criminal would reappear some day. But to so harm Zenith? StarDrifter looked back at his granddaughter, and his stomach curdled in revulsion at the crime that had been visited upon her.

"Zenith," he whispered, dropping to his knees before her again.

We cannot reach her . . .

"How did she come to be here?" StarDrifter asked harshly. "You said Drago was with her?"

"Her brother came with her, but has run off—"

What was going on here?

Drago was running from something. Something wrong at Sigholt.

"Drago was running from a misdeed, no doubt," the Goodwife put in, folding her hands over her belly and pursing her mouth, but the doe continued.

Zenith was with him—we do not know why—and Drago left her with us, hoping we could help her.

"And was he a party to her rape?" StarDrifter asked.

"No, good sir, we do not think so," the Goodwife answered. "But neither did he help her."

Stars, but he should never have left those children alone for so long! Why hadn't he visited?

They are not children any more, StarDrifter. All capable of choosing their own paths.

"Or fated," StarDrifter, his thoughts returning to what fought for control of Zenith's body and mind. Why Zenith? She had such a sweet and trusting nature—was that why she'd been chosen as a vessel for Niah's rebirth?

Who *was* this on the ground before him? Had it always been Niah? Or was Zenith a separate entity? A different personality?

StarDrifter shook his head slightly, hoping to clear it. "Why call me? What can I do?"

Drago said that she wanted to go to you.

StarDrifter frowned. "Why?"

Because you once told Zenith that you would always be there to catch her.

Except I wasn't, was I? StarDrifter thought. Should he take her? The island might be the worst place for Zenith if she was battling the reborn Niah.

But he had little choice, and, more importantly, neither did Zenith.

StarDrifter squatted down by his granddaughter and took her into his arms.

Strangely, she quietened a little as soon as he had gathered her against his breast.

"I'm here, Zenith," he whispered, and stroked her hair.

Suddenly she stilled, her breathing eased, and her entire body relaxed.

And yet her stillness did not ease StarDrifter's mind. Someone had won—but who?

"I will take her to the Island of Mist and Memory," he said. "Pray to both earth and stars that I am doing the right thing."

25

DragonStar

"Nothing?" Caelum said. *"Nothing?"*

Crest-Leader FeatherFlight BrightWing's expression did not change. "StarSon, we have sent scouts out to the feet of the Icescarp Alps, to the River Ichtar, and south as far as the Minaret Peaks. Nothing."

Caelum sat down heavily at the table in the map-room.

"Askam?" He did not even look at the prince, for he knew in his bones what the man would report.

"Nothing, Caelum." Askam spread his hands helplessly. "The patrols could not have scoured the Urqhart Hills more thoroughly if they'd done it on their hands and knees."

Caelum sifted through a pile of loose papers on the table. "And these . . . reports from Jervois Landing, Severin, most of the smaller hamlets between here and Carlon—even Gorkenfort! *Nothing!* No-one has seen him." Nor Zenith. Had WolfStar found her? Or was she hiding from their grandfather in some enchanted bolt-hole?

"Curse it!" Caelum sent the papers scattering across the table. "Where is he? Where could he have gone?"

Askam glanced at FeatherFlight. Caelum's nerves were strung as tight as a fishing line with a whale on its hook—and no wonder. Drago had disappeared completely. How? And how was it he'd managed to evade searchers that ranged from the strongest Enchanters to the ablest trackers?

By rights Drago should not have been able to escape more than a league or two . . . *if he* had *left Sigholt!* Was someone aiding him? Who? Why?

"He could have managed to get to Minstrelsea," Askam said slowly. "If he's in there . . ."

Caelum looked up sharply. "Stars, Askam! I should have you as a full-time adviser. FeatherFlight! Send word to Isfrael that Drago may well be within his domain."

FeatherFlight nodded, saluted, and left.

Caelum settled back in his chair. "Drago will never escape the eyes and ears Isfrael can call to his command. Askam, I thank you again . . . will you stay a week or two longer? I have need of a sharp mind about me at the moment."

"As you will, StarSon."

Caelum grinned at him. "And yet you fidget as if the most practiced whore awaited you in your bed . . . what is it?"

Askam returned the smile. "Master Horrald has been waiting for me at weapons practice this past half an hour. By the time I get there he will have broiled up a nice temper."

Caelum managed a laugh. Master Horrald was senior among the weapons masters at Sigholt—and not known for his sweet disposition. "Begone then, Askam, and ask Master Horrald not to cut you to ribbons, if only for my sake."

Left alone in the map-room, Caelum leaned his head into his hand and sighed. This last week had been distressful, and his nights had been filled with unsettling dreams of hunts that ran through forest and stars alike, and of huntsmen who ran down men, not animals.

It made him think for a moment . . . hunt. Could his mother's hounds . . . ? No, Azhure had told him a long time ago that the hounds could never be set to hunt mortals.

Caelum looked at his hands, twisting about the red-gold, diamond-encrusted ring on his right hand. It was not his father's ring—Axis still wore that—but an exact duplicate.

And Axis had taught him how to use it properly.

Enchanters wielded power by manipulating threads of the Star Dance, the music the stars made as they danced through the universe. For each purpose, a Song. For countless generations Icarii Enchanters had painstakingly discovered perhaps a thousand Songs they could weave from the Star Dance, but Orr the Ferryman had shown Axis that all an Enchanter needed to do was think of the purpose, and the diamonds on his ring would rearrange themselves to show him the particular Song to sing.

"Show me a Song for scrying," he whispered, and after an instant's hesitation, the diamonds on his ring rearranged themselves into a new pattern.

Caelum thought about the music his ring showed him. It would be a powerful Song, requiring him to manipulate a dangerous amount of the Star Dance, but he was powerful himself, and he could manage it.

He ran the Song through his head, absorbing the power of the Star Dance that flooded him, and directed that power to his purpose.

Instantly the room before him faded, and Caelum saw the plains of Ichtar stretching away to the west of Sigholt.

"Find me Drago," he whispered, and the view altered. His vision swept north until it danced among the peaks of the Icescarp Alps, then east and south, skimming over the gray-green tops of the Avarinheim and Minstrelsea.

Caelum felt giddy and nauseated with the amount of power he was being forced to wield, but was determined to see it through.

"Drago," he whispered, and the vision changed, and now he swept over the spires of the Minaret Peaks, now over Tare, now over Carlon.

"Drago!" he cried. "Find me Drago!"

He felt his body lurch, as if it had abruptly changed direction, and he saw the tranquil shores of the Island of Mist and Memory—there was a presence there . . . Zenith! Aha—so that is where she'd gone. Good.

But no Drago.

Caelum wondered if the Song was as lost as he. In desperation, he cried out one last time, now using Drago's birth name, thinking the Song required that.

"Find me DragonStar!"

In the space of a heartbeat, the entire world altered . . . and Caelum panicked. Tencendor had disappeared. Now he was lost, lost in a black void, and in this void he could sense a presence so infinitely powerful that he understood he would die if it found him.

"StarSon?" it whispered. "StarSon?"

Caelum could feel it reaching out for him, rushing toward him as if it were a great wind.

"StarSon!"

"No," Caelum whispered.

"You pitiful weakling, StarSon," the voice cried, and Caelum could feel the being *rippling* toward him. "Let me *hunt* you, let me *impale* you, let me violate your corpse, let me—"

"No!" Caelum screamed, and with the last of his willpower broke his contact with the Star Dance.

The Song ceased, and Caelum opened his eyes to the familiar surroundings of the map-room. His chest was heaving, his body covered in sweat, his hands trembling.

"Stars," Caelum whispered into the room, "was that *you,* Drago?"

That evening Caelum was visited by SpikeFeather TrueSong.

He appeared from nowhere, perhaps the door, but Caelum was not sure. The chamber had been empty when Caelum went to close the shutters at the window, yet SpikeFeather had been there when he turned back to the room.

"SpikeFeather!"

Caelum was unnerved by the birdman's sudden appearance. SpikeFeather carried about him an aura of subtle power.

Not Enchanter power, not anything any Enchanter had seen previously. Caelum assumed he'd absorbed it from Orr.

"StarSon." SpikeFeather bowed his eye-catching red head. "Has there been any news of Drago?"

"I am surprised that you have heard of such excitement secreted down in the waterways, SpikeFeather. Drago was still here, and RiverStar still alive, when you left to rejoin Orr."

"The waterways reflect many things, StarSon. And some of them have concerned the problems of Sigholt."

"You do not know Drago's whereabouts?"

"No, StarSon, I do not."

"But surely you could—"

"There is nothing I can do, StarSon. Drago is not in the waterways—that is all I can tell you."

Caelum sighed, and poured each of them a glass of wine. Stars knew he'd need it to sleep tonight. "Well, then, SpikeFeather. What news from the Star Gate?"

In the consternation surrounding RiverStar's murder and Drago's escape over the past week, Caelum had pushed to one side the strange tidings of the whispers beyond the Star Gate.

Now . . . now he wondered if they had anything to do with his frightening vision of this morning.

SpikeFeather sat down in a chair and sipped at his wine. "They still whisper and call, but they have come no closer. They seem to be holding their distance. Orr is tense, but he has sounded no alarm. StarSon, I would venture to advise that WolfStar was right. They pose no danger save to the over-curious mind who would be tempted to plunge after them."

"Through the Star Gate?" Caelum laughed incredulously—and a little too loudly. The Star Gate disconcerted him. He had seen his father, and numerous other Enchanters, stand at its rim, enthralled by the Star Dance and the universe it contained, but he always felt dizzy if he stayed there more than a moment.

SpikeFeather watched him, then shrugged. "No doubt the

issue of the children will become no more than a passing curiosity, StarSon."

"I do hope you are right," Caelum said, and abruptly stood to pour himself some more wine. "I do hope so."

He dreamed that night. He dreamed he was hunting through the forest. A great summer hunt, the entire court with him. His parents, laughing on their horses. His brother, Isfrael, and his sisters, even RiverStar. It was a glorious day, and they rode on the wind and on their power, and all the cares of the world and of Tencendor seemed very, very far away.

But then the dream shifted, changed. They still hunted, but Caelum could no longer see his parents or his brother and sisters. The hounds ran, but he could no longer see them either. The forest gathered about him, suddenly threatening.

And now even his horse had disappeared. He was running through the forest on foot, his breath tight in his chest, fear pounding through his veins.

Behind him *something* coursed. Hounds, but not hounds. They whispered his name. Oh, Stars! There were hundreds of them! And they hunted him.

They whispered his name. *StarSon! StarSon!*

Caelum sobbed in fear. *What was this forest?* It was nothing that he had ever seen in Tencendor. He cut himself on twigs and shrubs, fell, and scrambled, panicking, to his feet.

Something behind him . . . something . . . something deadly.

Running.

He heard feet pounding closer, he heard horns, and glad cries. They had cornered him!

Caelum fell to the forest floor and cowered as deeply into the dirt and leaf litter as he could.

But he couldn't resist one glimpse, and that one glimpse was enough to push him to the brink of insanity.

A man, clad in enveloping dull black armor, rode a great dark horse. In his hand he wielded a massive sword. The horse reared to a halt before him and, as it did so, Caelum found breath for one final scream.

"DragonStar!"

26

The Sack (1)

Drago moved south through Minstrelsea, not really knowing where he was going, only driven by some urge to go south, south, south.

During the day he crept within the shadows, avoiding the few Avar he heard coming down the forest paths, ignoring the brilliant birds and magical creatures that inhabited the forest.

Ignoring all but one. Drago had become aware on the second day after leaving Niah's Grove that the red doe followed him.

Damn her! Why follow him? Had she managed to contact StarDrifter? Was Zenith safe? The doe would not let him approach, so Drago had to continue on his way with his questions unanswered, trying his best to put her out of his mind, but wishing at every step that she would just leave him alone.

The evenings he spent gathering what fruit and berries he could from shrubs, and digging for the tuber roots he knew formed the subsistence food of the Avar. But he found little. One day he managed to catch a fish in a stream, and had to eat that raw because he did not have the implements for making a fire.

Its flesh was cold and slimy as it slid down his throat, and Drago choked and gagged, but forced it down. Disgusting as it was, Drago still preferred his current existence to the one he'd lived at Sigholt. Raw fish was surely better than lying in the corpse yard!

In the evenings, when he huddled beneath the overhang of some great-leaved plant, or in the exposed roots of the massive trees, when he had nothing but his thoughts for company, Drago reflected on his life.

It had been wasted thus far, he decided. He'd been kept trapped within the SunSoar family, trapped by their hatred and distrust, trapped by his reputation. He'd been allowed no role in the new Tencendor—and what role *could* he be given? Surely the black-hearted Drago would have only manipulated that role for his own gain and his brother's downfall!

Drago's bitterness, always a small, hard canker in his heart, began to expand. He could have been an Icarii Enchanter, a *SunSoar* Enchanter, yet here he was, running through the forest, falsely condemned of murder so Caelum could finally have the excuse to do away with him.

And so, late in the nights, Drago would hug his sack to him, and wonder if Caelum had missed it yet. And he would wonder further, how can I use this? How can I wield it? How . . .?

He dreamed he was hunting through the forest. A great summer hunt, the entire court with him. His parents, laughing on their horses. His brothers, Caelum and Isfrael, and his sisters, even RiverStar. WolfStar was there, too, grinning maniacally as he strode beside the horses in his billowing black cloak. It was a glorious day, and they rode on the wind and on their power and all the cares of the world and of Tencendor seemed very, very far away.

He shifted, uncomfortable, and the dream shifted with him.

He dreamed he hunted, and he rode a great horse. In his hand he wielded a weapon, the likes of which Tencendor had never seen before—not even the Wolven bow compared in strength and enchantment with this.

It combined the power of the stars with the power of the earth, and it sang as he swung it through the air.

Hunt, his mind whispered through the forest, and the hunt intensified.

His hounds—no, they were not hounds, they were something indefinably different—obeyed, and they put their noses . . . no . . . *beaks* . . . to the scent of the prey and they coursed and whispered and hunted.

They obeyed his every command.

Hunt! he cried again.

They sped through the forest, the quarry before them. Drago felt triumph seethe through his veins—he hunted through the entire realm and all ran before him: his parents, Axis and Azhure, cowering golden and scared; his brother Caelum, hiding at their backs; even Goodwife Renkin; and there was WolfStar, cursed WolfStar, his eyes widening in horror as he was cornered by . . . by . . .

Drago woke, shaking and sweating. What *was* it that he hunted with? Their names and the very concept of them lurked just out of reach. He should know, he *should,* but he didn't, and Drago almost cried with the frustration of it.

He shifted more comfortably against the tree and drifted back to sleep, and while his sleep was troubled by dreams, they were dreams of Zenith and his childhood, and no more did he ride to the hunt that night.

The farther south he moved, the more vivid grew the dreams of the hunt. Drago did not fear the dreams; rather, he found them intriguing. What were they telling him . . . that he should hunt down those who hunted him? At that thought Drago would invariably smile, or even laugh. He was not entirely sure the combined forces of Tencendor would cower to the ground in fear if he appeared, waving his sack over his head!

Nevertheless, Drago found he spent the days longing for the nights, longing for the dream where for once *he* was the one to hunt, *he* was the one with the power, *he* was the one who said, "Yes, you shall live, and, yes, you shall die."

And, although Drago often killed in these dreams, he never saw *who* it was he killed.

Sometimes Drago came close to tears as he stumbled along the paths of Minstrelsea. He thought of all he had lost. He had, apparently, been one of the most powerful Enchanters ever birthed—even WolfStar had said so. His name, DragonStar, had reflected that power. And yet his future had been destroyed so early.

But his mother hadn't actually destroyed his power, had she? She'd only reversed his blood order so that his human blood was dominant—except for Isfrael, all SunSoar children carried equal amounts of Icarii and human blood. That meant that somewhere within him still existed the Icarii Enchanter potential.

The day that Drago realized this his footsteps had dragged to a halt and he stood, thinking. Drago had thought he'd accepted his lot in life years ago . . . but now he was not so sure. What if he *could* retrieve his heritage, his potential?

What would it be like to live the life of an Icarii Enchanter?

As the dreams grew stronger, so the beasts that hunted for him grew more substantial in his mind, and so Drago's thoughts about regaining his Icarii power grew ever more dominant.

One night, tired, hungry, and cold, he curled about the sack and wished himself into dream.

He hunted, the horse striding powerfully beneath him. Before him ranged . . . ranged . . . Drago twisted and moaned. They were so close, he could almost see them. They hunted, they obeyed his every wish, and they were . . .

Hawks.

Drago relaxed in his sleep, and smiled. Yes, that was it.

They were not hounds at all, but they were hunting falcons, hawks.

Enchanted hawks.

Whispering. Whispering . . . *revenge*.

Drago woke into a clear-eyed clarity. He knew who these hawks were now. It was so obvious. So right. He should have realized days ago.

They were the children whom WolfStar had cast into the Star Gate. Roaming the interstellar wastes, crying out for revenge.

Looking for someone to direct them.

Was he that someone? Drago lay there and considered the matter. They were so much like him. Condemned to death before they'd had a chance to live. Condemned by WolfStar. And the more that Drago thought about it, the more he wondered if WolfStar had constructed the vision of RiverStar's murder that had condemned him.

WolfStar—they could all hunt WolfStar.

All the children needed was someone to bring them back through the Star Gate.

All they needed was a leader. Someone to direct them on the hunt.

Drago's mouth curled. Back through the Star Gate? He would die the instant he stepped through.

Maybe, but somewhere deep inside him was the blood of DragonStar, and maybe that would protect him.

Maybe once he stepped through the Star Gate, Azhure's curse would shatter and his blood order would be righted. He would regain his heritage!

"And this will surely protect me!" Drago said, his hands opening and closing about the object within the sack.

His eyes were alive with hope. He would get his revenge, and these hawks would be the ones to accomplish it for him.

Drago did not realize that what he guarded so jealously in the sack was manipulating his mind. It desperately wanted to get through the Star Gate, and it wanted Drago to go through as well. To this end it had been veiling Drago from the eyes of the farflight scouts for weeks, and over the past days had been speeding his feet along enchanted paths deep within the forest. Drago was moving faster than any human or Icarii had a right to move.

Drago did not know it, but he was being guided by a power far older and stranger than Icarii magic.

Behind Drago, day after day, trailed the red doe, pulled as much by the object in the sack as she was by worry about what Drago was doing.

She had been instrumental in its creation, and it had witnessed her death.

And, wrapped about its head, were still the remnants of the gown she had been wearing the day when Gorgrael had torn her apart.

So she trailed after Drago, fretting, not knowing what to do, who to tell, if to tell, wondering what he was doing, where he was going.

Pulled by the Rainbow Scepter.

27

Niah Triumphant

StarDrifter had laid Zenith on the bed in the spare chamber in the priestesses' quarters on Temple Mount, and then sat and waited. Zenith slept for two nights and three days. For most of that time she sweated and tossed, attended only by two of the priestesses and StarDrifter himself, but on the third day she calmed and slept soundly.

That evening she woke.

StarDrifter sat forward and took her hand. "Zenith?"

Her eyes fluttered, then opened, and she smiled at him. "You must be StarDrifter."

Something very cold and nauseating coiled about his belly. "Zenith?" he said, more hesitatingly this time.

"If you like," the woman who looked like Zenith said, and sat up in bed.

Automatically StarDrifter's hand reached to help her, but he pulled it back before he touched her.

"Where am I?" she asked.

"In the priestesses' quarters on Temple Mount."

Her entire face lit up. "I'm home! Oh, StarDrifter, I'm home!"

He tried to smile for her, but couldn't. This had been Niah's home, not . . . "You are not Zenith."

She eased by the bed and walked a little unsteadily to the window. "Look! There are the lavender gardens. Oh, StarDrifter, I have *dreamed* of being able to walk through those lavender gardens again!"

She turned back to face the Enchanter, and almost overbalanced as her wings caught against the windowsill. "Oh! I shall have to get used to these."

"You are Niah," StarDrifter said tonelessly. Somewhere a great anger was building, but at whom or what he did not know.

She paused in her inspection of her wings, and sent him a sweet smile. "StarDrifter, I know this must seem strange. Here I am, in what you perceive as your granddaughter's body. But," she walked over and knelt before him, taking his hands in hers, "I have always been here. What Zenith loved was because I had loved it first. Her dreams were but borrowings of mine. Her words and laughter were generated by my soul. Her—"

"I understand!" StarDrifter said, and pulled his hands from hers. He was angry at her, he realized. At Niah, not Zenith. But had Zenith ever existed?

"StarDrifter, do not mourn Zenith," the woman said gently. "She was but a shell waiting to acknowledge me."

StarDrifter's anger threatened to break forth, and he averted his eyes from the woman. "What am I to call you?"

"Call me . . . Niah. My death at Hagen's hands was but an interruption in my life. Niah is *my* name. And," her hands spread over her belly and a smile lit her face, "I am pregnant with WolfStar's child again. I am blessed."

StarDrifter stared at her. "He raped Zenith. How can you—"

"No," Niah said, and now her eyes were hard and determined. "No. Only Zenith perceived that as rape. I did not. WolfStar lay with me with my full consent and encouragement."

"Then *you* raped Zenith as much as WolfStar did!" StarDrifter shouted and stalked over to the door.

"Zenith was dying even then," Niah said. "If she felt pain, it was for her own death."

StarDrifter slammed the door behind him.

He walked to the southern cliffs of the Mount and stared at the wild seas beyond.

Was she right? Had Zenith never existed?

No, he could not believe that. He might not have seen Zenith much in recent years, but he'd known her well as a child and teenager. The Niah woman waiting back in that room had shown expressions and emotions that StarDrifter had never seen cross Zenith's face. No, there had been a Zenith. A different woman to the one who now used her body.

Which meant that, if she hadn't been completely destroyed, Zenith was still alive somewhere.

Trapped. Lost.

StarDrifter felt two emotions coursing through him. One, a desperate need to help Zenith. But the second was far more destructive. StarDrifter needed someone to blame.

WolfStar, certainly, for it was his machinations that had seen Zenith possessed by the spirit of the dead Niah. But in a vague and as yet undefined way, StarDrifter also blamed Azhure. Azhure had bred this trouble—but hadn't Azhure been bred by WolfStar and Niah?

StarDrifter stood at the lip of the cliffs and wondered what he could do.

After a while he realized he was crying.

28

River Crossing

The wind blew cold at Leagh's back, and the last of the Skelder birds had flown overhead two days ago. Now there was nothing but high gray cloud scudding above her, the thin sunlight shimmering on the weapons of the men who surrounded her, and the man who had lied to her by her side night and day.

He'd told her that he, Herme and Theod were making a point.

If Leagh wasn't so heartsick she would have smiled at that. Did Zared call seizing a castle "making a point"? What was he *doing*? Surely this would end in war?

She didn't understand his reasoning, and didn't understand his own sense of betrayal at the new taxes imposed by Caelum. And Leagh certainly didn't understand what Herme and Theod—and some eight thousand of their men—were doing here, either.

But most of all Leagh did not understand how Zared could have lied to her. "Come to Severin and be my wife," he had said, and then pulled her into his bed.

But they weren't traveling to Severin at all, they never had been, and she was not sure when they would happen across a public notary who could legalize her shame.

I feel like an army whore, she thought, keeping her face expressionless and her eyes dead ahead, traveling with a man who throws me apples in return for the use of my body.

Except that her body was worth a trifle more than that of the average army whore, wasn't it? Did he love *her,* or did he love the inheritance implanted in her womb?

For three days they had ridden south-west from the small valley where Zared had led her to view his . . . his army. There was no other word for it. It had been a military march, no comforts, no quarter given. They'd camped at night under the hard stars on equally hard ground, and the only reason she consented to lie wrapped in Zared's blankets was for the added warmth his body gave her.

At least that's what she told herself.

They'd risen each day before dawn, broken their fast on dry bread, warmed gruel and tea, and then mounted and ridden until mid-morning, when Zared had ordered an hour's halt. Then on to mid-afternoon, when they'd halt again, then ride until the stars came out and it was time to make yet another cheerless camp.

At least Leagh had been cheerless, but the men about her had seemed remarkably high-spirited.

What is it about war that makes men smile so? she asked herself each evening about the campfire. What is it about war that causes men to lust so?

She could find no answer.

Now they were approaching the Azle again after its great sweep west, and here they would have to cross into Aldeni. From there, Leagh supposed, they would ride due south and then east until they reached Kastaleon.

It was noon, and Zared decided they could accomplish the fording before dark. And then a day's rest the other side, he said, for this crossing would tax men and beasts.

At this point the Azle was still wide, but its waters had

deepened and were muddy and turbulent. Leagh sat her mare to one side as Zared had waved the majority of his men across—and with Herme's and Theod's men that must have amounted to at least fourteen thousand.

They struggled across slowly. Occasionally a horse and its rider would slip and be cast into the muddy waters. Both would disappear, then reappear twenty or thirty paces downstream, battling the current, battling for their lives.

All of those who fell managed to achieve the other bank—eventually.

All this Leagh sat and watched impassively, hunching further inside her cloak as the northerly wind grew sharper, wondering if even the Azle conspired against Askam.

Zared broke her reverie eventually, riding up to her and pushing the hood back from her face so he could see her eyes.

"Leagh? We will wait the night this side of the river. It is too late now to try and cross, and the river will be quieter in the morning."

She tightened her hands about the reins, and booted her mare viciously in the flanks. "No!" she cried as the mare bolted for the river. "I will go now!"

Even as the horse plunged into the icy water Leagh was wondering why she'd done such a stupid thing. It was her way, she supposed, of hurting him when he'd hurt her so badly.

"Leagh!" she heard him scream, and then she had no thought for anything else but the swirling, hungry river.

The horse sank to her belly almost immediately, half swimming, half plunging. Leagh was soaked to her waist as waves smashed against them. Gods! Why so strong this time of the year?

The mare struggled and snorted, plunging gamely forward, her neck outstretched, her eyes rolling, seeking the far bank.

They had fought perhaps halfway across when the riverbed fell away beneath them and both horse and rider were instantly submerged. Leagh felt herself being swept away from the mare and, her eyes tightly shut underwater, she struck out with a hand, grabbing a handful of mane.

The next instant both surfaced, spluttering, instinctively striking out. Leagh kept a firm grip on the horse, knowing that if she were swept away from the mare's strength she wouldn't be able to survive for long.

Was that Zared shouting? Or her imagination? Leagh could vaguely see men lining the far bank, but her eyes were blurred with the water and the cold and her own fear, and she did not know if they could help her.

She became aware that her grip on the horse's mane was slipping, and so she tried to wrap her fingers more securely, but they were cold, so cold, and they only fumbled ineffectively. Dimly Leagh was aware that she was sliding down the mare's body. She grabbed at the reins, and missed. She grabbed at the stirrup leather as it floated past her face, and missed. Her hands slid along the mare's rump until they finally tangled in the horse's tail, and she hung on with all her might.

Leagh might have made the far bank safely at that point, save that the mare, in her panic, kicked out, and one of her hind hooves struck Leagh in the rib cage.

Shocked by the blow, and then the flaring pain which made it impossible for her to breathe, Leagh let go, and was swept away by the waters.

Over and over she tumbled, the cold now as devastating and cruel as the waters, and Leagh—somewhere in a part of her mind that was still functioning—knew she was dying.

In her own way, she was happy. Better she die here than betray her brother and Caelum.

But then something grasped her hair, and then her waist. She tried to cry out, for whoever had her was paining her bruised ribs, but she choked instead, and that was so loathsome that she began to struggle . . . struggle against the man who held her and against the water that was trying to kill her.

Suddenly her head was out of the water and she heaved in a huge breath, then gagged as she coughed up gouts of muddy water. The man who had her now had found his feet, and was dragging her through waist-deep water, cursing with each step that she only hung limply on his arm, and then other hands had her, stretched her out on grass, and then rolled her onto her stomach and were pounding her back in an effort to make her cough up as much water as possible.

"Leagh?"

It was Zared's voice, and Leagh rolled over weakly. He was on his knees beside her, as soaked as she, and the wetness running down his cheeks was not all due to the Azle.

"Do you want to die that badly?" he asked, his voice hoarse, and she shook her head slightly.

"No," she whispered, and realized that she meant it.

That night the army camped a half-hour's ride south of the river, next to four or five small hills. Nestling among these hills was a shepherd's summer hut, deserted now, and there Zared carried Leagh to spend the night.

He dismissed those concerned men who hovered about, laying Leagh on a rough bed by one wall. Then he built a fire in the hearth, and set some food and wine to warm.

And then he came over to her, not talking, and stripped both her and himself of their wet clothes.

She protested, for the air was chill, but Zared took no notice, and once they were both naked he led her to the fire and rubbed them down with a blanket one of the men had left.

"Gods," he muttered as his fingers traced the bruise left by the mare's hoof, but found the ribs themselves relatively undamaged. To her shame, he then conducted a careful examination of her body, looking for other hurts, until he was satisfied that the bruise on her ribs was the extent of it.

He turned her around to face him, and cupped her face in his hands.

"Leagh, were you trying to hurt me by doing that? If so, then you succeeded. I thought you were dead."

She tried to drop her eyes, but Zared lifted her head so he could meet them. "Leagh, *were* you trying to hurt—"

"You *lied* to me!" she spat. "You have hurt me ten times more than I you!"

He winced. "I simply did not tell you my plans to—"

"You *said* we would ride to Severin and marry! Instead you drag me about with your army like a harlot!"

"I intend to marry you, Leagh! I—"

"And what is it makes you sure I still consent to marry you?" she said softly, and wrenched out of his hands.

To her anger, he roared with laughter. "Leagh! *Look* at us! Here we stand companionably naked, and after a week of sharing a bed and a passion. Do you think you have any choice?"

"If I say my shame was the product of rape," she said, pronouncing every word clearly, "then I would have every choice. My honor would be restored, yours tarnished. I would still have my choice of husband—"

"Even with your belly swelling with my child?"

"*If* it swells. And after the shock of that river crossing I have no doubt that I will lose any child conceived to this point. Any child conceived *after* this point can still be—"

"No! Leagh, I cannot believe you say this! Damn it, we love each other! How can you stand there and talk so calmly of ridding yourself of our child?"

"Because I doubt that you do indeed love me, Zared. Now I wonder if it is my lands you lust after more."

"How dare you say that to me?" he roared, and then cursed himself as he saw her flinch. He reached out for her, hugging her stiff body to his. "Leagh, I am sorry . . . but I could not believe you said that. Listen to me, as soon as I can find a notary we will marry."

She did not reply, and Zared rubbed his hands over her body, trying to arouse her. "Leagh, I *know* you enjoy my touch . . . why deny that?"

Again she did not answer.

"Leagh . . ." he murmured, kissing her hair, her cheek, her neck. "Be my wife. Do not punish me for the actions I have been forced to take to wive you. Did I not say that I would fight for you? Well, if I march at the head of an army now it is only for love of you. It was the only way I knew I could have you."

Leagh began to weaken, confused. Was that right? Was this all just for her? To convince Caelum to approve their marriage?

Or was there something else?

She murmured, trying to pull away from him, but again, as on their first night, he was too strong, and he pulled her down to the floor before the fire.

As he made love to her, Leagh thought she would choose to believe him. He had been rash and foolhardy, but he did love her, didn't he? And perhaps over the next few days she could gently persuade him to forget his crazed idea of taking Kastaleon and march back north. They could quietly marry in Severin, and there they would weather Caelum's certain anger.

Yes, she would persuade him to return to Severin. Once they were there, both Caelum and Askam would accept the inevitable.

29

The Ancient Barrows

Drago moved faster now that he knew where he needed to go. Sometimes he took food from an Avar camp. Not much, just whatever he needed to feed himself for a day or two. No-one ever spotted him—he moved like a night-shadow itself—and if it hadn't been for the doe following him, Drago believed he would have passed through Minstrelsea completely unnoticed.

The doe, Faraday, still worried him. He rarely saw her, but occasionally he heard a faint footfall behind him, or the rustle of a shrub as she passed. Two or three times he tried to shoo her away, and when he did that she disappeared for a while, but the next day he would again become aware of her presence.

He was still worried about Zenith, partly because the doe remained behind him. Was Zenith well . . . or consumed? He'd hated to leave her like that, but he hadn't the skills to help her, and just maybe StarDrifter or the priestesses on the island did.

Drago hoped StarDrifter would indeed be there to catch Zenith.

But if thoughts of the doe and Zenith ate at him, his dreams comforted him. Night after night he rode to the hunt, riding his great horse, the hawks to the side and ahead of him, and they sometimes slithered along the ground, sometimes flew through the air, but they always found their quarry. Drago grew to anticipate the final confrontation with his always nameless and faceless quarry. It would cower on the ground before him, and he would raise his sword, and plunge it down, and always at that point he would wake with an almost orgasmic ecstasy consuming him. He would lie awake for perhaps an hour, reliving every part of the hunt, remembering the thrill as the sword pierced the heart of his quarry, the ecstasy of its death.

And so he moved south.

It should have taken him many weeks, maybe even months, to reach his destination, but Drago found himself spotting landmarks that astounded him with the speed of their appearance. The Minaret Peaks (those he skirted as best he could, avoiding the tens of thousands of Icarii that thronged there), then the trading city of Arcen, just beyond the forest's western border.

Drago had no idea why he was moving so fast—or why the Avar or Isfrael hadn't confronted him yet.

Perhaps Caelum had decided to let him go. Drago's mouth quirked at that particular thought. "Caelum would be more likely to make love to Gorgrael's corpse," he muttered, grinning, "than let *me* pass unhindered."

Maybe his power wasn't trapped so deep, after all. Or perhaps his powers were resurfacing the farther he moved from his family?

Drago shrugged. It didn't matter, he was free, he had a purpose, and here on these green trails no-one spat at him.

Always the Scepter rode under his arm, safe in its sack.

And so, finally, some three weeks after he had fled Sigholt, Drago approached the Ancient Barrows. Here was where the ancient Enchanter-Talons had been buried so they could make their eventual way down to the Star Gate which existed beneath the tombs. Each barrow was an entranceway into the Star Gate itself, but Drago knew there were other passages secreted about these parts, passages more accessible than trying to dig down into one of the huge Barrows.

But where? And how well were they guarded?

Although Drago knew of the Star Gate, and had heard it described countless times, he had never seen it himself. Only Icarii Enchanters were allowed near its lip to reap the rewards of gazing into its depths. Drago had been kept well away.

But if Drago had not actually seen the Star Gate, nor knew the exact location of its entrances, then he'd heard rumors, and he'd heard Caelum and other Enchanters talking from time to time. And Zenith had occasionally chatted to him about the times she'd been down.

No, he could find it, but not tonight. Drago glanced at the faint stars twinkling through the forest canopy. Fifty paces before him the forest ended, for Faraday had planted around the Ancient Barrows to leave them easily accessible, but Drago ignored the call of the open spaces and crawled deeper back into the forest.

The lure of the dream beckoned.

The lure of the hunt.

* * *

Unknown to Drago, the doe curled up beside him as he slept, as she had curled up every night for the past week. She shared some of the dream, and shook, for she had good reason to fear the hunt.

But at least this time she was not the quarry.

She garnered from the man's dreams some of the memories that embittered him, and she sorrowed. This man was Axis and Azhure's child, and she loved both of them. Azhure as a beloved sister, Axis as . . . well, as a former lover. No longer did she harbor a passion for him, but he was a dear man to her and he and his concerned her.

Even if she rarely saw Axis or Azhure any more.

She knew why. They, like her, now traveled their own magical existence, and they rarely came back to the forest to see her. Azhure had once often come, but it had now been many seasons since Faraday had seen her. True, sometimes all the Star Gods came to dance in Niah's Grove, but Faraday did not approach on those occasions.

This man was their son. Faraday remembered that Azhure had been pregnant with Drago and RiverStar when Faraday had first met her. Even then Faraday had an inkling of the trouble these two babes would cause, and she'd later heard of Drago's crime against his brother.

And here he was, running through the forest, blind to its beauties, and with the Rainbow Scepter clasped beneath his arm.

That troubled Faraday. Axis had used the Rainbow Scepter to kill Gorgrael—

but not to save her

—and had then secreted it within Sigholt, intending to study it at more leisure one day. Faraday nuzzled the sack, dreaming and remembering. The five Sentinels, Jack and Zeherah, the seductive Yr, and the irrepressible brothers Ogden and Veremund, had stolen the virulent, strangely corrupting power from the hidden Repositories beneath the waters of the Sacred Lakes to create this Scepter. They had also given their lives. Faraday recalled that when Axis had wielded the Scepter, she'd heard echoes of the Sentinels' laughter in its flaring light—were their spirits still embedded in the Scepter?

The thought gave Faraday some comfort, but then she tensed as the man moved.

She relaxed slowly—he was only moving deeper into his dream. Running through the forest, hunting, setting . . . his hawks? What were they? Setting his hawks to the quarry.

What was Drago doing with the Scepter? Why had he taken it?

Should she do something? Tell someone?

But Faraday let the thought slip away. She so rarely spoke to anyone now. Even the once-constant shadow of the White Stag had faded; at the moment he ran the very upper reaches of the forests in the Avarinheim.

And as for Isfrael . . . the precious hours she'd spent with her child each year in Niah's Grove had been too few, and Isfrael had bonded to the Avar rather than her. Now she believed he barely even thought of her let alone sought her out.

Faraday's thoughts these days were generally vague. Deer-like. She thought about the trails and she thought about the choicest spots to nibble sweet grass and plump berries, but that was largely it. Until Drago had dragged Zenith into Niah's Grove, for months Faraday's thoughts hadn't been directed to anything more than the next grazing spot.

She thought briefly of contacting Axis or Azhure about the Rainbow Scepter, then let the thought drift away. She snuggled a little closer to the man, appreciating his warmth, and watched as he dreamed.

As he raised his sword to deal the death blow to his quarry, she rose and melted into the shadows.

Drago started out of his dream, breathing heavily, and clutching the Scepter to himself. He smiled slowly, remembering the satisfaction of his sword driving home to smash bone and cleave heart.

He could almost empathize with his father for spending so long at war. Was this how Axis had felt when he'd driven the Rainbow Scepter into Gorgrael's heart?

He lay for a while, then decided he may as well get up and make an early start. He finished the last of the malfari bread he had taken from an Avar encampment two nights previously, then stood up, brushing leaves from his cloak.

For a moment he stood there in the dim light, one hand scratching at his cheeks and chin. He had not washed or changed in weeks, and his face was thick with a new growth of beard.

But would any of that matter beyond the Star Gate?

No. Nothing would matter beyond the Star Gate save that he find the means to regain his heritage.

When I have refound my enchantments, he thought, I shall create for myself an image to suit my potential.

He grinned, and laughed at his vanity, and then he set off to look for a way down to the Star Gate.

In the end the entranceway to one of the tombs was not too difficult to find. There was a small encampment of Icarii within the Ancient Barrows, and Drago simply waited until he spotted two of them wing their way to a spot about two hundred paces to the south of the Barrows themselves.

Drago took his time approaching the spot where they'd landed. Not only did he have to travel on foot, but he had to keep to the edges of the forest as much as he could. Even that proved impossible as the Minstrelsea only extended some hundred and fifty paces south of the Barrows, and he had to cover the last fifty paces virtually crawling on his belly through the thick, knee-high grasses of the Tarantaise plains.

Every three or four paces he glanced at the sky, anxiously scanning for Icarii above.

But again luck was with Drago, and he managed to approach the entranceway to the passage without detection. There was a small mound of dirt, perhaps half as high again as a man, and below that was a black hole. From his hiding spot some fifteen paces from the entrance Drago could see a smooth-floored passageway extending down, torches flickering in its depths.

He wriggled deeper into the grasses and pulled some more over him. Would the Icarii come back out? Or had they gone down to keep guard over the Gate? Drago remembered Caelum sending SpikeFeather to stand watch with Orr, but he may have since placed another guard at the Gate.

Well, he thought, I shall cope with whatever and whoever is there as best I can. I shall—

His thoughts were cut off by a movement in the darkness of the passageway, and an instant later two Icarii stepped out. Drago breathed in relief; they were the two he'd seen go down earlier. Well, whatever they had gone down for, they were obviously not a change of guard.

They flew off, Drago hiding his face in the dirt and praying they did not spot him. There was a rush of wings, a movement of air high above him, and then there was nothing but the peaceful noise of the wind in the grasses.

Drago kept his head down until he had slowly counted to five hundred, then he cautiously looked about.

Nothing.

Gathering all his courage, and feeling for the first time a knot of fear in his belly, Drago grabbed his sack and ran for the entranceway.

Far behind him, the red doe stepped cautiously out from the shadow of the forest and trotted after him.

30

The Rainbow Scepter

The tunnel was cool and moist, and Drago pulled his cloak tighter about him. He was still nervous, but now that nervousness was tinged with excitement and a growing sense that he must step through the Star Gate soon, soon, soon . . .

He set off at a trot. The downhill slope was smooth, but Drago thought he would wind about in the bowels of the soil forever. His legs grew weak, and his breath short, and eventually Drago was forced to rest for some minutes before continuing at a slower pace.

He walked for what he thought was an eternity. Torches spluttered at infrequent intervals along the walls, and Drago wondered why there were not more of them. Surely the entrance into one of the greatest mysteries of Tencendor deserved a flood of glorious light?

He muttered as he stubbed his toe on an exposed rock, and stopped and rubbed it for a moment. Was this the entranceway to the Star Gate, or was it a trap for him? Had Caelum somehow guessed his destination? Had WolfStar spied out his whereabouts? Were there guards waiting around the next curve? Was *death* waiting around the next curve?

Drago felt his breath grow shorter still, and realized it was due to anxiety rather than effort. He stood a few minutes and deliberately calmed himself. No-one could know where he was. They would have seized him long before this. Neither Caelum nor WolfStar would have left him to wander if they'd known where to find him. No, no-one knew—

A footfall sounded in the tunnel below him and Drago

leaped into the shadow of one of the walls, his heart hammering. He stared frantically about, then slithered farther down the wall until he reached what shelter one of the wall's support beams gave him.

Perhaps if he stood very still, and made no sound . . . but this passageway had nowhere to hide, and even the fitful light of the torches would be enough to reveal him to any but the totally blind.

The tunnel had been carved out of soil and rock, and at the foot of the walls were small piles of rubble that had been left over from its construction. Drago bent down and selected a good-sized rock, feeling sick at the thought of having to use it.

The single footfall now resolved itself into a steady tramping. Just one, Drago thought. Just one. I can handle one if I have to. But his hand was slick with sweat, and he almost dropped the rock.

Whoever approached suddenly began to whistle, startling Drago so much he finally did drop the rock. It was a merry tune—Drago recognized it as a popular ballad often sung at Sigholt.

An Icarii, then?

His question was answered immediately as an Enchanter stepped around the lower curve of the tunnel. Drago knew her by sight and reputation, PaleStar SnapWing.

Stars! he thought, panicking, what am I going to do? She'll see me any moment! His mind came up with several frenzied excuses to explain his presence—he was on an errand for Caelum, he was looking for Zenith, he'd got lost on an afternoon stroll about Sigholt—but they were so ridiculous that even in his current predicament he had to fight the urge to laugh.

PaleStar would well know of his trial and subsequent escape.

She was almost level with him now, and Drago wondered if he could possibly wrestle her to the ground before she had a chance to use her Enchanter powers, or if she'd pin his back against the tunnel wall like a—

She walked straight past, still whistling, and continued up the tunnel.

Drago could not believe it. He stared after her, completely stunned. How could she have *failed* to see him? A half-blind old man would have spotted him easily enough, let alone an Icarii Enchanter with magically enhanced vision.

Stars, but he'd been only an arm's length from her!

Slowly he lowered his gaze to the sack under one arm, finally wondering if the Scepter had been aiding him all along.

Drago stared at it for a long time, then he eventually resumed his walk down to the Star Gate, no longer attempting to muffle his footsteps.

Farther up the tunnel the red doe also slunk against the wall as she heard PaleStar approach. She, too, watched in disbelief as the Enchanter walked straight by her.

Once Palestar SnapWing left him, Orr stood before the Star Gate and stared. He had taken the watch upon the Gate entirely upon himself. There was something very, very wrong. Something *beyond* WolfStar's story of the murdered, whispering children, but Orr did not know what it was. Unlike any Icarii or even human guard, Orr did not need rest or sustenance. So here he stood, as he had for weeks now, wrapped in his ruby cloak, staring into the depths of the Star Gate, listening to the poor, dead children whispering for vengeance.

WolfStar? WolfStar? We're coming . . . we're coming to hunt you . . .

And yet, something else, beyond that, and Orr wished desperately that he understood what it was.

There was a movement, and then a scuffle of feet, and Orr whirled about. A disheveled man had stepped into the chamber from beneath one of the archways. His eyes were wide, staring about the chamber.

"Where is it?" the man asked.

"Begone!" Orr said. "You have no right to be here!"

"Is this not the Star Gate chamber?"

"You have no right—"

The man ignored him, sidling around Orr and striding to the very center of the chamber.

Then he halted, transfixed by what he at first thought was a small pool in the center of the chamber.

Not a pool at all, but the universe. Beyond the rim of this circular wall wheeled galaxies and solar systems. Comets and asteroids chased each other through clouds of gas and vivid interstellar wastes. Colors, every imaginable color, swirled and shaded one into the next. It was frighteningly beautiful . . . and absolutely irresistible. The sack grew heavy and warm in his hands.

Outraged at this invasion, Orr reached out—

—and Drago spun around. "Don't stop me now!" he snapped.

"What are you doing?" Orr grabbed at Drago's arm, missed, and seized the sack instead.

He let go immediately and stepped back, appalled, his eyes round and staring at the sack. *"What are you doing with the Rainbow Scepter?"*

In desperation, thinking the Ferryman was going to lunge at him again, Drago drew the Scepter out of the sack and waved it at Orr. "Stay back!"

He was torn between watching Orr, and looking back into the Star Gate. He felt that it called to him . . . *Come to me! Come! Dance with me! Be my lover!* . . . and he was overwhelmed by an all-consuming need to step through.

Drago looked back at the Gate.

The instant he did so, Orr darted forward and grabbed the Scepter.

Something happened once Orr felt his hands touch the smooth wood of the rod.

Visions flooded his head.

A labyrinth. Darkness. He was trapped. No way out.

Hunting, hunters, questors.

Questors through the universe, hunting . . . hunting . . .

And something in the Maze. Something that watched for him. Something malevolent. Something that *writhed and twisted through the Maze, coming for him!*

Orr screamed and sank to his knees, although his hands remained tight about the rod of the Scepter. Drago tried desperately to pull it from his grasp, but the Ferryman's hands were unnaturally locked about the Scepter.

Qeteb.

The word, or name, Orr did not know or care which, filled his mind. It so intensified his terror that he flung back his head and screamed, *Qeteb!*

But Orr screamed with his power only, not his voice, and Drago did not hear him.

Although someone else did. Far above, Orr's apprentice, SpikeFeather, paused in his stroll about the roof of Sigholt and whispered, "Qeteb!"

Grail! the Scepter screamed at Orr, and this Orr also screamed in his mind.

Grail King!

And SpikeFeather repeated the words.

The red doe, crouched behind one of the pillars of the chamber, shuddered as a presence seeped through her.

And yet something *more* reached out to her, reached out via the Scepter although it emanated from somewhere else. Reached out and touched her. Spoke softly to her.

She shuddered again, and felt power seep through her.

Drago and Orr rocked back and forth, each struggling for control of the Scepter, back and forth, and both the Scepter and Orr continued to scream.

Beware the Grail King in the Maze!

"The Maze! The Maze!" Orr whispered. He let go the Scepter in horror.

Attend the Maze!

Drago heard nothing. No words whispered through his mind. All Drago knew was that Orr had finally released his grip on the Scepter. He spun it about and the cloth that had protected the head, which had been loosened in the struggle, flew off, and rainbow light flooded the chamber.

It pulsed about, searching, humming with intense power and, as it hit an archway on the far side of the chamber, it enveloped the small red doe.

The doe started, round-eyed but not scared, and fell to the ground. Her legs kicked, her entire body convulsed, and then she exploded. Blood, tissue, and bone fragments erupted about the chamber, but neither of the two combatants noticed, because Drago, in trying to correct his balance and stop Orr from seizing the Scepter again, unintentionally brought the Scepter down on Orr's head with a sharp crack.

The Ferryman fell to the floor, his wounded head smacking against the marble so hard it cracked open yet further, smearing blood and brain tissue across the floor.

Atop Sigholt, SpikeFeather started, and wondered what had happened that his contact with Orr was so abruptly broken.

Drago managed to regain his balance without falling into the Star Gate. Terrified by the pulsing light washing about the chamber, not knowing what he had unleashed, he slipped the sack back over the Scepter.

The light died instantly, and Drago took a deep breath. He stared, appalled, at Orr's body. As he watched, it suddenly glowed and then, stunningly, vanished, leaving only the ruby cloak puddled on the floor as any indication that Orr had ever existed.

Drago swallowed, then looked across the chamber.

There was blood everywhere. Fragments of fur, and bone.

And, in the middle of all this gore, lay a naked woman. She lay sprawled on her belly, her raised head toward Drago, and her green eyes were wide, and full of some emotion that Drago could not discern.

She stretched out a hand, then let it drop. "You are Axis' son," she said, and pushed herself into a sitting position. "He couldn't save me. He couldn't—or wouldn't. And yet you . . . look what *you* have done."

Then her eyes dropped. "And look at all this blood," she whispered. "Look, everywhere . . . that is *my* blood."

"I didn't mean to hurt you!" Drago said, thinking she was blaming him.

He grabbed Orr's cloak and threw it about the woman's shoulders. "There . . . you'll be warm now. Please, tell no-one I was here—"

Even as he said it, Drago knew she would tell. She had to. She was Faraday, and she was tied to his parents with bonds of love and suffering. She would tell.

"—please," he finished lamely.

Faraday raised her eyes and stared at him, and then said something that made no sense.

"I have to take WolfStar's place," she said. "And you must come with me."

"No! I cannot! I must—"

"You *must* come with me," she said more firmly, and clasped the cloak about her with one hand as if she were about to rise.

"No!" Drago shouted. "I am going through the Star Gate. I *must*! I—"

"Then if you do that," Faraday said, apparently unperturbed, "you must come with me when you get back."

"If I come back," Drago said, each word harsh with emotion, "it will only be to reclaim my heritage and to take my rightful place in Tencendor."

"Of course," she said, and smiled with extraordinary loveliness. "I would not have it any other way."

Drago opened his mouth to shout, but could find no response to her ambiguities.

Damn her! Why did she speak in such riddles?

He reached out a trembling hand, then snatched it back.

Then, before he forgot himself completely, Drago tucked

the sack firmly under his arm, averted his eyes from the strange expectation and—*curse* her!—confidence in Faraday's face, and ran toward the Star Gate.

He stepped onto the wall with one foot, then cast himself into the universe.

31

New Existences

There was pain, terrible pain, and a sensation as if every last breath and drop of blood were being squeezed out of him. He felt his chest explode. Then . . . then there was a nothingness for what seemed like a very long time.

Finally Drago—if he was still anything that resembled Drago—became aware that he was hanging suspended in a cold, dark space. No light, no warmth, no laughter. A vacuum of nothingness about him. Then he felt and saw stars, before he caught just the faintest snatches of what he thought must be the Star Dance.

Drago assumed this was the Star Dance, because none but Enchanters ever heard the Star Dance.

But whatever it was, the snatches Drago heard were so beautiful, so haunting, so powerful, that he felt cold tears slide down his cheeks.

How strange that he could cry when he was dead. Drago knew he was dead. He must be. The pain had been so terrible, and even now there were trails of it still running through his body.

Now, no doubt, he was on his journey to the AfterLife. At that thought Drago was overwhelmed with sadness. He did not want to die. His life had indeed been a waste.

For an unknowable time Drago wept in sorrow at such waste, and then, when his grief ended, he cast his eyes (or his awareness, Drago was not truly sure if he could still "see") about him. He drifted among stars, powerless. He recognized none of them. Even though Drago had paid attention to his childhood lessons on the patterns of the heavens, none of the patterns presented to him now made any sense.

But, of course, now he was drifting among them, not viewing them from the safety of the ground, and that made his perspective different.

It made everything different.

Drago wept anew. He clutched the sack to him, cuddling it, trying to let it comfort him, and suddenly realized that the Rainbow Scepter had gone. Destroyed, probably, in his leap through the Star Gate. Or lost to drift about the heavens, waiting for some other hand to pick it up.

What a waste his life was.

But just as Drago thought this, the stars reformed, whirling through the sky, twisted and rewoven by some powerful hand or force that Drago could not understand. He was caught up in a maelstrom, whirled about until the pain returned.

Who are you? Who are you?

Whispers, all around him. He had been consumed by a black cloud. It choked him, prodded him, invaded his mind, demanded that he answer.

Who are you? From where have you come?

"Drago," he whispered. "And I have come from Tencendor—"

Tencendor!

Triumph erupted about him, and in that instant Drago realized that he had succeeded. He had found those who would help him, and all his sadness dissipated in a heartbeat.

"I am alive!" he screamed through the universe, and that cry was taken up two hundred times about him.

Alive!

And then a voice, a different voice. Calm, gentle, benevolent. "Would you like to join the quest?"

"Yes, yes, yes," Drago cried. *"Yes!"*

* * *

Faraday sat on the floor of the Star Chamber, staring at the spot where Drago had thrown himself into the Gate, until she realized she was shivering with cold. She struggled to her feet, wrapping the Ferryman's cloak tight about her, and remembered the vision that had consumed her when she'd been struck by the light of the Rainbow Scepter.

She stood in a strange room, so strange Faraday felt disorientated and unsure. The walls, ceiling, benches and even parts of the floor were covered with metal plates, and these plates were studded with knobs and bright, jewel-like lights. Before her were the high backs of several chairs, facing enormous windows that . . . that looked out upon the universe.

One of the chairs before her swiveled, revealing a man in its depths. He was silver-haired, and his face was lined with care, but there was such youthful humor in his brown eyes that Faraday did not fear him. He wore a uniform made of a leathery black material, gold braid hung at his shoulders and encircled the cuffs of his sleeves, and Faraday saw a black peaked cap, also with gold braid about its brim, sitting on the bench behind him.

He stood, and held out both hands.

Without hesitation Faraday walked forward and took them.

"You are Faraday," the man said, his voice warm and lively, "and I have watched you for many years."

"Who are you?"

"Like you, I am a survivor," he said, and smiled. "But you may call me Noah. My friends . . ." his voice faltered, and his eyes glanced about the room, ". . . my friends once called me that, thinking to make me laugh. But it is an appropriate enough name, and I have made it my own."

"Where are we?"

He sighed, and released her hands. "I no longer know quite what to call this old girl," he said, and patted a wall almost affectionately. "She is a little different to what I once knew. This is . . . this is one of the Repositories."

"Ah! I know! The Repositories lie in the depths of the Sacred Lakes." And then Faraday frowned. "But the power of the Repositories was what killed the Sentinels. They came down here, and were so corrupted their skin blistered, and their hair fell out, and—"

"They visited the heart of the Repositories," Noah said hastily, "where lies the corrupting power you mention. The Repositories are larger than you can imagine . . . and mostly not dangerous."

Mostly, Faraday thought a little cynically. "Why am I here?"

"Because I want to ask something of you."

She did not speak, merely raised an eyebrow.

"I know that others have asked much of you, Faraday, and that you have endured pain and loss for your troubles on their behalf. Faraday, I dare to ask you again to commit yourself to Tencendor, and for your troubles I can promise you one of two outcomes. Either complete and lasting happiness and peace, or . . ."

"Or?"

"Or annihilation."

Faraday startled him by pealing with laughter. "Then I win both ways, do I not?"

Noah smiled gently. "I guess that you do, Faraday. I guess that you do."

"What must I do, Noah? Tell me and I will consider your request."

"Four things."

"Four? You ask a great deal, sir."

"You will not find them onerous, my dear."

"Then speak them, and I will make up my mind."

"First, be Drago's friend."

Faraday's eyes went wide with surprise. "Drago? But he . . ."

"He is not what most believe, Faraday." And then Noah leaned forward and whispered in her ear.

"Him?" Faraday stuttered. "I find that difficult to believe—"

"No, you do not." Noah laid a warm hand over her heart. "In here, you *do* believe it."

Faraday stared at him, then nodded. "I will be Drago's friend. That will not be an onerous task. What else?"

"Second, I want you to be Drago's trust."

"What do you mean?"

"My meaning will become clearer in time. Meanwhile, I ask only that you trust in *me* when I say that."

Faraday thought about it, then again nodded her head. "Very well, I will be his trust. What is third?"

"Thirdly, I wish that you bring Drago to me. As soon as you can, although that may not be for many long months yet."

"How do I reach you?"

"Go to the Silent Woman Keep. And trust."

Faraday grinned, but agreed. "And fourth?"

"Fourth, I want you to find that which is lost."

"I do not know what you—"

"Faraday," Noah said gently, "as we speak you are being transformed. It is the power of the Rainbow Scepter that transforms you, and the Scepter uses as its power the combined intelligence of the Repositories. No, let me finish. The transformation will enrich you. It will give you the power to find that which is lost."

"And what must I find?"

Noah shrugged. "Many things. Use the power as you see fit. But eventually, once Drago comes back, I will need you to find something that I mislaid. Something that Drago will need—my Katie's Enchanted Song Book."

"Katie?"

Immense sadness came over Noah's face. "She was once

my daughter, but that was long ago, and she and hers have turned to dust. Do this for me, please."

Faraday regarded him carefully. "You do not ask difficult things of me, Noah. I accept."

He leaned forward and briefly hugged her. "Faraday, I thank you! Once I meant to ask WolfStar these things, but he has misunderstood so many things and now I no longer trust him. I will hand Drago over to you instead. Oh Faraday, I do thank you!"

And she knew no more of Noah or of the strange room in the Repository.

So here she stood in the Star Gate chamber, committed again to someone else's quest, but this one Faraday could accept. At the end of it lay peace, whether the peace of happiness or the peace of death. Those were terms she could live with.

But she could do nothing for either Noah or Drago at the moment. Drago had gone through the Star Gate, and until he came back, her life was her own.

Faraday stilled at that thought. What was she to do with herself?

She did not particularly want to go back to the forests. She had not enjoyed treading the paths of Minstrelsea as a doe. The Mother had promised her peace in that form and, true, for a while she had found it. But she had also been trapped. She could not reach out to the ones she loved.

She had wanted to let Axis touch her, but the White Stag had not allowed it.

She would have liked to have held her child Isfrael in her arms, croon lullabies to him, but instead had been forced to watch him grow from behind the doe's eyes. Now he hardly ever thought of her. No-one ever thought of her. She had simply become a dream legend.

No-one thought of her any more.

She had done her dreadful duty for the Prophecy and for

Tencendor, and had been condemned to wander in doe form through legend. For an instant the memory of Gorgrael filled her mind. The feel of him tearing her belly out, then her throat, and all the while Axis locked in his duty as StarMan and doing nothing, nothing, nothing.

But now she had been released from that legend, hadn't she? She had a second chance, and time for herself—at least until Drago returned.

For what?

"To find that which is lost," Faraday murmured. "As I see fit. An easy task. Otherwise my life is now my own. To do what *I* want!"

"For what *I* want!" she repeated, and slowly straightened. That was a novel thought. Her life had been handed back to her, for *her* to direct as she willed.

She looked about the Star Gate chamber one last time. The blue light pulsed about the domed roof, and the sound of the star wind assaulted her ears, but she'd had enough of star mysteries. Now was her time. Finally.

She turned her back on the Star Gate, wrapped the cloak more securely about her nakedness, and walked slowly into the passageway.

She emerged into the dark, cold hours of the morning, and Faraday hugged the cloak gratefully to her. She let the cold air wash about her face, and suddenly she laughed and spun about.

"I am alive!" she cried, not caring who heard her. "I am *alive*!"

She could not remember ever feeling happier.

She stood and looked at the line of Minstrelsea to the north, considering. The forest had held her and nurtured her, and she could feel its welcoming pull. But it no longer felt like home.

She squinted into the dark and realized there was a figure standing there.

Goodwife Renkin.

Faraday shifted her weight from foot to foot. Did the

Mother wish to speak to her? But then she saw the Goodwife raise her hand and wave her good-bye. There was a lovely smile on her face, but she was too far away for Faraday to discern any other expression.

Good-bye, my Daughter. May the luck of the world finally spin your way.

"Good-bye, Mother," Faraday whispered, her eyes brimming with tears. "Good-bye."

Then she turned her back on the forest and walked south.

She walked until dawn, remembering only the warmth of the Mother's smile, and the blessing of her good-bye, then she stopped as the sun dawned, and she tried to think about where she should go.

Where did she want to go? Who did she want to see?

Zenith. She wanted to know how Zenith was. And StarDrifter. Drago's words that StarDrifter had said he'd always be there to catch Zenith had touched Faraday deeply, and she thought she would be glad to see StarDrifter again, too.

"South," she said, and laughed yet again. "South to the Island of Mist and Memory!"

She turned and strode across the Tarantaise plains, nothing but freedom before her.

32

The Questors

There was pain again, and darkness, and a time when Drago fell into an unknowing. And then he came to the realization that he was . . . asleep.

Warm and comfortable, and asleep. He rose slowly toward wakefulness, and as he emerged from his sleep the feeling of warmth and comfort increased until he thought he would cry with the joy that it gave him.

He lay, cocooned in warmth on a soft, fragrant couch. His eyes were still closed, yet he felt others about him. One of them approached—he heard soft footsteps—and Drago felt a smooth, warm hand stroke the hair back from his forehead. He smiled, still not opening his eyes, and heard a voice.

"He said his name was Drago." Rich, melodious, and full of power.

"He was drifting." Another voice, as powerful as the first, but with more of a lilt to it.

"He is a mortal," said yet another again, "and yet he has such a feel of enchantment about him."

"He stepped through the Star Gate—"

"And survived—"

"Why?"

"How?"

"Speak to us, mortal being. We know that you are awake."

"Share with us your secrets."

Drago opened his eyes, and they widened in wonderment as he beheld those before him.

There were five beings, human-like in shape, but with very pale skin and jewel-like eyes—all of different hues. They stood ranged before his couch in a semi-circle, their hands folded before them, their full, long pastel robes of plain cut. Behind them were pillars, and beyond those a garden of carefully spaced trees and close-mown lawn. There was something moving among the trees, but Drago could not make it out.

He frowned—*had* he gone to the AfterLife, and was this peaceful room the AfterLife he warranted?

"Nay, mortal man," one of the beings said. The only woman among them, and with sapphire eyes. "You are merely with us."

"Where am I?" Drago said, looking about. Strangely, he felt no fear.

The beings looked among themselves, and shrugged their shoulders. "It is difficult to explain," one said.

"It is a 'place,'" said another, and he shrugged uncomfortably. "A world, if you like. It is not our usual abode. Merely a necessary resting place on our journey."

Journey? thought Drago, but other questions took priority for the moment.

"And you are . . .?" He swung his legs over the side of the couch. He was still dressed in the clothes he had jumped through the Star Gate in, and Drago felt grimy and insignificant before these five beings.

"My name is Sheol," said the woman, and smiled. "This is Raspu," and indicated a dark-haired being with ruby eyes.

"I am your friend," said Raspu, and bowed. There was a faint suggestion of pitting and scarring under his luminous skin, but it accented his beauty rather than marred it.

Not knowing how to respond, Drago merely inclined his head.

"And this is Mot." Sheol indicated another of her companions, an ebony-eyed man who was painfully thin.

Drago nodded to him, and Mot smiled but did not speak.

"Barzula," and a being with unruly brown curls and golden eyes nodded.

"And finally, Rox." The last of the five, with black hair and ivory eyes, smiled and nodded.

"Who are you, Drago?" Raspu asked. "What are you? From whence have you come?"

"My name is Drago SunSoar," Drago said, and hesitated as the five glanced at each other. "You know the name?"

"Indeed we know the SunSoar name," Sheol said smoothly. "Please, continue."

"I am the son of Axis SunSoar and Azhure SunSoar." Again he hesitated, but the names apparently meant nothing to the five, for they gazed at him with bland eyes. "And I come from a land called Tencendor—"

"The land of the lakes?" Barzula interrupted. His tone was excited, eager, and Sheol laid a hand on his arm.

"There are lakes," Drago replied. "Four Sacred Lakes."

"Four!" the five exclaimed.

"Tell us about them," Rox said, allowing his eagerness to carry him forward a step.

Drago looked about at them, but decided they were only over-curious, rather than threatening. "There is little to tell, for they remain mostly mystery. Legend has it they were formed aeons ago in a fire-storm when ancient gods fell from the stars—"

"He *is* from the land," Barzula said, and his golden eyes blazed.

"Surely," Mot agreed.

"No-one has ever investigated their depths?" Sheol asked, and there was a strange light in her eyes.

"No," Drago said slowly. "Not that I am aware of."

He slid forward so that he was on the very edge of the couch. "*What* are you? And why these questions?"

"We are the Questors," said Raspu.

"And we quest toward your land of Tencendor," Sheol added.

Drago nodded slowly, thinking he understood. "You want something in those lakes . . . is that what you quest for?"

"Yes!" Sheol clapped her hands delightedly, but Drago thought it an oddly childish gesture for one of her obvious sophistication and power. "Yes, we quest for what lies at the foot of those lakes. Ah, Drago . . ."

As one their faces fell into sadness.

"Drago," Sheol continued, "before time had barely begun on your world we had something very precious stolen from us."

"Taken from us," the others echoed.

"By criminals, Drago. The Enemy. The Enemy stole from us and then fled through the universe only to come to grief on your world."

"What lies at the foot of the lakes could destroy you," Rox said sadly, but out of the corner of his eye Drago thought he saw a smile gleam momentarily on Barzula's face. But when he turned to check this, the Questor's face only reflected the sadness of the others.

"But we can remove it without harm to your people or your land," Rox finished.

"If you help us recover what is ours," Sheol said, "then we will be in your debt, and we will do anything in our power—"

Again Drago sensed vast amusement somewhere in this room, but he could not fix where it came from.

"—to aid you in your quest."

"*My* quest," Drago said slowly.

"My friend." Sheol slid down on her knees before Drago and took his hands in hers. "We felt you come through the Star Gate, and we felt the sadness in your heart. We cushioned you from death, and we sent our friends to collect you and bring you to us."

"Your friends?"

Sheol stood up and looked over Drago's shoulder. "Our beloved friends," she said very softly. "Behold, the Queen of Heaven."

Drago twisted about on the couch, and then froze. A woman had entered this chamber. She was not the most beautiful woman Drago had ever seen, although her dark hair and pale complexion were beauteous enough, but she carried about her such an aura of allure and power that Drago felt an instant attraction.

"You are a SunSoar," she said, and to his shock Drago realized she had the features and wings of an Icarii.

He nodded, realizing who she must be. "And you are StarLaughter."

She laughed, agreeing, then slid onto the couch beside him, hip to hip, her hand on his shoulder, her face close to his. Her eyes slid down over his body, and then back to his face. "Yes, I feel your SunSoar blood. Drago—what a strange name for a SunSoar—tell me your story."

Drago began slowly, not sure how to tell so much in a short space of time, but with StarLaughter's hand so hot on his shoulder, and her breath fanning across his cheek,

Drago found his words tumbling out. Whenever he paused to take a breath, she tilted her head to one side and murmured encouragement.

He told her about the Prophecy of the Destroyer and the fight between Axis and Gorgrael. He told her of his own birth, and of Azhure's punishment for his crime.

"My mother reversed my blood order, so that my enchanted Icarii blood was subjected to my mortal human blood.

"It was a cruel punishment," he added, "and it has been hard to live with. Sometimes I wonder what it *would* have been like to have been an Icarii Enchanter. I wish . . . I wish . . ."

"Ah," StarLaughter said, and leaned back to look at the Questors briefly. "And so you have leaped through the Star Gate, hoping to re-find your power. Well, death is always one way to find that which is lost. But tell me, what was your birth name? What was Drago shortened from?"

Instantly Drago remembered that she and WolfStar had named their unborn son DragonStar, and he glanced at her belly. Smooth. She had lost the babe, then.

"My name had been DragonStar," he said quietly.

He shocked her. StarLaughter leaned back and stared at him, her face paling, her chin trembling momentarily. Then she looked at the Questors. "That was *my* babe's name!"

"We know, Queen of Heaven," Sheol said soothingly. "How appropriate. How . . . fated."

She turned to Raspu. "Is he usable?" she murmured.

The mood among the Questors and StarLaughter changed abruptly. StarLaughter tensed and sat forward, Drago forgotten for the moment.

Raspu knelt down before Drago and took the man's face between his hands. "Peace, Drago. I will not harm you."

A tingling passed through Raspu's hands into Drago's body. It did not hurt, but it was not entirely pleasant, either.

Raspu drew in a long breath and sat back. "Yes," he said. "Yes he is. His Icarii power is still there, although cunningly hidden in twists and traps. But we can use it. He will be enough for the final leaps to the Star Gate."

StarLaughter laughed, a sound of pure exultation, and threw her arms about Drago.

"I *adore* you!" she cried, and Drago laughed with her. Everything was going to be all right.

33

StarLaughter

The Questors drifted off, claiming some matter they had to attend to, and Drago was left with StarLaughter.

"You are curious," she said, leaning back from him but keeping her hand on his shoulder. "Come with me and I shall show you this place."

Drago stood up, feeling a passing dizziness, but steadying himself almost immediately.

"You are still shaken from your journey through the Star Gate," StarLaughter said. "Stand a while, get your bearings."

Suddenly Drago remembered his sack. It lay on the floor by his feet and he bent down for it. The Scepter might be gone, but the sack's presence still somehow comforted Drago.

StarLaughter smirked. "What is it you dragged through with you from Tencendor, Drago? Here, let me see."

And she snatched it from him.

Drago tried to hang on, but StarLaughter had moved too quickly, and she hefted the sack in her hands.

"What is this?" she said, and thrust a hand in the sack. "What?"

She drew out her hand and it was filled with silver coins.

"What?" Drago echoed, and seized the sack from Star-Laughter. He emptied it out on the couch. All it contained was silver coins. Perhaps twenty-five or thirty. Almost dazed, Drago sifted them through his fingers. They were weighty, and each had stamped on one side a sword, and on the other a staff.

StarLaughter chuckled, and ran a hand through Drago's hair. "Did you think to pay for your passage, my delightful man?"

Where had they come from? Then Drago remembered the silver coin he'd found to pay the ferryman on the Nordra. Were they somehow connected with the lost Scepter?

"I carry my wealth about with me," he said lightly. "I trust no-one."

StarLaughter's face lost its humor. "Trust no-one," she said, and her voice had hardened as well. "Yes, yes. Trust no-one. That is a good plan. I trusted WolfStar, and look what *he* did to me."

She turned away, walking slowly toward the pillars, then whipped about, holding out a hand. Once again her face was lit with a smile.

"Will you come with me, Drago SunSoar? There are others you should meet."

Drago swept the coins back into the sack and tied it to his belt.

"We'll find you a bath and some clean clothes," StarLaughter said, linking her arm through his as he joined her. "I do not like the stink of sweat and dirt."

She wrinkled her nose at him, smiled and laughed yet again, and led him through the pillars.

There was a garden outside, and a sky and a sun, but all was different to anything Drago had ever experienced. The air was heavier, far more oppressive than even the Tencendorian summer, yet it was not hot. The sky was a dark purple, roiling with high clouds, and the sun shone weak silver, as if its own light were an effort it could not endure much longer.

The garden consisted of regularly distanced trees with large lawned spaces between them. The trees, like the light, seemed weak. Their trunks were spindly, their foliage sparse.

Some distance away, just out of Drago's vision, a cloud moved swiftly among the trees. Perhaps not a cloud, but whatever its true nature, it was dark and insubstantial, moving this way, now that.

"I can comprehend none of this," he said helplessly.

StarLaughter squeezed his arm sympathetically. "I understand your disorientation. This is a world far away from our home. A world distant from Tencendor. A world that would be but a bare speck, were you still gazing through the Star Gate from the safety and comfort of Tencendor."

"I have so many questions . . ."

"Then ask, sweet Drago," she said, leading him slowly through the trees. "Ask."

"What happened to me when I stepped through the Star Gate?"

She considered carefully before answering. "In a manner of speaking you died, but death is so unknown, and so largely misunderstood, that to use that expression will probably create illusions in your mind."

She paused. "You came through, you changed, and yet you are the same."

"But how did I get here?"

"The Questors felt you, as did my companions. The Questors, bless them, saved you as they saved us."

Us? "Saved you? StarLaughter, what happened to you and your . . . companions . . . after WolfStar threw you through the Star Gate?"

StarLaughter's entire body tensed, and her face hardened into a mask of utter hatred.

"We drifted, dead yet undead, for time unknown. We drifted, we hated, we lusted for revenge. But we were lost and helpless. Then," she took a deep breath and visibly relaxed, "then the Questors found us. Oh, Drago! We owe them so much! Look! Here are my friends, my companions, come to greet you!"

The cloud hurtled closer. Drago halted, wary, but Star-Laughter patted his arm and drew him closer, comforting.

"Be not afraid," she said, "for these are they who, with the Questors' help, brought you here."

Some fifteen paces from them the cloud resolved itself into a dense pack of moving bodies. They were Icarii, Drago saw, and yet not at all, but he could not quite discern why. They were the children WolfStar had sacrificed in his mad ambition. Some were as young as ten or eleven, others were nearing adulthood, but all had flat black eyes and expressions of implacable hatred.

There was something else, something Drago could not quite see . . . something . . .

As one they tilted their heads to the left, and regarded Drago. As one they fluttered, and twitched their heads to the other side. Curious. A strange murmuring arose from them, and then quieted.

As one, they shifted from leg to leg, and fluttered their wings behind them.

And as they tilted their heads, yet again as one, Drago had the impression of beaks and talons, although his eyes only saw faces and hands.

Abruptly he realized what it was about the children. They were more birdlike than Icarii.

They were a flock. A flock with a single mind.

"Revenge," StarLaughter said, and left Drago's side to scratch under the chin of the nearest child, and then to smooth back its hair from its forehead. "We all quest for revenge. My Hawkchilds and I."

She looked back at Drago. "What happened to us, Drago? We were betrayed. Our futures and our heritage were stolen from us."

A frightful murmuring arose from the flock behind her, and she waited until it had died down before repeating, "Betrayed, and our heritage stolen."

"Yes! As *my* heritage was betrayed and *my* future stolen!"

"Yes!" cried StarLaughter. "And as the Questors' heritage

was stolen from them by the Enemy. Don't you see, Drago? We are all the Betrayed, and we are all engaged in the same crusade. To recover that which was stolen from us!"

Drago stared at her, unable to believe his good fortune. These beings sympathized with him, they liked him, and they would help him recover his Icarii power. Drago was overcome with the idea that for the first time in his life he was no longer alone. Others had been as badly treated as he. He smiled, and then laughed.

Suddenly StarLaughter was in Drago's arms and he held her tight and kissed her passionately—it was the first time he'd ever held an Icarii woman. He was home. Revenge *would* be his!

From the garden StarLaughter led him back inside the building—Drago had only the haziest impression of a large domed structure—and into a chamber different from the one he had woken in. It was smaller, and obviously a living chamber.

"There is one more you must meet," StarLaughter said softly, and she led Drago to a crib.

She lifted a bundle from it, and beckoned Drago closer. "See?" she said as he stood at her side. "See? My son."

Drago looked, and swallowed instant revulsion. StarLaughter carried a baby in her arms, but he was not alive—though neither was he dead.

Drago frowned. The baby neither breathed nor moved. His skin was pale and waxy. His eyes stared wide open, as flat and black as Drago had seen in the faces of the children outside. Strange, disturbing eyes. The baby showed no reaction to StarLaughter.

"Pretty, sweet baby," StarLaughter crooned. She rocked him gently in her arms. "Sweet, lovely son. See my new friend? His name is Drago, and he will help us wreak revenge upon your father."

Suddenly, horrifyingly, she lifted the baby into Drago's

arms. He had to bite down nausea. His fingers grazed the baby's skin above the wraps, and it felt cold and clammy.

The baby's eyes stared straight ahead, unknowing.

Dead but not dead.

Hastily Drago handed the baby back to his mother. "He was born after you came through the Star Gate?"

"He slipped from my body with the shock, yes. But, see, Drago, is he not beautiful? Is he not lovely? My sweet, sweet son—what a man you will grow to be!"

StarLaughter sat down on a chair and bared a breast, lifting her child to suckle. She turned his head to her breast, but the baby's head flopped, and the nipple slipped from its unresponsive mouth.

StarLaugther seemed not to notice. She sat and crooned to her child as if he suckled vigorously, encouraging him, telling him what a wonderful, strong, healthy child he was.

Unable to turn away. Drago watched, sickened. After some minutes StarLaughter wiped the baby's mouth, even though there was no hint of moisture there, covered her breast, and placed the baby back in the cot.

"We'll leave him to sleep," she whispered, and drew Drago away. "He is growing so fast, he needs his rest."

Drago wondered if her experiences had left StarLaughter slightly unhinged. Could she not see what was wrong with the babe?

But maybe she couldn't bear to let him go.

Yes, some mothers were like that. Unable to let a dead child go.

But that child was not *quite* dead.

Drago shuddered, and StarLaughter frowned as she sat him down on a couch overlooking the garden.

"What ails you, Drago? Are you in pain? Hungry? Perhaps I should draw you a bath, you—"

"No, no, I am well, StarLaughter. Tell me," he forced the baby from his mind, "what did you mean 'usable' when you spoke to the Questors earlier? And how can I help you get back through the Star Gate?"

"Ah." StarLaughter snuggled close to Drago's body and put her head on his shoulder. Drago relaxed, enjoying the warmth. It had been a very long time since anyone had given him so much affection.

"The Questors and we are engaged in the same quest, my love," she said, and the endearment slipped naturally from her lips. "We seek what has been stolen from us. The Questors have been seeking, hunting, for much longer than have I and my companions. Aeons."

Drago remembered the legends of Fire-Night. They were ancient, telling of a time even before the original Enchantress founded the three human-like races of Tencendor. Perhaps the ancient ones, the Questors' Enemy, had been running for thousands of years even before they had crashed into Tencendor and created the Sacred Lakes.

"A long time," he said softly. "And they could not find what they wanted in all this time?"

"Oh, they *knew* where the Enemy had fled, but they did not have the power to break through the Star Gate, nor even to approach it."

She shifted slightly against his body, and for an instant Drago's mind was filled with possibilities that had nothing to do with regaining his power. But StarLaughter continued.

"The Questors need the power of someone *from* Tencendor to actually pull them to, and then through, the Star Gate."

"But you, and the children—the Hawkchilds—are powerful, surely. You are an Enchanter, and the children were all of great potential."

"Once." StarLaughter sighed. "Once. But we drifted a long time before the Questors found us, Drago. During that time our powers ebbed. The Questors have managed to use what was left of our powers to travel this close to the Star Gate, but no closer. But you," she looked up and smiled, "*you* have what they need. Your life force is so strong. *You* are going to get us through, Drago!"

Her hand rested on one of his legs, and she squeezed slightly.

"Me?" he said, trying to maintain at least the appearance of calmness. "How? I am useless as I am."

"The Questors can touch that part of you your mother buried so brutally. They can use it. Your power was not destroyed, only hidden. But what is important, my love," and her hand began to slowly trail up his thigh, "is that you *will* get us back through the Star Gate."

"But—"

"Not now, my beloved," she whispered, and sat up so she could kiss him. "Not now."

Her hand started to rub him, arousing with each motion.

"And will you regain me my heritage?" Drago managed to ask, his voice hoarse. "Can your Questors reverse my blood order? Make me once again an Icarii Enchanter?"

"Easily, my love," she said, "you shall be all that you want."

And then there was no more breath for words.

34

Of What Is Lost

From the Ancient Barrows, Faraday walked south through the grassy Tarantaise plains. She had never been so happy previously. Never. *Nothing* compared to this freedom she now enjoyed.

For that she thanked both Drago and Noah.

She did not know exactly what changes her transformation had wrought. Noah had said that the Scepter had enriched her, given her the power to find what was lost. But Faraday knew the changes went beyond that. From brief glimpses caught in streams she could see she looked like the Faraday who had died in Gorgrael's Ice Fortress, save that the lines of care and sadness about her eyes and mouth had gone. But if she *looked* like that Faraday, she did not know if she was quite the same woman.

That woman had labored in her service to the Mother and the trees. Now the trees waved in the sun far behind her and did not need her. They still loved her, Faraday could feel that, and she them. But they did not need her.

That woman had been torn to emotional and physical shreds by her love for Axis. Now she felt largely indifferent to him. The love had gone. She felt friendship toward Axis, but she did not know if she would ever completely trust him again. Even though Faraday knew he could not have saved her in Gorgrael's chamber, somehow she had always hoped he would.

But he hadn't. Gorgrael had torn her apart, and Faraday's love and regard for Axis had died with her.

The Mother still loved her, Faraday knew that, too. But she realized the Mother was willing to let her go.

Perhaps . . . perhaps her transformation into the doe had only been a stage, a transition. The Mother had promised her that for her service to the Prophecy of the Destroyer and the trees she would eventually run unfettered, and Faraday had supposed that when she had been transformed into the doe that promise had been fulfilled.

But in its own way, that had also been an entrapment, and Faraday had not been free to do as she wished.

"But for the moment I am!" Faraday ran through the grass, her arms outstretched, hair and cloak flying, laughing with sheer exuberance.

Once she had slowed down and caught her breath, Faraday turned her thoughts to the three people who now most concerned her.

StarDrifter. Her mouth curled in secret amusement as she thought of him. Axis' father. She did not know StarDrifter very well, but what she did know she liked. He was as arrogant as his son, but more open in that arrogance. If StarDrifter had a liking for something—or someone—then everyone knew about it. He would not have hidden a lover from Faraday, but would have confronted her with it. And yet, in that very confrontation, shielded her.

He was arrogant, but he also knew how to care. Faraday thought that the events surrounding Gorgrael's invasion of Tencendor had taught him responsibility and had deepened his sense of compassion. Now that he lived on the Island of Mist and Memory, leading the Icarii's worship of the stars and the Star Gods, he had more to think about than the relieving of his own desires.

Faraday had seen at once that he cared very much for Zenith, and she thought that no-one else had a better chance of helping the woman. Faraday sighed, and some of her happiness slid away. Poor Zenith. Another of Axis and Azhure's children caught up in some maelstrom not of their choosing or making.

From Zenith, Faraday's thoughts moved inevitably to Drago.

The evil rouge, the betraying child.

All true. And yet—more.

He would come back, and then she would see. She smiled.

And so Faraday walked on.

That night she dug out a hollow beneath the grasses, then curled up in the ruby cloak, and it kept her warm enough. The next morning she was awoken by her stomach growling in hunger.

She sat up, half expecting Goodwife Renkin to appear with a plate of sausages and eggs, but the Goodwife was nowhere to be seen.

"On my own," she said, combing her hair with her fingers. "Well, that is as it should be."

And so she rose and began once again to walk south.

In the mid-morning Faraday came upon an isolated farmhouse. Several fields ranged to the north and west of the farmhouse, and a herd of brown and cream cattle grazed on a hilltop some three hundred paces away. The house was made of faded mud-brick, with long low walls, and a well-patched thatch roof. A woman, the goodwife, was bent over in her vegetable patch beside the house.

Faraday stopped and looked, a half-smile on her face. The scene reminded her so much of the time the Goodwife Renkin had sheltered her and Timozel, on their way north to Gorkenfort.

I hope I can touch this woman's life for the better, too, Faraday thought, and walked toward the house.

"Goodwife?" she said softly as she stopped at the vegetable patch's boundary.

The woman jerked up straight, surprised by the voice.

"I mean you no harm," Faraday said, wondering what she must look like, barefoot, wild-haired, and naked underneath a rich ruby cloak.

"What do you want?" the woman asked, her eyes watchful but her tone reasonably friendly.

Faraday looked at her carefully. She was thin, and abnormally pale. Hard-worked, yes, but there was more . . .

"Take a small linen bag of stout weave," Faraday said, "and ask your goodman to fill it with iron filings. Put this bag into your stew pot, and eat well of the stew that you bubble in it. Keep the bag in that pot, week in, week out. When the linen decays, make another bag for the filings."

"Why?"

"In this way," Faraday said, "you will re-find your health, and your fertility. No more will your babes slip from your womb in the first month or two after conception."

The woman's eyes filled with tears. "Lady, I do thank you. How may I repay your kindness?"

"Well," Faraday said hopefully, "do you have an old dress that perhaps you no longer need, and a pair of boots?"

And so, now comfortably booted and robed, Faraday walked on. As the sun dipped into mid-afternoon she came across a band of horse traders. They drove before them a herd of some forty horses, mostly yearlings, bound for the markets of Carlon far to the west.

Their leader, a rough-whiskered middle-aged man, pulled his horse up and stared at her.

Faraday felt no fear, and she merely returned his regard, a small smile on her face.

"Who are you?" the man asked roughly.

"My name is Faraday," she said.

"You are a long way from any village," said another man, pulling his horse up beside that of his leader.

Faraday nodded, but said nothing.

The men, three now, sat their horses and stared at her. The possibilities in the barren plain were endless. Rape, and then a murder to silence her. Perhaps rape, and then a quick sale in the unquestioning markets of Nor.

Faraday looked at them, trusting.

One of the men slid from his horse, handed the reins to his companion, and walked over until he stood less than a pace from Faraday.

"You're a very beautiful woman," he said.

"Thank you."

"Here," he said, and handed her his purse. "Take what you want."

"Thank you very much," Faraday said, and graced him with her warm, lovely smile. She slid several coins out, then handed it back to the man.

As he took it she said, "Your wife has lost most of her youth, hasn't she?"

"Yes. How did you know that?"

Faraday shrugged away the question. "She is unhappy, because along with her youth she feels she is losing you."

The man shifted uncomfortably.

Faraday placed her hand lightly on the man's chest. "Your wife's youth lies in your heart." She patted his chest gently. "Only you have the power to give it back to her."

He stared at her, then nodded, understanding. "You are very wise."

Faraday laughed. "No, good sir, I am merely repaying the debt I owe you."

And with that she slipped the coins into a pocket, and walked away.

The three men sat their horses for a very long time, watching her.

South, south, ever south. A week after she'd met the horse-traders Faraday veered south-west, heading for the province of Nor. With the coin the horse-trader had given her she purchased food from the isolated homesteads she occasionally passed, but otherwise Faraday kept away from habitation. She enjoyed her solitude. At night she wrapped herself in the ruby cloak and slept dreamlessly, a small smile on her face.

Once in Nor Faraday met many more people. Nor was the most populous of Tencendor's provinces and, in many ways, the most intense. Its vividness showed in the characters of the Nors people themselves, in their clothes, the way they decorated their homes, and in virtually every aspect of their lives. Convention was anathema to the Nors people, they lived and loved at a pace and with a fervor the other Acharites often had trouble accepting.

Faraday loved it. These people were *alive,* and she reveled in them.

In upper Nor she decided she'd had enough of walking, her boot soles were growing ever thinner, and so she decided to find passage south on a merchant's cart.

She waited for a day by the side of a road, watching trading traffic going by, waiting for the right merchant. Finally, toward evening, she spotted a man walking beside a cart loaded with pottery and pulled by four sturdy horses.

"Good sir," she cried as the cart came level with her.

"Aye?" the man said carefully, looking her up and down. He was thin and brown-haired, still young, but with the hunched shoulders of one far older.

"Good sir, I wonder if you travel to Ysbadd. I would go there."

The man's eyes narrowed. He wondered how she would pay. He had no taste for whores, and she did not look as if she could pay him the coin such a journey deserved.

"You have lost trade recently," Faraday said. "I can tell you how to find it again. That should be worth the cost of my journey."

"What—"

"It is your brother's doing. He was jealous at your initial success at carting these pots," and Faraday waved her hand at the cart, "and has spread the tale that you trade only in weak and defective vessels."

The man regarded her steadily. It would not be past Holt to do such a thing. "And how do I regain this trade, fine lady?"

"Guarantee your produce. Offer to replace every faulty vessel that you sell—or have sold—with a sound one."

"But that would cost me—"

Faraday grinned. "Only if you *have* been trading in faulty vessels, Jarl."

Jarl wondered how she knew his name. But he thought on what she'd said, then smiled himself. "You have a sharp mind, lady. What should I call you? It is many days travel south to Ysbadd."

Faraday let him help her climb into a spare space on the cart. "My name is Faraday, Jarl. Have I earned my journey?"

"You have indeed, Faraday, you have indeed."

* * *

Ysbadd left Faraday breathless. If she had been any younger she thought she might have clapped her hands in glee. She nodded good-bye to Jarl in the main square, where he was loudly proclaiming his new idea of guarantee, and she wandered the streets for hours. The city was a riotous mixture of gaudy spires and fat domes, intermixed with cool shaded walks and parks. People thronged the streets and markets, colorful in scarves and beads, and waved from windows, shouting greetings to strangers and family alike.

As a girl Faraday had always been warned to be careful of Nors people by her thin-mouthed mother. Nors morals were not what the staid northerners agreed with. Yet wandering through the streets, Faraday decided that for all their fun-loving and indulgent lives, the Nors people were basically good-hearted.

By dusk she felt hungry, and so picked a food stall where, in return for her fill of beef stew and fresh bread, she told its proprietor where he could find the gold tooth he'd lost during a drunken party several weeks ago.

Having eaten, Faraday asked directions to the port and, once on the wharf, she walked slowly to and fro, eyeing the ships, until she finally climbed aboard a vessel with dusky pink sails and black eyes painted in the center of each canvas. A deckhand asked her what she wanted, and she said she wanted to see the Master.

"For passage?" the deckhand asked.

"Yes. I have heard you provision for a voyage to the Island of Mist and Memory."

"Oh aye," the deckhand muttered. "We provision, all right, but I doubt we'll be voyaging anywhere in the near future."

"Nevertheless, I would like to see the Master of the vessel."

"Very well," the deckhand said, and led her below.

"Go away!" a voice shouted when Faraday knocked politely on the cabin door.

"I believe," Faraday said clearly, "that you've lost your nerve."

There was utter silence on the other side of the door.

"I have come to help you find it again," Faraday said, and folded her hands and waited.

After a moment the door opened.

35

SpikeFeather's Search

"Send someone else to watch the Star Gate," SpikeFeather told Caelum, "for Orr has gone."

That is all he said, for since his apprenticeship to the Ferryman SpikeFeather had developed a secrecy about him that had not been there previously. SpikeFeather knew there was something wrong, and he knew Orr had disappeared, but until he knew exactly what had happened he was not going to waste Caelum's time with speculations.

Once SpikeFeather had been an ordinary Icarii, not even an Enchanter. Just a birdman who did his best at whatever he'd been assigned to. More by accident than design, SpikeFeather had found himself commanding the Strike Force during the last months of Axis' campaign against Gorgrael, but he had not truly felt comfortable in the position, and once peace had settled over Tencendor, he'd handed the position of Strike Leader to DareWing FullHeart.

Besides, he owed a life to the Ferryman.

SpikeFeather had spent many years in the Overworld after his pact with the Ferryman in return for Orr transporting the children to safety, but fifteen years ago Orr had summoned SpikeFeather to the waterways.

There, Orr had begun to teach the birdman.

SpikeFeather was never quite sure *what* the Ferryman taught him.

It was not magic, for SpikeFeather remembered no spells and had no power to wield them in any case.

It was not the explanations to great mysteries, for SpikeFeather never remembered feeling very enlightened.

Orr had mostly just talked, generally about what he had seen and heard over the past millennia—and over fifteen years he had barely managed to scratch the surface of his experiences.

SpikeFeather only spent a few months of each year in the waterways. Orr often told him that he needed to spend as much time reflecting as he did absorbing, so in those months he spent in the Overworld, SpikeFeather wandered about Sigholt, sometimes talking with one or two of the SunSoars, mostly just thinking.

SpikeFeather had been standing atop Sigholt when Orr's terror struck him. Apart from a few disjointed words, nothing had reached him but that terror.

Terror? SpikeFeather had not known Orr to be capable of such emotion.

Now SpikeFeather sat in a small flat-bottomed boat in the center of a vast underground violet lake. Above him soared an immense domed roof of multifaceted crystals.

Where was Orr?

SpikeFeather did not know. He had called, but Orr had not appeared.

SpikeFeather could try to look for him, but if the past fifteen years had taught SpikeFeather anything it was that the waterways of the Underworld were so vast that to search for someone without a clear idea of where they might be would be to search in vain.

So SpikeFeather searched for clues in the words that Orr had sent him.

Qeteb. SpikeFeather frowned, rolling the word about his mouth until whispers echoed off the crystal roof.

Qeteb.

He did not know it. Nothing Orr had ever said in the past

alluded to a Qeteb. It meant nothing in any of the languages SpikeFeather knew. All he knew was that with the word, Orr had passed across the knowledge of indescribable terror.

SpikeFeather shivered.

Qeteb meant nothing. What else? Grail. Grail King. Beware the Grail King in the Maze.

Only one word had some association for SpikeFeather. Was the repeated Grail a reference to Grail Lake? If so, then what?

SpikeFeather tried to think it through, but found no answers and came to no conclusions. Orr had never mentioned anything about the Sacred Lakes, and yet . . . yet . . . wasn't there a mystery about them?

SpikeFeather sighed, and turned his mind to the other word.

The Maze. Orr had sent the message, "Beware the Grail King in the Maze." And then, "Attend the Maze!"

The Maze? The Maze?

Where was Orr, where *was* he? SpikeFeather needed to find him, to get him to explain what this Maze was, and why SpikeFeather had to attend it. And why had Orr been so terrified of this Qeteb, and the Grail King?

SpikeFeather sighed. Even if he was almost certain he would never find Orr amid the meanderings of the waterways, he needed to try. He took hold of the oars and began his search.

The waterways was a world both magical and physical. Thousands of leagues of actual physical waterways wound about underneath Tencendor and the surrounding oceans, but the magical waterways extended far further. Those Icarii Enchanters who knew how, and who commanded enough power, could manipulate the waterways to mirror the various melodies of the Star Dance. If an Enchanter sang a Song to accomplish his or her purpose, then someone with the knowledge could travel a waterway that matched the pattern of the Song to accomplish the same purpose.

It was cumbersome, but possible.

But not for SpikeFeather. He was not an Enchanter, and Orr had never taught him the magical secrets of the waterways. So SpikeFeather traveled the waterways the most difficult way of all, by the strength of his own muscles and the labor of his heart.

He had no idea where to start looking for the ever secretive Orr, or for this Maze, or for any way to approach the Grail Lake via the waterways. The only one of the Sacred Lakes he knew the path to was the Lake of Life, and that was only because Orr had needed to show him an easy way to travel between Sigholt and the waterways.

So SpikeFeather rowed. He followed his instincts, and when that got him nowhere he followed his frustration and anger.

Where was Orr? What had he been so terrified of? What was wrong?

Who or what was Qeteb? The Grail King? The Maze?

SpikeFeather rowed. He rowed through caverns where gray stone cities lay smothered in cobwebs. He rowed through forests of glass and enamel. He rowed along waterways that were lined with weed, and some that were lined with figures carved from ice. He passed strange creatures embalmed in limestone, and others stranger trapped in petrified wood.

But he did not find Orr.

Finally, after many days, SpikeFeather sat in his flat-bottomed boat in the center of the violet lake and wept. He had failed Orr in his hour of need. He had proven a failure as a pupil, and an even worse failure as a friend.

Orr had trusted him with those words and phrases, as he had trusted him to know he was terrified, perhaps unto death, and yet SpikeFeather could not help him.

Eventually SpikeFeather raised his eyes. There must be *something* he could do.

Who else had spent time with Orr in the waterways? Axis SunSoar had, but Axis SunSoar would reveal nothing of what he had learned from the Ferryman.

But there were others. The Lake Guard. As children they'd spent a night with Orr on their way from Talon Spike to Sigholt. No-one knew better than SpikeFeather how strangely time passed within the waterways. What if those children had spent one night of Overworld time in the waterways, but a year of Underworld time?

The children had been changed, all agreed on that. They were apparently loyal to Caelum, but did they in fact care more for . . .

"Orr," SpikeFeather whispered. The Lake Guard *must* know something! And if not, then would they not help search for Orr?

Yes, surely.

Suddenly glad-hearted, SpikeFeather grabbed at the oars and rowed for the Lake of Life.

It was an arduous journey, and he was close to exhaustion when he emerged onto the moonlit lake. But once he'd moored the boat close to Sigholt he managed to wing his way to the roof with alacrity. Answers waited, and Orr needed his help.

There was no-one about as SpikeFeather made his way down to the quarters where slept WingRidge CurlClaw, the captain of the Lake Guard.

SpikeFeather tapped at the door gently, not wanting to startle the birdman, but was startled himself when it swung open to reveal WingRidge sitting at a table.

"Greetings, SpikeFeather," WingRidge said.

"You knew I was coming," SpikeFeather said, slipping into the room and closing the door behind him.

WingRidge shrugged. "I was merely passing the night with my memories. I thought you had gone back to the waterways, SpikeFeather."

SpikeFeather was in the act of sitting down opposite the captain when he saw the embroidered device on the birdman's uniform as if for the first time. A complicated knot—but weren't all knots simplified mazes?

SpikeFeather slowly sat down and looked WingRidge in the eye. "I had to come back."

"Really?" WingRidge leaned back and poured them both some wine. "How so?"

SpikeFeather briefly explained what he had experienced atop the roof of Sigholt, and the sense of terror that Orr had passed across to him.

"Terror?" WingRidge became suddenly very watchful. Orr had been standing guard at the Star Gate. What had he seen? Heard?

"I could not understand it. It was a terror so great it was almost formless. With the terror he passed across some words."

"Yes?"

"Qeteb."

WingRidge slowly put his glass down and stared at SpikeFeather.

"Beware the Grail King in the Maze." SpikeFeather watched WingRidge's reaction carefully, then leaned forward and tapped the birdman on the chest. "You *know* of what I speak!"

WingRidge nodded, his eyes shifting as he thought quickly. If Orr had been at the Star Gate, and if he knew of Qeteb, then he could only have known by two means. Firstly, he'd discovered Qeteb by a means as yet beyond the Star Gate. But WingRidge didn't think that the case, for he'd have known—*all* would have known—if disaster was that close. No, Orr had likely found out via the Scepter that Drago carried, and that meant the Maze wanted Orr and, through him, SpikeFeather, to know.

It also meant that Drago had likely stepped through the Star Gate. WingRidge almost smiled with satisfaction, then remembered SpikeFeather sitting impatiently before him.

"Then the time *is* nigh," he said slowly, and did not know whether to feel excited . . . or terrified.

"Tell me!"

"Most of it I cannot, SpikeFeather."

"WingRidge, Orr also told me that I must attend the Maze."

WingRidge stared at his glass, his eyes carefully veiled.

"Curse you, WingRidge, I *need* to know where to find this Maze . . . this Qeteb!"

WingRidge laughed harshly, utterly devoid of humor. "No, no, you *never* wish to find Qeteb!"

SpikeFeather, exhausted and emotionally drained, lost his temper. "What demon do you owe your cursed loyalty to, WingRidge? What—"

"*Never say I owe my loyalty to a demon!*" WingRidge screamed. Leaping to his feet, he sent the table crashing to the floor with one furious twist of his wrist. "I owe my loyalty to the *StarSon*! Not to any damned demon!"

His fury stunned SpikeFeather back into silence.

WingRidge took a deep breath and calmed himself. "I offer my apologies, SpikeFeather. You are closely associated with Orr and the waterways, and it was you who first brought us into contact with the Underworld. For that I, as all the Lake Guard, remain in your debt."

He paused, and rubbed his eyes. When he looked back at SpikeFeather they were rimmed with dread. "If the Grail King stirs, then so I *must* speak. Especially since the Maze appears to require your presence. Yes, I owe you some explanation. Please, will you help me right this table so we may sit in comfort again?"

SpikeFeather assisted him, then they sat, each silent on his side of the table.

After a while WingRidge began to speak in a quiet, even tone. "When you left us with Orr we floated only a small distance with the Ferryman before he left us to continue our own way. The boats we sat in were magically guided, and all we had to do was sit and sing to get to the Lake of Life."

"But—"

"But someone else came to us down in the waterways, SpikeFeather, and told us of a mighty secret."

"Who?"

Silence for a long time. Then, very quietly, "WolfStar SunSoar."

"Ah!" SpikeFeather exclaimed. "Will this WolfStar never leave us alone?"

"He showed us a great mystery," WingRidge said, a trifle defensively.

"He manipulated you."

"He showed us the Maze," WingRidge said. "And he showed us our purpose."

"Your purpose?"

"To serve the StarSon as best we might."

And well you show it, SpikeFeather thought, for sometimes you barely give Caelum the time of day. "Where is this Maze?"

WingRidge hesitated. "Very well. You have reason enough to know. Look," and, pulling a piece of parchment to himself, WingRidge drew a plan with swift, dark strokes.

36

Kastaleon

As the autumn thickened with clouds overhead, Zared moved on Kastaleon. He did not want to initiate a war, he did not want to evoke images and memories of invasion or treason, he only wanted to make a point. And so Zared did not invade Kastaleon with an army, or even an armed force, but with a relatively small group of men.

By the first week in Bone-Month Zared had his army stationed at a point some two leagues to the north-west of Kastaleon—a morning's ride away. Zared was tense and worried, as were Herme and Theod. Had they managed to pass unnoticed through Aldeni, or did the captain of Kastaleon have intelligence of their movements? Would his arrival be a surprise, or quietly awaited? Zared had done his best to keep the army to uninhabited stretches of Aldeni, and Theod had spread the word among his people that the least said about any sightings of Prince Zared and a force moving south the better . . . but Zared well knew that a single loose tongue could mean a trap awaiting him at Kastaleon.

Even a vengeful Caelum.

A vengeful Leagh was bad enough. After they'd moved away from the almost disastrous river crossing at the Azle, she'd spent days—and long nights—pleading with him to turn back to Severin. Marry me there, she'd said, rubbing her naked body against his, and we will ride out Caelum's anger. And if there are further disputes between you, then surely Council would be the best place to reason them out.

When he'd continued to refuse to turn for home, Leagh had become angry. Again she'd accused him of lying to her, deceiving her.

"And deceiving your parents' trust in you," she said several nights ago, "for they believed you'd remain loyal to the Throne of the Stars."

That had been too much, and Zared, furious, had moved his sleeping roll away from her for the rest of the night.

His fury was also tinged with guilt. What would she do when she learned that he was intent on reclaiming the Acharite throne, and on regaining the Acharites their pride? She would certainly then believe he only loved her for her inheritance. That was wrong, Zared told himself during the rest of that long, lonely night, for he *did* love her, and as much for her wit and charm and strength of character (which he currently cursed) as her lands.

Zared admitted to himself that part of Leagh's appeal lay in her inheritance, and that inheritance could not possibly be divorced from his current crusade. It was naive of her to think otherwise.

But this evening, as he watched his men set up camp above Kastaleon, Zared sighed, and vowed to make peace with Leagh as soon as he could. Gods knew what would happen if she refused to marry him . . .

Before Zared ate his evening meal he sent fifty men to Kastaleon in groups of three or four. They were garbed as traders or itinerants, and would be able to pass unnoticed among the crowds that gathered about Kastaleon. The castle was not simply a defensive structure, but it also served as the point where Askam imposed his tariffs on the Nordra River. No vessel could slip by Kastaleon unnoticed or unchallenged. All stopped, all were inspected, all were taxed. With the trade, and just the general traffic along the roads leading to and from the grain lands of upper Tencendor, there was generally a large number of people moving past or through the castle and the settlement surrounding it; his fifty would attract no undue attention.

Zared gave them that night and the first part of the following morning. Close to noon he led a force of some five hundred men south; the bulk of the army staying behind. The intelligence Zared had received showed that Askam had about one hundred and twenty men stationed at Kastaleon. Not many. After all, this was peace time.

He glanced across at Theod, who looked excited, and Herme, who was considerably graver.

At Zared's stare, Herme shrugged. "You have no choice, my Prince. You *must* demonstrate how deeply Caelum has insulted you, and how he cannot afford to ignore the issues that threaten Tencendor's peace."

But do *I* threaten Tencendor's peace by this action? Zared wondered. Will it stop at Kastaleon, or will it spread ripple-fashion throughout the entire land? But it was too late to back down now; already some fifty of his men were waiting inside Kastaleon, and they would cause mischief enough even if Zared turned for home at this very moment.

So Zared waved his men out.

They now carried the Prince of the North's standard, and Zared himself rode at the head of the column dressed in clearly visible insignia. If he had wanted to keep his approach through Aldeni quiet, then he needed to ride into Kastaleon openly.

The captain of the watch spotted them a thousand paces from the castle. He peered through the afternoon sun, trying to catch a glimpse of the standard, then his eyes widened.

"The Prince of the North approaches," he cried. "Form an honor guard!"

"Curse his hairy stones!" the captain muttered as he climbed down the ladders to the inner courtyard. Zared might have sent a forward scout to warn of his arrival. No doubt he would expect a full banquet and noble entertainment in the hall tonight. Well, he'd have to think again. Kastaleon hardly had the facilities to—

His thoughts were cut off by a clatter of hooves across the drawbridge. Zared, with some two hundred and fifty men, swarmed into an already crowded central courtyard.

The captain frowned. Why were they deploying so? One would think they were almost . . .

He snapped to attention as the Prince himself reined his horse to a halt before him.

"Welcome to Kastaleon, my Lord," he said. "May I inquire as to the purpose of your visit?"

"Certainly," Zared said pleasantly, dismounting and pulling the gloves from his hands as he walked the few steps between himself and the captain. "I have come to seize your castle, sirrah. Your surrender, please."

The captain's mouth dropped, unable to believe what he'd just heard. "But . . . but . . ."

Then training took over, and he snapped out of his fugue. "Hartley!" he shouted, turning to look for his second-in-command, "we are under—"

The hilt of Zared's sword crashed into the back of his skull, and the captain collapsed to the pavement. The rest of the courtyard was in uproar. Men had come to their senses at the same time as the captain, and many had drawn swords and moved into defensive positions.

But it was too late, the invader was already inside!

And worse. The fifty men Zared had sent in earlier were causing chaos and distraction within the buildings, shouting false orders, seizing weapons, locking men in barracks and storerooms. The two hundred and fifty Zared had brought into the castle with him quickly subdued the soldiers within the courtyard and on the walls, while outside Kastaleon another two hundred secured the immediate riverfront, wharf and approach roads.

Kastaleon was Zared's.

That evening he summoned the captain of Kastaleon's guard. The captain was sullen and subdued, nursing a dreadful headache and a worse case of resentment.

"I am sending you north," Zared said as soon as the captain stood at some sort of attention before his desk.

"I am not yours to command," the captain muttered.

"Nevertheless, I am sure you would like StarSon Caelum and Prince Askam informed of my actions?"

The captain stared silently at him.

"Yes, I am sure you would. Well, I would like you to take a message to Caelum for me."

The captain continued to stare at Zared.

"I am *ordering* you to carry a message to Caelum!" Zared snapped, and the captain nodded curtly.

"You will inform Caelum that I have seized Kastaleon in part compensation for the loss of trade Prince Askam's exorbitant tariffs on river cargo have caused me and most of Western Tencendor. Nevertheless, I am a generous man, and I will be prepared to forget the loss and hand Kastaleon back into Prince Askam's care once Caelum is prepared to negotiate the matters I discussed with him in Sigholt. Please repeat what I have just said."

The captain hesitated, then repeated the message.

Zared sat back in his chair. "Good. You will ride north with all possible haste."

"Are you invading the West?" the captain said.

Zared noted the lack of a title, but understood the captain's attitude. No doubt Askam would not receive news of his failure to defend Kastaleon with much good cheer.

"Not if I don't have to," he said. "Now, get you gone from here. There is a horse and an escort waiting."

Once the captain had gone, Herme emerged from a shadowy corner. "The first act has been played out in this war of nerves, my Prince. And now?"

Zared thought for some time. "I don't want Caelum receiving intelligence that Kastaleon is surrounded by an army fourteen thousand thick, Herme. I will keep the five hundred here, but the rest . . . the rest I want to start to move," he hesitated, "move them inland to the Western Ranges."

Herme nodded. Within striking distance of Carlon. Whatever Zared was saying publicly, he'd been thinking of Carlon. Well, if he truly wanted the throne, Kastaleon was never going to be enough. "Do you think Caelum *will* move against us, Zared?"

"Frankly, I doubt it." Zared stared into the flames of the fire in the hearth across the room. "I think your counsel that he would do anything to avoid a serious confrontation was wise. But just in case . . . just in case. Who knows what Askam might push him into? If I have to stand and fight I do not want to do it here. Kastaleon is not built to withstand a siege, and this is a bad place to stage a battle. I need to be prepared for . . ."

"For?"

"For whatever else might eventuate . . ."

"My Prince—"

"I saw that man's face, Herme. He hated me. Until a few

moments ago this was all such an academic exercise. Too easy. A routine deployment. But I very much fear we may have to fight this one out, Herme."

"Most of the Acharites will fight for you, Zared! You fight for them, for their pride!"

"I most certainly hope so," Zared said very softly, his gaze still unfocused in the flames. "I most certainly hope so."

As Herme left the room Zared saw Leagh standing in the gloom of the door. The expression on her face was very cold.

After a moment she presented her back and walked away.

37

The Leap

He woke to the feel of StarLaughter's fingers trailing down his body, and he smiled, although he kept his eyes closed. But she had seen the smile, and she laughed, low and jubilant, and bent her mouth to the task of arousal even as her fingers slipped lower.

Drago continued to play at being asleep. This must be true happiness, surely. Here no-one hated him, no-one constantly threw infant misdeeds in his face, and here the distractions were only ever of the pleasurable kind.

Here power beckoned, and life as a SunSoar Enchanter seemed a tangible certainty rather than a hopeless dream.

Here everyone lived only to regain what they had been robbed of, and Drago reveled in the single-minded atmosphere of revenge. Revenge? No, he didn't want to think that. All here only wanted what had been wrongfully taken from them. Restitution, perhaps. Satisfaction, certainly.

"StarLaughter," he murmured, and reached for her.

Here his lover was no kitchen girl, but a powerful Enchanter, and the wife of the most powerful Enchanter-Talon of all. He did not know why she loved him; it was just enough that she did, and Drago was grateful.

When they were done, and StarLaughter had exhausted him, Drago drifted back to sleep. He dreamed of the hunt, of riding through the forests, riding down all in his path, invulnerable in his armor, riding until he had his quarry at the point of his sword, and then *on* the point of his sword. That felt very good. Very good indeed. Even StarLaughter could not make him feel that good.

Drago rolled over, half asleep . . .

. . . and rolled against something cool and clammy.

He recoiled immediately, leaping into full wakefulness. It was the baby, StarLaughter's damned not dead, not alive child that should have been decently interred four thousand years ago.

Repulsed, Drago rolled completely out of bed and stood looking at him.

StarLaughter carried the babe everywhere, offering him her breast when they sat down, apparently unaware that the child did not breathe or move or blink.

He just lay, and stared with his undead eyes.

StarLaughter crooned constantly to the baby, whispering words of love and encouragement, and her attention to the child sickened Drago.

He leaned down, hesitated, then poked the baby in the ribs.

The baby rolled a little at his touch, but otherwise made no response. And yet . . . yet Drago had the strangest sensation that somehow the baby had filed away that minor insult. Locked it away in some dark room of its mind where it kept all experiences. Kept it until it could be examined with . . . with more *life* and some decision made as to the response it merited.

Well, Drago tried to joke to himself, if the infant hadn't made any response in the past four thousand years, doubtless he wouldn't any time soon.

"My baby," crooned StarLaughter behind Drago, and he jumped guiltily. Had she seen?

Apparently not. "My beautiful boy," she said, and picked up the baby, cuddling him to her. "See how he grows!" and she looked to Drago for confirmation.

"A very beautiful boy," he finally said. Why didn't she accept that the baby was . . . wrong?

But maybe all that had kept StarLaughter going these past millennia was the baby. Maybe she kept him to stoke her hatred and need for revenge.

But Drago discarded that thought almost as soon as it crossed his mind. No, StarLaughter seemed genuinely to believe that the baby was alive.

"Come, my love," she said, and Drago realized she was speaking to him. "Come walk a while with me."

Drago dressed, in finer clothes now than those he'd arrived in, although he knew not from where they had come, clasped the sack of coins to his belt, and escorted StarLaughter and her strange undead child into what Drago had come to call the orchard.

Orchard it was not quite, for no fruit drooped from the branches of these strange anemic trees, and the sun shone only fitfully from amid the roiling violet clouds, but orchard conjured up images of peace and happiness for Drago, and it reminded him of home.

That surprised him, for he had not thought to so miss Tencendor. But miss it he did, and he could not deny he would be glad to go back through the Star Gate. It would be good, he thought, going back cloaked in so much power people would envy him, rather than revile him.

The cloud flitted through distant trees, and Drago turned to watch them. StarLaughter called them her Hawkchilds, and the name suited them. She may have retained her Icarii resemblance and her loveliness, but the children had changed in the wastes. They *looked* Icarii enough, with their delicate features and their jewel-like wings, but at the same time they had developed such a quintessence of bird, of predatory bird, that they appeared more the flock of hunting hawks than the crowd of children. Whatever childlike qualities they'd once possessed had been lost in their transformation to birds of prey.

Hunting hawks, not children.

Drago smiled and held out his hand as the cloud drew closer. It whispered, a constant undertone of WolfStar's name repeated over and over, and the children—the hawks—wheeled this way and that, as if of one mind, one heart.

The cloud approached him as if it would envelop him, but it halted at the last moment, the two hundred staring at him with their heads on an identical tilt, their eyes identically dark and curious.

StarLaughter smiled. "See how they come to you, Drago. Will they hunt for you, do you think, when we return to Tencendor?"

He rubbed under the chin of the nearest creature. She tilted her head, leaning into his hand, and smiled and closed her eyes, enjoying the attention.

"I hope so," he said. "Do you know I dreamed of the hunt? Even when back in Tencendor?"

"You must have felt us, even then, my love. You and we are bonded. Linked by our need to regain what is rightfully ours."

"The dream is stronger here," Drago said. Some nights it left him exhausted, breathless, but always, always with such a deep sense of satisfaction it was pleasure in itself.

He dropped his hand, and the creature drooped, dipping her head, wanting more.

"Later," Drago said, and waved his hand.

Whispering their disappointment, the flock wheeled off, racing cloudlike through the trees, whispering, whispering, whispering.

"The Questors," StarLaughter said, and Drago followed her eyes.

They waited between the pillars of their chamber, and Drago felt a knot of excitement form in his belly. The Questors were so powerful, and yet so benevolent in that power, that Drago felt privileged they allowed him to share their time.

"Drago," Barzula said as he and StarLaughter joined them. "How the children adore you." He smiled, and grasped Drago's hand.

"They are . . ." Drago searched for the right word, "so determined."

Barzula's smile faded. "Determined. Yes, as are we. Please, do sit down."

Drago had not had much opportunity to talk with the Questors since he'd arrived. StarLaughter had been his constant companion, and the Questors had kept largely to themselves.

He sat, with StarLaughter and her child, on the same couch he'd originally awoken on.

The Questors sat before him, ranged on a semi-circle of plain wooden chairs.

"We thought we would begin our return journey soon," Sheol said without preamble.

Drago breathed deep in excitement. Soon! "I cannot wait to return, to regain what I have lost."

"Nor can we," Mot said, rubbing his skeletal hands up and down his thin arms.

"What did the Enemy steal from you?" Drago asked. "It must be very valuable that you have hunted so long and so hard after it."

"Think *you* to steal it from us?" Raspu said, and everyone, including StarLaughter, grinned. "I would not counsel that at all."

"No, no, not at all. I was just curious. What *did* the Enemy steal from you?"

"Ah," Sheol said, and her face fell in sadness. "The Enemy stole something very precious from us. *Very* precious. We call it . . . we call it the Grail."

"Ah," said Drago, understanding. "Grail Lake, of course. What you hunt is buried beneath Grail Lake. Well, I can show you where that is."

"Thank you very much," said Barzula.

Drago missed the sarcasm. "But what *is* the Grail—"

"It is none of your concern," Rox said, and his voice was so heavy with threat that Drago recoiled. "The Grail is *ours*!"

"Of course. I was just curious—"

"Curiosity can be dangerous," Sheol said, her voice as implacable as her companion's. "Fatal."

"I will not steal what is yours," Drago said, his own anger stirring in the face of the threat. "Have I not had enough stolen from me not to wish further loss on you?"

In the blink of an eye the demeanor of the Questors altered. Friendliness and companionship radiated from each of them, and StarLaughter slipped an arm through Drago's, pulling him closer to her.

"We do not mean to doubt you," she said. "But what we all hunt is precious to us."

Drago let himself be soothed. "And I will have my blood order reversed and my power restored if I aid you?"

"Assuredly," Sheol said. "We can do that for you. All we need from you is to help us through the Star Gate."

"You will be so powerful," StarLaughter whispered against his ear, "that no-one will dare laugh at you or taunt you again."

Drago relaxed. "But I am concerned that you use my Icarii power to help you. What if you use it all up? I *need* that power, and I—"

"Be still." Sheol slipped from her chair, and Drago suddenly realized that all the Questors had stood, and were now surrounding him.

"We will leave you what you need," Sheol added. "Be very sure of that."

"Are you certain?" Drago started to rise, but hands clamped down on his shoulders and head, and he was forced back to the couch.

"This will only hurt a little," Sheol said, and then they began.

* * *

She was wrong. It felt like they tore his flesh apart and then ripped into his soul. He felt as if a hundred fish hooks had been sunk in his heels, and then pulled up through his body. As if a ravenous rat had been let loose in the spaces of his body and told to eat its fill. He felt himself explode so slowly he could count the particles of flesh as they skimmed by his eyes.

It hurt.

At no time did he lose consciousness. He sat, awake and aware, through the entire ordeal.

He wished for death. Nothing would be sweeter than death. Sweet, blissful, total annihilation.

He realized it was over when he became aware that the five Questors were back in their semi-circle of chairs, and Star-Laughter sat beside him. She stared at him curiously, her breast bared, its nipple hanging over the baby's unresponsive mouth.

He stared back at the Questors, unable to form any words, but wanting to know why . . . why had they done that?

"We have leapfrogged closer to the Star Gate," Sheol said, her voice echoing as if it came from behind an ice wall. "Look!" And she threw out a hand at the world beyond the pillars.

Slowly, every movement agony, Drago looked to where she pointed. At first he thought nothing had changed, but then he realized that the world beyond *had* altered. The trees were still there, but now they were so stunted they were barely shrubs. Now no mown lawns spread between them, but red, cracked desert. Now a silvery-white sky hung over them, and two giant red suns ebbed low on the horizon.

Pain throbbed through him, and Drago fought to remain conscious.

"Five more leaps and we will be there," Raspu said conversationally. "Do you think you will survive?"

38

Zenith Lost

StarDrifter walked slowly up the rise toward the Temple of the Stars, every step heavy with sadness. Not only for Zenith's problems, but also for RiverStar. News had reached him from visiting Icarii about her murder, and of Drago's involvement. And now apparently Drago had disappeared. Two granddaughters lost, and a grandson fled. What was happening to his family? StarDrifter wished his power could stretch as far as Sigholt so that he could see down its secretive corridors.

The Temple rose into the morning sky, a great violet beacon that speared into the clouds. Stars danced in its midst, but StarDrifter found little even in that beauty to comfort him these days.

She stood there, hands folded before her, her wings folded less than gracefully against her back, staring into the beacon.

"I wish I could step in there," she said, and sighed.

"No-one save Enchanters can enter the Temple," StarDrifter said unnecessarily. But Zenith could have entered. His granddaughter could have entered.

Niah had apparently lost whatever powers Zenith had enjoyed.

StarDrifter shivered. Maybe it was catching. Over the past few days he'd felt as though some of *his* power had slipped away, as well. It was more than perturbing.

Niah turned and smiled at him. "Oh, StarDrifter, it is enough that I am alive to see it. When I was First here it seemed an impossibility that the Icarii would ever return, or that the Star Gods would walk among us again. But here I am, and I am alive to see it, after all."

StarDrifter averted his eyes. She had been here five weeks, and in that time Zenith had not said a word, nor had StarDrifter seen her in an expression, or a single movement. Niah was in undisputed control of this body and this mind.

She said that she had always been Zenith, and Zenith her. That all that had happened was that "Zenith" had realized her true identity.

But StarDrifter did not believe that. He saw before him a completely different woman, different in movement, expression, and personality. If Zenith *had* been Niah all this time, then he should not have seen this massive change.

So if this entity occupying Zenith's body was not Zenith, then where was Zenith?

Niah walked about the Temple, beckoning StarDrifter to follow, and he somewhat reluctantly did so. In normal circumstances he knew he would have liked this woman, but not now. Not now she had destroyed or trapped his granddaughter.

Damn WolfStar to eternal night, StarDrifter thought, his expression remaining neutral, and damn Azhure with him for encouraging his obsession with Niah. Damn her for damning her own daughter.

Niah led him about the Temple and then down the grassy slope toward the southern cliffs. She stopped some twenty paces from them, adjusting her wings awkwardly in the stiff breeze.

"Lift them out for balance, as I have," StarDrifter said, and Niah glanced at his white wings extended part-way out behind him.

"I wish they would go away," she said. "I hate them. I cannot adjust to them."

And no doubt Zenith also finds it hard to adjust to whatever torment she has been subjected to, StarDrifter thought.

Without thinking he took one of Niah's wings in his hand, intending to lift it into position for her.

"Don't you dare touch me!" she hissed and spun away, almost overbalancing with the weight of her wings.

"I was only trying to help," StarDrifter said, keeping his voice even.

"I am sorry," Niah said stiffly. "It was concern for my baby only that made me speak so."

Her hands rested on her belly, and StarDrifter involuntarily glanced down at them. And curse that baby that had been got on Zenith's unwilling body.

StarDrifter knew Niah encouraged WolfStar back into her bed night after night. A feeling, a presentiment whenever the renegade Enchanter was with her, the expression on Niah's face in the morning, all told him that WolfStar visited her whenever he could.

StarDrifter felt sickened by it, but there was little he could do. He was powerless in the face of WolfStar's own ability, and he could hardly lock Niah up for taking a lover to her bed.

"I dreamed last night," Niah said unexpectedly after a few minutes' silence. She was staring out to sea, the wind whipping her black hair to tangle in the upper feathers of her wings.

"Yes?"

"I dreamed that I was trapped in a small chamber underground, so restricted I could not stretch my wings, could not fly. I called and screamed for help, but no-one heard."

She shivered. "No-one heard."

Niah turned her head and smiled at StarDrifter. "I must have been remembering when I was locked in death, don't you think? Awaiting rebirth. I was pleased when I awoke."

No, StarDrifter thought, that was Zenith calling for help, and you woke and trapped her into yet more darkness.

"Ah." Niah wrapped her arms about herself. "This breeze has grown cool. I shall go back to my quarters, I think, and perhaps find one of the priestesses to talk to."

"Do you resent not being First any longer?" StarDrifter asked suddenly.

Niah tipped her head back and laughed. "Oh no! I shall use this life for other purposes, methinks."

And then she was gone, and StarDrifter was left to watch her walk toward the Temple with eyes and heart smoldering with loss and resentment.

He flew, for Zenith's sake as much as his own. He lifted off the cliffs and soared sunward on the thermal rising from the combined heat of island and temple beacon.

It was only there, high in the sky with just the seagulls and the sun to observe, that he let himself cry. He had lost a granddaughter, yet still her body was paraded before him, *used,* to remind him every moment of his loss. She had been stolen, and abused in that stealing.

He soared higher and higher, until the island became only a speck far below him. Perhaps it was time to leave the island, find a different purpose in life. He could not bear staying to watch Niah give birth (and to *what*? An Enchanter? Surely, if Wolfstar fathered it, and if Zenith's Enchanter powers were latent in her body), or to watch WolfStar himself croon over the baby.

No, he should leave. Perhaps stay with FreeFall and EvenSong for a while in the Minaret Peaks. But that would be a useless life, and here at least he had some use.

I have failed her, he thought. I have failed Zenith. I should have been able to help her.

Slowly he spiraled downward, thinking only to secrete himself in his room for reflection, when he swept over the northern cliff face of the Mount. A cart had dropped off a visitor at the foot of the steps and she was now climbing upward.

Impelled by curiosity more than anything else, StarDrifter made another pass over the steps—and almost fell out of the sky in surprise.

Faraday stood there waving at him.

She climbed to the top and StarDrifter alighted before her, sweeping her into a great hug.

"StarDrifter!" Faraday laughed breathlessly, and pulled herself out of his grasp. "Whatever is it?"

She sobered as she saw the expression on StarDrifter's face. "What's wrong?"

He took a great, sobbing breath. "I've lost my granddaughter."

They shared tales in StarDrifter's quarters, Faraday sitting close to the Enchanter, holding his hand, comforting him.

"Is she lost or is she gone?" she asked eventually.

StarDrifter told her of Niah's dream. "I have to believe she is still there, Faraday."

Faraday smiled and patted StarDrifter's hand. "Well, if Zenith is lost we shall just have to find her again."

39

The Maze

SpikeFeather moored his boat to the dusty gray rock and studied the city before him. WingRidge had drawn a plan of the waterways, directing him to this cavern.

"Find a way down," WingRidge had said, and then remained obstinately silent.

What is it about the Icarii race, SpikeFeather thought irritably, that so predisposes us to mysteries? No doubt WingRidge thought there was value in making SpikeFeather toil in finding his way to this forgotten Maze, but SpikeFeather thought WingRidge could just as easily have told him directly.

He stood in one of the largest caverns in the waterways. It soared high above his head, so high SpikeFeather could not see its roof in this dimness, and extended so far back that Spike-

Feather was sure he could fly for an entire day and not reach its limits. Most of the cavern was taken up with an ancient city so old that the stone of walls and pavement had bleached into a colorless gray. Cracks webbed their way through wall and road alike, and rock dust lay thick over every flat surface and clung in damp draperies to the walls. The buildings were massive, fourteen, fifteen levels high, SpikeFeather guessed, and each level spacious enough to plant a field of grain in. Doors of petrified wood hung at odd angles, shutters lay in piles beneath windows and littered the roadways.

It was a place, not of death, but of nothingness. People (*who?*) had once lived, loved, laughed and died here. But there was nothing left. Nothing to remember them by save these memory-less buildings. The entire purpose of their existence had been lost forever.

SpikeFeather shook himself out of his maudlin thoughts. He reached into the boat and drew out a dry brand—Orr had insisted he always carry a torch with him in case he found the need to explore the caverns. Well, now SpikeFeather had the need. He lit the brand and, carrying it high, walked into the city.

Down, WingRidge had said, so SpikeFeather walked slowly through the streets, looking for an entrance to a cellar, or steps leading down . . . *something*. But no matter how hard he looked, and how many buildings he explored, he found no trapdoors or stairwells.

Down. But how? Only the need to find Orr and to explain his terror kept SpikeFeather looking even when tiredness began to slow his steps. He did not know how far he'd wandered through the city, or how much time had passed, when he came upon a curious symbol scratched into the pavement.

It was a diagram of a knot—a maze.

It was the same symbol that the Lake Guard wore on their tunics.

SpikeFeather squatted down and studied the symbol. It showed a stylized maze, a walled circular center space with twists of corridors about it, eventually leading, once the dead ends had been negotiated, to an exit. SpikeFeather looked at the exit, then looked to where it pointed. There was an alleyway leading away from the main street.

SpikeFeather stood and walked down the alleyway. Some seventy paces down he found another symbol scratched into the pavement, and this time the exit from the maze pointed down a wide avenue.

SpikeFeather followed the sign until he found another symbol, and another, and then another.

He paused, and looked about. He was back in a street that he knew he'd been down hours ago—and yet there had not been a symbol here then. And look! The next indicated street was another that he'd previously explored. He realized he was retracing his steps, and the maze symbols also crisscrossed each other, so he was partly retracing the original pathway the symbols had told him to take.

SpikeFeather stood and thought. Lost? Misled? Or something else?

He remembered something Orr had taught him. The waterways formed patterns in the same way that sung music did. Were the symbols leading him in a complicated dance? Were the patterns he formed with his steps a kind of magical dance—an enchantment?

Yes, yes, that was it. The symbols were forcing him to form a pattern, and when that pattern was completed . . .

SpikeFeather hurried down the street indicated. Now that he knew what was happening he did not hesitate. He felt rejuvenated, excited. How much longer before he completed the pattern—the enchantment—that would show him the Maze?

As it turned out, not long. Three more symbols, three more turns, and the enchantment slipped into place.

SpikeFeather walked into a large rectangular stone-flagged market area, an area he had crossed four times already in his quest for the Maze. But this time there was something different. This time almost all the stone flagging had disappeared to make way for a massive set of stairs leading down, down, down.

"Down," SpikeFeather whispered, and began his descent.

He climbed down the wide, winding stairwell until his legs screamed in protest. This was longer and more arduous than any of the stairwells SpikeFeather had traveled in order to reach the waterways from the Overworld. The incline of the stairwell was deceptively mild, but after hours of traveling and turning, SpikeFeather had learned to curse it.

He stopped, paused, and laughed wryly to himself. What was he doing? Had his years with Orr fuddled him so completely he'd forgotten his wings?

Still smiling ruefully, SpikeFeather spread his almost-forgotten wings and spiraled down the stairwell.

In two turns he came to the end, and he wondered if he'd passed some kind of test.

There was a high corridor, extending perhaps some hundred paces before him. It was lined with columns carved with strange picture symbols that SpikeFeather glanced at but did not pause to investigate. He strode down the corridor, through the archway at its end, and stopped . . . stunned into complete immobility.

He stood at the lip of yet another staircase, but he could well see where this one led. Before him spread a city—but it was more than a city. It was also a maze. A labyrinth. And it was massive beyond comprehension.

There was a wall, some thirty paces high, that ran about it, but directly before SpikeFeather, at the foot of the staircase, was a gate.

SpikeFeather walked slowly down the stairs. Like everything else associated with this Maze, the gate was huge. It stood twenty paces high, and ten across. It was arched with great blocks of stone guarding twin closed doors of solid wood. There were no handles, no locks. SpikeFeather cautiously laid a hand on one of the doors and pushed.

It did not budge . . . but the instant that he'd laid his hand on the wood SpikeFeather had felt rather than heard a distant tinkle.

As if glass had broken.

SpikeFeather was no fool, and Orr had taught him well. He knew what that was. These gates had been warded. An enchantment had been laid over them to warn someone if they were touched.

Warn who?

Warn of what?

SpikeFeather spun about, unsure what to do. Should he run? Get out? Should he—

"Well, well. I always thought it would be Caelum who found this Maze," said a voice, "or at the very least Axis."

WolfStar SunSoar stepped down from the arch of the corridor. "But, no. It is SpikeFeather TrueSong. The Ferryman's apprentice. A birdman with no business here at all. What do you do here, birdman?"

40

The Maze Gate's Message

"How did you find this place?" WolfStar said, walking down the steps.

"The Lake Guard drew me a diagram."

WolfStar stopped on the last step and raised his eyebrows. "The Lake Guard? But they were ever sworn to secrecy regarding this place."

"They are afraid that the Grail King stirs."

"What?"

WolfStar rocked badly enough to make him almost lose his balance. Then, in a movement so fast it was a blur, he was on top of SpikeFeather, a hand buried in the cloth of his tunic, another in SpikeFeather's hair. *"What?"*

"The Grail King in the Maze," SpikeFeather forced out between teeth clenched in fear. "Qeteb. The Maze. That is all I know."

Qeteb? he wondered amid his fear. Was that the name of the Grail King? Of whatever was trapped in the Maze?

"And how is it that *you* know these things, SpikeFeather TrueSong? You are an apprentice Ferryman," WolfStar spat the phrase with unconcealed disgust, "and not even an Enchanter. You have no right to know these things, nor to be standing before the Maze itself!"

As briefly and as quickly as he could, SpikeFeather told WolfStar of the message—and the terror—Orr had passed across to him.

"I have been looking for Orr as much as the Maze, WolfStar. Do . . . do you think he might be in there?"

Despite WolfStar's still fierce grip, SpikeFeather managed to tilt his head slightly toward the Maze.

"In there?" WolfStar let SpikeFeather go and the birdman relaxed. "In the Maze? No, I do not think so. He would not be able to enter. Caelum is the only one who can."

"Caelum?"

WolfStar ignored the question. "I need to retrieve the memory of the night Orr sent you that message, SpikeFeather. Be still . . . this will not hurt."

WolfStar buried his hand in SpikeFeather's hair again, holding him still. The Enchanter initiated the Song of Recall, faltered, then recovered, and SpikeFeather felt the memory of Orr's terror and words sear up through his mind.

Strangely, for SpikeFeather had thought WolfStar lied, the enchantment did not pain him in the slightest. The sensation was unusual, but not unpleasant. The memory of Orr's words and emotions tumbled through his mind, and he could feel WolfStar playing with them, reviewing them from every angle and, SpikeFeather shivered, traveling back down the memory to its source.

To the Star Chamber.

"Stars!" WolfStar cried, and again let SpikeFeather go.

SpikeFeather stumbled, but as he caught his balance WolfStar cried, "Look!"

Before them the gray haze of the vision appeared. In it Orr

struggled at the very lip of the Star Gate with Drago SunSoar. Both were shouting, struggling for possession of something wrapped about with an old cloth of strange shifting colors . . .

WolfStar groaned and sank to his knees. SpikeFeather, dragging his eyes away from the vision for an instant, could not believe the horror on the Enchanter's face. *What was it that so terrified Orr and WolfStar alike?*

"He has the Rainbow Scepter," WolfStar mumbled. "That carrion bastard Drago has the Scepter!"

Orr had his hand about the smooth wood of the rod.

"It speaks to Orr," WolfStar said tonelessly. "The Scepter acted as a conduit for the power of the Maze. The Maze was the source of the knowledge and the words, SpikeFeather. Not Orr. Orr knew nothing of this place or what it contained."

"The Scepter spoke to—?"

"It must be terrified. Look, see how they struggle! The Scepter has passed the terror to Orr, and he to you. Oh, mercy! Drago, I should have killed you myself!" WolfStar lowered himself into a crouch, almost as if he thought to spring into the vision itself.

Now Drago had pushed Orr away, and he spun the Scepter about his head. The cloths had fallen off it, and rainbow light spun about the chamber.

Then, amid the violent struggle, the Scepter came crashing down on Orr's head, and the Ferryman collapsed on the floor.

"No!" SpikeFeather cried, and reached uselessly into the vision.

"Yes!" WolfStar said. "See how practiced Drago has become at murder? He tried with Caelum, succeeded with RiverStar and see how he now does Orr to death!"

Orr breathed his last, and with that the vision faded.

But not before WolfStar had caught a glimpse of the red doe watching from the pillars. *Faraday?*

WolfStar slowly straightened from his crouch. Had Faraday seen what happened next?

"Did Drago step through the Star Gate with that Scepter?" WolfStar asked no-one in particular. "Did he?"

"WolfStar, what is happening? Is Orr dead? What *is* this Maze? WolfStar, *tell me what is happening!*"

WolfStar's eyes slowly focused on SpikeFeather's face. "Well, why not. The Maze itself seemed to want you to find it. Perhaps the Lake Guard were right to trust you. Yes, Orr is dead—"

SpikeFeather wailed.

"Oh, stop your grieving! He had outlived his time and has at least performed one valuable service in relaying the Scepter's warning."

"WolfStar! Tell me what is—"

"If you will be quiet for more than one moment then I will!" WolfStar took a deep breath. "Good. Now, this Maze has stood here for many thousands of years. Tens of thousands of years. Until I told the children who have grown into the Lake Guard, none knew about it save I. Not even Orr or any other Charonite."

"Did you learn of it beyond the Star Gate? Is it one of the mysteries you brought back with you from the dead?"

WolfStar thought about again rebuking SpikeFeather for the interruption, but decided against it. "In a sense you are right, for I first learned of the Maze beyond the Star Gate. The Maze itself managed to reach me—I know not how—and inducted me into certain knowledges. Largely it was the Maze's power that enabled me to come back."

"And you have kept its secrets since you returned? For three thousand years?"

WolfStar nodded.

"Then why show the children I rescued from Talon Spike? Why did they become the Lake Guard?"

WolfStar frowned, for he knew there was something between the Maze and the Lake Guard he was not privy to. "The Maze asked to see them, and so I brought them here."

"Yet Orr, as all the other Charonites, never knew of the Maze?"

WolfStar was growing tired of the incessant questioning—why did the Maze need to see *this* irritating birdman of all people?

"They were not required to attend the Maze, SpikeFeather, and thus it never informed them of its presence."

WolfStar's mouth curved in secret amusement. "Did you realize that we stand directly under the Grail Lake? This cavern lies far below the depths of the lake."

SpikeFeather looked startled, his eyes darting nervously upward as if he expected to see faint trails of moisture seeping down the cavern roof far above.

"SpikeFeather, did you have a chance to examine the gate itself?"

WolfStar walked to the stone arches surrounding the gates, SpikeFeather a step behind him. As he got closer, SpikeFeather saw that the stone was covered in the same strange characters as the columns in the corridor leading to the Maze had been.

WolfStar glanced at SpikeFeather. "Can you read them?"

"No, I can't . . . no, wait. This, and this . . . they are pictorial representations of . . ."

"Ideas and conceptions, SpikeFeather. The ancients wrote in language that did not use letters as we know them, but actually drew different symbols to impart ideas. If you remember that, then the translation does not become too difficult, although it will take you some months to master it fully. But for now I shall translate. See, the inscription starts here."

WolfStar squatted by the foot of the arch, his finger tracing upward, and began to read. The Gate told of a time when four craft from a world very far away crashed into Tencendor, so long ago that the land had a different and now long-forgotten name. The creatures within the craft had died, but the craft had survived, burying themselves into the land, the depressions they created eventually forming the Sacred Lakes.

"The waters of these lakes borrowed an infinitesimally tiny amount of the residual power left from the crafts' impact, but enough to make them deeply magical. The true magic, however, lay far deeper under the waters."

WolfStar paused, knowing SpikeFeather was not ready for it all, yet.

But then, who was?

No, there were others who needed to know first—yet even before he told them. WolfStar needed to discover if the vision had been correct, if Drago had truly stolen the Rainbow Scepter.

"The craft contained various items," WolfStar said. "Items that the creatures who had originally driven the craft had . . . appropriated . . . from some others. I am afraid that these others will one day come back for them."

And if the shit-rotted Drago *had* gone through the Star Gate with the Scepter then they might very well be on the move now.

WolfStar stilled, a frightful coldness creeping over him. Over these past few weeks he had noted an annoying weakness in his power. Not much, just a trifle, but it was there. Witness the minor problem he'd just had with the Song of Recall. Was it because . . .? No! No! It could not be!

Gods, but he needed to know what was happening!

"WolfStar? WolfStar?"

WolfStar broke out of his reverie. "Yes?"

"If these 'others' come back, WolfStar, do we let them take what is theirs?"

WolfStar slowly shook his head. "No. No, we do *not* let them take what they want. We fight until Tencendor itself is charcoal, if necessary, but we do not let them take what is theirs. Look." WolfStar pointed to a symbol above the cornerstone of the arch. It was a star, surmounted by a sun.

WolfStar smiled gently. "StarSon."

"The Lake Guard said they owed their loyalty to the StarSon."

"Yes, they would protect him above all else."

"Why did you say only Caelum could enter this Maze? And why is StarSon mentioned on this archway?"

WolfStar thought very hard, then decided a portion of the truth would not hurt. "SpikeFeather, the Rainbow Scepter is made partly from the power of the Mother, but in great part it uses as its power the energy of the four craft themselves. The energy that powered the craft also enlivens the Scepter. The Scepter is very closely tied to the craft, with what the craft protect, and is thus closely tied to this Maze which is an outgrowth of one of the craft. Axis SunSoar used the Scepter to destroy Gorgrael, but he used only a tiny proportion of its power to do that. SpikeFeather, I believe the Scepter can also be used, if need be, to destroy what lies at the heart of the Maze."

"And StarSon?"

"I believe StarSon is the only one who can wield it. Caelum . . . I have always loved that boy, but when I knew also how he, or his descendants, might protect Tencendor against the horrors that seep through the Star Gate, my love grew three-fold."

WolfStar suddenly turned around and stared furiously at SpikeFeather. "And now that *carrion* has stolen the Rainbow Scepter! Has he also taken it through to the TimeKeepers? Has *he*?"

Before SpikeFeather could form any answer, WolfStar disappeared, leaving behind him as many questions as he had answered.

Most particularly, SpikeFeather realized, he had carefully steered the conversation away from the subject of the Grail King and Qeteb.

41

A Town Gained, a Scepter Lost

"He's *what?*" Caelum whispered.

"Taken Kastaleon?" Askam shouted, rising, from his chair.

The captain shifted uncomfortably. "He argues it is in part compensation for the losses your trading tariffs have caused him and Western Tencendor, my Prince. But," the captain moved his gaze back to Caelum, "he says he will hand Kastaleon back if the StarSon is prepared to negotiate on the matters that Prince Zared raised when he was here for Council."

"How could you have lost Kastaleon?" Askam said. He cared not for whatever message Zared had sent.

"My Prince, I had no reason to suspect that the Prince of the North meant to seize the castle. I greeted him in the courtyard with the respect he is due, and instead found myself invaded. StarSon," again he looked to Caelum, "I did not realize we were at war with the North."

"Neither did I," Caelum muttered. "How many men did Zared have with him?"

"Perhaps five hundred, StarSon. Only lightly armored."

Caelum looked to Askam, still red-faced and upset. "Is Kastaleon stocked and weaponed for a siege, Askam?"

"What? Oh, ah . . . no. It could stand a few weeks, perhaps. But not long, and not with only a few hundred men."

Caelum looked back to the captain. "Thank you, Captain. You are dismissed. But do not leave Sigholt yet. I have no doubt that Askam will demand a few more answers from you than I have."

The captain nodded unhappily. He bowed to Caelum and then Askam, and left the map-room.

Caelum sat silent, needing a few minutes to think. By the Stars! What had driven Zared to act so?

"It is Rivkah's bad blood," Askam said in an undertone. "First Borneheld, and now Zared."

Caelum looked up sharply. "You forget that I carry Rivkah's blood, too."

Askam flushed. "My apologies, StarSon. But Borneheld tore this land to pieces in his quest for the throne of Achar. Committed murder to do so. Zared now appears intent on doing the same."

"I never thought he would go this far," Caelum said, looking tired and worried. "Taking over Kastaleon? What did he think he would accomplish?"

"My Lord, I request formal permission to lead a force to retake my castle."

"No, no. Let us think this through a moment, Askam."

"My Lord—"

"Askam, I am *not* going to rush into an ill-considered response. Now, sit."

Caelum turned his face slightly to one side as Askam sat down. What worried him the most was what Zared might be prepared to do next—and who might be prepared to support him in it. FreeFall and Yllgaine would never support Zared's rebellion—for that is what it was—but what about the human peoples in their territories? Did Zared have good reason to act so precipitously? Caelum remembered Yllgaine saying he'd heard murmurs from among the humans regarding the throne.

"Askam, *did* Zared have a point about the peoples in the West and North murmuring that they wanted their throne restored to them?"

"No, I have never heard a word about it," Askam said, but Caelum noticed that he spoke too quickly and would not look him in the eyes.

Caelum dropped his gaze again, thinking. Askam would

have good reason to deny that his people were agitating for a restored Acharite king.

Were the human peoples truly muttering about needing a king of their own?

Caelum repressed a shiver. If the people were willing to back Zared there was so much else a King of Achar could restore as well. The hatreds and divisions between the Icarii and the Avar and the Acharites. How well *had* the humans accepted the return of the Icarii and Avar into southern Tencendor? Not well, if they wanted their own monarch back. And if they wanted their king back, then what else might they consider resurrecting? The Seneschal? A limited war to wrest lands back from the Avar and Icarii?

This time Caelum did shiver. He could all too easily envision a King of Achar leading to another Wars of the Axe and the eventual destruction of Tencendor. Another thousand years of hatreds and bleakness and exile.

How could Zared even *think* of asking for the throne of Achar? Didn't he realize the implications? Or did he realize only too well? What else did Zared have planned? A request for the Minstrelsea to be leveled once he had the circlet of king firmly on his brow?

Caelum took a deep breath. This was not just a crisis, but a test. The first real test of his reign. All Tencendor would be watching to see how he coped.

What would his father have done?

"We have to act," Caelum said, and Askam jerked his head up from his own contemplations.

"How so, StarSon?"

Caelum did not answer immediately, but rose from his chair, walked to the door, and asked the guard to request Strike Leader DareWing FullHeart to attend him immediately.

"Caelum? What do you plan?" Askam said as Caelum walked back and sat down again.

Caelum looked at him, and Askam was stunned to see

what appeared to be fear in his eyes. "I plan to quash Zared once and for all," Caelum said quietly. This is what Axis would have done. "His push for power represents too many evils for me to watch it go by quietly. My father battled for years to reunite Tencendor in the face of Acharite opposition. I cannot lose it for him in just one generation."

There was a movement at the door, and the Strike Leader entered.

"Ah, DareWing, sit down."

DareWing, a birdman with sharp brown eyes and saffron wings, sat himself opposite Caelum. "StarSon?"

Caelum briefed DareWing on the situation. "I have to act, DareWing. I cannot let this pass."

"I agree, StarSon, but surely—"

"*Damn it!* I cannot believe he would do this!" Caelum said. "Not with all the old hatreds so fresh in our minds. Well, if he has attacked *us,* then we shall attack him. DareWing, ready the Strike Force."

DareWing shot an anxious glance at Askam, but Askam's own face was lit with excitement, and DareWing knew he'd have to fight this on his own.

"StarSon, would it not be better to ask the advice of the other Five Families?"

"No time to call them, Strike Leader. I shall have to rely on my own judgment."

DareWing took a deep breath. Gods! "Perhaps the StarMan."

"*I* sit the Throne of the Stars, DareWing! My father has little to do with the world of mortals. This is *my* decision!"

DareWing tried one last time. "StarSon, at least discuss this with a wider circle. To use the Strike Force to attack humans in Kastaleon—well, nothing could be more guaranteed to provoke old hatreds."

"Ah," Caelum said tonelessly, "I do not intend to throw you at Kastaleon, DareWing. I want you and your Strike Force to take Severin for me."

"But—"

"Seize it as Zared has seized Kastaleon."

"But—"

"Do it, DareWing! I want to see your battle plans this evening! Now, leave us!"

DareWing rose stiffly and bowed.

"DareWing," Caelum added as the Strike Leader walked to the door.

"Yes?"

"I want no word of this to get out. Severin *must* be taken by surprise."

DareWing nodded curtly, and left.

"A city for your castle, my friend," Caelum said. "I intend to grind Zared into the dust for his stupidity. For this piece of foolishness Zared will lose his seat of power."

"Good." Askam sat back. "You will not negotiate with Zared? You are not considering his rash request?"

Caelum grimaced. "A King of Achar is the very last thing that Tencendor or I need, Askam. Rest easy, your lands will be safe. I shall send word that I request Zared to stay at Kastaleon while I summon the other Heads of the Five Families to meet at the castle to discuss the throne—peace, Askam! I simply do not want Zared moving anywhere else until *I've* had time to move. If he believes I'm prepared to negotiate he'll stay in Kastaleon."

Caelum smiled grimly. "By the time I've finished with him, no-one will support him."

"When do we ride for Kastaleon, StarSon?"

"As soon as DareWing sends word that he has secured Severin. A few days, no more. And within a month, Askam, no-one will want to offer Zared so much as an apple in case it be construed as support."

DareWing FullHeart led the Strike Force himself, saddened beyond measure that the StarSon had asked him to do this. Severin was a lovely town, bustling and open-hearted. It had no idea of the forthcoming attack, no reason to expect it.

DareWing did not lead the full twelve Wings of the Strike Force. Severin would offer no resistance, and six Wings would do as well as twelve.

Besides, once word of this filtered through Tencendor, who knew where else the Strike Force would be required? Damn Caelum for reacting this savagely, DareWing thought, *damn him!* Why couldn't he have talked with Zared first? Surely this could have been solved around the negotiating table?

But he obeyed anyway. Not to do so would be worse than complying with his order.

DareWing attacked, if such a maneuver could be called attack, at dawn. The townsfolk were only just waking up, and most were still fogged by sleep. The militia were cold after a night's watch—and, DareWing noted, were sparse anyway. Zared must have moved most of his forces farther south.

No-one offered much resistance. The six Wings dropped out of the dawning sun, subduing the watch with virtually no bloodshed. As had been the case in Kastaleon, the watch assumed that the Icarii dropping out of the sky were on a friendly, if puzzling, mission and did not offer any resistance until too late.

Once the militia were subdued, DareWings ordered guards be placed at the main roadways, public buildings, and informed the mayor personally that for the moment Severin was under martial law. StarSon Caelum's martial law.

"What?" the mayor spluttered over his eggs and toast. *"Why?"*

"You have not heard what Zared has done?" DareWing asked.

"No." But the mayor narrowed his gaze, and DareWing wondered if he had guessed.

"He has seized Kastaleon from Prince Askam, claiming it as compensation for the people of the West and North. As reprisal, Caelum has ordered Severin seized."

"He can't do that!"

"Nevertheless," DareWing said, "he has. Now, I require a tour of the town and what fortifications and weapon stores it has. Immediately, if you please."

The mayor pushed aside his toast and eggs and stood up. As he did so he glanced at his wife hovering in the kitchen doorway. She nodded slightly, and backed silently into the kitchen.

"This way," the mayor said, and pushed past DareWing to the front door.

"Severin is taken," the farflight scout reported to Caelum, standing in Sigholt's central courtyard.

"Good," Caelum said, and turned to Askam. "Then we ride for Kastaleon in the morning. Will we be able to get there before word reaches Zared of the Strike Force's action?"

"Yes, StarSon. Severin is slightly closer to Kastaleon as the raven flies, but we can use the river transports on the Nordra. They await us at Gundealga Ford as I speak."

"Good, then see to the final preparations."

Caelum strode back inside Sigholt, irritated at his inner uncertainty. He *knew* he was doing the right thing. Surely. What else could he do? Negotiate with Zared over the throne of Achar? Never! A king of Achar would only ferment the hatreds of the past.

But would Zared do such a thing? Did he not say that he only wanted to create a ceremonial position?

"No," Caelum muttered aloud as he strode along the corridors toward his private apartments. "If not Zared then his son, or his great-grandson. I cannot allow even the seeds to be sown, let alone watch the harvest ripen into despair."

Caelum opened the door to his apartments, and stopped short in shock. "*WolfStar!*"

He slowly closed the door behind him. "Why are you here, WolfStar? Is it the children? Are they closer?"

"No," WolfStar said shortly and far too sharply, and gestured impatiently. "Caelum, where did your father secrete the Rainbow Scepter?"

"Is that for you to know. WolfStar?"

"Tell me!" WolfStar stepped forward.

Caelum stiffened, but held his ground. "The Rainbow Scepter is none of your—"

"Confound your objections, boy! I oversaw its birth!"

"But the Scepter was my father's, and through him, mine, and I would know why it is you want to see it."

WolfStar breathed deeply, tendons standing out on his neck. "Yes, you are correct—the Rainbow Scepter *is* yours by right and, by the Stars! I hope you will have the chance to use it!"

Caelum frowned, but WolfStar went on.

"I want to see it, Caelum StarSon, because I have every reason to believe it is no longer here."

"What?"

"I think Drago has stolen it. I am sure of it."

"No," Caelum whispered. "No. It cannot be!"

Zared's treachery had pushed Drago from Caelum's mind over the past few days. He'd had patrols out looking for his brother, and had sent word throughout Tencendor for everyone to be on the watch for him, but no-one had heard or seen anything.

Now his nightmare came rushing back, and for an instant Caelum felt himself impaled at the end of DragonStar's sword. *Had he seized the Rainbow Scepter?*

Was that the cry of the hunt he could hear?

How would Drago manage to seize the Scepter?

Was that the thunder of the black horseman in the distance?

If Drago had it, what could he do with it?

"Caelum!" WolfStar said, and seized Caelum by the elbow, shaking him. "Where is it hidden?"

Caelum struggled with, and then mastered, his unreasoning fear. "Come with me," he said, and led WolfStar into the corridor. They moved down until they reached a smaller hallway branching off to the left. It had several doors either side, but Caelum ignored them.

He walked to the end of the hall, and stopped at a wall of gray stone.

"Where?" WolfStar said.

Caelum did not answer, but instead hummed a snatch of music. He waited, frowning, then hummed it again.

"What—?" he began, but before he could say any more the wall shimmered, then dissolved, revealing a small chamber.

WolfStar glanced sharply at Caelum, but for the moment he walked silently into the chamber. It was bare, save for red-plastered walls and a small window high in one wall. The oakwood floor revealed no trapdoors.

"Where?" he repeated.

Again Caelum did not answer, but again hummed a melody. This time he did not have to repeat it.

A shelf appeared on the back wall, and on that shelf was a beautifully worked silver casket.

"My father had this made to house the Scepter," Caelum said. "He meant to study it, explore it, but it always reminded him so much of Faraday's death he never did."

He paused, the casket in his arms, and looked at WolfStar. "Drago could *never* have stolen the Scepter," he said. "The enchantments that hide this casket are powerful indeed."

Enough for you to falter over, thought WolfStar. Or is there something else wrong, Caelum? Why stumble so badly?

"Open it," he said.

"No-one knew of these enchantments save my father and myself," Caelum said, delaying the inevitable. "No-one knew where the Scepter—"

"Open it!"

Caelum's eyes dropped. He took a deep breath, then the fingers of his right hand pressed into a secret catch on the side of the casket.

The lid sprung open.

Revealing nothing but the scarlet, silk-lined interior.

The Scepter was gone.

"Stars!" Caelum cried, and for an instant he could almost *feel* the tip of the sword slicing through his chest, *feel* the taste of Drago's bloody malevolence in his mouth.

"WolfStar . . . WolfStar, there is *no* way that Drago could have stolen this! No way! He can't—"

"Nevertheless, the fact is he *has*!"

WolfStar stood thinking, shifting a little from foot to foot, then faced Caelum with such a look of dread that Caelum's stomach clenched.

"My boy," WolfStar said very softly. "Over the past weeks, has your power remained untainted? At full strength? You needed to try that enchantment twice to enter this chamber . . ."

"There has been a minor disturbance. But I thought it only because I have been so concerned with my cares that I—"

"By all the stars in heaven," WolfStar whispered, his face blanching, "it *has* begun!"

And then he vanished.

Caelum stood, alternatively looking helplessly at the spot where WolfStar had vanished and at the empty cache.

What did WolfStar mean, "It has begun"? And what should *he* do?

For a very long time Caelum stood there, the empty casket in his arms, not knowing what to think or do next.

How had Drago managed to get in?

What could he do with the Scepter?

"Gods," Caelum eventually whispered, his face ashen. "It *has* begun again. Drago has set his sights on my murder, it seems. Where are you, Drago? What do you plan?"

Did he ever dare sleep again?

WolfStar strode through the archways surrounding the Star Gate chamber, startling the two Enchanters standing watch there into anxious exclamation.

"Oh, be quiet!" WolfStar snapped, "I am not here to eat you!"

He walked to the Star Gate and stood silently, wrapping his golden wings about him, cocooning himself against the terror he half expected to be rushing toward it from the other side.

But there was nothing.

Nothing save the whispers of the children.

We're coming . . . we're coming, WolfStar!

"They're closer," one of the Enchanters dared to say. Both of them had backed a safe distance away.

WolfStar shot her a furious look, but she was right. They *were* closer. Significantly closer.

But still far away, WolfStar tried to reassure himself. Besides, it was not the children that so worried him.

Was there a hint of anything *else* approaching the Star Gate?

WolfStar bent his entire power and concentration to the task. Listening, feeling, probing.

But even WolfStar's power, extensive as it was, was not enough to feel anything else.

Was it because there *was* nothing else?

Or was it because . . . they . . . were using the approach of the children to mask their own approach?

WolfStar shuddered. He didn't know whether the slight diminution in his own power—and it *was* only slight—had any real connection with those who waited beyond the Star Gate. WolfStar didn't even know if Drago had gone through the Star Gate. Had he murdered Orr, then fled back down one of the passageways in terror? Was he lurking in the waterways somewhere? *Where was the Rainbow Scepter?*

The red doe. Faraday. *She* had been here. She would know.

WolfStar tried to concentrate, tried to think it through. If—and only if—Drago had gone through, then would he have survived? Unlikely. But even if he had snapped out of existence, that left the Rainbow Scepter floating lost amid the stars . . . lost for any who cared to pick it up and make use of it.

"We need that Scepter," WolfStar murmured. "Caelum—*Tencendor!*—has no chance without it. None!"

Confound that piece of rotting carrion! *What had happened?* And what if . . . they . . . were approaching behind the children?

What should he do?

He needed far more power to scry them out than he commanded. "The power of the Circle," he said to the puzzled Enchanters.

And he needed to know if Drago had gone through the Star Gate, or if the Rainbow Scepter was still in Tencendor.

"Faraday," WolfStar said, and vanished yet again.

The two Enchanters looked at each other, shaken beyond measure at the renegade Enchanter's visit, and wondered what *they* should do.

42

ForestFlight's Betrayal

Zared narrowed his eyes against the late afternoon sun and stared into the sky. A stiff northerly breeze, redolent with frost, ruffled his black hair. He shivered and pulled his cloak closer. An Icarii approached from the north-west, his wings shuddering with the effort of coping with the wind.

"He is not armed," Herme murmured by Zared's side. They stood atop Kastaleon's walls, awaiting Caelum's reaction. Indecision? Action? Retreat? They knew not what, and the unknowing was driving all to short tempers.

"Even *I* could deal with a single armed Icarii," Zared said.

"Of course," Herme soothed. "I did not mean—"

"I know you did not," Zared said, dropping his eyes from the Icarii momentarily. "I apologize for my tone, Herme."

Herme nodded, accepting the apology. They had heard nothing for . . . what? It was over two weeks since they'd taken this isolated pile of stones. In that time Caelum could have done anything.

The Icarii circled lower and one of the guards called out a challenge.

The Icarii answered, his words lost in the wind for Zared and Herme, but the guard waved the Icarii toward where they stood.

"It's one of the Lake Guard," Zared said, every muscle in his body tensing as the Icarii dropped down toward him.

"Caelum's answer," Herme said, laying a hand on the hilt of his sword, even though the birdman was unarmed. "They wouldn't fly about Tencendor for anyone else."

"Hail, Prince Zared," said the Icarii, landing gracefully some two or three paces away from them. He was a striking birdman, with brilliant blue plumage and eyes and luminous white skin. "My name is ForestFlight EverSoar, and I—"

"You come from Caelum?" Zared said shortly.

"Indeed, my Prince. He has instructed me to greet you well in his name, and to—"

"Oh, get on with it, man!"

"My Prince, StarSon has instructed me to say that while he abhors your actions, he has reluctantly conceded that talks on the throne of Achar must proceed. Accordingly he bids that you wait here until he can summon the other Heads of the Five in Council at Kastaleon."

Zared looked at the Icarii carefully. "He is summoning a Council to meet here?"

"At this very moment, my Prince," ForestFlight said, unblinking.

Zared looked to Herme. "Well?"

Herme chewed his lip. "You seem to have startled him

into some good sense, Zared. Although, gods knows, Askam must be furious."

Zared nodded. "Well, nothing for it but to wait for the Council to arrive, I suppose. ForestFlight, I thank you, please avail yourself of the hospitality of Kastaleon before you leave. ForestFlight? You may leave. Now."

ForestFlight stood his ground.

"Go, birdman!" Herme snapped, sliding his hand back around the hilt of his sword.

"Of course, there is that which Caelum very carefully instructed me *not* to tell you," ForestFlight began.

Zared and Herme stilled. "Yes?" Zared said.

"StarSon would very much like you *not* to know that eight days ago six Wing of the Strike Force took Severin, nor would he like you to know that even as I speak he and Prince Askam lead a force down the Nordra to retake Kastaleon and take you, the Duke of Aldeni and the Earl of Avonsdale into custody prior to your trial for high treason against the Star Throne. And we all know, do we not, Sir Prince, how well Caelum conducts trials."

Zared could hardly breathe. He stared at ForestFlight, standing perfectly calm before him, and he struggled to come to terms with what the birdman had just declared. "Severin is taken?"

"Yes, my Prince. It has been sealed, no-one can leave. That is why you have not heard."

"And Caelum is leading a force to Kastaleon? How many? Where are they now?"

"Some five thousand, Prince Zared. And barring shoals and accidents, they will land during the dark hours of tomorrow morning. His message is a lie. Caelum is determined that the throne of Achar will never be resurrected."

Zared stepped forward and took the Icarii's chin in his hand. "And why are you telling me this, ForestFlight?" he said softly. "Why should I trust you? Is not your complete loyalty to the StarSon?"

ForestFlight wrenched his chin away from Zared's grasp.

"I answer to no-one save my captain," he said. "WingRidge gives me my orders. I do not know why he requested I tell you this. You may believe me or not, as you choose."

And with that he leaped into the air with a powerful beat of his wings. Zared grabbed at him, but missed. He cursed, then put a hand on Herme's arm.

"No, my friend. Do not shout to the guard. Their arrows would never hit him now, and nor would I want them to."

"My Prince? What do you think we should do? Was that a false message from Caelum?"

"I don't know. But can we afford to ignore it? And Severin? *Taken?*" Gods! He'd not expected that of Caelum! Zared felt guilt bite deep that an innocent town suffered for his ambition.

There was a shout from the courtyard below. They looked down. Theod stood there, beckoning urgently. By his side stood a trader Zared recognized from Jannymire Goldman's coterie.

"Luck? Or design?" Zared muttered, but stepped onto the ladder anyway.

"Severin was taken over a week ago," the trader, Bormot Kilckman, said bluntly.

"And how do you know—" Zared began, his voice roughened with frustration, when Kilckman thrust a cage at him. Inside was a small, gray pigeon.

Zared recognized it instantly. "Mayor Iniscue's bird," he said softly, then explained to Herme and Theod. "Mayor Insicue's wife keeps a score of these courier birds, trained to fly to various locations."

"This one landed at Carlon two days ago," Kilckman explained. "It had a message tube attached with the bare fact of Severin's capture inside. I caught the next riverboat for Kastaleon."

Zared looked to the skies again, half expecting to see ForestFlight still circling above. But he was long gone . . .

back to the StarSon he apparently served so badly. There was nothing there save dark clouds scudding in from the north-west.

Bad weather, then.

"So Severin is indeed lost," Herme said. "Is then Caelum a few bare hours away?"

"What?" exclaimed Theod.

Zared ignored him for the moment. "We must assume so, Herme. I cannot afford not to."

Herme nodded, and quickly told Theod what they'd learned from the Lake Guard.

Theod paled. "Four or five thousand men? Where would he get that—"

"Askam sent a thousand of his own men to Sigholt," Zared said. "Perhaps he thought he'd need them at Council. And Caelum has always had a good force stationed at Sigholt. Coupled with the force he could have called in from Jervois Landing . . . yes, Caelum could easily have five thousand."

"We'd never hold against five thousand," Herme said bluntly. "Can we recall our major force from the Western Ranges?"

Zared shook his head. "It would take too long, far too long, and in any case I do not want to make a stand here."

"Sir Prince," Kilckman said, "what will you do?"

"Caelum thinks I will be here, awaiting his decision. He thinks to attack, probably at dawn tomorrow."

"We have less than fifteen hours," Theod put in.

Zared stood, thinking, the others watching impatiently.

"We have to leave here," he said.

"For where?" Theod and Herme said together.

"Carlon."

No-one looked surprised. "Yes," Kilckman said. "Carlon is your safest destination. Five thousand would not be enough to take Carlon from you."

"But if Caelum is only a few hours behind us," Herme asked, "what chance—"

Zared grinned. "*Every* chance, my friend. Theod? Once you played a prank on the Prince of Nor's younger cousin during his fifteenth name-day feast . . . do you remember it?"

Theod slowly smiled. "Yes, yes I do."

"Then I think we will not only have a surprise waiting for Caelum and his five thousand, but the means to delay them here some hours, if not days. Yes?"

Theod laughed. "Yes!"

"What *is* going on?" Herme asked.

Zared slapped him on the back. "Come, my friend. I shall explain shortly, but first we have to get our men out of here. I want this castle cleared, the trap set, and us to be on the road for Carlon within five hours. Herme, I need you to send word to our forces waiting in the Western Ranges to move to Carlon. Kilckman? Master Goldman said that the traders and guilds of Carlon would back me in whatever way they could. Can you fulfill that promise?"

"Aye, Sir Prince." Kilckman's eyes gleamed. "What can I do for you?"

"Prepare the way, Kilckman. Leave now. Take the fastest boat if you have to. And . . ." Zared paused. "And ask Goldman if he will ensure that there will be an appropriate street welcome. He will know what I mean."

Zared walked down the hallway leading to the private apartments in Kastaleon's Keep.

The Keep was very quiet—everyone was outside preparing for departure—and the sound of his steps echoed eerily.

He stopped outside the door to the main apartment, knocked quietly, then entered without waiting for a reply.

Leagh was sitting on a bench by a window that looked down into the courtyard. She glanced up as he entered, then swiftly turned her eyes back to the window.

She did not speak as Zared walked across the room and sat down beside her.

He looked out the window—the courtyard was a-bustle with activity.

"We are pulling out of Kastaleon," he said. "Tonight."

Leagh finally looked at him.

"Caelum comes," she said coldly. "And with an army. No wonder you run."

Zared flinched. "Yes, Caelum comes, and I would prefer to meet him on better terms than those I have available here."

"So where do we run?"

"We *move* to Carlon."

"Carlon? But—"

"Leagh," Zared leaned over and took both her hands.

She stiffened, but did not pull them free.

"Leagh, I have lied to you, and I have been dishonest with you, and for that I must ask your forgiveness."

"I don't think that I—"

"Wait, let me finish." He shifted his grip slightly, holding her hands more firmly, and he looked her straight in the eyes. "There is far more to my struggle with Caelum than trade problems. At Council I . . . at Council I also asked that the throne of Achar be restored to me."

"*What!*" Leagh pulled her hands from his and leaned back, utterly shocked.

"Leagh, *listen* to me! For some time now representations from Carlon and the West have pleaded with me to restore the throne of Achar, restore the Acharites' pride and nationhood."

"I don't believe you!"

"Damn it, Leagh! Why do you think Theod and Herme ride with me?"

"For their own gain?"

"Ah! Leagh, did you never walk beyond your own apartments in your palace in Carlon? Have you never listened to the hearts of those who thronged the streets?"

She was silent, but she dropped her eyes.

"Leagh, there is far more involved than you or I, or my quarrel with Caelum and Askam. This involves an entire people, *their* wants and needs. Leagh . . . my love . . . I ask you to say nothing at this time. I hope that when we arrive in Carlon you will see that this is not of my wishing, but of the wishing of a people."

"My loyalties—" she began.

"Your loyalties and your responsibility should *always* be to your people, Leagh. Not to me, not to Askam, not even to Caelum."

"My loyalty is to the Throne of the Stars, as should yours be!"

"No," Zared said very softly, and took her hands again. "Our loyalty should always be to the people we represent, to those who look to us for leadership and protection. Leagh, I need you to understand this. I do *not* seek the throne of Achar through personal ambition, but through the wishes of the Acharites and a need to right the wrong that has been done to them, not just the unfair taxation burden that only the Acharites have been forced to shoulder, but the fact that Axis stripped our people—*our* people, damn it!—of their nationality and pride."

"And me?"

"You? Leagh, I love you heart and soul, and for that reason alone I want you as my wife. But I also love you for what you represent—a chance for the rift between West and North to be healed."

"You want the lands of the West!"

"If it would help reunite the Acharites as a people, then, yes, I do," he said bluntly.

She was silent, trying to absorb his words.

"Leagh," he said, "I have been utterly honest with you here today, and I regret that I have not been previously. You and I are not carter and laundress, with no responsibilities other than those our honest occupations demand. We both represent massive numbers of people and vast areas of land. Of course those responsibilities impinge on our relationship, and on how we view each other."

He sighed, and lifted one hand to cup her face. "Leagh, I

love you as a woman first and foremost, I love your strength and your courage, your wit and your laughter. I also know how advantageous a marriage between us would be, not personally, but to the *people* we represent. Do you know what I am saying?"

She nodded. "We are man and woman, but we are also greater than that. We cannot regard marriage as a personal contract, but as a contract between people."

"And so," he said softly, "we must take into account the wishes of our own people in our marriage. Leagh, I want you for my wife. When we get to Carlon I hope that you will see that *your* people want me for your husband. Will you accept their wishes in your answer?"

She thought a long time, staring vaguely out the window.

When she finally looked back at him, Zared could see tears brimming in her eyes.

"If Carlon wants you as King, Zared, if I think that the people of the West want what you do, then, yes, I will be your wife."

Zared relaxed, and leaned forward and kissed her.

"Then don your riding clothes, my love, for tonight we ride."

43

Faraday's Lie

Niah linked her arm with Faraday's as they strolled through the orchard. "I am so glad we have this opportunity to talk," Niah said, and gave Faraday's arm a gentle squeeze.

"You are?"

"How long have you been here? Ten days? And in that

time I have barely seen you. I have had to learn your history from the gossip of the priestesses' table."

Faraday laughed. "I cannot imagine they painted a pretty picture of me!"

"Oh, but you are wrong! The priestesses admire you enormously. The First told me that, with Azhure," Niah paused to take a proud breath as she said her daughter's name, "you were primarily responsible for Axis' success against Gorgrael."

Faraday's face lost its laughter, but Niah did not notice.

"You planted out the entire Minstrelsea by yourself? And the Avar were yours to command?"

"It wasn't quite like that—"

"And you wielded such power! Faraday, I am in awe."

"You also had your part to play."

Niah shrugged. "I bore a daughter."

"And you died for her."

"You died for Tencendor."

They walked some way in silence, each lost in her own thoughts. Only once they reached the southern cliffs did Niah resume the conversation.

"And, having died, here we both are. Free to do as we will, free on this beautiful and magical island."

"One of us is not quite free." This was the opening Faraday had been waiting for. She had spent much time with StarDrifter, talking with him about Niah, wondering how best to free Zenith. This was a risk, but it had to be taken.

"Oh?" Niah said, and halted, pulling Faraday to a stop beside her. "And how are you not free, Faraday?"

"It was not myself of whom I spoke," Faraday said gently, looking Niah in the eye.

Niah dropped her arm from Faraday's. "I have done nothing wrong."

"We have both come back from the dead," Faraday continued. "But I have not taken over someone else's—"

"I have not 'taken over someone else'!" Niah countered. "I am *me,* I always have been! I—"

"Niah—"

"Zenith never existed! She was only waiting to realize her true self. Me!"

"Niah, please, hear me out. I do not mean to make you angry, but—"

"I am *no-one* but Niah! I never have been!"

"StarDrifter tells me that your mannerisms are different, the way you react to things, even your laughter. You are not the same—"

"My handwriting is the same! My tastes! Do not argue that—"

"Niah! Listen to me!" Faraday's voice was unusually sharp, and Niah subsided.

"Niah, can you not see that Zenith was a different woman? She loved to fly, you loathe it—why, if you were always her? Do you not remember how it felt to soar?"

Niah was silent, her face set in stubborn lines.

"Niah, believe me, I do not begrudge you your grab at life. It—"

"It was promised me! And can *you* stand here and begrudge me my second chance at life when . . . how many chances have you had? Two? Three?"

"I have never taken over someone else's life," Faraday repeated. "I have retransformed within the same world and within the same existence. Niah . . . in the manner of things, whoever dies is always reborn at some point. A soul inhabits the empty shell of a growing fetus. A soul cannot—should not—inhabit an already occupied and whole body."

Niah turned her back to Faraday, staring out over the choppy gray sea.

"Niah, surely you can see that merely by waiting—"

"I have waited long enough!" Niah yelled, still refusing to look at Faraday. "WolfStar promised me that I would be reborn, and I have! And this time into a SunSoar body so that he *can* and *will* love me for eternity!"

Faraday sighed quietly. In this Niah was right. To live an eternity with WolfStar would require SunSoar blood to hold him.

"But it does not solve the problem of Zenith," she tried again.

Now Niah did face her. "Zenith never existed," she said firmly. "Never. There was only me, waiting to be acknowledged."

Then her face changed. It lit up, radiating joy and she stared at Faraday as if she were the only meaning in Niah's life.

Faraday frowned, then realized Niah was staring at a point some distance beyond herself.

Niah gave a glad cry, picked up her skirts, and rushed past Faraday into WolfStar's arms. "Beloved!"

Faraday silently cursed. Not only at WolfStar's untimely intrusion—had he appeared thinking that Faraday might persuade Niah to relinquish control of Zenith's body?—but also at Niah's sheer determination. Was Zenith still there? Faraday did not know, and she wondered if StarDrifter's faith that Zenith still existed was warranted.

Despite her irritation, Faraday composed herself, and faced the lovers.

Niah was wrapped in WolfStar's arms, locked in a passionate embrace. Faraday raised an eyebrow. Was this love on WolfStar's part, or simple lust? She did not know if he was capable of true love.

As if reading her thoughts WolfStar raised his face from Niah's and grinned at Faraday. "Again she bears my child," he said, his voice hoarse with what Faraday recognized as triumph. "And this one I shall raise myself, not leave for some dirt-trodden Plough-Keeper to mismanage."

Niah wriggled against WolfStar's body, such a wanton act that Faraday blushed.

"What? *Here,* my love?" WolfStar laughed. "Did I not sate you last night?"

"A pregnant woman always craves love," Niah murmured, her hands running down WolfStar's body.

Faraday turned her face aside, unwilling to watch the spectacle Niah was making of herself. And she a former First Priestess!

Eventually it was WolfStar himself who gently disentangled himself from Niah's embrace. "Now is not the time, my love. I must speak with Faraday."

Niah murmured, but she let WolfStar go.

The instant WolfStar was free of her, his entire demeanor changed. He assumed power as others would assume a cloak, his violet eyes darkened and became more intense, his entire bearing more autocratic.

"What happened to Drago?" he demanded.

Faraday just stared at him.

"You were in the Star Gate chamber when Drago killed Orr."

"I was in the chamber when Orr died," she agreed.

"Drago had the Rainbow Scepter."

Faraday was silent.

"Didn't he?"

"I was terrified," Faraday said, her eyes not leaving WolfStar's face. "Terrified by the violence, the terror, the death. I did not notice what he was carrying."

"You did not *notice*?"

You were the one who sent me through Prophecy to die for Tencendor, Faraday thought, her mind closed to his probing. She held his stare. You sent me to die, *others* released me. I owe you no loyalty.

WolfStar swallowed his anger. Well, perhaps she had not noticed. "What happened to him, Faraday? Did he step through the Star Gate?"

"I cannot know exactly what happened, WolfStar. I was so terrified, and some power beyond my knowing was tearing me apart, retransforming me back to this," her hand indicated her own body. "I did not notice where—"

"Tell me the truth!" WolfStar snarled, his anger strengthened by his fear. *Tell me the truth!* he raged through her mind.

He was terrifying, almost beyond control, and so Faraday shivered, and confessed.

"He ran back through the passageways, WolfStar. Which one I am not certain. But he must be in Tencendor somewhere."

WolfStar stared at her. Was she telling the truth? He did not know. Could she withstand his need for the truth? He did not know . . . and all that he did not know was making WolfStar a very, very frightened man.

"Ah, bah!" he said, and, in his manner, vanished.

Niah let out a low cry of disappointment, and threw Faraday a resentful look.

"Well?" StarDrifter asked Faraday as she walked into his quarters.

Faraday ignored him for a moment, then sat beside him on the bed. "Niah will not willingly relinquish Zenith's body," she said. "And in this she is aided by WolfStar."

"You saw WolfStar?"

Faraday nodded, her expression unreadable.

"What did he want? What did he say?"

Faraday hesitated. "Later, StarDrifter, later. For now we must concentrate on finding Zenith."

"Can you do it?"

"Yes." Faraday's voice was now much stronger, and she looked StarDrifter unhesitatingly in the eye. "Yes, I can. But persuasion will not work. We must find a stronger means to free your granddaughter."

"And the sooner the better." StarDrifter sat back, his face creased with worry. "Every day I can see the Niah woman grow stronger. And that baby . . ."

Faraday stared at him. "Yes . . . the baby! StarDrifter, you have given me an idea."

And she leaned forward and kissed him on the cheek.

44

. . . And Sixty-Nine Fat Pigs

Caelum stood in the cold pre-dawn air, watching the preparations about him. He had slept badly; in truth, he had not slept at all, for fear DragonStar would hunt him down in his dreams. Now his eyes were shadowed, his movements hesitant, and nerves fluttered in his stomach. This would be his first military action. Stars, he thought to himself. I am over forty years old, and by my age my father had battled from coast to coast and won a realm. I? I have but listened to the tales.

True, he had trained all his life for this moment. Not only his father, but every battle-hardened captain, human or Icarii, had been brought in to give the StarSon lessons. He had spent most mornings of his life at weapon practice.

And until this moment he had thought it would all be unnecessary. How could Tencendor ever slip back into war, even in *his* lifetime?

"I want to see the bastard *flayed*!" Askam muttered at his side. Before them he could just make out the rising hulk of Kastaleon, although he knew Caelum's Icarii vision could see in far more detail. "Is he there, watching for us?"

"The castle is quiet, Askam. I can see a few guards atop the walls, but even they are more likely asleep than not. No doubt Zared is asleep in his bed, dreaming of how he can persuade the Council to accept his ambition."

His mouth twisted grimly. "I predict he will awake to something of a surprise. Askam, are the units ready?"

"Aye, StarSon. They moved into position an hour ago, as stealthy as stalking cats. When will you give the word to send in the forward scouts? It lacks but an hour until dawn, and soon the castle will be rousing."

Caelum hesitated, the nerves in his stomach flowering into full-blown nausea. But he was determined to show Zared—nay, all Tencendor—that he could captain as well as his father. Forward scouts? No, he would work it better.

"Keep the scouts back, Askam. We will ride into Kastaleon in full force. Zared does not expect us, and those guards atop the walls are all but asleep."

"Caelum!" Askam stared aghast at him. "It is surely prudent to send in scouts first? Make sure that—"

Caelum turned from his contemplation of Kastaleon and snapped at Askam. "I know what I am doing! I can cloak us in enchantment so thick that Zared and his men will not see us. They are not expecting us, are they? That fort is as quiet as a grave. Why waste time on forward scouts?"

Askam chewed the inside of his cheek. What Caelum said was true enough, and if he could cloak them in enchantment . . . Askam suddenly smiled at the thought of finding Zared abed, waking to discover the tip of Askam's sword at his throat.

"As you order, StarSon. Shall we move out immediately?"

"Wait a moment. I have to cast the enhancement."

It sickened him even more that he must mask the approach of his units with enchantment, but if it gave them an edge . . .

Axis had never fought under cloak of enchantment.

Caelum thrust the thought aside. He was *not* his father, and surely Zared had brought sneakiness upon himself. Caelum twisted the ring about on his finger, although he did not need it to show what Song to sing for a cloak of invisibility. He had used the Song only recently and it was fresh in his mind, but the action calmed Caelum's nerves. He ran the Song through his mind, then coldness swept over him.

The Song had required significantly more power than when he'd last sung it. Why? Caelum remembered WolfStar asking whether he'd noticed a taint in his power. What was happening? Was it just nerves that had made him expend so much more energy on the Song this morning, or was it something else? Something considerably bleaker? What?

"It is done, Askam. Move them out."

They had moored their boats four hundred paces north of Kastaleon, hidden both by the darkness and a sharp bend in the river. Over the past hour Askam had sent troops out to surround the castle as best they could without actually being seen. Now, he sent out the order for them to move in.

He and Caelum mounted their horses and set off down the main approach road. No-one within the castle would be able to see or hear them, and there was no reason to try to be quiet. Askam dug his heels into his horse's flanks, sending the beast skittering across the roadway.

"Peace, Askam," Caelum said. "We will be there soon enough, and Kastaleon will soon be back under your control."

"I want to wake Zared with the point of my sword—"

"Enough, Askam!"

Askam subsided into silence as they covered the last hundred paces before the castle. There was still no reaction from within, even though soldiers were pouring in through the gate. Askam smiled a little at the thought of Zared's surprise on waking at sword-point.

It would be very, very good finally to see Zared *fail* at something.

Askam wondered if Caelum would strip Zared of his lands for his misdeeds. Would *he* then receive some? What? Askam wondered . . . Severin . . . the gem mines? All his debts could be solved with one signature if he got the gem mines.

The next moment gem mines were forgotten as they clattered across the bridge and into the castle. Askam shouted orders to his captains, then he and Caelum dismounted.

"It's too quiet," Caelum said, looking about. "Even with this enchantment someone should have noticed something . . . *bumped* into one of us, for Stars' sake! Askam . . . shouldn't there be more guards about?"

Before Askam could answer, one of their men ran from the stables. "StarSon! The stables are empty!"

An awful premonition gripped Caelum. What should he do? No horses . . . did that mean . . .?

"Check the barracks!" he called, and reached for his horse again. Should he mount? What should he order? What would his father have done?

There was a faint shout from atop the walls. "Dummies, StarSon! There are no men up here!"

Caelum shot Askam a wild look. What . . .?

"The barracks are empty, StarSon!"

"They've gone!" Askam cried, unnecessarily.

"Well, at least you have your castle back," Caelum murmured, trying to think it through. Should they secure the castle or ride after Zared? But which way had he gone? How *long* had he been gone? Caelum cursed. Why hadn't he brought any Icarii with him? Axis would never have made this mistake.

"Perhaps—" he began, and then the world exploded about them.

For minutes all he knew was a dreadful shock. He was blown off his feet, his horse beside him. About him were screams and grunts, choking smoke, sharpnel flying through the air, a stifling heat that went on and on and on, and the smell of charcoal and burned flesh.

Caelum rolled onto his side and gagged. The stench of burning meat filled his entire body and he couldn't get it out. Screams cut through his mind, tore into his soul. *Gods! What was going on? Why wouldn't the screamers shut up?*

A hand grasped his shoulder and rolled him over. "StarSon? Are you all right? Oh, praise the StarMan, you live! Get up, my Lord, you have to get up . . ."

Caelum allowed himself to be dragged to his feet. Every muscle felt torn, every bone broken, but he found he could walk easily enough. Perhaps he wasn't close to death, after all.

The hand dragged him forward. Caelum hoped that whoever the hand belonged to knew where he was going, because Caelum could not see a pace in front of him in this red, smoke-filled hell. He bent over and choked again, and found his eyes not a handspan from a corpse that had literally been blown apart. There was red flesh and white bone fragments, but nothing else recognizable.

His stomach roiled again, and the hand now grasped his hair and hauled him forward.

They stumbled through the gate—or what was left of it—and fell head-first into the moat.

The bridge had gone.

The icy shock of the water brought Caelum to his senses as nothing else could have done. He spluttered and fought his way to the surface, blinking the water out of his eyes. Beside him a foot soldier likewise spluttered—it must have been this man who dragged him out of the inferno—and Caelum looked back to the castle.

What he saw appalled him. The castle had been blown apart. The outer walls had great holes rent in them through which smoke and flames now poured. The Keep no longer existed—there was only blackness where once that had stood. Men and horses, some of them on fire, careened out of the smoke and flames and fell into the water.

"Stars!" Caelum whispered, unable to come to terms with what he saw. "Oh . . . *Stars!*"

Eight hundred paces away on a small hill, Theod stared, appalled, at the carnage. How had Caelum ridden into the castle with his entire force without being seen?

Enchantment, no doubt.

But why hadn't he sent in forward scouts first? Every war leader was trained to do that. No-one rode blindly with their full force into an unknown situation.

The charges had been rigged so that they would be set off when the first scout reached the cellars. Yes, a few men would be killed, but the main object had been to destroy the castle and all riverboats moored beside it. Caelum would be delayed several days until he could get more boats.

But the man had taken his entire force inside!

Neither Theod nor Zared had foreseen—even imagined—such stupidity. Or such carnage.

How many dead? Theod sat behind his covering bush and gaped, trying to come to terms with the disaster.

His man-at-arms finally found his voice. "Gods, my Lord! What . . . what did you pack into those cellars?"

Theod swallowed and managed to speak. "Wood, nails, pottery, fire powder, eighty-five barrels of resin cracked and left to spread . . . and sixty-nine fat pigs. It was the pork fat that gave the explosion such potency."

"But," the man stumbled, "why did Caelum lead his entire force in? Why didn't he send scouts in first?"

"As any competent captain *would* have done," Theod said grimly. "Come on, man. We've got to get out of here. Zared needs to know what's happened."

He grabbed the man's sleeve, and they both ran for their horses.

Caelum eventually found the strength to swim for the shore, where for an hour he sat shivering and watching the sun rise over the devastation. Survivors slowly stumbled from the castle, fell into the moat, and swam to shore. A few score, perhaps, no more. There had been five hundred men still outside the castle when it had exploded. Some of those had died from rocks and shrapnel catapulted out of the inferno, but most had survived. That left him, what? Six hundred out of the five thousand he'd brought sailing down here.

Six hundred.

His first military action, and he had lost ninety per cent of his command.

And not one kill for it.

Even Gorgrael and his enchantments, even the Gryphon

falling out of the sky, had not been able to inflict such calamity on Axis.

And yet Caelum had lost *ninety percent* of his command to a meager force of humans!

He rose unsteadily to his feet and walked slowly among the groups of men lying on the grass. Most were injured to some degree, some horrendously so, and Caelum knew they would not live. Here and there he stopped and stared, the men he looked at staring back, but he said nothing and eventually he walked on.

Damn Zared to eternal fire!

At one group he stopped, then dropped to his knees. "Askam? Askam?"

His friend lay unconscious in a pool of blood. One of his men sat by him.

"He lives, StarSon. Just."

Caelum nodded dumbly. That Askam lived at all amazed him. His left arm had been blown completely off.

45

The Enemy

He lay in bed, trying to find his courage. The Questors had used him for two leaps, each more painful than the last, if that were possible. And today, another one.

Why did they cause him so much pain? StarLaughter murmured in her sleep by his side, and turned over. Drago glanced at her. She slept peacefully enough, but *she* did not have to endure . . .

Although StarLaughter had, she assured him last night. She and all the children WolfStar had cast to their deaths had been used in this way.

"Me more than most," she'd murmured comfortingly to

Drago last night, "for I was more powerful and more highly trained than any of the children."

"But they stopped using you . . ."

"A long time ago, my love."

"Why?"

"Eventually our life force lost its potency. You are so useful because your life force is still so strong. You are only recently come through the Star Gate."

Drago thought briefly about the baby. He was surely evidence that one's life force ebbed considerably after four thousand years beyond the Star Gate.

"The Questors find it so easy to follow your trail back," StarLaughter said, and then she paused and smiled at him. "We are so close, my love. Three or four more leaps and we shall be at the threshold of the Star Gate."

Three or four more leaps. "Will you survive?" Raspu had asked. Drago didn't know. He didn't know if he could endure the pain.

"They're draining me of all my power," Drago said. "Is all my potential as an Enchanter being burned up? Am *I* being burned up?"

"Hush, lover," StarLaughter whispered, holding him tight. "They will not drain you completely. They use only a small portion of your potential. When we tumble back through the Star Gate, your blood order will be reversed and you will come into your full potential as an Icarii Enchanter. The Questors have promised, and they will hold by that promise."

"Are you sure?"

"Very sure. Why would the Questors lie to you?"

"I don't know," Drago said slowly.

"Then trust them."

The Questors were waiting for them in their circular chamber. Outside shone a world of pure gold, the Hawkchilds spinning about the trees in an agitated cloud, whispering, whispering, whispering.

"Quick!" Sheol said, her voice brusque. "The interstellar winds are propitious for a giant leap. If we manage this, we may only have to do two more leaps instead of three."

Sheol and Barzula thrust Drago onto the couch, and then all the Questors were crowding about, their hands heavy on his head and shoulders.

Mot smiled benevolently. "This won't hurt—"

"Much," finished Rox, and all five Questors laughed, then bit deep into Drago's soul, deeper than they'd ever gone before.

Pain seared through him. He arched his back in a silent agony—and felt some part of him dying, burning as though caught in a great conflagration. He'd never felt this so strongly before, but he knew what it was. The Questors *were* destroying his power. They had lied to him.

They were destroying him.

He screamed.

They leaped.

Into a world where there was no clear definition between ground and sky, where light and rain melded as one, where there was no color save gray, no joy, no life, no ease of mind. The children whispered in a gray shadow through the trees—now petrified stone in this grayest of worlds—and StarLaughter sat and crooned to her undead child. The Questors laughed and spoke words of praise and comfort to Drago, and he outwardly let himself be comforted and reassured that yes, they did love and need him and no, they were not engaged in bleeding him to a useless hulk.

DragonStar SunSoar, Icarii Enchanter, would live again, they cried—and then they all laughed. They *howled* with laughter, and Drago stumbled away from them, deep into the forest of petrified stone, where he sank down against a tree and put his head in his hands.

Eventually he sat up and idly fingered the contents of his sack. The coins felt comforting, and Drago let his mind go blank as he sat there on that alien world, watching with unseeing eyes as the strange children leaped and cried amid the fossilized wood, and as StarLaughter sat smiling with the Questors, jamming her useless nipple yet again into the child's mouth.

And Drago slipped into waking dream.

He dreamed of the hunt, and he felt the thrill of power surge through him. The forest slid by amid the thunder of hooves, and the hunters whooped with joy, sensing their quarry near. The children—the Hawkchilds—had been loosed and were swooping through the forest. The prey was frantic. Who? Drago wondered. Who?

The hunt surged forward.

Yes, everything *would* be all right. The Questors did not lie to him. They would not drain him completely, and his Icarii powers *would* be restored when they leaped through the Star Gate.

And then the entire perspective of the dream changed. Suddenly Drago found himself running through the forest. His heart was pounding, his legs were trembling with fatigue, cold sweat bathed his face and body. His breath rasped through his chest and throat—he couldn't breathe at all! Trees loomed to either side, closing in on him, tightening about him.

Behind him a clarion sounded. Shrieks of joy reached out to him. The hunters were closer! There was a rustling and roaring in the trees—the Hawkchilds had spotted him!

Drago fell into thorn bushes and then scrambled out, blood pouring from a dozen deep cuts to his face and arms.

On the forest path behind him galloped a great black horse with an even darker rider. His armor absorbed light, but the point of his lance reflected it—it was a beam of light, coming straight for Drago's chest.

He stumbled, and then fell.

He twisted onto his back, trying to scrabble away, but the horseman had reined his beast to a halt before him and Drago felt the lance in the center of his chest.

With every breath he felt the point slide in deeper.

The pain was horrific.

"Who are you?" he screamed.

"I am DragonStar, come back from death," replied the horseman, "and I hunt the Enemy."

And he leaned his entire weight on the lance.

Drago lurched into consciousness, his breath rasping into his chest in preparation for a scream.

But it never came. He managed to control it, but he sat there for a very long time, remembering the feel of that lance as it had sliced through his lungs and heart.

46

The TimeKeepers

"There is trouble in Tencendor," Axis fretted, rubbing his hands before the fire. "I can feel it. Caelum . . . Caelum has encountered trouble."

"I, too, can feel it," Azhure said, and shook out her thick black hair, letting it stream out in the wind that ran down the Icebear Coast.

There had been disturbances recently, disturbances they had felt in the very fiber of their beings. In their power.

With nothing else to blame it on, they thought it a product of the disharmony within Tencendor.

"But," Azhure glanced at Axis, "we can do nothing. Tencendor is Caelum's to do with as he will. Leave it, Axis, he will manage."

Across the fire Adamon nodded. "Leave it, Axis."

Axis sighed. "Yes. I will leave it." He smiled wanly and looked about the group of Star Gods. "Did you have as much trouble leaving your mortal concerns behind?"

Flulia laughed. "Oh, my! I remember Adamon had to snatch me from my old laundry. I could not bear the way the new laundress starched the sheets."

Adamon smiled. "I told her that a god had no business amid the washing. Flulia became quite angry, as I recall. She actually stamped her foot."

Everyone laughed, and Pors leaned forward. "I chased the brown-legged frogs of Bogle Marsh through my dreams for a thousand years after I achieved my place with Adamon and Xanon. I missed them desperately. What you and Azhure are going through, Axis, is nothing unusual."

Axis' smile faded a little. "Then pray I do not fret at you for the next thousand years."

There was quiet as the gods stared into the flames of the fire, remembering their individual experiences on the journey from mortal to immortal, then Adamon spoke up.

"There is good reason why I have called us all here together this night. Xanon and I," he took his wife's hand, "are worried. Look!"

Adamon threw his free hand over the fire in a sudden motion. Instantly stars became visible in the flames—comets, solar systems, galaxies. Axis thought it was like looking into the Star Gate, save that the lure of the Star Dance was mute here.

"Look," Adamon said again, but now his voice had lost its urgency, and was soothing, hypnotic. "Look."

His hand swirled over the fire again, and then yet again, and the flames roared higher. Every galaxy was exquisite in its detail, every movement of the stars faultlessly performed.

"Beautiful," Azhure murmured.

"Beautiful," Xanon echoed, "save here," her finger pointed, "and here, and here."

As her fingers moved, the flames danced and what they revealed made the others, save Adamon who had seen this already, gasp with horror.

Spreading through the universe, like a thin trail of blight, was a black shadow. It was as yet only tiny, and hardly noticeable—the others might well have missed it if it had not been for Xanon—but . . .

"It is coming directly for us!" whispered Nors, appalled.

"For the Star Gate," Adamon said. "Yes."

"How long has this been visible?" Axis asked.

"For less than a day," Xanon replied. "Adamon and I noticed it last night."

"It's moving toward us with frightening speed," her husband said. "Look, this was where it was when first we noticed it, and then, while we watched, it leaped forward, through this galaxy, and this, then came to rest here."

"What is it?" Azhure twisted her hair nervously into a knot. "Is it the children?"

"Partly," Adamon said. "They come with it. We can hear their whispers louder than ever before. But they are not driving it. They are not the power behind it."

"Well . . . what *is*?" Axis asked. He remembered how he'd felt when Jayme had first told him about the invading ghostmen from the north. Then he'd had a premonition of disaster. But that was nothing compared to the foreboding that now swept through him.

Adamon shook his head. "I do not know. I have no knowledge of what it is. I can *feel* its power, but I do not understand it. What is worse, see how it has blacked out an as yet tiny portion of the stars? Axis, do you not feel what that has done to you?"

Axis stared into the flame-vision, then his entire body went rigid.

"Axis?" Azhure murmured, and laid a hand on his arm.

"By the Stars themselves," Axis said hoarsely, "it has cut out the sound of the Star Dance from that area!"

"Yes," Adamon said. "And if it comes closer, it will block out yet more of the Star Dance. What if, the heavens forbid, it blocks out *all* of the Star Dance?"

Each present was silent, appalled. If that happened, then all power based on the use of the Star Dance would cease. All Icarii magic and enchantment would wink out of existence.

The Star Gods would become mortal.

"What is it?" Pors fretted. "What is it?"

Adamon shook his head helplessly. "I cannot know, I have seen nothing like this before. Nothing! I do not even have a name for it!"

"Well, I do," a voice put in from the wastes behind him, and the gods turned about, startled.

WolfStar SunSoar stood there, a black cloak wrapped about his body, despair on his face.

"They are the TimeKeeper Demons," he said. "And they are coming for what was stolen from them."

There was utter silence for the space of several breaths.

Then Adamon rose to his feet. "And how is it that *you* know of them, WolfStar SunSoar? Have your misdeeds beyond death yet to impact on Tencendor? Do your sins bring these TimeKeeper Demons to ravage *us*?"

"No, Adamon. I know of the TimeKeepers, but, for once," he managed a small grin, "I am not responsible. May I sit?"

Adamon hesitated, then nodded, sitting himself.

WolfStar sat as close to the fire as he could, wrapping his cloak tightly about him.

"The TimeKeeper Demons are trouble," he said. "Trouble loose in the universe. Catastrophe if they break through the Star Gate."

"You met them beyond the Star Gate?" Axis asked. "Are they coming for *you*?"

WolfStar shook his head. "No, and no, although I think that with them they bring the children I threw into the Star Gate. I became aware of the TimeKeeper Demons in my time beyond the Star Gate, but their exact nature, name and purpose I discovered only after I had returned.

"First of all I should explain who, or rather, what, the TimeKeeper Demons are. They are a harmonious group of six demons, each of whom roams—hunts—through a particular period of the day or night. They are known as the Time-

Keepers because no-one keeps such assiduous track of the passing hours as do they. There is Mot, the Demon of Hunger. He hunts at dawn. Barzula, the Demon of Tempest, hunts at midmorning. Sheol, Demon of Despair, hunts at midafternoon. Dusk belongs to Raspu, the Demon of Pestilence. And the night belongs to Rox, the Demon of Terror. They hunt for souls, for sustenance, and they prefer to call themselves the Questors. They quest, but always hunger, tempest, despair, pestilence and terror ride in their wake."

"You said there were six," said Narcis.

"The sixth is the reason the other five TimeKeepers have been battling for tens of thousands of years to find their way through the Star Gate into Tencendor. In their own way the five I have described are terrible enough, but the sixth is the worst of all. He is their leader, their father, their savior. They are nothing without him."

WolfStar paused and stared into the fire, but no-one spoke to disturb him. Finally he lifted his head.

"His name is Qeteb, the Destruction that wastes at midday. He is the Midday Demon. The others will nibble at your soul, but Qeteb will steal it and rape it for eternity."

"Qeteb is *here*?" Adamon said. "He is somewhere in Tencendor? *That's* why they are coming?"

"In a manner of speaking, Adamon. But let me tell the story. The TimeKeeper Demons, Qeteb among them, once ravaged free on a world far, far from here. There was a race on that world who were determined to break their power—and this they did. One day they trapped Qeteb—I can only imagine the courage and fortitude it took to do this—and they dismembered him. I talk not of a bodily dismemberment, but a dismemberment of his life, so to speak. They separated warmth, breath, movement and soul from his flesh, and they fled with them. They fled through the universe, using craft that had been designed for interstellar travel—"

"They used *craft*?" Xanon interrupted. "How . . . cumbersome."

WolfStar shrugged. "They had a different kind of power to what we know, Xanon. Well, they fled through the universe on a journey that itself took many tens of thousands of our years. It ended here, on Tencendor. They crashed through the barriers that separated Tencendor from the universe—"

"Creating the Star Gate!" Adamon cried.

"Yes, creating the Star Gate. Their four craft, for they used a different craft for each of Qeteb's life parts, crashed into Tencendor, blasting out the craters that filled with the waters of the Sacred Lakes."

"So the Lakes take their power from the remnants of the craft of these ancient ones?" Azhure said.

"Yes, although the craft are very much intact. The creatures within them died, but buried beneath the Lakes are what the craft have become in order to protect Qeteb's life parts."

"So how is it," Zest asked, "that these Demons approach now? Is it just that their journey has taken many tens of thousands of years, and is only now reaching its culmination . . . or is it . . ."

"Something else," WolfStar said. "You have seen the path of darkness they have left behind them in the past day. You have deduced how they block out the Star Dance as they draw closer—we have all felt a diminution in our abilities over the past weeks. They are now moving faster than they ever have before. I believe there is a very good reason for that speed . . . and for all of us to fear their imminent arrival."

"What reason?" Axis hissed. His hand groped momentarily at his side, as if he still had a sword there.

"I think Drago is leading them to the Star Gate," WolfStar said directly.

For the second time that night there was utter silence.

"What?" Axis whispered.

"Drago?" Azhure said, as ashen-faced as Axis.

"That filth, curse the day he was conceived, has murdered Orr and leaped through the Star Gate."

Murdered Orr?

"But I don't understand," said Axis. "Drago has no powers. The Star Gate would have killed him. And even if he *did* survive and find his way to these Demons, how is it that Drago has the power to catapult them through the stars like that?"

WolfStar looked Axis in the eye. "Because his father did not have the foresight to hide the Rainbow Scepter where it could *never* be found! In a room in Sigholt, by the Stars! You might as well have hung it on a pole outside the front gate!"

There was instant uproar about the fire. Axis leaped to his feet, yelling at WolfStar. Azhure jumped up with him, hanging on to his arm, trying to calm him, yet sending a myriad of questions toward WolfStar at the same time. Silton and Narcis were also on their feet, shouting not only at WolfStar, but at the entire heavens in general.

"Be quiet!" Adamon thundered, and silence fell upon the company.

"Be silent," he repeated. "Now, I am going to ask WolfStar a series of questions, and I want *no-one* interrupting." He shot Axis a furious glare and he subsided, Azhure at his side.

"Good. Silton? Narcis? Your places, if you please. WolfStar," Adamon turned to the Enchanter, who had remained calm in the face of all the anger directed his way, "how is it that the Rainbow Scepter can help the Demons move so fast?"

"Because it is in large part composed of the power of the craft of the ancient ones. I assume the Demons are using that power to catapult themselves forward."

"How do you know that Drago has the Scepter?"

WolfStar explained about the message Orr had sent from the Star Gate chamber. He recalled SpikeFeather's vision for them, and the Star Gods watched in horror as Drago fought Orr, then killed him with the Scepter.

"The Scepter has gone from Sigholt, Axis," WolfStar said. "Of course, if the enchantments that were *supposed* to hide it had been worked better—"

"Enough, WolfStar!" Adamon snapped. "But we did not know that Drago stepped through the Star Gate—"

"Faraday was there," Axis put in, his voice quiet. "Did you not see her watching from the pillars?"

"Yes," WolfStar said. "Faraday was there. She is now on the Island of Mist and Memory, inhabiting her human form once again."

Axis and Azhure both jumped. *With StarDrifter?*

"And you saw her?" Adamon asked.

"Yes. She . . ." WolfStar hesitated, "she said that Drago fled through one of the passageways after murdering Orr. She said he must still be in Tencendor. But I do not believe her. I think she is lying to protect Drago."

"Why would she do that?" Azhure asked. "She has no reason to like or admire him."

"I do not know why, Azhure. But Faraday was lying, I am sure of it, and I think the certain proof lies in the trail of darkness we can see spreading through the stars. The Demons are on their way. Suddenly. With such power and vigor as they have never shown previously. I can only assume that, yes, Drago has passed over the Rainbow Scepter to them."

"He ever had a twisted mind!" Axis said viciously. "Look, Azhure! Look at what he has done now! Subduing his Enchanter powers did nothing. You should have—"

"Killed him?" Azhure cried. "Do *you* think you could kill your own flesh and blood?"

"I *disown* him as my flesh and blood," Axis said, more angry than Azhure had ever seen him. "And yes, I could kill him for what he has tried to do to my family, for what he *has* done to my family, and what he *will* do to Tencendor! My friends," Axis looked about the circle, "don't you understand what will happen if these TimeKeepers come close enough to block out the Star Dance completely? They will ravage at will! *No-one* will be able to stop them!"

He threw a furious look at WolfStar. "Is this your mad, bad blood outing itself, renegade? Is this your virulent inheritance tearing apart my family and my land? Did I fight for *nothing*? Did—"

"I have had nothing to do with either the Demons or with Drago's actions!" WolfStar cried. "I will tear him apart myself should I meet him before you!" He gained some control of himself and lowered his tone. "Believe me, Axis, all I *ever* wanted was the best for this land. For Tencendor."

"Again, enough," Adamon said. "WolfStar, all about this fire can see what these Demons do to the stars. There is a wake of such sadness behind them that I wonder what they will do to Tencendor if they manage to come through the Star Gate."

"Without Qeteb they will wrap this land and its peoples in disease, starvation, storms, depair and terror such as it has never seen before, not even under Gorgrael. *With* Qeteb to lead them, the TimeKeeper Demons will turn Tencendor into a dark wasteland, all its people slaves—automatons—to their whims. And, as Axis said, without the power of the Star Dance behind us, none of us can stop them."

"*None* of us?" Axis asked, once again in control of himself. "Then is there nothing that can be done to counter them? Did these ancient ones, the Demons' 'Enemy,' leave us any means by which to protect ourselves against the cargo they left among us?"

WolfStar nodded. "In a manner, yes. Each site is protected by a series of measures against the Demons returning to recover Qeteb's life parts. The site under Grail Lake is the most heavily protected of all, for it is there that Qeteb's soul is buried. In a cavern beneath the lake lies a Maze—an extension of the craft that has grown there during the thousands of years since it crashed."

"Grown? Grown?" Azhure said. "Explain."

WolfStar was silent for a while, trying to find a way to convey what these craft actually were. "I do not understand them completely, Azhure. All I can say is that these craft are not dead, but neither are they alive. They are aware of the world and of the circumstances about them. Let me explain. In this cavern under Grail Lake lies the Maze. It protects Qeteb's soul and is, in its own way, highly magical. A massive gate protects the entranceway to the Maze. About this gate is a stone arch, and on this arch are characters that explain what measures can be taken against Qeteb. For aeons the gate made only vague mention of a champion it referred to as the Crusader. Then, forty years ago, the gate *named* the champion."

"Who?" Adamon asked.

Everyone save WolfStar looked at Axis.

"Caelum," WolfStar said.

"Caelum?" Axis said. "But surely *I* would be better—"

"No, Axis," WolfStar said firmly. "The Maze clearly states that Caelum StarSon is the one who can best protect Tencendor. StarSon, it says. Ah." His entire face softened. "It knew even before you proclaimed Caelum your heir and gave him the title StarSon outside Tencendor. Axis, Azhure, *you* have bred the champion."

"WolfStar," Axis asked very softly as horrid realization hit him, "was it the Maze which taught you the Prophecy?"

"Yes."

Axis found it difficult to ask the next question. "Are you telling us that the Prophecy was a manipulation designed primarily to breed the Maze its champion?"

"Yes. *And* to create the circumstances and environment that would shape him into the Crusader the Maze wanted."

Axis stared at WolfStar, appalled. Had he and Azhure fought through so much only to provide the Maze with suitable breeding stock?

"There is always a deeper purpose to every life," Adamon said softly. "And to breed a son like Caelum is a purpose worthy enough, surely."

"But we have also bred the traitor to undermine his chances," Azhure said bitterly. She remembered the Beltide night when she and Axis conceived Caelum. She remembered how she'd been caught up in a magic far more powerful than herself. Had the Maze been there, twisting and manipulating? Had they had no free will that night? "Why would Drago have done such a thing? *Why?*"

"He had been sentenced to death," Pors said emotionlessly. "He chose the best means he could to save himself."

"I do not care what should have been done about Drago in the past," Adamon said, "or what mistakes were made in his upbringing. What we all need to do now is to consider how best to cope should these Demons come through the Star Gate."

"We must help Caelum," Azhure said. "Train him as best we can. Axis, surely you would be best for that."

"As I," WolfStar put in, and stared at Axis.

Axis conceded. "As all of us. I do not know how well Caelum will cope . . . he has had so little experience . . ."

"There is one thing more I should tell you," WolfStar said. "One more thing that Caelum will need to use against Qeteb."

"Yes?" Adamon asked.

"The Rainbow Scepter. The Maze clearly connects the StarSon with the Scepter. Again and again the symbols for the StarSon and the Scepter are intertwined, made as if they are one. No doubt Caelum must wield the Scepter to drive back the TimeKeeper Demons, or to defeat Qeteb should he be reconstituted."

Axis laughed harshly. "Well, then, why don't we just prepare a greeting party with wine and food at the Star Gate? Drago has betrayed his brother and Tencendor with consummate skill. We are doomed."

WolfStar shrugged a little. "Axis, we need to train Caelum, and he needs the Rainbow Scepter."

"Oh?" Adamon said. "Do you suggest that we go through the Star Gate after it? None of us," he waved at the other Star Gods, "can do it, for we are so peculiarly tied to this world. Who else . . . you?"

WolfStar shuddered. "No, not me. Our only chance to regain it is when the Demons come through the Star Gate—*if* the Demons bring it back with them."

"We wait until they are *here*?" Axis said.

WolfStar nodded. "If we cannot stop them beforehand,

then that is the only option left to us. And then to find some means to snatch it back. I'm sorry. It's all we can do."

"But how can we combat them for the Scepter?" Azhure cried, despair all over her face. "By the time the TimeKeeper Demons are here they will have completely blocked out the Star Dance. We will be as ants before their power! And Caelum? What chance has he against these Demons with all his power gone? I can't see—"

"Azhure, my dear, be calm," WolfStar said gently. "We will get the Scepter back for Caelum. By whatever means we can."

47

Niah's Grove

Faraday paused at the door to Niah's room, listened, then pushed it open. She moved wrapped in an aura of dream, so she made no sound, and she was virtually indistinguishable from the shadows. Every day Faraday found different uses for her newly enriched power, and this current trick was a most useful accomplishment.

The room was dark, filled only with the sound of sleep. Faraday stood a while, catching her bearings, learning the layout of the room, memorizing the patterns of the bed, chests, hanging robes and mirrors.

Then she moved silently toward the bed.

Niah lay there. Alone. Faraday had more than expected to find WolfStar here tangled with her, their bodies a mass of damp flesh and twisted feathers. But WolfStar had abandoned his lover for this night. No matter. Faraday could act whether WolfStar was here or not.

She sat on a stool by the bed and watched Niah sleep. The woman slept awkwardly, not sure what to do with her wings.

They hung to either side of the bed, drifting across the floor, Niah's naked body pale and vulnerable in the faint moonlight. Waiting, perhaps, in case WolfStar found the time to visit.

Faraday's eyes rested on Niah's belly. There was only the faintest suggestion of a roundness there—it was far too early in the pregnancy for any noticeable swelling yet. Faraday leaned forward, and placed both her hands on Niah's belly.

The woman stirred, and Faraday whispered soothingly to her, quieting her, sending her deeper into sleep.

Once Niah had stilled, her breathing now so quiet and slow Faraday knew she was lost in her dreams again, she began to knead her fingers into Niah's belly. Probing. Deep. Looking, sensing, for the baby.

There. The slight hardness of the thickened walls of her womb. All depended on . . . yes! Faraday sensed the life force growing there. A girl child. Good. Very good.

"What a lovely baby," she whispered. "So healthy. Such a willing receptacle."

Then she lifted her hands from Niah's body and sat back. She opened her mind to dream, seeking that which was lost.

She opened her mind to Niah's Grove. Of course. Here Zenith had last drawn breath, here Niah's old body moldered, here Niah had finally consumed Zenith altogether.

Faraday looked about the grove that she could see in the shadow-lands of dream. Like all things in the shadow-lands, the grove was insubstantial. The forest faded in and out of view beyond the ring of nine great trees. Faraday had planted these trees herself to honor Niah's memory, and now she regarded them wryly. Perhaps she should not have been so willing. This grove and this grave had harbored Niah's spirit as a scabbed wound harbors infection.

Here Zenith had lost her fight.

Faraday wandered slowly about the grassy ring. Moonwildflowers grew here in abandon, thicker around the center. Here Axis had brought Isfrael to see her. Here Azhure had wept over her lost mother. Here. On the site of Smyrton.

Perhaps we should have left it, Faraday thought. She remembered the day Azhure had loosed her power to raze Smyrton to the ground. She remembered the foul wind that had swept over them. Infection again. Had it befouled Niah, tied to this spot . . . waiting, waiting, waiting?

She raised her head and looked about. "Zenith?" she whispered, the whisper echoing strangely about the trees. "Zenith?"

There was nothing, but Faraday was patient. If there still *was* a Zenith, then here she would be.

"Zenith?"

Faraday sat in the very center of the grove, ringed by Moonwildflowers, and waited. She sat, and absorbed the stillness of the shadow-forest about her, and listened to the air as it moved damply about her.

A movement. There, to her left.

Very, very slowly, for Zenith must be truly lost and frightened, Faraday turned her head toward the movement and smiled. After a moment, she lifted her arm and held out her hand, palm uppermost.

Zenith.

"I do not know where I am."

Zenith, come sit with me.

Another movement, stronger this time, and a form rose from the grass at the edge of the trees. It was wraith-like, almost apologetic, but it was Zenith's form.

"I am lost."

"Surely, sweetheart." Now Faraday used her speaking voice, and widened her smile. "Come to me. Let me show you the way home."

The form drifted toward her. She wrung her hands, and tears slid down her cheeks. "I do not know what to do."

"Here." Faraday patted the grass. "There is space here."

The form drifted across and sank down beside Faraday. She was so ethereal that Faraday thought gossamer would seem like iron scaffolding beside her.

Zenith. There was not much of her left. Niah had almost won. A week or two more, and she *would* have won.

Faraday folded her hands in her lap and gazed serenely at this apparition. "Poor Zenith. Would you like me to show you the way home?"

"Who are you?"

"Oh!" Faraday almost forgot herself and laughed, but she stifled her merriment before it could find voice and frighten Zenith away. Zenith had never seen her, and had never known her human form.

"I am Faraday, Zenith. Once Duchess of Ichtar, once Queen of Achar, now just Faraday, owner of her own soul and destiny."

The apparition smiled wistfully. "To own your own soul and destiny . . . that must be true happiness."

"Ah, it is, Zenith; it is. I was bound by the Prophecy of the Destroyer, bound by my guardianship of the trees, bound by the Mother and by my love for your father for too long. Now I am free."

What was left of Zenith nodded. "I am glad, Faraday. I did not envy your role in the Prophecy."

"And I would that you be free, too. Do you want that?"

"Niah is too strong. I tried to fight her . . . but she was so tenacious, so determined."

"She had the strength of the grave behind her, my dear, and you could not fight that. You did not have that experience. Then. Now, of course, Niah has made a ghastly mistake in banishing you to the one place where you *can* obtain the experience and yet *still* return. Zenith," Faraday's tone turned brusque, "I have a plan."

"Good," Zenith said, and her tone finally made Faraday laugh.

"Yes, extremely good. Niah has taken your body to the Island of Mist and Memory. There she continues to deepen her affair with WolfStar—"

Zenith turned her head aside.

"—and grows his child within your womb. Zenith, that child will be your savior."

"I do not want it!"

"Undoubtedly not. It is a product of rape—who could love a child of that? And who knows what WolfStar and Niah can breed between them? Listen to me, Zenith. You must fight."

"How?"

"Can you still feel Niah? Feel the presence of her?"

Zenith nodded.

"Very well. Eventually we will use that child for our own ends, and that infant girl shall be your savior. But first we must get you back to your body. Back to what Niah has claimed."

"I don't understand."

"Zenith, this shadow-grove is but one part of the shadow-lands that mimic entirely the world of waking. We can travel through these lands, travel toward the shadow dormitory of the priestesses where lies Niah."

Zenith looked puzzled, but that puzzlement was underlaid with hope. "Tonight?"

Faraday smiled sadly. "Nay, child, not in one night, although we will make a start tonight. It will take us many, many nights. But get there we will, and we must get there before some other spirit inhabits the baby-child within Niah."

"How long do I have?"

"A month perhaps. I shall come back each night and help you."

"A month only to walk to the Island of Mist and Memory?"

"Every step we take in the shadow-lands equals fifteen in the world of waking. We travel much faster here." Faraday smiled wryly. "It is one of the advantages of wraithdom, I suppose."

"Then we had best begin."

Faraday stood, then helped the Zenith-apparition to her feet. "My dear, the closer we get to the Island of Mist and Memory, the harder Niah will fight."

"She will be aware that I approach?"

"Not as such—that's why we move at night, only when she sleeps—but she will know something is wrong. Her own sleep-mind will raise barriers for you, try to prevent you. Zenith, there will come a time when each step you take toward the island will be agonizing. It will go on for night after night. Can you face that?"

Zenith laughed, low and bitter. "Do I want life? Come Faraday, let me lean on you, and we shall take this first step."

48

Carlon's Welcome

"Still nothing from our rear?" Zared asked Theod yet again as they sat their horses a half-hour's ride northeast of Carlon.

"No, my Prince," Theod said. "Caelum must be suffering from shock. He has not sent so much as a scout after us. Not," he said glumly, "that he has many to send."

Zared turned away from Theod, his thoughts bleak. When Theod had caught him up with the devastating news that Caelum had ridden his force straight into Kastaleon without so much as a dog to scout the place out, and had thus suffered the full force of the explosion, Zared had blanched.

"How many?" he had asked quietly.

"Between three and four thousand dead at least, my Prince. And scores more injured nigh unto death."

"Caelum?"

Theod had not known, but Zared refused, *refused,* to consider Caelum dead. Besides, had Caelum died Axis would surely have known and acted.

Why in the name of every god in existence hadn't Caelum sent in a scouting party first?

Zared had been prepared to risk five or six deaths, much as he regretted them, but he had yet to come to terms with the horror of three or four thousand dead. All he'd wanted to do was destroy Kastaleon and hold Caelum up for a few days. What he *had* done was create a situation where war was unavoidable.

His hands were tied, and through his own action. He could either surrender himself—an idea anathema to the proud Zared—or he could work to make his position unassailable.

His doubts had been blown away as forcibly as most of Caelum's force. He now had *no* choice. He must make himself King of Achar, with Leagh at his side. Once King he could hopefully rally the support of hundreds of thousands of Acharites feverishly loyal to their resurrected monarch.

Even Caelum might think twice about setting the Strike Force on the entire West and North.

At the least, Zared thought with only the tiniest degree of humor, he might think about sending in a scouting party first. Frankly, Zared was amazed that six days after the destruction of Kastaleon, the Icarii Strike Force was still not yet wheeling down on him from the sky.

"I would have set *everything* I had after me had *I* been Caelum," he muttered. "What in the name of all gods is he up to?"

They had moved south fast from Kastaleon. Desperately fast. They'd ridden a day, then commandeered riverboats to carry them toward Carlon. This morning Zared had ordered the boats to put to shore, and land his men so they could ride the final league.

Zared hoped that Goldman had been right in saying Carlon would support him, and that western Tencendor would rise up to back his claim to the throne. The last thing he needed was to ride into an apathetic city.

"She still does not know?" Theod said softly beside Zared, breaking his thoughts.

Zared glanced over his shoulder. Leagh was several lengths behind him, riding with Herme. Zared reined his horse closer to Theod's.

"No. I have not liked to tell her. Who knows if Askam lives or dies? It would be cruel to tell her."

Theod looked at him with concern, thinking to say more, but Zared's gaze was now fixed on the road before them.

"Look! Is that Goldman?"

A group of five horsemen had ridden from Carlon's gates, still some three hundred paces distant. Two outriders carried poles from which fluttered pennants and standards.

"Look," Theod said, "they bear the standards of Carlon . . . and of Zared, Prince of the North."

Zared felt his muscles relax a little; he had not realized he was so tense until this moment. He pulled in his own horse, then waved his column to a halt.

There was a movement to his side, and Herme and Leagh rode up.

"Goldman," Zared said, indicating the riders, but Leagh said nothing.

The group of riders covered the distance to Zared at a brisk canter. It was indeed Jannymire Goldman, with four well-dressed companions.

"Prince Zared," Goldman said, reining his horse to a halt three paces from Zared, "I offered the support of the traders and guilds of Carlon, and here it is. May I present Mayor Gregoric Sandmeyer, and the Guild Masters of the Wool, Fish and Grain merchants' guilds."

Zared raised his eyebrows. A powerful coterie indeed. "And do you also present me Carlon, Master Goldman and Mayor Sandmeyer? I have at my back a force of some five hundred men. Hardly enough to overrun Carlon's walls should I be forced to do so."

"I think you will hardly be 'forced,' Prince," Sandmeyer said, bowing deeply from his saddle. He was a barrel-chested man, with strong features and startling eyes. "Carlon—indeed, Achar—eagerly awaits you."

Then he turned to Leagh, and offered her another, if smaller, bow. "My Princess, I am glad to see you again. It has been too long. And you ride by Prince Zared's side. If I may be so bold, for many know that the Prince has been petitioning for your hand for many a long year, may I ask if you ride as his wife?"

"Not yet," she said shortly. Sandmeyer was being too forward. "I have yet to come to a decision."

"I see," Sandmeyer said softly, and looked at Goldman.

"I think, Princess," Goldman said, "that Carlon's reception may make your decision a little easier for you."

Zared had hoped Goldman would organize a welcoming crowd, but he had never envisioned the tumultuous welcome that Carlon put on for him.

As they urged their horses forward, Zared became aware of a muted roar. Initially it puzzled him, but as he drew closer to the main gates he realized—with absolute astonishment—that it was the thunder of a crowd tens of thousands strong.

He looked at Leagh—they now rode side by side at the head of the column, the others having drawn back—and saw that her face was pale, as astonished as his.

And then they were inside the gates, and inside a maelstrom.

The noise of the crowd was overwhelming, and Zared had to grab at the bridle of Leagh's mare as it shied in fright. One of Carlon's militiamen ran forward, and took it from him, and Zared leaned back in the saddle, trying to absorb the sights and sounds before him.

Carlon's streets were lined ten-deep with people. Others crowded balconies and roofs. Everyone was waving something, whether ribbons or pennants or banners; some were the rose and gold of his familial standard, others were the royal blue and scarlet of the Acharite throne.

As one, they roared his name.

"Zared! Zared! Zared!"

Atop the shouts of the crowd came the trumpeting of horns—scores of them—and the beating of drums and the clashing of cymbals. The noise bounced off walls, echoing wildly through the streets and then into the sky.

Zared stared, then he laughed, almost overwhelmed with the emotion poured out in his welcome. He spurred his horse forward and waved, and the noise, if possible, tripled.

Leagh, riding at a more sedate pace behind him, was utterly stunned. She could hardly comprehend the sights and the sounds. She had seen nothing like this before. Nothing. Even Caelum's crowning on the shores of Grail Lake had been a sedate seventh-day picnic compared to this.

Askam had never pulled a crowd of more than a thousand onto the streets, but Leagh thought that Carlon's entire sixty thousand must have abandoned home and work and school to pay homage to Zared.

And that was what it was, she realized. Homage, not welcome.

Before her the crowd surged, trying to follow Zared's progress. He had been mobbed, but did not seem afraid. Instead he was laughing, and leaning down from his horse, grabbing hands, touching faces.

"King Zared!" the crowd now roared. *"King Zared!"*

Then the mob were crowding her, too, and she heard them call out her name.

"Leagh! Leagh! Queen Leagh!"

Some ten paces in front of her, separated by hundreds of people, Zared swung his horse about and caught her eye.

Leagh stared at him, shaking. She had never realized . . . never realized . . .

* * *

They were led, eventually, to the dazzling ancient Icarii palace on the highest hill in the city.

Not to the Prince's palace.

The Icarii palace had been the one used by the former Kings of Achar, passing into the hands of the SunSoar family once Axis had destroyed the throne.

Now, apparently, it would again be used by an Acharite king.

There, in the Chamber of the Moons, Carlon had prepared a reception for Zared that was only slightly less restrained than the street welcome.

On the dais sat a throne, a perfect replica of the ancient throne of the Acharite kings. Leagh stared at it in amazement—how long had they been preparing for Zared? The throne was the patient work of a master craftsman, several masters, for exquisite wooden carvings had inlays of gold and silver and scatterings of precious gems.

How had I never known? she thought to herself, still dazed, as Zared took her arm and led her to the dais. How had I never known?

Zared would not use the throne, saying it could wait until he was crowned, but he stood on the dais, Leagh at his side, Herme, Theod, Goldman and Sandmeyer slightly behind him, and received the well-wishers of Carlon.

First there were representatives from the guilds, all of whom knelt before Zared and promised him their support.

The city militia stood forth and did likewise.

Representatives from each of the major blocks of Carlon came forward, some with their wives and children, and proffered their support.

And from the nearer rural areas came the rural guild masters, there, as all the others, to offer Zared their wishes and their loyalty.

Leagh was a little amazed that even the rats had not sallied forth from their sewers to pledge *their* allegiance as well.

"Prince Zared," Goldman finally said, standing forth so that he could address Zared. "Have you any doubts as to the loyalty of your people?"

"No, good Goldman," Zared said softly. "This is more than I ever dreamed possible."

"Do you have any doubts as to their wishes, my Prince?"

"No, Goldman. I do not."

In a dramatic gesture, Goldman dropped to one knee, put a hand over his heart, and dipped his head in obeisance.

"Zared, will you accept the loyalty of your people? Will you accept the wishes? Will you assume the throne of Achar?"

There was utter silence in the chamber, and Zared looked slowly about, not only at the people who waited for his answer, but also at the chamber itself that had witnessed so much violence and death during Axis' war with Borneheld.

"I was born to the throne of Achar," Zared said, his voice ringing to the very peak of the brilliant blue-enameled dome itself, "and so I will assume it."

The chamber erupted. Goldman waited until the noise had died down, then he looked at Leagh. "And will *you* accept the wishes of the Acharites, Princess?"

She stared at him, then Zared leaned across and took her hands, turning her to face him.

"Will you be my wife, Leagh?" he said. "Will you be my Queen?"

She looked at him, studied his face, and knew she had no choice. "Yes, Zared," she finally said, "I will be your Queen."

49

Caelum amid the Ruins

Caelum had viewed the disaster of Kastaleon for a full week, and yet still he could hardly credit his eyes. The castle was a ruin—no longer smoking perhaps, but the piles of cold, useless stone were as painful to gaze upon as the burning wreckage had been.

What remained of his command was still camped about the ruins. Six hundred men, many still abed from their injuries. Straggly tents, ragged horse lines, and morale that was as damp and gray as the moat most had been forced to swim through to survive. Beyond the camp site, thousands of sad mounds stretched into the distance. Graves. Reminders of the treachery Zared had visited on him.

"How could he have done it?" Caelum muttered, but no answer occurred to him as it had not occurred to him every time he'd asked himself that question over the past week.

He turned from his useless contemplation of ruins and camp and walked toward a tent set aside from the others. A guard outside saluted as Caelum approached, but Caelum noted the guard's eyes slid away, refusing to meet his.

Lingering grief for his comrades, Caelum told himself.

He lifted the tent flap and entered. It was dim inside, too cool, and Caelum thought about asking a servant to light the brazier. He half turned back toward the tent flap, intending to ask the guard to fetch someone, then thought better of it and lit the brazier himself.

"Caelum?"

Caelum closed the brazier hatch. "You're awake, Askam. Did the herbal brew not work?"

Askam struggled into a sitting position on his bunk. "The pain has dulled, but my left hand itches abominably. Ah!" He spat into a corner of the tent. "The ghost of this arm haunts me, Caelum! Will it never leave me in peace?"

Caelum sat down on a stool close to the brazier and watched Askam warily. He did not know the words needed to comfort the man, but he suspected that Askam would accept no comfort. All Askam wanted was revenge. Revenge for his castle, revenge for his arm. He had lost more weight in the past week than Caelum had thought possible any man could do. The skin hung gray and slack from Askam's bones, his eyes were red-rimmed with pain and exhaustion, and the fingers of his remaining hand constantly trembled.

His breeches were stained by wear and the exudate from the crusty bandages about his torso.

Askam could hardly bear the pain when the bandages were changed and, to Caelum's knowledge, they had not been touched these past three days.

There was a sweet stench in the tent that could not entirely be explained by the fragrant wood burning in the brazier.

"You should rest, Askam, perhaps eat more. And someone should surely clean your—"

"I will bite off the hand of the person who dares touch me!" Askam snarled, and Caelum reflexively jerked back on his stool.

"Askam—"

"I will flay the skin from Zared's body with my remaining fingernails for what he has done!"

To that Caelum had nothing to say.

"When do we move? What *else* of mine has he seized?"

"We cannot move while you still lie so weak, Askam."

Askam lurched to his feet. He swayed alarmingly, but threw off Caelum's concerned hand and managed to find his balance.

"I can ride, Caelum. And it was not my sword arm that was stolen."

"You can hardly stand," Caelum said carefully. "And the lack of your left arm will severely hamper your sword balance."

"*I can fight!* When do we move?"

"I have not yet—"

Whatever Caelum was about to say was halted by a movement outside the tent, an exclamation of surprise, and the lifting of the tent flap.

Axis SunSoar, God of the Star Dance, entered the tent.

Caelum gaped at him, then enveloped him in a huge hug. "Father!"

Axis briefly returned the hug, then pushed Caelum back.

He looked almost as gray as Askam. "By all the stars in creation, Caelum, *what has happened here?*"

For eight days the Star Gods had talked, argued, and studied the black stain in the universe as also the slight taint that each felt in their powers. What to do, and how?

Finally they'd decided that Caelum had to be told what was happening. If the saving of Tencendor rested on his shoulders, then he needed to be informed.

Thus Axis had materialized just outside Kastaleon, focusing his Song of Movement on the faint tug of his son's blood.

When his vision cleared from the enchantment, the sight that met his eyes caused him to cry out in shock.

The destruction appalled him. He'd had no idea of any war being fought on Tencendorian soil. He, as his companion gods, had been so consumed by the problem of the TimeKeeper Demons he'd paid no attention to the daily travails of Tencendor.

Besides, Caelum now ruled, and Caelum needed to be left alone to rule as he saw fit.

But what in the name of all Stars had happened here? There were graves . . . thousands of them! For the first time in a week all thought of the TimeKeeper Demons and their potential for utter disaster had fled from Axis' mind.

Now Axis grasped his son's shoulders, as worried by the pallor of his skin and the dark circles under his eyes as he was by the destruction and death outside. "Caelum? What has happened here?"

But it was not Caelum who replied.

"Your *brother*," Askam almost spat the word, "has committed such treachery that this land has not seen in decades."

Axis ignored him, his eyes still locked with his son's. "Caelum?"

Caelum glanced at Askam, then took his father's arm and steered him outside.

Askam made as if to follow, but faltered at the first step and sank back to his bunk again. He muttered Zared's name as his head hit the pillow, and even he was not sure if the word was a curse or a promise.

"Zared had seized Kastaleon as part of his quest for the Acharite throne—" Caelum began.

"What?" Axis exploded, then subsided as he noticed small groups of men turning to stare at them.

Damn Zared into a thousand pits of fire! Damn Rivkah for breeding him!

Caelum nodded. "Even with the mention of the throne, Father, it seems that the hatreds of the past have flared into war. Zared claimed that the human populations felt slighted, that they needed their throne back."

"Stars," Axis muttered. "Was all I fought for in vain? Had he no *thought*?"

He took a deep breath and calmed himself. "What did you do?"

"I raised five thousand men and came here to personally supervise his expulsion. But . . ."

"But it did not go well for you, did it, my son? I assume Zared does not lie in any of those graves."

Caelum hesitated, then shook his head. "We approached stealthily. I hid the force under cloak of enchantment—"

Axis glanced sharply at him.

"—and I thought us to be safe enough. The castle was quiet. I thought Zared and his men asleep. But as we entered the courtyard . . . once most of us were in . . ."

Caelum turned to his father and shared with him the vision and experience of the explosion.

Aghast, Axis halted him. "You led your men into a trap, Caelum! Did you not think to send scouts . . . make sure all was as it seemed before you blithely marched your entire force inside?"

Caelum flushed. "All seemed well, Father! How could I have suspected such foul—"

"As easily as Zared anticipated *your* approach, Caelum! Why were you not more careful?"

Axis took a deep breath, averting his eyes from his son's face. "Did you not think to parley first?" he asked in a quieter tone. "Zared would have talked. His seizure of Kastaleon was just a theater to gain your attention."

"What? Look at this, Father!" Caelum waved a hand at the ruins. "Is that 'talk'?" He turned to the field of graves. "Are they 'theater'?"

"I might have done the same had I heard a force of five thousand approached, Caelum!" Axis snapped. He paused, and collected himself. It was no use expending his anger at Zared on his son.

"You are right," he said. "He should not have gone to these extremes. Where is he now?"

"Ah, he, ah . . ." In the first shocking aftermath of the explosion Caelum had not thought to determine Zared's position, and in the past two or three days he had been so plagued by his nightmares it seemed that whenever he blinked he saw the point of the sword screaming down toward his heart.

Gods, why hadn't he acted quicker? How was it that Drago could so destroy his mind from whatever hole he'd secreted himself in?

"You *have* sent farflight scouts to search him out, Caelum . . . haven't you?"

Caelum licked his lips, then wished he hadn't. "I left half of the Strike Force in Sigholt, the other half in Severin."

"Severin?"

"I thought it best that, at the least, Zared could lose his seat of power for his treachery in seizing Kastaleon."

Axis only just managed to stop himself from swearing. "You have started a civil war, Caelum!"

"It was not *I* who started it!"

Axis stared at his son, fighting back the words. A parley, open discussions about whatever grievances Zared had, and restitution to Askam for the seizure of Kastaleon would have solved the entire problem. But, no. Caelum had felt the need for dramatic action. Had he not taught his son better?

And he had just marched his entire force into enemy territory without scouting first?

Axis turned away, pretending a careful study of the ruins. How could he revile his son for the actions he'd taken? Caelum had no experience of war, and little of diplomacy. The now-dead Duke of Aldeni, Ronald, had warned Axis many years ago that peace did not breed good kings or war leaders. Well, Axis hoped that Caelum would learn from this experience.

Stars knew he was going to need it.

"Caelum," he said quietly, facing his son again, "Zared is not the only problem you and Tencendor must face."

Briefly he told his son what WolfStar knew about the Sacred Lakes and the TimeKeeper Demons. He did not tell him that WolfStar claimed Caelum was the only one who could battle against the Demons. *That* Caelum did not need to hear right now.

What Caelum had heard was bad enough. He stared at his father. "Tell me the implications of the TimeKeepers' approach!"

"They will destroy our power, Caelum. Already they blot out the Star Dance from a tiny portion of the universe. If they get close enough to the Star Gate then they will cut out the music of the Star Dance completely."

"But that will mean . . . that will mean that all Enchanters in this land will lose their powers! Every . . . every . . ." Caelum stared at his father, not able to say it.

"And every Star God, Caelum. Every Star God."

Caelum shook his head, trying to comprehend this torrent of bad news. No wonder the problems he'd been experiencing with his own powers. And it would only get worse? He tried to imagine life without the ability to hear or use the Star Dance, and found he could not do so. "Why do they approach so fast? Why now?"

And even as he asked the question, he knew. Drago.

Drago had taken the Rainbow Scepter through the Star Gate to these Demons!

Yes, Axis answered in his mind. "He leads them," he continued in his speaking voice, "no doubt in some plan to finally wrest control of Tencendor from you. Stars knows he was ever ambitious!"

"Father," Caelum whispered, "have you dreamed of the hunt recently?"

"No. Why?"

Caelum told his father about his dreams, about being hunted through forest and plain alike by the horseman dressed in his enveloping dark armor.

"It is DragonStar," Caelum said, "and always he hunts me down, and always he impales me on his sword."

His eyes were haunted, terrified. "Now Drago leads Demons to destroy us. Drago's infant pact with Gorgrael was the least of his horrors, wasn't it, Father? He will never rest, never, until he can kill me."

"Caelum, listen to me." Axis took his son's shoulders and forced him to meet his stare. "We will prevail. We have time to prepare. The Demons are far off yet."

Axis could feel Caelum trembling beneath his hands, and his power could detect the memories rushing through his mind. Stars! He had not realized Drago exerted such a hold over Caelum.

"Caelum? We *will* deal with this."

"Yes. Yes, you are right." Caelum straightened and subdued his doubts. "But first I must deal with Zared."

"Yes." It will give you experience, Axis thought. Experience and confidence.

"Do whatever you think best, Caelum."

"I'll battle it out, then," Caelum said. "Zared has lost the right to parley."

Axis frowned, then nodded. "If your judgment tells you that is the right course, then take it."

Then he caught himself. What was he thinking? Was he about to sacrifice his brother in order to hone his son's skills? But Caelum had been right to say that it was Zared who'd started this. Zared had drawn the first blood.

Was Tencendor worth a brother? Axis had to stop a grim smile. He'd killed two brothers already to accomplish his dream. The death of another to preserve it was no great sacrifice.

Was it?

"If you need advice, Caelum, never hesitate to ask."

Whatever doubts Caelum had exhibited earlier had now apparently vanished. "I will deal with Zared on my own, Father. Zared is my problem. But," his mouth quirked, "Drago is something I may need a little help with. With him, and with these Demons, I do invoke your aid."

Axis smiled, and put his arm about Caelum's shoulders. "Go deal with Zared, and then we shall scheme to put Drago away for an eternity."

50

The Shadow-Lands

At first Zenith moved easily through the shadow-lands. Every night Faraday came to her, took her hand, and encouraged her farther south. The journey was painless through shadow-Skarabost. They left the forest quickly—for the shadow-Minstrelsea was an unnerving place to remain—and traveled the great grain plains of Skarabost. Insubstantial men and women tilled the fields and the vegetable patches, their every movement slow and deliberate, their eyes always turned away from the two women who moved among them.

Once they reached southern Skarabost, Zenith found her steps increasingly painful. It was Niah's unconscious mind, Faraday explained, throwing up defenses against Zenith's approach.

"It will become ever more painful," Faraday said, and Zenith turned her head aside. Painful or not, she was determined to recover her body and her life.

Their journey slowed. Each night they covered less ground, even though Faraday bent every art and skill and encouragement she could. Night by night, step by step, the pain increased.

"What are these shadow-lands?" Zenith asked one night to keep her mind occupied with something other than the pain.

"The world of dream is as real as the world of waking, Zenith. But few know of its existence. Even when they dream, they barely skirt about its edges."

"How did you know of it?"

Faraday was silent a long while before she answered. "You do not know how I was transformed back into human form, and I do not think I am able to explain it all to you. But a force such as I have never known seized me, changed me, and enriched me. Over the past two months I have explored my new power, and one of the avenues it opened for me was into the shadow-lands. Zenith, that is not much of an explanation, but it is the best I can do."

Zenith nodded and accepted it.

Despite the questions she asked to keep her mind from the pain, by the time they neared the shadow-Carlon, Zenith had bitten her lip red with the effort of not crying out.

But what the two women found at the site of Carlon and the Grail Lake drove the pain from Zenith's mind.

They stood and gaped.

"What is it?" Zenith asked, leaning on Faraday's arm.

Faraday stared ahead. "It is a maze," she said, and some part of her knew that it was somehow connected to Noah.

They stood on a small rise from where they should have been able to see Grail Lake and Carlon rising in splendor on its shore. But a gigantic maze had replaced both lake and city. Where once had been water were now twisting stone-walled avenues and alleys, blind cul-de-sacs and trick doorways. It was massive, easily a league from side to side and perhaps two long. At its most western aspect the Maze rose as if it climbed a small hill—and there rose Carlon, as it would have risen beside the lake. But it was not quite the same Carlon. Its streets had twisted into a maze-like tangle as well, its buildings and spaces merely an extension of the maze below.

"Look," Zenith whispered, and pointed.

"Yes," Faraday said. "I see them."

Tens of thousands of people scurried in the Maze that filled the site of the lake and overwhelmed Carlon. Most of the activity was in the section of the Maze that had once been Carlon, but many hundreds had somehow found their way into the lower Maze. But whatever section they were in, the people ran this way and that, frantic even in the dream-like shadow-lands. Many carried bundled belongings, or children. Some ran headlong into stone walls and fell senseless to the ground. Others lent each other aid to climb the walls of the Maze, only to tumble into a section of labyrinth more frustrating than the last. Others looked over their shoulders as if they were being pursued, others still checked the position of the sun, almost lost in a haze, as if their lives depended on it.

"I don't understand," Zenith said.

"Look!" Faraday cried, and pointed.

At first Zenith could see nothing beyond the scurrying people within the Maze, but then she saw that one entire section of the Maze had emptied. Emptied, save for a man running. He was frantic, casting his eyes over his shoulder, bouncing off walls in his terror, falling and scrambling to his feet in the one breath. He was bloodied and tattered, and it appeared that he had been fleeing a very long while.

"And there," said Faraday softly.

Zenith again looked where she pointed. There were a group of horsemen, five or six, led by a man in dull black armor atop a great black horse. In his hand he wielded a massive sword.

Zenith felt nauseated. "Look, they are gaining on him."

The hunting party were only a few bends away from their quarry now, and in the space of three breaths they had cornered him in a cul-de-sac.

The man fell to his knees, his hands outstretched, but whether in denial or pleading Zenith could not tell.

The black horseman spurred his mount on, reining it to an abrupt halt.

Then he waved his sword once about his head.

"DragonStar!" Zenith and Faraday heard the hapless victim call out, and then he said no more, for the horseman drove the blade through his chest, then again through his belly, and then the horseman was standing in his stirrups, screaming his victory, blood scattering in small drops about him as he waved his sword about.

"Tencendor is mine!" he screamed. *"Tencendor is mine!"*

"Drago?" whispered Zenith.

Faraday paused. "On the horse? Maybe, maybe not, but do not dwell on it, Zenith. All will be well."

She took Zenith's arm and urged her forward. "We'll give the Maze a wide berth," she said, "and we will be safe."

51

The King of Achar

Zared wandered slowly through the ancient Icarii palace of Carlon. After the Wars of the Axe this palace had been the home of generations of Kings of Achar. Here they had wived and sired their heirs. Here they had surveyed their kingdom, cast their decisions. Here they had conspired to keep the Forbidden—the Seneschal's word for the Icarii and Avar—locked behind the Icescarp and Fortress Ranges.

Here once, but no more. Zared paused by the window of

one of the chambers. Grail Lake lapped quietly under the chill morning sun. Today, the first day of Frost-month, would be his wedding day and his crowning day.

He smiled slightly, thinking of Leagh, and then his smile broadened as he thought of what the afternoon would bring. A circlet. A ring of office. A realm. Achar.

The circlet and ring were here in Carlon. Rivkah had kept them in Severin for many years, but in her old age had succumbed to sentimentality and had caused them to be held in a quiet and secretive storage here in Carlon. Their ancient home. Where they belonged.

And now here he was. His ancient home. Where he belonged. It felt so right. He may have stumbled to this point, but once here . . .

Zared turned back into the chamber. It was spectacular—far more so than in Priam's or Borneheld's day. Once Axis had gained control of Tencendor he'd caused the palace to be restored to its ancient Icarii splendor. Every chamber had a domed ceiling, enameled in jewel-like colors, each dome sparkling with representations of stars or, as in this chamber, dancers drifting through the sky.

Zared strolled into the center of the chamber, deep in thought. Once Icarii, then seized by the Kings of Achar as their own. Restored by the half Icarii, half human StarMan. Now . . . now back to the Acharite throne.

As Zared wandered, Leagh sat very still at her mirror table, looking at her reflection. From early morning her maids had labored on her body, her face, her hair, her robes. Now here she sat, minutes from her wedding, and a few hours from a crowning.

She could not stop the lingering doubts. Oh, how she wished she had either Askam or Caelum to talk to, to ask advice from, to beg for forgiveness! She loved Zared, and she accepted that the . . . the Acharites (how clumsy that word sounded on her tongue and in her mind!) wanted him as their king. But was that necessarily right for Tencendor?

Should the throne be restored?

"Gods," she whispered at her reflection. "What will Askam do when he discovers my actions? What will *Caelum* do?"

But it was too late. She now had no choice. She had promised Zared that she would accept the will of the people, and so she must.

"He has been honest with me," she said, more firmly now, "and so I must be honest with him."

And with that she rose.

"My Prince!" enthused Wilfred Parlender, Carlon's Prime Notary. "It is indeed an honor to be asked to officiate at the wedding of our Princess to the heir to the throne. Prince, know that Carlon wishes you well! Even now the streets are lined with revelers."

Zared repressed a smile and fidgeted with his embroidered gloves. He felt uncomfortable in this finery, but a marriage such as this had to be observed with due formality.

He looked about him. Scores of people lined the walls of the Chamber of the Moons, but Leagh had not yet made her appearance. She was late. Why? Zared was struck by the horrible thought that she'd changed her mind and had fled the palace.

Back to Caelum? Zared's fidgeting grew more noticeable. Where was Caelum? What was he thinking? Zared had expected some reaction from the StarSon before now—but nothing. Maybe Caelum had died in the explosion—no, that could not be. His fairy blood would have protected him, and there had not been a vengeful Axis to deal with.

Not yet.

"Peace, my Prince," Gregoric Sandmeyer murmured in his ear. He stood slightly behind Zared, acting as chief witness. Behind Sandmeyer ranged sundry nobles, Theod and Herme chief among them, Master Goldman and his entire family, all the guild masters, their wives, and the most important craftsmen, businessmen, and notables of Carlon. Zared had requested their presence. He needed credible witnesses who could attest for ever afterward that this was a legal marriage, with Leagh giving free and willing consent.

"Peace," Sandmeyer said again. "The entire city of Carlon stands behind you, Zared."

"*Achar* stands behind you, my Prince," Goldman added. "The demonstration you saw in the streets yesterday is but a fraction of the support you enjoy throughout Achar. Every man, woman and toddling child will rally to your name. Do not fear."

Zared was about to answer when there was a rustle at the door, and the servant standing there nodded to Parlender.

"She arrives!" Parlender said breathlessly, his chubby face perspiring from high excitement.

Leagh entered the room, splendid in gold and rose, and Zared loved her for wearing his colors. Her eyes sought his, and she smiled at him sweetly.

Zared smiled back, and held out his hand. It will all be well, he thought as she walked toward him. It *will* be.

"Zared," she murmured as she joined him, and dropped her eyes demurely, although a smile remained on her lips.

"My Lady," he said, "you are more beautiful than the sunrise."

She blushed at the flattery, but accepted it anyway. There were many in the room more beautiful than she, but a woman was allowed to believe any fantasy she liked on her wedding day.

"Ahem." Parlender cleared his throat. "My Prince, Princess, would you like me to begin?"

Zared lifted his eyes, smiled, and nodded.

* * *

Leagh thought the rite the most beautiful she had ever witnessed, let alone participated in. Zared stood by her side, so striking she thought she would never be able to catch her breath again, so sure, so confident, speaking the vows with a measured yet potent voice. She knew that many people crowded the Chamber of the Moons, but she was aware only of Zared and the lesser presence of Prime Notary Parlender.

Leagh had not thought to be this entranced. She had been so uncertain this morning, but the instant she had seen Zared standing, waiting for her, all her doubts had vanished. The sun shone so bright, the waters of Grail Lake sung to her from the open window, and the brief glimpse of joyful Carlonese crowding the streets made her heart swell with happiness.

It will all be well, she thought, it truly will. She would enjoy being Zared's wife, raising their children, growing old and contented with him. Zared's parents had been deeply in love, and Leagh was beginning to hope that she and Zared would also enjoy that depth of love and commitment.

It *will* all be well.

Zared had spoken his vows, and now he turned to her. He held her hands, and his eyes smiled at her, and Leagh knew that everything would be glorious, and that the small sadnesses and irritations that struck every marriage would hardly dim the happiness of their union.

"My Princess," Parlender said softly. "Do you give your free and willing consent to marriage with Prince Zared?"

She smiled, and felt the pressure of Zared's grip increase in response. "I do hereby give my consent freely and willingly," she said clearly, "and gladly and unhesitatingly."

Parlender spoke the vows for her to repeat, but now Leagh was hardly aware even of him. All existence was centered about Zared's smile, and the warmth and pressure of his hands.

And it was done. The crowds, inside the chamber and outside in the street, cheered and yelled. Music swelled, Zared bent down to kiss her, and now Leagh knew she dared have no doubts at all, for there was no undoing their marriage.

To her surprise, Zared hurried her with almost indecent haste from the Chamber of the Moons to their prepared apartments, where he proceeded to bed her.

"Why?" she gasped as he drew her into his embrace, slipping his hands down to worry at the tiny hooks of her gown.

"Why not? It is two weeks at least, since we have bedded, and I hunger for my wife."

"But this afternoon is the crowning, and I will wear this same gown, and I will have to bathe and dress all over again, and—"

"Oh, do be quiet, Leagh," and he slid the fine gown from her shoulders and she gave in to his persistence.

Perhaps there was some final legal point that stated a consort crowned beside her husband had to be a formally *bedded* consort.

Whatever, she spoke no more, and wrapped her now-bare arms about her husband as he slid the rest of her clothes into a puddle about her ankles.

They lay for an hour only, and then servants hurried into their chamber—causing Leagh to blush as they discovered her naked—and began to wash and dress man and wife for the crowning. Abandoned clothes were snatched from the floor, and hurriedly cleaned and pressed. Hair was brushed and dressed, maids re-powdered and rouged Leagh's face, man-servants shaved and scented Zared's cheeks and chin.

And so they walked in stately procession back to the Chamber of the Moons.

There a somewhat attenuated crowning took place. In previous years, the Brother-Leader of the Seneschal would have crowned the heir, but the Seneschal and the Brother-Leader were no more. There was no other official with the same stature—neither the Lord Mayor nor the Master of the Guilds was appropriate.

So in the end it was Theod, Duke of Aldeni, as highest-ranked nobleman present, who lowered the golden circlet on Zared's head, and slipped the amethyst ring of office onto his finger.

And then he dropped to one knee, and bowed his head. "Long live the King!" he cried, and the cry was taken up in the Chamber, as in the streets where again, it seemed, the sixty thousand had gathered to welcome in their monarch.

Then Zared lowered the lesser circlet on to Leagh's brow. She opened her eyes wide as it settled; it felt cold, and unusually heavy.

The responsibilities of Queen, she thought, and then the thought was driven from her head as the air again rang with the jubilation of the crowds.

"Long live the Queen!"

Oh gods, she thought, what have I done? I have just participated in a ritual that has wiped my brother from his position as Prince of the West!

She'd never thought about that before. What *had* she done?

Then, as in ancient ceremony, the nobles present came forward to pledge to their king their homage and fealty. Theod first, and then Herme. Baron Marrat of Romsdale was noticeably absent, but several other minor nobles presented themselves. The guild and craft masters again promised their allegiance, and the same procession of people who the day previously had confessed their loyalty now bent before Zared once again.

After the seemingly endless procession had ended, Zared took Leagh's hand and led her to a balcony where they received the acclaim of the Carlonese.

The swell of joy and sound almost overwhelmed Leagh. Zared smiled and waved, but for some minutes all Leagh could do was stand and stare. Thousands—*tens* of thousands—stood and cheered, their joy was patently unfeigned and unpurchased.

He was right to chastise me for not walking about the

streets of my own city, she thought, for I never knew they hungered this much for their lost king.

Leagh raised her hand and waved, and gradually came to distinguish individual voices among the general hubbub.

"My Lady Queen," an old woman cried out directly below her. "Rule wisely and well!"

"An Acharite King and a Queen—at last!" another cried.

"A cheer for the King and his Queen," shouted yet someone else, and the wave of sound swelled into meaningless noise and almost overwhelmed Leagh.

She swayed, and felt Zared slide his arm about her waist and support her against his own body. "It's what they want," he whispered. "If it hadn't been their desire, then I would not have dreamed of claiming my right."

He kissed her, delighting the crowd, and then Leagh felt a hand on her shoulder.

Whose? she wondered, for Zared had both his clasped about her waist.

And so she raised her head, and looked, and cried aloud with fright.

Axis SunSoar stood behind them, a hand on each of their shoulders.

The crowd screamed, loving it—there was the StarMan! Even the Star Gods blessed the marriage and the crowning!

But Leagh was much, much closer to Axis, and from the expression on his face she wondered that he did not tumble them to their deaths in the crowd below.

Zared stiffened. "What do you here, brother? Have you come to impart your best wishes?"

"Inside!" Axis hissed, and his hands tightened to the point of pain.

Leagh glanced at Zared; his face was white with anger.

Without a word they walked back into the Chamber of the Moons.

"Out!" Axis shouted into the crowded chamber, his entire power as God of Song behind his voice, and the chamber emptied within moments.

"You are stupid beyond belief!" Axis seethed, turning back to face Zared and Leagh. "Zared, how could you *do* this? How could you betray all that I had worked to achieve? How—"

"How could *you* betray your mother's people as *you* did?" Zared shot back.

Leagh looked between the two men, both furiously angry, and retreated a step.

"I always knew you would betray me," Axis said, quietly now. "*Knew* it from the moment I heard Rivkah was pregnant again. You have inherited your father's 'loyalty,' Zared. Magariz was ever willing to swap masters for expediency's sake—"

"He followed where his heart told him, Axis. I but do the same!"

"The Kings of Achar deserve to lie forgotten!"

"Not according to the Acharites."

"Then damn them! Is all I did in vain? Did I not fight Borneheld to the death in this very chamber," Axis' arm swept in a violent arc, "to save this country and *all* its peoples from utter destruction? Damn *you,* Zared, am I always to be troubled by disloyal brothers?"

"You were ever prepared to fight for what you thought was right, Axis. I am only doing the same. I claim my rightful heritage back from your destruction of it."

"You will send—*have sent*—men to the grave to do it!"

"How many men did *you* send to the grave in the pursuit of *your* dream, Axis?"

"You will tear this country apart again, Zared! What will you demand next? The resurrection of the Seneschal?"

Zared's temper finally broke. He buried his fist in the front of Axis' tunic and hauled him close. "You are my *brother,* Axis, not my god! Go strut your fine-sounding phrases and ideals with your immortal companions, but do *not* tell me what is best for the Acharite people *because I don't believe you have any bloody idea!*"

Axis grabbed at Zared's arm, staring fiercely at him, but before he could speak Leagh stepped forward and spoke calmly.

"My husband speaks wisely, if intemperately, Axis. Can you not hear the cry of the crowd? They believe they need their king as much as the Icarii their Talon, or the Avar their Mage-King."

"And it is plain to see, Leagh," Axis said, his eyes not leaving Zared's face, "that *you* have not inherited the loyalty of *your* father. Belial was ever a true friend to me. I had expected the same of you."

He finally tore himself free from Zared and faced Leagh. "Do you not care that your brother lies crippled due to the actions of your husband?"

"Askam?" Leagh's face was stricken. "*Crippled?* Zared, what does he say? What does he mean?"

Axis answered. "Lady, do you not know that Zared caused the death of thousands at Kastaleon? Do you not know that men *burned* for his ambition? Caelum and Askam were caught in that conflagration. They barely survived."

Leagh felt as though she might faint. She stared at Zared, a hand to her throat. "Is what he says true, Zared?"

"Leagh, I did not tell you, for I had no way of knowing if Askam lay dead or alive. I—"

Leagh looked back at Axis. "Askam is crippled? What do you mean?"

"He has an arm torn from him, Leagh. He will be maimed for life for his loyalty to Caelum. And yet here you are. His sister, who he thought loyal to him . . . who *Caelum* thought loyal! Were you forced into this marriage, or were you a free and willing partner to Zared's treachery? What did he tempt you with? A crown? Power? How did he buy your support in this . . . this *foul* deed?"

Leagh looked between the two men, both now staring unblinking at her, both demanding her loyalty, both demanding that she choose. All she would have to do to escape this marriage, and escape Zared, would be to claim she'd not been a willing partner to the marriage. Claim she'd been forced to consent.

All she'd have to do is lie.

But had not Zared lied to her? *Why hadn't he told her about Askam?* Gods, what should she do?

"Answer me!" Axis snapped.

"I . . ." she began, then she took a deep breath and squared her shoulders. "I went willingly into my marriage, Axis."

"Then willingly you shall share the same fate as Zared!" Axis snarled, then whipped about to his brother. "Caelum leads Tencendor now, Zared, and he swears he will lead an army to your destruction! Curse your misled ambition, Zared! Tencendor needs to be united now as never before! Ah! I shall leave you to Caelum. This is not my fight any longer!"

"If Caelum comes after me—and by coming after me he comes after all Acharites—he will aid in the destruction of your own dream," Zared said quietly. "All Caelum had to do, all *you* had to do, was to admit that the Acharites deserve as much pride as do the Icarii, or the Avar, or the Ravensbund. If Tencendor now slides into war, Axis, then know it is a war that SunSoar blindness has started."

Axis stared at him, his face working with his fury, then with an abrupt motion of his hand, he vanished.

His presence and anger stayed for longer. Zared and Leagh stood motionless for some minutes, waiting for it to dissipate, then Zared slowly turned to Leagh.

"Lady," he said quietly, taking her hand and kissing it. "I do thank you."

Leagh snatched her hand from his, her entire face contorted with an emotion he could not read.

"You said you would be honest with me," she said, "and then you set the trap that almost killed my brother."

And she turned her back and left him standing there.

52

Voices in the Night

He lay in bed, and listened to the sound of the strange, cold world outside, and the gentle breathing of the strange, cold woman beside him.

If he had ever believed StarLaughter loved him, or even regarded him well, he no longer labored under that misapprehension.

She used him, as did the Questors. As perhaps also that frightening, vacant baby who even now lay uselessly attached to StarLaughter's breast.

Lying there, looking with sightless eyes into the night.

Drago lurched out of bed before he gave in to the overwhelming desire to snatch the baby and throw him with all his strength through the open window. Would the baby bounce when he hit the hard stone ground outside? And once he had bounced and rolled, would he just lie there, and stare, stare, stare?

He stood trembling, making sure that he'd not woken StarLaughter.

No. She slept as soundly as ever.

Slowly he relaxed, taking deep breaths and stretching the muscles of his back and shoulders. It was deep night—he had hours to himself if he wished, and yet hours to do what? There was nothing to do in this bizarre existence save wander amid the petrified stone forest outside and listen to the flock of children whisper for revenge as they swept swift and shadowlike through the trees.

Perhaps the Questors sat, awaiting some conversation. Drago did not know what they did with themselves through the night hours, but he suspected they did not sleep. More than likely they just sat in their semi-circle of chairs. Watching.

Drago shivered and walked over to the chair where he'd draped his clothes the night previously. He hunched into a light robe, then his eye fell on the sack of coins.

He hesitated, then snatched the sack from the chair and wandered over to the archway that led into the stone-frozen garden.

In the distant night he could make out a blacker shadow whirling through the trees.

Drago dragged his eyes away from the Hawkchilds, and sat down on the floor, his back against the pillar of the arch, his knees bent, the coins tumbling out of the sack into his lap.

He picked one up and studied it in the poor light. What did it mean, this staff on one side and the sword on the other? Why had the Scepter transformed itself into *coins*? Had the Scepter meant to do that, or was it an unwanted consequence of the leap through the Star Gate?

He rolled the coin slowly through his fingers, gradually relaxing, the questions drifting away in his mind. He leaned his head back against the cold stone of the arch, and again dreamed of the hunt. But this time he watched as . . .

the doe fled panicked through the forest, the hunters gaining on her, the hounds (birds?) at her heels. In an instant they had her down, and she was torn apart in a flurry of frantic kicking hooves and blood spraying through the . . .

Drago's eyes flew open, his heart pounding, and he stared about the chamber.

Nothing. All was quiet. StarLaughter lay as if stone herself, the infant staring into the void from her breast.

He turned his head. Outside the children wheeled through the stone forest, hunting . . . would they hunt *Faraday* if they returned?

Surely not. Surely. They only wanted WolfStar. They would leave Faraday alone. Wouldn't they?

But who did the Questors hunt?

You may have to protect her, as she will protect you.

Drago jerked halfway to his feet, staring wildly about him. That voice, an old man's voice, had echoed through his mind but had also seemed to whisper through the spaces about him.

We are grateful, Drago, that you served to free her.

Another voice. A woman's voice, seductive and humorous.

Thank you.

Now several voices all at once. Drago stared about, his mouth dry with fear, not moving only because he did not know which way to flee. He recognized the touch of power, and loathed it. Were these the Questors, come to taunt him?

No.

"Who then?" he whispered. "Who?"

Silence.

We were once free, then gave our freedom to serve the Prophecy and make the Scepter.

Drago remembered tales of the five Sentinels, and dimly recalled his father saying once that they had given their lives to make the Scepter. Hadn't they been burned . . . or something?

Once we were the Sentinels, but no more.

Drago slowly settled back on the floor, his muscles still tense, every sense alert. He rolled the coin between his fingers again, feeling its smooth, cool metal surface.

Drago, you have done some reprehensible things. The voice of a stern man. Authoritative. Jack.

Drago grimaced. Another father figure to hound him and remind him of his mistakes.

Truly reprehensible things. The woman again, laughing. *But nevertheless,* you *are very intriguing.* Yr, the seductress.

The coin stilled in Drago's fingers. His legs tingled, warm, as if a large cat had brushed against them.

Now the voices continued apace, but they talked among themselves rather than to Drago.

Freed from that damned Scepter!

At last!

Given our freedom.

Freed to the Stars.

They continued to chatter, moving into what Drago thought nonsense. Arguments about the lengths of donkeys' ears, or the precise color of Faraday's gown. They talked a great deal about freedom and choice, and then got deep into a debate about whether choice was freedom or imprisonment. He may not have followed their chatter or their reasoning, but Drago listened anyway. They were surely argumentative, but they were also amusing and intriguing, and just the sound of their voices gave Drago a sense of well-being and peace.

And somehow they seemed to give just a little hope.

She comes!

Be still!

Unpanicked but warned, Drago folded the coin into the palm of his hand, and arranged his robe so that it hid the pile in his lap.

"And what does my fine man do here on the floor?"

StarLaughter sank down beside him.

"I couldn't sleep."

"Ah." She ran a hand through his hair. "My poor man. The Questors will not need you in the morning. Shall we sit and talk? Or shall I teach you how to hold my baby just so when I give him a bath?"

"Talk," Drago said hastily and then, to distract her hand which was creeping to his lap, he said the first thing that came to mind.

"Did you play like this with WolfStar?"

She sat back, her hands still now, her face hard. "I loathed him then, as I loathe him now."

"But surely . . . you were both SunSoar . . . you must have loved—"

"I *never* loved him!" she spat.

"No, of course not. He must have been rabidly mad, even then."

She was silent a while before she spoke. "He was attractive enough, and sometimes he made me laugh. But he was in the way."

"What do you mean?"

StarLaughter looked at Drago carefully, as if assessing him. Then, "I always thought I would have made a better Talon. I intrigued against him—fool WolfStar! He thought I was so sweet, so pliant! He thought of me as a bedmate and a breeder. Nothing else. I *hated* him for that. So I planned to replace him."

Drago thought of his own bid for power, and then shuddered at the thought that he and StarLaughter might be so much alike. "You did not succeed."

And, he thought so suddenly he almost jumped, you did not succeed, and I did not succeed, and maybe it was better that way.

"Succeed? He threw me to my death!" StarLaughter said. "*And* our child, our baby." She glanced back to the bed where, Drago was grateful to see, the infant still lay. "He was no father to my baby."

"No." Drago wished he had not mentioned WolfStar. Gods, had he been this bitter? This loathsome?

"He betrayed me!"

"Yes."

"Twice over, the crow!"

"What do you mean?"

"He betrayed me twice over. First by casting me to my death . . . then by lying with another. You bear his blood. I can feel it. Who did he betray me with?"

Drago hesitated. "With a woman called Niah. She was First Priestess on the Isle of Mist and Memory."

StarLaughter laughed, but it was ugly and harsh. "The First? He seduced the First? What did she bear him, a son or daughter?"

"A daughter. My mother, Azhure."

"Ah." StarLaughter was silent for a while. "Then you have given me another name to hunt."

Drago forgot the coins. "My mother? You can't!"

"My, my. I thought you loathed your mother for what she did to you. But never mind. I do not mean your mother. I mean Niah. The adulteress. I shall hunt her with as much appetite as I shall hunt WolfStar."

Drago suddenly remembered Zenith. "StarLaughter, Niah is dead. She was but human. Forget her."

StarLaughter turned her beautiful head and regarded Drago carefully. "Death means nothing, Drago. Surely you have learned that by now. Niah exists somewhere, and wherever she is I shall find her and destroy her. Adulteress."

"She did not know who WolfStar was, StarLaughter. She meant you no harm. Hunt WolfStar if you will, but leave Niah alone."

"She bore a child." A live child. "I was left to rot amid the stars, left to bear my child as best I could."

By all the stars in heaven, Drago thought, if ever I get back through the Star Gate I *am* going to live life as a humble carpenter or water carrier. If StarLaughter is an example of what happens to someone when they crave power and revenge, then I think I shall put aside all thoughts of power. Life is enough.

"*My* baby should be WolfStar's heir!" StarLaughter added.

"And so it shall be," a soft voice said from the shadows, and Drago tensed.

Sheol stepped forth, the other Questors behind her. "And what is the title of the heir to the throne, Queen of Heaven?"

StarLaughter looked inquiringly at Drago. "What is it now, Drago?"

"StarSon," Drago mumbled.

"StarSon!" Mot cried. "Perfect! Son of the Queen of Heaven, StarSon, heir to Tencendor!"

"Heir to Tencendor," Rox said, and smirked. "Once he's caught his breath, of course."

Wild laughter rang out and Drago's heart hammered in

terror. He shuffled the coins back into the sack under cover of a fold of his robe.

"The Queen of Heaven's child," Barzula chortled. "StarSon! And so we wish and so it shall be. A StarSon such as has *never* been before."

53

An Army for the Asking

Four weeks after the disaster of Kastaleon, Caelum stood alone on the windswept plain of northern Rhaetia and wondered at his father's courage. He, too, must once have felt this alone, but from somewhere he'd found the strength to best both Borneheld and Gorgrael—and Timozel and every other traitor the star-damned Prophecy had thrown his way.

Except Axis hadn't quite disposed of the one who really mattered, had he? Caelum's eyes swept the sky, searching the stars hidden behind the sun's brightness. Drago was out there somewhere, communing with his companion demons, plotting again for the destruction of Tencendor.

Demons that could dull the Star Dance? Wipe Icarii enchantments from Tencendor? Caelum shuddered, and tried to put from his mind the growing tarnish he could feel in his own powers; every day he had to reach harder to hear the Star Dance. His mother and father and WolfStar would see to that—they *must*!

Ah! What was he doing? Why did he let his fear of Drago consume him so? With considerable difficulty, Caelum cast Drago from his thoughts. He had treachery more close at hand to deal with.

Over the past weeks travelers had brought news from the West. Zared. He had "seized" Carlon, with the help of the

Princess Leagh, and had declared himself King of Achar. Or was that King of the Acharites? Caelum did not care about the stylistic distinctions. All he knew was that Zared now styled himself King of Achar—the Carlonese, at least, cheered him through the streets—and that Caelum would need a war to wrest the West back from Zared.

A war. Well, if he had to go to war to bring peace back to this land, then he damn well would. Besides, wasn't that what everyone expected him to do?

He sighed, and his eyes filled with tears. But war was the last thing, the *very* last thing that Tencendor needed. Why couldn't they have peace for longer than a lifetime? Why couldn't the hatreds and ambitions of the past lie peacefully in their graves? Why should *he* have to deal with something he thought his father had ended?

I wish I hadn't been born first, he suddenly thought. It would all have been so easy if I hadn't been born first. But only bleakness lay in following that train of thought, and Caelum forced his mind back to his current difficulties.

He turned and surveyed the plain at his back. Over the past two weeks he'd moved his five hundred south to this point just above the low mountain range of Rhaetia. He'd finally managed to re-establish contact with the Strike Force in Sigholt, and now most were flying south to join him. They'd be here in a few days. Caelum had ordered several units from Sigholt to free the Wings currently in Severin; they should join him shortly as well.

So at least the Strike Force was on its way—but not much else.

From the West reports drifted in that Zared, aided by Theod and Herme, had a force that numbered close to fourteen thousand and was growing each day. Word about Zared's seizure of the Acharite throne had spread faster than a contagious disease, and Caelum had received information that Acharites from Ichtar, Zared's home province, as well Theod's Aldeni and Herme's Avonsdale, were moving south to join their new King in Carlon.

Caelum should have expected nothing less from those provinces, controlled as they were by their treacherous overlords. No doubt many had been threatened with seizure of lands if they did not support their lords. But men from Romsdale—whose lord, Baron Marrat, supported Caelum—were also reportedly on the move to Carlon.

Have I judged wrong? Caelum wondered. Do these men crave a human King and an Achar more than they crave a SunSoar-led Tencendor?

But even if they do, he reasoned quickly before his doubts crippled him, they should not be allowed to have it. No, this rebellion must be stopped *now,* before it went too much further.

He walked slowly back toward camp. The West and North, traditionally the areas from which the majority of a ground force could be recruited, were largely lost to him. That left Nor in the south, and the vast eastern territories, governed by FreeFall, Talon of the Icarii, in conjunction with Isfrael, Mage-King of the Avar. In the spring or summer he could also have called on the Ravensbundmen, but now they were lost in the northern icepacks, hunting their seals.

Nor. Prince Yllgaine had sent word that he rode to Caelum's side. But it would be some weeks before Yllgaine could get a force to help Caelum. Normally Yllgaine would have sailed troops up the Nordra, save that the traitorous Carlon sat on the waterway like a spider waiting to snatch at them, so they were coming north on horseback instead. Another three weeks at least. At least. It was not easy to raise an army in an hour or two.

And the rest of the east? There were the populous plains of Skarabost and Arcness. But populated with Acharites—and how many of them might elect to slip past Caelum and run helter-skelter for their shiny new King?

That left the Avar and the Icarii.

Caelum's boot heel caught in a small hole and he cursed as he tripped and almost fell. Had it come back to this? Avar and Icarii against the Acharites? It was the Wars of the Axe all over again, save for the name.

And all due to the damned ambition of Zared. Axis should have done *more* to ensure that line stayed dead and buried than just declare the throne destroyed. Rivkah should never have been allowed to bear that child. Never.

Caelum shivered. In the time it'd take him to raise a force capable of striking back, Zared would have consolidated his own position. Ample time for him to raise more mischief to tear the realm apart.

He quickened his stride. In a few weeks he would meet what forces Marrat could muster, as well as Yllgaine's horsemen, in the northern plains of Arcness. Between then and now he had to raise what he could from the Icarii and, possibly, the Avar. Although what his strange half-brother would give him was debatable.

Askam stood waiting for Caelum just beyond the camp's perimeter. He had gained strength over the past weeks, although his face was still unnaturally thin and prematurely lined. Askam had not found pain the best of companions. His jacket sleeve flapped uselessly in the wind; Askam refused to pin it out of the way, saying that he did not want to hide Zared's cruelty from the world. Of all the major players, Askam had lost the most from this sudden descent into hostility. Virtually the entire West had abandoned him for Zared.

Along with his sister.

"When do we move out?" he asked.

"Are you rested enough?"

"Dammit, I am not an invalid! *When?*"

Caelum let his eyes drift over the mountains to the southeast. The Minaret Peaks.

"In the morning," he said. "At dawn. You and I to the Minaret Peaks. DareWing will meet us at FreeFall's court. Unit commander Froisson will lead the rest of the force into the Rhaetian hills to await our return in their shelter."

"The Icarii will assist us," Askam said, his voice cracking.

Caelum looked at him. "I surely hope so."

"FreeFall is family. He *must* help you!"

Zared is family, too, yet see what he does, Caelum thought. But he smiled and clapped Askam on his right shoulder and led him back to their tent.

The Minaret Peaks had once been known as the Bracken Ranges, but that was before Faraday had planted out the Minstrelsea forest that crowded their slopes, and before the Icarii Enchanters had recovered the ancient cities that had lain buried under enchantments during their thousand-year exile. Now the ranges that ran from eastern Rhaetia to the Widowmaker Sea were crowded with minarets and spires that rose from the magical forest of Minstrelsea. It was a beautiful and mysterious region of Tencendor, and Caelum regretted that war had brought him here for the first time in almost fifteen years.

He should have left Sigholt more, he realized as he and Askam cantered their horses toward the first of the trees. He should have showed himself more to the peoples he led. No wonder the greater number of humans now flocked to a man they could—at the very least—put a face to.

The paths of the forest were cool and calming, and Caelum ordered they rein their horses back to a walk.

"Why?" Askam demanded. "We have no time to saunter along these paths, StarSon. We are on a mission of war, not a picnic."

"Nevertheless," Caelum said, "Minstrelsea does not like horsemen rushing about her paths. Do you not hear how she sings? Can you not feel her beauty?"

Caelum's Enchanter powers opened him to the more magical of Minstrelsea's songs, but he knew that ordinary mortals could well sense—if not completely hear—the music that floated about the trees. He let it relax him, let it comfort him.

His eyes drifted to the strange creatures that cavorted in

the shadowy spaces and light-dappled glades. Diamond-eyed dragons crawled along branches and luminescent badgers snuffled beneath bushes. And others, yet stranger.

Askam pulled his horse back with bad grace. Stars! But it would take them six weeks at this pace!

But he had underestimated the magic of Minstrelsea. It was not yet gone noon when he noticed an Icarii birdman standing in the center of the path before them.

"StarFever HighCrest," Caelum said, pulling up his horse as he recognized FreeFall's Master Secretary of the Palace. "I greet you well."

StarFever bowed low. Every last speck of him, whether feather or robe, was a saffron orange. "And I you, StarSon. The Talon received word two days ago of your visit, and he and his wife have been eager to meet with you."

Caelum tried to ignore Askam's obvious impatience at StarFever's long-winded speech; StarFever had gained his position for his skill at protocol, not his reticence.

"It has been too long since I last visited the Spires, StarFever."

"Then let me lead the way, StarSon," and StarFever turned and strutted in stately fashion down the forest path.

Caelum cautioned Askam into patience with a sharp glance, and they pushed their horses after the Master Secretary.

StarFever led them deeper and deeper into the forest. After some time Caelum noted that while trees still soared to each side of the path, shapes also humped just under the moss-covered soil, too regular to be natural. A few more minutes down the path low structures began to snake their way through the trees, and then resolve themselves into walls that soared toward the sky.

"Gods!" Askam breathed, his impatience forgotten as he realized that massive buildings filled the spaces between the trees—yet harmonized so completely with the forest that they added to the impression of space and light between the trees. Their walls were of pastel-colored stone, sometimes shading toward pink, sometimes toward mauve, sometimes toward gold, and they curved and fell and soared into arches and cloisters and columns and spires.

"The minarets reach at least three hundred paces into the sky," Caelum said in a low voice to Askam as StarFever led them off the path toward a wide archway. "And tunnels and chambers are carved deep into the mountains themselves. The Minaret Peaks are honeycombed into Icarii wonders. Have you never been here?"

Askam shook his head, dismounted where StarFever indicated and handed the reins to a man of solid build and dark eyes and skin. An Avar. The people of the forest.

Caelum noticed Askam watching the Avar man, and wondered if this was also the first time he'd seen one of the forest people. The Avar rarely ventured out of their forest homes, whether the Minstrelsea or the Avarinheim, and many Acharites were initially wary of their formidable build and fierce expressions. But the Avar lived peaceful lives, deeply attuned to the cycles of the seasons and the needs of the earth.

StarFever bowed to the Avar man. "I thank you and yours for your help, Heddle. Will you keep the horses well until StarSon and his companion return?"

Heddle nodded, his eyes skipping over Askam to rest on Caelum. He inclined his head, but he did not bow. "You are welcome among the trees, StarSon."

Caelum thanked him, then he and Askam followed StarFever into the world of the Spires.

This was truly an Icarii wonderland. The walls of the wide and high passageways glowed with a soft radiance that owed more to magic than any lamp. Above their heads flew jewel-bright Icarii, and through the doors and archways they passed could be glimpsed chambers and spaces that led even deeper into the mountain. Soft murmurs of voices and music drifted through the air.

Why did I leave it so long before coming back? Caelum

wondered again, and before he could answer his own rhetorical question, StarFever had led them into an enormous chamber underneath one of the spires, and FreeFall was hurrying to greet them.

FreeFall hugged Caelum, then turned to Askam.

"By the Stars, Askam!" he said, shocked. "What has happened to you?"

"He lost his arm in the explosion that destroyed Kastaleon," Caelum put in before Askam could respond.

FreeFall swung his violet gaze back to Caelum. "Not only Askam's arm, but over four thousand lives were lost, I believe."

Caelum nodded soberly. "Whatever Zared packed into the cellars of that castle was murderously spiteful."

FreeFall sighed, and beckoned Askam and Caelum over to a round table situated directly under the spire. Caelum glanced upward as they approached. Smooth walls adorned with gold and silver swirls fled upward toward a speck of blue sky at the apex of the spire. Even Caelum, with his Enchanter heritage and Icarii blood, felt a moment of dizziness.

He looked down, and there was FreeFall's wife, EvenSong, to greet him.

EvenSong smiled and kissed him on the cheek. "It has been too long since you have visited our home, Caelum." She turned, exclaimed over Askam as FreeFall had done, then indicated the chairs about the table.

DareWing FullHeart was already waiting for them, and greeted Caelum and Askam as they sat down.

"I have heard the news from the West," FreeFall said without preamble. "I can hardly believe that Zared would have gone so far." He glanced at Askam's empty sleeve again, and Askam smiled bitterly.

"Another Borneheld has swept down from the north," he said.

"Hardly Borneheld," EvenSong put in softly, her eyes steady on Askam.

"What difference?" Askam said. "Did not both seize the

throne through vileness and treachery? Does not Zared seek to tear the realm apart as once did Borneheld?"

"No," EvenSong said, more strongly now. "I will *not* credit that Zared is another Borneheld, Prince Askam. He has done wrong, surely, and for that he must pay, but he does not have the narrow mind and the cruelty of—"

"You were not there to see Kastaleon torn apart," Askam cried, scraping his chair back. "You did not have to endure the smell as four and a half thousand screaming men burned in that inferno!"

"Askam," Caelum said, "be still. EvenSong, Askam makes a good point. *You* did not have your arm torn off, nor did you have to watch the graves being dug for your command."

"This is counterproductive," FreeFall said as EvenSong dropped her eyes. "I care not whether Zared takes after his elder and unlamented brother Borneheld or not. What I *do* care about is making sure that Tencendor regains peace as soon as possible. I find no joy in contemplating the resurrection of Achar and all that it implies."

Caelum placed both his hands flat on the table. "Quite. FreeFall, EvenSong, this must be resolved by action, not diplomacy. It has gone too far to be solved with words."

"No action ever goes so far that it can't be solved by—"

"Nevertheless," Caelum snapped, stopping EvenSong dead. "I cannot ignore the fact that Zared is raising an army in the west, and I cannot ignore the fact that he claims he will not relinquish the throne unless he is forced to do so. Dammit! What is it about brothers that they torment the SunSoars so?"

There was silence as Caelum restrained his anger. "This will *not* be solved with words," he said again, staring EvenSong in the eye, "but with war. As Zared prepares for war, then so must I. DareWing?"

DareWing straightened on his stool. "The Strike Force are within two days of the Rhaetian hills, StarSon. They will arrive well rested, ready for action."

"You cannot use the Strike Force against humans!" EvenSong cried. "Axis was ever loath to do it."

"I will do as I must, EvenSong."

"But that *would* open the scars of the past as nothing else would, Caelum. You cannot do it!"

"EvenSong makes sense," FreeFall said. "I did not want to see Zared take the throne of Achar, but using the Strike Force to retake Carlon is . . . too dreadful to consider."

Caelum sat silently, remembering his earlier thoughts that this could all too easily disintegrate into another Wars of the Axe.

"What else can I do?" he eventually asked. "What? There is no ground force I can use to defeat him because the majority of the north and west swings behind Zared. FreeFall, even the Strike Force may not be enough. Not to take a city the size of Carlon—or even Arcness, should that also decide to throw in its lot with Zared. And the Strike Force, impressive as it is, cannot patrol the entire realm."

He looked about the table, then let his gaze rest once again on FreeFall. "I need more, FreeFall. Will the Icarii help me?"

FreeFall's eyes widened, and he looked at his wife before replying. "Caelum, cannot the Lake Guard help? They are at least six hundred, and as skilled at arms as the Strike Force."

"I am wary about taking them from Sigholt." Caelum had begun to wonder if the Lake Guard had some connection with the craft at the foot of the Sacred Lakes. For the moment, he preferred to keep them where they were in case they could provide information about the TimeKeepers or, more importantly, in case they might somehow be able to help against that danger. But he did not want to tell FreeFall that. As yet only himself, WolfStar, SpikeFeather and the Star Gods understood what was threatening from the stars. No-one within that group wanted to spread the knowledge until they understood more clearly the nature of the peril.

"Well, then," FreeFall said, sharing another, more anxious

glance with EvenSong. "What about Nor? Ysgryff brought some nine thousand to Axis' cause, as I remember."

"That was forty years ago. Of those nine thousand most are dead, and Yllgaine did not keep up the same level of military preparedness that his father did. After all," Caelum continued bitterly, "we *all* thought to have entered a time of peace. Yllgaine can send me perhaps four thousand. No more.

"FreeFall, I *need* the assistance of the Icarii. Every one of the adults has spent a few years in the Strike Force. There must be thousands among you who could be retrained to fight."

"No!" FreeFall banged his fist on the table. "Caelum, understand this. I abhor what Zared has done, and I fear it beyond words. But I fear more what would happen if I mobilized the Icarii nation against the Acharites. I think I would prefer to see Achar reborn in the West before I set Icarii against human again. Caelum, we are *all* children of the Enchantress."

"So tell me what you will do, Talon of the Icarii," Askam said, leaning forward over the table, his eyes glittering, "once you see men falling down in worship of the Plough in Zared's West? What then, Talon?"

"Artor is dead," said FreeFall. "There is no need to fear the worship of the Plough."

"But the hatreds that built the Seneschal may only be simmering beneath the surface. What else might they build? What other Seneschals?"

"*You* must know!" FreeFall snapped. "As you are Acharite yourself! Tell *us,* Askam, what to fear!"

"Peace!" Caelum cried into the tension. "I do not want us warring against each other! FreeFall, I accept your answer. For now." His voice hardened. "But know that I may well return and *demand* your aid if I find myself desperate enough for it. I am StarSon, I sit the Throne of the Stars, and I can damn well order you to provide what you will not willingly give!"

FreeFall blanched and sat back. Caelum leaned forward and stabbed a finger across the table. "You gave your homage and fealty to my parents, and that homage and fealty extends to me. Do not underestimate me, FreeFall. I can and will demand it of you if I have to."

DareWing, who had been watching and listening in silence, regarded Caelum with speculative eyes. StarSon had been indecisive and unsure in the early weeks of this crisis, but in the past hour DareWing had seen Caelum show more spirit than he had in months. Well, some men needed a crisis to push them into their full potential. Was Axis' blood finally making its mark on the man?

FreeFall nodded stiffly. "As you will, StarSon."

They sat silently, staring, until EvenSong smiled a little too brightly. "And what other news, Caelum?"

Caelum looked away from FreeFall reluctantly. "My other nemesis, Drago. I have reason to believe that he passed through Minstrelsea some weeks ago. Have you any reports of him?"

Both EvenSong and FreeFall shook their heads. "It is strange," EvenSong said, "that he was not noticed. Many feet walk the paths of Minstrelsea, seen and unseen, and there would be many eyes to mark his passing. But we have heard nothing. If Drago was moving south, then perhaps he took a route other than Minstrelsea."

Maybe, Caelum thought, then thrust Drago to the back of his mind again. His father would deal with him. "Is Isfrael within the northern groves?" he asked FreeFall.

FreeFall nodded slowly. "You do not think of asking him for aid? The Avar would hardly—"

"I must," Caelum said quietly, "since the Icarii refuse." This was a journey Askam could not participate in. Caelum used his power—and he had to expend such an effort!—to transfer into the northern groves of the Avarinheim forest where Isfrael had his court.

The forest was silent, watchful. Caelum walked slowly through the outer groves, nodding to the few Avar standing about their edges. They watched him suspiciously, turning to murmur to their companions as he passed.

There were several score Avar in the Earth Tree Grove itself. They stood about in small, silent groups before the stone circle that ringed the massive Earth Tree. As Caelum stepped into the grove, they all turned to stare at him, their dark faces impassive, their hands folding before them.

Keeping his own face expressionless and his gait steady, Caelum walked into the open space before the stone circle. He glanced at the watching crowd, then looked at the stone circle. Just inside he could see Isfrael, sitting a wooden throne placed underneath the Earth Tree herself. Standing slightly behind his right shoulder was Shra. Taking a deep breath, Caelum walked underneath one of the stone arches and stopped a few paces away from Isfrael's throne.

"Brother," he said by way of greeting, and inclined his head.

"What do you here?" Isfrael asked bluntly, and Caelum suppressed a wince. Should he have asked permission before stepping into these groves? No! Why should *he* of all people?

"Zared has proclaimed himself King of Achar and—"

"So I have heard," Isfrael said.

It did not occur to Caelum to wonder *how* Isfrael had heard.

"So now we have a King of Achar again," Isfrael continued. "What are his intentions?"

"Who knows what he plans," Caelum said. "And who knows if your forests are safe. I go to stop him now. And thus to my purpose—"

"No."

"You don't know what I—"

"I know. Our father asked the same of the Avar, and he was denied as well. I will not help you in this war. We are not a fighting people."

"You owe me loyalty!"

"I owe you *nothing*! I have never offered fealty and homage, Caelum. Not to you, not to our father."

"Isfrael, please . . ."

"No."

"What if Zared comes to destroy the forests?"

Isfrael studied Caelum carefully. "I do not think Zared would do that."

"But—"

"Zared is your problem, Caelum, not mine. He does not become my problem until I see the sparkle of axes in my forests. I will *not* send my people out to fight someone else's war. Do you understand?"

"Then damn you, too," Caelum said bitterly, and turned his back on his brother.

Isfrael sat and watched Caelum stalk toward the edge of the grove, and then fade out of view as he worked the Song of Movement.

"He has a lot to learn," Shra said softly.

Isfrael thought for a while before answering. "He will always do his best," he finally said, "although I wonder if his best is going to be good enough."

There was a step behind them, and an Icarii birdman emerged from behind the Earth Tree.

It was WingRidge CurlClaw, Captain of the Lake Guard.

"I do thank you," he said, bowing deeply before Isfrael.

"I would not have helped him in any case," Isfrael said. "The Avar will *never* take up weapons and stalk the field of war."

Isfrael paused and watched WingRidge carefully. "You are an interesting young man," he said eventually. "And you serve your master well."

"I am bound to his service," WingRidge said. "But it has been hard sometimes."

Isfrael nodded sympathetically. "He will understand that eventually," he said, then waved the birdman away.

54

Journeying through the Night

Faraday slipped quietly into the room and sank down into the chair by Niah's bed. The woman was alone. Over the four weeks of nights that Faraday had come in here, she had occasionally found WolfStar tangled about Niah, but his visits were becoming rarer, and Faraday supposed he had more urgent business elsewhere.

Niah was sleeping badly. She murmured and tossed, and by the sheen of the moon Faraday could see that the woman was perspiring lightly. One hand lay resting on her by now slightly distended belly.

No doubt she feared sleep, yet did not know why.

Faraday smiled, and prepared herself to enter the dream world. Every night Zenith took another step closer, every night Niah was pushed just that bit closer to the baby. Step by step.

Closer to entrapment.

Faraday closed her eyes.

When she opened them again she found herself in the misty world of the shadow-lands.

About her bustled—and yet drifted—the dream reflection of Ysbadd. People moved from shop door to window, from street corner to boudoir, from wharf to storeroom. All moved slowly, hesitatingly, as if they had forgotten their purpose, and yet somehow all arrived at their destination.

Faraday wandered the streets, ignoring, and being ignored by, all those who drifted past her.

Ah, there was Zenith. Under the awning, its canvas flapping inconsonantly in this most visionary of domains, where she had stopped last night, unable to take another step.

Faraday moved to her side. "Zenith."

Zenith lifted her eyes and stared at Faraday. Then she smiled, slowly and hesitatingly. She had only been smiling since the plains of Tarantaise. It was a good sign.

Faraday took her hand, and then leaned forward and hugged her. "Niah worries, yet does not understand the reason for it. She walks through her days, her eyes flitting over her shoulder, gasping at breezes in shadows. She is losing, Zenith. She *is* losing."

"And the baby grows?"

"Healthy and ever receptive. But we must be quick, for the baby is approaching the stage of its growth where it can be inhabited by a spirit. And you and I know which spirit we want to inhabit it."

Zenith nodded, and looked down the street. "I feel stronger tonight, Faraday. I can surely walk to the wharves."

"Good! Zenith, if you can walk to the wharves, then I can find you passage. Imagine, all the way to the Isle of Mist and Memory! For once you need take no steps."

Zenith gave an almost predatory smile. She could sense victory, and it lent her strength. She had no guilt about what she was going to do. Niah had felt nothing but triumph in possessing her and in spiriting her into this dream-world prison.

"Then let us make a start," she said and, leaning on Faraday, she took a step forward.

The way was fraught with difficulties. As with each night's journey over the past two weeks, Zenith found every step agonizing, so difficult that her breath wheezed in and out of her lungs, and her fingers dug into Faraday's arms and shoulders with the strength of her distress. Some steps Faraday thought Zenith was about to collapse, but then Zenith would somehow find the strength to stumble forward. They moved through the streets, each movement a torment, no other thought on their minds but that Zenith must lift one leg and put the next foot forward, and then transfer weight to it, and then find the strength to use it to spring her into another step, and then another, and so onward, ever onward. Until finally . . .

"Faraday, I cannot go on! This must be it for tonight. I am sorry, I cannot . . ."

"Look, Zenith!" Faraday grasped Zenith's chin in fierce fingers and forced her head up. "See? Five more steps and we are at the wharf!"

"Five steps too many, Faraday. Tonight I must rest here. I must. I—"

"Then prepare to live your life, your *eternity,* locked in this shadow-world! The baby grows apace, Zenith. We cannot leave it too much longer. A week, ten days at the most, and some other spirit will inhabit it! I cannot keep them at bay for much longer. Get to the wharf, Zenith, or I swear I will not return tomorrow night!"

Zenith wailed, and Faraday's heart turned over in sorrow and pity for her, but she let none of it show on her face.

"Move!" she hissed. "Now!"

And Zenith put another foot forward, screaming with the pain, but Faraday urged her on, and somehow she got another foot forward, even though her leg was trembling so badly Faraday thought it would never bear her weight.

But it did, and then they were only three steps from the wharf.

Again Faraday's fingers bit painfully into Zenith's face. *"Look!"*

And Zenith raised her head and looked.

There, bobbing in the gray sea, was a boat. A small boat, a lantern in its prow. A flat-bottomed ferry.

Zenith took another step, and bent double and groaned with the pain. But again she raised her head and looked.

"Where did that come from, Faraday?"

"It had lost its owner," Faraday said. "And, lost, it needed a purpose. So I summoned it. Come, two more steps."

They were two more steps that almost tore Zenith apart, but she took them. She sobbed as she sank down on the ferry's cushions, and Faraday climbed in beside her and cast off the rope from the wharf.

"I will ride with you a way," she said, "before I return. And tomorrow night . . . tomorrow night I will greet you at the pier of Pirates' Town. Oh, Zenith, there, there. No need to cry, it will soon be over. All will be well soon, I promise."

She took Zenith's head and placed it in her lap, and she let Zenith sob until she fell into an exhausted sleep.

Faraday sat there a long time, watching the gray waters drift past, lost in the shadow-sea between the coastline of Nor and the Isle of Mist and Memory. She sat there until she felt the approach of dawn in the world of the waking, and then she vanished, leaving Zenith to travel the shadow-seas by herself.

The dawn was still and cold, and Faraday stood at the lip of the southern cliff of the mount, seeming not to notice the thousand-foot drop beneath her. She shivered, more in delight than discomfort, and wrapped her arms about herself. She loved standing here, looking out into the great southern ocean, watching the waves roll in, feeling the salty wind push back her hair.

It smelled of freedom. If she wished she could step off the cliff and die, or she could turn and walk back to the priestesses' dormitory for breakfast.

Which?

She laughed, reveling in the fact that she *had* a choice, and felt rather than heard StarDrifter land on the grass behind her.

She half turned her head and grinned. "Come to save me, StarDrifter?"

He returned her smile briefly, took the step between them and wrapped his arms about her.

"You're cold."

"I'm alive."

His arms tightened, and Faraday relaxed back into them. Faraday shared a deep companionship with StarDrifter. A friend, she thought, for all life and through all future lives.

"Zenith is closer," she murmured, and his arms tightened.

"Where?"

"Drifting the shadow-seas between Nor and this island."

"When?" His voice was tight, anxious.

"I hope to find her on the shadow-pier of Pirates' Town tonight."

"And then it will be only days until she reaches the Mount?"

"Only days, StarDrifter. You will have your granddaughter back soon."

"Axis and Azhure should be caring for her, helping her to find her way home."

Faraday was silent for a long moment, then she shrugged in his arms. "*We* love her, StarDrifter, and *we* help her."

They stood a while in silence, then Faraday became aware that StarDrifter was distracted, and very, very worried.

"What is it?" she asked.

StarDrifter stood back. "Faraday, at dawn one of the priestesses hurried into my chamber. She had disturbing news."

"What?"

He took a great breath. "There is something wrong with the Temple of the Stars."

55

The Blighted Beacon

StarDrifter led her up the small rise toward the Temple of the Stars, and Faraday realized as soon as she saw it that something was indeed badly wrong.

The Temple was constructed entirely of a great beacon of cobalt light that speared into the sky. Within the light, stars danced and swayed.

But today a dark stain also danced and swayed within the light. It had cut a great swathe through the beacon, consuming ribbons of stars and, in two instances, entire galaxies.

"What is it?" StarDrifter whispered. "What? I can feel it reflected in my own soul, and it mutes the sound of the Star Dance. Faraday, I have not thought to worry you, but over past weeks I have felt something wrong with my own powers, and all the other Enchanters on the island have felt much the same. I had wondered if it was WolfStar, perhaps, playing his tricks, but now I realize it has been caused by this . . . this *cancer* that eats its way through the stars. See how the beacon flickers! What is it?"

Faraday chewed her lip. Had Drago somehow done this? No, she thought not . . . not with what Noah had told her about him. But Drago was surely, surely caught up in it.

"What is wrong," StarDrifter cried, "to have caused this?"

"What is wrong, StarDrifter?" Axis' angry voice said behind them. "Demons come to destroy the Star Dance and ravage this world, that is what is wrong. And Drago leads them."

Faraday and StarDrifter turned around. Axis and Azhure stood a few paces away. Both their faces were hard, their eyes angry.

Axis shifted his gaze from his father to stare at Faraday. The last time he'd seen her in the flesh had been in Gorgrael's chamber, watching him rip her to shreds in a futile attempt to stop Axis from destroying him.

And here she stood again, serene, lovelier than he remembered, and standing too familiarly close to his father. Axis had thought himself immune to jealousy, had thought himself over his love for Faraday, but now he found himself seething with some undefinable anger. Faraday . . . and his *father*?

"Faraday?" Azhure asked. "What are you doing back in human form?"

"I'm free," Faraday said.

"How?"

"Azhure, what does it matter 'how'?"

"Ah!" StarDrifter said impatiently. "Axis, explain *this*!" And his hand swept toward the blight in the beacon.

Speaking in short, terse sentences, Axis told Faraday and StarDrifter what the Star Gods had learned from WolfStar. Demons. TimeKeepers. Come for Qeteb. Their approach blocking out the Star Dance. A future bleaker than the worst black ice.

StarDrifter stood appalled, his mind racing to comprehend what Axis was telling him. A future without the Star Dance? Without enchantments?

Faraday, on the other hand, nodded quietly to herself. It explained a great deal to her about Drago.

Azhure saw her reaction, and her mouth thinned. "You saw Drago," she said. "In the Star Gate chamber."

Faraday sighed. "Yes."

"Do you know what he has *done*?"

Faraday blinked at the anger in Azhure's voice. "No. Tell us, what has Drago done?"

"He has murdered RiverStar—" Axis said.

"I have heard he was so accused," Faraday said quietly.

"—*and* Orr and he is now well on the way to destroying all I have built, all *we* fought for—"

"*And* died for," Faraday observed.

"Drago is intent on the utter destruction of Tencendor!" Axis shouted. "See that blight? It is Drago's doing!"

"No," Faraday said quietly. "I cannot believe that."

Axis battled with his fury. "How is it that *you* stand there, Faraday, with your face so serene, and condone all that he has done!"

Faraday raised an eyebrow. "I? Condone?"

"You have protected him," Azhure said, her tone flat. "You told WolfStar that he had fled back through one of the passageways that connects the Star Gate with the outer world. Yet we *know* he went through the Star Gate. Why did you lie to protect him?"

Faraday stood silent, thinking of how she could answer. So many people misunderstood Drago. His parents. Caelum. WolfStar. Faraday could not blame them, for as yet they did not understand what she did. Yet she had no right to reveal Noah's confidences, to explain that Drago was not quite the enemy most thought.

She almost smiled. Sometimes it paid to lie down with the enemy.

"I thought," she eventually answered, her voice very even, "that Drago deserved to be protected by someone, just as Zenith deserves to be protected and loved."

Azhure blinked. "Zenith?"

Axis ignored the sudden change in topic. "*Drago,*" he hissed through clenched teeth, "currently leads a group of murderous Demons to the Star Gate so he can gain Tencendor for his own!"

"Only Caelum can face them," Azhure added. "Yet he needs the Rainbow Scepter—and Drago has handed it to the Demons!"

"Then you have a troublesome puzzle to solve," Faraday said lightly. "But how can StarDrifter and I help? We have our own problems here."

"Damn you!" Axis cried, and looked at his father. "StarDrifter? Every Enchanter's powers are fading, as are ours! This *is* going to become your problem, whether you like it or not."

"Faraday," StarDrifter said softly. "Perhaps it would be best to tell Axis what you can."

She shrugged, and looked at Axis. "What do you want to know, Axis?"

He suppressed a movement of irritation. "Tell us what else you know about Drago," he said. "What did he say? What did he do? What is his purpose?"

"Drago has ever kept his purpose to himself, it seems," Faraday replied. "He did not share his innermost secrets with me, Axis. In fact, he hardly said a word."

Axis turned away, furious with Faraday that she had lied yet again, furious that she had allied herself with his cursed son. Was this just another revenge to pay him back for his betrayal of her? Was she prepared to watch Tencendor torn apart to gain her feminine satisfaction?

"Axis," StarDrifter said, "what can we do? About the Demons, about the loss of power, about . . ." and he gestured toward the beacon.

"Ah." Axis' face lost all its anger. "StarDrifter, at the moment no-one truly knows. But know that the Star Gods will do our best. If you can help, then I will contact you."

StarDrifter nodded, understanding Axis' frustration—the frustration of every Star God and Enchanter in this land—and there was silence between the four for a while. Then the Enchanter lifted his head and looked back at his son and Azhure.

"Axis, Azhure," he said. "There are other matters that we must discuss. Do you not want to ask after Zenith?"

"Zenith?" Azhure said, frowning at the change of topic. "I do not even know where she is."

Faraday stared at her. Were Axis and Azhure so lost in their antipathy for Drago that they had ignored their youngest child's problems?

"Zenith is here," she said. "In a manner. Azhure . . . did you know that she carried within her the seed of Niah's soul?"

Azhure had the grace to look uncomfortable. "I suspected, Faraday, but I did not tell her."

"Why not?" StarDrifter cried out in frustration.

"Because I did not know when, if ever, Niah would claim ascendancy, StarDrifter. There was no point in speaking until then."

"Well, it has happened," Faraday said softly. "Zenith has been consumed by Niah's spirit. Azhure, don't you care for your daughter?"

"You know nothing!" Azhure snapped, angered. "Zenith was *always* Niah. If anything, I am glad she has attained her true identity."

StarDrifter, already tight and anxious over the news Axis had revealed, lost his temper. He couldn't believe the indifference Axis and Azhure showed to Zenith's pain and struggle. "Zenith was ever her own woman," he said. "What exists in that body now is so different to Zenith that I cannot imagine you can claim that Zenith was always Niah. Zenith is lost! Your *daughter* is *lost*! How can you stand there and say you are *glad*?"

"StarDrifter, you cannot understand, or you would share my gladness," Azhure said. "Niah was promised rebirth—you read the letter yourself."

"But not at the expense of my granddaughter!" StarDrifter shouted.

"I sincerely hope you are not making Niah's welcome a difficult one, StarDrifter." Her voice was very stiff.

Faraday put a warning hand on StarDrifter's arm. "We are doing everything in our power to ensure she receives the appropriate hospitality," she said.

Azhure looked at them carefully. "Do not meddle in what you do not understand," she said very slowly. "I *forbid* it."

There was commanding power and stinging rebuke in that last phrase, and StarDrifter knew that if it had not been for Faraday's hand on his arm he would not have been able to resist it. As it was, he was incapable of speech, and was glad when Faraday answered.

"We will only ever do what is best for Tencendor," she said. "Believe that."

There was uncomfortable silence between the four of them, then Axis finally spoke.

"StarDrifter, I will call on you once we know how best to resist the Demons. Faraday, I wish you well."

And then they were both gone, and Faraday and StarDrifter were left alone before the blighted beacon.

"Faraday," StarDrifter said, "was it true what they said about Drago?"

"No," Faraday said softly. "Drago is as lost as Zenith is." She paused. "Zenith is not the only SunSoar child in need of some assistance."

She turned and took StarDrifter's hand. "Will you trust me? More importantly, will you trust the faith I have in Drago?"

StarDrifter thought about that a very long time. "Yes," he said finally. "If you ask it."

56

Discussing Salvation

Drago lay under the gently swaying tree, so consumed by agony he could barely draw breath. He had stumbled blindly out here after the leap, not sure what kind of world he was walking into, and had fallen only when he'd walked straight into the coarse-barked tree.

He was aware that somewhere a sun shone, and that warmth bathed his right leg where it extended from the shadow of the tree. He was aware there was a gentle breeze, for the branches of the tree rustled and swayed above him. This world also had a rather pleasant scent about it. But everything else was lost in the sea of pain.

Sheol had patted him once they were done, pleased, and said that only one more leap remained.

And then they would be at the Star Gate.

One more leap, and then one to get *through* the Star Gate.

But Drago was certain that he would not survive another leap, and he was not even sure if he would manage to survive the effects of this one.

In the distance he heard soft laughter, and an excited voice. One of the Questors, and then StarLaughter's husky tones. Kind souls that they were, the Questors would give him time to rest. Recuperate. Enjoy the sun.

Drago would have laughed had he the strength. He knew they would drain him into a useless, dead hulk. They would consume his power, and then they would consume his life.

Quite. Do you know what you aid, Drago?

Drago really didn't care at this precise moment. He wished the Sentinels would go away. He wished he had never stolen the Scepter. He wished he had died when he threw himself into the Star Gate.

But still his hand stole to the sack at his belt. It never left him now. Even at night it lay within easy reach.

Do you know what you aid, Drago?

Drago hated the persistence of the voice. Over past days and nights he'd occasionally heard the five Sentinels nattering between themselves. Now it was the leader of the group, Jack, who spoke to him.

Drago, do you know—

"I care not!" he whispered fiercely. "Leave me alone!"

Demons, Drago. Demons who will devour Tencendor.

Drago was silent. He didn't want to hear it.

Imagine, you are the agent by which such destruction will be visited on Tencendor.

"Go away."

There was a rustle behind him, and a movement, then a brief wind and shadow as the flock of Hawkchilds rushed past and then disappeared again among the trees.

You are in danger, Drago.

Drago amost laughed, but could not find the energy. "Tell me something I do not know."

They have hurt you already. That was the voice belonging to the older woman, Zeherah. Drago felt a soothing warmth spread through his body, partially alleviating the pain.

He gasped, and straightened a little. "Will you help me? I do not want to die."

Why do you think we should help you?

"Because if I die, then you will fall into the hands of the Questors. So you must save me to save yourselves."

They burst into loud merriment. *We* are *saved!* cried Zeherah. *We have no need of your assistance!*

"You will if you want to get back through the Star Gate."

We do not want to go back. An older male voice, perhaps Ogden or Veremund.

"What? You *must* go back. You are the Rainbow—"

No, we are not. True, our physical forms once went into its making and we resided in it for long years, but we have been freed from it now. You did that for us, Drago. By jumping through the Star Gate with the Scepter you freed us. Now we can wander the stars if we choose.

"Then why are you still here?"

Because we regard you benignly and because we want to ask you a question.

"What?"

Are you prepared to aid Tencendor and your brother Caelum?

Drago was silent long minutes before he replied. "I realized," he finally said, "how alike StarLaughter and I are, how alike the Hawkchilds and I are. We have all been disinherited, our lives and heritages destroyed. My friends, I did not like the comparison. I do not want to be like them. Yet . . . yet at the same time I cannot ignore the harm Caelum has done me. I did not kill RiverStar, and yet he would not believe my denial. He *wanted* me dead, and so he found me guilty. Help Caelum? I don't know."

There was a silence, then Jack spoke sadly. *See how* you *have harmed Caelum, Drago SunSoar.*

Drago found himself caught up in a vision—someone else's vision. He was staring through a child's eyes, staring at the sky above Sigholt.

Do you know with whose eyes you see, Drago?

No, no! he cried in his mind.

Yes! Who is he, Drago?

Caelum. I see through Caelum's eyes.

Yes. Watch and feel with Caelum, Drago, as your infant malevolence strikes home.

With Caelum, Drago found his eyes locked onto a nightmarish creature plunging out of the sky. Gorgrael! He heard a shriek of primeval terror, and realized it came from Caelum. He felt despair sweep through Caelum; despair and horror as the boy realized that Gorgrael had come because DragonStar wanted him dead.

Betrayed by his own brother, betrayed to this horrifying creature.

There was a sudden movement, and Drago felt Caelum's nurse, Imibe, snatch him. She turned away, trying to protect Caelum with her body, but Gorgrael had capered across the roof.

"Fool!" Gorgrael hissed, and raked his talons down Imibe's face.

Caelum did not feel those talons, but his despair darkened and ran rampant until Drago thought the boy would surely die from it.

Warm blood—Imibe's blood—trickled down his body.

There was a flood of foul breath, and a flurry of movement, and Imibe was torn to shreds by Gorgrael's claws.

And through all this blood and death and despair, Drago could feel one overriding emotion—triumph. *His* triumph. His infant, malevolent triumph, *surging* across the rooftop from where he was bundled in Cazna's arms.

And Caelum felt it, too. Caelum felt it and his whole

world broke apart, because brothers should not do this to each other. All he'd ever wanted to do was love Dragon-Star, play with him, explore the world with him, grow into adulthood with him, and yet all DragonStar wanted to do was see him torn apart, see him *die,* and for that purpose DragonStar had allied himself with the most hated creature in Tencendor.

Now Gorgrael's claws grasped Caelum's body, and Caelum could no longer cope with the enormity of Dragon-Star's betrayal.

He lost consciousness, and Drago thought it was over.

But no, it had just begun, for Caelum woke to more horror as he found himself trapped in Gorgrael's Ice Fortress, trapped with Gorgrael leering over him and running cruel talons down his body. The torture went on and on, for days upon days, the pain riddling his body, the despair biting deeper.

Caelum knew it would never end, and he could not understand it, when all he'd ever offered DragonStar was love.

For your sins, for your pride and ambition and your over-weening hatred, a good woman died and your brother was fatally scarred for life. Your brother has been crippled by your malevolence, and by the memory of that attack. If we let you live, are you prepared to aid Tencendor and Caelum?

57

While WolfStar Lay Sleeping

She sat weeping, disconsolate, as the ferry bobbed and bumped against the pier of shadow-Pirates' Town. About her pirates and their wives and chickens moved slowly, trancelike, not aware of her, not caring.

Zenith did not think she had the heart to continue. Was

life worth all this effort and pain? Why not let Niah have her life and be done with it.

"Ah, Zenith! There you are. Here, take my hand. Let me help you from this ferry."

Zenith raised her eyes. Faraday was kneeling on the pier, leaning down, a hand extended, a lovely smile on her face.

"Take my hand, Zenith."

Zenith sat and wished it would all be easier.

"Take my hand, Zenith."

Zenith sighed, prepared for the pain, and took Faraday's hand.

They crept through the streets of shadow-Pirates' Town, each step agony. The mist of the shadow-world made everything seem so unconnected that Zenith wondered if she had any existence at all.

"StarDrifter is waiting, Zenith."

"StarDrifter?"

"We are on the Island of Mist and Memory. You forget, this is his home. Tomorrow night you will be close enough to him that he can join us."

"Join us?" Zenith stumbled as her toe caught a rock, and she spent a moment crying in despair.

Faraday hugged her close. "Assuredly, sweet girl. His power has not been strong enough for him to join us earlier, but here, StarDrifter can reach us."

Zenith almost smiled. "I would like that."

Faraday smoothed back Zenith's hair. "And so would he. Come, another step. Yes, that's it. And yet one more. Tonight I would like us to reach the long road that leads to Temple Mount. And from there, only a night or two more."

Suddenly she laughed, the sound ringing through the mist, giving substance and meaning to Zenith's existence.

"Fancy, Zenith, how Niah must be trembling in her sleep! Do you know that your mother came to see her during the daylight hours? They spoke for some time."

Zenith showed the first spark of interest that Faraday had seen in her for a very long time. "Really? What did Azhure want? What did she say?"

"She crooned over her mother, and Niah told her how wonderful it was to be reborn, and she patted her swelling belly, and said that the baby grew apace. And . . ."

"And?"

"And Azhure asked her why her eyes were so ringed with shadows, and Niah said that her sleep was troubled with strange dreams, undoubtedly a result of her pregnancy."

Faraday paused, and helped Zenith for a while in silence. When she did resume speaking, her voice was hard. "Neither mentioned you, Zenith. Neither mourned you."

The next night, as Zenith sat in her half-existence beneath a great drooping malayam tree at the edge of the jungle that covered the southern half of the island, she heard footsteps, and then laughter. She raised her head, wincing at the effort.

Down the road from Temple Mount, their steps light and joyous, walked Faraday and her grandfather, in all his silver and golden splendor.

"StarDrifter!" she cried, and he bent down and pulled her into his arms and held her so tight that Zenith knew she must be alive, after all.

"StarDrifter believed in your existence when all others did not," Faraday said quietly to one side. "It was he who convinced me to look for you, Zenith. It was his belief in you that kept you tied to this shadow-land, his belief in you that did not let you wink out of existence."

Zenith burst into tears and held StarDrifter as tightly as he did her. Every tear left a trail of pain down her cheek, but all she felt was the strength of StarDrifter's love and belief.

He believed in her more than she had believed in herself.

She burst into fresh weeping, and StarDrifter murmured to her, stroking her hair, her wings, her back. He looked over her head at Faraday, standing weeping herself now.

"Thank you," he whispered. "Thank you so very much." For this moment StarDrifter had put aside his concerns about the beacon and the Demons. Zenith was all that mattered, Zenith was his entire world, and nothing, nothing else, held any relevance.

That night they reached the foot of Temple Mount.

Niah retired to her chamber early, wishing WolfStar would come to her. She could not shake the feeling of dread that lay so heavy across her shoulders, and yet she knew not what caused it.

Was it fear for the baby, so vulnerable at this early stage of development?

Niah wandered about her chamber, unwilling to go to bed, yet not knowing why she feared it so much. She paused by the bed, her hand twitching at the coverlets, then she moved away again, her head high, eyes searching.

"WolfStar?" she said, but he did not answer.

Niah knew he had a great worry that kept him occupied somewhere else, but just tonight . . . tonight she wished he could have been with her. She wished that—

"Niah?" His voice, husky with desire, broke into her reverie and he stepped from the shadows.

"WolfStar!" She flew into his arms, and he laughed and kissed her.

"What ails my love? Why call with such desperation?" He kissed her, and laughed at her fears of the night.

"No desperation now that you are here, WolfStar. Oh, hold me, tell me I am safe!"

"Forever in my arms," he whispered, and carried her to the bed. "Forever I promised you, and forever it shall be."

Faraday, wrapped in power and the darkness of the chamber, sat and watched them. She cursed Niah for calling WolfStar this night, and she cursed WolfStar for answering.

Would it make a difference? Faraday did not know. She had gone to Zenith in the shadow-lands before now when

WolfStar lay sleeping at Niah's side . . . but tonight was the night that Zenith hoped to step from the shadows into the light.

It would be dangerous under the best of circumstances. And WolfStar's presence made it close to the worst of circumstances. What if he woke and realized what was happening? He surely had the power to banish Zenith completely, not only from this world but from the shadow-lands as well. Banish her to a place where Faraday would never be able to find her.

Where she would be lost forever.

There was a silent movement at the door, and Faraday turned her head slightly.

StarDrifter.

He walked silently to her side, and she lifted a hand and took one of his.

In this room, with WolfStar present, they could not even use the mind voice without waking him.

Faraday summoned her power, and she and StarDrifter entered the shadow-lands.

Through the night they toiled with Zenith up the thousand steps to the plateau of Temple Mount. On flat ground Zenith found every forward movement agonizing; on a flight of steps her pain was close to being unbearable.

But she was determined. Tonight. Even if WolfStar lay there sleeping.

StarDrifter and Faraday put their arms about her, and lent her their love, and she took another step.

They stood outside Niah's chamber. Zenith was shaking with fatigue, but her mouth was a thin line of determination, and her eyes glittered with hatred.

For Niah, for the woman who would destroy her.

Tonight she would end it.

Faraday met StarDrifter's eyes, then she nodded at Zenith.

StarDrifter put his hand on the handle and pushed open the door.

Zenith lifted her head and stared.

Stared at the Enchanter lying tangled with *her* naked body. Stared with loathing at *her* hand resting on *her* swollen belly.

Zenith's lip curled, and she growled, and . . .

Disappeared.

Frantic, StarDrifter clutched at Faraday. Her fingers dug tight into his arm, cautioning him into utter silence, and then she dragged them back into the world where WolfStar and Niah lay sleeping peacefully on the bed.

Except now, as they discovered when they opened their eyes in that world, some of that peace had dissipated.

WolfStar still lay sleeping, but Niah had gone rigid in his arms. Her eyes had opened wide and were staring at the ceiling, although Faraday and StarDrifter knew she saw nothing.

Niah's entire body trembled . . . and then *rippled*. Rippled again, and then jerked.

WolfStar stirred, and Faraday again grabbed at StarDrifter and pulled him back into a darkened corner, cloaking them in power.

WolfStar opened his eyes, blinked, and looked at Niah.

She lay still now, one hand curled protectively over her belly.

WolfStar smiled, stroked the hair back from her brow, and settled back into sleep.

When he had relaxed completely, the woman on the bed opened her eyes and stared into the corner where Faraday and StarDrifter stood.

It is done, she whispered in their minds, and the hand that had rested so protectively over her belly now rose, clenched into a tight fist, and slammed down hard.

Zenith rolled over and gagged, but she raised her hand again, and struck herself as hard as she could.

WolfStar rolled over, rising out of his sleep, and, desperate now, Zenith half fell out of the bed, grabbed at a heavy candlestick on a table, raised it, and drove it into her belly.

This time she could not help but cry out with the pain.

StarDrifter could bear it no longer. He leaped from the corner, leaped from the protecting cloak of Faraday's power, and to Zenith's side. "Zenith!"

WolfStar roared into full wakefulness. Not yet grasping the full import of what was happening, though understanding that something was dreadfully wrong, his power reached out and slammed StarDrifter into a far wall.

Zenith backed away, inching from the bed on her buttocks and hands and feet.

Even from the corner Faraday could see the spasms that quivered across her belly.

"Hurry, Zenith, *hurry!*" she whispered.

Zenith moaned, and doubled over, clutching at her belly.

"Niah!" WolfStar was at her side. "Did he hurt you? What has he *done*?"

"The baby!" Zenith gasped, and rolled completely over, moaning again.

She left a pool of blood gleaming behind her.

"Niah?" WolfStar whispered again, his mind refusing to believe what was happening. "Niah?"

Zenith grunted, once, twice, and then a third time. Her fingers scrabbled at the floorboards. She grunted again, curled into a tight ball.

WolfStar bent over her, and then somehow sensed Faraday in the corner.

"Help her!" he cried.

Faraday smiled. "With pleasure," she said, and bent down to Zenith's side. She was grateful her heavy hair hung down to hide the satisfaction that crossed her face.

Zenith, her hands bloodied, pushed Faraday back, then grabbed at something between her legs.

Then, in a move so appallingly fast WolfStar had no hope of stopping her, Zenith seized the tiny, bloody body and struck him across the face with it.

"Take your lover," Zenith screamed, *"and enjoy her into eternity!"*

WolfStar backed away in confusion and horror.

Zenith hefted the tiny, battered body once more and flung it at him.

It hit his head with a sickening wet smack, and then flopped to the floor.

WolfStar, his face smeared with blood—and worse—slowly lowered his eyes.

There, lying at his feet, was the undeveloped body of a tiny baby girl. Bruised. Battered. Unmoving. Unbreathing. Her skull crushed beyond all repair.

"Niah," Zenith said flatly, her eyes glittering hatred. "Dead at last."

58

As Clear as a Temple Bell

Beyond the Star Gate darkness swirled among the stars like tainted smoke. Entire galaxies had been lost, star systems obliterated, the very music of the Star Dance itself dulled.

The observers knew that the universe itself was in no danger, it was just that the closeness of the TimeKeeper Demons to the Star Gate meant that it was hard to see beyond their influence to the stars.

But that knowledge was no help—especially when the Star Dance itself was so muted by the Demons' presence.

"Look how close they come!" Adamon cried. "How long before they totally block out the Star Dance?"

Axis lifted his eyes from the horror in the Star Gate and stared at him. He'd never seen Adamon anything other than totally composed. To now see him so agitated was in itself almost more terrifying than witnessing the TimeKeepers creep so close to the Star Gate.

"How long before all Enchanters—and *us*—lose touch with the Star Dance?" Adamon said, more quietly now.

"WolfStar," Axis said, determined to try to find something that could aid them. "You can use the Dark Music. Has that been dulled by the approach of the TimeKeepers, too?"

WolfStar ignored the question. He stared into the Star Gate, his expression so bleak that Axis thought he looked as though hope itself had been torn from him.

"WolfStar?" he asked softly.

WolfStar's head snapped up. *"What?"* he snarled.

"I asked if the Dark Music has been dulled by the approach of the TimeKeepers."

WolfStar took a deep, shuddering breath. "I apologize. My thoughts were . . . elsewhere. But, to answer your question, yes. If we can't prevent these Demons breaking through the Star Gate *soon* then we shall shortly be powerless to do so at all. And if they do break through, then nothing will prevent them ravaging at will."

And my son leads them, Axis thought numbly. My *son*! He brings the destruction not only of Tencendor, but of the Star Gods and every Enchanter alive with it.

"What of Caelum?" Axis said. "If we lose all power, then so will Caelum. How can he stop them then?"

WolfStar shrugged. "I'm sure we can find some way to get the Scepter back for him—"

"Hope will not win this day," Axis said. "I, for one, have had enough of this vacillation. WolfStar, it is time we studied this Maze Gate. And then it is time we actually *did* something. Will you take us there?"

WolfStar nodded, and turned away.

SpikeFeather started as the three suddenly appeared at the head of the steps leading down to the Maze. He'd spent the past few weeks either trying to decipher the Gate's message—an uneasy task at best—or wandering the waterways, trying to access the sites of the other craft. The search had been a miserable failure, and his attempts to decipher the Gate not much better.

It was a most frustrating Gate.

Beside him sat WingRidge. WingRidge had appeared a few days ago—his fifth visit in the time SpikeFeather had been down here—although the captain had maddeningly refused to say what his exact business was. In fact, it was infuriatingly impossible to get WingRidge to say much at all.

Yet even so, the lines of worry about his eyes and mouth were far easier to decipher than the mysteries of this Gate.

Adamon and Axis walked down the steps slowly, unable to conceal their amazement at the sight of the city-maze before them. Everything within the city—streets, buildings, roofs, doors, windows—formed part of an incredibly intricate labyrinth. It stretched into a hazy distance, leagues of twisting, winding madness.

"How could *anyone* find their way through that?" Axis whispered, stopping halfway down the steps and staring.

"The idea was that nothing should ever find its way *out* of it," WolfStar said.

"Qeteb's soul lies in there?" Adamon said.

WolfStar nodded. "Somewhere. If they need to reconstitute him completely then the Demons must hunt it down."

And suddenly, as clear as a temple bell on a snowy night, WolfStar knew what he had to do. Life parts lay scattered all over Tencendor—just waiting to be used. On any dead body that needed reviving.

Niah!

Axis studied him carefully, wondering at the emotions raging across WolfStar's face. "So the Maze is intended not only to keep Qeteb *in,* but to keep the Demons *out.*"

WolfStar composed himself; whatever had distracted him now seemed put aside. "Partly."

He hesitated, then indicated that they should join Spike-Feather and WingRidge by the Gate. "But I think the Maze serves other purposes as well—although I have never been able to decipher exactly what. Ah, wait!"

WolfStar stopped Adamon and Axis on the final few steps. "Look!" He pointed toward a distant quarter of the Maze. "Those streets and that tenement complex are new. The Maze is growing. Faster than I've yet observed it."

Adamon glanced at Axis. "In response to the approach of the Demons," he muttered, and then they negotiated the last five or six steps and joined an awed SpikeFeather and an impassive WingRidge.

SpikeFeather bowed deeply to Adamon and Axis, murmuring a greeting.

"Peace," Adamon said. "We have not come to disturb your contemplations, SpikeFeather, but to scry out this Gate for ourselves. And you," he turned to the captain of the Lake Guard, "are WingRidge?"

WingRidge inclined his head.

"WolfStar tells us you are devoted to the Maze."

"Devoted to the StarSon, Adamon," WingRidge said.

"Then why are you not above ground helping him in his battle with Zared?" Axis asked harshly.

WingRidge's composure did not falter. "I, as the entire Lake Guard, serve the StarSon as we see best. Sometimes, Axis, that way is not immediately apparent to outsiders."

Axis held his tongue, although he resented being called an outsider. He knew from his own experiences that many who acted in the best interests of Tencendor sometimes took mysterious paths whose purposes were not immediately apparent.

"The writing has shifted," WolfStar murmured, moving to the Gate. "Changed."

Axis and Adamon followed him, and studied the mysterious characters. They were so alien, almost incomprehensible—yet scattered symbols made a subtle sense.

"Here," WolfStar said quietly. "And here, here, and here, and yet again here."

Axis followed his finger. WolfStar pointed to identical symbols that depicted a star surmounted by a sun. "StarSon," Axis said.

"Caelum," WolfStar agreed. "The Gate mentions him again and again."

"WolfStar," Adamon said, stepping back so he could view the entire Gate. "Does the Gate show what must be done?"

"Yes," WolfStar said.

WingRidge regarded him wryly. Yes, the Gate *does* show what must be done, he thought. But have you got the translation right, oh vaunted Enchanter?

"Well, what does the Gate *say*?" Axis asked.

WolfStar studied it closely. "It shows Caelum," he said quietly, "battling to save a world disordered by the Questors. Here it speaks of peoples lying down in the streets to die of despair, here they capitulate to terror, here to hunger. It speaks of a world where the Demons run rampant, where Qeteb rises from the grave, where hope and joy exist not even in memory."

"And yet if Caelum—if *we*—lose our powers when the Demons break through the Star Gate, then how can he master them?" Adamon paced back and forth. "What hope has he?"

"The Rainbow Scepter contains its own powers," WolfStar said. "With that, with the power of the ancients, Caelum *can* master them! Remember the ancients managed to contain Qeteb in the first instance. Adamon, Axis, that Scepter is our only hope. See how the Gate intertwines the symbol of the StarSon with that of the Scepter time and time again! The Scepter *must* be Caelum's only hope. Our power is likely to be useless before the Demons and certainly before Qeteb. But with Caelum wielding the Scepter . . ."

"And yet Drago has the Scepter, and uses it to help drag the Demons through the Gate and enslave us all." Axis' voice tightened in frustration. "And Caelum is entangled with Zared."

"Axis," Adamon asked very quietly, speaking as tactfully

as he could, "*can* Caelum deal with this threat? He has so very little experience."

Axis opened his mouth, then snapped it closed again. Finally, reluctantly, he spoke. "Caelum needs the experience and, dammit, the *confidence* of winning this conflict with Zared. He must deal with Zared on his own, and he *must* win. He needs to be trained to deal with the Demons and Qeteb—but I dare not drag him away from his fight with Zared. To do that would totally destroy his confidence."

"And there would be no need for Caelum to meet these Demons if we manage to stop them first," Adamon said.

WolfStar looked away from the piece of script he was studying. "What do you mean?" And if the Demons *were* stopped, would that give him free rein to gather together the life parts he needed?

"I am talking of warding the Star Gate so the Questors cannot break through—even if they hammer on the other side."

"Can we do that?" Axis asked.

Adamon suddenly looked very tired. "It would take all our remaining power, and then more. Axis, we would need the help of a hundred of the most powerful Enchanters, as well as Isfrael's assistance."

"The trees," Axis said. "We will need the magic of the trees behind us."

"We will need *everything* we can bring to bear to stop these fiends," Adamon said quietly, "Because if we do not stop them at the Star Gate, then I fear they will turn Tencendor into a wasteland of desolate souls in their quest to reform Qeteb."

"I pledge my every power, my last effort, in the building of those wards," WolfStar said fiercely. "We *must* stop the Demons!"

59

Zenith

Weakened both physically and emotionally, Zenith still found the strength for laughter and optimism. She sat with Faraday and StarDrifter on the upper steps of the empty Assembly Chamber. The wind stole gently about them, carrying with it the scent of flowers and mown lawns.

Zenith took Faraday's hand, turning it palm uppermost in her own. "I find it difficult to find the words to express my gratitude, Faraday."

"You do not need to." Faraday kissed her cheek softly. "I have thanks enough to see you sitting here smiling."

StarDrifter sat slightly apart from the two women, a soft expression on his face, loving both of them. He loved Faraday for finding Zenith and bringing her home, and he loved Zenith for her slight of WolfStar. StarDrifter loathed WolfStar, hating his dark influence on so many lives, his power, his self-righteousness. How could an Enchanter who had murdered hundreds, and sent yet more to dreadful deaths, who had *manipulated* with such ease, still earn the admiration and respect of so many?

After Zenith had flung the dead fetus in his face, WolfStar had picked it up gently from the floor, held it in his hands, then raised his head to Zenith. He'd said nothing, just looked at her, and then, the fetus still in his hands, he had walked calmly out the door. None of them had seen him since.

StarDrifter sincerely hoped WolfStar didn't have the power to resurrect that fetus. Zenith had twisted its neck as it was being born, and had then crushed its skull. That should be enough, surely, to kill the most persistent of spirits.

"Faraday," Zenith said suddenly, breaking the comfortable silence that had built up between the three of them. "What happened to Drago?"

"Oh! I'd forgotten that you wouldn't know. He stepped through the Star Gate, and he took with him the Rainbow Scepter."

"He had the *Scepter* with him?" Zenith's eyes opened wide. "He carried that sack so tight and close . . ."

She turned her head slightly so she could see StarDrifter. "But, grandfather, surely the Star Gate would have killed him?"

StarDrifter thought carefully before answering. "What happened to Drago when he stepped through is largely conjecture, Zenith. Your parents think he went through to aid the TimeKeeper Demons."

"The *who*?"

StarDrifter and Faraday explained what they knew.

"Poor Drago," Zenith said quietly when they'd finished. "I cannot condone what he has done, but . . ."

"But," StarDrifter edged down the steps between them so he could sit on the other side of Zenith, "but you aided his escape from Sigholt."

"Aided it, yes," Zenith answered, thinking of the peculiar role the Lake Guard had played in that escape as well.

Faraday glanced at StarDrifter, then back to Zenith. "Why?"

"Because I do not believe he killed RiverStar."

"Why innocent?" StarDrifter asked. "Was he not found by RiverStar's body, knife in hand? Did not the Song of Recall show him to be the murderer?"

Zenith's eyes focused on the star-map mosaic in the chamber floor far below them. "I cannot explain it, StarDrifter, beyond saying that the Song of Recall was conjured by WolfStar, and I had seen already how deeply Wolf-

Star loathed Drago. He would have done anything to see him convicted and executed."

StarDrifter nodded. He could understand why Zenith would not trust WolfStar . . . but did that make Drago any the less guilty? But Faraday had asked him to have faith in Drago, and if she believed in him, then StarDrifter thought that he could too.

"And if not Drago, then who?" Faraday asked. "Zenith, you must have *some* suspicion. Neither StarDrifter nor I were there."

"RiverStar claimed she had a new lover, very powerful, very potent. She said she loved him, and wanted to wed him. I think he may have murdered her. If not, then why hasn't he come forward? Why so secretive?"

"She was SunSoar," StarDrifter said. "She could have loved only SunSoar or been sated by a SunSoar." He shrugged slightly. "It is the nature of our blood."

Zenith raised her eyes from the mosaic floor and studied her grandfather. "Did you ever lie with her, grandfather?"

The directness of the question discomforted StarDrifter. "For many years I thought I loved Azhure. I did not know why then, because it took us years to discover that she, too, was SunSoar. But I lusted after her, I adored her, I plotted to snatch her from Axis.

"Of course, I did not succeed, and when Caelum was born I realized that I never would. So I swore to myself over Caelum's birth-bed that I would take Azhure's first daughter for myself."

He paused, remembering. "When RiverStar was thirteen, she came to my chamber one night, flaunting her naked body and, even at that age, her experience. I was repelled. I could hardly believe that reaction in myself, for RiverStar is—was—almost sexually irresistible, but I was repelled nonetheless."

"Well," said Faraday. "RiverStar had found a new lover. And SunSoar . . . *perhaps*. Who? FreeFall? Axis?"

"No!" StarDrifter cried. "First blood is forbidden!"

"I doubt that would have stopped RiverStar getting what she wanted," Zenith murmured.

Faraday ignored her. "Caelum? WolfStar? And what about Isfrael?" *No!* she thought, stricken, not my son!

"Drago himself?" StarDrifter said, trying to distract her.

Now it was Zenith who was horrified. "*Not* Drago! I would almost be willing to believe she'd bedded our father before I'd accept the idea of Drago."

"You like him very much, don't you," Faraday observed softly. "Why?"

Zenith spoke without thinking. "Because I trust him. He was nothing but kind to me, and in moments when he thought not to be observed, he was kind to others. I cannot explain it, but on some fundamental plane of my being I do trust him."

"And yet," StarDrifter said carefully, "as a child he showed himself to be completely untrustworthy."

"What he did as an infant was reprehensible," Zenith said. "No-one can condone his alliance with Gorgrael. For that he was punished, and dreadfully, considering that no lasting harm was done to Caelum, nor even to our parents or Tencendor by his actions. To have his Icarii blood disallowed . . ."

She halted, trembling. Magic and enchantment was so much a part of her Icarii heritage, as it was StarDrifter's, that neither found it possible to contemplate a life without it. And yet, wasn't it due to Drago's actions that she *was* being forced to contemplate such a life?

"But what was abhorrent in Drago's subsequent life," Zenith finally went on, "was that neither Axis nor Azhure took the chance to rebuild or reform his soul. He was further punished every day of his life for his infant crime. He was never loved, never hugged, always reminded that he was the most vile of creatures—and yet he could not even remember what he had done to deserve such treatment! Drago was constantly reminded that he was vile and untrustworthy—yet he could not know why."

StarDrifter stared at her. He'd never thought of that. Neither, he wagered, had Axis or Azhure.

"If he has continued to be surly, even bitter," Zenith said softly, looking at her grandfather, "then it is because he has never been allowed to be anything else. Who knows who or what the real Drago is? Or what he was capable of becoming? Our parents slammed him into a mold and kept him there. Eventually he conformed to that mold. Our parents never gave Drago the love and affection that would have redeemed him."

"Everyone was too ready to accuse him of RiverStar's murder," Faraday said.

"Because not to accuse Drago," StarDrifter said, his face paling with horror at what he was about to say, "would be to suspect another SunSoar male."

"Who?" asked Faraday. "Who?"

"Of our entire family," Zenith said softly, "StarDrifter was the only one not present in Sigholt when RiverStar died."

"Niah?"

The voice broke the quiet between them.

"Axis!" StarDrifter leaped to his feet. Would his son *never* leave him to finish a conversation in peace? Axis was walking down the few steps from the top of the Assembly Chamber to meet them. His face was mildly puzzled.

"Niah?"

His daughter rose smoothly to her feet and faced him. "I am Zenith."

He stared at her. "What happened?"

"Niah lost her battle with life," she said very quietly, holding his stare. "I lived."

"But you *are*—"

"No!" Zenith abruptly shouted. "I am *not* Niah! I am your daughter!"

"Then where is Niah?"

StarDrifter could not believe he was hearing this conversation. "Niah has returned to the grave, Axis. Loved and remembered—but dead."

Axis did not move his eyes from Zenith's face. "Your mother thought that—"

"She was wrong."

"She believed that—"

"She should have believed in *me* more."

Axis was quiet. Then, "I heard some of your conversation before I made my presence known. Zenith—you *helped* Drago escape?"

"Someone had to help him."

"Do you know what you have done? Drago now leads the—"

"I knew that someone should have helped Drago, Father! That someone should have been you or Mother, many years ago. If there was a murder committed in Sigholt, then it was not only RiverStar's!"

A muscle twitched in Axis' cheek. He stared at Zenith a heartbeat longer, then switched his gaze to StarDrifter's face.

"In order to cope with Drago's treachery, StarDrifter, I must enlist your aid."

"You know you have it. What can I do?"

"By assisting to ward closed the Star Gate—if we can do it. *If*. The Circle of the Star Gods will not be enough. We need the most powerful Enchanters, as well as Isfrael and the Banes of the Avar peoples, to help construct our defense. StarDrifter," his voice became gentler, "I need you. Now. At the Star Gate. We have to move fast."

"You have me."

"Who else do you have here on the Mount to help?"

StarDrifter named some ten or eleven Enchanters, and Axis nodded.

"Then let us not linger, StarDrifter. The Demons quest closer."

* * *

Zenith and Faraday stood side by side watching as Axis and StarDrifter hurried away.

"He did not ask *me* to help," Zenith said quietly.

"True," Faraday said, then she grinned. "But do not fret, Zenith. I have something just as helpful and, methinks, much more fun for us to do."

She laughed at the expression on Zenith's face. "Come now, Zenith. Did you think that I would let us linger here while the saving of Tencendor awaited?"

60

Old Friends

"Faraday? What do you mean?"

Faraday stood up, then grabbed Zenith's hand and hauled her to her feet. "Imagine the scene at the Star Gate, Zenith. Hundreds of Enchanters and Banes. All wasting what little power they have left to ward the Star Gate. Or fighting whatever it is that comes through. Do you think they will spare a moment's thought for Drago?"

"And," Zenith said softly, thinking it through, "what if RiverStar's real murderer stands there? Waiting for Drago?"

"I would not place a large wager on Drago's life then, my sweet. Besides, from what I have heard, Axis and Caelum would be glad enough to see him dead and put aside for good. Do you trust *anyone* there?"

"I would trust StarDrifter."

Faraday slowed as they walked down the steps into the center of the Assembly. "Yes. Yes, so do I. But StarDrifter alone will be of no help—especially not if all Icarii Enchanters lose touch with the Star Dance. Zenith, can you feel the fading of the Dance?"

She nodded. "I feel it like a wound. It . . . it lessens me."

They reached the mosaic circle of the Assembly and walked arm in arm toward one of the exits. "Faraday, how are we going to reach the Ancient Barrows? My father might be able to spirit StarDrifter and the other Enchanters there, but I don't have the strength—"

"Hush," Faraday said. "I have some old friends we can rely on." She grinned. "If they still remember me."

By the time the women had reached the dormitory, Axis, StarDrifter and the other Enchanters had gone.

"He wasted no time," Faraday murmured. "And neither shall we. Zenith, fetch yourself a cloak, beg us a small bag of food from the kitchens, and we will be on our way. Meet me at the top of the steps in an hour."

Then she kissed Zenith's cheek and was gone.

Zenith collected a thick green cloak from her chamber, sliding a feather and hair comb into its pocket, then begged a basket of food from the thin-faced cook in the kitchens. The man, despite his morose face, had a kind heart that did not require too many explanations, and he filled a large basket with enough food to see the women through several days.

"I thank you," Zenith said as he handed the basket over, and then she was gone.

Faraday was waiting for her. "Are you sad to be leaving here, Zenith?"

Zenith looked over her shoulder at the temple complex and the great beam of cobalt light that speared into the sky from the Temple itself. There were streaks of gray through it.

"No, I am not. I do not think I ever wish to come back here. This place reeks of Niah."

Faraday nodded, then led the way silently down the steps.

From the base of the steps it was a day and a half's walk to reach Pirates' Town on the island's northern harbor. They walked briskly, but not at a pace that would overly tire them, resting every two hours and taking turns to carry the basket. Faraday brought nothing with her save a magnificent ruby cloak that Zenith thought she had seen before. But when she asked Faraday, the woman only smiled and changed the subject.

They rested the night under the eaves of the thick jungle that covered most of the island. It was warm, and the women's cloaks were useful more as mats than blankets. They spoke late into the night, Zenith hesitatingly asking Faraday about her life as the daughter of Earl Isend, then as Borneheld's wife. She was not sure if Faraday would want to talk about it, but she did not seem to mind, and for the first time in her life Zenith heard the story of the Time of the Prophecy of the Destroyer from a perspective other than her parents'.

"You must have loved my father very much," Zenith remarked softly as Faraday finished.

Faraday thought about that a long time—so long Zenith had assumed she wanted to escape the question by pretending sleep.

"I was young, impressionable," she finally said, "and Axis was everything a young and impressionable girl dreamed of." She gave a low laugh. "*Every* young girl in Achar was more than half in love with him, I think. And then I was caught up in the Prophecy, so much rested on my role, that I was consumed by joy that it should have been *me* whom the Prophecy had picked. But," her voice turned sourer, "I did not know then what a dreadful price I would have to pay. That the Prophecy required my death to fulfill its purpose."

"You died so that my mother could live," Zenith said.

"Yes. But I am not bitter about that. Azhure, as Axis, as *everyone* including Gorgrael, was as much a victim of the Prophecy's manipulations as I."

"But you were transformed into the doe. I saw you occasionally when I was a child and Azhure brought Caelum, Isfrael and myself into Minstrelsea."

Faraday reached out and touched Zenith's cheek. "And I saw you, too, Zenith. I envied you your freedom—of course I did not know about Niah's legacy then."

"*My* freedom? But I thought you the most carefree of creatures—"

Faraday laughed harshly. "I was trapped by the forest, trapped by my timidity, trapped by my form. Drago," her voice altered, "Drago freed me with the Scepter as much as your father trapped me with it. With his careless wielding he cast off all the chains of Prophecy and fate that had bound me. Free. I was finally free."

There was quiet between them a long time, then Faraday quietly said goodnight, and rolled over and went to sleep.

Zenith stayed awake a good deal longer.

By noon the next day they had reached Pirates' Town. It was a thriving port town, populated by brightly scarved, gleaming-knived pirates who plied the southern seas seeking rich merchants and Corolean bullion ships. Beside them strode their hard-eyed wives, and thousands of thin-flanked dogs and scrawny chickens.

"Has no-one ever thought to put a stop to the pirates?" Faraday whispered, her cloak clutched tight about her as they wandered down the main thoroughfare. For a thousand years the pirates had served to guard the secrets of the Island of Mist and Memory, but she thought that now Tencendor had been freed from the grip of the Seneschal life would have been more tightly regulated on the island.

"I mean," she added, "they don't still . . . pirate . . . do they?"

Zenith laughed. "I'm afraid they do, Faraday. Neither Axis nor Caelum has been willing to try and restrain them, beyond insisting they keep their ships away from Tencendorian waters. Besides, the pirates prefer the rich pickings off the Corolean shores. Still," she nodded a greeting to a pirate wife wringing the neck of a chicken on her front doorstep, "I know Caelum has had to deal with more than one complaint from the Corolean ambassador about them."

Faraday went a little green at the sound of the chicken's neck cracking. "You like it here?"

"I spent many weeks of each year on the island when I was a girl. StarDrifter often sent me down here for a few days. Once—although don't tell StarDrifter this—I even went out on a pirate ship for two days."

Faraday stared at her with round eyes. "I did not think you such the adventurer, Zenith."

Zenith shrugged. "Oh, I grew out of it."

"I wonder." Faraday grinned. "Oh look, here is the wharf."

Zenith looked about. "There's a ship over there swinging supplies aboard. If they're going to Nor they may well take passengers. Did you bring any coin with you? I forgot in our rush to leave."

"No coin required," Faraday said quietly, and pointed to the very end of the main pier. "Not for this ferry trip."

There bobbed the small flat-bottomed ferry that Faraday had provided for Zenith in the shadow-lands.

Zenith suddenly remembered where she'd seen the ruby cloak before. "The cloak, the ferry, these are Orr's!"

Faraday nodded. "He has no need for them now. Come. The ferry shall carry us smooth and calm to Nor."

And so it did. Faraday sat in the prow, the hood of the cloak cast back, her chestnut hair streaming out behind her, her face calm and beautiful as she looked into the distance. To each side of them the Sea of Tyrre raised fat waves that swelled the height of two men above the ferry.

And yet that ferry sailed smooth and calm through the heavy seas as if it glided across the still surface of an ornamental pond.

Zenith sat farther to the rear of the ferry, her eyes shifting from Faraday, to the waves, then back to Faraday again. She knew the woman wielded power, but she did not know of what kind it was. Zenith knew of the power of the trees and the earth, and she could sense it whenever Banes wielded it in her presence—but this was so different. Faraday used a source of power that Zenith had never experienced before.

Faraday turned her head slightly so she could see Zenith from the corner of her eye. "It is simply different, Zenith. It is the only way I can put it."

"And you feel no diminishing as the Star Gate clouds over?"

Faraday shook her head. "This is not related to the stars, nor even to the trees or the earth."

She lifted her shoulders in a wonderfully evocative shrug, smiled, and turned back to the seas before them.

The ferry glided on.

Within two hours of setting out from Pirates' Town, the ferry sailed into the port of Ysbadd. A normal vessel would have taken a day at least to sail the distance. Zenith just accepted it.

Faraday stepped calmly off the ferry, climbed the ladder on the side of the wharf, and waited for Zenith to join her. Zenith looked back at the ferry, bobbing gently against the wharf, then looked up to see Faraday already halfway down the wharf. Sighing, she hurried after her.

"How are we going to get to—" she started, but Faraday waved a hand lightly.

"We go to the market, of course, and we shall find what we need there."

Zenith rolled her eyes and gave up asking. No doubt Faraday would discover a ferry on wheels that could glide them to the Ancient Barrows.

Not quite a ferry on wheels, but something equally astounding, and something Zenith recognized immediately from all the tales she'd heard about Faraday.

Faraday had led her into the bustling, hot, heavy-aired market square in the center of Ysbadd, and then stood looking, a small frown on her face.

"Ah," she finally said. "There. The livestock section."

Faraday walked over to a far corner of the square where stood lines of oxen, horses and three short-haired dromedaries from Coroleas. She walked slowly, looking down the lines, her frown deepening, a mystified Zenith at her shoulder.

"Ah!" she cried as she saw the vendor. "Good man, I am looking for something I have lost. Would you perchance . . . ?"

The man, barrel-chested and red of face, stared at her, then his face cleared and he smiled and bowed. "My Lady. Yes. I wondered when you would claim them. They have been eating me out of my best oats."

And he waved a hand to the overhang of a canvas awning.

Underneath it, harnessed lightly to a dainty blue cart, stood two white donkeys.

As they caught sight of Faraday they twitched their ears, and one gave a low bray of welcome.

"Oh!" Faraday cried and, hurrying over, hugged and patted both the donkeys.

Zenith approached more slowly, smiled, and wiped the tears from her eyes.

Old friends, indeed.

61

An Army of Norsmen

Feblone Aszrad, silk merchant and bastard son of a Corolean soldier seeded during the Tencendorian wars of forty years past, pulled back his horse and swore. His laden mules would be crippled if they were forced off the road surface and into the uncertain gullies on either side.

And he had buyers waiting impatiently in Carlon's markets and palace halls for this silk.

But he had little choice. Swearing again, but a little more

softly this time, Aszrad waved to his muleteers to hurry their charges into the side gullies.

"But carefully!" he roared as a long-haired youth jerked at the lead mule and almost pulled it off its feet. Damn these Nors boys! They were useless for anything save sloe-eyed dancers and entertainers.

Useless, that is, until they reached their manhood. Aszrad's eyes slipped to the dust approaching from the southern reaches of the Tarantaise road. Here, if he was not mistaken, came a goodly force of Nors knights.

And bound for where?

Not Carlon, that much was certain. Not for Zared.

Aszrad reined his own fine-boned stallion off the road, holding his breath as the horse's hooves rattled on the loose scree, then relaxing a little as the stallion found its footing and stepped into one of the gullies. Aszrad turned around in the saddle, checking to make sure the train of mules was safely out of the way of the approaching force, then dismounted to watch as it thundered past.

The Nors knights were famous for their silent, cruel warfare. They were good, very good. If they fought *for* you. Aszrad winced as the first ranks swept by, narrowing his eyes against the dust, clinging to his stallion's reins as it pulled back in fear.

The force was heavily armored, but moving quickly despite it. Burnished gold, copper and bronze plating glinted and sent reflections of sun-fire slanting about the landscape. Banners, pennants and lance tassels snapped in the breeze of their passing, saddle cloths flapped, weaponry—in full display—sat easy and ready to hand in practical leather scabbards, sheaths and quivers. A bright force, but a fighting force.

Aszrad blinked and counted the units as they rode past. Twenty-nine! By the great multi-armed Baba himself! If those units were the full three hundred men, then that was almost nine thousand!

Nine thousand?

"For Caelum, no doubt," Aszrad murmured. "Nine thousand to Caelum's aid. And all bright and ready for war. What will my Lord Zared do against such as these?"

As most merchants in Tencendor, Aszrad favored Zared, not only for his free trading policy along the River Nordra, but for his decisive action in *freeing* trade along the river. As the last of the units thundered past, Aszrad turned to one of the muleteers.

"Bring me a carrier bird," he said.

"Nine thousand!" Zared crumpled the note in his hand and flung it into a far corner of the reception room. About him were ranged sundry captains and lieutenants of the force he had managed to raise thus far, Herme and Theod standing slightly to one side.

Leagh, forgotten, sat embroidering by a window.

Her head was bowed in concentration over her silks, but her fingers moved slowly and clumsily.

"Where?" Theod asked.

"A league south of Tare, riding north," Zared said. "About forty leagues due west from Carlon."

"And the note?" Herme said. "How old is the information?"

"A day only." Zared sat down heavily at a table with maps and lists of units and supplies scattered about it. "An armored force that heavy and vast could ride perhaps three leagues a day."

"They're riding through a rich agricultural area of Achar—" the captain caught himself, "—of Tencendor, sire. There are enough barns and provisioning stores in Tare and western Arcness to feed an army twice that size. Perhaps, sire, they could be moving even faster."

"I thank you for your optimistic assessment of the situation, Grawen," Zared said dryly, then sighed. "But you are most likely correct. He would be riding to join Caelum. Herme, any fresh intelligence on Caelum's force?"

Herme stepped to the table, scrabbled about for the map he needed, then jabbed a finger down on northern Arcness, just below the Rhaetian ranges. "Intelligence of last night put Gaelum's force here. About fifteen leagues south of the Rhaetian ranges, heading due south. Now some four thousand men he's scraped together from Skarabost and Arcness, although not Arcen itself. And the Icarii Strike Force are with him—another two thousand."

But worth ten thousand, every man in the room thought. An air-borne force held a frightful advantage over a ground force—and the Strike Force had kept their wits and skills ever since Axis had taken their training in hand during the wars against Gorgrael's ice creatures.

"And how old is *that* intelligence?" Zared said wearily. "Gods, but I wish I had some of Caelum's farflight scouts to aid me. But, no, I must rely on men who ride a week to pass me information so old that it is almost useless. Caelum could be close to Carlon by now."

Herme looked at Zared carefully. "This information *is* less than a day old, sire, and came by birdman."

"Again," Zared said softly.

Leagh paused in her embroidery.

"A member of the Lake Guard, sire," Herme said, "although I disremember his name."

Zared stared at Herme. These Lake Guard were proving remarkably disloyal. Three days ago had come a very private message from WingRidge CurlClaw, telling Zared a little about the Demons that threatened. Even as vague as it was, the information was so explosive and so terrifying, Zared had shared it only with his closest commanders.

"The information tallies with what we know from other sources, sire," Herme added.

Zared rose and paced about the room. "Why do the Lake Guard aid us?" His eyes swept the entire room, seeking an answer. "Why? Are they not devoted to the StarSon? I cannot but think a dreadful design behind their so-called aid."

Was the information about the demons meant to dissuade

him from causing Caelum further problems? Was it meant to force him to sue for peace so Tencendor could face the threat united? Were the Lake Guard actually working *for* Caelum, rather than betraying him?

"Their aid saved us at Kastaleon," Theod said.

Leagh gave up any pretence of embroidering and lifted her head to listen. The Lake Guard had betrayed Caelum—and Askam—at Kastaleon? Her brow furrowed.

"Still . . ." Zared hesitated.

"We have to believe it," Herme put in. "Dammit, Zared, we *have* to."

"Is the birdman still here?" Zared asked.

"No. He left as soon as he had delivered the information."

"Very well." Zared made his decision. "We trust the information. So, if Caelum rides fifteen leagues below the Rhaetian ranges, how long will it take the Norsmen to reach him?"

Herme worked it out. "At three leagues a day, and allowing necessary days to rest the horses, I would say ten to twelve days."

Zared chewed the inside of his cheek. His eyes fell on Leagh and his eyes softened, although his expression remained hard.

"I cannot allow that force to merge with Caelum's," he said quietly. "I cannot. With the Norsmen and the Strike Force, Caelum would be almost invincible."

"Sire," Herme said, "would it not be better to stay here? Have Caelum come to us, try to take Carlon?"

"I will not risk the people of Carlon to Strike Force attack," Zared continued, remembering Severin. "And besides, if we can prevent the Norsmen joining Caelum then he will be seriously weakened."

"But Caelum isn't best—" Theod started.

"I am not going to rely on his bad generalship forever," Zared said to him. "Even Caelum has to start learning at some point. Herme? What numbers do I command now?"

Herme glanced about at the others in the room. In the five weeks since Zared had taken the crown thousands had flocked to Carlon. Many soldiers, many just enthusiastic peasants. Even the rumour of a King of Achar had been enough to put many thousands of feet on the roads to Carlon.

"Seventeen thousand," Herme said. "Fourteen thousand regular forces, three thousand men half-trained with the pike and sword. The regular forces are horsed, the three thousand mostly are not."

"Herme, Theod, I want the fourteen thousand ready to ride in the morning, the rest to follow as best as they are able. I am going to stop that Nors force before it reaches Caelum."

He looked about. "Questions?"

62

The Warding of the Star Gate

Isfrael stood at the edge of the forest and shuddered. He tipped his head and rubbed one of his horns against a tree, finding calmness in the touch of velvet to bark. Only the desperate summons of the entire Circle of the Star Gods had made him venture to the very edge of the forest in these dark times. Isfrael found himself more and more uncomfortable in open spaces as each year went by. Even the relatively closed spaces of the Ancient Barrows were almost as distressful as the stone of Sigholt.

At his side Shra sent him a sympathetic glance, but did not take his arm as she would have done in private. "The Barrows are a place of magic, Sacred One," she said. "You will feel more comfortable underground."

His teeth gleamed. "I doubt it. I wish I had not been summoned from the trees."

"The need is great," Shra murmured. "Else why would the Star Gods call you?"

"They blame Drago," Isfrael said, and tilted his head as a stag does when it scents the wind. "They say he stole the beloved wood and uses it to lead the Demons through the Star Gate."

He snorted. "But WingRidge tells me that Drago is innocent of my sister's murder, and that WolfStar has misunderstood crucial aspects of the Maze's message."

"But the threat of the Demons *is* real enough, Sacred One," Shra said, her eyes on the figures moving about the Barrows in the distance.

"Yes, the threat is real enough."

Shra nodded, but did not speak further. It was the only reason Isfrael had consented to come. He might not have moved to aid Caelum, but Isfrael would not deny the plea of the Star Gods.

Isfrael turned slightly so he could see Shra. More than any other woman, even more than his mother or Azhure, she was the one who had shaped his childhood. She might not now exert such an influence over him, but Isfrael loved and respected her very much.

"Whatever happens, Shra," he said, his voice unusually soft, "I will keep the trees safe."

She smiled. "I know, Sacred One." She paused, then changed the subject. "Have you heard where your mother is?"

They were unsure of Faraday's whereabouts. The Scepter had hidden both her and Drago so skillfully that neither Isfrael nor Shra, nor any one of the Avar, knew that she had traveled south to be retransformed at the Star Gate itself.

Isfrael's expression darkened. "No, and I do not—"

He was interrupted by a golden and silvered Icarii Enchanter alighting before them, his white wings almost luminescent in the moonlight.

"StarDrifter SunSoar!" Shra bowed, the heels of her hands to her forehead, but Isfrael just stared hostilely.

"Your mother is well, Isfrael," StarDrifter said, greeting both of them with the same gesture Shra had used. "And was, the last time I saw her, on the Island of Mist and Memory."

Isfrael's entire body jerked. *"She left the forest?"*

"She had other paths to explore," StarDrifter said, regarding Isfrael carefully. In the ten or fourteen years since he'd last seen him the Avar had clearly won dominance. Not even the hint of a feather. There was now little or no SunSoar left in the Mage-King. "Perhaps once we are done about the Star Gate I can explain further. But rest easy for now—she is well, and loved."

Isfrael shrugged, pretending some indifference. "She had the choice to leave, and she took it."

"Isfrael, Bane Shra," StarDrifter said, "I—nay—all of us currently here are glad of your arrival." He glanced behind Shra. "Have you brought Banes with you?"

"Thirty-seven," she said. "Almost all our Banes. I hope your project will not put them in danger, StarDrifter."

"The Star Gods' project, not mine," StarDrifter said. "And there *will* be danger if these Demons manage to break through the wards and into Tencendor."

Isfrael's eyes gleamed. "It is said that your power fades, StarDrifter. Is that so? Are all Icarii Enchanters fading into insignificance?"

StarDrifter winced—Isfrael almost seemed delighted at the thought. "Yes, it is true. As the Demons gather close to the Star Gate their darkness shields us from the Star Dance. If we cannot push them back . . ."

"And my father? And Azhure? And the other Star Gods?" Isfrael said. "Do they fade as well?"

"Not as badly as the Enchanters," StarDrifter said. "Not yet."

"Not *yet*. Well, so they desire my—*our*—help?"

"Yes, Isfrael," StarDrifter said quietly. "Tencendor needs your help."

There was movement and the sound of voices among the fires surrounding the Ancient Barrows, and StarDrifter stood back and waved with his hand. "Sacred One, we need your presence."

Isfrael looked, shrugged, and walked forward, Shra at his side and the other Banes following in a silent, dark group.

The twenty-six Barrows spread in a huge arc from west to east. When Axis reclaimed Tencendor, Enchanters had erected a graceful bronze obelisk in the center of the arc. It still stood there, spearing into the night sky, a bright blue flame in the shallow pan at its apex.

But now there were hundreds of smaller bronze tripods set up, forming a perfect circle that enclosed the Barrows. Enchanters stood by each waist-high tripod, their eyes closed, hands folded over breasts, wings tucked neatly behind them, deep in concentration, reaching for every note of the Star Dance they could still hear.

The outer ward, StarDrifter whispered in Isfrael's and the Banes' minds, and they nodded, watching closely as they moved through to the inner circle.

There stood several more Enchanters, slightly to the side of a man and a woman who exuded power.

Isfrael bared his teeth in the semblance of a smile. "Adamon and Xanon," he said, and inclined his head slightly at the two Star Gods.

"It is good of you to answer our plea," Xanon replied gravely, "when your concerns lie so deep in the forests."

"Here, or at the Star Gate itself?" Isfrael asked without preamble.

"At the Star Gate," Adamon said, and Isfrael noticed the dark circles under his eyes. "The chamber itself will form the strongest ward."

"And how do we descend?" Shra asked. "I have heard that there are many tunnels, but all take hours to negotiate."

"Ah," said a voice to one side. "But I have lent my assistance."

And WolfStar stepped into the light.

Isfrael literally snarled. "What do *you* here, you lurking rabid wolf?"

To one side StarDrifter smiled.

WolfStar raised an eyebrow. "I *help* here, TreeSon." It was not quite what WolfStar had in mind to call Isfrael, but even WolfStar thought it prudent not to call the Mage-King a twig-encrusted joint of venison. He shot a glare at StarDrifter.

"Peace!" Adamon snapped. "Isfrael, WolfStar has opened one of the Barrows—"

"Mine," WolfStar said.

"—and cleared the stairwell so that we may travel quickly and easily down it. An hour of steps, that is all."

"Then let's commence," Isfrael said, "before I lose patience and break for the trees."

And he shouldered past both Enchanters and gods and stalked toward the open Barrow.

Axis stared into the Star Gate. The stain had not only spread, but thickened during the past few days. How much longer? He did not know. These days he lived with a constant tight knot of fear in his belly. He had not lived with such fear for a very long time, not since he was a youth first riding with the Axe-Wielders, and even then he'd not felt anything this intense.

About him were ranged Azhure, the five other Star Gods, and several score Enchanters—the most powerful of the Icarii nation. The chamber was already crowded, but as he heard steps from one of the entrance tunnels and raised his head, Axis realized it would be tightly packed with bodies once the Avar Banes had squeezed themselves in.

Well, that would not matter if between them they managed to construct a warding strong enough to keep these damn Demons—and his renegade son—beyond the portal.

Isfrael stepped into the chamber. Like StarDrifter, Axis had not seen him in many years and he could hardly believe the degree to which Isfrael had absorbed the power of the trees. In manner and appearance he reminded Axis vividly of the power that drifted about the Sacred Groves and the Horned Ones who inhabited them.

Isfrael caught sight of his father. He stared, unsure of how to react. Finally he stepped forward, looked into the Star Gate, then raised his eyes back to his father and simply nodded.

"Will you help us, Sacred One?" Axis said. "Daily our power fades, as does that of the Icarii Enchanters. We need your help."

Isfrael tilted his head, pretending to think. "Do the trees need to fear what comes through that Gate, StarMan?"

"Do you *know* what threatens through that Gate, Mage-King?" Silton, God of the Sun, stepped forward. "Do you want despair and pestilence riding the trees as they will ride the plains? Terror and Famine lurking in the shadows of the glades as they will in the homes of Icarii and human? Do—"

"Enough!" Isfrael snapped. "I will help, otherwise I would not be here. StarMan," he turned back to his father, "when this ward is worked, must I and my Banes stay to maintain it?"

Axis shook his head. "Not all, three or four, perhaps. Once built, the ward will take only a fraction of the builders to keep it in place."

"And when the Demons start to bulge through?" Shra asked very quietly. "What then?"

"Then we stand here in force, Isfrael," Xanon said. "All of us."

Isfrael shook his head. "No. Not I. Not Shra."

"But—" Axis began.

"*Not* I, *nor* Shra, *nor* the greater number of the Banes!" Isfrael snapped, turning on his father. "We will help build this ward for you, and we will keep several Banes here to maintain it, but if those Demons bulge through then I am keeping the majority of the Avar safe within the forests. You may think that you have the means to prevent this tragedy which stains the night sky, but I have my doubts! And, doubting, I prefer to keep me and mine under the protection of the forests!"

"Then we may well fail!" Axis shouted, unable to believe that Faraday's son would let him down this badly. "If we need to push the Questors back, prevent them from bulging through, then *we need every magic worker within this land here to aid!*"

"I will only do what was asked of me," Isfrael said quietly, and Axis winced. "To help build and to offer Banes to maintain the ward. Nothing else."

"You know how we," Axis indicated the Circle of Star Gods, "and the Enchanters rely on the Star Dance for our power. If the Demons get so close as to be able to bulge through the Star Gate, then they will likely cut us off from our source of power completely! We *need* the power of the trees here then!"

"No," Isfrael said, and folded his arms across his bare chest.

"You offer as much help as the Avar did during the majority of my campaign against Gorgrael," Axis snarled, unable to stop himself.

"And it was *my* mother who died for you, and the Song of the Trees that splintered apart Gorgrael's army for you."

"Then help us now, damn you!"

"No."

"Why?"

"I have my reasons."

"Oh!" Axis turned aside, furious. Damn the Avar for turning against him yet again!

"If I and most of the Banes were to be killed here trying to maintain the ward against an invasion of the Demons—as I believe we would be—then the forests would be left vulnerable. Axis, my first loyalty and responsibility is *always* to the forests, whatever else slithers and creeps across the plains."

"Stop this," Adamon interrupted quietly. "Let us build the ward. Who stays to protect it, or reinforce it, can be decided later. For now, please, let us build the ward before it is too late."

They worked through the night, exhausting themselves in the process. From the forests, Minstrelsea and the Avarinheim, and from the Earth Tree which guarded the forests, Isfrael and the Banes called forth the power of the Mother, of the soil and of the seasons. It swept down over the land, majestic music, as powerful as a sea-maelstrom and twice as terrifying, and it was gathered up by the Enchanters who encircled the Barrows and funneled down the stairwell to the Star Gate chamber itself. There, Isfrael, powerful beyond belief, and aided by Shra and the other Banes present, caught the music and fashioned it into a translucent dome of jade-green, its diameter a perfect fit for the low circular wall about the Star Gate, and then he manipulated it so that it hung over the Star Gate itself, its edges resting on the wall. The translucent dome picked up the sound of the Star Dance that still—only just—filtered through the Star Gate, magnifying it, then spinning it about the chamber to be caught by the Star Gods and the Enchanters. From the music of the Star Dance they fashioned a dome similar to Isfrael's, except it was of a lovely silvery sheen, and this they placed over the jade dome. The two domes fitted perfectly, jade and silver swimming together in rivers of power, humming with life and intent.

It was all they could do.

"Will it work?" whispered Azhure.

Axis, exhausted, slid his arm about her.

"It will have to," he said. "Or else all is lost."

The Demons stood on the balcony of their many-pillared chamber and they looked into the sky. Above them the once-blue firmament had transformed into swirling streams of jade and silver.

"A ward!" cried Sheol, and clapped her hands.

"How pretty," said Raspu with a sneer.

"And how very, very useless," murmured Mot. "How utterly, indescribably useless."

And then they all burst into shrieks of merriment that echoed about their chamber, and then about the orchard, and then speared into the sky to fret against the enchantments warding the Star Gate.

63

Leagh's Loyalties Divided

"Everything will be for the best, Leagh," Zared said, his hand cupping her chin gently. "Believe that."

Her eyes slipped away to watch the preparations in the central courtyard. Men scrambled, horses fidgeted, weapons gleamed. The scraping of metal against metal, and steel against cobble, irritated her beyond measure.

"I do hope so," she said quietly.

"If I leave you in charge of Carlon, Leagh, will you be true?"

Her eyes returned to his face. True to whom? "I will do what I think best," she said.

"I am your husband."

And you almost murdered my brother. "I know that. I know where my duty lies."

"You took vows to be true to your husband."

"I know that!" But what if I now regret those vows, Zared?

What should he do? Zared thought. He could leave Herme or Theod in Carlon, for control of the city needed one of the highest-ranking nobles, but he could ill afford to leave either of them behind. But could he trust Leagh? He remembered how she'd defended him to Axis, and he quieted his thoughts.

He leaned forward and kissed her briefly. "Keep well, Leagh." Keep true.

"And you, husband."

He mounted, then glanced at her once more before turning his horse's head for the gate. "Herme! Pass the word! We move out!"

Fourteen thousand men took over two hours to move through the cheering, crowded streets of Carlon and then swing north for the ford above Grail Lake. Leagh spent most of that time atop the battlements, thinking.

Whom *did* she owe her loyalty to? Askam and Caelum, or her husband and the ecstatic crowds in the streets? Who was right, and who not? Was Caelum wrong for not listening to the needs of the people? Was Zared right in seizing and then destroying Kastaleon? Crippling her brother but not telling her?

The units moved northward along the shore of Grail Lake in a sinuous column. The sunlight glinted off metal and silken banners. Leagh knew Zared rode at the forefront, although they were so far away now she could not see him.

An army of Achar rode again. A King of Achar rode at their head.

And she, the Queen, was left behind to rule in the absence of her lord. Strange that she did not feel very much like a Queen.

What should she do?

The easiest thing would be to just stay here and oversee the daily bureaucratic decisions of the major city of the realm. Smile at the mayor. Hold out her hand for the occasional ambassador to kiss. Listen with sympathy to the petitions of street urchins and aggrieved housewives.

But that would be too easy.

Leagh felt the heavy load of responsibility and guilt on her shoulders. How many nights now had she lain by Zared's side, listening to him gently breathe in sleep, wondering if she committed treason against Caelum by doing so? Did she betray Caelum by giving herself so willingly night after night to Zared, or would she betray her husband if she turned him a cold back?

Ah! Why was love never easy?

She owed Zared responsibility and loyalty, but she also owed her brother and their overlord, Caelum. How many times had she sat at her father's knee and listened to his tales of the dreadful struggle Axis had to unite Tencendor and defeat Gorgrael? If she stood back quiescent, watching while Zared single-handedly destroyed that unity, would she then bear as much guilt as he?

What came first, the wishes of one race among many, or the integrity of a nation?

Leagh could not bear the thought that Caelum no doubt found her as guilty as Zared, yet neither could she bear to think that Caelum and Askam's force might well decimate Zared's. She did not want to wear the weeds of widowhood yet.

Leagh lifted her hands and wound her hair into a heavy rope over her shoulder. Her fingers twisted until her hair was tangled and knotted. She did not notice. Her eyes were still fast on the now-distant army riding north.

What would happen when—*if*—they met the army of Norsmen? Would Zared die? If he succeeded, would Caelum set the Strike Force to his destruction? And if Zared then succeeded again, would Tencendor be torn apart in a bloody civil war of retribution, Icarii against Acharite? Age-old hatred nurturing new-found malice?

Leagh's fingers stilled, and her eyes filled with tears. Whatever decision she made, whatever she decided to do, she would commit treason against either husband and people or brother and overlord.

She lay in bed awake, unmoving, until late into the night. The palace lay still and quiet. Everyone was abed, fast asleep after the excitement of the day. She rolled her head to one side, looking at the empty pillow beside hers, pristine and lonely in the moonlight. Where was Zared now? Where Caelum?

"Ah!" she exclaimed softly, and sat up. She paused in the moonlight, then got out of bed, grabbing a robe to wrap about herself. She missed Zared. She wished he was here.

Leagh walked into their robing room, rummaging about in closets and drawers until she found what she needed. Breeches, small enough to fit her form. A simple worsted shirt and jacket; leftovers from a time when she'd once ridden to the hawks in the plains above Carlon. Belial had liked to do that, and she'd not gone a-hawking since he'd died. After the jacket a cap, under which she twisted her hair, and then some sturdy boots.

Pausing to study herself solemnly in a mirror, she couldn't help smiling. She looked like a country boy. A messenger, perhaps. Well, in a sense that's what she was.

From her apartments Leagh crept silently down halls and stairwells until she reached the courtyard. Guards dozed at their posts; no-one expected action in Carlon. Not yet.

Holding her breath, she hurried across to the stables and walked silently down the central aisle, searching out the mount she wanted. There. A dark bay Corolean mare, fine-boned and swift, gentle-mouthed and great-hearted.

Leagh soothed the mare with light strokes, then swiftly saddled and bridled her. Her heart thumping, feeling sick from the tension, Leagh led the mare from the stables, fearing with every step that the mare's hooves would rattle or strike a spark from the cobbles.

But nothing.

In the courtyard Leagh paused again, looked about, then led the mare through the gate.

The guard in his dark niche jerked at the movement of air, but did not wake.

Damn you! Leagh thought. You should be more alert! What if we were attacked? What if Caelum sent the Strike Force?

But just this once she needed them dozing. When she got back—if she got back—then things would be different.

Leagh mounted several blocks away from the palace and kept the mare to a walk through the streets of Carlon. There were some people about, street sweepers and bakers hurrying to early morning ovens, but they all assumed she was but a messenger boy, off on some errand.

No-one stopped her.

Once through the main city gates Leagh turned the mare's head for the north and pushed her into a canter and, once past the last curve of wall, into a flat-out gallop.

The road was clear and smooth, but the way ahead was treacherous and fraught with difficulties.

By the time the sun was above the horizon Leagh had left Carlon well behind. She turned the mare onto a series of farm tracks that she remembered from her hawking days. They led roughly due north, and would harbor no awkward questions from strangers. The Nordra lapped and laughed to her right, glinting rose and gold in the early morning sun, and the water fowl chirped and fluttered as she rode by.

The army had been out a day before her, but she could move faster than it.

She rode until mid-morning, alternately cantering and trotting the mare, and sometimes running alongside her. Then she stopped by an isolated farmstead, and paid the Goodwife for a mug of milk and a sandwich. Rested, she and the mare continued north beside the Nordra.

They reached the river crossing as evening fell, and the ferryman asked no questions of the quiet rider who paid passage.

She rode for five days, rode until both she and the mare were almost dead with exhaustion, rode until she spotted the campfires of the army ranged in a wide, shallow valley.

"Thank the gods," she whispered, and booted the mare forward for one final effort.

She saw as she neared that the camp was a hive of activity. Men milled about, horses were being readied.

War. Was she in time? Or too late?

A guard challenged her, then had to step forward and catch her as she fell from the mare's back.

"Princess Leagh!" he said, almost dropping her in astonishment as he caught sight of her face.

She tried to smile, but failed. "Good man," she whispered, her exhaustion making her shake uncontrollably. "Is the Prince Askam to hand? And StarSon Caelum? I must speak with them. Urgently."

64

A Dagger from Behind

Zared pushed his force hard. Maybe too hard. From Carlon they rode north, swimming their horses across the relatively shallow and peaceful Nordra half a league above Grail Lake, then headed due east for a day and a half before swinging north again for another four days' ride.

The trail of the Norsmen's passage was clear; dirt trampled with steel shoes, edges of roads flattened, the banks of watering streams and edges of ponds muddied and ruined.

Zared desperately wanted to catch the Norsmen before they combined with Caelum. He still hoped that he and Caelum could come to some negotiated settlement, although he knew that might well be a forlorn hope after the disaster of Kastaleon. But if Caelum had the Nors force to back him, then Zared very much feared he would brook no negotiation. Especially not with a one-armed Askam at his back.

Zared's mouth twisted in a wry smile as he squinted

against the sun on their seventh day out. Askam had never cut a very prepossessing figure, and one sleeve hanging loose and flapping would hardly improve his image.

"Sire!"

Zared straightened in the saddle and squinted even more. There was a plume of dust ahead of him, resolving within a few heartbeats into a bedraggled rider.

Ormond, one of the forward scouts he'd sent out before dawn.

"Well?" Zared asked sharply as Ormond hauled his exhausted horse to a staggering halt.

"Half an hour ahead of you, and swinging back. They have two farflight scouts with them. They saw me. I am sorry, sire."

"Damn," Zared muttered. Herme, Theod and several of his captains crowded their horses about, trying to hear the news.

"Their readiness?" Zared asked Ormond.

"Good, sire. They are fresher than us, despite their travel."

"How do they disperse themselves?" Herme snapped.

Ormond swung red-rimmed eyes at the Earl. "My Lord, I rode as if I had the damned after me when I realized I'd been spotted. But I think they were turning in arc formation."

"Are you *sure*?" Zared asked. "I must dispose my force accordingly if they ride in arc—"

"Sire," Ormond said. "I can only relate what I saw as *I* turned to run before the sun. It appeared to me that the Norsmen turned in arc formation." He shrugged tiredly. "But that may be only for the turn back. Who knows how they ride now."

"I thank you, Ormond." Zared dismissed the man, then consulted with the others. "Well? What do you think?"

"Spear," Herme said instantly. "If they *do* ride arc formation."

"I concur," Theod said, and several of the captains nodded.

"Why?" Zared asked Killingrew, one of the younger commanders who was yet to prove his worth.

"The center of the arc will be weak," Killingrew replied. "If we hold the spear formation we could break straight through."

"And leave our flanks vulnerable to the arms of the arc closing," Theod said. "Zared? What think you?"

Zared stared into the heat-encrusted afternoon as if it could give him inspiration. Sweat trickled down his back, but he was only dimly aware of the itch. "They will be here soon," he said softly. "Look." He indicated a faint haze in the distance. "They ride."

He peered intently. "That dust haze is wide. I think they still ride in the arc. They would have wanted to turn as quickly as they could, race for us, catch us unawares if possible, and the arc would be fittest for that purpose."

Suddenly he was all activity. "Theod, Killingrew, Urnest, ride back and start shaping our column into spear formation. *Fast*. Set the supply mules and spare horses free if you have to. Herme, wait here with me. I need your advice. Fikness, I need you to send several scouts four or five hundred paces ahead to signal once the Nors force gets closer. Bonnime, find me eight or ten riders. If I need messages to get back through the force then I'll need to do it fast. Move!"

The commanders scattered.

The forces met as the sun sank into rose-colored finery over the distant Nordra. The shining, metal-plated Norsmen, visors down, lances tucked under arms, grim-silenced riders galloping to engage the traitor's force; the stolid Acharites, fighting once again under the banner of their King—and this time proud to be doing so.

As Zared had predicted, they met in a clash of spear and arc. The Acharite force had formed itself into a three-pronged spear, twenty-seven riders wide at its head, forty-nine at its widest point, the shaft seventeen riders wide. They galloped to the fray, trusting in the lead riders' sight and pace, nerves jangling as the dust thickened about them.

The Acharites met the Norsmen in a mangle of spear, sword and pike in the very center of the Norsmen arc. It shattered, being only five riders deep, but it shattered at a dreadful cost to the Acharites. Swords and spears were no match for a well-held lance that was three times as long as the height of a man. Once those lances were past, the Acharites could turn and fight faster than the Norsmen—but again, the Norsmen were better plated and armored, and even as the fray got down to the meat and blood of sword to sword and mace to mace, the Norsmen more than held their own, even improved upon it.

And Zared's force was tired, very tired. He'd pushed hard to get this far this fast, and his men had ridden into battle without sufficient rest or preparation.

But they were determined, and they had a leader they believed in, which was perhaps a little more than the Norsmen had.

They battled until the evening darkened into night. Zared, exhausted, swung about on his horse, trying to see through the gloom what the state of battle was.

There were shouts and cries, the thud and screech of weaponry, but it was too damned dark to see what he should do—

Something landed on the back of his horse. A strong arm slid about his throat, another pricked a dagger through the joints of his breast-plate.

"Call your men off," a voice hissed, and Zared heard the inflections of Icarii arrogance.

"Call your men off, Prince of Treachery, for you have lost. Even now the Strike Force wheels down. Hear the wind of their descent? *Feel* the prick of their vengeance?" And the dagger slid in deeper, tearing into flesh, and Zared groaned.

The Icarii clinging to his back laughed, low and harsh. "Your wife told us of your arrival, Zared. Even now she sits waiting with her brother and StarSon. Sipping wine, no doubt, and laughing at your fate."

Now the dagger slid to critical depth and Zared gagged.

"Call your men back!"

And he did, although his every thought was with Leagh's treachery, not the battle grinding to a halt about him, nor the dagger wedged to its hilt in his side.

65

A Brother to Die For

They stood there in their confident semi-circle, the five Questors and the Queen of Heaven, cuddling her life-lacking son in her arms.

Their eyes were directed to a spot far above them, shimmering in the violet night-sky.

Star Gate.

It glowed with the strength of the enchantments warding it, lightning streaked jade and silver, a bulge in the stars.

A doorway.

"How nice of them to so brighten it for us," Sheol murmured, and she laughed with Barzula, and slipped her arm through his.

"One more leap and we reach its rim," Mot said. His arms were stringy in their thinness, and he kept them wrapped about his skeletal form, but his face was well-fed and satisfied, and his eyes glowed with victory.

"And then one more push *through*!" cried StarLaughter, and she bounced the undead child in her arms. "Through!"

Raspu leaned over and took the baby from her. He crooned and hummed to him, and stroked his clammy cool brow. "Soon," he said, and squeezed the child in his enthusiasm.

"What first?" asked Rox, leaning over to stroke the child's cheek. "Breath or warmth?"

"Warmth," said Sheol. "For it is a precondition of all the others."

"And warmth is . . . ?" StarLaughter said, watching over Raspu's enthusiasm lest he damage her beloved son.

"Cauldron Lake, my Queen of Heaven," Rox answered. "Warmth is burried in its depths."

"Can you conquer it?" StarLaughter raised her eyes first to Rox's face, then to Raspu's.

They grinned, feral, confident. "Assuredly, sweet mother," Rox said. "We have been waiting a long time, after all, and we know enough of the Enemy to be certain of their tricks. We think we can be sure of their wards and embellishments."

"And the Star Gate?" Drago had hitherto been sitting cramped in a shadowy corner. Now he rose and took a hesitant step forward. "Can you negotiate the wards about the Star Gate?"

As one the Questors turned to stare at him. Then, in tune, they smiled.

"We will shatter them," Sheol said, and suddenly hissed, her eyes bright and fierce.

Drago took a frightened step backward. "But—"

"Think you that these pitiful wards can counter *us*?" Mot roared, the sound stunning coming from his bony frame. "We will *quest* through the wards!"

"Poor boy," StarLaughter said softly. "Look how frightened he is. Go away, frightened boy. We have no need of you yet."

Drago sank down on the floor as the Questors turned back to contemplation of the Star Gate. His hands gripped the sack.

He was going to die, he knew it.

Stupid, stupid fool for thinking these creatures would be his friends.

He should have stayed home.

He started. Home. Tencendor? Yes, he supposed it was home. He wanted to go home.

They will kill you. You know that.

I know that, Drago answered in his mind.

We can help.

Drago felt the bitterness of life-long rejection well within him. No-one helps me.

Zenith did.

Zenith. He wondered if she was well, or if Niah had overcome her. I wish I could have helped *her,* he thought.

We know. There was deep sadness in their voices. *Now it is your turn to help. Are you prepared to help Tencendor?*

Drago's thoughts drifted. He remembered the Tencendor of his youth. Sigholt, keeper of bad memories and resentments. Carlon, all silver and gold, but petty in its preoccupation with pleasure. But then he remembered the forests. He thought he'd always hated the forests, but they had never hated him. Surprisingly. He remembered a stream he had crossed when he was about nine or ten. It had been an insignificant stream, but it had flashed agreeably, and the sound of its waters had been beautiful. He remembered the loveliness of smooth flowing plains and the peace of a herd of cream-colored cattle grazing in the sun. He remembered his grandfather, StarDrifter, sitting on the edge of the cliffs of Temple Mount, explaining some mystery of the breeze as he ignored his grandson's surliness. He remembered the laughter of someone—himself?—watching the antics of a courtyard litter of kittens.

Let us show you something, said Veremund, and a vision filled Drago's mind.

He saw a landscape which had been brutalized by a cruel wind—and something else.

He saw crazed cattle, hunting in feral packs, craving the taste of blood in their mouths.

He saw people wandering disconsolate through this barren landscape. They were thin, and scabbed, and they tore listlessly at their rags and moaned as they wandered.

They were despairing.

He saw Icarii, huddled about scathed rocks of the Icescarp

Alps. They shivered in a bitter wind, their eyes sunken, haunted, even the memory of beauty lost to them.

Their wings lay in tatters along their backs, and they no longer knew the meaning of the word "music."

He saw the Avar, sitting lump-like under a relentless sun. No shade. No trees. And yet somehow forced to live nevertheless.

Beside them rotted the carcass of a stag, white hairs blowing across the land.

The Questors can do all of this? he wondered. How?

The Demons' greatest ally is that which already exists in people's souls. Terror. Despair. Tempest. Anger. Greed. Lust.

Gods! thought Drago. And resentment and bitterness. They have used what was in me to further their own cause.

Yes. They let him think a moment. *Will you aid Caelum, Drago?*

Caelum? He thought of his brother as a child, screaming in despair at his brother's treachery, knowing he was to be the sacrifice for his brother's ambition. If a brother could betray him this cruelly, then what could he ever trust again?

In Caelum, Drago thought, I seeded uncertainty. If I hadn't destroyed Caelum's security on the rooftop of Sigholt, then Caelum would doubtless meet the Questors with the golden confidence that should have been his inheritance. I shattered Caelum's future and I stole his heritage, Drago realized, as much as I believed others stole mine.

Yes. See the devastation across Tencendor. See the lives, the hopes, the enchantments lost. See Caelum waver helpless in the winds of indecision. It will *happen. Nothing you can do can save it. Unless . . .*

Drago knew what they meant.

Unless . . .

He thought of that stream, of the peaceful cattle, of StarDrifter's patience, of Zenith's courage, of Caelum's terrified scream that day long past.

Will you offer your life to aid Caelum and Tencendor, Drago?

Yes, he thought. Yes, if I can save my home. He sat there for long moments, watching the Questors murmur and laugh among themselves, passing the undead child back and forth, back and forth.

Oh gods, what *was* he loosing on Tencendor?

Yes. Yes, I am prepared to die to save Tencendor.

For the first time in his life Drago smiled unaffectedly. It lightened his face, softened his eyes. Kill me then, he thought, before the Questors have a chance to use me again.

The Sentinels' laughter rang in his ears. *No! Too easy! Your life is now vowed to Tencendor and to your brother, vowed to the fight against the Demons. You will live past the Star Gate. Believe us.*

"And you? Will you come back with me? I know Faraday would like to see you again."

And it would be good to see her again, too. But, no, we will not come back. We will see you through, then we will stay this side to drift forever more among the stars. Now, tell us, do you know this pretty lullaby?

A sweet tune slipped through Drago's mind, and there was something so soothing about it that he relaxed completely against the pillar he leaned on. No, he thought, I do not know this tune.

Then learn it, Drago, for it will keep you well.

Drago, running the melody through his mind, had no idea that this was the lullaby that Goodwife Renkin had sung to the seedlings to make them spring into life as the trees of Minstrelsea. All he thought, as he let the melody sweep through him, was that it was something he wished his mother could have sung to him had she ever rocked him to sleep at night.

StarLaughter glanced at Drago, and frowned. He looked unexpectedly at peace with himself, his eyes half closed, his body relaxed. Then she shrugged and turned away. No matter if he went to his death with a smile on his lips rather than a scream. Just so long as he proved useful to the end.

"But what time of day would be best?" Sheol said at her side, and StarLaughter turned her thoughts to the Questors' conversation.

"Afternoon?" Sheol continued. "An afternoon filled with despair?"

"Dawn?" suggested Mot, hungrily. "They will be fogged by sleep. Easy eating."

"Night!" cried Rox. "When nocturnal terrors strike easily!"

"Let me quench them with tempest," said Barzula. "Let me tear their limbs from them and tumble them over the plains like a scattering of dust. Morning."

StarLaughter smiled, and cuddled her child close. This was the music she craved, not the Star Dance.

"Nay," Raspu said. "Let it be dusk. I shall cover their bodies with boils. They shall be too busy scratching at the scabs to halt us."

Sheol looked at StarLaughter. "Your choice, Queen of Heaven," she said softly, reverently. "When?"

"Mid-afternoon," StarLaughter whispered, staring into Sheol's sapphire eyes. "Despair will destroy them more than anything else I know. Strike during mid-afternoon."

Again, as one, they turned their eyes heavenward.

The nearest Enchanters to the Star Gate gazed into its depths and shuddered. WolfStar stood at the rim, as did Flulia and Pors. Azhure stayed under the shadow of one of the arches, not wanting to look, but drawn by the dreadfulness emanating from the Gate. Axis stood atop the very wall surrounding the Gate itself, staring down.

There was no lure now, only horror.

Darkness swirled beyond the Star Gate, almost obliterating the Star Dance entirely. Even the Dance of Death was fatally reduced. Azhure and WolfStar, the only beings alive who could make use of the Dark Music, could barely hear it.

Every creature within that chamber, Enchanter or God, could feel their powers ebbing.

"Look how they swarm," Axis said quietly to no-one in particular. "What can we do?"

He looked up, and those within the chamber saw that his eyes reflected the darkness swirling at his feet.

Despair beckoned and tugged at their souls.

No hope.

66

In Caelum's Camp

The birdman wrenched out the dagger, and Zared collapsed back against him, almost fainting with the agony of it.

Leagh!

The Icarii slid back over the horse's rump, catching Zared as he half fell, half slid after him. He lowered the man none too gently to the ground.

The birdman, Strike Leader DareWing FullHeart, looked about. All around, men were laying down weapons as members of the Strike Force spiraled down from the darkened sky.

All the Strike Force were dressed in black. None save Enchanters could have known they were there.

DareWing looked down. Zared had half raised himself, a hand to the wound in his side, black blood seeping through his fingers.

"Leagh?" he asked.

"She told Caelum you were coming," DareWing said. "She must have ridden out within hours of your own departure. Almost killed herself and her mount in her effort to warn StarSon."

Zared slipped back to the ground, his vision momentarily swimming. He had trusted her. But she had betrayed him.

"Ah," DareWing said above him. "Here are the first of the

wagons now. Here, you! Take this man to StarSon's camp. Caelum himself will want to question him."

Rough hands reached down, and Zared almost screamed with agony as they threw him into the back of a dusty wagon.

Water sloshed in his face, and Zared jerked into wakefulness. Where was he? There were sounds about of horses, and feet, and the clink of metal.

A camp.

"Get up."

Zared slowly raised himself on one hand, wincing as the pain stabbed through his side again. He blinked, clearing his vision. A camp, night, men moving purposefully about.

Another standing in front him, beside the open-trayed wagon.

Askam.

A guard stepped forward from behind Askam and hauled Zared roughly off the tray and onto his feet. He stumbled, catching at the rim of the wagon wheel to steady himself; loss of blood had made him dizzy. The other hand he kept clutched to his side.

Askam reached out with his remaining hand and struck Zared a heavy blow to his head.

It was enough to topple Zared to the ground, and Askam buried a steel-tipped boot in his injured side as he curled up.

This time Zared could not prevent the cry, and Askam grinned. "That was for my arm, traitor," he said, and swung his leg for another blow. "And *this* is for the four thousand who died at Kastaleon!"

Zared screamed, unable to believe he was still alive. He dimly saw Askam prepare for another blow—surely the one which would kill him—when another man stepped up behind Askam and laid a restraining hand on his shoulder.

"Have him carried inside my tent," the man's voice said.

Caelum.

Zared fainted.

When he came to again he was inside a warmly lit tent. A command tent, for it had desks and chairs and scattered maps about its interior. Of everything in the tent, Zared had the most opportunity to study its rich blue and cream carpet, for his face was almost buried in it.

He wondered if his blood had stained it beyond repair.

A hand, rough but not unkind, rolled him over. "He's awake."

Zared blinked, trying to focus his vision, trying to remember the voice. Marrat. Baron Marrat. He must have finally managed to join Caelum after all. Zared vaguely found himself wondering about the logistics of that. Marrat would have had a long journey from Romsdale.

"Well, King of Achar," a quiet voice said. "Look to what kingdom you have come."

Zared managed to pull himself into a sitting position, leaning back against a wooden chair. Caelum stood about a third of the way across the tent, dressed all in black, arms folded, his hair neatly combed back, staring at him with an undeniably hostile face.

Slightly behind and to one side of him stood Askam, the sleeve of his jacket trembling slightly in the air.

Behind Askam were several guards and one or two commanders, DareWing FullHeart (come to peruse his handiwork, Zared thought numbly), and behind this group, sitting wan and shocked on a chair, her hand to her mouth, eyes round and horrified, was his wife. Leagh.

He held her eyes for a moment, and wondered that she was not smirking. Surely this was the fate she had worked to bring him to?

"How many?" he asked.

"Eight hundred and seventy-nine of yours," replied

DareWing. "Dead. Another thousand injured. Of the Norsmen, about the same."

"Eight hundred and seventy-nine," Zared repeated softly, and looked Leagh direct in the eye. "Dead."

She blanched, but said nothing.

"And more would have died," Caelum said, moving across to a chair and sitting down, "had your wife not moved to warn us of your arrival."

Zared did not shift his stare from Leagh's. "I was moving to protect my people," he said, and finally looked at Caelum, "from your invasion."

"They are not *your* people!" Caelum said. "They are Tencendorians all!"

"They are Acharites first and foremost," Zared retorted. "I was protecting their hopes and wishes."

"You simply sought to mask your own ambitions in the color of peasant dreams," Caelum said more moderately. "Well, now both your ambitions and simple peasant dreams lie buried in the dust of western Arcness. Your 'army' awaits my command, the traitors Herme and Theod, as the other commanders in your force, await my judgment, as do you. I will decide your fate in the morning."

"The Acharites will not answer to your command, Caelum," Zared said, fighting back the urge to gag with the pain that had now grasped his entire torso in hot pincers. He swallowed, his voice hoarse with the effort. "They will only ever respond to my voice."

"*I* am the StarSon," Caelum said, leaning forward. "They have no choice!"

"Strip them of choice, Caelum, and you strip them of the willingness to obey. You should know that. Or wasn't it in the textbooks on the art of wise governance that my brother showered you with?"

Caelum sat back, his face expressionless. "Get him out," he said, and two guards reached down and hauled Zared to his feet.

Again he shamed himself by crying out, and from somewhere within the fog of his own agony he heard Leagh echo his pain.

They threw him in a rough pen made of wickerwork wound between uprights of slender timber. As a prison it was not very substantial, but it was ringed with guards, all standing facing inward with swords drawn, so Zared sank to the dirt in the freezing night air and concentrated only on drawing breath.

"Zared?" A whisper. Herme. "Zared, oh gods! How badly are you wounded?"

Zared did not have the strength to reply. He vaguely heard other voices murmuring about him, Theod and several of his commanders, but then there was a movement, and he felt Herme and the others step back.

"Zared." A soft voice. Leagh.

He reached within himself for the strength required to open his eyes and stare at her. She was on her knees beside him, her hair tumbling loose about her shoulders, her face lined with horror for his pain. She reached out a trembling hand, terrified to even touch him, then snatched it back.

"I did not think you would betray me," he said. "I misread you."

She began to cry, silently, hopelessly. "Zared . . . I . . . I came . . . I came only to beg Caelum to talk with you. I could not," she paused and gulped, wiping away her tears with the back of her hand, "I could not bear to see Tencendor riven apart like this. I thought Caelum and Askam would listen to *me* of all people! I only wanted to make him see reason, see that he ought to talk with you."

"Instead you have seen your husband riven apart," he said. "See?"

He reached out and wiped his fingers down her cheek, leaving bloody trails. *"See?"*

Leagh began to shake uncontrollably. The blood had smeared the corner of her mouth, and she could taste its coppery bitterness. "Instead, Caelum took what I told him and sent the Strike Force to tear you apart as you met the Norsmen! Oh gods, Zared, I did not mean for this to happen. Not to you!"

He stared at her tears and shaking shoulders, and reached out a hand. "Leagh. Leagh . . . I do not know what to do."

She grabbed at his hand, clasping it between both of her own. He could feel her entire body shaking through the contact.

"Leagh. I do not know how I can bear this pain any longer."

67

Caelum's Judgment

Caelum slumped wearily in a chair in his tent. He had won his encounter with Zared, but felt little satisfaction from it.

Gods, what should he do with the man? Four thousand had died screaming in the burning disaster of Kastaleon—but could he blame Zared for that? No. He should have sent in a scouting party first. That disaster was as much of his making as it was of Zared's.

"Of course," Caelum said wryly into the empty tent, "Zared made the fatal mistake of assuming he was up against a capable commander."

By rights, Zared was a traitor. By rights, he should hang from the gallows in the morning—along with Herme and Theod.

But could Tencendor risk losing one more man when it faced such devastation from the Star Gate?

Axis had spoken in his mind earlier. The Star Gate was warded, but no-one knew if it would hold. Axis had shared the sight of the Demons bulging behind the ward; Caelum had been appalled.

Tencendor could not afford civil war now. Every effort had to be concentrated on holding the Star Gate. Axis had asked for his help, and within a day Caelum intended to lead the combined force as hard as he could for the Ancient Barrows. He did not know what it could do against these Demons, or what part it could play in holding the warding, but an army surely could not hurt.

Caelum dropped his head into one hand, trying to rub the tiredness out of his eyes. How could everything go so wrong in only a few short months? Zared initiating rebellion, Demons threatening through the Star Gate, Drago escaping and haunting his dreams with promises of revenge, and RiverStar lying cold and bloodied on the floor of her chamber.

"Oh gods!" Caelum whispered, wishing he had not thought of her. "RiverStar!"

And he bowed his head and wept.

Askam stood tense and furious, unable to believe what he'd just witnessed. He had spent the night organizing Caelum's force to be ready to march east toward the Ancient Barrows, and was now trying to get Zared's men to obey as well.

Trying.

Gods! Why would they not listen to him?

"Lads," he tried. "Has not Caelum granted you your lives? Is it too much to ask that you now serve him?"

The soldiers standing before him stared insolently.

"Damn you!" Askam said, tiredness and frustration breaking his temper. "Obey me or—"

"Or *what,* my Lord?" asked the soldier standing before him. All Zared's commanders were penned and guarded. Only the common soldiers faced him now—surely their lives in exchange for obeying their *true* lord was a fair enough deal?

"Or *what*?" the man repeated. "Imprison us? You'd need all the cattle yards in Tencendor to do that. Set your men against ours, perhaps? Then you'd lose half your force by daybreak. Prince Askam, we owe our loyalty to one man only. The King of Achar. Zared."

"And if we discover him dead at dawn," shouted a voice farther back in the throng of men crowding before Askam, "then by the gods you'll not be long to follow him into the AfterLife!"

Askam paled, with anger rather than fear. "Your self-styled King has no kingdom, no power, and lies in a cattle pen himself. You have no choice but—"

"We have *every* choice," said the soldier, very calmly, and at a motion of his hand the crowd behind him swelled and surged forward.

"Zared!" they cried. "King Zared!"

The noise jerked Caelum out of his fitful slumber.

"What's that noise?" he said, rising from his chair as a captain burst into the tent.

"My Lord StarSon! Mutiny! Zared's men have rebelled!"

"Then get Zared in here . . . *fast!*"

Damn, he thought as the captain ran from the tent. I should have foreseen this.

The tent was surrounded by shouting, milling men—Zared's men as well as Caelum's Norsmen—by the time several guards dragged Zared forward. Leagh, disheveled and tear-streaked, followed as close as she could, Herme and Theod under escort directly behind.

Zared looked barely alive. The guards sat him in a chair and he slumped forward, only Leagh's quick hands saving him from falling straight out again.

"Stars!" muttered Caelum. He knelt by Zared's side, took a fistful of his hair in his hand, and pulled his head up.

Zared stared at him with sunken, pain-filled eyes. His skin

was gray, covered with a sickly sheen. His flesh was cool to the touch.

"Get a surgeon in here, now!" Caelum said, and a soldier ran from the tent.

Caelum turned back to Zared. "Zared, do you still have your senses about you?"

Zared managed a weak smile. "I thought *you* thought I'd lost them a long time ago."

Some of the lines about Caelum's eyes relaxed in relief. If he could still joke then there was life in him yet.

The surgeon arrived, and Caelum stepped aside to let the man examine Zared; none of Caelum's powers could aid healing. The surgeon pulled away the rough bandage that Leagh had wound about Zared's torso and probed, none too gently.

Zared yelped in pain, and Leagh grabbed at his hands, lest he interfere with the surgeon.

"Shush, my darling," she whispered, but Zared turned his head aside.

Leagh's eyes clouded with pain. She had thought only to be doing the right thing. She had thought that Caelum would surely listen to her plea for a negotiated settlement. But no, he had used the information she'd brought to try and kill Zared. And now Zared thought her the betrayer.

Perhaps he was right.

"The wound is deep, and has caused some serious internal lacerations," the surgeon said. "But the blade was clean, and I do not think the wound will putrefy. Here, I will stitch it, and bind it, and as long as he does not engage in too much strenuous activity over the next week or so, he will probably heal, although this side will likely always be stiff."

He reached down into a sack he'd brought with him and pulled out a pouch of instruments. Chatting away, apparently completely oblivious to the tensions within the tent, he stitched Zared's wound up in several layers, starting with the deep muscle and working back to the skin.

Zared grunted at the first touch of the needle and forceps, and then winced at each successive jab that slid toughened catgut through his flesh, but he managed to endure the ordeal with little fuss.

"Are you sure . . . ?" Leagh asked as the surgeon bound Zared's side tightly.

He shrugged. "One can never tell with wounds of this type. But if he's survived the past few hours, and there appears to be no serious internal bleeding—although the blood he's lost externally will seriously weaken him—well . . . I make no promises, but if I were you I'd place no orders for widow's weeds, either."

Leagh thanked him, then shot a furious look at Caelum and at Askam, who'd walked into the tent while Zared's wound was being stitched.

The surgeon packed up his pouch and left, to Zared's murmured thanks.

There was a small silence, then Caelum sat down in his chair, and looked at Askam and Zared.

"This stupidity has gone far enough," he said. "I am sickened by the death and by the futility. Tencendor now faces annihilation through the Star Gate, and yet my two most senior princes fight over taxes and petty circlets of power. I have had enough!"

He took a deep breath. "You two will put these problems behind you. *I* need you, *Tencendor* needs you—*both* of you—to face the Demons who threaten through the Star Gate. *Do you understand me?*"

His furious eyes swept the tent. Zared, and then Askam, nodded.

"Your differences are laughable compared to what the entire realm faces. Zared, are you prepared to accept my command? I need a united force against these Demons. Zared," Caelum's voice softened, "only one man can command."

"I need reassurances," Zared said weakly. He cleared his

throat, then went on in a stronger voice. "I need to know that you *are* prepared to sit down and discuss not only my grievances, but the grievances of the Acharites as a whole."

"And what of *my* grievances?" Askam said, stepping forward. "What of this?" He flapped his empty sleeve. "What of my palace and my rights and my castle and my *lands* that have been usurped? Caelum, I demand this man's head!"

"No!" Leagh cried.

"Whore!" Askam hissed, and she recoiled.

"If she has betrayed you, then it was through my trickery," Zared said quietly. "Take your venom out on me, Askam, not your sister."

Leagh shot him a grateful look, but he still refused to meet her eyes, and her face fell.

"Enough!" Caelum barked. "Zared, I am prepared to sit down and discuss all grievances, but only after we have defeated the Demons."

"And Theod and Herme," Zared said. "What of them? And my other commanders? Caelum, they have only followed my orders. Again, I say to you what I just said to Askam. Take your venom out on me, not them."

"And will they follow my orders?" Caelum asked.

"If I ask them," Zared said quietly, meeting Caelum's eyes.

Caelum's jaw tightened. *If Zared asked them.* Well, it was enough. He nodded.

"When this is all over," he said, "when we have *won* against these Demons, then perchance we will have time and energy for these petty quarrels. But not now, *not* now. Do you understand me?"

Grudgingly, and staring at each other, Zared and Askam nodded.

"Good," Caelum said. "Then I expect all of you to work under my command. Tomorrow you ride for the Ancient Barrows."

68

Toward the Star Gate

They left at dawn the next day.

Both commands, now uneasily united, had endured forced marches in preceding days that had driven most men and horses near to exhaustion. Now again they marched.

They had no choice.

If Zared had been fully fit, keeping the peace might have been an impossible task. But he was so weak, and still in so much pain, that he quietly accepted what Caelum said and passed on the orders to his command.

His own command was not quite so compliant. Indeed, it was hard reconciling two forces of over ten thousand each to the fact that if on one day they had fought as foes, the next they had to march as comrades. Caelum had little choice save to keep the two forces apart as much as possible. That meant that Zared's men led the column, the Strike Force wheeling overhead lest they decide on some mischief, while Caelum's ground forces and the Norsmen marched behind.

Caelum had briefly toyed with the idea of having Zared's force march behind his. Briefly. He hoped he could trust the man; in fact, he was sure that he could. But Zared's thousands were a little too volatile for his liking, and he far preferred to have them before him than behind him.

They'd pulled out taking only the minimum necessary for survival. Tents, spare supplies and blankets were left in sad piles on the western Arcness plains. Men could sleep wrapped in saddle blankets, the Icarii in their wings. All could survive on two simple meals a day for the time it would take them to reach the Barrows.

* * *

It is Gorgrael all over again, Caelum thought, remembering back to his infancy and the battles against the Destroyer's forces. Again as the winter snows threaten we march to a war.

It seemed as if the forty years of peace had never been.

Zared sat on his horse at the head of his army. It meant that he proved the point at which the easterly wind broke its force, but that wind also somehow kept him in his saddle. He was still in some pain, but not so weak as he had been. The surgeon had given him wads of stringy vegetable matter, impregnated with drugs, to chew, and they both helped to dull the pain and give him strength. Slightly behind him, astride the bay mare she'd taken from the palace stables, rode his wife.

All Leagh wanted to do was take Zared in her arms and rock and soothe him, but how could she do that in front of twenty thousand men? And Zared would not allow it anyway.

His stiff back was punishment enough for her naive stupidity.

She should have ridden to her husband instead. Then at least the Norsmen may have had no warning. Then at least a birdman would not have dropped from the sky to plunge his dagger into her husband's body.

"I will not leave you now," she whispered, and the wind snatched her words away. "Not ever again."

The column marched on.

They marched through the day until the evening air had settled and cooled about them. Then Caelum sent word to the front that they were to halt and settle as best they could among the grasses and gorse bushes of the Arcness plains.

Gustus rushed forward to help Zared from his horse, reaching him before Leagh had a chance to dismount herself. When she reached Zared, she saw that his clothes were stained with pink discharge and that his eyes were bright with fever.

She said nothing, but she cleaned his wound, rebound it, made him eat and drink something, and only opened her mouth to protest when he rose.

"I must speak with my commanders," he said roughly, and left her alone by their horses and the piles of tack.

She blinked back tears, wrapped herself as best she could in a saddle blanket, and waited.

They rode for the next five days. Due east, then angling south-east. Dawn to dusk. Nothing for it but to follow the man in front, and to hope that he knew where he went.

At night, when men still found time from their tiredness to talk, they wondered.

On the sixth night out, Zared stood talking quietly with Herme, Theod, Gustus and Killingrew.

"Sire," Killingrew said, "the men want to know what they march to meet." None of Zared's command had ceased to call him sire. Caelum was angry about it, but he could not stop the freedom of men's mouths.

Damn Caelum, Zared thought, for not telling them. The problem of the Demons was to be kept a SunSoar mystery, apparently. At the least, it was to be kept from the human races. The Icarii knew, and apparently so did the Avar, but Caelum expected the Acharites to march to what might well be their deaths with no knowledge of *why*.

And what could men do against Demons? And Demons such as these? Zared wondered at the benefits of marching the only army in Tencendor straight into the jaws of interstellar Demons.

Zared grew more disturbed by the minute. He looked at Killingrew. "Do *you* know what we march to meet, Killingrew?"

Killingrew looked at Herme, then nodded unhappily. "Aye, sire. Most of the commanders do."

"And what is your advice then?"

Killingrew took a deep breath. "Sire, the men need to be told."

"I agree. I do not like this forced march into obvious horror without telling them." Zared stepped back so he could the more easily look about the camp. His wound had healed over well the past few days, although it plainly still troubled him.

"Look," he said. "Men mutter about their campfires. Do they discuss their wives and sweethearts back home? No, I think not. Dammit, Caelum is go-ing to have more than Demons to worry about if he doesn't rectify the situation."

Not to tell the men is to insult them, he thought, especially as the Icarii and Avar knew and were undoubtedly making preparations in every home against possible invasion.

Black resentment gripped him. "I must speak with Caelum," he said. "Now. Herme, will you accompany me?"

"Gladly, sire."

"And I!" cried Theod.

Zared managed a small grin at the man's enthusiasm. "Nay, Theod. You stay here. I'd hate your general good cheer to force even Askam to smile."

And, to the accompaniment of his commanders' laughter, Zared and Herme strode away to Caelum's campfire.

"StarSon?" Zared said. "I need to speak with you."

Caelum looked up from his plate of dried vegetables and stew. He glanced at Askam, on the other side of the fire, then nodded. "Sit down."

Zared and Herme sat down cross-legged before the fire, Zared wincing as the half-healed wound tugged at his insides.

"Caelum. The men need to be told what they ride to face."

Caelum chewed on a mouthful of food, then swallowed. "It would be worse to tell them."

"What? Worse? How so, StarSon?"

"What *could* I tell them? That some unknown demonic force threatens from the stars? That Drago SunSoar leads them, no doubt to feed his own ambition? That would only make them fear, Zared."

And fearing, Caelum thought, would make them more readily desert the fragile peace now holding these two forces together.

"They fear *now,* Caelum. They understand that something is badly wrong—why else such a forced march? They also understand that the threat is deadly. For the gods' sakes, Caelum, tell them! They deserve to know."

"Curse you, Zared! Accept my judgment as you accepted my command. I am tired, and—"

Zared swept an arm about. "*All* of us are tired, Caelum. But the majority of the men out there are being unnecessarily frightened."

"They would be *terrified* if they knew the details, Zared."

Zared turned his face away.

Herme watched him, then spoke himself. "StarSon, I have led men for many years. I *know* men."

He paused, wondering how to put this diplomatically. "StarSon, you have spent so much time locked in Sigholt that perhaps you cannot remember what it is that ordinary men think and fear. At the moment, they fear that they are being led into a deadly danger that they know nothing about."

"All I ask of them is that they obey orders," Caelum said fiercely.

"But—"

"If I tell them, Herme, they will run screaming into the night. Curse you, Herme, Zared! Will *you* not follow orders?"

Zared held his temper in check. "Caelum, I beg you. Tell these men what they ride to meet. You think they will run screaming into the night if you tell them the truth, *I* say that not telling them will make them desert you far earlier."

"With you at their head, no doubt," Askam said sarcastically.

"That will be enough, Askam!" Caelum said and threw his plate down. "Zared, you may leave."

Zared hesitated, then rose, indicating that Herme should do the same. He paused, stared at Askam's slight smile, then marched off.

* * *

Zared fumed all the way back to his campsite. Just before he reached it, he turned to Herme. "Call a meeting of all my commanders," he said. "Moonrise, at my fire."

Herme nodded, and walked off.

Zared sighed, rubbed his eyes—gods! When would he recover his strength?—and walked the few remaining steps to his campfire. Perhaps he should talk with Leagh, too, but he'd been too tired even to do that.

He walked into the circle of light about the fire, then stopped dead in amazement. Sitting with Leagh were two other women, one Icarii, one human.

"Zenith?" he said wonderingly, then turned in confusion to the other woman. He'd never seen her before in his life.

"Who are you?"

His voice was rougher than he meant, but Zared unaccountably felt discomforted by the woman. She was lovely, yes, but there was something more about her.

A power.

"My name is Faraday," she said, and rose gracefully, holding out her hand. "And I apologize for disturbing the peace of your fire."

"You're legend only!" Zared said, so shocked he did not think to take the woman's hand.

"And that is indeed a sad epitaph for a living breathing woman," Faraday said. "Please, I will not harm you." She waggled her fingers a little impatiently.

Zared realized his rudeness and hurriedly took her hand, wondering that he could still remember the courtly graces in this most incongruous of settings.

"My Lady Faraday, I only meant that your bravery and courage have reached legendary proportions within Tencendor."

She smiled prettily. "And do you not have a greeting for your niece?"

Zared let her hand go, stepped about the fire and enveloped Zenith in a bear hug.

"Zenith! Whatever happened to you? I'd heard you disappeared from Sigholt—"

She leaned back in his arms. "It's a long story, Uncle. I left with Drago . . . willingly. But, look at you, Leagh has told us that you have been injured."

"I am healing, Zenith. What . . . what are you *doing* here?"

Zenith let him go and indicated they should sit down again. Zared hesitated, then sat next to Leagh.

Her eyes widened in surprise.

Faraday noted, then smiled gently at Zared. "I have heard you now wear the crown of Achar, Zared. King Zared and Queen Leagh—this can hardly be the court you imagined." She looked about her.

Zared suddenly remembered that Faraday and her husband, Borneheld, had been the last reigning monarchs of Achar. He opened his mouth, but he did not know what to say.

"Say nothing," Faraday said. "I care not for crowns now. Zenith and I," she took her friend's hand, "have both come back from the dead, in a manner of speaking. Now we have other things to worry about than titles and crowns."

"Faraday, Zenith, what *are* you doing here?"

"Well, first," Zenith said with a hard gleam in her eye, "we have come to comfort your wife, Zared. It seems she has been unhappy."

Zared dropped his eyes. "We have not made a good start to our marriage."

"Then do something about it," Faraday said sharply. "Both of you are mortal, and have no time to chase each other through successive aeons trying to make up for mistakes hundreds of years old."

Zared suddenly laughed, surprising himself. He took

Leagh's hand, interlacing their fingers. "I am sorry," he said, and smiled at her.

"And I. I should have thought before—"

"Hush," he said and, leaning forward, kissed her gently on the lips.

"Good," Faraday said. "Now as to what other purpose Zenith and I have . . . well, all of it you need not know, but we are on our way to the Ancient Barrows."

"As are we."

"Yes, as are you. But I think your mission a sad error."

Zared looked at the two women carefully. "But Caelum says that his father thinks we can help."

"Axis does not always know what is right or not," Faraday said. "Frankly, I don't think Axis really knows *what* to do. He just feels comfortable with an army surrounding him. It is the influence of his youth, I suppose."

She shrugged, and looked at Zenith. "You explain, Zenith."

Zenith nodded, studied her hands for a few moments, then raised her eyes gravely. "Zared. Do you know what comes through the Star Gate?"

"Demons," he answered. "Creatures from within the stars themselves, for all I know. And WolfStar's nemesis. All the children he murdered so many thousands of years ago."

Zenith nodded. "And they bring dreadful powers, for all we know—but, frankly, we do not truly know *what* they bring. But did you know that their approach is seriously sapping the Icarii Enchanters' powers?"

"What do you mean?"

"Over the past weeks I have felt my Enchanter powers fade. The Star Dance itself is diminishing, faltering."

"But, how—"

"Shush, Uncle, and let me finish. As these Demons approach, their influence is clouding the Star Gate itself. The Star Dance cannot get through, and without the Star Dance, we *have* no powers."

Zared stared at her, aghast. There was a step behind him,

and Herme, Theod and several of Zared's commanders appeared.

"Not now," he began, but Faraday stopped him.

"No. They need to hear this as well. Please be seated, gentlemen."

Somewhat bemused, the men sat down, crowding about the fire.

"Go on, Zenith," Faraday said.

She spoke slowly, emphasizing each word. "The approach of these Demons is not only stripping the Icarii Enchanters of their powers, but also the Star Gods. By the time the Demons break through, all Enchanters, as Star Gods, will have lost their powers completely."

There was utter silence.

It was Leagh who finally answered. "But that would be . . ." she frowned, trying to come to terms with the concept. "Unthinkable. Tencendor with no magic?"

"Some will remain," Faraday said. "In the trees and forests, although we cannot know how the Demons will affect them in the long term. And within . . . several other creatures. But nothing will compensate Tencendor for the loss of the Enchanters' power, nor that of the Star Gods."

All the men present glanced between themselves. They were all loyal to Zared, and to the concept of a reborn Achar, but they were also men who had lived most if not all their lives within close proximity to the Icarii and to the magic and rites of the birdpeople. Many of them had traveled to the forests, and had felt the power there. They might have been only mortal, but they knew and recognized the worth of enchantment.

"Zared, gentlemen, listen." Zenith leaned forward now, her voice sharp, demanding to be believed. "When the Star Dance fades completely, then there will be *nothing* that can prevent those Demons coming through. Nothing."

"Then . . ." Zared's voice trailed off.

"Then you are all riding to certain death!" Leagh cried,

and grasped Zared's hand yet harder. "Is that what you're saying, Zenith?"

"Yes. I am afraid so."

The commanders present exchanged fearful glances and shared murmured words.

"We can't ride on," Zared said.

Faraday shook her head very slowly and deliberately.

"Damn it!" Zared whispered, trying to think.

"Zared, is there any way you can persuade Caelum to turn about?"

Zared looked at Faraday. "I doubt it. He is convinced that Axis needs us at the Star Gate."

"Lady Faraday," Theod said. "What can we do? Are you saying that *nothing* can ever be done about these Demons? That our land is to be condemned to . . . what?"

Faraday and Zenith had a fair idea to what Tencendor would be doomed when the Demons broke through, but they had no intention of telling these men that. They had to leave them some hope.

"We cannot know," Faraday said gently. "But we fear very much. We may not have answers, but we have advice, and we beg you to listen to it."

"And that is?" Herme asked.

"You are currently about four or five leagues due north of the Silent Woman Woods. My friends, I think that for the moment the trees will provide your best cover. We think the Demons will leave the trees well enough alone for the time being."

We *hope,* she thought.

"And our families?" Gustus asked, his voice tight and angry, although his ire was not directed at these two women. Damn Caelum to a worm-ridden AfterLife! The majority of the men still didn't even have the vaguest idea about the danger threatening the Star Gate, let alone *this* horror!

"On our way north," Zenith said, "Faraday and I met with several groups of merchants moving north, some to Carlon, some to other centers. We gave them what advice we could without unduly frightening them. The last thing we wanted to do was to create panic."

"And that advice is . . . ?" Killingrew asked. He had a wife and two young children awaiting him in Carlon. Right now he felt like abandoning everything and rushing home to see to their safety.

"There will be certain times of the day when it will be horrific to go outside," Zenith said. "More than dangerous. Dawn and dusk, all through the night. Mid-morning and mid-afternoon. And, eventually perhaps, midday."

If we cannot succeed, Faraday thought. If we do not succeed, then midday will be the most terrible time of all.

"But if people stay indoors during those bad times, if they shutter windows and doors, then they will survive."

"But what sort of life is that?" Zared said angrily. "There will be only a few hours each day when people can go outside, when fields can be tilled, when—"

"It will be a *life,*" Faraday said. "During those times we have said, the Demons will roam."

"But what can we do?" Herme threw up his hands in despair. "Can we battle these fiends with sword and steel?"

"No," Faraday said. "I do not think so—but, hush! I do think I can find a way. I am sure of it."

"What?" Zared asked. Both his hands were wrapped about Leagh's now.

"Zared, forgive us if I do not explain now," Faraday said. "I am still unsure of my path, and there are unexplainables I cannot foresee.

"What I ask of you," she continued, "what I *beg* of you, Zared, is to save as many of these men as you can. Get them to the Silent Woman Woods as *fast* as you can, because that is the nearest shelter for a body this size. I think there is less than a day remaining before the Demons attempt to break through. Once there, wait for us. But, hark me true, *do not go near the Cauldron Lake!*"

"Why?"

"Because I fear the Demons may visit. Zared, they come into Tencendor for what lies at the bottom of the Sacred Lakes. And Cauldron Lake is so close to the Barrows."

Zared was too depressed to ask any more questions.

"Wait for us in the northern Silent Woman Woods," Zenith said quietly. "We will return to you there. Believe in us."

Faraday looked about the circle of light. "Believe in us, all of you, for at the moment we are all that you have left to believe in."

No-one spoke for many minutes. Zared rested his face in his hands, Leagh holding his shoulders, trying to give him some comfort.

Zared's misery was mirrored by most of his commanders. They could comprehend none of this, and yet they believed and trusted these two women without exception.

"Where do *you* go now?" Zared finally asked of Faraday and Zenith, raising his head from his hands.

"Us?" Faraday said. "Why, we go to the Star Gate, of course. There is someone we have to meet there."

69

The Fading of the Dance

StarDrifter stood in the chamber of the Star Gate and mourned. He leaned against one of the carved pillars, one wing wrapped about it for support, and grieved for the fading of the Dance. His whole life had been lived to its beat, all his laughter attuned to its merriment, his entire purpose bent to its tune.

Now, slowly, surely, inevitably, it faded.

He did not look into the Star Gate itself, because he knew what he would see.

Swirling bleakness, consuming their vision of the universe.

Black doom, streaked with shrieks of lightning that was itself blighted and cancerous.

Demonic voices, laughing at the dwindling of the Star Dance.

Whispers.

We're coming for you, WolfStar.

He looked across the chamber. WolfStar stood there, just beyond the huddled Circle of the Star Gods. His face was gray, his breath too rapid for calmness.

We're coming for you, WolfStar.

And the worst thing of it was that their coming was inevitable.

StarDrifter looked back to the wards above the Star Gate. How bright and powerful they had once seemed! Now the wards were fading and warping. Grayness slunk over them, a reflection of the blackness seeping closer through the stars, but also a reflection of the fading powers of the Enchanters and Star Gods.

StarDrifter had never imagined what it would feel like to be . . . human. No power of any sort. No joy in touching with the Star Dance. But StarDrifter had a truly dreadful feeling that he would know *exactly* what it was like all too shortly.

A human with wings. That is all he would be.

StarDrifter lowered his head and wept.

We won't be able to stay here, thought WolfStar. He was wrapped in misery at the loss of both the Star music and the death of the woman he loved.

How could Zenith have done that?

We won't be able to stay, he thought. He wouldn't be able to stay. Too dangerous—the children, StarLaughter (and, by the Stars! what kind of revenge would *she* seek?), the Demons. He knew he must run far and fast if he was to have any hope. If Niah was to have any hope.

But for now, he thought, I shall just stand and witness the final hours of Icarii Enchantment.

It deserves that honor, at least.

Zared, Leagh and the commanders farewelled Faraday and Zenith as starlight faded into daylight.

The two women had left the pair of white donkeys tied to a gorse bush beyond camp. Now they untied them, climbed into the small blue cart, and waved as the donkeys cheerfully trundled their way east toward the distant dark line of Minstrelsea and the Barrows.

"Those donkeys," Herme murmured. "It couldn't be. It *couldn't*!" He shook his head. It just couldn't.

"Herme?"

Zared's voice broke into his thoughts. "Yes, sire?"

"Caelum has ordered the pull-out. So mount up the men and, as soon as the order is given to ride out, do so. I will ride back to Caelum, try to persuade him. Herme, once you see that I have reached him, give the order for the men to turn their horses due south. And ride. I want you within the Silent Woman Woods by afternoon."

"But you'll—" Herme began, but was cut short by a wail from Leagh.

"Zared, no! He'll not let you go!"

Zared took her shoulders and held her gently for a minute. "Leagh. Go with Herme. Take that wonderful mare of yours and ride like the wind."

"I'll not leave—"

"Yes, you *will*! Leagh, I will join you. I promise. I'm not ready to die yet, not out here on this open plain like a dog." He grinned wanly. "Trust me."

She leaned her forehead into his chest briefly, feeling his heartbeat.

"Yes, I trust you," she said, smiling through her tears. "And this time I'll do as you say."

"Good girl. Herme?"

"As you order, sire. But you follow us, damn it. You hear?"

Zared laughed. "As *you* order, Earl of Avonsdale! Now, get those men mounted. Inform them . . . inform them that once they're safe within the Silent Woman Woods, I'll tell them what's going on."

Herme saluted. "Aye, sire."

Zared looked about, nodded at the other commanders, kissed Leagh briefly, then turned to his horse.

"What's he up to?" Caelum muttered as Zared rode straight for him, his horse at a flat-out gallop. Behind him his men had mounted up and were moving out.

Caelum checked the skies. Most of the Strike Force were aloft, their myriad black specks circling far above.

A month ago he would have been able to pick out the buttons on their uniforms.

He squinted, then waved at who he hoped was DareWing.

The speck circled lower.

Zared reined in his horse. "Caelum! I must speak to you."

"What do you here? Your place is at the head of your men."

"I have heard disturbing news about what it is we meet at the Star Gate, Caelum."

"His title is StarSon," Askam corrected.

Zared flicked Askam a scathing glance, wishing for the first time that the blast at Kastaleon had done a better job.

"Nephew StarSon," he said dryly, "I am concerned about the situation at the Star Gate."

"Your task is not to be concerned, Zared," Caelum said. "You vowed that you would accept my orders. Zared . . . please . . . Axis needs us there."

I did not *quite* get around to that vow, thought Zared, for the conversation was deflected. But now was not the time to quibble over such delicacies. "I have heard news that makes me question the decision, whether yours or Axis', to ride pell-mell for the Star Gate, Caelum."

Caelum raised his eyebrows. He hoped DareWing would land swiftly.

As if in answer to his thought, a shadow swept over them and DareWing FullHeart alighted to stand by Caelum's horse. "StarSon, what is it?"

Caelum inclined his head at Zared. "Zared has heard disturbing news, it seems."

Several other of Caelum's commanders had drifted closer. One of them shaded his hand, looked into the distance, and cried, "StarSon! Zared's force is wheeling to the south!"

"Stars in Heaven!" Caelum shouted. "What other treacheries do you have for me, Zared? DareWing, set the Strike Force—"

"Wait!" Zared yelled. "DareWing, commanders, *listen to what I have to say to you!*"

"Then say it *fast*!" DareWing growled, his wings tensed for flight, "before I set my birdmen's arrows to your men's backs."

Zared locked eyes with Caelum. "All the damned Enchanters in this realm, all the Star Gods as well, have all but lost their powers. DareWing, there *is* no Icarii enchantment to protect us at the Star Gate! The Demons will break through with the ease of a babe clutching at a fistful of jelly! *If we ride to the Star Gate we will all die!* They," he flung a hand in Caelum's direction, *"will not be able to save us!"*

"You lie!" Askam shouted. "Seditious words to mask your own cowardice! DareWing, set your Strike Force to—"

"Demons?" muttered one of Caelum's junior commanders.

"Then prove you still have your powers, StarSon Caelum SunSoar. *Prove* to me and to all your men here that you *still have your powers!*" Zared yelled.

DareWing turned slightly and looked Caelum full in the face.

"I am only trying to protect my men, Caelum," Zared continued more moderately. "I am a commander who will flee if it means that the majority of my command will survive to fight the next day. *I* do not make rash judgments and mistakes."

Caelum recoiled, but said nothing.

"Enough!" DareWing snapped as Askam reached for his sword. "StarSon, does Zared speak truth?"

Still Caelum said nothing, staring at Zared.

"As the Demons approach," Zared said quietly, "their darkness clouds the Star Gate, blocking off the sound of the Star Dance. DareWing, *you* know what that means. Without the Star Dance . . ."

DareWing looked more intently at Caelum. There had been more to the crisis at the Star Gate than he'd been told. He'd felt it with every instinct he'd gained as a member of the Strike Force for over sixty years. He'd battled Skraelings, Gryphon and humans, and he'd learned enough to trust his instincts. "StarSon?"

Caelum suddenly slumped in his saddle. "He speaks truth, DareWing."

A muttering rose behind him, but Caelum paid it no attention. "Zared, where did you hear this?"

"From the Lady Faraday and from the Princess Zenith. Zenith confirmed the almost absolute loss of her powers."

"Faraday!" DareWing exclaimed. He had met her on many occasions when she had been Queen of Achar, and her role in the replanting of the forests, as her willingness to die for Axis, gave her almost godlike status in DareWing's eyes, and in those of so many other Icarii.

"My father asked us to ride for the Star Gate," Caelum said slowly, but without any conviction. Faraday had returned? And *Zenith*?

"Axis was distraught, and had not thought it through," Zared said. "He was acting on battle instinct alone. Caelum, DareWing, there is nothing we can do at Star Gate save witness our own deaths."

"Damn you!" Askam cried, fumbling with his sword. Curse his one-handed embarrassment! "Does no-one have the courage to ride to the Star Gate's aid?"

Zared wheeled his horse out of the way. "There is nothing stopping *you,* Askam."

Askam looked at Zared, looked at the now almost deserted expanse of plain before them, then looked at Caelum. "Can't you save us?"

"No, Askam," Caelum said slowly, looking at Zared rather than Askam. "No, I cannot, and mayhap the Star Gods cannot either. Zared speaks wisely. My friend, I should have listened to you last night. DareWing, set the Strike Force after Zared's men—"

Zared straightened in alarm.

"—to escort them to shelter." Caelum rose in his stirrups and waved to his commanders. "Turn your men for the Silent Woman Woods. Now! Then ride . . . *ride!*"

His commanders were shouting orders as soon as the word "Silent" had left Caelum's lips.

70

Leap to the Edge

A hand seized his arm, and hauled him to his feet. Drago cried out, but did not resist. It was time. His only sadness was that he lost his dream of a gentle pasture somewhere in Tencendor where a shallow stream ran over smooth-backed rocks and pebbles, reflecting a carefree sun and the faint shadow of the afternoon moon.

Fully awake now, Drago almost let his terror claim him. Terrified, not only for himself, but for what his bitter treachery was bringing to Tencendor.

He wondered if there was anything he could do to save Tencendor.

Trust us.

But he was given no time to trust. The Questors dragged

him into the center of their pillared chamber. Outside the sky was awash in silver-streaked emerald.

Gods! How close *were* they to the Star Gate?

"Not close enough," said StarLaughter, and cuddled her child close. One of its arms flopped out of the wrap, and Raspu reached over and absent-mindedly tucked the flaccid limb back into safety.

"Now," Sheol said conversationally, "has come the time to use you all up, Drago SunSoar."

"You promised me that you'd see my blood order reversed!" Drago no longer believed in their promises, but he was desperate to buy himself some time.

"Did we?" asked Mot, one eyebrow raised, his mouth slack and moist with anticipation. "*I* cannot remember it."

"Nor we," echoed the other Questors in well-rehearsed chorus. "Never."

"Never," whispered StarLaughter. She tossed her head, and sneered. "I confess myself unsad over the matter. For a SunSoar, you were a lackluster lover."

She frowned, and put a finger to her pursed lips. "Well now, doesn't that make me think. Perhaps you are *not* a SunSoar after all!"

She pealed with laughter. "Use him! I am anxious to get home!"

And the Questors reached out.

It was agony. They made no attempt to spare him. Pain *ravaged* through his body, destroying vessels and tissue, burning and roping out of control.

He was dying, he knew it. And somehow, he was glad of it. He would not have to face what he had betrayed. His father's anger. His brother's terror. A land ravaged by disease and hunger and despair.

And more, if these Demons managed to put Qeteb back together again.

The pain increased. It bubbled and boiled through him.

Drago felt himself explode as if in slow motion. He thought he actually saw bits of his tissue and organs spray about the chamber until the Questors and StarLaughter were covered in it. The children—the black-winged and visaged Hawkchilds—were clinging to pillars, writhing on the floor, sucking and licking, their hands clawed and scrabbling. Some of them, he observed with dying clarity, seemed to be growing beaks.

Well, too late for curiosity now. He was only a disembodied mind, watching with casual interest the disintegration of his body.

Had all the men and women and creatures who had died so his father could attain his dream of a reborn Tencendor suffered the way that he did now?

"I am so *sorry*. I wish I had been a better man."

We regretted. We were consumed with regrets. It is nothing unusual. Use your grief and regret, Drago.

How?

You will help Caelum and Tencendor?

Yes, yes, yes.

In any way you can?

Yes, yes, yes.

Then listen to the Song we make.

And Drago opened his eyes, and blinked, and the Questors were gone, and the children and StarLaughter and her abominable baby were gone, and in their place stood a group of five people, three men and two women, their faces kindly and caring. One of them, an old, plump man with wispy white hair, reached out a hand in a farewell gesture.

"Farewell, Pilgrim," he said. "Remember us from time to time."

StarLaughter licked the blood off her fingers, tipped back her head, and screamed with joy. All were coated in blood, all licked, scraped, slurped in their efforts to consume as much of what had once been Drago as they could.

It tasted good.

More importantly, it tasted of power.

Sheol lifted her head. Her chin was slippery with blood. "We are here," she said tonelessly.

They looked about. All traces of the chamber had gone. The orchard had gone. Any semblance of a world had gone. They stood surrounded by darkness, their feet standing on cold, flat nothingness. But over them, pulsating with energy, hung the Star Gate.

Through it they could see four or five faces staring down at them.

As they watched, the emerald and silver warding sighed, shimmered, and died.

"What time of day is it?" asked StarLaughter.

"Just gone noon," Sheol whispered. "Not long now. Prepare yourselves."

She clicked her fingers, and whistled to the flock of children swarming to one side.

"Come, come, my chicks. Spread your wings, taste the feel of the air. Soon you will be free to quest."

Axis gagged, partly at the sudden cessation of the Star Dance—he had felt this only once before when he had "died" in the ice fields north of the Murkle Mountains—and partly in horror at what he could see through the Star Gate.

Pitch darkness, but there was a *something* within that darkness.

It bulged.

"It's over," said Adamon, just behind him. "It's all over."

Axis looked away from the horror in the Star Gate and gazed about the chamber.

The Circle of Star Gods were here.

Useless.

Some fifteen Enchanters, including StarDrifter, were here.

Useless.

Even WolfStar was still here.

And he was as useless as the rest of them.

"What can we do?" Axis said, desolate. Azhure moved to his side and put her arms about him. She buried her face in his shoulder. She could not yet believe that all they were, all they had fought for, was teetering on the brink of absolute disaster.

"It is my *son* who has brought this on us!" Axis cried, and Azhure's arms jerked tighter about him.

"My son!" And he screamed, arching his body back, the scream reverberating about the now pale, shadowed dome.

"No," WolfStar said, stepping forward. "Blame the ancient ones who left us these repositories of misery. Blame *them* if you must blame anyone, Axis."

"But—"

"WolfStar is right," StarDrifter said tiredly from his corner. He had never thought to witness the day when he would support WolfStar. "Drago was only a means. The Demons would have found a way to get through eventually."

"Then damn all stars in the universe that it had to be during *my* lifetime!" cried Xanon.

That drew a shaky laugh from Adamon. "Beloved, our lifetimes were—*were*—once forever. Of course they came during our lifetimes."

"But not forever any more," Azhure said, lifting her head and wiping the tears from her eyes. She'd only had forty years to live with immortality, but forty years had been enough to develop an affection for the everlasting.

"No," Axis whispered. "Not forever at all. Mortal once more."

He looked about the chamber, and laughed bitterly. "All of us! *Mortal!* Plain men and women. No power. No magic. No enchantment. *No Star Dance!* What shall we do in this new world, Azhure? Crawl about roofs replacing thatching to make ourselves feel useful?"

"Axis," StarDrifter said, finally moving forward to look into the Star Gate. He grimaced, swallowed, and looked away. "That is enough. What we must need discuss now is what we *do* now. These Demons ready themselves to break through. What do we *do* about it?"

"We can do nothing," WolfStar said.

"We must be able to do *something*!" Axis protested.

WolfStar shook his head, and looked at Adamon.

"Axis," the once-God of the Firmament said, "they will slaughter us when they break through. They will want to ensure that we never, never rise again. They will want free rein through Tencendor."

"But the Scepter!"

"We will find another day to snatch it back," Azhure said. "Adamon is right. If we are all bunched into this chamber when the Demons break through, then they will slaughter us all. Better to flee now so we can live to aid Caelum in his quest."

"Caelum," Axis suddenly said. "Gods! I asked Caelum to ride for the Star Gate!"

"You cursed fool!" WolfStar cried. "He's our only hope and you told him to ride *here*?"

"I thought an army would be useful . . . I thought . . . oh *damn* it! I did *not* think! We've got to warn him."

"How?" StarDrifter said dryly. "Do you suggest we run or fly to him? Will we have time?"

"Enough!" Adamon said, taking charge. "We all need to get out of here, *fast*. I do not know how we are going to counter these demons, but I *do* know that we will be more useful alive than dead."

"True," WolfStar said. "We must leave. Now." And he took a step toward one of the archways.

"WolfStar!" Adamon grabbed him by the arm. "I do not particularly care where you go, but for the moment you go nowhere near Caelum! With these Demons come over two hundred raging souls questing for *your* personal destruction. I do not want to risk them finding you with Caelum although, by the Stars, I truly don't care whether or not they find you at all!"

"Oh," WolfStar said, "I have enough to keep me busy for the moment without bothering Caelum."

Axis took Azhure's hand. "Azhure and I will go to him, Adamon. He is our son."

Adamon nodded. "Be careful." He grinned wanly at the stupidity of that remark. "Be careful, all of you. Run to whatever place you think safe. Later . . . later I will send word to you. We will regroup. We *must,* if Caelum is to prevail. Now, I suggest that we start to move. *Now!*"

The chamber of the Star Gate lay empty. Outside the sun dipped toward the west. The afternoon winked and woke.

Shadows suddenly started to shimmer over the dome of the chamber again.

But they were not blue—rather, black.

Beyond the Star Gate lay only blackness. But it was a blackness that rippled and writhed. Faces and hands and claw-tipped wings pressed against it, seeking to create the rent through which to enter.

Despair waited.

71

The Sack (2)

The two white donkeys, in their own indefinable way, accomplished more than any horse or even birdman could. As the noonday sun faded into afternoon, the little blue cart pulled up at the edges of the Minstrelsea forest just above the Ancient Barrows.

"Faraday?" Zenith said. She sat uncomfortably, more afraid than she'd ever been in her life. She felt only emptiness where once had been the Star Dance. She was useless. A husk instead of a living entity.

"Hush, Zenith. We will be safe within the forest."

Faraday climbed down from the cart and unhitched the two donkeys, leaving them free to browse about the undergrowth. She patted their necks and whispered to them, then turned back to Zenith.

"I want you to stay here with the cart and donkeys," she said.

Zenith blinked. "But I thought . . . at the Star Gate . . . you'd need me."

She stopped, thought, and then smiled sadly. "But I am somewhat useless, am I not?"

Faraday took her hand between both of hers. "You are not useless, but you would be dead there, Zenith."

"And you?"

Faraday paused before answering. "What I have has not been affected by the cessation of the Star Dance, Zenith. I have enough to protect me."

"I hope so, Faraday. How can you know what you will face when the Demons break through?"

Faraday smiled suddenly, brilliantly. "Zenith! I have been through so much. I have been rent and torn and reborn too many times to fear death again. I doubt the Demons will worry me over much. And Drago will need me."

"Drago . . . who knows if he is even still alive?"

Faraday's smile died and she dropped Zenith's hand. "Given where he has gone, and what uses him, I doubt very much that Drago will come back through the Star Gate 'alive.' But however he comes back, it is all we will have to work with. Now, rest here, Zenith. I shall come back. I promise."

And then she was gone.

Faraday walked quietly but briskly toward the Ancient Barrows. About her the forest was still. Waiting. The birds had roosted; she could see rows of them lining the branches of the trees, all looking south-east toward the Barrows.

They knew what was coming.

As did the other creatures of the forest. They lay or crouched unmoving amid the undergrowth, humped shapes in dark shadows. All, as the birds, aligned south-east. Waiting.

The trees' Song, normally such a beautiful undertone to the forest, now hummed and buzzed with agitation. Beneath the murmuring of the individual trees, Faraday could hear the angry hum of the Earth Tree herself, far to the north in the Avarinheim.

What would happen, she wondered, when the Demons broke through? Would the trees attack? Or would they just watch?

It depended, Faraday supposed, on how the Earth Tree herself perceived the Demons. Would she see them as a threat to the land, or just to the people—and the plains people in particular? If so, then the Earth Tree and the forests might leave well enough alone.

Perhaps she might even be glad that the Plains Dwellers, as the Avar still tended to refer to the Acharites, were being decimated.

But the Icarii were affected, too. Deeply so, since they had lost the Star Dance.

Faraday shook her head. There was no point in trying to second guess the trees' reaction.

There was a step to one side, and Faraday halted.

Goodwife Renkin stepped out from the trees. Still dressed as ever in the country worsted draped inelegantly about her coarse frame, she nevertheless exuded the power of the Mother.

"I do not like this, Daughter," she said without preamble.

"What can you do, Mother?"

"Watch."

"But—"

"I cannot know *what* assails us, nor what I or the trees can do about it until it moves among us, Daughter. Tell me, is Axis' son Drago responsible for this?"

"Is he responsible for the fact the sun sets each night? Is he responsible for the rain that batters your trees?" Faraday took a deep, angry breath. "Drago is a pawn. He is being used by the Demons to enter this world, but the Demons would have come eventually anyway, with or without him."

Better *with* him, she thought, better by many, many lives.

The Mother eyed Faraday curiously. "And what will you do, Faraday? You move through these trees with purposeful step."

"I will *help,*" Faraday said. "I am discontent with just watching."

She approached the spaces about the Barrows cautiously. There was no sign of activity, and they would have appeared abandoned were it not for the heavy air of tainted expectation that lay over them. She shuddered, wrapping her arms about herself.

The blue flame above the bronze obelisk stuttered and flickered, sickened nigh unto extinction.

"Drago," Faraday muttered, reminding herself that it was, indeed, necessary to go down the tunnel.

She flicked a glance at the sun. Gods, but it was sinking toward mid-afternoon!

Fighting the nervous impulse to retch, Faraday lifted her skirts and ran toward the tunnel entrance leading to the Star Gate. It was too late to rely only on her legs now, and so as she fled inside the black mouth of the tunnel, Faraday wrapped herself in Noah's strange, ancient power.

Sheol tipped back her head and howled.

All the Questors, as well as StarLaughter and the now

beaked children who huddled close, were wrapped in consuming darkness. There was no sense of any world about them now, they were suspended in time and space just below the Star Gate.

Sheol abruptly swallowed her howl and looked about her at the others. Her sapphire eyes glittered with power and hunger, momentarily lighting up her companions.

"It is time," she hissed.

The other Questors murmured, while the children shuffled in excitement, but StarLaughter gave an incoherent cry and jiggled the child agitatedly in her arms.

Raspu reached out to her and laid his hand on her shoulder. "Quiet, Queen of Heaven. Our time is nigh. Soon your child shall live and breathe again."

StarLaughter stared at him with wild eyes. "Soon?" she whispered.

"Soon," he murmured, kissing her brow. "Very soon."

"Now," said Sheol and, lifting her arms, called to bear all the residual power the Questors had drained from Drago.

About her the children shrieked and wailed.

As one, every statue in the chamber of the Star Gate cracked. Fissures ran from feet through the bodies, then splintered to run to the tips of each outstretched wing.

There was a sound, as if of a sigh, and then small chips of marble began to fall to the floor.

Faraday, huddled in the gloom behind one of the archways, put her hands to her mouth in horror.

They would destroy the chamber? She had not thought this.

And then another thought, more frightful than the last. Would they then destroy the Star Gate itself?

"No!" she wailed between her fingers, and rocked back and forth in agony. *No!*

The Star Gate began to boil. Faraday could not see it from her hiding place, but she could *feel* it. The blackness within the Star Gate was boiling as surely as a fetid soup over the fiery pits of the AfterLife.

Within the chamber the atmosphere thickened and warmed.

Faraday crept one or two steps closer, the limit of her courage. Everything within her screamed to flee before it was too late—but she could not. Drago would be lost without her, and Tencendor would be lost without Drago.

Then humps, lumps, shapes—she did not know how else to describe them—rose through the Star Gate. Scores of them, rising as if through swamp of thick black mud, their true nature cloaked by the as yet enveloping blackness.

"Gods, gods, gods," Faraday whispered, unable to help herself. She sobbed, choking on words, and she had to drop her eyes to gather her courage.

When she raised them she was numbed with horror. Through the Star Gate, she did not know how, were emerging black, winged shapes. There were many scores of them. Hundreds of them.

Faraday flattened herself against the tunnel wall, hiding from the strange black orbs that had replaced their eyes.

She knew they had to be the children, but they no longer looked like children, and only their wings connected them with their Icarii heritage.

In every other respect they appeared gigantic black hawks. Only . . . only that at the tip of each wing groped a scrawny, clawed hand, and the beaks were more mouths than horn. Mouths with enlarged, protruding upper lips that had hardened into a sharpened beak at their center.

They might be more bird than Icarii, but they had retained their mouths with which to cry WolfStar's name, and hands with which to grasp their prey.

Now they had emerged fully from the Star Gate, and shucked off what remained of the gloom that had been their birthing membrane. They fluttered, ran, hopped, and flew about the chamber in disordered horror. They clutched, clawed and pecked at their companions in anger and frustration as they collided and careened about in their mad chase about the too-small chamber.

There was a whisper, and the children—*hawks*—halted.

"Hunt."

And again. *"Hunt."*

Faraday pressed her hands against her ears now, for she could not bear to hear that voice again.

The hawks exploded into purpose. They turned for the archways that led upward to the twenty-six Barrows and rushed through. There was a noise, a strange wailing, and Faraday realized it was the sound of the Hawkchilds surging through the tunnels and apertures leading up from the chamber into the Barrows themselves.

The Barrows exploded. They burst apart in a shower of earth and gorse and rock, sending gouts of material several hundred paces into the air.

And from the wreckage of each Barrow erupted the black shapes of the Hawkchilds, higher yet than the rocks and earth, straight up.

Zared's men, the accompanying Strike Force throwing fluid shadows from overhead, had fled through the morning and into the afternoon. By the time the northern border of the Silent Woman Woods loomed before them, men were clinging in weariness to saddles, and horses had blood dribbling down their legs from scrapes where they'd stumbled to their knees in exhaustion.

Behind them, at a distance of perhaps a hundred paces, rode Zared himself, and behind him at another half a league came Caelum and his force.

The Strike Force, as all Zared's men, were safely within the Woods when Zared pulled his horse to a halt some forty paces before the first of the trees.

He dismounted, patted the beast, and slapped its rump,

sending it trotting toward the forest. Then he turned and watched Caelum riding toward him.

As he waited, Zared felt an oppressiveness settle over his shoulders. He shuddered, and looked about, but did not know to what to attribute it.

Then his eye caught the sun. Mid-afternoon.

He dropped his gaze and beckoned urgently at Caelum. "*Faster!*" he screamed.

Caelum, as every man behind him, dug boots into exhausted mounts and gained a last spurt of speed. A few of the riders outpaced Caelum, but Zared stood his ground as they thundered past him and into the trees.

"Thank the gods," Zared said as Caelum pulled up beside him. "I thought you would not—"

There was an earth-shattering roar to the south-east, and Caelum's horse had to fight to keep its feet.

"What . . . ?" Zared said, and Caelum half stood in his stirrups and shaded his eyes so he could peer toward the Ancient Barrows.

"Merciful Heavens," he said, then slumped down into the saddle.

"What is it?"

"The Barrows have exploded."

"Then they are coming—"

"My parents are there," Caelum said in a curiously toneless voice.

"You cannot help them now!" Zared yelled. About them horses and men ran for the trees with forgotten reserves of strength. "Quick!"

Zared grabbed at the reins of Caelum's horse, but Caelum shook himself and reached down a hand.

"It will be faster if you ride behind me, Zared," he said quietly.

Zared stared at him, then grabbed his hand and swung up behind his nephew.

* * *

Faraday slowly raised her face from her arms and looked back into the crumbling Star Gate chamber. The black forms of the Hawkchilds had gone, but they had been only a prelude to the true horror about to step through.

Faraday didn't so much see the Demons, as she was *aware* of them.

A man with bones that stuck almost through his skin stepped through first. He paused, looked about, and burped through his gluttonous smile. Mot.

Faraday was almost overcome with an overwhelming sense of hunger, a hunger so deep she knew she would hack off her own foot to assuage it. She fought it with whatever power she could bring to bear, and it slowly faded into a persistent ache in the pit of her stomach.

The man leaned back into the swirling, nauseous mess within the Star Gate and aided another of his companions into Tencendor.

Faraday began to itch, her eyesight blurred and she felt her blood slither toward every orifice of her body. Her skin twitched, and pustules simmered eagerly beneath its surface.

Raspu, Demon of Pestilence, hugged his companion, and together they aided Barzula, Tempest, through the Star Gate.

Faraday felt something rush through the tunnel toward her. Air, fire, water, ice-stones the size of her fist—where had they all come from? Instinctively she fought back, and the storm dwindled and died.

Mot, Raspu and Barzula turned toward the shadows where Faraday lay huddled.

"What was that?" Raspu said.

"I felt power," Mot said.

Barzula took a step toward the archway. "Unusual—is not the Star Dance dead?"

Mot caught at his arm. "No time. It does not seek to harm us. And look, Rox emerges!"

Faraday was crushed by a sense of terror so extreme she almost voided her bowels. Surely she could not survive in the face of this! She slid to her belly on the dusty floor of the tunnel and whimpered, her hands clutching at the detritus about her.

Somehow she held on to her reason.

After long minutes she looked up. Four figures stood about the rim of Star Gate, gazing into it. Then one, the thin man with the loathsome face, suddenly reached down and grabbed a hand.

Faraday slowly sat up in astonishment as a lovely Icarii woman emerged, a strangely sluggish baby in her hands.

Who?

Barzula leaned forward, and kissed the woman on her lips. "Welcome home, Queen of Heaven."

Faraday frowned. Queen of Heaven? Could this be Star-Laughter? And the child? WolfStar's son?

Then another woman stepped through, throwing something into a darkened corner of the chamber as she did so, and this time Faraday could hardly control the despair that swept over her.

No-one would survive. It had all been useless. Axis and Azhure would die arthritic middle-aged fools in the desert wasteland that had once been Tencendor. StarDrifter would suicide into bloody oblivion, Caelum would be torn apart by dogs, and Zenith would be used by bandits until they tired of her, tore off her wings, and threw her over a cliff. Within a generation, it would all be lost. No-one would—

"Stop it!" Faraday hissed to herself. *"Stop it!"*

She battled the vision, appalled by its severity. If she, who still retained power after the loss of the Star Dance, could hardly repel this despair, then what chance did the ordinary folk of Tencendor have?

Gods, but she had to do something to help this land before all *was* lost!

"There, again!" Mot swirled about, his bones seeming almost to clank with the abruptness of his movement.

"Power," said Barzula.

Sheol frowned, irritated at this distraction. "StarLaughter? Can you recognize the power being wielded?"

StarLaughter concentrated, rocking the child absentmindedly in her arms as she did so. "No," she said slowly after a moment or two. "No, I cannot. It is not Icarii power, nor what I know of the Avar, or even the Charonites."

She shrugged. "It is negligible, in any case. Perhaps it was originally left by the Enemy when they crashed through."

"Can we use it?" asked Rox.

StarLaughter shook her head. "It is almost . . . directional power. I can find no other way to describe it. Ignore it. It is no threat to us, and we cannot use it. Sheol, what do we do now?"

"We use the final reserves of Drago," Sheol gestured impatiently to what she had discarded on stepping through the Star Gate, "to move to a more congenial site. Come!"

She clapped her hands, and the Demons, with StarLaughter and her child, vanished.

But if Sheol had vanished, then the sound of her hands continued to reverberate about the chamber.

Statues crumbled into piles of useless rubble. Archways groaned, and almost a third of them collapsed while the others wavered and creaked. The Dome split into five sections with one almighty crack.

Faraday, terrified but knowing she had only one chance, rushed from her hiding place. She looked about frantically, shielding her head with arms and hands.

There!

The object Sheol had discarded as she stepped through the Star Gate.

Faraday hurried over, tripping and almost falling over a tumbled statue. Whatever the nature of the object, it was now shrouded in gray dust and small rocks. Faraday worked with her hands, dusting and pushing aside the rubble.

When she had uncovered it, she sat back on her heels, unmindful of the chamber shattering about her, her face expressionless.

Before her lay a sack of bones, wrapped about with skin.

Faraday reached out a trembling hand and touched the disgusting thing fleetingly.

She drew her hand back, grimacing. The skin felt cold and clammy.

Poor Drago to have come to this. Digested and spat out as this pitiful clump of skin and bone.

She reached out her hand once more. This time she did not pull her fingers back as she touched the skin. This time she softly stroked the remains, running her hand over as much of it as she could.

"Poor Drago," she whispered, ignoring the great rock that crashed not half a pace away from her. "Poor, sweet, lost Drago. Where are you now? Come home, Drago. Come home."

She fancied that the skin grew warm under her hand, and firmer to the touch.

But the bones still shifted and scraped each against the other in their sack.

Faraday remembered the sack that Drago had clutched so desperately when he'd entered this chamber weeks (months?) previously. Now *he* was the sack, but now he possessed the power that the original hessian sack had contained. Faraday understood that very clearly, and she hoped Drago would be able to come to terms with it also.

"Poor, sweet Drago," she murmured. "Come home. Come back to Faraday."

It did not occur to her to pick him up and rush him from the chamber before both were forever crushed in the grave it was rapidly becoming.

Eventually she looked up and realized the danger. The chamber was collapsing into itself—already the Star Gate was half full of rubble.

Faraday's eyes filled with tears. So much beauty to be destroyed! She remembered when Jack and Yr had brought her, a naive and foolish young girl, to this chamber. She had been deeply moved by the beauty and lure of the universe beyond the Star Gate, and deeply moved that something this beautiful, this magical existed beneath the dusty plains of Achar.

Now it was being destroyed. Within a few minutes at most, the beauty and power would be gone forever.

Faraday's hand stilled.

Within a few minutes all would be destroyed—but she still had those few minutes.

And this chamber and the Star Gate were magical. Not as much as it had once been, for now the music of the Star Dance had been stilled, but there was still power here.

She turned slightly back into the chamber, one hand on the skin and bones, one hand outstretched toward the Star Gate.

And she concentrated, concentrated on pulling all the power left in the chamber into her, combining it with what she herself was, and then channeling it into the skin and bones.

Then she felt something. She looked at the sack, gasped, and shuffled back a pace.

It was filling out.

It filled, then lengthened, widened, then filled some more. Again it stretched, and now the buds of arms and legs became visible. They filled and lengthened, and then Faraday saw the head.

It was Drago's head. His face firmed and fleshed out. It was Drago's face, although somehow different.

Indefinably different.

His transformation completed itself, and Drago crouched there, blinking in confusion, his hands patting distractedly at his nakedness.

Faraday put her hand on Drago's shoulder and shook him as hard as she could.

"Drago!" she said sharply. "Drago! Pay attention! It is time we were gone from this place."

He groaned, shuddered, and made as if to stand up. But

his muscles were still weak, and he had to try three times before he managed.

Meanwhile rocks fell about them in an increasing crescendo of destruction. Faraday glanced at the dome above them—there were now dark gaps between the five sections. When it came down, as it surely would, the entire chamber would be lost.

"Drago! Come *on*!"

"Faraday?" He reached out with a hand, and she grabbed it, hauling him to his feet.

"Yes. Now, *come!* We will die if we stay here!"

"Faraday? Faraday, there is something I must get."

"Drago!"

He paused, ignoring Faraday's attempts to pull him away, then he hurriedly pulled his hand from hers and bent back to the rubble.

"Drago! *We've got to get out of here!*"

"Wait," he mumbled, feeling with hands that were cut and abraded by the loose rocks about him. "Wait."

He grasped the end of something and pulled it free. "Ah!"

Faraday stared at it. It was a rosewood staff, very plain, curved into a shepherd's crook at its tip.

Drago hefted it in one hand, and with the other grabbed Faraday's. "Run!"

They escaped just as the Star Gate chamber finally collapsed. The five sections of the dome fell inward, landing within the Star Gate itself.

They filled it completely, jutting out in jagged spires.

An instant after the dome collapsed, the walls fell inward, covering what remained of the statues and the low circular wall.

The Star Gate and the chamber that had housed it for countless millennia was no more.

* * *

On the Island of Mist and Memory the sickly cobalt beacon that speared skyward from the Temple of Stars flickered, flickered again, then abruptly died.

The temple and Star Gate were dead, the Star Gods were made mortal, Enchanters were as ordinary birdmen. Icarii magic was no more.

The Dance had ended.

The Demons crouched atop one of the destroyed Barrows, StarLaughter at their side. Above them wheeled the Hawkchilds. Suddenly they veered to the north, vanishing in the haze of dust from the destruction amid the Barrows.

"They hunt," Raspu said, then looked at Sheol. "Now it is time for you to feed, my dear."

Epilogue

The Wasteland

It was mid-afternoon in Tencendor, and despair ruled. In Carlon a boy carting fruit to the market let his load drop from his back and watched expressionlessly as it rolled down the gutter.

It was no use. He would never rise above the rank of fruit-carter. He saw himself as an old man, his back bent and bowed by seventy years worth of oranges and apples, his old age a helpless mess of pips and bruised, rotting fruit skins.

He threw himself under the wheels of a driverless wagon careering around the corner of the winding street.

A Goodwife of western Tarantaise was outside hanging her washing when despair swept the land. She paused, and silent, hopeless tears slid down her cheeks.

At her feet a toddling girl sobbed.

The Goodwife looked down. What life was her daughter destined for? Marriage to a man who abused her at night and cursed her by day? A life spent wringing wet washing amid the never-ending rain?

What kind of life was *that*?

Sniffing loudly, swallowing her tears, the Goodwife reached down to her daughter, lifted her skyward, and twisted the washing line about her neck.

She left her hanging there with the washing, choking amid the sad, wet, flapping sheets.

Then the Goodwife went inside to see to her infant son.

* * *

The Icarii birdman was drifting the thermals high above the plains of Skarabost when he suddenly realized his life was pointless.

There had been no use in re-creating Tencendor. The StarMan had wasted his time and the Icarii nation's energy in battling Gorgrael.

The StarMan hadn't killed *every* Skraeling, had he?

No, some had escaped. Some had fled north again, doubtless there to breed and whisper revenge.

No doubt Skraelings were even now massing in the northern tundra to nibble and whisper their way south again.

The birdman had been present at the massacre of Earth Tree Grove, and his mouth was filled with the memory-taste of blood smeared over feather and flesh chewed to mincemeat in seconds.

It had been pointless. They would all suffer the same fate again.

He wailed, flipped over on his back, and watched the sun diminish in size as he plummeted to the ground.

He died impaled on a rake left outside by a careless harvester.

Cattle went mad in their fields. Sheep screamed. Pigs grunted and stampeded.

However, some stilled, as if listening. Then the cattle began to raven, and the pigs to plot.

For hours rubble continued to collapse inward from the destruction that had been the Barrows. There was a steady drip, drip, drip of rock and earth onto the pile of masonry that had filled the portal created so long ago by the flaming craft of the Demon's Enemy.

Nothing more could pass through to harry Tencendor.

Nothing could escape.

There was no music.

Nothing save the slow settling of the rubble and the cold, silent, broken, half-buried wings of the marble statues.

The Avar withdrew deep into their forests and prayed to their horned gods and to the Mother that she might have the strength to repel the invaders. The Acharites huddled inside tightly shuttered homes, apartments and palaces and wondered when it would be safe to scurry outside again.

In the Silent Woman Woods some twenty-four thousand men looked to the east and saw nothing but darkness and rubble. They turned to look at each other, and saw nothing but darkness and rubble reflected back by their companions' eyes.

"Courage," said Zared, and bent down to Caelum, sitting head in hands at his feet. "Courage."

Under one of the trees of Minstrelsea, Axis gathered Azhure in his arms and held her as tight as he could. Everything had been so bright. Gorgrael had died, his family had grown laughing and frolicking in Sigholt. Now it was all dead. Tencendor lay under the rule of the TimeKeeper Demons. Gorgrael had been a child's creation next to them. The Dance had gone, the Star Gate was no more. There would never be any magic or Song or music again.

No matter what they did, no matter how potent Caelum proved against the Demons, the music and the Dance were gone.

Azhure took a tremulous breath and raised her head. "What now, beloved?"

He smiled bitterly. "Now? Now we relearn our limitations. We learn all we can about these Demons. We help Caelum."

He paused. "Now we start all over again."

But in his mind, a mind Azhure could no longer share, Axis thought, *When I finally meet Drago I will tear his life apart with my bare hands for what he has done to this land.*

* * *

Under the first trees of Minstrelsea, Faraday pulled her cloak tight about her and looked at the man crouched in the half-light by her side.

"Can you feel the despair sweeping Tencendor?" she asked.

He looked up. "I am responsible for it."

Faraday remained silent.

He cast his eyes slowly across the wasteland beyond the trees. "Who am I?"

"You know that."

"Yes." He sighed. "I am the Enemy."

Glossary

ACHAR: the realm that once stretched over most of the continent, bounded by the Andeis, Tyrre and Widowmaker Seas, the Avarinheim and the Icescarp Alps. Now integrated into Tencendor.

ACHARITES: one-time citizens of Achar, now referred to only as humans. Caelum has banned the use of the term "Acharite."

ADAMON: one of the nine Star Gods of the Icarii, Adamon is the eldest and the God of the Firmament.

AFTERLIFE: all three races, the humans (Acharites), the Icarii and the Avar, believe in the existence of an After-Life, although exactly what they believe depends on their particular culture.

ALAUNT: the legendary pack of hounds that once belonged to WolfStar SunSoar and ran to the hunt with Azhure. They are all of the Lesser immortals.

ALDENI: a small province in western Achar, devoted to small crop cultivation. It is administered by Duke Theod under the overlordship of Prince Askam.

ANDAKILSA, RIVER: the extreme northern river of Ichtar, dividing Ichtar from Ravensbund. Under normal circumstances, it remains free of ice all year round and flows into the Andeis Sea.

ANDEIS SEA: the often unpredictable sea that washes the western coast of Achar.

ARCEN: the major city of Arcness. It is a free trading city.

ARCNESS: large eastern province in Achar, specializing in pigs.

ARTOR THE PLOUGHMAN: the now disbanded Brotherhood of the Seneschal taught that Artor was the one true god. Under His sway, the Acharites initiated the ancient Wars of the Axe and drove the Icarii and Avar from the land. Artor was killed by Azhure and her hounds.

ASKAM, Prince of the West: son of Belial and Cazna. Askam is a close friend of StarSon Caelum.

ASZRAD, FEBLONE: silk merchant of Carlon, bastard son of a Corolean soldier.

AVAR, The: ancient race of Tencendor who live in the forests of the Avarinheim and Minstrelsea. The Avar are sometimes referred to as the People of the Horn. Their Mage-King is Isfrael.

AVARINHEIM, The: the northern forest home of the Avar people.

AVENUE, The: the processional way of the Temple Complex on the Island of Mist and Memory.

AVONSDALE: province in western Achar. It produces legumes, fruit and flowers. It is administered by Earl Herme under the overlordship of Prince Askam.

AXE-WIELDERS, The: once the elite crusading and military wing of the Seneschal. Once led by Axis as their BattleAxe, the Axe-Wielders are now completely disbanded.

AXIS: son of the Princess Rivkah of Achar and the Icarii Enchanter StarDrifter SunSoar. Once BattleAxe of the Axe-Wielders, he assumed the mantle of the StarMan of the Prophecy of the Destroyer. After reforging Tencendor Axis formed his own house, the House of the Stars. He now drifts as the Star God of Song.

AZHURE: daughter of WolfStar SunSoar and Niah of Nor. She is married to Axis and is now Goddess of Moon. During the time of Prophecy, Azhure used the Alaunt to hunt and kill the Plough God Artor, and summoned the power of the trees to destroy Gorgrael's army.

AZLE, RIVER: a major river that divides the provinces of Ichtar and Aldeni. It flows into the Andeis Sea.

BANES: the religious leaders of the Avar people. They wield magic, although it is usually of the minor variety.

BARROWS, The Ancient: the burial places of the ancient Enchanter-Talons of the Icarii people. Located in southern Arcness, the Barrows guard the entrance to the Star Gate.

BARZULA: a Questor.

BATTLEAXE, The: once the leader of the Axe-Wielders. The post of BattleAxe was last held by Axis. *See* "Axe-Wielders."

BEDWYR FORT: a fort that sits on the lower reaches of the River Nordra and guards the entrance to Grail Lake from Nordmuth.

BELIAL: lieutenant and second-in-command in Axis' army during the fight against Gorgrael. Belial is the father of Askam and Leagh. Now dead.

BELTIDE: *see* "Festivals."

BERIN, Baron: a minor nobleman of Romsdale.

BETHIAM, Princess: wife to Prince Askam of the West.

BOGLE MARSH: a large and inhospitable marsh in eastern Arcness. Strange creatures are said to live in the Marsh.

BOOK OF FIELD AND FURROW: the religious text of the now disbanded Seneschal.

BORNEHELD: One-time Duke of Ichtar and King of Achar. Son of the Princess Rivkah and her husband, Duke Searlas, half-brother to Axis, and husband of Faraday of Skarabost. After murdering his uncle, Priam, Borneheld assumed the throne of Achar. Now dead.

BRACKEN RANGES, The: the former name of the Minaret Peaks.

BRACKEN, RIVER: the river that rises in the Minaret Peaks and which, dividing the provinces of Skarabost and Arcness, flows into the Widowmaker Sea.

BRIDGE, The: the bridge that guards the entrance into Sigholt is deeply magical. She will throw out a challenge to any she does not know, but can sometimes be tricked.

BRIGHTFEATHER: wife to RavenCrest SunSoar, former Talon of the Icarii. Now dead.

BROTHER-LEADER: the supreme leader of the Brotherhood of the Seneschal. The last Brother-Leader of the Seneschal was Jayme.

CAELUM STARSON: eldest son of Axis and Azhure, born at Yuletide. Caelum is an ancient word meaning "Stars in Heaven." Caelum now rules Tencendor.

CARLON: main city of Tencendor and one-time residence of the kings of Achar. Situated on Grail Lake.

CAULDRON LAKE: the lake at the center of the Silent Woman Woods.

CAZNA: wife to Belial, mother of Askam and Leagh. Now dead.

CHAMBER OF THE MOONS: chief audience and sometime banquet chamber of the ancient royal palace in Carlon. It was the site where Axis battled Borneheld to the death.

CHARONITES: a little-known race of Tencendor who inhabit the UnderWorld.

CIRCLE OF STARS, The: *see* "Enchantress' Ring."

CLANS: the Avar tend to segregate into Clan groups, roughly equivalent to family groups.

CLOUDBURST SUNSOAR: younger brother and assassin of WolfStar SunSoar.

COHORT: *see* "Military Terms."

COROLEAS: the great empire to the south of Tencendor. Relations between the two countries are usually cordial.

CREST: Icarii military unit composed of fourteen Wings.

CREST-LEADER: commander of an Icarii Crest.

DANCE OF DEATH, The: dark star music that is the counterpoint to the Star Dance. It is the music made when stars miss their step and crash into each other, or swell up into red giants and implode. Only WolfStar and Azhure can wield this music.

DAREWING FULLHEART: senior Crest-Leader and Strike Leader of the Icarii Strike Force.

DISTANCES:

League: roughly seven kilometers, or four and a half miles.

Pace: roughly one meter or one yard.

Handspan: roughly twenty centimeters or eight inches.

DOME OF THE MOON: a sacred dome dedicated to the Moon on Temple Mount of the Island of Mist and Memory. Only the First Priestess has access to the Dome, and it was in this Dome that Niah and WolfStar conceived Azhure.

DRAGONSTAR SUNSOAR: (also known as Drago) second son of Axis and Azhure. Twin brother to RiverStar. DragonStar is also the name of the son StarLaughter SunSoar was carrying when she was thrown through the Star Gate by her husband, WolfStar.

DRIFTSTAR SUNSOAR: grandmother to StarDrifter, mother of MorningStar. An Enchanter and a SunSoar in her own right and wife to the SunSoar Talon. She died three hundred years before the events of this book.

EARTH TREE: a sacred tree to both the Icarii and the Avar.

EARTH TREE GROVE: the grove holding the Earth Tree in the northern Avarinheim where it borders the Icescarp Alps. It the most important of the Avarinheim groves and is where the Avar (sometimes in concert with the Icarii) hold their gatherings and religious rites.

ENCHANTERS: the magicians of the Icarii people. Many of them are very powerful. All Enchanters have the word "Star" somewhere in their names (except Caelum and Zenith).

ENCHANTER-TALONS: Talons of the Icarii people who are also Enchanters.

ENCHANTRESS, The: the first of the Icarii Enchanters, the first Icarii to discover the way to use the power of the Star Dance. The Icarii revere her memory. This title is occasionally given to Azhure.

ENCHANTRESS' RING, The: an ancient ring once in the possession of the Enchantress, now worn by Azhure. Its proper name is the Circle of Stars, and it is intimately connected with the Star Gods.

ENEMY, The: the name given by the Questors to the ancient ones who crashed into Tencendor during Fire-Night.

ESCATOR: a kingdom far away to the east over the Widowmaker Sea. There is some intellectual, diplomatic and trade traffic between Escator and Tencendor.

EVENSONG: daughter of Rivkah and StarDrifter SunSoar, sister to Axis and wife to FreeFall SunSoar.

FARADAY: daughter of Earl Isend of Skarabost and his wife, Lady Merlion. Once wife to Borneheld and Queen of Achar, then Tree Friend, Faraday wandered the forests in doe form after being killed by Gorgrael.

FERNBRAKE LAKE: the large lake in the center of the Minaret Peaks. Also known by both the Avar and the Icarii as the Mother.

FERRYMAN, The: Orr, the Charonite who plies the ferry of the UnderWorld. He is one of the Lesser immortals.

FESTIVALS of the Avar and the Icarii:

Yuletide: the winter solstice, in the last week of Snow-month.

Beltide: the spring Festival, the first day of Flower-month.

Fire-Night: the summer solstice, in the last week of Rose-month.

FIRE-NIGHT: *see* "Festivals."

FIRST, The: The First Priestess of the Order of the Stars, the order of nine priestesses on Temple Mount. The First, like all priestesses of the Order, gave up her name on taking her vows. Niah of Nor once held this office.

FIRST FIVE FAMILIES, The: the leading families of Tencendor: led, in turn, by Prince Askam of the West, Prince Zared of the North, Prince Yllgaine of Nor, Chief Sa'Domai of the Ravensbund and FreeFall SunSoar, Talon of the Icarii.

FLULIA: one of the nine Icarii Star Gods, Flulia is the Goddess of Water.

FLURIA, RIVER: a minor river that flows through Aldeni into the River Nordra.

FORESTFLIGHT EVERSOAR: a member of the Lake Guard.

FORTRESS RANGES: the mountains that run down

Achar's eastern boundary from the Icescarp Alps to the Widowmaker Sea.

FREEFALL: son of BrightFeather and RavenCrest SunSoar, husband of EvenSong SunSoar and Talon of the Icarii.

FROISSON: a unit commander in Caelum's force.

GATEKEEPER, The: Keeper of the Gate of Death in the UnderWorld and mother of Zeherah. Her task is to keep tally of the souls who pass through the Gate. She is one of the Lesser immortals.

GOLDMAN, JANNYMIRE: Master of the Guilds of Carlon. One of the most powerful non-noblemen in Tencendor.

GORGRAEL: the Destroyer, half-brother to Axis, sharing the same father, StarDrifter. Axis defeated him in a titanic struggle for control of Tencendor forty years before current events.

GORKEN PASS: the narrow pass sixty leagues long that provides the only way from Ravensbund into Ichtar. It is bounded by the Icescarp Alps and the River Andakilsa.

GORKENFORT: a major fort situated in Gorken Pass in northern Ichtar.

GRAIL LAKE: a massive lake at the lower reaches of the River Nordra. On its shores are Carlon and the tower of Spiredore.

GRAWEN: a captain in Zared's army.

GREATER, The: the nine Star Gods.

GRYPHON: a legendary flying creature of Tencendor, intelligent, vicious and courageous. Gorgrael re-created them to defeat Axis, but they were all destroyed by Azhure.

GUNDEALGA FORD: a wide, shallow ford on the Nordra, just south of the Urqhart Hills.

GUSTUS: captain of Zared's militia.

HAGEN: once a Plough-Keeper in the (now destroyed) village of Smyrton, who was husband to Niah and stepfather to Azhure.

HANDSPAN: *see* "Distances."

HEAVORAND, BRANSOM: a merchant from Carlon.

HERME, Earl of Avonsdale: son of Earl Jorge, mentor of Duke Theod of Aldeni and friend to Prince Zared.

HORNED ONES: the almost divine and most sacred members of the Avar race. They live in the Sacred Grove.

HSINGARD: a ruined town situated in central Ichtar.

HURST, KARL: a wool trader from Carlon.

ICARII, The: a race of winged people. They are sometimes referred to as the People of the Wing.

ICEBEAR COAST: the hundred-league-long coast that stretches from the DeadWood Forest in north-western Ravensbund to the frozen Tundra above the Avarinheim. It is very remote, and very beautiful.

ICESCARP ALPS: the great mountain range that stretches across most of northern Achar.

ICESCARP BARREN: a desolate tract of land situated in northern Ichtar between the Icescarp Alps and the Urqhart Hills.

ICEWORMS: massive worms of ice and snow created by Gorgrael in his battles with Tencendor.

ICHTAR, DUKES of: once cruel lords of Ichtar, the line died with Borneheld.

ICHTAR, The Province of: the largest and richest of the provinces of Achar. Ichtar derives its wealth from its extensive grazing herds and from its mineral and precious gem deposits. Ruled by Prince Zared.

ICHTAR, RIVER: a minor river that flows through Ichtar into the River Azle.

ILFRACOOMBE: the manor house of the Earl of Skarabost, the home where Faraday grew up.

INISCUE, Mayor: Mayor of Severin.

ISABEAU: first wife of Prince Zared. She died in a hunting accident ten years before current events.

ISFRAEL: Mage-King of the Avar. Son of Axis and Faraday.

ISLAND OF MIST AND MEMORY: one of the sacred sites of the Icarii people, once known as Pirate's Nest.

The Temple of the Stars and its complex are situated on a great plateau on the island's southern coast.

JACK: senior among the Sentinels.

JARL: a pottery trader of Nor.

JERVOIS LANDING: the small town on Tailem Bend of the River Nordra. The gateway into Ichtar.

JESSUP, BARON: a minor nobleman of Avonsdale.

KASTALEON: one of the great Keeps of Achar, situated on the River Nordra in central Achar.

KEEPS, The: the three great magical Keeps of Achar. *See separate entries under* Spiredore, Sigholt, and Silent Woman Keep.

KILCKMAN, BORMOT: a trader of Carlon.

KILLINGREW: a young commander in Zared's army.

LAKE GUARD, The: a militia composed entirely of the men and women whom SpikeFeather TrueSong rescued as children from Talon Spike when it was threatened by Gryphon. They escaped via the waterways, and were changed by their experience. The Lake Guard is dedicated to the service of the StarSon.

LAKE OF LIFE, The: one of the sacred and magical lakes of Tencendor. It sits at the western end of the HoldHard Pass in the Urqhart Hills and cradles Sigholt.

LEAGH, PRINCESS: sister to Askam, daughter of Belial and Cazna.

LEAGUE: *see* "Distances."

LESSER, The: a term given to creatures of such magic they approach god-like status.

MAGARIZ, PRINCE: husband to Rivkah, Axis' mother, and father to Zared. Now dead.

MAGIC: under the influence of the Seneschal, all Artor-fearing Acharites feared and hated the use of magic, although their fear is now as largely dead as the Seneschal itself.

MALFARI: the tuber that the Avar depend on to produce their bread.

MARRAT, BARON: Baron of Romsdale.

MAZE, The: a mysterious labyrinth underneath Grail Lake.

MAZE GATE, The: the wooden gate into the Maze. Its stone archway is covered with hieroglyphics.

MILITARY TERMS (for regular ground forces):

Squad: a small group of fighters, normally numbering under forty and usually archers.

Unit: a group of one hundred men, either infantry, archers, pikemen, or cavalry.

Cohort: five units, so five hundred men.

See also "Wing" and "Crest" for the Icarii Strike Force.

MINARET PEAKS: the Icarii name for the Bracken Ranges, named for the minarets of the Icarii cities that spread over the entire mountain range.

MINSTRELSEA: the name Faraday gave to the forest she planted out below the Avarinheim.

MONTHS (northern hemisphere seasons apply):

Wolf-month:	January
Raven-month:	February
Hungry-month:	March
Thaw-month:	April
Flower-month:	May
Rose-month:	June
Harvest-month:	July
Weed-month:	August
DeadLeaf-month:	September
Bone-month:	October
Frost-month:	November
Snow-month:	December

MOONWILDFLOWERS: extremely rare, delicate violet flowers that bloom only under the full moon. Closely associated with Azhure.

MORNINGSTAR SUNSOAR: StarDrifter's mother and a powerful Enchanter in her own right. She was murdered by WolfStar SunSoar.

MORYSON: brother of the Seneschal and a disguise once used by WolfStar.

MOT: a Questor.

MOTHER, The: either the Avar name for Fernbrake Lake, or an all-embracing term for nature which is sometimes personified as an immortal woman.

MURKLE BAY: a huge bay off the western coast of Tencendor, its waters are filthy, polluted by the tanneries along the Azle River.

MURKLE MOUNTAINS: a range of desolate mountains that run along the length of Murkle Bay. Once extensively mined for opals, they are now abandoned.

NARCIS: one of the nine Icarii Star Gods, Narcis is the God of the Sun.

NECKLET, The: a curious geological feature of Ravensbund.

NIAH: of the once baronial family of Nor. Mother to Azhure, Niah was seduced by WolfStar SunSoar and murdered by Brother Hagen. Niah was the First Priestess of the Order of the Stars.

NINE, The: *see* the "Star Gods." ("The Nine" can also occasionally refer to the nine Priestesses of the Order of the Stars.)

NOAH: a man associated with the craft under the lakes.

NOR: the southernmost of the provinces of Achar. The Nors people are far darker and more exotic than the rest of the Acharites. Nor is controlled by Prince Yllgaine.

NORDMUTH: the port at the mouth of the River Nordra.

NORDRA, RIVER: the great river that is the main lifeline of Achar. Rising in the Icescarp Alps, the River Nordra flows through the Avarinheim before flowing through northern and central Achar. It is used for irrigation, transport and fishing.

OGDEN: one of the Sentinels, brother to Veremund.

ORDER OF THE STARS: the order of nine priestesses who keep watch in the Temple of the Stars. Each priestess gives up her own name upon taking orders.

ORMOND: a soldier in Zared's army.

ORR: the Charonite Ferryman.

PACE: *see* "Distances."

PALESTAR SNAPWING: an Icarii Enchanter.

PARLENDER, WILFRED: Prime Notary of Carlon.

PIRATES' NEST: for many centuries the common name of the Island of Mist and Memory and still the haunt of pirates.

PIRATES' TOWN: the town in the northern harbor of Pirates' Nest—or the Island of Mist and Memory.

PLOUGH, The: under the rule of the Seneschal each Acharite village had a Plough, which not only served to plough the fields but was also the center of their worship of the Way of the Plough.

PLOUGH-KEEPERS: the Seneschal assigned a Brother to each village in Achar, and these men were often known as Plough-Keepers.

PORS: one of the nine Icarii Star Gods, Pors is the God of Air.

PRIVY CHAMBER: the large chamber in the ancient royal palace of Carlon where Achar's Privy Council once met.

PRIVY COUNCIL: the council of advisers to the King of Achar, normally the lords of the major provinces of Achar. This council has been replaced in Tencendor by the Five, the leaders of the First Five Families.

PROPHECY OF THE DESTROYER: an ancient Prophecy that told of the rise of Gorgrael in the north and the StarMan who could stop him. It is now forty years since the time of the Prophecy of the Destroyer.

PUMSTER, NETHEREM: Master Bell-Maker of Carlon.

QETEB: the Destruction that wastes at Midday.

QUESTORS, The: a group of five beings who quest for what the Enemy stole from them.

RAINBOW SCEPTER: a weapon constructed from the lives of the five Sentinels, the power of the craft that lie at the bottom of the Sacred Lakes, and the power of the Earth Tree. Axis used it to destroy Gorgrael.

RASPU: a Questor.

RAUM: once a Bane of the Avar people, now the sacred White Stag.

RAVENCREST SUNSOAR: once Talon of the Icarii people. Now dead, killed in the Gryphons' attack on Talon Spike.

RAVENSBUND: the extreme northern province of Tencendor.

RAVENSBUNDMEN: the inhabitants of Ravensbund.

RENKIN, GOODWIFE: a peasant woman of northern Arcness who is often a disguise for the Mother. The Goodwife helped Faraday plant out Minstrelsea, finally leaving to wander the forests.

RHAETIA: small area of Achar situated in the western Minaret Peaks.

RIVERSTAR SUNSOAR: third child of Axis and Azhure. Twin sister to Drago (DragonStar).

RIVKAH: Princess of Achar, mother to Borneheld, Axis, EvenSong and Zared. Married to Prince Magariz. Now dead.

ROMSDALE: a province to the south-west of Carlon that mainly produces wine. It is administered by Baron Marrat.

ROSCIC: Chamberlain of Askam's Household.

ROX: a Questor.

SACRED, GROVE: the most sacred spot of the Avar people, the Sacred Grove is rarely visited by ordinary mortals. Normally the Banes are the only members of the Avar race who know the paths to the Grove.

SACRED LAKES: the four magical lakes of Tencendor: Grail Lake, Cauldron Lake, Fernbrake Lake (or the Mother) and the Lake of Life. According to legend, the lakes were formed during Fire-Night when ancient gods fell through the skies and crashed to Tencendor.

SA'DOMAI: Chief of the Ravensbundmen, son of Ho'Demi.

SANDMEYER, GREGORIC: Mayor of Carlon.

SEAGRASS PLAINS: the vast grain plains that form most of Skarabost.

SENESCHAL, The: once the all-powerful religious organization of Achar, now non-existent. The Religious Brotherhood of the Seneschal was extremely powerful and played a major role, not only in everyday life, but also in the political life of the nation. It taught obedience to the one god, Artor the Ploughman, and the Way of the Plough.

SENTINELS: five magical creatures of the Prophecy of the Destroyer. Originally Charonites, they were recruited by WolfStar (in his guise of the Prophet) in order to serve the Prophecy. They gave their lives to form the Rainbow Scepter.

SEPULCHRE OF THE MOON: a cave on Temple Mount, the haunt of the Star Gods.

SEVERIN: a new town built by Prince Magariz as the replacement capital of Ichtar. Now Zared's base.

SHEOL: a Questor.

SHRA: now the senior Bane of the Avar. As a girl she was saved from death by Axis.

SICARIUS: leader of the pack of Alaunt hounds. One of the Lesser.

SIGHOLT: one of the great magical Keeps of Tencendor, situated on the shores of the Lake of Life in the Urqhart Hills in Ichtar. Home of the SunSoar family.

SILENT WOMAN KEEP: one of the magical Keeps of Tencendor, it lies in the center of the Silent Woman Woods.

SILENT WOMAN WOODS: ancient woods in southern Arcness, now joined to the Minstrelsea.

SILTON: one of the nine Icarii Star Gods, Silton is the God of Fire.

SKARABOST: large eastern province of Achar which grows much of the kingdom's grain supplies.

SKRAELINGS: creatures of the frozen northern wastes who fought for Gorgrael.

SKYLAZER BITTERFALL: a member of the Lake Guard.

SMYRTON: formerly a large village in northern Skarabost, it was destroyed by Azhure for its close association with the Plough God, Artor.

SONG OF CREATION: a Song which can, according to Icarii and Avar legend, actually create life itself.

SONG OF RE-CREATION: one of the most powerful Icarii enchantments which can literally re-create life in the dying. It cannot, however, make the dead rise again. Only the most powerful Enchanters can sing this Song.

SORCERY: *see* "Magic."

SPIKEFEATHER TRUESONG: once a member of the Strike Force. SpikeFeather is now Orr's apprentice, since offering his life to the Ferryman as payment for safe passage for the Icarii children he rescued from Talon Spike.

SPIREDORE: one of the magical Keeps of Tencendor. Azhure's tower.

STAR DANCE: the source from which the Icarii Enchanters derive their power. It is the music made by the stars in their eternal dance through the heavens.

STARDRIFTER: an Icarii Enchanter, father to Gorgrael, Axis and EvenSong. He now lives on the Island of Mist and Memory.

STARFEVER HIGHCREST: Master Secretary of Talon FreeFall's palace in the Minaret Peaks.

STAR FINGER: the tallest mountain in the Icescarp Alps, dedicated to study and worship. Formerly called Talon Spike.

STAR GATE: one of the sacred sites of the Icarii people, situated underneath the Ancient Barrows. It is a portal through to the universe.

STAR GODS: the nine gods of the Icarii. *See separate entries under* Axis, Azhure, Adamon, Xanon, Narcis, Flulia, Pors, Zest and Silton.

STARLAUGHTER SUNSOAR: wife of WolfStar, murdered and thrown through the Star Gate four thousand years before current events.

STARMAN, The: Axis SunSoar.

STARS, HOUSE of the: Axis' personal House.

STARSON: the title Axis gave to Caelum.

STRAUM ISLAND: a large island off the coast of Ichtar and inhabited by sealers.

STRIKE FORCE: the military force of the Icarii.

SUNSOAR, HOUSE of: the ruling House of the Icarii for many thousands of years.

TAILEM BEND: the great bend in the River Nordra where it turns from its westerly direction and flows south toward Nordmuth and the Sea of Tyrre.

TALON: the hereditary ruler of the Icarii people (and once over all of the peoples of Tencendor). Generally of the House of SunSoar.

TALON SPIKE: the former name of Star Finger.

TARANTAISE: a rather poor southern province of Achar. Relies on trade for its income.

TARE: small trading town in northern Tarantaise.

TARE, PLAINS of: the plains that lie between Tare and Grail Lake.

TEKAWAI: the preferred tea of the Ravensbund people, made from the dried seaweed of the Icebear Coast. It is always brewed and served ceremonially.

TEMPLE MOUNT: the plateau on the top of the massive mountain in the south-east corner of the Island of Mist and Memory. It houses the Temple Complex.

TEMPLE OF THE STARS: one of the Icarii sacred sites, located on the Island of Mist and Memory.

TENCENDOR: once the ancient name for the continent of Achar before the Wars of the Axe, and, under Axis' and now Caelum's leadership, the reforged nation of the Acharites, Avar and Icarii.

THEOD, Duke of Aldeni: grandson of Duke Roland who aided Axis in his struggle to unite Tencendor. Friend of Prince Zared.

THREE BROTHERS LAKES, The: three minor lakes in southern Aldeni.

TIME OF THE PROPHECY OF THE DESTROYER: the time that began with the birth of the Destroyer and the StarMan and ended with the death of Gorgrael.

TREE FRIEND: a role Faraday played during the time of the Prophecy. She was instrumental in bringing the forests behind Axis.

TREE SONG: whatever Song the trees choose to sing you. Many times they will sing the future, other times they will sing love and protection. The trees can also sing death.

TYRRE, SEA of: the ocean off the south-west coast of Achar.

UNIT: *see* "Military Terms."

UR: an old woman who lives in the Enchanted Woods. For aeons she guarded the transformed souls of the Avar female Banes.

URBETH: an immortal bear of the northern wastes.

URQHART HILLS: a minor crescent-shaped range of mountains in central Ichtar. The hills cradle Sigholt.

VEREMUND: one of the Sentinels, brother to Ogden.

WARS OF THE AXE: the wars during which the Acharites, under the direction of the Seneschal and the Axe-Wielders, drove the Icarii and the Avar from the land of Tencendor and penned them behind the Fortress Ranges. Lasting several decades, the wars were extraordinarily violent and bloody. They took place one thousand years before current events.

WAY OF THE HORN: a general term sometimes used to describe the lifestyle of the Avar people.

WAY OF THE PLOUGH: the religious obedience and way of life as taught by the Seneschal. The Way of the Plough was centered about the Plough and cultivation of the land. It was all about order, and about the earth and nature subjected to the order of mankind. Some of the Icarii and Avar fear that many Acharites still long for life as it was lived according to the Way of the Plough.

WAY OF THE WING: a general term sometimes used to describe the lifestyle of the Icarii.

WESTERN MOUNTAINS: the central Acharite mountain range that stretches west from the River Nordra to the Andeis Sea.

WHITE STAG, The: when Raum transformed during the time of Prophecy, he transformed into a magnificent White Stag instead of a Horned One. The White Stag is the most sacred of the creatures of the forest.

WIDEWALL BAY: a large bay that lies between Achar and Coroleas. Its calm waters provide excellent fishing.

WIDOWMAKER SEA: vast ocean to the east of Achar. From the unknown islands and lands across the Widowmaker Sea come the sea raiders that harass Coroleas.

WILDDOG PLAINS, The: plains that stretch from northern Ichtar to the River Nordra and are bounded by the Fortress Ranges and the Urqhart Hills. Named after the packs of roving dogs that inhabit the area.

WING: the smallest unit in the Icarii Strike Force consisting of fourteen Icarii (male and female).

WING-LEADER: the commander of an Icarii Wing.

WINGRIDGE CURLCLAW: Captain of the Lake Guard.

WOLFSTAR SUNSOAR: the ninth and most powerful of the Enchanter-Talons. He was assassinated early in his reign, but came back through the Star Gate three thousand years ago. Father to Azhure.

WOLVEN, The: a bow that once belonged to WolfStar SunSoar and was used by Azhure when she rode to the hunt.

XANON: one of the nine Icarii Star Gods, Xanon is the Goddess of the Firmament, wife to Adamon.

YLLGAINE, PRINCE: Prince of Nor, son of Ysgryff.

YR: one of the Sentinels.

YSBADD: capital city of Nor.

YULETIDE: *see* "Festivals."

ZARED: Prince of the North, son of Rivkah and Magariz.

ZEHERAH: one of the Sentinels, wife of Jack.

ZENITH: youngest daughter of Axis and Azhure.

ZEST: one of the nine Icarii Star Gods, Zest is the Goddess of Earth.

An excerpt from

Darkwitch Rising

BOOK THREE OF
THE TROY GAME

BY Sara Douglass

Now available in paperback

1

Gog Magog Hills, Cambridgeshire, and Oatlands Palace

Weybridge, England

Simon Gautier, Marquis de Lonquefort, gripped the armrests of the wildly rocking carriage and grinned lascivi-
usly at his current mistress, Mademoiselle Helene Gardien,
itting across from him. She was sixteen, with the face of an
ngel and the body of a whore, and she was shrieking with
eigned terror, although whether at the wild movement of the
arriage or at the wanton expression on his face, Lonquefort
lidn't particularly know—nor did he particularly care. Out-
ide the driver had whipped the team of horses into a frenzy,
nd they plunged recklessly down the forest track, their
ooves and the abused wheels of the carriage marking each
lip, each hole, and each rock that pitted their way.

Lonquefort was a man who disdained sedateness, in every
ispect of his life.

His uncle, and his guardian since the death of his father,
ad sent Lonquefort for a season to the austere colleges of
Cambridge in an effort to wean him from the fleshly delights
of his native Paris. But Lonquefort was a man not to be out-
witted, and in July of this year of our Lord 1629 he arranged
or the passage of Helene across to England. She was young,
liable, tender and fresh, and she shrieked delightfully
whenever Lonquefort buried himself within her pleasures.

Which explained why Lonquefort had hired carriage and
driver for this day expedition to the Gog Magog Hills four
niles south of the university city: the Cambridge dons were

starting to complain about the noise. What better to calm their shattered nerves and to indulge his own wanton desires than to take Helene in the center of some stubbled field, or the incline of some gentle hillside slope, where she could scream to her heart's content and he could . . .

Oh, God, he was going to have to stop the carriage soon!

As Helene pursed her sweet lips for yet another shriek, Lonquefort glanced outside. He'd been told the Gog Magog Hills were gentle rolling hills, cleared by years of grazing, yet the view which met his eyes contradicted all reports he'd heard.

Forests crowded about, thick and dark.

Lonquefort frowned.

Helene shrieked.

Lonquefort looked at her.

She gave another cry, and jumped slightly in her seat, her breasts jiggling just enough that her nipples slipped briefly, tantalizingly, into view above the frothy lace of her bodice.

Lonquefort forgot the strangeness of the forests.

"Stop!" he cried, his voice so thick with desire he could barely manage the word. "Stop, I command you!" He lifted his cane, banging its golden head against the roof of the carriage.

Outside the driver swore as he hauled on the reins in an effort to stop the violent, plunging motion of the horses.

Lonquefort couldn't tear his mind away from the violent, plunging efforts *he* would soon be engaged in. As the horses finally came to a halt, he leaned forward, grabbed Helene by the hand, flung open the carriage door, and hauled her outside.

"Wait here," he said to the driver.

Lonquefort managed to get Helene twenty or thirty paces inside the tree line before his lust overcame him. He pulled her to him and tore her bodice apart. He grabbed at her breasts, bruising them, then pushed her first against the broad trunk of a tree, then down so that she lay beneath him amid the leaf litter of the forest. He bit at her neck, and her breasts, and his hands grabbed at her skirts, fumbling in his haste.

Oh, God, oh, God, he'd never wanted her this badly. Never! Never!

Helene cried out, but he took no notice, and did not realize that the tone of her voice had changed from the provocative to the terrified.

She beat at his back and his shoulders, trying to push him away.

He took no notice.

Helene grabbed at his hair, intending to pull it until he pulled away from her, but instead her fingers encountered not fine, powdered brown hair, but the soft velvet of antlers.

Lonquefort thrust deep, and Helene, gasping with horror, felt not her lover, but the heat and strangeness of a wild beast. No, no, of a beast so untamed she felt as if she would die from the force and horror of it.

Lonquefort's movements became frenzied, and Helene lay quiescent beneath him, shocked beyond resistance. Her face was devoid of its usual rosy color, her eyes wide and staring, her injured breasts heaved, her breath whistled in her throat, her hands now clutched behind her at the bark of the tree, preferring to find comfort there before the pelt of the creature that was mating her.

Then, suddenly, wondrously, she was at peace, and she sighed and closed her eyes. While the beast above and inside her still felt wild, he no longer seemed strange, or frightening, and she lifted down her hands from the bark of the tree, and buried them within his pelt, and she whispered, "Anything for you. Anything."

And she felt then, within the pit of her belly, the beginning of something incredible, and Helene knew that her life as a girl was done for.

She sighed once more, and was replete.

* * *

"Madam?"

Henrietta Maria, queen of England, looked up from her embroideries, and put a practiced smile on her face.

"My good lord," she said, rising, then sinking in a deep curtsy, "I had not expected you."

Charles I looked at his wife, repressed a sigh, then instantly hated himself for his impatience. Other men managed with wives they found difficult to love, and so must he. Besides, she had been ill, had miscarried of a child, and doubtless some of her coolness could be ascribed to her aches both of body and of spirit.

At this thought Charles looked a little more closely at his wife. Sweet Lord Christ, she was only sixteen, and yet her face was drawn and lined almost as if she had lived through twice those many years. There were shadows under her dark eyes, her cheeks were pallid, and her hair had lost the luminosity that he remembered from their awkward, fraught wedding night.

What kind of man were he, then, to have brought a girl to this extreme of weariness? What kind of husband, to look in irritation on a woman, and judge her unkindly, when she had just lost a precious child? What kind of king, if he could not care for this most important of his subjects? What kind of lover, if he could not make her smile?

Now Charles smiled himself, and the expression was unexpectedly kind and warm, wiping away much of the aloofness which Henrietta Maria found so intimidating.

"You and I have made a poor start to our marriage," he said, "and I am sorry for it."

The false smile froze on Henrietta Maria's face, and Charles could see the confusion in her eyes. They had spoken nothing but banalities to each other in the entire first year of their marriage. This degree of forthrightness, *and* spoken so winsomely from a man prone to the most frightful bouts of stuttering, patently had caught her off guard.

Charles suddenly felt a most unexpected wave of mischievousness wash through him. She *was* but a girl, after all.

Why had he not remembered that? His smile warmed, his ntire face relaxed, and he was rewarded with the slightest of aws in his wife's own expression.

Charles glanced behind him. "We would be alone," he aid, and with those words, and a wave of his hand, he dis-nissed from the royal presence the entire bevy of ladies-in-vaiting, valets, diplomats, secretaries, and courtiers who ormally attended every waking moment of king and queen.

Henrietta Maria's face grew uncertain.

"Am I so unkind a husband," he asked, holding out his rm for her, "that you must look so suspiciously upon me vhen I seek a moment or two alone with you?"

"You are not unkind," she said, slipping her arm through is as he led her for a gentle stroll down the splendid gallery f Oatlands palace.

"Then, if I am not unkind then I have most certainly een—" He paused awkwardly, his speech struggling to naster the word. "—ungracious."

She did not reply.

He stopped, and turned to her, cupping her small face be-ween his hands.

Her muscles tensed beneath his fingers.

He lowered his face until it was but a finger's distance bove hers. "I have no doubt that as I speak, our courtiers nd ladies, indeed, half the realm, stand huddled against the ther side of the far door, ears pressed against its hardness, vondering what we do alone in here. What do *you* think they magine?"

His voice was light and teasing, and as its reward, he felt er face relax slightly.

"Perhaps that we discuss great matters of state," she said, er voice low.

"Perhaps, but, no. I think not. What else might they con-sider?"

"Perhaps that you rebuke me for some childish wrong."

"I hope not," he said, his voice and face now sober, "for hat would be a stain on my soul, and I am most sorry I should ever have given them the fodder to imagine such a thing.

"*I* think"—he lowered his face that final distance between them and planted a soft kiss on her mouth—"that they imagine we sit in silence on our cold thrones, and stare out the windows at the stiff, formal gardens, and wish to ourselves that we were anywhere else but in each other's presence."

"I sincerely hope not," she said, "for that is *not* what I wish right now."

"Then perhaps they imagine that I have been so overcome by my desire for you—"

Her cheeks stained even rosier.

"—that I have begged for solitude so that I might enjoy my wife's love."

"My lord—"

"Perhaps even now they think I have borne you to that bench by the window—"

She giggled.

"—and there avail myself," his voice grew deeper, a little hoarser, and she could hear real admiration within it, "of your sweet, wondrous white flesh. What say you, wife? Shall I?"

"My lord! It lacks but an hour until noon. We cannot—"

"Parliament may plot to make my life a misery," he said, "but it has not yet passed that act which forbids the nation's monarch from making love to his much-admired wife during the daylight hours."

"You admire me?"

"Most particularly during this beautiful hour before noon. What say you, wife. Shall we? That bench looks right inviting."

"But . . . But they'll *know*!"

His only answer was to kiss her neck, and lay his hand on her bosom.

"Charles . . ." she said, and he heard the weakness in her voice, and it encouraged him to turn tease into reality.

And so, atop a beautiful brocaded bench set into one of the great windows of the gallery at Oatlands, Charles I of England made love to his young wife while their courtiers crowded the door outside and a shaft of sunlight broke through the clouds and clothed the couple's soft movements in gold.

Although this was not Charles and Henrietta Maria's marriage night, it *was* the day on which they made their marriage, and it was also the day during which they conceived one of the greatest kings that England would ever know.

Far away in London a fair-haired, hazel-eyed boy in his midteens raised his face to the sky. He was tall for his age, and too thin for his height, but he held himself gracefully nonetheless, and his face already held hints of the handsomeness it would assume in maturity. He stood in one of London's innumerable back alleys, hidden in shadow. At his side stood a solemn-faced toddling girl of some eighteen months. She was a pretty little thing, with soft brown eyes and silvery hair, but her prettiness was marred by a blank look of terror in those dark eyes, and she stood tense and fearful, as if expecting a blow at any moment.

The boy held her by the hand, and, as he lowered his face, he gave her flesh a squeeze, painful enough that the girl gave a low gasp, her eyes filling with tears.

"Do you feel it, Jane?" said the boy. "Do you know what has happened?"

She made no reply save for two great fat tears that rolled down her cheeks.

The boy squatted so he could look directly into her eyes. "You *do* feel it, don't you? Brutus is back, your lover when you were Genvissa. He's reborn, and growing contentedly in a queen's womb. Not a bastard, *this* life. Tell me, pretty Jane, do you think he'll want you? Do you think he'll ever stoop to love *you,* dirty street urchin, Asterion's whore?"

More tears flowed, and the boy nodded slowly. "Aye. You know he's back, and you know he'll never touch you. So sad, pretty Jane."

She spoke, this tiny girl, with the voice of a child much, much older. "Let me go, Weyland."

"Never," Weyland whispered. "You're mine, now. You and all your talents.

2

Paris, France, and St. James's Palace

London

On the twenty-ninth of May in 1630 Helene Gardien went into labor at daybreak, delivering her child six hours later. Her lover, Simon Gautier, the marquis de Lonquefort, was in residence at the Parisian townhouse where he'd installed his mistress and visited Helene two hours after he'd been informed of her safe delivery.

This was his first child, and he was curious, if somewhat apprehensive and more than a little annoyed. All he'd wanted from Helene was sex, not responsibility.

"Well?" he said as he inched up to the bed.

"A boy," Helene said, not looking up from the child's face. "See, he has neither your eyes, nor mine, but those of a poet."

Neither your eyes nor mine. Lonquefort instantly seized on her words. Could he claim the child wasn't his? Not his responsibility?

Then he looked at the baby, and was lost. The baby's eyes *were* different, for while both Lonquefort and Helene had blue eyes, this infant had the deepest-black eyes Lonquefort thought he'd ever seen in a face. But it wasn't their color that immediately captivated Lonquefort. The boy's eyes *were* those of a poet, Lonquefort decided, for they seemed to contain knowledge and suffering that stretched back aeons, rather than the two hours this boy had lived in this painful world.

"He will be a great man," Lonquefort pronounced, and Helene smiled.

"I will call him Louis," she said, then hesitated. Poet or not, the boy was a bastard, and Helene was not sure whether she should name him for his father.

But who was his father, she wondered as the awkward silence stretched out between them. Lonquefort, or that strange beast she'd envisioned riding her in the forest?

"Louis," Lonquefort said, then he grinned. "Louis de Silva, for the forest where we made him."

Helene laughed, her doubts gone. The forest had made him, indeed, and so he should be named.

"I shall settle a pension on him, and you," said Lonquefort. "You shall not want."

"Thank you," Helene said softly, and bent her head back to her poet-son.

As Helene relaxed in relief, another woman, far distant, arched her back and cried out in the extremities of her own labor.

Henrietta Maria, queen of England, lay writhing in the great bed draped with forest-green silk within her lying-in chamber off the Color Court of St. James's Palace. About her hovered midwives and physicians, privy councillors and lords, all there either to ensure a safe delivery or to witness the birth of an heir.

Elsewhere within the palace Charles I paced up and down, praying silently. He was riven with anxiety, more for Henrietta Maria than for concern over the arrival of a healthy heir. Over the course of the past nine months, as his wife's body had swelled, so also had waxed Charles's regard and love for her. Now he could not bear the thought that she might suffer in childbed.

As the palace clocks chimed noon, one of the privy councillors hurried toward Charles.

"Well?" demanded Charles.

"You have a healthy son," the man said. "An heir!"

"And my wife?"

"She is well," said the councillor, and Charles finally allowed himself to relax, and smile.

"A son," he said. "He shall be named Charles."

"Of course," said the councillor.

Charles went to his wife, assured for himself that she was indeed well, then turned to look at the child one of the midwives held.

He studied the baby curiously, then folded back his wrappings.

"By Jesus!" Charles exclaimed, and looked back at Henrietta Maria. "Are you sure you *are* well, my love?"

She grinned wanly. "He was an effort, my lord. But, yes, I am well. He did not injure me."

Charles looked back to the baby. *By God, look at the size of him!* He was a giant, surely, with great strong limbs and a head of long, tight black curls. Charles reached down a hand and, as he did so, the baby reached up his own right hand and snatched at a golden crown embroidered on Charles's sleeve.

"Observe!" said the midwife. "He was born a king, truly! See how he grasps for what shall be his!"

Then both the midwife and Charles cried out, for the baby's hand tightened about the crown, and tugged at it, tearing it away from his father's sleeve.

"I shall have to watch my back, surely," Charles said with a forced laugh, "in case this son of mine decides to snatch my crown before his time."

The midwife prised the torn piece of material out of the infant's fist, and he began to wail.

"You shall surely die abed, an aged and beloved king," murmured one of the physicians. "This is no omen to be feared."

"Of course not," said Charles, but at that moment the room darkened as a cloud covered the sun, and the only one in the chamber who did not shiver in dread was the baby.

* * *

Weyland Orr brought his little sister Jane to stand outside the octagonal-towered gatehouse of St James's Palace among the other crowds awaiting news of the queen's delivery. Most of the crowd prayed for a prince; Weyland and Jane *knew* the child would be a prince. A king reborn.

Weyland hoisted Jane in his arms so that she could see through the gates into the Color Court off which, the crowd was reliably informed, the queen labored in her chamber.

See, Genvissa, in that tumbled mess of ancient buildings Brutus-reborn draws his first breath, while you sit, caught in the arms of Asterion, knowing you'll never feel Brutus' arms about you again. Will he come looking for you, do you think, once he has control of those infant legs of his?

Weyland laughed, softly, tormenting Jane with his thoughts. *No, of course not. He'll want his precious princess, Cornelia. He won't want you, particularly after what I have planned.*

Weyland sent a series of images skidding through Jane's mind, and the girl began to cry.

Weyland hugged her to him. "There, there," he whispered, playing the part of the affectionate brother to perfection. "All will be well. I shall look after you."

Then he lifted his head. A nobleman had walked to the gates, and now shouted to the crowds.

"A son! A son! The queen has been safely delivered of a healthy son!"

The crowd roared, and Weyland cheered with the best of them.

In his arms, the little girl wept.